For Ian who is the strongest man I know.
Your journey is only beginning,
but you will go far and wide.
Just mark my words.

And for Madaug and Cabal.

And for Steven who has walked through the fires of hell
and come through them ever stronger, and who will
rise like a phoenix to heights unparalleled.
Let no one ever tell you who you are.
You know and you will defy all those
who stand in your way.

STYGIAN

Stygian

SHERRILYN KENYON

piatkus

PIATKUS

First published in the US in 2018 by Tor Books,
an imprint of St Martin's Press, New York
First published in Great Britain in 2018 by Piatkus
This paperback edition published in 2019 by Piatkus

1 3 5 7 9 10 8 6 4 2

A CIP catalogue record for this book
is available from the British Library.

ISBN 978-0-349-41333-4

Printed and bound in Great Britain by Clays Ltd, Elcograf S.p.A.

Papers used by Piatkus are from well-managed forests
and other responsible sources.

Piatkus
An imprint of
Little, Brown Book Group
Carmelite House
50 Victoria Embankment
London EC4Y 0DZ

An Hachette UK Company
www.hachette.co.uk

www.littlebrown.co.uk

STYGIAN DAWN

Tears blinded Braith as she stared through the bars to see what they'd done to her once proud husband. While all the Sephirii beings were ethereal and beautiful, none were more so than her precious Kissare. Yet they had beaten him to the brink of death. Had sliced his white wings from his muscular body and left him a broken shadow of the fierce warrior he'd been.

Even so the fire of life returned to his warrior's gaze the moment he saw her through his matted white hair. Empyreal hair that contrasted sharply with the blackness of hers.

"Apollymi," he breathed, using an endearment that in his language meant "the light of my heart."

From the moment they'd first met, he'd refused to call her anything else. Unlike the others who scorned and mocked her for a monster to be feared, Kissare alone knew her for something more than the pit of utter darkness that would devour the world whole, and laugh while she did it.

And they were right. She hated everything and everyone.

Except for him.

He smiled at her in spite of his pain. "You shouldn't have come here."

"I had to." Choking on her grief, she cupped his face through the bars. "I drugged Atticus and have stolen the key." She released him so that she could pull it from the folds of her cloak and unlock his prison to free him. "We can—"

"Nay," he said, cutting her off. He placed his bloodied and bruised hand over hers to stop her from setting him free. "I cannot leave. It's the only way to protect you and Monakribos."

She sobbed at the mention of their young son, who'd been crying himself to sleep every night as he asked after his absent father. Kissare and Monakribos were so close. From the very hour of Monakribos's birth, Kissare had been there for him. Had never missed a single night of tucking their son into his bed to sleep—provided the babe hadn't fallen asleep while nestled in his father's arms.

Until the other gods had learned that Kissare was the father of her child.

Damn Kissare's brother for his loose, treacherous tongue! A tongue she'd nailed to the ceiling over the betrayal that had caused Kissare's arrest.

Not content to stop there, she'd also nailed both of Tisahn's testicles beside his tongue as he screamed out for a mercy she'd refused to show him. Then she'd grown him two more balls just so she could rip those off and nail them up as well. Pity the weakling had died before she'd had a chance to give him a third set.

Worse still, her pathetic sister had hidden his corpse from her so that Braith couldn't resurrect him and torture him longer. ...

Wretched bitch! She'd get Cam back for that one day, even if it was the last thing she did.

While it was fine for the male gods to have children with the female Sephirii, or any other whore they dredged up from the lowest pits for that matter, it was considered sacrilege for a male Sephiroth to impregnate any goddess he served.

But in her heart, Braith had only loved Kissare and their son. In all these centuries, Kissare alone had been the one who'd made her laugh. His had been the sole company she'd sought. Whenever she'd been despondent, he'd comforted her. When she'd needed friendship, he'd always been there. No excuses. No delay.

Her best friend.

Her *only* friend.

Now ...

"I don't know how to live without you, Sare. I don't *want* to live without you."

"Shh," he whispered before he placed a tender kiss to her cheek. "You are a goddess. The most beautiful of all. You lived centuries before my birth and you were fine without me."

"No. I survived and endured. I was cold and unfeeling. The last thing I want is to be cast back to that lonely hell I used to call home."

"And now you have a baby who needs his mother."

She choked on a sob. "He needs his father, too." How would their son ever learn kindness without Kissare? She could teach him nothing save murder, torture, and hatred.

Those were all she understood.

He buried his hand in her dark hair and locked gazes with her. "The other gods will never leave us in peace, Polli. You know that. We've broken their sacred law, and they are a hateful lot. My execution will make amends. Better they punish me, alone, than you and Kree. ... But I will come back for you. I swear it. No matter what it takes. Death can't keep us apart. Nothing can. I love you too much to stay away."

Through the pain, she believed him. If he said it, it was true. He'd never once lied to her. It wasn't in him to do such.

"How will I know it's you?"

He took her hand into his and placed it over his heart so that she could feel its fierce, strong beat beneath her palm. "You will know, and you won't doubt me. Ever. You'll see."

"Then I will wait for you. No other shall ever touch me. You will forever be my only heart." She turned her hair snow white to match his and to honor him and his noble sacrifice.

For her and their son.

Never again would her hair be any other color, and she would sit in black—to mark her darkness—until his return.

He gave her a sad smile. "You will always be my precious Apollymi." He kissed her lips. "Now go before they find you. Raise our son and never let him doubt how much his father loves him. One day, I will return for you both. You can count on it."

Her heart shattered as she nodded and let go of his hand. "I will wait for you! Forever!" She turned and walked away, fearing the future. And knowing what she would do if the gods dared keep them apart.

June 25, 9527 BC

Apollymi the Great Destroyer burst from the depths of her hellish prison to set fire to the entire earth, intending to scorch it back to its primordial ooze.

Her wrath was implacable.

And no one was immune.

Waves crashed over continents and sank them overnight to the bottom of the oceans. Roiling black clouds obliterated the sun. All life upon the human earth was threatened with extinction.

Even the very gods trembled in fear.

Why? Because those gods of old had banded together once more to take from her the one thing she'd loved above all others. Again. The only one she'd allowed them to lock her in prison to save.

Her second born son.

The sole child she'd hidden in the world of man, hoping to spare him from their cruelty and slaughter.

And like his brother before him, he had been persecuted by the gods. No mercy had been shown him.

No kindness.

Instead, her own pantheon had allowed humanity to abuse him and had gone out of their way to stalk him until they'd succeeded in brutally murdering him just after the eve of his twenty-first year.

As with Monakribos before him, he'd been deprived of his father's love.

Deprived of his mother's protection.

Now ...

She would have her vengeance!

In a furious blood quest for atonement, Apollymi had set upon her own pantheon first, annihilating every god who'd cursed her child.

Until she reached the final two in Katateros.

There, the ancient goddess sent the force of her winds to knock both Symfora and her daughter, Bet'anya, into the bright foyer of the theocropolis where the Atlantean gods had once held their immaculate parties, and their meetings that determined the fates of mankind, along with those of Apollymi's beloved sons and husband. She stalked them like the predator she was, intending to feast upon their souls for what they'd done.

"You killed him. All of you!"

Symfora—their goddess of death and sorrow, who was as dark in coloring as Apollymi had been before they'd interfered with her first and only love—shook her head. "We didn't kill your son. He still lives."

Narrowing her swirling silver eyes as her white hair cascaded around her lithe body, Apollymi curled her lips. "My Apostolos was slaughtered this morning by the Greek god *you* invited into *my* lands." A god who had killed her son and then cursed all the Apollite people to die painfully at age twenty-seven.

Symfora's eyes widened in terror. "I *never* welcomed Apollo here. That was a decision made by you and Archon."

"Shut up!" Apollymi blasted her into oblivion for speaking a truth that speared her with guilt. She refused to be blamed for what had happened to her child.

The gods had betrayed both her sons, Monakribos *and* Apostolos! And she was done with them.

Now alone in the wake of her mother's fate, Bet'anya faced Apollymi without any help whatsoever. Her dark caramel skin turned pale. The Atlantean goddess of wrath, misery, and the hunt was the last one standing.

She would be the last one to fall.

But as Apollymi reached for her, she hesitated at the sight of Bet'anya's distended belly. The much younger goddess was pregnant. About to give birth any day by the looks of her.

In that moment, rage and pain warred within her heart. Most of all, compassion flared deep as she felt the pangs of a mother who'd lost her child, not once, but twice. How could she deliver such pain to another?

Her breathing labored, Bet'anya met her gaze levelly, without fear or deceit. Of all the goddesses in Katateros, she was by far the most beautiful. Half Egyptian and half Atlantean. Her exotic features were sharply chiseled, and framed by a wealth of thick ebony hair that set off her almond-shaped eyes to perfection. Apollymi could see why the Egyptians called her Bethany. In Atlantean, Bet'anya meant "keeper of misery," but in her father's language, Bethany meant "oath of grace."

A far more fitting moniker for such a fetching creature. "I didn't incarcerate you or hunt your son, Apollymi. I took no part in their cruelty. The one time I thought I'd stumbled upon your son in the human realm, I came to you with that information and not the others. I never breathed a word to them against either of you." Tears choked her. "You know it's true. I came here today to leave this pantheon forever so that I could have my own baby in peace, away from their politics. Please, do not do to me what I did not do to you."

The girl was right and Apollymi knew it. No matter how much she wanted Bet'anya's blood, she couldn't kill another innocent baby. Especially not on *this* day. Not while the soil was still damp and stained with the blood of her own son. "Who among the gods is his father?"

"The father's mortal. Human."

Human . . .

There was something Apollymi would have never suspected from a goddess she knew hated that disgusting species even more than she did. "His name?"

"Styxx of Didymos."

For a moment, Apollymi couldn't breathe as her rage renewed itself with a vigor unprecedented.

Of all the mortals, in *all* the world, *that* was not the name to give her.

Not today.

Not after she'd seen through her son's own eyes the life

he'd lived and what had been done to him because of *Styxx of Didymos* ...

Damn him! For Styxx was the prince she'd chosen to bond with her own son to protect him from the gods who'd been hell-bent on killing her precious Apostolos. The human twin brother who was supposed to have protected her child and his birthright!

Instead, Styxx had stood by and allowed her son to be slaughtered and betrayed. Of all men, he was the very human whose throat she wanted most to personally rip out!

She felt her eyes turning from silver to red as her Destroyer form took over.

Bet'anya stumbled away and wrapped her arms around her belly to protect her baby. "Please, Apollymi ... my baby's innocent."

"So. Was. Mine!"

Both of them. And yet her sons had been given death sentences by the gods.

All of them.

Before she could stop herself, Apollymi reacted on instinct.

And she returned to the goddess what her pantheon had done to her.

In the blink of an eye, she ripped Bet'anya's son from her belly with a furious scream.

Bet'anya staggered back and fell to her knees. Gasping, she stared at her unmoving son in Apollymi's hands, and she reached out to touch him.

But Apollymi wouldn't have it. No one had shown her an ounce of mercy. Not once.

Therefore, she delivered it back, full force. She blasted Bet'anya away and turned the bitch into a statue like all the others. Let her sit out eternity in a fathomless void where she could hear and see, but never again move or be part of any world. It was what they all deserved for what they'd done to her.

What they'd done to her children.

Then Apollymi looked down at the tiny infant in her hands and started to discard it as they'd done her son.

To toss him into the sea like he was garbage. Without a second thought so that he could die.

But because he was the son of Styxx, it was as if she held her own son in her arms. He looked like her Apostolos.

Identical, in fact. Every last part of him was the same. His tiny little fingers and toes.

His lips that had never had a chance to call her mother . . .

Tears filled her eyes as she remembered that day, twenty-one years ago, when Apostolos had been ripped from her womb and taken from her. So small and fragile.

Just an innocent babe in need of love . . .

And she remembered when Monakribos had been so tiny and sweet. When all he'd done was beg for his father's love after they'd stolen his father from both of them and left them lost in their grief. Powerless to keep the world from crushing them with its unkindness.

"Just like you," she whispered to the baby. "They were helpless, too."

No one had taken pity on them.

For her sons, alone, she'd allowed her powers to be bound. Had allowed the gods to lock her into a dark, hollow prison until she'd lost what little sanity she'd had.

Her tears formed crystals on her cheeks as they fell silently and her grief shredded a heart she'd never wanted to begin with.

Damn you, Kissare, for making me feel love.

Because of him, the goddess of destruction was not without feelings. Her heart was shattered and she was devastated. And no matter how much she hated Styxx of Didymos, she couldn't bring herself to kill this baby who looked so much like the creature that had fathered him.

A baby who looked so much like her precious Apostolos who wasn't supposed to die so very young.

So very brutally.

More tears blinded her as she struggled to breathe past the pain that lacerated her heart.

I will protect you, little one. You will grow to be a strong, fine man.

"Out of darkness comes the light. From the loins of this Stygian hell, you are born and you will be called Urian—the flame of our new people. And one day, you will be my blade. My vengeance upon them all. They took my son from me, and I will take theirs from them. Together, my precious Flame, we will destroy the human race, and all the gods of this earth."

But first, he would have to be reborn in the land of the mortals and from the belly of a mother who would have no idea of who or what she carried ...

What this child's destiny would become.

And Apollymi knew just who his new temporary mother would be. What father would be the best to mentor him to manhood.

Aye, the world of man would tremble before them all.

June 26, 9527 BC

Dawn

Strykerius Apoulos cringed in horror as he heard the screams of a thousand Apollites dying in utter agony. Why hadn't they listened to him when he'd told them to take cover, and heed the warnings of the priests and priestesses?

Because no one wanted to believe their creator had turned against them over something they'd taken no part in. Something they'd been innocent of.

They continued to believe in a god who hated them. One who had not only turned his back on them but cursed them in his callousness.

Throwing his head back, Stryker roared with the injustice of it all. How could the entire Apollite race be damned over the actions committed by a mere handful?

Yet that was what they were facing.

Total extinction.

By the hand of *his* own father. Brutal annihilation over a slaughtered whore his father had barely tolerated. One who would grate the nerves of a saint. It was so unfair.

"Stryker?"

He winced at the sound of his wife calling to him. Though she was beauty incarnate, with blond hair, perfect blue eyes and features and curves that were the envy of every woman born, including his aunt Aphrodite, he cringed every time Hellen came near. Not because she wasn't desirable but because he'd never wanted to marry her. Yet to please his Olympian father who'd cursed his race, he'd abandoned the real woman he'd loved. Left her cursing his very name so that he could appease his father by taking Hellen for his bride and leaving Phyra forever.

So much for wedded bliss. And familial obligations.

"Stryker, come quickly! Please! Something's wrong with the children!"

Terror seized him at the panic in her voice.

Nay! Surely his father had spared his own grandchildren ...

Are you an idiot? Since when does Apollo give two shits about you, *never mind* your *children?*

Granted, that was true—still, Stryker didn't want to believe that his father would be *this* reckless.

Or stupid.

While his father might not care about him or his children, surely Apollo wasn't suicidal ...

If he and all his children died, so would the god who'd tied them to his life.

That was his thought until he ran into the nursery to find his children writhing and throwing up. Their little bodies were shaking as they sobbed and moaned in absolute agony. It was a pain he knew well, as he'd gone through it himself only hours before as he'd transitioned into the very monster his father had made him.

Tears welled in his eyes as he saw a cruel truth he couldn't deny.

His father hated them all, without mercy or compassion.

"Seal the windows! Now," Stryker growled at his pregnant wife and the two female servants who were assisting her.

They rushed to obey his orders.

If the rays of the dawning sun touched their children, it would kill them instantly. For that was the curse of his father, Apollo. Henceforth, no Apollite was allowed in the Greek god's domain. If Apollo caught any who possessed one drop of their blood out in the light of day, he would singe them to the bone and kill them instantly.

Why? Because the Apollite queen, Stryker's birth mother, in a fit of jealousy had ordered the death of Apollo's Greek mistress and the bastard son she'd birthed for the Greek god. As further punishment for the queen's atrocious crimes, Apollo had cursed all of her people to feed from each other's blood—they were damned to know no other sustenance.

But the worst of all ... no Apollite would ever again live past their twenty-seventh birthday. While they would now age faster than humans from the moment of birth, on the morn of their twenty-seventh year, their aging cycle would speed up even more and by the end of that day, they would painfully die of old age and decay into dust.

No exceptions. No alternatives.

Anyone who held a single drop of Apollite blood.

That was his father's mandate. And it applied to all of them. Including Stryker and his children—Apollo's own grandchildren.

Horrified, he gathered his four young sons into his arms to comfort them, even though there was no solace to be had. "Shh," he breathed.

Like him and their mother, they were all golden-haired and fair, with tawny skin and bright cheeks. Said to be the pride of their grandfather who'd turned his back on them.

Hellen held their daughter, Dyana, against her shoulder. And to think, they'd actually named her for Stryker's aunt, Artemis—Apollo's twin sister. The thought turned his stomach now. How could he have ever honored any of his paternal family?

I won't go against my brother, Strykerius. Not even for you. Do not ask me for help again.

How he hated that Olympian bitch for her selfishness. His only prayer now was that Artemis would one day lose something she held as dear to her as he held his children.

"Baba!" Archimedes whined as he held his stomach and dry heaved. "It hurts so much!"

"I know, *m'gios.*" He kissed his son's brow and rocked him in an effort to soothe his pain. "Just breathe."

Theodorus didn't say a word as he buried his little face in the folds of Stryker's cloak and cried harder. Likewise, his twins, Alkimos and Telamon, whimpered and moaned. Their matching curls were damp and tangled with sweat as they held on to him for dear life.

Hellen's features turned as pale as her hair. "They're cursed, too, aren't they?"

Stryker's gaze fell to his toddler daughter, who was an exact copy of her beautiful mother. Sick to his own stomach, he nodded as he watched Dyana's pale eyes turn dark, and his sons' teeth elongated into pairs of fangs like the ones he'd grown just hours before.

Since the children had gone the whole day without mutating, and because his wife was Greek and didn't share his Atlantean blood, Stryker had assumed his father had spared his grandchildren from the curse. How stupid of him to think for one minute that his father would actually care.

Hellen let out a soul-deep wail as she realized that their children would never again be allowed to see the light of day without it killing them.

Or eat a bite of real food.

That Stryker would leave her a widow in only six years, and that she would be reduced to begging in the street for a mercy no one would give. Because he was cursed by the gods, and she was the mother of his half-bred spawn, everyone would hate her. The Apollites because she was Greek, and the Greeks because she'd married an Apollite and bred with him. People were ever cruel. They both knew that well.

For the first time ever, Hellen glared at him with fury in her pale blue eyes. "Why did your mother have to send out her soldiers to slaughter Ryssa and her son?"

"Because my father's an unfaithful, horny idiot!" And Apollo couldn't take five seconds to tell Queen Xura that Stryker was alive and well, and being raised in Greece by his priestesses. Rather Apollo had left Xura to believe that Stryker had been slaughtered by the gods because they feared he might be the prophesied infant of the goddess Apollymi, who was destined to overthrow their pantheon. Hence the reason Xura was so jealous that Ryssa's son had been allowed to live after hers had been "killed."

Leave it to Stryker to have two such unreasonable parents. His mother's answer to jealousy hadn't been to simply kill Ryssa and be done with her. On no, it'd been to tear her and her son into pieces. And his father hadn't been content to just kill Xura and her soldiers in retaliation.

Nay, never something so simple as that.

The god of moderation had lost his mind and struck out at the entire Apollite race as if they'd all been guilty of the slaughter. And once such a curse was spoken, there was no way to undo it.

Ever. As Stryker had quickly learned, as every god and priest had concurred.

Apollo's word was final.

"We're damned," Stryker whispered under his breath. No one would help him. While he'd never deluded himself into thinking for a moment that he was surrounded by anyone other than a bunch of selfish assholes, this more than confirmed it.

Everyone was out for themselves. They were only his friends until he turned the other way. They took what they could grab and left, and quickly forgot what they owed him. What he'd done for them.

His head swam from the horror of it all as he glanced to Hellen's swollen belly. She would birth him another son any minute now. With his own Apollite powers he could feel the strength of the boy's soul stirring.

A cursed child.

And that made his anger ignite to a dangerous level.

Fuck this! His indignant rage renewed its venom. "I won't let this happen!"

Whatever it took, he would save his children.

Hellen looked up at him. "What are you saying?"

Stryker handed his sons over to their mother. "I'll be back."

Her jaw went slack. "The sun's dawning. Where are you going?"

"To find a way out of this nightmare."

She shook her head as her skin paled even more. "But—"

Stryker ignored the hysteria in her voice and kept walking. Contrary to what she thought, he wasn't headed for suicide.

Earlier, he'd tried all the Greek gods he knew. Even though he was family, they'd all turned him away by saying there was nothing to be done.

Yet through it all, one other had called out to him. Assuming hers was a vengeance cry, he'd ignored her call out of fear. It had to be a retaliatory trap. After all, why would she help him when his own family refused to?

Her lust for his head was reasonable. His father's pantheon had destroyed hers and cursed her people to die. It only made sense that she'd want to destroy Apollo's son to get back at the god. She had no way of knowing that Stryker was hated and despised by his father.

But now everything was different. And he was desperate enough to take the gamble that she might be willing to do something while the others ignored his fate.

This was the best hope he had.

The only hope, really.

And he had nowhere else to go.

No one wanted him. No one cared.

I'm alone in this world.

Then again, aren't we all?

Making sure to stay to the shadows and out of the daylight, he picked his way through the lush island home he'd once loved. Now he hated it for its alliance to his father. But he was grateful that at one time, it'd belonged to the Atlanteans before the Greeks had conquered this paradise and taken it from them. Because today, he needed that connection to the prior gods.

Not that there was much left. Most of their old buildings and temples had been destroyed—burned to the ground during battle and afterward as a show of Greek might.

All except for one village that not even Apollo had dared to touch.

Apollymia.

Said to have been under the protection of the great Apollymi. The goddess of destruction was so revered and terrifying that the fearful Greeks had allowed nature to reclaim her beloved village. Because everyone, god and human alike, feared the goddess so. Even after she'd been defeated, not one piece of the village had been pillaged or plundered. Left completely untouched, it lay like a time capsule, completely empty as it'd been the day the Greeks had arrived and the Atlanteans had abandoned it.

Sadly, time had been unkind to the structures that had caved in or that were overgrown with weeds and brush.

As a boy, Stryker used to run and play through the ruins here, seeking some connection to his mother and her people, aching to know something of that side of his blood.

One day while exploring, he'd discovered a forgotten temple of the goddess who'd once protected this place. For reasons he still didn't know, he'd come here to sit and talk to the goddess who ignored him as much as his father. Yet even as a boy, he couldn't help wondering what the island people had done to cause Apollymi to abandon them so. Had it been hubris? Neglect?

Or simple divine capriciousness that caused her to turn her back on her people?

When it came to Apollo, it took nothing to make him abandon those who worshiped him.

Stryker hoped that wasn't the case with Apollymi. *Please be better than my father . . .*

Terrified she wasn't, Stryker prayed even harder that her summons wasn't a trap. That maybe, against all odds, she would come to his aid in spite of how the others had treated him. Surely, the Atlantean goddess of destruction hated his father as much as he did . . .

Her hatred of the Greeks was legendary.

Stryker had barely reached the ornate gold-covered doors of the old temple before the sun began scorching him.

His legs burning, he shoved at the doors that protested his entrance with stubborn defiance that seemed determined to have him combust on the doorstep. Their rusted hinges creaked mightily from all the decades of disuse, neglect, and decay. But he wasn't about to let them win this. Even more stubborn than the doors, he pushed harder until they gave way, then rushed into the soothing darkness that succored his ravaged eyes and blistering flesh.

Breathless, he used his cloak to put out his smoldering skin that bubbled and boiled. He hissed at the bleeding, festering wounds on his legs that would no doubt leave vicious scars. So be it. He'd heal.

Grimacing in pain, he cursed his father again and wished the bastard dead a thousand times over.

"May you roast in Tartarus, you rat turd!" His voice echoed, sending several birds into flight and other animals he didn't want to think about scurrying for cover.

Disgusted, Stryker glanced about the decaying mess. It was even worse than it'd been the last time he'd ventured here years ago. The cobwebs were so thick now, they hung like hollowed-out curtains from one column to the next. No vessel or burner remained intact. Nor statue. The once pristine marble lay like crumbs on the earthen floor. Even the main statue in the center of the temple where Apollymi's worshipers had gathered to pay homage to her had been cracked to such a state that Apollymi held no arms, or crown.

Her once beautiful face was contorted into a condemning sneer, yet remained intense and terrifying. Her mercury eyes seared in the dim light.

Truly, the goddess of destruction had long ago abandoned this place and not looked back.

Damn it!

Not that it mattered. He couldn't go home until nightfall. So he might as well attempt this. Not like he had anything else to lose, other than six more years of misery.

Praying for a miracle he doubted would ever come, Stryker headed for the broken altar that stood at the foot of the broken statue where the goddess sat upon an ebony throne made of skulls and roses. With eyes of chipped silver, she stared down at him as if she could see straight through his very soul.

Maybe she could.

Since Stryker was born of a god and had visited them many

times over the years, he'd never been nervous in the presence of divinity before. Yet something about this one made him extremely uneasy. Perhaps it was her ruthless reputation.

Or something more. A sense of foreboding that said her reputation wasn't one of boasting, like his father's. That hers was actually understated.

Either way, he swallowed hard as he lifted his arms to invoke her.

"Apollymi Magosa Fonia Kataastreifa ... " He cut open his forearm and made a blood offering on her altar to let her know that he was most serious in this matter. "If you can hear me, my goddess. I have come in answer to your summons, and I implore your divine aid. Please, akra ... I need you and I offer you my life, my soul, and my sword. For all eternity."

Nothing happened.

Why should it?

He was half Greek and her enemy. For centuries, his people had warred against hers. Why should an Atlantean goddess care what happened to him and his children when his own father didn't?

You knew this was bullshit. You shouldn't have bothered.

Disgusted that he'd ever believed for a moment that someone, anyone, would help, he started for the doors, intending to try to find a way home again.

"Why did you wait to come here, son of Apollo?"

Stryker froze at the sound of a fierce, yet melodic voice. One that sent shivers over him.

As he began to turn back toward the statue, the temple doors flew open. A fierce wind plastered his clothes against his body and forced him to grab the column at his side to keep from being blown outside into the deadly rays of the sun. Out of the dark shadows appeared the outline of a tall, graceful woman.

One with glowing eyes made of swirling silver. They were filled with a fury that matched the rage in his own heart.

Ribbons of white-blond hair twisted around her body as if they had a life of their own. She appeared wild and fierce in a ghost, wraith form, the very epitome of the ruthless goddess she was purported to be.

"Goddess Apollymi?"

She curled her lips. "You think another would dare step her foot inside my temple and dare my wrath?"

Given her temperament? Only if they were profoundly stupid.

"Now answer my question, Greek dog!"

Stryker met her gaze levelly, knowing that this particular goddess couldn't abide cowardice in any form. "I delayed because I thought you were asking me here to kill me. And I apologize profusely, akra, if that was an incorrect assumption. Now, I've come to ask your guidance and benediction. I throw myself on your mercy."

She laughed. It rolled through her temple like thunder and caused part of the ceiling to crash down around him, threatening his life with more daylight as it streaked ever closer to his body.

But he was desperate enough to pay it no heed. "Please, akra. I come here to beg vengeance against my father."

Her laughter died instantly. "Why should I believe you?"

"Because I'm also the son of the Atlantean queen he slaughtered."

"You never knew Xura. Your father took you from her womb before you were born, and you were raised in Greece among his priestesses. Why should you have loyalty to your mother or to me?"

Stryker flinched at the truth. But there was a lot more to it than that. His childhood had never been happy. In truth, it'd been bitter and miserable. One he held against his father and hated him for. "Among women who lived in terror of my father and his capricious moods, and who had no love of me because of him. Only fear that I might prove no better a man than what sired me. I assure you, akra, I hold no loyalty to any of them. They never brought me anything other than heartbreak and misery."

The wind settled down as she raked a suspicious glare over his body. She swept him from head to toe as if trying to gain insight to his character. "You come to me with an offer of loyalty while telling me that you're loyal to none?"

She was right. He'd never given it to anyone. The closest he'd ever come was Zephyra. His first wife had been the one he'd intended to die beside. To this day, he owed his fealty solely to her.

But his father had seen to it that he'd had no other choice than to let her go. More to the point, that Stryker had been forced to make Phyra hate him forever.

"I freely admit that I'm worthless, akra." Stryker drew a ragged breath at a truth he didn't want to face. "In all honesty, I care nothing for myself or anyone else ... except for my children. They're all I have that I value."

He prayed that she saw the truth of his heart in his eyes. "And my father has damned them. I beg you, please spare them, and I will do *anything* you ask me. And I mean anything at all. Take my life. My soul. Whatever it is you ask, I will do without hesitation. Just don't let them die. Not like this. Not for something they took no part in. Again, I beg you, akra. And I have never begged for anything. Not from anyone."

"And that is why I called to you, Strykerius. I knew we could come to an accord. That our hatred for Apollo would be enough to bind us."

With a sweeping grace, she crossed the room so that she could stand before him. There was a light that shone from her so bright that it was almost blinding to his Apollite eyes, and it forced him to lift his hand up to shield them.

Her ghostly fingers cupped his chin. "Aye, Strykerius. I can show you how to live past Apollo's decree and thwart his curse. But the cure is ofttimes worse than the malady. However, if you are brave enough, and can suffer the taste of it, you and your children will have life eternal. Walk by my side and serve me, and I will show you how to claim the entire world. Together, we will rebuild what they've destroyed. Fight with me and the world shall belong to the Atlantean gods once more, and the Greeks will choke to death on *our* wrath."

The hairs on the back of his neck prickled at her words. Bargains with the gods never worked out well for the weaker party. He knew that better than anyone.

Yet for his children, he would barter with the darkest powers in existence.

Apollymi.

"I will do as you say, akra"—he made sure to use the Atlantean word for "lady and mistress" to placate her ego—"Forever."

A warm smile curved her lips as she manifested a beautiful golden chalice. With one long black nail, she cut open her wrist and bled into it, then offered it to him. "Drink, *m'gios*. If you dare. And I shall reveal my realm to you. There you and your children and people can live where the daylight will never again harm you. From this day forward, you shall be as my son. A member of my pantheon, and an Atlantean god. I will show you the key to Apollo's destruction, and together we will make your father pay and you will regain everything he took from you."

Stryker wrapped his cold hand around her cup and nodded. "Here's to the future. May it rain nothing save the blood of the gods and humanity for all eternity."

June 29, 9527 BC

Apollymi froze as she heard Strykerius's panicked voice shouting for her aid. Throughout her despised Kalosis hell realm, all was quiet instead of the loud celebration that had been taking place only moments before.

For days now, the remnants of the Apollite race who'd agreed to join Strykerius for their war on humanity had descended here to pick out homes and start new lives in this realm where Apollo's deadly sunlight could never reach them.

As they settled in, Strykerius had been busy with the birth of his twin sons—the first Apollites born after their grandfather's curse.

Now something was terribly wrong.

She flashed herself to Strykerius's side where he and his wife had taken up residence in the smaller temple next to hers. Hellen lay in their bed, still too weak to stand after birthing her sons.

While his wife held one infant in her arms, Strykerius stood to the side with Urian—the baby that Apollymi had ripped from Bethany and placed in Hellen's womb so that the Greek whore could birth him without anyone else knowing. It was a secret Apollymi intended to keep to herself forever.

Yet by the stern frown on Strykerius's face, Apollymi knew something had gone wrong with the child she'd hand-chosen to be her vengeance upon the world.

"What is it?"

His face ashen, Strykerius drew a ragged breath. "We're losing my son."

The grief in his voice tugged at her heart, and that caused her fury to rise. Urian would *not* die. Apollymi had made a vow to that.

Before she could rethink her actions, she took the baby from his hands. He was much smaller than the other infant they'd named Paris. Because of the disaster that had come from her combining Apostolos's life force with Styxx's, Apollymi had refused to do that with Paris and Urian—she would never again make *that* mistake. Instead, she'd bonded Urian to Paris's and Strykerius's DNA only enough to mask the baby's origins, never knowing that Apollo would be cursing them just hours later when she did so.

Sadly, prophecy and foresight weren't among her powers.

Yet now that she stared down at the infant who struggled to live, she wondered if she'd made a grave mistake in not tying his life force to that of his twin brother.

For Strykerius was right. Unlike Paris, Urian wasn't thriving.

She glanced over to his brother, who was pushing away from his mother's breast and fussing about it. An odd thought occurred to her. "How much has he eaten?"

"Nothing." Hellen choked on a sob. "Neither has Paris. They both refuse to suckle."

Apollymi wanted to curse the woman's stupidity. But then, she was a Greek. Intelligence from her was too much to hope for. "They don't want your milk, *human*," she spat at her.

She lifted her index finger to her lips and bit the tip until she broke the skin. Then she placed it into Urian's mouth.

He opened his dark eyes and quickly began to suckle her fingertip as he quieted down. Color returned to his skin.

Apollymi let out a relieved breath. She was right.

Apollo was a bastard.

Grateful that she'd saved this child, Apollymi withdrew her finger before her blood mutated the babe further. As it was, it turned his dark eyes to blue.

Relieved that his life was spared, she handed him to Strykerius. "He needs Apollite blood to drink. They both do. Because of the curse, they can't suckle the breast milk of a human mother."

Strykerius sighed in gratitude. "I hadn't thought of that. Thank you, akra."

She inclined her head to him. "Tell the others with newborns.

Most likely they will all need blood with their mother's milk, even if their mothers are Apollites. No doubt your father intended for the infants to die off."

Apollo was a heartless prick like that.

Tears swam in Apollymi's eyes as she remembered the way she'd found her own son . . .

Gutted by Apollo's callous hand. Dumped into the sea for the beasts to feast upon.

She clamped her teeth together to keep from screaming as the need for vengeance rose up and demanded she rip out Apollo's heart and devour it. Something that would damn the very world into oblivion. And she would gladly see it burn. Gladly rip down every god in existence. That would be the only thing that would placate this pain in her heart.

Utter destruction.

Patience, dear Braith. Patience. Akou aimassorai, ni aday-akopa'ia—*Though I am the one bleeding, I will not be broken.*

Anekico ler aracnia—*Victory to the spider.*

The one good thing to come from Apollo's curse was that the Apollites aged much faster than humans now. It wouldn't take Urian eighteen to twenty years to reach maturity.

He'd be there in only ten.

Then he would be ready to train for war and she could send him after her enemy.

One day, Urian would bring her the head of Apollo.

And return her sons to her, as well.

August 9, 9524 BC

"Can you see it? Is it there? Can you see the sunlight, Urian?"

His heart thumping with nervous anticipation, Urian grimaced at the brightness. Holding his breath, he peeked around the corner of the crevice where he and his twin brother were hidden by the deep, dark shadows that had protected them all their young lives. Against all rules and dictates, and dire consequences and threats, they'd snuck out from the portal hours ago and had waited for the dawn to come.

Now it was upon them and they couldn't wait to finally see what no Apollite their age or younger had ever seen before.

The sun!

"I think so, Paris." Urian's heart rate picked up its pace as he smiled in eager anticipation. All his life, he'd dreamed of this moment.

Seeing daylight!

Just once. He could only dream of its warmth. The brightness. The glowing magick of it. They all tried to imagine what it was like. Their parents had tried to explain it, but it wasn't the same as actually experiencing it for himself.

A simple thing, really, when one thought about it. Humans saw it all the time. Even cockroaches and rodents. But for those like him and Paris, those born to the Apollite race, it was forbidden.

Now they were on a tantalizing quest. To discover this unknown secret that humans possessed.

Urian had to know what it was.

Even if his father beat him black and blue for defying their laws, it would be worth every blow.

"What's it look like?"

"Golden." Like Paris's hair.

Even though they were twins, they weren't identical. Urian's hair was colorless white, while his brother held the enviable shade that others preferred and often remarked upon as perfection.

The only thing Urian was perfect at was finding trouble.

And he found that a lot.

"Strange."

"What is, Uri?"

"The sun," he mumbled.

"How so?"

For one thing, it was much smaller than he'd thought. Screwing his face up, he tilted his head to study it with a stern frown. "It seems to be moving. Coming closer."

Too close, he realized with an alarmed gasp.

"How so?"

Ah, crap! *That's not the sun!* Panicking, Urian squeaked and turned toward Paris only to discover they had nowhere to run for safety.

"Uri?"

He clamped his hand over Paris's mouth and dragged him tight against the wall to hold him there.

"Paris! Urian!"

He winced at his father's deep, guttural growl. Aye, he knew *that* tone well. As did Paris. It was so fierce and angry that it caused his brother to instantly wet himself.

And Urian's leg in the process.

Disgusted, he shoved Paris away out of habit. Only to remember too late why he'd been holding him to begin with.

Urian silently cursed both their stupidities.

"There you are!" His father's steps headed straight for them. "Where's your brother?"

Paris instantly pointed in his direction and outed him. Faithless turd! Unlike his best friend Davyn, Paris had never held any loyalty whatsoever. He'd turn in anyone to save his own skin.

Growling low in the back of his throat, their father handed Paris off to Trates, his second-in-command, before he snatched Urian out of his spot so that he could glare down at him with a glower that had set even their fiercest warriors fleeing in terror. And who could blame them? Almost seven feet tall, Strykerius was a massive, muscular beast of a male. The son of the god Apollo, he held even more powers than the rest of their cursed race. And while all Apollites and Daimons were born fair-haired, his father had chosen to dye his long locks jet black. Something that made him appear even more sinister and lethal than all the others combined.

But Urian was braver than most. Lifting his chin, he faced his father in spite of his fear and blinked slowly. He kept his hands at his sides, clutched into fists, even though he knew his spanking was imminent.

"You know I'm going to beat you for this transgression."

Urian nodded. "I expected no less."

"Three lashes for every year you've lived."

"I'll survive nine strokes."

"From Trates."

Fierce and loyal, Trates never hesitated at anything his father asked of him. Urian knew those lashes would hurt, yet they would cut him as much as they did Urian, for Trates couldn't stand harming a child. That weakness was something his father hated about his second, and it was one he tried constantly to strip out of his soldier.

Urian couldn't stand the thought of harming Trates for something that had been his bad idea. It wasn't fair that they both should suffer. "From Xedrix."

His father's jaw dropped. "The Charonte demon?"

Urian nodded. "He won't pull back from the punishment. It's what you want, is it not?"

That set his father back and caused his jaw to drop even more. "By the gods, you are a cheeky little bastard, aren't you?"

"Cut from the same cloth as my baba ... at least it's what Mata tells me."

One corner of his father's lips curved upward in wry amusement as his anger seemed to flee. "At least I know that's not *your* piss on your leg. ... Paris's?"

"I'd rather not say, Baba."

His father narrowed his eyes, then lifted him up into his arms. "I should beat you for what you've done. You could have been killed!"

"I just wanted to see the sunlight."

"And I want to see my sons grow to be men, Uri. Do you understand?"

He nodded.

Fisting his hand in his hair, his father held him against his chest so tightly that it actually hurt. "Baba! Pain! Pain!"

His father let out a fierce sigh. "You don't know what real pain is, Urian. And I pray to the gods that you never do. You've no idea what horrors await you in this world. Terrible things I can't protect you from."

Urian placed his hand to his father's bearded cheek. "Don't worry, Baba. I'll keep you safe from them."

His father laughed. "I believe you will." Then his features turned stern and his eyes red as anger darkened his brow. "But you are *never* to venture near sunlight again. Do you hear me?"

"Yes, akri." He switched to the Atlantean term for "lord and master" that he'd learned from Xedrix and the other Charonte who shared Kalosis with them.

"Are you being sarcastic with me?"

Urian wrinkled his nose devilishly, knowing he'd been caught. "No, akri. Never."

His father growled and squeezed him. "Oh, you little scamp!" He set him down on his feet. "Off with you! Get cleaned up and head to bed!"

"Okies." Urian ran through the portal that took him back to the central hall in Kalosis where they lived, and where his father normally sat, waiting for any strays who might venture into their realm. The dark hall was completely empty and eerily quiet at this time of night. Which was a shame since he was starving because earlier his baba had been gone, and no one had wanted to feed him. They were all too afraid of his weird eyes. Only his baba didn't seem to mind the fact that Urian wasn't like other Apollites.

He should have asked to be fed ...

Oh well.

His stomach rumbling, Urian headed toward the hallway that led to his room.

"Urian?"

He froze at the stern, melodic voice he knew, but one they weren't supposed to ever speak to directly. That, too, was against the rules.

Yet no one had ever said what to do if the goddess spoke first. Surely it would be rude to ignore her ...

"Akra?"

Apollymi appeared in the hallway right in front of him. "Would you like to see sunlight?"

He bit his lip in indecision, unsure of what his father would say. He'd told him to go to bed. But he also said that they were to always obey their goddess ...

Smiling, she held her hand out toward him. "I promise this one won't hurt you, and you won't get into trouble for it. Come, child."

Too thrilled to say no, he ran to her and took her hand into his. She screwed her face up at the urine on his clothes. "Your brother is disgusting."

He wouldn't argue that, since Paris had a habit of wiping things on him that oft caused Urian to beat him.

As soon as her hand closed around his, he was clean and fresh again. "Thank you, akra!"

"You're very welcome." She led him through her halls to her dark garden and toward a pool in the back where black roses bloomed all around and scented the air with their crisp sweetness. Urian wasn't sure how they managed to grow in the darkness, but for some reason, those flowers thrived in the shadows.

Two of Apollymi's winged Charonte demons stood guard on each side of her magical marbled perch. Their beautiful brightly colored flesh made them appear inviting and kind, but he knew firsthand that those looks were very deceiving, as the Charonte were a vicious warrior race more prone to eating anyone or anything who came near them than striking up a friendly conversation.

Neither made a sound or a move as Urian and the goddess drew near the rippling pool of black water. If he didn't know how much they loved to eat stray little boys, he'd have thought the demons statues. But Urian was well versed in how much the Charonte lived to dine on wandering Apollites they found in places where the Apollites shouldn't venture in this domain, as his father had often threatened to feed him to one whenever he or his brothers misbehaved.

Even so, he sucked his breath in sharply at the beauty of them and the goddess's garden. "What is this place, akra?"

"My special looking glass. 'Tis a mirror where I can gaze out and see the world above and what happens in it."

"Oooo!" He leaned over and reached with one finger to touch the black water that ran backward up the stone wall instead of down, toward the pool. "How does it do that?"

Wrinkling her nose at him, she winked. "Magick!" she breathed.

He giggled.

With a kind smile, she took a seat on the marble at the side of the pool and motioned for him to join her.

Urian skipped to her side.

Reflected in the midnight ripples of the pool's water, he saw the deep sadness in her silver eyes as she looked down at him and brushed her hand through his straight hair. Hair that was as white as hers. "Why are you so sad, akra? Is it because I'm not as handsome as Paris?"

She pulled him into her lap. "Don't be silly, Urian. You're far more handsome than your brother could ever be."

"Not what others say."

"They're wrong."

He would argue that, but even he knew better than to argue with a powerful goddess who could kill him with a sneeze. "Then what hurts your heart?"

She brushed her hand across his cheek in a gentle caress that caused the Charonte demons beside them to stir in nervous alarm. "You remind me of a boy I once knew. He was curious like you and forever getting into trouble."

"Was he named Urian, too?"

"Nay." She touched him lightly on the nose. "He was named Monakribos. But I called him Kree."

Those were strange names. "What happened to Kree?"

A tear fell from her cheek where it turned into a bright diamond against her pale skin. Urian marveled at the sight of it. "He fell in love, Urian, and the gods killed him because they are cruel. You must promise me that you'll never fall in love. For love is a stupid, harmful emotion and it destroys everything it touches."

"That's what Baba says, too. He says that love makes people crazy and weak."

She nodded in agreement. "He's right. Your father is a very wise man."

"Then I shall never love."

"Good boy." Kissing his head, she leaned down to dip her hand into the black water of the pool so that she could stir it in a circle. "Now close your eyes, Urian, and think about the sun you want to see."

"But I don't know what it looks like."

"You don't have to. The pool knows your heart and it will find what you most desire, and show it to you."

Urian made a large O with his lips at the thought of something so incredulous. It was good to be a god and have such tools. And it was why he didn't understand why his grandfather had been so cruel as to curse them. How could anyone squander such gifts? He'd never understand how anyone could toss away things so precious.

And speaking of . . .

Closing his eyes, he did as the goddess instructed, then opened his eyes to see the rippling waves forming a beautiful landscape awash in vibrant colors the likes of which he'd never seen before.

They were unlike anything he'd ever imagined. Glorious! But the bright light hurt his eyes terribly.

He lifted his hand and squinted in pain. Tears swam in the corners as he tried his best to study every detail.

"*That's* the sun, Uri."

"It's blinding."

"It can be." She stirred the water again so that the light was less intense and he could see it better.

Urian lowered his hand. "Have you ever seen it, akra?"

"I have."

"Did you like it?"

She shrugged. "In truth, I thought nothing of it, one way or the other."

"Then do you miss it?"

Her sadness grew as she let out a ragged sigh. "It's not what I miss."

How could she not? "Then what?"

"You're too young to understand the pain that haunts me. Sadly, you won't always be and that saddens me most of all."

Urian didn't understand her grief, but it ran so deep that he felt it. Wanting to comfort her, he stood up on the edge of the pool, put his arms around her neck, and hugged her close.

Both of the Charonte stepped back.

Apollymi tensed at first and then held him tightly against her breast. She rubbed his back and laid her head against his shoulder. "Anytime you want to see the sun, you come to me, Urian, and I will show it to you."

"Okies. And anytime you need a hug, akra, you come to me and I will give you one." He pulled back to smile at her.

She cupped his face in her cold hands. "Your father's right, you are a scamp. And you shouldn't tell him about this."

That only confused him. "Why not?"

"He wouldn't like it. Best to keep our meetings a secret between us, okay?"

Urian nodded. "Okies."

She held her hand up. "We need to swear on this."

He spit on his hand. "Okies, akra."

She bit her palm until she was bleeding. "A blood oath is stronger than spit."

His stomach rumbled at the sight and smell.

She arched her brow at the sound. "Are you hungry?"

"Very."

Apollymi held her hand out for him. "Then go ahead and feed, Uri. That will be our bond. Let no one know of it. And you will be like Achilles. Made stronger than the others of your kind. Even though I'm not an Apollite, my blood can feed you. And it will keep you safer, until the day comes when you will repay me for it."

Urian was too hungry to think about what he did, but the moment he tasted her blood, he realized that he would never be the same ...

March 20, 9522 BC

My baba's dying . . .

Urian couldn't breathe or think as he ran through the darkness. Blinded by tears and pain, he wasn't even sure where he was headed as he sought an escape from the death that constantly stalked his people.

He didn't even know what had happened to his father. All he knew was that they'd brought him home a few minutes ago, barely alive. Everyone had been angry and screaming as they sought to stop his father from bleeding before he died of it.

So much blood . . .

He'd never seen his father weak before. Never seen him so pale and trembling. Even now, the image of Trates carrying his father through the door was seared into his mind.

How could the fierce and mighty Strykerius be unable to stand on his own?

And though he knew his parents didn't love each other, his mother had taken his father's bruised and bloodied hand and wept. That alone had told him how dire his father's condition was.

When Urian tried to see him, Archie had shoved him out of the room. "No one wants you here, Uri! Go away!"

The doctor had concurred. "You're underfoot, boy! Move!"

And so he'd run out the door, into the street. With no destination in mind, he'd just kept going. Now . . .

His lungs ached from the crisp chthonic air that kept them safe. The muscles of his legs protested his long sprint, while his grief choked him with a vicious grip that threatened his own life. Unable to deal with it all, he collapsed on the damp ground and gave vent to all his misery that screamed out in silent agony.

He couldn't lose his father. Not like this.

I love you, Baba!

Suddenly, something shifted near him in the darkness.

Urian sat up on the dark ground with a gasp and a hiccup. "Wh-wh-who's there?" he demanded, his authority undercut by his ragged tears.

Something warm brushed against his cheek so fast that he couldn't see it. He could only feel it swipe at his tears, like a warm, dry lick. And it left in its wake a glass figure in his lap. One placed there so gently that he barely felt the drop against his linen chiton.

Confused and baffled, Urian picked it up to see an image of a small soldier, perfectly formed. It was amazing. So real and detailed that he half expected the man to move. The hoplite even had a spear and shield.

Sniffing back his tears, he drew a ragged breath and wiped his eyes.

Do you feel better now?

Urian glanced around at the soft, sweet voice he heard in his head. "Who are you?"

I'm the guardian of the Atramentian Falls. You're not supposed to be here, you know. The goddess would punish us both if she knew you'd trespassed into her special sanctuary. I'm supposed to eat anyone who dares cross the dark borderlands.

Urian scowled at the worlds. *Eat?*

That piqued his curiosity immediately. "Are you one of the Charonte?" They had their own lands here in Kalosis where they didn't normally interact with his race, unless Apollymi was angry and set them loose as punishment. And while he couldn't quite remember which direction he'd run, he was rather certain he wouldn't have been so stupid as to head toward *their* section.

Only Paris and Theo were that dumb and suicidal. Urian always took care to give the demons a wide berth.

Nay, I'm not a Charonte.

He arched a brow at that. Not a Charonte?

What else was there?

Clutching his gift, Urian pushed himself to his feet so that he could peer into the shadows where he'd seen the movement earlier. "Are you a god?"

A soft, gentle laugh sounded in his head. *You shouldn't come any closer. Else you'll be afraid.*

Of what? "Why? Are you a monster?"

Indeed. Hence why I eat children who come into my domain.

More curious than ever, Urian glanced down at the soldier in his hand. Strange that a monster would give him a present while he'd been upset. It seemed incongruous and thoughtful for such a beast. "You must be a lonely monster, then."

Pardon?

Wiping his nose on the back of his hand, he drew another ragged breath. "Just that you don't seem scary, is all." Rather, she was nice.

He felt the air around him stir again.

I assure you, if you saw me you'd be quite terrified.

Urian snorted at the challenge. "Bet I wouldn't. Show yourself."

At first, he didn't think she'd meet his dare. Not until the brush in front of him began to shake.

And not just a little.

A lot.

An awful, *awful* lot. The ground beneath his feet shook so much that he was unbalanced by it. Just how big was this monster?

Urian wasn't sure what he'd expected, given her warnings. But it definitely wasn't the large, silvery-gold orange dragon in front of him.

"You're beautiful." Those words were out before he could stop them. After all, it might not be the smartest thing to call a dragon beautiful given that they liked to be thought of as fierce. Yet he couldn't help it. She was.

For that insult alone, she might eat him.

He swallowed hard as he waited for her anger to manifest.

Instead of being offended, she pulled back in surprise. *Beautiful? You think me pretty?*

"Well ... yes. Hasn't anyone ever told you that?"

She shook her head. *Are you not afraid of me?*

"Not particularly. But that's because my brother says that I don't have enough sense to be afraid of anything."

She laughed. *What's your name,* pido?

"Urian. And yours?"

Sarraxyn.

It was as beautiful as she was, and it sent another hot wave over him. He moved closer and held his hand out toward her. "Nice to meet you, Sarraxyn."

She reached out to brush against his skin.

Urian expected her scales to be cold and slimy. Yet they were surprisingly warm and soft. "You smell like lilies."

You are a cheeky one, aren't you?

"That's what everyone tells me."

Her black wings twitched as if she were silently laughing. *You'd best be on your way, Urian.*

Too bad he didn't want to. He'd rather stay and talk to her. But he was smart enough to know better than to stay where he wasn't wanted. "Very well, but thank you for my gift."

You're most welcome, Lord Urian, and have no fear. Your father won't die tonight.

He gasped at her words. "What?"

She inclined her head to him. *Part of what I guard is the goddess's sacred tree of life. She already sent Xedrix here to fetch sap to save your father's life. By the time you return, he should be much improved.*

With a cry of relief, Urian launched himself at Sarraxyn and hugged her. "Thank you!" He gave her a tight, giant squeeze before he ran off to check on his father.

Only he didn't go far. After a few steps, he came rushing back to her. "You're not a monster, Sarraxyn. You're beautiful!" With a quick kiss to her scaly cheek and a shout of happiness, he dodged away.

Sarraxyn watched in baffled awe as the Apollite ran off. Her jaw slack over his actions, she waited until he was out of sight to return to her human form. Still, the warmth of his hug and kiss clung to her skin.

No one had ever shown her such affection before. No one.

Few had ever been kind. Only a small handful of her brothers—Falcyn, Max, Illarion, Hadyn, and Gadryn.

In fact, it'd been her own brother, the bastard Malstrom, who'd sold her to the Atlantean war god, Misos, to serve here in his realm. The last thing she'd ever wanted was to be enslaved as an eternal guardian for the sacred Haxyn where she wasn't allowed to see anyone or do anything other than rot in absolute loneliness.

She hated this dark, dank realm of eternal night. While dragons were supposed to be solitary, she wasn't quite the same as others of her ilk. Most females weren't. They were more social than the males of her species. And she more so than even the average female drakos.

To be enslaved here without family or friend made this more of a hell realm than it already was. Damn the Atlanteans for their cruelty.

The Charonte were the only visitors she ever had, and they came rarely. Maybe once every century.

Urian had been the first "human" she'd seen since . . .

She couldn't remember. That was how long it'd been. And she couldn't remember a more fair, handsome one.

Like her, he appeared young. Though she wasn't really sure how Apollites aged. He could be older than dirt, for all she knew. Like some of the gods who appeared as children, even though they were thousands of years old.

It was why she preferred to live her days as a dragon. In that form, no one knew she was just a girl. Plus, as a dragon, she was a lot stronger, which was much safer for her as she was less likely to get eaten by something larger or meaner.

Her brother Veles had drilled that into her with iron spikes. *Whatever you do, Xyn, remain a drakoma! They can't harm you easily. Stay strong. Above all, stay alive!*

'Course, Veles hated his human form. Just as he hated all humans.

And everyone else, too. Especially the gods who'd cursed them and their mothers.

Normally, Xyn agreed with her brother. She didn't care for others herself. They were too quick to betray. Quicker still to strike the first blow, and she had no time for that.

But Urian had been a nice, brief distraction from her boredom and loneliness. Seldom did anyone or anything venture here. Not even a cockroach.

Sighing, she shifted back to her alternate body before the goddess happened to spy upon her and catch her away from her post. That would never do.

Apollymi was a terrible mistress. Demanding and fierce. Ever harsh whenever she felt someone was slacking. And in particular she seemed to hold a grudge against Xyn.

Yet this time, Xyn had something more to do than count the pebbles lining the ground around the base of her tree. She had a handsome, fair-haired boy to think about.

One with vivid blue eyes and a beautiful smile.

"Don't eat the boy! While tasty, he won't be worth the indigestion. And he's probably gamey-tasting, too."

Xyn had to force herself not to laugh at Urian's bold and outrageous declaration in the still darkness. She'd sensed him the instant he'd returned to her grove. There was no mistaking that unique scent of leather and male. It had filled her nostrils the moment he came near her lair.

That was the beauty of her kind. Nothing and no one could hide from them. And it was also their curse given the propensity of many humans to avoid a regular bathing routine.

However, this particular male smelled delectable. He made her want to nuzzle him ... which would probably terrify him if he knew that.

Just as it did her. So instead, she wrinkled her nose and headed through the thick copse of trees to see what it was he wanted with her.

Xyn froze as soon as she caught sight of him in the small clearing, holding what appeared to be a rather large crystal. Had he stolen it?

What did you do?

Setting it down, he shrugged. "Do you know how hard it is to find a gift for a dragon?"

No. We're quite easy. We eat anything smaller than us. That tends to leave a lot.

Her flippant comment made him nervous. "Oh ... well." He cleared his throat as he gestured toward the crystal. "Um, I didn't go there with my shopping. In my experience, parents tend to get a little cranky if you try to steal their children and use them as sweetmeats for dragons." Scratching at his neck, he hastened to the large crystal near him. "But I asked around and the elders all said that dragons like shiny things, so I found you this."

He struggled to carry it closer to her.

Xyn smiled. *It's lovely. Thank you!*

"You're welcome. It was the least I could do since you saved my solren."

Warmth spread through her at his thoughtfulness. It was remarkably kind. And even more rare. *It was my pleasure ... for once.*

He paused in his struggle to grimace at her. "What do you mean?"

Just that I normally don't care for the people I help. Yet for you, I'm glad I was able to do something.

"Ah." There was a peculiar note in his voice. "So I was right. You are lonely here, aren't you?"

She wanted to deny it. But what was the use? The truth was apparent to even the most dense. And it wasn't like she had so many to speak to about it, anyway.

Aye. Terribly.

Urian leaned against his gift and sighed in the most adorable fashion. Perhaps it was her loneliness speaking, but she found him absolutely enchanting. And gorgeous.

Worse was the peculiar desire she had to be human around him. To take his hand and stand uncommonly close. She'd never had such a desire before. But she wanted him to look at her the way the men looked at the women they hungered for.

That was something that could be deadly to them both, as the goddess would never allow her to fraternize with anyone.

"Can I tell you a secret?"

Xyn forced her thoughts to return to a more reasonable, and much safer topic. *Sure.*

Glancing around as if afraid someone might hear him, Urian stepped closer to speak in a soft whisper. "I'm lonely, too. A lot." He pressed his lips together. "Do you think it might be okay if I come and visit you sometimes so that we can be lonely together?"

She bit back a laugh at his words. He was so unbelievably

charming and hilarious. And though she should send him on his way, she couldn't quite bear the thought of not seeing him again.

So she made a very bad decision that she prayed she wouldn't one day regret. *We'd have to be careful not to get caught. The goddess would be terribly upset if she learned I was allowing someone near her tree, or her waters.*

"What do you suggest, then?"

Xyn hesitated. This was a bad idea. She knew it with every part of her being. And yet she couldn't stop herself. Was it honestly that bad that she wanted a friend?

Didn't she deserve to have someone? Anyone?

Before she could stop herself, she spoke words she prayed wouldn't come back to harm either of them. *You can come on Áreos when the goddess is in mourning for her son. No one disturbs her during that time, and she never ventures out. All is silent in the land.*

Neither of them should ever get caught then. It was the one day of the week when Apollymi kept to her schedule and held it sacred. Nobody dared to disturb her on that holy day.

Urian nodded. "Hesperus Hour." Like the day, that hour was the most sacred time when the goddess would tolerate no interruption on pain of death.

Not even Stryker would dare to encroach on it.

We can visit then and none will be the wiser.

Urian's smile lightened her mood instantly. "I'll see you then, my dragon."

Happier than she had a right to be, and to a level that actually scared her, she didn't speak as she watched him run away.

I'll see you, my friend.

But in her heart, she had a terrified feeling that this wasn't going to end well for either of them.

June 19, 9516 BC

"She'll be a beautiful bride."

"Don't make me rip out your throat, Trates."

Urian choked on his laughter as he saw the raw fear his father's wry threat wrung from Trates, who quickly excused himself so that he could put as much distance between himself and Stryker as possible. Not that he blamed him. His father was in a rotten mood, and had been for the last few days since Tannis had announced her intentions of tying herself to a worthless bit of Apollite trash.

In fact, no one wanted Tannis to marry Erol. Especially their father, and this engagement party was thoroughly pissing off everyone.

Even though she was a full-grown woman who was fully developed thanks to their Apollite curse that had her appearing the same age as a human in her late teens or early twenties, she was still only twelve years old.

As her father, Stryker couldn't get past her real age, and the fact that had they not been cursed, he would still have a few more years with her at home. Which was why he was insisting on a long engagement. Something that had left his daughter, her future groom, and Tannis's future in-laws complaining.

Aside from their father, Urian and his mother seemed to be the only two who agreed about the long engagement. But then Urian hated Erol. He was a massive beast of an arrogant bastard, and they had a long history of fighting between them.

Then again, Urian had a long history of fighting with most everyone.

His mother sighed as she hugged Urian's arm. "I can't believe I'm losing another baby so soon."

"I'm sorry, Mata." He jerked his chin toward his father, who was sharpening a knife while glaring at Erol. "Though I'm thinking if Solren has his way, there won't be a wedding. Maybe just a wedding feast ... "

She laughed. "There are times when I simply adore your solren, Uri." Patting his arm, she stepped away as if she knew her human blood tempted him in spite of his deep love and respect for her. She adjusted her cloak higher around her neck. "So ... who here has *your* fancy?"

Urian felt the color rising in his cheeks at a question he always dreaded. Especially since it made his stomach rumble from hunger. It seemed ever his destiny to starve. Even though he was in a room full of walking meals. But there wasn't anyone here who would feed him.

"Haven't found anyone yet."

"You're still not being fed?"

He didn't miss the note of panicked fear underlying her question. It was a secret he and his father had intentionally been keeping from her ... and everyone else. The fact that his father had a handful of loyal men he forced to bleed so that he could bring their blood to Urian in bladders or cups. While it wasn't the same as eating the way Apollo intended Apollites to feed, it kept Urian from starving to death.

The one advantage to it was that it left him a bit edgier than the others.

Leaner and meaner, as the humans would say. Because he was perpetually hungry, his senses were sharper. His powers stronger—more focused. And he was always angry and looking for a fight.

Except where his mother and sister were concerned. And of course the goddess. But that was simply because he knew Apollymi would rip out his throat if he ever showed his temper around her.

Luckily, Tannis called his mother away at that moment and saved him from having to answer as his sister took her home for the small meal she'd prepared for their mother to eat. Since their mother was the only one here who required food, Urian, Tannis, Paris, and Davyn took turns cooking meals for her.

Apollymi always made sure she had vegetables, fruits, and fresh meats. And they took it as a source of pride to make sure their mother was well cared for.

And protected from any threat.

Restless, Urian drifted through the crowd in the dark hall where many of their community had gathered to celebrate his sister's news and feed. Which meant the hall was quickly turning into an orgy, so parents were covering the eyes of their smaller children and rushing them home. No doubt that was really why Tannis had called their mother away. They were all careful to keep their human mother separate from any of their "parties." Aside from the fact that the way they ate tended to horrify her, as a non-Apollite she could easily find herself someone's prime course—and the witness to Urian's first massacre, as he was rabidly protective of his mother and sister to a frightening level. While his father might sharpen the knife, Urian was a little too quick to use it.

Another reason no one would feed him. His temper was quite legendary among their people already.

As were his powers.

Davyn staggered over to him. By the glazed and dazed appearance of his eyes, it was obvious he'd been feeding quite a bit already and was more than a little blood-drunk. Licking his fangs, he smiled as he draped himself against Urian's back and rested his chin on Urian's bare shoulder. Because they'd grown up together, he alone held no fear of Urian.

Or much of anyone else.

"Hey, brother Uri. Sure you don't want to join us?" His hand drifted a little too far south, toward the hem of Urian's short chiton.

Urian laughed as he extricated himself from Davyn's hug and sloppy grope. "You're a little too happy, Dav, and Paris doesn't share. Believe me, I know. I still have a bruise from the last time I hogged too much blanket. Given the ass-whipping I took from that, I'd hate to think what he'd do if he found his boyfriend draped all over me."

Davyn tsked. "I know you're hungry. Don't you get tired of drinking reheated blood? Wouldn't you like someone fresh to eat?"

His breathing turned ragged at an invitation that was extremely hard to say no to. Every part of him was attuned to the scent of Davyn's blood. To the hunger inside him to feed.

However . . .

I won't be an asshole.

Not to his brother.

And definitely not to Davyn, who would be horrified if he were sober. Davyn would *never* act like this if he weren't high from the bloodlust. Paris should have known better than to have fed him and left him alone to find his way home. It'd been a stupid thing for his brother to do. Davyn was too young and inexperienced to have been abandoned in a crowd where someone could easily prey on him.

"Tell you what, Davy. Let's find Paris, shall we?"

"Ooo, three of us, frolicking. Good idea. I like that even better!"

"Yeah." Urian draped Davyn's arm around his shoulders and led him through the crowd to hunt for his twin.

Yet the sight and smell of the others feeding while he was starving and this close to a willing donor . . . it was torture. And it made his stomach rumble with need. Not to mention, other parts of his body reacted with a disturbing hunger of their own that he didn't even want to contemplate.

"Where did you leave Paris?"

Davyn was almost unconscious.

Urian had to shake him awake. "Davyn! Where did you leave my brother?"

"In a room."

Oh, that was so unhelpful. Had Davyn been sober, Urian would have slapped him. Instead, he sighed in irritation. It was a good thing Davyn was the only friend he had or the temptation to gut him would have been harder to resist.

Unsure of how to best handle this, Urian decided to find his brother Theo, who had taken his wife and children home the moment the first set of clothing had started coming off. While Theo was far from prudish and had been known to participate in some of the most lascivious parties ever thrown—as had Theo's wife, Praxia, prior to their marriage—Theo's eldest child was a daughter and he was extremely protective of her virtue.

Not to mention, Theo's home was the closest to the hall so it made sense to head there first and start with him.

After Urian's insistent knocking, a barely dressed Theo answered the door with an annoyed frown. Given his brother's state of dishabille and the redness of his throat, Urian would say Theo had been in the midst of his own sexual encounter with Praxia.

Something further confirmed by the bite in Theo's bark when he growled at Urian. "What do you want?"

He blinked slowly, just for maximum annoyance as that was a moral imperative whenever dealing with one of his older siblings, then he spoke slowly, drawing out his words to again irritate his brother as much as possible. "Apollo's death. Apollite domination over the world of mankind, and an end to our curse. But at the moment, I'd settle for you returning your attitude to whatever asshole gave it to you, and finding Paris."

Urian caught Davyn as he began to slowly sink sideways to the floor and helped to right him. "Our good and thoughtful brother abandoned Davyn and vanished to who knows where, to do who knows whom. Can you lend us a hand and watch over Davyn while I try to find the stupid bastard?"

Davyn finally stopped trying to grope Urian long enough to scowl at them both. "I don't want to sleep with Theo, Uri. He's an asshole. Let's find Paris. He's very cuddly."

Urian passed a see-what-I-mean stare at his older brother.

That took the edge off Theo's anger. "How long has he been like this?"

"Since I found him."

Theo rolled his eyes at Urian's sarcasm. "And Paris left him in this condition?"

"You're making all *my* points, genius." Gah! Was he the only member of his family who possessed a functioning brain? There were times—like this—when Urian suspected he might be hoarding the only one capable of any semblance of reason in his whole sibling gene pool.

Smirking, Urian gave him a peeved glare. "Davyn's right. You are an asshole."

With a disgusted sneer, Theo grabbed Davyn by his chalmys and pulled him deeper into his home before he called out to his wife. "Prax? Get dressed. I need you to watch Davyn until we return."

"Where are you going?" she called from the other room. There was no missing the irritation in her shrill tone.

"Just do what I say, woman!"

Urian paused at the door. "You shouldn't talk to her like that. She's the mother of your children, you know." Not to mention, she put up with Theo when Urian couldn't imagine why.

"Mind your own business, Uri. This is my house and I'll run it as I see fit."

Oooh, leave it to Theo to default to the same cave logic that had made all of them resent their father. "And your solren would have your ass if he heard you speaking to your wife in that tone."

Theo's nostrils flared with anger as he pinned on his chalmys.

Ignoring his brother's anger and disgusted by his behavior, Urian looked past Theo to where Praxia was coming down the stairs to take over watch duty. "We're going to look for Paris. As soon as we find him, I'll bring Theo back."

Maybe not unbruised, especially if he kept lipping off, but . . .

"Thank you, Urimou."

Respectfully, he inclined his head to her, then made his exit.

As soon as they were outside Theo's house, Theo grabbed him and slammed Urian against the wall of his neighbor's home. "You ever do that again, and I'll—"

Urian punched him in the gut. "Don't threaten me, Theo. I'm not a child anymore."

Theo used his powers to knock him back and choke him.

With his own psychic blast, Urian broke his hold and struck out, letting his powers have full rein of his fury. He knocked Theo careening down the street without touching him.

Because his powers were so much stronger than anyone else's, Urian knew better than to put them on display. That was why this was the first time he'd ever fully unleashed them in front of anyone, other than Apollymi.

But he was too angry and hungry tonight for restraint.

And too late, he recovered his control and temper to realize that there were a lot of witnesses on the street tonight for his outburst. Too many who'd been coming and going from the celebration.

Shit. He turned around slowly to see the horrified stares that condemned him.

Always.

If anyone else had shown such massive power, they would have been applauded for it. Considered great and praised.

Not him. Nay, never the son with freakishly white hair born to Stryker and his *Greek* bride. The one with eyes unlike other Apollites. He was to be feared and ostracized for things he didn't do and couldn't help.

I really am born cursed.

This was no exception to his humiliation and misjudgments. Already, he could hear their whispers around him.

He's a freak!

How can anyone so young do that?

What's wrong with him?

I told you he was to be avoided! You see what he can do! It's unnatural!

Even when Urian tried to do the right thing, it always turned against him. Somehow he ended up on the wrong side of any matter in the eyes of their people. It never failed. They always judged him the bad guy.

Just like now.

They never saw the truth of him.

Everyone stared at him as if he should be punished, when

all he'd been trying to do was help his twin, Davyn, and his sister-in-law.

When will I learn?

He was the Anti-Midas. Everything he touched turned to shit, and the injustice of it burned raw in his belly.

If that weren't bad enough, he saw Paris among those wanting his head on a spike for the outburst—and Paris was completely fine, and standing with their brother Alkimos. *I should have known . . .*

No good deed goes unpunished.

"Urian? What is this?"

He cringed as his father appeared by his side.

Before he had a chance to answer, Theo pushed himself to his feet. "I was doing him a favor, Solren, and this is the thanks I get for it. He assaults me without reason."

Their father returned his attention to him. "Is this true, Urian?"

Urian glared at Theo. "I had my reasons."

That answer didn't sit well with his father, who cast them both a disgusted sneer for having brawled in the street like two common hoodlums and not the princes they were supposed to be. "Then elaborate."

Holding back his outrage, he gestured toward Theo. "You sired an asshole, Solren. I was trying to cull him down to a mere shit-for-brains."

"Urian!" his father growled.

He straightened his chalmys over his chiton with a nonchalance he definitely didn't feel, especially while the others continued to smear his semirespectable name. All Urian wanted was to leave while he could. To be left alone by everyone.

Instead, he forced himself to stand as if it didn't bother him at all. He'd never give them the satisfaction of knowing how much their condemnation scalded his heart and scarred his soul. "I took issue with the manner in which he spoke to me, and sought to teach him a more respectful tone. I've had it with his high-handed tactics and I refuse to be talked down to anymore, by him or anyone else."

Theo curled his lip. "You see, Solren! He's a recalcitrant brat. Instead of indulging his disrespect all the time, you need to be spanking his spoiled little ass."

Their father shook his head. "Nay, Urian's right. The world and people will treat you how you allow them to. I won't punish him for having the temerity to stand up to you, Theo. Especially when I know you have the ability to fight back and that you've never hesitated to strike him down whenever you think you've been slighted by him or anyone else."

Theo sputtered indignantly. Finally, he curled his lip as he raked a glare over Urian. "One day, Solren, you will regret the fact that you didn't keep a tighter leash on your favored pup. Mark my words. He's a rabid little bastard who's loyal to no one but himself."

Luckily, their father knew better. He passed a meaningful glance toward Theo's home. "Careful, *m'gios,* too often when confronted, we condemn ourselves in our anger. So think twice before you spew venom to taint your brother with the shadows of your own sin. For hate is a boomerang that once it's cast out has a nasty way of coming back to the one who threw it, and more oft than not, it cripples the hand that first unleashed it."

A tic started in Theo's jaw. "Fine. Coddle him. You always have. It's half of what's wrong with him." And with that, he headed home.

Yet the crowd remained. Staring, whispering.

Condemning.

Urian felt their judgment as if it were a living, breathing beast crawling all over his skin. And he deplored the sensation. Why couldn't he be more charming like Paris?

Everyone loved and adored his twin.

Yet it seemed the harder he tried to be liked, the less inclined they were to do so. So he'd given up trying and had just reconciled himself to their hatred and disparagement. To his sullen solitude. It was easier that way. Better to reject them before they had a chance to slap him down and risk this sick feeling he currently had in his stomach that churned it sour.

"Don't listen to him, Uri."

He barely caught himself before he rolled his eyes at his father's most commonly uttered phrase for these situations. Despite what his brothers thought, their father would backhand him if he showed any form of disrespect. Stryker wasn't known for his patience with anyone or for brooking any form of insubordination or insolence.

Especially not from his children.

"Aye, sir."

His father caught him roughly by the hair at the nape of his neck and forced him to look up until he met his gaze. There was a stern yet loving glow in those swirling silver eyes that now matched those of their goddess—a result of Apollymi's having saved his father's life that night when Urian had first met Sarraxyn after his father had almost died in a confrontation with Apollo. It was why his father couldn't feed him anymore. Not without it converting Urian not only to a Daimon like his father but also bonding their life forces together and allowing his father to see through his eyes. To know his thoughts and emotions. Because his father held the blood of two gods, it gave him a lot more power than any of the other Apollites or Daimons.

Truly his father was like no other.

And neither was Urian.

"You listen to me, *pido*, and take these words to heart. Damn them for what they think. For that is something you can *never* control or change. What you do have authority over is your own reaction to their spiteful words, and they have no value in your world unless you will it so. The only opinions that should ever matter to you are those of the people you love. The people *you* deem worthy of your concern. To the rest, close your ears and close your heart. Because if they don't care what damage they do to your life, then you don't care what damage you wreak to theirs. Blood to blood. Fang for fang. Remember, Urian, a smart man strikes the first blow, but it's the wise man who strikes the last one. Understand?"

"Aye, Solren."

He pulled him against his shoulder and hugged him close, then kissed his head. "I love you, *pido*," he growled deep against Urian's ear. "Don't you ever forget that."

Urian nodded as he clutched his fist in his father's cloak and held tight to him, grateful for his support.

With two powerful pats to his spine that left him bruised, his father released him and stepped back. "Now go. See to your business."

"Aye, sir." Urian headed for Paris and then slugged his brother so hard, it sent him straight to the ground.

"What the hades!" Paris sat up and rubbed at his jaw. "Have you lost your mind?"

Urian glared at him. "That's for being an asshole. Find Davyn and don't leave him again. Next time you're this stupid, I'll stab you for it, and take your boyfriend from you—you don't deserve someone as good and decent as Davyn if you're going to run off and abandon him when he's unable to fend for himself."

Paris pushed himself to his feet as Urian walked away. "I'm not the ass, Urian! You are!"

Without stopping, Urian scoffed. "You are wrong about that, *adelphos!* And you'd best make a sacrifice to the gods tonight that I don't decide to one day embrace the demon all of you think lives inside me. I promise you, the day I let that beast out . . . you will all be running for cover."

December 15, 9515 BC

"Baba! Do something! You can't let Matera go and leave us!"

Urian wanted to echo his sister's frantic words, and inside he was screaming just as loudly as Tannis's whining drone, but he knew better than to say a word of protest out loud. For one thing, he wasn't sure his father wouldn't knock him through a wall for it.

While Stryker could be a loving and doting father, he never tolerated that kind of nasal complaining from his sons. At least not from anyone other than Ophion. For some reason, Ophie got away with bitching.

The rest of them ...

I'm raising men, not boys. By the gods, you will be soldiers who do me proud. I will not stomach cowering dogs to represent my household in this world. I'll see you to Hades myself before you embarrass me like that!

It was a common Stryker tirade they all knew well.

So Urian stood with a ramrod spine as his mother kissed their cheeks with tears in her eyes. "It's for the best. Truly." She swallowed hard. "I dare not stay here any longer. Not as the sole human among the growing number of Daimons in Kalosis." She glanced nervously at their father.

Urian couldn't blame her, and it spoke volumes about how much she loved them that she'd stayed here as long as she had, given how many eyed her with hunger in their eyes. Their father had turned Daimon almost eight years ago—which said a lot for him that he'd been able to resist feeding on her soul all this time. Because Hellen of Kalosis held one of the strongest spirits of any human Urian had been near. The warmth and conviction of her life force called out to the beast in him and made him salivate every time she drew near. It was only his own love for her that kept her safe in his presence.

And the fact that the rest of the Apollites and Daimons here feared his family, and knew what they'd do to any who harmed her, kept her sacrosanct and safe in their midst.

Yet she was right. Every single day she lived among them came with a growing risk.

Apollite marriages were ones of necessity. Given the brevity of their life span and the fact that they could only live off each other's blood, they married young to start families as soon as they reached physical maturity, and so that married couples could supply each other with nourishment. Especially since feeding heightened their hormones to a frightening level after puberty and caused them to become extremely aroused anytime they ate. As a result, they were incapable of feeding from family members—another revolting bonus curse Apollo had thrown at them.

Even Daimons, like his father, had to feed on blood. While the human souls they took prolonged their lives, it did nothing to quench their blood-hunger that needed Apollite plasma. And since Daimons could no longer sire children after their bodies converted from Apollite to a living dead state, and Hellen had been unable to nourish her children with her human blood, their mother had served no purpose in this realm, other than to tempt Daimons to kill her for her soul.

Had their father loved her, it might have been different. Then he might have been willing to fight to keep her at his side.

But while their father respected her as their mother, his feelings went no further. Stryker wouldn't allow anyone to disrespect her or speak badly to her or about her. Yet that was as much as he was capable of showing her in terms of affection. Theirs had been an arranged marriage forced on him by Apollo and one he'd never wanted. All of his children knew that. In fact, he went days when he wouldn't even look in her direction.

Something they were all very much aware of, and it pained Urian to see his mother's plight. The constant sadness behind her smiles that never faded. Or the longing in his father's gaze whenever he thought of his first wife Apollo had forced him to divorce.

Their mutual torment was so bad that Urian had often wondered if he and his siblings had been conceived the only times his father had ever managed to have sex with his mother. So when she'd proposed leaving Kalosis to return to the human realm a few days ago, his father had begun immediate preparations. Stryker had done everything to hasten the journey but pack for her.

With her beautiful features contorted by grief, his mother cupped Urian's face in her hands. "I hate to leave my babies. But all of you can come see me, anytime you want. You know that. You'll always be welcome wherever I am. I'll make sure to keep a dark place that's safe." Biting her lip, she glanced between them. "You will come see me?"

Urian nodded. "I'll come."

"I know you won't break your word." She kissed his brow. "My precious, Uri. You'll watch after your brothers and sister for me?"

"Don't you trust *us*?" Archie asked defensively.

She tsked at him as she stepped over to her eldest. "You know I do. But you have your own wife and child, now, and another on the way. Urian's still at home."

"'Cause no one will have him." Theo cast an evil smirk toward Urian that cut him all the way to the bone.

Normally, Urian would have lashed out and struck him, but he was too grief-stricken over his mother to bother.

"Theo!" Their father cleared his throat sharply in warning.

Alkimos, who was leaner, like Urian, but whose features were identical to Stryker's, took up the torment. "Why are you so angry, Solren? We all know Urian's still a virgin."

All his siblings burst out laughing at him over that, adding even more blows to his ego.

"Enough!" their father roared.

Urian felt his gut shrivel at the mockery his brothers knew went straight to his heart.

Which was why they did it. Bastards!

"Freak," Alkimos whispered in his ear.

Urian ground his teeth, tempted to slug him for that insult, but then he knew he'd be the one to get into trouble for striking the first blow—which was what his brother wanted. They were forever taunting him to violence.

He had no idea why he was so different from his brothers, yet there was no denying it. It was as if everyone could feel it and they all reacted to something he couldn't understand or help.

Like he was defective.

His mother returned to hug him, and that only made it worse. Because he knew she wouldn't be here tomorrow to make it better when they started this shite with him. Tomorrow, he'd be alone with their cruelty without her precious balm to soothe it.

Urian fisted his hands in her cloak, choking on the words he wanted to say. He wanted to beg her to take him with her, or to stay so that he wouldn't feel so alone and unwanted.

Both would be selfish and dangerous.

Closing his eyes, he winced at the memory of what had prompted her departure.

The Daimon who'd been trapped in Kalosis too long.

Urian and Paris had been walking with their mother, to shop for fabric so that she could make Tannis a new chiton. Both of them had been complaining mercilessly over the task neither had wanted to be dragged into.

"Why isn't Davyn doing this?"

Paris had smirked at him. "You're such an ass. He doesn't like to shop any more than you do."

Their mother had rolled her eyes. "Would you both stop complaining! Your sister needs something pretty. Erol is too nasty to her. It's time she had something to make her smile again. I don't like seeing my children so unhappy."

That had only made Urian screw his face up more. "Then why are we here again?"

Before she could speak, he'd heard the outraged bellow. "Human!"

Three seconds later, the Daimon had attacked, aiming to rip out their mother's throat.

Paris had grabbed their mother while Urian cut the Daimon off and prevented him from reaching her. He'd been prepared to kill the Daimon without hesitation. Luckily, it hadn't come to that.

No sooner had Urian reached for his sword than his father appeared to stab the Daimon through the black mark over his heart. As soon as the blade penetrated the stain left by the human soul he'd consumed, the Daimon splintered into pieces.

Urian had stepped back in relief, but his mother had been shaken to the core. And this time, she hadn't calmed down.

Rather, their mother had become more withdrawn and fearful than ever before.

The unspoken truth had grown like a monster they could no longer deny. If she remained, it was only a matter of time before her soul became too great a temptation for someone else. She couldn't stay here in this realm anymore.

If Urian went with her to live, and one of the humans learned he was an Apollite, she would be killed for being his mother.

He knew those horror stories as well as his mother did. Humans burned alive any man, woman, or child they caught harboring an Apollite. To humanity, such a person was worse than a Daimon. They were traitors and heretics. And used as examples to scare off anyone else who might take mercy on any of his people.

I have to let her go.

For her sake as well as theirs.

Yet it was so unfair. She was his mother and he wanted to keep her with him as long as he could.

She felt that way too. Her reluctance to leave was evident in the way she held on to him and his siblings.

"Come to me anytime you need to," she whispered in his ear. "I will always have a safe place for you, my precious baby."

Urian nodded. "I love you, Mata."

She tightened her arms around his shoulders. "And I love you more, my Urimou." Kissing his cheek, she let go and stepped over to Paris.

Paris drew a ragged breath as she straightened his chalmys and repinned it with his fibula. "My child . . . you've never learned to properly drape a cloak."

His brother smiled down at her. "If I did so, you wouldn't feel useful."

With a wistful smile, she smoothed it down with her hand. "You will watch over Urian for me? Make sure the others don't hurt him?"

"You know I will. He gets on my nerves, but he is my twin. Besides, Davyn likes him better than me most days, anyway."

She laughed at that. "Where is Davyn?"

"Outside with the wives."

"Good. I didn't want to leave without seeing him."

Sick to his stomach, Urian stood back while she finished saying her good-byes and waited for the next wave of hell he knew would be unleashed.

It came a few minutes later, as expected. The instant his father announced who'd be escorting their mother to her new home in the human realm.

"All right, Urian. You have six hours to see her settled. I expect you back long before dawn."

Archie cursed and sputtered in outrage. "Why does Urian get to go and not one of us?"

"The goddess willed it so."

"It's not fair!"

The look on their father's face would have quelled anyone with a brain.

Sadly, Archie was missing that vital organ as he continued complaining.

Finally, their father cut him off with one sharp glower. "And I don't care, Archimedes. Now step aside and let them leave."

Urian sighed at the glares he collected as he and Trates, along with two other Daimons, left through the shimmering portal with his mother.

Out of the four of them, he was the only one who could command the limani portals that led to and from Kalosis. A gift not from their father as the others all assumed, but from Apollymi herself when he'd been a boy. Oddly enough, his father hadn't questioned why the goddess had bestowed it upon him. Rather he accepted it without comment.

Urian had never asked when Apollymi told his father about that gift, and his father hadn't volunteered it. Instead, his father had just accepted the fact that one day Urian had shown up with the key to open the portals and not once had they spoken about the what-for or why.

But then his father was good at that. Especially when it came to the gods. Stryker barely questioned anything the gods did.

Not wanting to think about that, Urian closed his eyes as they fell through the vast nothingness that bridged the worlds together. He hated traveling this way. It left him disoriented and sick to his stomach. But it was the only way to leave Kalosis.

When they finally arrived and stepped out into the dark human world, it was near a small, stone cottage on the edge of a majestic Greek cliff. A huge full moon lit the olive-scented landscape with buttery shadows that danced across a dark, crested sea. Because it'd been so long since she last saw anything more than the dull, dreary gray of their realm, his mother gasped. Tears filled her eyes.

"Mata?"

She placed her hand on his shoulder as the wind blew her pale blue veil from her hair so that her blond curls sprang free from her braids. "I'm all right, Uri. They're tears of joy that your father remembered the details of my home from when I was a girl. It looks just as I told him so many times."

Grateful that she was happy, he carried her case toward the small cottage door. It was nestled in the midst of a good-sized farm that should sustain her quite well. There were apple trees aplenty, along with a small vineyard and livestock. He could hear the cows that would easily provide her with the milk she loved to drink that had been so hard for them to procure for her in Kalosis.

He headed to the cottage and opened the wooden door for her, then pushed it wide with his elbow.

She went in to inspect her new home while he waited outside and set her case on the ground at his feet.

The Daimons who'd come along to help secure her moved to stand at his side so that they could peer inside the cottage. "May we come in, akra?"

She turned toward them with a smile.

"Nay!" Urian snapped the moment his mother opened her mouth to say aye.

The smile on her face died instantly.

As did the joy.

He quickly tempered the anger in his tone as he used his foot to push her case through the threshold. "Never invite a Daimon or Apollite into your home, Mata. Remember that you are always safe inside the doorway. We cannot enter so long as you haven't granted us permission to be there." Another curse of his grandfather to ensure that they couldn't go where the gods didn't want them.

Something that left all of them feeling even more unwanted and outcast than they already did. All it did was ram home that they were less than humans. Less than animals. In the eyes of the gods, his people were the lowliest of life forms, unfit for even the most basic form of shelter or care.

Their lot in the world was to be spurned and ridiculed throughout their absurdly short lives.

"But, Urian—"

"Nay, Mata." Tears choked him at a necessity he hated that would keep him from his mother forever. Yet it was for her protection. "Not even I'm worth it. We will meet elsewhere when I come to visit. I beg you to keep your home safe. From *all* of us. Even me."

Because the truth was that when the hunger was bad enough, when the day came and he went Daimon, she wouldn't be safe even around him and he knew it. No human soul could ever be safe near a Daimon.

No matter how much they loved them.

Tears flowed down her cheeks as she realized that he had no

intention of ever staying with her. That he didn't trust himself not to give in to the Daimon that he would one day become. She returned to stand outside with him. "I will miss you so much! Won't you stay?"

He crushed her against his chest, wishing to the gods that he could. "I have no way to eat here." It would be even more difficult than it'd been for her to eat in Kalosis. At least there, the Charonte and Apollymi had shared his mother's diet. There had been a variety of food for her to choose from. Maybe not milk, but most other things had been in abundance.

An Apollite or Daimon in the human realm was only asking for trouble as they needed another of their kind to feed them.

His mother glanced over to Trates and the others. "Your father didn't wait until his twenty-seventh birthday to turn Daimon. Can't you turn early?"

"Mata," he chided, "I'm too young. And I'd still need to feed." Not to mention, he could turn trelos—the Daimon madness that caused them to kill indiscriminately. If he did that here, she would never be able to stop him from harming her. As a human, she was too weak and tiny.

The thought of destroying his own mother was more than he could stand.

With a ragged sigh, she nodded. "I just hate the way they treat you in Kalosis, and I blame myself for it."

"Why?"

"Because I'm human. I keep thinking that if I'd been an Apollite, too, you wouldn't be different and they wouldn't spurn you so. You should be married . . . "

Urian shook his head. "Mata, don't."

"Don't what? Worry about my son? Telling a mother not to worry about her son, Urian, is like telling someone not to breathe."

He laughed. "I shall be fine. I swear."

"And I shall worry about you, every minute of every day that I live. But with that worry, know that I love you ten times more."

"I know. Just as I love you, too." He glanced over his shoulder to where the others waited. "You should go in and make sure you have everything you need. I'll wait here until I see you light the fire. Solren said that he'd arranged for servants to come on the morrow. They'll bring food and supplies and everything you need."

His father hadn't wanted those servants to be here on her arrival for fear that they might realize Urian and the others were Apollites and Daimons, and harm her for it.

These days, too many Apollites preyed upon the humans just for shits and giggles. After Apollo's curse and the destruction of Atlantis, those who'd managed to survive had taken a sick pleasure in rampaging against the Greek humans in an all-out frenzy.

While human blood couldn't sustain or feed them, it slaked their thirst for vengeance and sated their need to strike back at the gods who'd cursed them. Not to mention the crazed trelos Daimons who were insane killing machines. Without conscience or restraint, they didn't care who they tore apart. Their basic motto was, "Give me somebody."

The treli wreaked such havoc as to spawn all manner of grandiose stories and legends among the human populations about Apollites and Daimons. It went a long way in spreading fear and suspicion, too.

For their melees and sprees alone, it was a wonder the humans hadn't been on an eternal quest to exterminate them all.

His mother glanced over to the others. "Could you please step away so that I might have a moment alone with my son?"

Trates and the others moved off.

Taking Urian's hand, she switched to Greek so as to give them even more privacy from what the others might overhear. "I know that your feedings bother you."

"Mata ... " He tried to pull away, but she held him in place with a grip so firm that the only way to break free would have caused her harm, and *that* he refused to do.

"Listen to me, Uri. I know how much this embarrasses you. That you haven't had a live feeding since you hit puberty ... "

She cupped his cheek and forced him to look at her, even though he was mortified by this topic.

And she was right. Because of the color of his eyes and the fear the other Apollites had of him and his father and grandfather, no one was willing to pair with him in any way. They were terrified of what other defects he might carry.

"There is *nothing* wrong with you. You're a good boy. A wonderful son. Your father and I are so proud of you. And one day, you will find a woman who sees that, too."

He swallowed hard as pain choked him. It was a deep-rooted misery that had planted itself firmly inside his soul long ago and wouldn't let go no matter how hard he tried to pry it loose. "I was born a twin, Mata, and yet I feel so alone. Shouldn't I feel as if I'm part of *something?*"

She tsked at him. "You were born almost an hour apart. Unlike Paris, you wanted to come into this world feet first. You were most insistent upon it, in fact. Took an act of the goddess to get you to change your mind and reverse yourself so that I could birth you. And then you wouldn't feed. But for Apollymi, we would have lost you that first day. The goddess knows, you've been stubborn every day since. Like your father, you've always wanted to do things on your own terms, with a courage I envy you for. *Never* lose that. Especially given what you'll be facing, all too soon."

Her pale eyes turned serious. "I pray every night that your father finds another way to end this curse Apollo has placed on you and your siblings. I curse all the gods for it, and for the fact that they do nothing to help you. Damn them!"

He gaped at the venom in her tone. Never had she used such language or raised her voice while speaking of the gods before. His mother had always been a gentle, kind soul.

Unless someone threatened her children or they broke a rule. Then she could make his father look weak.

"Life isn't fair and it's been exceptionally cruel to my children. But don't let it sour you. No matter what, Urimou. Enjoy every breath you have, whether a handful or billions. You fight for every one. And when others seek to knock you down, you rise up and know that only *you* can defeat you. Never give anyone power over you, not for any reason."

Nodding, he led her hand to his lips and kissed her knuckles. "I will come visit as often as I can." He meant that, and he prayed it was a promise he could keep. Though he never intended to stay long or step inside her house, he could come and see her from time to time.

"I'll be here. You know I will and my hearth will always be warm and waiting for you."

Just as his heart would always heat up with warmth for her.

Urian reluctantly let go and watched as she went inside and closed the door. The latch fell with an echoing sound of finality that cut deep to his soul.

His throat tightened even more as he waited for her to get the fire started. And with every heartbeat, he ached more, hoping he could keep his promise and that he would see her again.

But the life of an Apollite was an uncertain thing. Especially whenever they ventured into the land of the humans. Those who'd made it down to Kalosis had come with terrifying tales of the war between their two races. Of entire Apollite villages being raided during daylight hours where the humans would drag them out into daylight, just to watch them burn.

Humans weren't content to let them die at twenty-seven. They wanted them gone completely. Their age didn't matter. Apollite infants had been seized from their cradles and thrown from city walls to sizzle and die beneath the sun they'd been banned from. Suffocated in their cribs. Drowned.

Or worse.

Their women and children had been tied to Apollo's outdoor altars and left in the sun to blister and die at dawn. The men had been beheaded and ritually sacrificed like animals for slaughter.

Unbelievable stories of horror abounded. Just when Urian thought they couldn't get any worse, someone came in with one that topped the last one he'd heard.

And it was nothing compared to what the Greeks did to the humans they found who helped his people. He couldn't imagine what they'd do to his mother for birthing them.

Trates came forward as he rejoined his men. "Are you all right, *kyrios?*"

He blinked at the question. Like all the Apollites and Daimons in Kalosis, Trates called him "my lord" in Atlantean. A formality his father insisted upon.

Urian nodded. "Just worried about my *mata.*"

The light finally began to cast shadows in the cottage. She pulled back a curtain to wave at him. Even though he knew she couldn't see him, he returned the gesture.

Summoning a portal, Urian made sure that his voice carried so that the others with him would hear it. "If anyone ever harms her, I will make what the soldiers did to Ryssa of Didymos and her son look like a gentle caress in comparison to the vengeance I will wreak upon them and their families."

The haste with which they ran into the portal assured him that they not only heard his words, they believed them.

Good. Because he had every intention of carrying them out. His mother might be human, but she was his mother and he would see her safe, no matter what.

Yet as he looked back one last time to see her loving face framed by candlelight, a horrible feeling of dread went through him. *Please, don't let this be a mistake ...*

And don't let this be the last time I see my mother.

Heartsick with fretful worry and anxiety, he followed them to Kalosis.

While his men went home, he ventured to the dark garden where no Apollite was allowed to visit. It was a trek he'd been making every week since the night he'd met Sarraxyn.

Yet this wasn't Hesperus—the time of night when they normally held their meetings. Not that the risk mattered to him tonight. Urian needed his best friend.

His only friend, really. Other than Davyn. But he had to share Davyn with Paris, and though Davyn was a good friend, Urian knew that in the end, Davyn's loyalty would always lie with Paris above him. As it should.

Xyn was solely his. He shared her with no one else. Ever. She was always there when he needed her, through thick and thin. And he had no idea how he'd have made it through his life without her.

Everyone should have their own pet dragon. Even if she did threaten to eat him about half the time.

And those were the times when he didn't get on her nerves.

Since he was intruding at an unscheduled hour, he made sure to spread his scent wide, and to make more noise than he normally would.

"Xyn?" he whispered loudly into the darkness, needing her more now than he ever had before. "You there?"

"Where else would I be, Uri? Not like I can hide."

He froze at her voice coming from an external source. That was a first. He hadn't known she even had real vocal cords until now.

"So why are you here? 'Tis not Áreos."

He cleared his throat of the painful knot her question wrought. "My mother left Kalosis tonight, to return to the human realm, and I could really use a friend."

She appeared by his side. Her scales flowed in the darkness like a vibrant wave that sparkled through the moonless night. *You could get us both in so much trouble.*

"I know. I'm sorry to be so selfish." He just couldn't help it. He needed her.

It's fine. You're upset. You shouldn't be alone when you're hurting.

And neither should she. Yet she never had anyone around her at all. Not for anything. Urian reached up to cup her jaw and lean against her long, warm neck. He'd never understood why that comforted him the way it did, and yet there was no denying how the mere sensation of her scales against him soothed the beast inside his heart. No one ever made him feel like she did. She was his dearest friend. "I asked Apollymi about freeing you."

She went still in his arms.

"You were right, Xyn. She didn't like it."

I'm surprised you're still in one piece.

So was he. In fact, Urian cringed at the fury of her violent reaction. "I'm surprised she didn't feed me to Xedrix. I swear I saw him break out a dish of sauce for it."

And he had. The goddess's eyes had turned blood red and her winds had knocked Urian back so fast and furiously, he was amazed every bone in his body hadn't snapped.

She laughed. *Thank you for trying.*

"I'm not through. I will find a way to free you yet. It's not fair for both of us to be cursed here."

She flicked at his hair with her tail. *But at least I'm cursed here with you.*

He scoffed at something she always said. How she could remain positive, he'd never understand. "That's not much of a bright side. Especially to hear my brothers tell it. Or my sister. They'd say it's the worst sort of hell."

Xyn scoffed, then vanished so fast that Urian stumbled forward without her to lean against.

"Sarraxyn?"

She appeared a few seconds later. *I made you something.*

Her words shocked him. "You didn't have to make me anything."

Aye, I did. The moment you told me that your mother would be living in the human realm, and I knew you'd be venturing to it all the more ... She gave him a gimlet stare from her serpentine eyes. *I know you, Uri. Ever you find trouble, even when it should be hiding. You can't help yourself. So it had to be done or else you'd be skewered in no time.*

There was truth to that. "So what did you get me? Human-away spray?"

He'd meant that as a joke.

It wasn't spray. Rather she manifested a suit of golden-orange armor that appeared at his feet. Using her tail, she lifted it for him to see and inspect. *It's made from my scales, so it's stronger and more resilient than any human- or Apollite-made armor.*

No mortal or immortal weapon can pierce it. Nor will any fire harm you so long as you wear it.

Tenderness flooded his heart at her thoughtful gift. His jaw went slack as he fingered the dragon's head that was set in the center of the hauberk. "It's beautiful, Xyn. How can I ever repay or thank you enough for this?"

By never getting hurt. I should be terribly put out should something happen to my only friend.

Stepping forward, he gently kissed the tip of her snout. "I'll do you one better. I'll make sure you go free!" And that she never got into trouble for something he did.

With that thought in his mind, he gathered his armor and headed off into the darkness before someone told Apollymi he was here and he got her punished for it.

With every step, he swore to himself that he'd free her. It was the least he could do!

Xyn didn't move until Urian was out of sight. She should be thrilled he was determined to free her. At one time it was all she'd dreamed of.

Now . . .

All she wanted was Urian. Somehow over the years of their weekly visits she'd fallen quite in love with her shy Apollite boy who hadn't so much as kissed her.

And he was the one thing she could never have.

You are a fool, Sarraxyn.

Her brother, Veles, would be the first one to drown her if he ever learned she'd done something so suicidal as give her heart over to one of his ilk. And she didn't want to even contemplate what the goddess Apollymi would do if she learned of it.

This relationship was all kinds of impossible.

In her heart, all she could see was Urian. She wanted no future without him.

Yet she could see no future with him. At all. It just wasn't possible and she knew it.

"We're doomed," she whispered. And still she couldn't stop herself from doing it.

March 5, 9514 BC

"Urian! I wasn't expecting you! What are you doing here?"

He barely caught himself before he exposed his fangs over his own thrill that his mother's adoring smile caused. "It's your birthday, Mata. You had to know that I wouldn't miss it."

No matter the danger.

Rising up on her toes, she hugged him tight. Urian closed his eyes and savored the one thing he'd missed most about not having her in Kalosis anymore.

His mother's loving embrace. He'd missed it so much that he'd barely been able to wait until nightfall to seek out her cottage and visit. His eagerness had caused Xyn to even tease him.

"I can't believe you're here! It's so wonderful to see you!"

He shrugged as he handed her the small basket in his hands that contained a gift from him and one Xyn had made from her scales as well. His dragon was always thoughtful that way. She took care to save every scale that she shed and put them to use.

"I only wish I could have come earlier or that I could stay longer."

With warm blue eyes, she brushed his hair back from his face. "My precious Urimou." She jerked her chin toward her cottage. "Why don't—"

"Nay, Mata," he said, quickly, stopping her before she invited him into her home and broke the one cardinal rule he insisted on for her safety. "You mustn't."

"You're being silly about that."

"I don't want to chance it."

"Hellen? Are you all right?"

"I'm fine, Memnus. It's my son come to visit."

Confused by the note in her voice he hadn't heard before, Urian stepped back as an older man came outside with a lantern.

"Your son?"

Urian cursed silently as the old bearded man, who was dressed in a brown chiton and woolen cap, headed straight for them.

He froze the moment his buttery light struck Urian's new armor that Xyn had given him, and he realized how tall and muscular Urian was. His jaw dropped. "Why ... I didn't realize your boy was a soldier."

An amused glint hovered in his mother's eyes. By necessity, all Apollites were. Either they learned to fight or they died. "He is, indeed. As are all my sons—like their father."

The old man's eyes glowed with warmth. "I know you're proud of them." He held his hand out in friendship. "Why, you remind me of Prince Styxx, you do. Spitting image of him, you are."

Shaking his arm, Urian scowled. There was only one person he'd ever heard who held that moniker. "Styxx of Didymos?"

"Aye. Best military commander ever born. I served with him when I was young. Was there for his first battle at Halicarnassus. And I'll never forget it." Snorting, he shook his head. "He looked like nothing more than just a scrawny snot-nosed brat—and his helm was so loose upon his head it appeared it would ring like a bell in battle if it got struck. And we were all mocking him when he rode out to rally us on a horse what probably cost more than most armies did in them days. And who would have blamed us, really? A rich little prince bratling with no battle experience whatsoever. We figured we'd all be dead by nightfall by his lack of leadership experience. We thought it an insult that he was there to command us. But he showed us, he did. Never have I seen courage like what he showed them Atlanteans that day. None of us had. He had the strength and cunning of the gods themselves. The sword skill of Ares. The strength of mighty Atlas. He bowed to no one. It's why I wear the badge of our army to this day."

Urian arched his brow as the old man pulled the chain from around his neck to show him a medallion that held a red enameled piece. In the center was a black phoenix rising with the words "I defend" over its head.

The old man grinned proudly as he pointed to it. "That there's the emblem for the Stygian Omada, it is."

The piece fascinated Urian as he traced it with his finger. "Stygian Omada?"

"Aye. It's what we were called back in the day. Achilles had his Myrmidons. Jason his Argonauts. Styxx had his Stygiai. And proud I am that I was one of them." He pulled it from over his head and pressed it into Urian's fist. "Here. You should take it."

Urian was stunned by the gift. "Nay, sir. I can't take something so precious."

"Go on, I insist. Please. I never had a son or a grandson, and my daughters and granddaughters are tired of my old war stories, they are. Before I die, it needs to go to a warrior who will bring it honor again. His Highness would have approved of this, he would."

Urian frowned at his words and the heartache they betrayed. "You speak as if the prince is dead."

The old man's eyes turned dark and sad. "Unfortunately, he is. Taken by the gods far too soon, he was."

Urian gripped the medallion. He felt terrible for the older man. That was too sad. "I'm sorry."

Tears swam in Memnus's eyes. "Thank you. 'Twas a terrible day, indeed." With a ragged sigh, he patted Urian's arm. "But here, I've intruded enough. You spend time with your mother. It was nice meeting you, young Urian."

"And you." Urian held up the medallion. "Again, thank you. I shall treasure it!"

Smiling, he headed back to the house.

As soon as he was gone, his mother fisted Urian's hand over the medallion. She turned a set of worried eyes toward him. "Word to the wise, my precious, keep this away from the goddess and especially your father."

"Why?"

"Styxx of Didymos was no friend to either of them. He was the blood brother to Princess Ryssa."

Urian's stomach slid to his feet at the news. "Apollo's mistress?"

"The same. And he died the day she did. Some claim by the hand of Apollymi. Others say that it was Apollo who killed him. Either way, he was only well loved by his soldiers. The ones he conquered ... they didn't like him at all."

That went without saying.

Still, he was curious about the legendary prince commander. "Did you ever see him?"

She shook her head. "I only knew him by reputation. But what Memnus said was true. He was beloved by his men and ruthless in battle. No one ever defeated him."

Wow ... Urian could admire that. And it made him very interested. Like his father, he respected anyone who could stand strong in battle. The more anyone could learn about strategy, the better.

But first, he had a birthday to finish celebrating.

Then he'd focus on infuriating his father and the goddess who protected them. He planned to irritate Apollymi until she agreed to free Xyn or she killed him for the effort of it.

July 24, 9513 BC

"I really hate *that* bastard."

"Now, now Archie, don't be hating just because he kicks your ass every time you step into the arena."

Archimedes shoved at Davyn so hard, Davyn staggered back into Paris. Both of them burst out laughing. When Archie moved forward to strike his much smaller friend, Urian flashed in behind him to catch his hand.

He'd had it with his brother's bullishness and attitude. Especially today.

"You want to hit someone, *adelphos*. Return to the field and pick up your sword. I'll be more than happy to knock you down a few more times until your temper's spent. But you're never to lift a hand to Davyn."

"Fuck you, Urian!" Archimedes, who'd just been defeated by Urian in a sword match, charged at him.

"Archimedes!" Their father's furious shout quelled his anger instantly. "What are you doing?"

His face swelled up into a sullen pout. "You're always yelling at me for my temper ... why don't you ever go at *him*"—he jerked his chin toward Urian—"for his arrogance?"

Their father cut a steel glare toward Urian, who arched a brow in response to it as if daring them both. "I would, if he were in the wrong. Now go cool your heels or else *I'll* be the one you'll face in the arena."

That succeeded in calming down the massive brute who was second in size only to their father.

Even though Urian was practically a full-grown man due to his Apollite blood, he still lacked a few inches of being as tall as the two of them and doubted if he'd ever measure up completely. While his muscles were well-defined and honed, he tended toward a leaner, faster build than his father's, Paris's, and Archie's bulkier builds.

As did Davyn.

The two of them were about half the girth of the rest of them. Still, they could hold their own. What they lacked in all-out brutish strength, they made up for in speed and dexterity.

Satisfied that Archie was done shoving Davyn around, Urian retrieved his shield from where he'd dropped it when he'd rushed to protect his friend.

"Halt!" The fury returned to his father's voice and froze them all to the spot.

Urian didn't move or breathe as his father came over and pulled his shield from his arm. But his brothers were all grateful they weren't the ones under fire—wretched dogs. They broke apart and even had the nerve to smile in relief.

And too late Urian realized why he was the one blessed with this unwanted attention. His shield was emblazoned with a rendition of Styxx's black phoenix rising, and encircled by a Greek key pattern with the words "I defend" written above the phoenix's head.

Shit, I should have changed that emblem more . . . When he'd redesigned it, he'd thought he'd disguised it enough.

Major miscalculation there.

Just as his mother had predicted, his father's eyes and nostrils flared with anger. "This is the emblem of the Stygian Omada. The army that belonged to Styxx of the House of Aricles!"

For the merest heartbeat, he considered lying. But he'd always been honest in all things, especially with his father.

Judge me for what I do, not for the lies you hear from my lips, for I will not lie or from those of another about me . . .

That had always been his motto. He wasn't about to change it now.

"I know, Solren." Urian had stopped calling Stryker Baba a long time ago. "Baba" was for children and "Solren" was what men called their fathers.

"He was an enemy to Atlantis. You know this, Urian. Why, in the name of the gods, would you choose to fight under such a banner?"

Because I'm an idiot. That seemed the only logical reason given the amount of fury his father showed over this.

But Urian knew *that* answer would get him backhanded, so he checked his sarcasm and went with the truth. "He was one of the greatest military commanders to ever grip a sword, Solren. One who was barely older than I am now when he won his first battle at Halicarnassus, and that was against the gods themselves. And he was an enemy of Apollo. Just like us."

The more Urian read about the man, the more he admired him.

"And our akra hates him as much as, if not more than, any of those gods. If you value your life, *pido,* burn that shield and *never* say his name around her. Do you understand me?"

Oh . . . That was important information to have.

"Aye, Solren. I'll—" Urian's words broke off as someone screamed out.

They all turned to see a large, burly male covered in blood. His eyes wild, he was obviously out of his mind and seeking any victim he could find.

"Trelos!"

Urian cringed as the cry went up among their people. Cursing, his father shoved Theo aside, drew his sword, and headed immediately for the deranged man. Paris and Davyn did the same.

He picked up his shield and went to lend a hand with the others who were rushing to defend their people. The trelos Daimon began attacking any and every Apollite he could reach.

Man, woman, child, it didn't matter. He went for them all.

And with every bite, there was always a risk he could prematurely turn one of their people into a Daimon like him—one who had to rely on human or Apollite souls to elongate their lives or else they would decay into dust.

Which was what had driven him insane. For that was the chance every Apollite took whenever they decided to thwart Apollo's curse in the manner that Apollymi had taught them.

It was the risk no one ever mentioned or talked about, except in hushed whispers or fearful tones whenever they thought the goddess or his father couldn't hear them.

It was hard enough to make the decision to become a true predator who lived off the life force of other sentient beings. To consume their souls so that you could live one more day past your curse.

It was quite another once you realized that every soul you consumed came with the very real possibility that it could drive you insane and turn you into this crazy, mindless beast that might cause your friends and family to be forced to put you down, with extreme prejudice.

But his people had no choice. Once the trelos madness took hold, there was no way back.

Death was the only option, as a new soul only worsened the madness of the previous one. Urian felt terrible for the beast, but his feelings didn't matter when it came down to it.

Trelos Daimons posed as much a risk to the Apollite population as they did to the humans. They were akin to a rabid animal that killed indiscriminately. Without mercy, compassion, or comprehension. Therefore, he had to put aside his own emotions and help destroy them.

"Where is that bitch!" the trelos screamed. "I want the throat of the goddess who turned us into this!"

Stunned and shocked, Urian drew up short as he heard lucid words. It was the first time a trelos had said anything remotely sensible while in this state.

His father moved to cut off the trelos's path to Apollymi's palace.

For once, his father was no obstacle. With an astounding ease of motion, the Daimon knocked his father aside and slammed Archie into Davyn. Then he picked up Paris and threw him into Theo. Both of them crashed to the ground, tripping three others in the process.

Urian barely cut the trelos off before he reached Apollymi's doors. "Don't." With a move he'd learned from studying

Styxx's journals and diagrams, he used his shield to press the Daimon backward.

The Daimon slung him to the side with the unexpected force of a Titan. It was so great that for a moment, Urian feared the bastard had torn his arm from its socket.

That hadn't been in the manual.

Urian hit the ground hard but refused to stay there. No one would ever keep him down. Not for anything.

Rather, he quickly rolled over with his shield and in one fluid motion sprang to his feet. Prepared for war, he held his ground, but he knew his legs were wobbly. He only prayed that it wasn't obvious to anyone else.

Especially the beast he faced.

With a loud, furious roar, the Daimon moved to wrest the shield from his arm. Afraid that this time he might actually lose his limb, Urian let it drop and stabbed him in the side. The trelos screamed and staggered back. His breathing labored, Urian unsheathed his kopis and stepped forward to slice upward with a stroke that landed straight in the center of the Daimon's chest to hit the black mark where the human souls he'd feasted upon had gathered to form a giant stain over his heart. Instantly, the Daimon burst apart, showering them with a fine golden powder.

More relieved than he wanted to admit, Urian barely suppressed his nervous laughter. Mustering as much bravado as he could, he used his arm to wipe away his sweat and tried his best to act nonchalant about his victory. As if he did this kind of thing all the time, instead of it being his first real victory in battle.

But inside, he was turning cartwheels.

Who's the Daimon-slayer? I'm the Daimon-slayer. Kiss my ass, bitches!

Archie began cursing him while the crowd around them cheered his name. His father smiled proudly. Yet in all honesty, and in spite of his relief, Urian was more shocked than anything. Stunned he was still standing and that his strike had worked.

Given the size and immense strength of the Daimon, he was

lucky he wasn't bleeding on the ground, lying next to his shield in pieces.

Come to think of it ...

Where was his shield?

Urian scowled as he realized it was nowhere to be seen. *What the ... ?*

"You were amazing!" His father clapped him on the back and hugged him.

As did Davyn and several others who rushed to congratulate his victory.

Until they realized that Apollymi and her Charonte stood in the open door of her palace, glaring at them.

That cut short everyone's revelry and merriment. A scowling goddess usually did.

Especially when it was Apollymi. No one wanted to come under her scrutiny, as those who did usually met with a massive calamity of some sort.

Even Urian swallowed hard as he prayed that her expression wasn't directed at something he'd done. He could literally feel his testicles trying to climb back inside his body.

"How did that Daimon get so close to my domain?" Oh yeah, that tone was chilling.

His father rubbed nervously at his neck. No doubt his own nuts were shriveling, which made Urian feel better about his. "He came through the portal, akra."

She folded her arms over her chest, with a sarcastic sneer. "You were supposed to be monitoring it, were you not, Strykerius?"

"I was, akra. Forgive me."

Her gaze narrowed dangerously as a wind began to stir through Kalosis, warning them of her temper. They all dreaded whenever the goddess did that. "It appears these treli are becoming problematic for us. We need someone who hunts them. A group who can make certain they are dealt with before this happens again."

"Agreed." His father glanced to Trates, who paled instantly.

Apollymi also turned toward Trates, who shrank back from

her stare as if she'd shot fire from her eyes at him. "Gather forty of your best warriors, and designate them as an elite force to hunt them down."

"I will, akra." Trates's voice actually cracked. He cleared it before he spoke again. "We'll have an Illuminati guard you, and the portal to make sure no other comes this close again."

"You do that. And make sure Urian is among them."

Urian's stomach hit the floor. Why was he drawn into this?

His father's eyes widened. "But he's just a *pido*, akra."

"A boy who succeeded where the rest of you failed. Do not underestimate your son, Strykerius. Even at his tender age, he's already among the best of your fighters."

He barely caught the groan in his throat. *Great . . .*

Urian could already feel the ass-kickings that were headed his way as he met his brothers' angry glares. *Single me out, goddess. Not like they don't already resent my father's favoritism that he never seeks to hide. By all means, add yours to it, and put another target on my back.*

If his father wanted to know why he was such a good fighter, all he had to do was start by counting how many sons the man kept producing whenever he dropped his loincloth. Sons who took aim for Urian's head whenever they were left alone. Even Tannis was known to take a whack at him from time to time, if he let his guard down around her.

And she had incredible aim with her shoes. Thank the gods she didn't sharpen the heels.

Oh, to have been an only child . . .

But no, he had to have been born to fertile parents.

Theo shoved his shoulder into Urian's back as he walked past, letting him know they would have "words" later.

Beautiful.

There were times when he truly felt as if he were an outsider in his own family.

This was definitely one of them. Especially when he caught the snarled-up grimace that contorted the features of his own twin as everyone began dispersing.

Damn. It was particularly bad when even Paris resented him. Davyn passed him a sympathetic stare before he followed after Paris.

Urian ...

He didn't react to those summonses he'd learned long ago only he could hear. Sadly, this one didn't come from the one who brought him joy. But rather from the one who scared him witless.

Suddenly, he felt as if he were being watched. His skin crawled with the sensation. He rubbed at his neck and glanced about until he caught sight of a petite blonde he'd never seen before. She was stunning.

And the moment their gazes met, she quickly rushed off and vanished with the crowd.

Damn it! He'd give anything to find out who she was. But right now, he didn't dare. Not while he was being called.

His little timid rabbit would have to wait.

Taking care to make sure no one saw what he was doing or where he was headed, he made his way through a hidden back door, into Apollymi's palace and down the hall that led to her private garden where she spent most of her time by the pool she'd first shown him many years ago when he'd been a small boy seeking daylight. A pool he'd visited many times in secrecy since that fateful dawn.

He slowed as he drew near her position.

As always, she was breathtaking in her beauty. Ethereal and strangely serene in her sadness that tugged at his heart. He'd never seen anyone so graceful.

Her long white-blond hair was dressed in tiny braids that coiled around her face in an intricate style that framed her delicate features. The back of her hair had been left free to fall in waves over her thin, pale shoulders. Her long black gown fanned out across the dark stones, blending with it as if she were part of the landscape. A cold, brittle piece that would mercilessly crush anyone who dared disturb her.

Someone sane would run as far away from this place as they could. But he'd been summoned, and so running seemed more like suicide. Therefore, he stepped forward so that he could kneel before her and bow his head. "Akra."

She pulled her hand from the black waters and wiped it off in the folds of her gown. "You were incredibly brave today, Urian. A credit to your solren."

"Thank you, akra. I try."

"No, Urian. You succeed." She rose to her feet so that she could approach him. A peculiar air hung around her. One that was unfamiliar to him and left him puzzled as to her mood, which was even more somber than normal.

Cocking her head, she narrowed her gaze. "Should we discuss this?" His shield appeared between them.

Urian's eyes widened as he realized why she was angry at him. *Ah ... crap, not this again. Why didn't I listen to my mother?*

"I meant no disrespect, akra."

Instead of anger, a strange light danced in her pale, swirling eyes. "None taken, but I imagine your solren was quite put out by it."

That was a mild way of stating his mood. "He said you would be livid."

She pursed her lips. "I have to say that Styxx of Didymos was no friend of mine. And I find it ... *odd* that you would admire such a beast, given what he did to Atlantis."

Urian shrugged. "He was strong and resourceful. Fearless."

"And he almost marched his army up the steps of Katateros, into the hall of the gods."

"So it's true?"

She nodded. "But for an act of treachery on the part of Apollo, Styxx would have defeated Atlantis, and this would have been his home. He would have ruled us all."

"Is that why you hate him?"

"Nay, child. My reasons run much deeper than that. And are far more personal." Her grip tightened on the shield until her knuckles turned as white as her hair. But after a moment, she let out a ragged breath. "However, I won't take your hero from you. A boy should always have someone he looks up to. Someone he aspires to be. And as much as I hated that bastard while he lived in the mortal world, I will grant you that he was fair to his men in war. An undefeated commander in battle. There's nothing wrong with acknowledging that even a mangy dog has noble traits when he's not scratching his fleas or licking his balls."

Urian wasn't sure how to take that last bit. Especially when a moment later she changed his shield so that Styxx's phoenix merged with her dragon emblem to form a unique chimera of the two.

A Daimon symbol.

With a motherly smile, she held it out toward him. "Here, *m'gios*. You shall form a Stygian Omada of your own and lead it for me. Your army will eclipse Styxx's and be remembered long after his is nothing more than a forgotten memory."

Stunned and amazed, he gaped at her graciousness. "Thank you, akra. I shall do my best to honor you both."

"I know you will." There was a longing in her gaze that he didn't understand. It lingered with a haunting pain.

As he started to leave, she stopped him.

"Answer me another thing, Urian."

"Akra?"

"I know why your brother Paris has no interest in wenching, but I've noticed that you refrain as well. Yet not for the same reasons. Why?"

He felt heat sting his cheeks as this inevitable question came up yet again. Why was everyone so fixated on his diet? Or lack thereof? It was bad enough that he was embarrassed by the fact that he was alone. Why did everyone have to keep making him explain it?

"Did you swallow your tongue, *pido?*"

"I think I died of shock, akra."

She tsked at him. "Have you no answer for me? Or, like Paris, do you prefer the company of men as well?"

"In truth, I prefer to keep to myself, akra."

Her look turned dark and foreboding. "You're lying, Urian. You should never lie to a god. We can smell it on you."

Shame filled him as he fidgeted with the edge of his shield. This was the one thing he'd never liked to speak about.

To anyone.

"Urian?"

He glanced up to meet her swirling silver gaze. "You know that I'm not like the others."

"How do you mean?"

"They fear me, akra. Because of my eyes, they say that I'm even more cursed than the others."

"Your solren has spoken to me of this foolishness and I've told him to pay it no heed. Neither should you."

Tears choked him as his humiliation rose up again to burn like an inferno. "Easy for you to say, akra. And for Solren. But it's hard when I'm the only one here who has to take my meals from a cup. And everyone knows it."

"I see."

But it was Urian who felt the pain and shame of it all. "That is why I keep to myself. . . . which is fine. Really. I've no desire to father children and watch them be faced with the decisions we have to make. I would much rather be alone."

At least that was the lie he tried to convince himself to believe.

She moved to stand beside him so that she could brush her hand through his hair with a tenderness no one would believe her capable of. But she'd never hesitated to show it with him. At least whenever they were alone.

Sadly, she and his father were the only two who weren't afraid of him.

And Davyn. For some reason, he'd always been a good friend.

"Poor child."

He shifted uneasily under the weight of her sympathy. "Why are my eyes blue, akra?"

She cupped his cheek in her cold palm and turned his face so that he met her gaze. "Because you are special, Urian. Not cursed. *Special*. Never doubt that."

"I don't feel special." He felt like a bastard stepchild. Hated and unwanted.

She tensed and pulled back as if something had disturbed her. "Your father's looking for you. You'd best go before he worries."

Nodding, he lifted his shield and bowed to her, then turned to leave.

"Urian?"

He paused and looked back over his shoulder. "Aye, akra?"

"Never doubt your destiny. Greatness isn't something you feel. And it's not taking up a challenge or a fight that you know you'll win. Greatness comes when you're scared and yet you take action against a greater foe, while others cower in terror and allow themselves to be victimized and do nothing to protect themselves or others. What you did today, both for Davyn and for me ... that was greatness. And that you have in spades."

His heart swelled with pride. Whenever she spoke of such things, he could almost believe it. "Thank you, akra."

She smiled and this time it reached her frozen eyes. "Trust in your destiny, Urian. For it will find you. Even if you hide from it."

September 3, 9512 BC

Xyn drew up short as she found Urian in their usual meeting spot on a blanket he'd spread out near the dark falls that fed part of Apollymi's mirror. While that part wasn't unusual, the fact that he'd brought food with him was, especially since he could neither eat nor drink it. This was something he used to do for his mother while she lived here.

Not for her.

What is this?

Smiling, he pushed himself to his feet. "Happy birthday!"

She scowled at his words, confused by them. *Pardon?*

His smile widened to where she could see his fangs. "Well, since you don't know when you were born and you always take care to remember the date of my birth, I decided that I'd give you one of your own. So I designate today as yours. Happy birthday, Xyn."

Tears blurred her vision at his kindness. Worse? Tenderness choked her. She didn't know what to say. No one had ever been so thoughtful before. She almost changed out of her dragon form and back into her human skin, but caught herself.

There was no telling how he might react. While he knew she had a lot of powers, he didn't know the full extent of them. And she'd never bothered to tell him that she could make herself appear human. In fact, there was much she'd kept from him out of fear of what he'd think and how he'd react if he knew the truth—such as who her parents really were.

He would hate me forever.

That she couldn't bear. Urian was all she had in this world where she was cut off from everything and everyone. He was her only friend. Apollymi had seen to it that even with her extensive powers, she couldn't Bane-Cry to her brothers to help her. She had no escape.

No hope.

Urian was her sole comfort. Her light in this abysmal darkness. The irony of that, given his name, wasn't lost on her. And it was only part of why he meant as much to her as he did.

"Are you crying?"

She blinked the moisture away, not wanting him to see her weakness. *Of course not. The stench of you is what makes my eyes water.*

Urian laughed. He never took offense at her teasing because he knew she didn't mean it. She could never really insult him. "I don't believe you."

You should. When was the last time you bathed, anyway?

Tsking, he shook his head at her as he feigned insult. "Fine then, I shall eat this alone."

You don't eat.

"Oh yeah. I forgot."

Flopping down by his side while taking care not to harm him with her dragon's body, she nosed at the food, which actually was very tasty. *Thank you, Uri.*

Urian smiled at his irritable dragon. He didn't know why he found her cantankerous nature so amusing when such demeanor from his brothers drove him to outright violence.

Yet he adored her.

Everything about her, even her insults.

And he loved doing things for her whenever he could. Large or small, it made no never-mind to him.

Happy that he'd pleased her, he climbed onto her back and lay against her spine, between her wings so that he could scratch between them where she couldn't reach.

She let out a contented sigh and spread her black wings wide on the dark grass. Her sides began to vibrate in a soothing way that was a dragon's equivalent to a purr. The first time he'd discovered it, she'd almost rolled over and killed him.

Now, they'd found a happy compromise that allowed him to scratch her back and her to lie peacefully without causing him injury.

The tips of her wings fluttered in time to her purr.

Urian stretched out along her spine. "So what did you do all week?"

She scoffed. *Ate. Bathed. Slept. Circled the garden. Slept a bit more. Thought about setting fire to Apollymi ... you know, the ushe. What about you?*

"Fought with my brothers. Fought with my sister. Was punished by my father for fighting with my siblings. Trained to fight. Was lectured on why fighting was bad, which confuses the hades out of me. Got snubbed a few dozen times by everyone around me. You know, the ushe."

Sorry.

"It's fine. I don't mind. Kind of used to it."

I hear the lie in your tone.

Yeah, and he felt the lie in his knotted gut. How he wished it didn't bother him. "And here I thought I was being subtle."

She turned her head so that she could look at him on her back. *So what do you want, my Uri?*

He sighed wistfully. "I don't know. When I was little, I wanted to see the sun. To walk out into daylight. Now ... I want to rip out Apollo's throat."

Don't you want a family?

Urian shook his head. "I have all the family I need. Most days *more* than I want."

She laughed. *But what about love? A woman of your own?*

That was beyond him. No female would ever feed him. He'd given up all hopes of *that* useless dream and reconciled himself to his cold meals. Which disturbed him most of all. As Theo and Archie kept pointing out, he was destined to die an unwanted virgin. "I don't believe in love. At least not what the poets peddle."

You're young.

Perhaps. But there was no way to miss the disdain and suspicion that hovered in the eyes of everyone he met. Or to miss hearing their whispered hate. How he cursed his superhuman ears that allowed him to pick up every syllable of their vicious gossip.

He sat up on her spine. "What? You disagree about love?" Of all creatures, he would have assumed she'd be with him on this topic.

Aye. I know the love of which they speak.

"Then you're lucky."

Xyn fell silent as she thought about it and realized that Urian was wrong. She wasn't lucky to love him. Not as long as he felt the way that he did about the subject.

Not as long as he thought of her as his pet and had no idea how very human she was beneath her scales.

To love someone born of another species, who didn't believe in it, was without a doubt the cruelest fate ever devised by the gods who hated them all. And she wished she could tear out her heart and stop it from beating. Because as long as it beat, it would always beat for a man who would never return her love to her.

October 17, 9512 BC

Missing Xýn and wishing he were with her, Urian paused as he saw his sister on a stoop near one of the abandoned temples of the old gods who'd once called this realm home. Diafonia's temple. The Atlantean goddess of discord. Born to the rulers of the underworld, Misos and Thnita, she and her sister Pali—goddess of strife—used to walk the human realm, where they would set humanity and the Atlanteans at each other's throats. Just for fun. And usually for no other reason than they were bored.

He'd never understand that kind of cruelty. Any more than he'd understand his grandfather for cursing them.

It also baffled him why Apollymi would choose Pali and Diafonia as her favorites, given their cruelty. Yet even so, that hadn't been enough to spare them from her wrath when she'd rained down her vengeance against her family.

It was said those two goddesses had been among the first to fall.

Which made Urian's blood run cold. Treachery never knew any limits. It always came in the darkest of night and from where you least expected it.

From the hand of the one you trusted most.

No one could ever be trusted. Especially not with your life or well-being.

Not wanting to think about *that*, Urian headed for Tannis, who appeared upset over some matter. She hadn't looked this despondent since their father had forced her to change her name from Dyana to Tannis because he refused to have her go by a name that honored Apollo's sister who'd abandoned them to die.

As soon as his shadow fell over her, she looked up with a startled gasp, then settled down in relief.

He scowled at the sight of her utter misery. "Are you all right?"

She dabbed at her wet cheeks. "Fine."

He didn't believe that lie for an instant. "Last time you said that to me, it preceded your hurling a shoe at my head. And the other at my groin."

The latter of which had landed true and caused him endless suffering that still made him flinch.

His reminder almost succeeded in making her smile. Or perhaps that came from the urge to launch another shoe at him. "That's because you were annoying me at the time."

"Am I annoying you now? I just need to know if I should be ready to duck and cup ... or not."

She laughed, then choked on a sob.

He instantly sobered. "All right, I know you're not fine." Worried, he knelt down at her side. "What's wrong?"

Her lips trembling, she reached out for his red chalmys and clutched it, then blew her nose into the thick wool.

Okay, that was disgusting and under normal circumstances he'd take serious issue with her actions. Tonight, however, he forced himself to be patient with her and not cringe too much. "You're really lucky you're my sister and crying. Otherwise I'd kill you if you were one of my brothers. Or *anyone* else."

She looked up at him so that only her eyes were visible over the scarlet material. With one dainty sniff, she finished wiping her nose off on his cloak before she lowered it. "Sorry. Would it help if I said it's one of the reasons you're my favorite brother?"

Scoffing, he glanced down at his soiled garment. "Not really. Mostly, because I know that for the lie it is. You much prefer Paris or Ophie."

"That's not true." She rubbed the wool together, trying to remove some of her damage.

Urian unpinned it. "Here. You might as well take it now. I've no further use for your snot rag." As he moved to fasten it around her shoulders, he paused at the sight of the bruising on her neck. Her throat had been brutally ravaged. "Who did this to you?"

Panic flared in her eyes. "It's nothing."

Anger rose up from deep inside and temporarily blinded him. "Erol?"

When she didn't answer, he knew the truth. Damn her husband. She'd only been married a week.

A week!

He felt the heat stinging his cheeks as he stood.

"Urian, no!" Tannis grabbed his arm. "What are you about?"

"Honor. Decency. And fair play. Same things your father taught *you*. We don't pick on those weaker than us. *Ever*." He felt his fangs cutting into his lips as he spoke—that was the degree of his rage and how much he wanted to taste the blood of his brother-in-law.

Tannis shot to her feet. "They already think you're a freak, *adelphos!* If you attack Erol over his husbandly rights—"

"I can't control what others think. And I don't give a shit what they think of me. But I can stop him from hurting you." Urian grimaced at the rawness of her throat as his fury continued to mount. There was no way he would let this go unpunished. It wasn't in him. It just wasn't. "I will not see you like this. Not because he can't control himself."

He gently extricated his arm from her grasp, then headed for the hall where her husband normally passed the time with his friends. They oft gathered there, hoping for a stray Apollite or human to fall through one of Apollymi's portals so that they could prey on them.

Which said it all about their mind-sets.

And with every step he took, his mood darkened so that by the time he entered the dismal hall, he was ready to taste blood and break some bones.

Just as he expected, Erol sat near the front, at a table where he was surrounded by a group of young men. All laughing and having a grand time while Tannis had been left to weep alone.

If he hadn't been furious before, that alone would have pushed him to homicide.

Worse? Two of those writhing beside him in drunken revelry were his own brothers. Telamon and Theo both drank from the veins of women they were passing between them. Xōrōn or blood-whores. Men and women who sold themselves to be used as food by other Apollites and Daimons.

Drunk from the blood and lust that came from overfeeding, Telamon looked up to see Urian's approach. He pulled back from the half-naked woman in his lap, causing her to whimper in protest. "Little brother, Uri . . . what are you doing here? No one wants you."

That caused Theo to withdraw from the woman he was screwing while feeding. Pity it wasn't his pregnant wife who no doubt was at home, wondering where her husband was so that she could have her dinner.

And none of them seemed to care about the fact that their brother-in-law had no better morals than they did when it came to their sister.

Other than the fact that the lecherous bastards didn't beat *their* wives. If he was ever lucky enough to find a woman who'd have him, he'd be loyal to her and treat her with respect and care. Not gallivant around like some insatiable satyr.

Damn them all!

With a furious snarl, Urian seized Erol and snatched him from the whore he was treating more kindly than he had Tannis and backhanded him.

The much larger Apollite cursed before he attempted an undercut to Urian's jaw. Urian blocked the punch and countered with a fist to Erol's gut that caught him hard in the breadbasket. He staggered back, wheezing. Doubling his hands, Urian brought them down hard against Erol's jaw, then again into his throat. Enraged beyond control, he was intent on the man's utter destruction.

Honestly, he wanted to gut him with his sword and it was a hard temptation to resist.

After that, Urian lost count of the punches as he unloaded his rage against the much larger beast. All he saw was his sister's neck and her tears. Her sobs rang in his ears.

Damn them straight to Tartarus!

Until he felt his father pulling him away.

"Stop!"

His breathing ragged, Urian blinked hard as he realized how many people had gathered to witness his fury.

Tannis was there, screaming at him while everyone else stood in stunned silence.

Erol lay on the floor, covered in blood and sobbing.

"What is wrong with you?" Theo glared at him.

He was cursed. Sun deprived. Everyone hated him. Most days he hated himself. He needed better hobbies.

In puberty. With assholes for brothers. And a dragon for a best friend.

And he had a hangnail.

Really, the list was endless.

But most of all, Urian refused to back down or apologize. It just wasn't in him. Instead, he kicked at Erol's feet. "If he ever lays another angry hand to Tannis or puts another bruise on her body, even by accident, so help me, Apollymi, I'll rip out his heart and feed it to him!"

That succeeded in getting his father's attention. "Excuse me?"

Urian jerked his chin toward Tannis. "Look at what he did to her neck. Then criticize me and tell me I'm wrong."

Tannis stopped screaming immediately. Cringing at their father's approach, she clutched Urian's chalmys higher against her throat.

But their father was having none of that. "Show me."

"It's nothing, Baba."

Not even her use of "Daddy" could placate his mood or weaken his resolve. Their father's eyes turned blood red. "Lower it and show me your throat. Now!"

The moment she did, the hall cleared as everyone realized this was about to turn deadly. Everyone rushed to safety lest they take any of the fallout. Theo and Telamon scrambled to dress.

"We didn't know, Solren." Telamon gulped audibly.

Without a word, he turned to face Urian. "Take your sister home."

"Baba," Tannis sobbed. "What are you going to do?"

"Don't you worry. Just leave with Urian. And take the others with you. Now!"

Urian inclined his head respectfully. He knew better than to speak a single word when his father was like this, lest he find himself the scapegoat. Yet he knew his siblings were all pissed off at him. Not that there was anything new about that. It seemed a perpetual state for their ongoing relationships.

A fact proven the moment they were clear of the hall.

Theo was the first to strike him on the arm. "Can't you ever mind your own business?"

"Yeah!" Telamon shoved him from behind. "Why are you always meddling in our affairs? You're such an asshole!"

Tannis slapped at them. "Leave him alone!"

Urian wasn't sure who was the most stunned by her actions: his brothers or him.

Especially when she reached out and kissed his cheek. "Thank you, Uri. I know you were protecting me and I, for one, appreciate it."

Damn ... how bad had Erol hurt her? "I love you, Tanny."

"I know. Love you, too." She turned to glare at Telamon and Theo in turn. "And shame on both of you for the way you act. Neither of you has even asked if I'm all right. You're such bastards!"

When she started to leave, Urian reached out and took her hand. "You want to stay with us tonight?"

Her lips trembled. Then she cast another shameful look toward his brothers. "You hate Urian for the way Solren dotes on him and you blame Urian for it. Instead, look to yourselves. This"—she gestured between them—"is why Urian holds the place he does with our parents. He thinks of others and is aware of everything around him while the two of you never see anything more than your own uselessness. You're selfish and petty!"

Taking Urian's hand, she pulled him toward home. "Aye, Urian. I'd rather stay with you and Solren, tonight. I've no use for the others."

Stunned beyond rational thought, Urian didn't speak as they headed home to the temple palace that was second in size only to Apollymi's.

Adjacent to the goddess's, it'd been the one their father had chosen as his residence on his arrival here. Ironically, it'd belonged to the wife of Misos, the god of this underworld hell realm, when the Atlantean gods had called Kalosis home—which was why it had a back hallway that connected it to Apollymi's temple.

Because Thnita had been the queen of Kalosis, her palace was almost equal in size to the one Apollymi currently resided in. But from the stories others whispered, he knew that Apollymi hadn't always lived there in that palace. At one time, she'd been a prisoner here in Kalosis, though he had no idea where the other gods had kept her sequestered during those days.

Or how they'd managed to keep her contained. It must have surely been fun for them to try to restrain a goddess so powerful.

Once as a boy, Urian had made the mistake of asking Apollymi where her cell had been in those days.

That was the night he'd learned that her eyes didn't always stay their swirling silver. Nor did her hair remain white-blond.

He'd seen the true form of the Destroyer. And according to her pet Charonte, Xedrix, Urian was the only one not demon-born who'd ever survived an encounter with her in that state and lived to tell it.

Lesson learned. Apollymi didn't like to be questioned. And never, *ever* mention her imprisonment. At least not if one wanted to continue breathing.

In fact, between her and his father, he'd learned not to question people at all if he wanted to remain healthy. Let them volunteer what they wanted you to know.

It was much safer that way and resulted in a lot less bruises. Physically and mentally.

Therefore Urian remained quiet as he led his sister through their ornate marble hall, toward the back where their rooms waited. No one had touched hers since her marriage.

Just as they'd left their mother's room exactly as it'd been on the night she'd gone to the human realm. In their mother's case, all save their father would drift in here, seeking the comfort of her presence. The memories of her warmth. It was their way of preserving her memory and paying honor to her whenever they missed her more than they could bear.

When it came to Tannis, their father had made it clear that in the event she needed a haven from Erol, she was to have her room here to withdraw to, at any time, and that none of them should ever encroach on it. Since she was the weakest member of the family, it was their job to protect her from any and all threats.

"Tanny!" Ophion came running up to hug her the moment she came through the door.

Atreus and Patroclus were right behind him.

Laughing, she hugged them each in turn, calling them by name.

Urian snorted. "I still don't know how you can tell Atreus and Patroclus apart. I gave up and simply refer to them as 'twin' most days."

"Uri!" she chided. "That's mean, especially coming from someone who *is* a twin."

"Aye, but I look nothing like Paris." That was the beauty of being a fraternal set.

"It's all right, Tanny. Atreus and I don't mind. Solren gets it wrong about half the time himself. We just don't bother to correct him."

Cupping Patroclus's chin, she tsked. "Perhaps we should write your names on your clothes."

Ophion scowled at Urian as he noted the bruises on his face. "Another fight?"

Urian didn't comment. "If you'll excuse me ..." He stepped past them so that he could head for his room at the end of the hallway.

Once there, he closed his door, but still he could hear them gossiping about him.

"Leave him alone, Tanny."

"I need to return his chalmys."

"I wouldn't. I'm sure Urian's going to feed and you'll just make him mad if you intrude."

Urian heard her pause in the hallway just outside his door with Ophie.

"Oh!" Tannis gasped. "I didn't know Urian had found someone."

"He hasn't," one of the twins whispered loudly.

Clenching his teeth, Urian bit back a curse as he glanced toward the chilled bladder his father had left for him by his bed. He'd had no idea that his younger siblings had figured out what he was forced to do in order to live.

Damn you, Apollo.

And damn me.

Pain and humiliation shredded him that he was relegated to this. Not even a xōrōn would accept money to feed him. How sad was that when even a whore couldn't be bought? He was a complete outcast even among other outcasts.

Urian shoved the bladder into a drawer. He'd rather starve than resort to it.

Honestly? He'd rather die.

Disgusted and ashamed, he pulled his dagger out and drew it across his forearm until he'd opened a deep slice to alleviate some of the pain he felt. Yet it no longer soothed him the way it once did. The agony now ran too deep.

And that was the problem. His lows kept getting lower and his highs kept getting lower, too.

At this rate of rapid descent, it wouldn't be long before he'd have to fall down in order to get up.

More than that, his father would have conniptions if he saw him cutting himself again. He'd already threatened to tie him to a rock like Prometheus if he saw so much as a single scar on his skin.

"So help me, Urian! I'd beat you, except you seem to like the pain of it too much for it to be a deterrent!"

It was true. No one could break him because he was already shattered. In so many, many ways.

Suddenly a shadow fell over him.

Expecting his father or one of his irritating brothers, Urian looked up, ready to battle.

Until he realized it was Tannis materializing in his room, and he saw the sympathy in her dark eyes.

With an expression of deep sympathy, she covered his hand with hers and pulled the dagger back from his arm. "Little baby, what are you doing?"

Even more ashamed by her loving care that didn't scold or judge, he dropped his gaze to the floor, unable to look her in the face. The ache inside him was so great that at times it felt as if it would swallow him whole. It was like some great beast that gnawed at him, threatening to devour what little was left of his soul. "I'm too young to be this tired, Tannis," he whispered. He was sick of the way the others treated him. Of the lies they told behind his back and of how they watched him—with malice, jealousy, and hatred when he'd done nothing to warrant it.

It was what made him lash out in violence. He wanted to beat the world down as much as it tried to do to him. Most of all, he just wanted to be left alone.

Sliding onto his bed, she drew him into her arms and held him. "I know. Everyone expects you to be strong and to act like a grown man and you're just a boy, Urian. Yet you were never allowed to be a child."

It was true. They always had to be on guard. And because they appeared to be grown, everyone treated them that way, but inside, they were still kids. At least that was how he felt.

"Do you feel old enough to be married?"

She shook her head. "There are parts about it I like. Parts of it that scare me." She sighed. "I imagine it's like you in the ring. Do you feel ready for real battle?"

"Sometimes. You know, I've been battling Theo's and Archie's hairy asses for years."

She snorted. "Not the same and you know it."

"So you say. It's gotten pretty bloody at times." And at the mention of blood, he became acutely aware of how hungry he was. How near her veins were to his lips. It caused his stomach to rumble.

Tannis's eyes widened. "How long has it been since you last fed?"

Unlike humans, they didn't call their nourishment eating. It wasn't the same. At all.

What they did was primal and raw in a way humans would never understand. It was more a ritual. Not that he would know, since the only thing he was intimate with was a cold, nasty sheepskin bladder.

Urian shrugged.

"You don't feed every day?"

"Why bother? It's not like it's ever filling, anyway."

"Urian!"

He let out a tired breath. "Don't, Tannis. You've no idea what it tastes like. It's disgusting." He pulled the bladder from the drawer where he'd thrown it and held it out to her.

She gingerly took it and, after a dainty sip, gagged on the foul taste.

"Told you so."

Pressing her hand to her lips, she handed the bladder back to him and shuddered. Still unable to speak, she nodded and then coughed. "You win. That's revolting."

"I know."

Tears filled her eyes. "I wish I were a warrior. I'd kick all their rears for being mean to you and force them to feed you."

"That's called rape, sister. I'd rather starve."

She took his hand into hers. "I'm going to help you find someone. I promise."

How easy she made it sound. Not even bloodlust or intoxication could override their innate mistrust or fear of him. It left him so lonely and isolated. He felt like such an outsider. Like an enormous freak. So much so that the only one he could relate to was a dragon . . .

"Wish you luck with that."

"Tannis!"

She jumped at their father's roar.

Urian tightened his grip on her hand. "You want me to come with you?"

"Nay. Best I go face the beast alone. I talked him into this godforsaken marriage. While I might only be a daughter, I did inherit the same degree of backbone as my brothers." Smiling sadly, she kissed his knuckles and released his hand. "A marriage for you soon, I promise."

Those words hit him like a fist to his gut. "Just one better than yours."

"Ha, ha. That was low, Urian. Even for you."

"Sorry. Couldn't resist."

She blew him a kiss before she flashed herself out of his room to confront his father and find out if there was anything left of her husband.

Sighing, Urian leaned his head back against the stone wall and closed his eyes. His father's muffled voice was strangely comforting in its anger. Not because of its fury but because of the love that fueled it. Stryker would never be this riled over anything else. He was a passionate man.

"Damn it, Tannis! I told you not to marry that piece of shit!"

Urian smiled at Tannis's calm, sweet voice. "Am I a widow, Baba?"

"Nay, but I doubt you'll ever be a mother."

Urian laughed. And with that, he craved a visit with his own mata. It felt like forever since he'd last seen her.

Getting up, he used his powers to dress in his armor—something his father insisted they do if they ever left Kalosis. They were also supposed to go out in groups. Never alone.

A minimum of four. More was even better. His father was that paranoid, especially when it came to his sons. Stryker wanted no one to take a chance on being jumped by the humans or gods who hunted them.

That was the only order of its kind that Urian defied. And only when he visited his mother.

Not because he was reckless but to protect her. The fewer who knew where she lived, the better. She was too vulnerable and the last thing he wanted was to make her a target for someone who might need a quick soul to elongate their life. Daimons got desperate and when they did, no one was safe. They would prey on anyone.

Man, woman, child.

Infant.

His siblings could find her if they desired. And while it might be selfish, Urian always preferred to see her without them. Only Tannis didn't hog his time with her. She would selflessly share their mother whenever they visited, and not try to belittle or upstage him.

Not even Paris was so kind.

Besides, he had Xyn's armor and so long as he wore it, he couldn't be harmed. It was like being wrapped in her arms, and he felt safe and comforted in a way that defied explanation. Normally whenever he was upset, she was the one he sought.

But tonight, he wanted his mother's comfort more.

Leaving his room, Urian went to the chest where they each placed things they wanted to take to their mother on their visits and put them in a small basket. It was something they all did for each other as a favor. Then he walked down the narrow passage, toward Apollymi's section of the palace where he knew none of his family would be, as they feared the goddess even more than they feared their father. And there he opened a portal to the human world. It was the only safe place to do so without risking detection. If one of the others here detected the rift, they'd attribute it to either Apollymi or one of the Charonte, who weren't supposed to use the portals, but sometimes they did so at the behest of the goddess, or whenever some human or the demon-broker, Jaden, summoned them out.

The channel began as a cold shift in the air, then a shimmer of glowing particles that swirled faster and faster until they congealed to make a large hole that united the two worlds. The light was blinding to those who lived in darkness. And like moths to a flame, it drew them toward it.

As soon as Urian stepped through, he realized that it was later than he normally visited his mother's cottage. Closer to the middle of the night, judging by the height of the moon in the clouded sky.

Still, his mother usually kept her cottage lit until well past the midnight hour in case one of them happened by.

The moment he stepped into her realm, Urian shivered at the unexpectedly cold air. That was one thing that was hard to get used to in the human world. The difference in climate. The weather in Kalosis was steady, year round. Never too hot. Never too cold. It didn't rain.

Out here . . .

Brr . . .

Blowing into his hands, he stamped his feet against the ground, then paused as he caught a peculiar sound from inside the cottage. It was a high-pitched laugh followed by a deep moan.

Urian's eyes widened at intimate sounds he knew all too well.

His mother had a lover.

Time froze solid and came crashing down around him until he couldn't breathe or think. His heart hammered hard in the center of his chest. How could this be?

Part of him wanted to storm into that cottage and tear them apart like an angry child. To gut the man who dared to defile her so. To demand she return and apologize to his father for humiliating him when he was the one who provided for her and cared for her welfare.

But the man in him understood her loneliness that had to be debilitating at times. The fact that while his father did provide for her material well-being, he'd never once cared for her emotionally. Stryker hadn't even ventured here a single time since her exile to speak to her or ask if she needed anything. The way he'd left her had been cold and callous.

That part of her life their father left entirely up to them to see after. So no, he couldn't blame her for wanting this.

Needing companionship.

Still . . .

Heartsick that she'd moved on with her life away from them, Urian knew what he needed to do. He set the basket down that he'd brought for her and removed the necklace she'd given him.

His mother deserved to be happy without the threat or taint of her Apollite family hanging over her head. She was human and this was her world.

It wasn't theirs. It could *never* be theirs.

"*S'agapo*, Mata," he whispered. *I love you.*

With tears in his eyes, he touched the door of her cottage, knowing that this would be their final good-bye.

It was for the best. She was human.

He was an Apollite.

Forever cursed. Forever damned. His mother would have to be darkness from this day forward. Better now than later.

As Apollymi had told him, love was a weakness that no one needed. He wasn't a child any longer. He was a man. A warrior. Time to throw his toys away and embrace the soldier his father had raised him to be.

I am the light who will lead my people.

He couldn't change what he was. Nor could he deny his destiny. Nay, the time had come for him to embrace his fate.

Alone.

June 10, 9511 BC

"I can't believe I let you morons talk me into this."

"Zeus almighty, Archie ... enough! No one invited you!" Paris paused to glare at him before he passed an irritated glare at Urian. "One more gripe and you have my permission to knife him where he stands."

Theo put his hand over Archie's mouth. "How 'bout I strangle him?"

"That'll work." Paris draped his arm around Davyn. "Now show some respect and shut it already."

Archie continued to make sounds of discontent as they moved in relative silence through the forest toward the village where Davyn's sister and brother-in-law lived.

Urian didn't say anything as they trudged along. While it annoyed him that Archie was here, it was actually very typical of his brother's behavior. Davyn had wanted to come out and be with his family in their village for a couple of days, and as a matter of course, Paris had insisted on being with him to make sure Davyn didn't do this alone.

No one should be left alone to watch a family member die.

Needless to say, while they might attempt to kill each other most of the time they were together, they weren't about to let anyone else have that honor. And it was too dangerous for Paris and Davyn to run solo in the human realm without them. While Davyn might claim his family could take care of themselves, they didn't believe it.

In it for one. In it for all.

So here they were, en masse. Pissed off and sniping at each other.

As Xyn would say, *the ushe.*

"What is this Cult of Pollux stuff again?" Ophion asked.

Unlike the rest of them who remained blond, he had chosen to dye his hair black, like their father.

"In a word? Idiotic!"

"Archie!" Paris renewed his stern glare. "Stop!"

"It's fine, Paris. He's not exactly wrong." Davyn handed Ophion a small medallion that contained an interlocking circle pattern on it.

Ophion scowled at the piece. "What's this?"

Urian tried to keep the disdain out of his own voice since he actually agreed with Archie, for once. "Everyone in their community wears that emblem as a sign of solidarity that they intend to honor their pledge. Or they wear it on the night when they come together to be with the family member who's abiding by the vow they took that they won't commit ritual suicide to avoid Apollo's curse and go Daimon. That they'll sit there on their twenty-seventh birthday and decay as the god intended them to." Alkimos's and Telamon's eyes widened in horror. "Archie's right! They're idiots!"

"Thank you. Finally someone who agrees with me."

Theo snorted at Urian's words. "I often agree with you. I just don't admit it out loud 'cause I don't want anyone else to think I'm an idiot like you."

Urian's laughter died as he smelled fire all of a sudden. The scent hit each of his brothers at about the same time.

As did the crackling sound of it. The clashing of steel and screams . . .

In unison, they went into battle mode and formed a phalanx, pulling on their helms and locking their shields into place. Out of habit, Urian took the weak end. As the strongest fighter among them, he'd volunteered for it years ago. The eight of them present were a well-practiced unit when it came to war, especially against humans.

Unlike Davyn's family and their village, the sons of Strykerius weren't Anglekos—the term reserved for Apollites who'd taken a vow never to use their psychic powers or superior strength to harm humans.

They were Spathi. Ruthless. Cold. In it for blood and bone. Loyal only to Apollymi, and hell-bent against the human race and anyone who threatened an Apollite or Daimon. It was why their emblem was a dragon over a sun. The sun being the mark of Apollymi the Destroyer, and the dragon for their father, Stryker.

And as they came up to the village under the cover of darkness, Urian saw what caused the noises and odor.

Human soldiers had annihilated the Apollites who lived there and were still pillaging and burning everything and everyone they could find.

With an anguished cry, Davyn almost broke rank and started forward, but Paris caught him and held him back.

"Nay, love. In the name of vengeance. Remain calm or they'll have us, too."

Something proven as the humans saw them and rallied to attack.

Theo came around so that they formed a circle. Urian frowned at his brother, who cast him a smug sneer.

"What?" Theo asked in an offended tone. "I might think you're an obnoxious little shit ... which you are, Uri. But you are my brother. Be damned if I'll see you die by a human hand."

"Aye," Archie growled. "And I'm not about to go home and tell Solren I let you die. He'd skin us all."

Urian laughed as his brothers let out a war cry and countered the first strike against them and the impenetrable wall they presented to their enemies. He struck with his kopis and his powers, using both to drive the humans back and knock them from their feet as they attacked him and his brothers.

They had intended to remain in a circled phalanx, but in a matter of minutes, the humans had broken them apart with their assault, especially those who were coming at them in chariots with javelins. Urian twisted as one of the charioteers came by and slammed a whip down across his shield. It caught against the edge, yanked him forward, and wrested him away from their protection.

Even so, Urian used his powers to lock the chariot's axle and sent the bastard who hurt him flying.

As he turned to engage his next attacker, a bright blue flash caught his eye.

It was a blond child, running.

His jaw went slack. Especially when he noticed the boy trying to run into a burning cottage.

Shit!

Urian flashed himself to the child's position so that he could grab him to protect the boy.

The moment he did, the boy sank his fangs straight into Urian's hand.

Definitely Apollite and not human.

"Hey!" Urian flashed his own fangs at the boy to let him know whose side he was on.

Tears flowed from the child's eyes as he realized Urian was an Apollite and not a human out to harm him. "Please help! My mata and sister are trapped because my mata's blind and my sister won't leave her!"

Glancing around, Urian saw that the boy wasn't safe either. Not in the cruel sea of madness that surrounded them. The humans were brutal and those fighting them weren't a bit better. "All right." He pushed him toward some brush. "Stay low. I'll be right back."

The boy ran like a rabbit while Urian rushed into the building. Even over the roar of the fire, he heard the girl weeping and pleading with her mother as she tried to save her. He headed for them.

Covering his mouth and nose with part of his chalmys, he picked through the burning building, dodging embers and falling planks as best he could. He'd always been afraid of fire. It was another thing that could easily kill them.

The smoke burned his eyes while he stayed low and felt his way along the floor until he found the girl next to her mother, who was barely conscious and wounded terribly. It was obvious the humans had taken their time abusing her.

And the moment Urian touched the woman, she screamed and began swinging wildly at him.

"Shh, you're safe. I've got you." He unpinned his fibula and removed his cloak, grateful to the gods that Sarraxyn had made his armor flameproof. Strangely enough, it managed to even keep his body cool in the oppressive heat of the place.

"He's an Apollite, Mata. He's got fangs like us."

The woman broke down into horrendous sobs as she clung to him unexpectedly.

"I'm going to wrap you in my cloak and teleport you both out. All right?"

She nodded weakly.

Urian quickly covered her naked body and then flashed them from the burning building to where the boy should be waiting for his return, hopefully well hidden, under cover so that no one had discovered him and hurt him while he was gone.

As soon as the three of them were outside, the boy ran over to them from his hiding place in the hedges. The girl grabbed on to her brother and held him tight. "Geras! I thought you dead!"

The boy answered with a scream.

His heart hammering at the alert, Urian turned to see what had him alarmed.

A human was running toward the children. He set the woman down with his powers and barely caught the armor-clad man before he could reach them. Urian manifested a sword and pulled his shield from where he'd left it. The shield flew through the fire and fighting to ricochet to his arm and fasten itself into place.

Knocking the human back, Urian sliced the human's arm with his short sword, then turned and caught him with the edge of the shield. In one smooth move, he turned and came around again to slice through the human's throat with his kopis.

The human let out a gurgled cry as he staggered back and fell to the ground to die.

After double-checking to ensure that the man was dead, Urian fastened his shield to his back and returned to the mother and children. Since the woman was blind and had been through enough trauma for one night, he made sure to explain to her what he was doing before he touched her. "I'm taking the three of you to a place where you'll be safe and the humans can't reach you. Do you trust me?"

"Aye," their mother breathed, clutching his cloak tighter to her ravaged body.

"My name's Urian."

"Xanthia. My children are Geras and Nephele."

Disgusted with what had been done to them and wanting blood for it, Urian knew he had to stay focused on the task at hand. "Bear with me, good Xanthia. Now brace yourself. I'm about to wrap my arms around you to pick you up. Nothing more." He carefully embraced her naked and bruised body and tried not to think about what had been done to her. The ruthless violence the poor woman had needlessly suffered. Damn the humans for this, and the pathetic Apollites who'd thought they could live in peace with such animals. "If you're ready?"

She nodded.

Urian tried to be as gentle as he could as he lifted her.

The moment his arms tightened around her, she choked on a sob and almost fought against his hold.

"I'm not going to hurt you."

"I know," she breathed.

But knowing something and not acting upon it were two entirely different things. He knew that better than anyone.

Summoning a portal, Urian realized he had to be quick or her panic would get the best of her, and if she began fighting him in the portal, it could kill them all.

The moment it opened, the children shrank back in fear.

"It's all right," he assured them. "The light won't hurt you. It's not sunlight. We're going to a land where no one will harm you. I swear it on my life and honor." He held his hand out to Nephele. "Take my hand and hold tight and hold on to your brother."

She bit her lip in uncertainty.

"It'll be fine," Xanthia whispered. "I think we can trust this one."

How sad that the girl's tiny hand still trembled as she took his. That was what bothered him most—that a child so young would fear this much. She should only know trust and good things in life. As should all children.

No one should know such betrayal and pain. Least of all a child.

Choking on his rage, Urian made sure the children wouldn't pull away and harm themselves, and then he walked them through the glowing light.

Their screams echoed in his ears as the portal swept them from the human realm to Kalosis. Not that he blamed them. It was startling the first time through, when you didn't know what to expect. Though it wasn't much better even when you did.

Not to mention, it was completely jarring when he landed in the center of the banquet hall, where his father sat on his throne with a stern glower that said he was only waiting there to devour whatever fool came through the shimmering mist to land at his feet.

One made doubly worse because his father had no idea that any of his sons had left their dark domain that night.

"Urian? What the hades is this?" His father's glower went from him to the beaten, naked woman, then to her children.

Aye, that was the face of a monster from legends that parents used to frighten children. Not even Urian was sure his father wouldn't kill him.

The children shrank back from that coarse bark with loud screams. Not that Urian blamed them. He'd seen grown men wet themselves before his father's wrath.

Kneeling, he gathered them to his chest while he kept Xanthia balanced against him. "Shh, children. It's fine. Stryker is my solren. He won't harm you."

Him, on the other hand, his father might beat for such blatant disobedience.

Nephele calmed down first. "Your baba?"

He nodded. "Don't worry. He always looks fierce. But he only eats humans." Smiling, he rubbed at Geras's back. "He has a lot of sons and grandsons. I promise he's not angry at you. I'm the one he wants to spank."

That succeeded in making the boy laugh. "B-b-b-but you're a man. A fierce warrior who saved us!"

"Not to my baba. Trust me. In his eyes, I'm no bigger than you are."

Nephele leaned over to her mother to whisper loudly. "Mata, his baba's a Daimon! And he's humongous!"

"Shh, Neph. That might offend him."

Urian rose with Xanthia in his arms. "Their village was attacked by humans. I need Tannis to help with them. The lady is severely hurt."

His father's simmering glower darkened to a murderous level. "Where are your brothers?"

"Fighting."

"Trates!"

Urian cringed at the rage in his tone. "Solren—"

"Not one word from you until I get back. See to her and the children. Open the portal for us so that I know where you left your idiot brothers, and don't you dare return to the fighting or so help me I'll geld you where you stand to make sure you never stray from home again!"

"Aye, sir." Urian obeyed without question.

As soon as his father and a group of Illuminati were gone, he glanced down at Geras. "Like I said, he still thinks I'm your age, bit. And brainless to boot."

Eyes wide, Geras clutched at Nephele's arm while Urian led them from the hall toward his home. He used his telepathy to call for his sister so that she could meet him in the palace and have the beds waiting.

Luckily, she was at the door with Archie's wife when he arrived. He would have teleported them, but given how weak Xanthia was and the fear of the children who cringed at every shadow they passed, he didn't want to risk doing more harm or trauma to any of them.

Tannis gasped as soon as she caught sight of their bedraggled states.

Tall and lithe, and the epitome of beauty, his sister-in-law winced at the shape they were in. He'd never understand how Archie had been so lucky as to land a wife so beautiful or kind. Or why, having done so, the idiot would ever cheat on her. Yet his brother strayed constantly for reasons only Archie knew.

"Welcome, little ones. I'm Hagne. Why don't you come with me and I'll see you cleaned up while they tend your mata? I have hot water and toys waiting for you." She cast a sympathetic, pained grimace toward Urian. "Are you all right?"

He nodded.

Her frown deepened. "Was Archie at least living when you left him?"

"Aye."

"Thank the gods. 'Cause I want to be the one who kills him when he gets home."

That was so messed up, but honestly, he couldn't blame her for it.

Without a word, Urian carried Xanthia toward the bedrooms.

Tannis rushed ahead of him. "You can put her in my old room. I've already had the servants ready a bed. She'll be more comfortable there."

Since Urian knew his "guest" couldn't see who was around them, he explained it for her. "Xanthia, this is my sister Tannis. I'm surrendering you to her care. She's extremely gentle ... at least to those who aren't her brothers. And a good, kind lady to all." Urian took her into Tannis's room and laid her tenderly on the bed. "You'll be in the best of hands."

As he started to withdraw, Xanthia caught his arm. "Thank you."

"Think nothing of it. Rest now. I'll make sure your children are well cared for until you're better." Feeling horrible for what they'd done to her, he patted her hand reassuringly and released her, then headed back to the receiving hall.

Hagne was ordering servants to draw more hot water for the children to have a bath, and to bring clothing. As soon as she saw Urian, she pulled him aside. "Their father was killed in front of them. Did you know that?"

He winced at the thought of the nightmares they'd have for the rest of eternity. "Nay. I didn't really get a chance to ask about their father. Things were happening too fast when I found them." Anger and grief choked him. "Did they see what happened to their mother?"

"I don't think so. From what I gathered out of watching them and listening, the boy's father tossed him out the window and had him run into the stable when the humans came into their home. The boy looked back to see his father die. The girl, too, then she was hidden in their cellar by her mother in time to keep her out of their hands."

"Thank the gods." Otherwise Nephele would have been raped, too.

Suddenly and without warning, Hagne slapped him.

His cheek stinging, Urian gaped at her. "What was that for?"

"What were you doing there, anyway? With *my* husband!"

Glaring at her, he rubbed at his abused jaw. Damn, she could hit almost as hard as a man.

Then again, she hit harder than a couple of his brothers. "Escorting Davyn to see his brother-in-law on his twenty-seventh birthday, which starts at dawn. He wanted to be with his sister when her husband died. He didn't want her and their children to be alone for it."

She slapped his arm where it was bare between his armored sleeve and vambrace. "You thoughtless ass! I could kill you *and* Paris! Damn you both for your stupidity!"

Grimacing, he sputtered as he moved out of her striking range. Damn her for her long arms and their reach. She was like a toddler who could manage to stretch three times the expected distance. "Why? Archie hates us."

"Hades's loincloth, he does. He can't get along with you and your twin because you're just like him, but he loves the two of you more than his own life. He'd die if anything happened to either of you, hence his stupidity in going along tonight, instead of staying home where he should have been."

Still unable to believe a word of it, Urian gaped at her.

"Archimedes Strykeros? Big asshole? You know? The brute who spends his days trying to pummel me into the ground? Who holds me down and farts in my face?"

"Aye. The same disgusting creature." She wrinkled her nose in distaste of his vulgarity. "Believe it or not, he's trying to toughen you up so that no one can hurt you."

"Oh, I don't believe that for a heartbeat."

"Well, you should." Hagne punched him in the arm one last time before she headed toward the children.

Grimacing at the pain, Urian let out a fierce sigh. Damn, if it wasn't his brothers beating his ass, it was one of his sisters. He couldn't win for losing.

"Uri?"

Great ... now it would be Tannis's turn to have a go at him.

He couldn't wait to see what he'd done to piss her off and how she'd retaliate as he headed back down the hallway.

His stomach tightened with every step until he reached the room where he'd left her. He put his shoulder against the door to push it open.

Tannis was inside, next to the bed.

Urian drew up short, confused by the scene. "You needed me?"

"Aye." She jerked her chin toward Xanthia. "Do you know where her husband is?"

He lowered his voice to a whisper. "The humans killed him."

Tannis winced in sympathetic pain and sighed heavily. "She's weak and needs to feed. Have you any of your blood to spare for her, then?"

He had to force himself not to curl his lip, but Tannis was right. Xanthia was in no shape to feed the way an Apollite normally did. "I'll see if any's still fresh. It tends to go rancid fast." That was the worst part about his father's forced donations. They were only good for a few hours. Maybe a day, if he was lucky.

Urian left them and went into his room. He headed to the small stone chest where he stored his blood bladders and unsealed the most recent one.

Gingerly, he sniffed it.

Oh yeah, that was some foul shit there … not that it was ever particularly appealing. Blood chilled quickly once it left a body. Began to decay almost instantly. Within minutes, the metallic taste worsened.

After an hour, it was nauseating.

But beggars couldn't be choosers. So he carried it to his sister and handed it over.

"It's not much. She can have it all, though." He was used to starving.

"Thank you."

Inclining his head, Urian had barely reached the door when Xanthia began retching over the taste.

"You have to drink it," Tannis insisted in that frustrated tone she normally reserved for him. "If you don't, you'll die."

"I … I can't!" She sobbed as she pushed it away and retched again.

He knew the feeling. It was definitely an acquired taste, and she was used to fresh blood.

Urian hesitated as he debated what to do. His sister was right. Without blood, Xanthia's body wouldn't heal, and she had children to feed. While they could take the blood of others, Apollite children usually preferred to feed from those they knew and were comfortable with rather than take blood from a stranger. Blood exchanges were up close and personal. Not something a young one wanted to do with someone they'd just met. That type of recklessness didn't come along until puberty and accelerated hormones that craved getting laid by whatever was "handy."

Children normally only wanted their parents to hold them while they fed, especially since they tended to drift to sleep right after.

Nephele and Geras had lost one parent tonight. They couldn't afford to lose another.

Before he could stop himself, he returned to the bed and began unlacing the vambrace Xyn had made for him. "Here."

Even though Xanthia couldn't see him, she looked up, startled.

As did his sister.

Tannis scowled. "What are you doing?"

"It'll be fine," he assured them both. "I can feed her from my arm." He saw the terror on Xanthia's face even though her sightless eyes had no idea if he was sincere or not. "My sister can stay to ensure your safety and well-being. I won't touch you. Just take what you need so that you can feed your children."

Tannis shook her head. "Urian ... it'll weaken *you*." Her gaze dropped to the gashes in his arm where his armor hadn't covered him and he'd taken a few cuts from swords. "And you're wounded."

"I'll be fine, Tanny." Those wounds needed a few stitches. He'd had worse injuries training with his brothers.

Xanthia pulled the covers up to her chin. "Your wife won't mind?"

"I don't have one."

"You're a Daimon?"

"Nay, I'm still an Apollite. You won't be harmed." He placed his arm just in front of her so that she could feel the heat of it. "It's here when you're ready. I promise I won't come any closer. You're as safe as if your solren were feeding you."

"My brother is a man of honor. He won't break his word."

After a few more seconds of hesitation, Xanthia lowered the blanket and reached out to gingerly finger the flesh of his forearm. His skin tingled from the delicate sensation of her exploring the length of his limb.

Her breath stirred him even more and made him harder than he'd ever been before as she licked her lips and gently fingered his flesh for a tender spot to bite.

Urian closed his eyes and braced himself for the pain. He had no idea what to expect. It'd been so long since he last fed naturally that he couldn't remember what it'd felt like. He knew that it was supposedly an entirely different sensation after puberty. But he'd always assumed that the hormonal surge was only felt by the one who fed.

He was wrong.

The moment she sank her fangs into his skin, his entire body came alive as if he'd been struck by lightning. Every single nerve ending he had drew taut. Worse, her feeding caused him to harden even more. Made him crave her with an unimaginable lust.

Dear gods . . .

He trembled from the force of it all.

For the first time, he understood what a trelos must feel like before he or she went on a killing spree. Because this, *this* was madness.

His breathing turned ragged as he fought down the urge to take her right then and there. Fisting his other hand, he forced himself not to move. He didn't dare.

And that was the most difficult thing he'd ever managed in his entire life. Every single molecule in his body wanted to feed and take her. It was an innate need so overwhelming that he had no idea how he was able to resist it.

Tannis's cheeks turned bright pink as she visibly grew more uncomfortable with each passing heartbeat. "I'm going to check on the children." She practically ran from the room.

Still, Urian didn't move.

He didn't dare.

Xanthia licked and sucked at his arm, growling as she drank in a more and more frenzied pace. She began to claw at his skin with her nails.

Those sounds, combined with the smell of her rose-scented hair . . . all he wanted to do was bury himself deep inside her until he was covered with her warmth and scent, and lost in it.

Worse, he wanted to feel her lips on his neck. To taste her blood in turn . . .

Stop it! You're not an animal!

No, but he felt like one at the moment. The demon in him slithered and salivated.

Until she sank her nails into his biceps and went completely still.

With a startled gasp, she looked up at him.

Her jaw dropped and quivered. The sight of his blood on her lips beckoned him even more. She licked at it, then reached up to touch his chin in startled alarm. "H-h-how can I see you? What are you?"

Equally stunned, he gaped. "Pardon?"

Squinting up at him, she drew a ragged breath and fingered his jaw. Her gaze was filled with incredulous wonder. "I was born blind ... " She glanced around the room. "Until now, I only saw the vaguest of shadows. The irony of being banished from daylight was that I'd never seen it, anyway. Not that I was really old enough to remember those days." Xanthia let out a nervous laugh as she returned her gaze to his. "You're so beautiful. How can I see you ... or anything else?"

It was Urian's turn to laugh bitterly at her words. "As you said, *mibreiara*, you've been blind your entire life. You have no one to compare me to. Believe me, I'm nothing special." He moved to step away, but she caught his arm and kept him by her side.

"Thank you, Urian." Tears swam in her eyes. "There's nothing I can do to repay you for what you've done for us ... for me."

"Urian!"

He grimaced at the thunderous snarl he knew intimately.

The color faded from her cheeks as she shrank back into the bed. "Your solren?"

Nodding, he grinned at her. "Wish I could say his bark is worse than his bite. Sadly, it's much milder."

And before he could move, the door crashed open to admit one insanely furious Daimon.

The expression on his father's face mirrored one of Apollymi's explosive tantrums that normally resulted in numerous dead bodies exploding around them in a brilliant show of Daimon powder or Apollite entrails. It was the type of fury that normally sent Trates scurrying into a corner for cover. And over his father's shoulder, Urian could see Paris imploring him from the shadows to cover his brother's ass.

What the hades had happened now?

"You're the one who insisted your brothers go?"

Hardly. He hadn't given a shit, one way or the other. Paris had been the one determined that Davyn not go alone, and Urian had been guilted into joining them by his twin, who had wanted company for the trip.

Once Urian was confirmed, Theo had been the first to insist, and then Ophie had piled on. After that, Theo had drafted Alkimos and it'd just escalated from there.

Still Paris begged and pleaded with him in silent gestures he made behind their father's back. There was obviously something going on here that he'd missed. Something very important to his twin.

You know this is going to get your ass into all kinds of shit. Otherwise Paris wouldn't be acting like that.

Yeah, he did.

That alone made him want to knock his brother's teeth down his throat. Why did they put him in this position? Just once he wanted to be a traitorous ass and hand them over to his father for punishment.

Sad to say, he wasn't. And he hated that he had no self-loyalty. That his loyalty to them always took precedence over his self-preservation.

Urian narrowed his gaze at his twin. *Oh, you owe me, you flea-turd!* He used his powers to project his thought to his brother.

Paris blew him a kiss.

Tempted to return it with an obscene gesture, or a knife throw, Urian forced himself not to react. "I'm not sure how to respond to your question, Solren." Mostly because he didn't want to lie to him.

His father backhanded him so hard that for a moment he feared he might actually lose consciousness.

Or a few teeth.

As it was, he rebounded into the wall and barely caught himself against the chest there. The oil lamp rattled and almost fell to the floor.

"Telamon lies near death. You'd best pray to the gods that

he survives. You ever walk away from a battle again while your brothers are still fighting, and so help me I'll gut you for the cowardice!" He grabbed Urian up by his hair and slung him toward the door. "You abandoned family for a stranger! How dare you!" He kicked him through the threshold.

Because he knew no words would save him, Urian locked his jaw, put his hands up to his face, and prepared himself for the beating to come. Damn Paris for this. And for not warning him. This was the one thing that drove their father to insanity and Paris knew it. Thanks to Apollo and the fact that the bastard god had always neglected their father and put everyone and everything above him, Stryker couldn't stand for them to ever make that mistake. Or anything close to it.

Blood above all.

Urian hissed as the blows rained down over his body. His father had no idea what he was doing. This wasn't about punishing him as much as it was about lashing out at his own father. It was pure unadulterated hatred.

And it stung him to the core of his soul, even through his armor.

Mostly because he couldn't protect himself. He refused to strike his father. For any reason.

"Strykerius!" A wave went through the room, knocking his father away from him.

Panting and weak from the blinding pain, Urian lay on the floor, shaking. He ached from head to toe while Apollymi materialized in the room between them so that she could glare at his father.

"What are you doing?" she demanded. "Do you plan to kill one son because another was injured? In what rational world does this make sense?"

His father pushed himself to his feet as sanity returned to his eyes. Finally in control, he knelt beside Urian and brushed his hair back from Urian's stinging cheek, eye, and jaw so that he could cup his face and survey the damage he'd wrought. "I'm sorry."

Like I give a shit.

Pushing his father away, Urian rolled over and stood on legs that didn't really want to support him at all. In that moment, he hated his father with every part of his being.

Hated his twin even more. Damn them both for this. He'd done nothing to deserve it and he was tired of taking the brunt of their aggression. Tired of being beaten when all he'd done was try to help someone.

"Urian ... "

Not wanting to hear it, he ignored his father, and he continued on to his room. He forced himself to close the door gently with his powers, even though he'd rather slam it. But the last thing he needed was one more ass-kicking tonight for violating another house rule.

He was too weak to lose even as much as one more drop of blood. His breathing ragged from the agony, he wiped at his nose and spat the blood out of his mouth into the basin he used for washing, then rinsed his mouth. Damn, it hurt. That blood had loosened his fangs. Not that *he* needed them.

Still ...

The air stirred behind him. He tensed, expecting it to be his father or brother.

"Are you all right?"

His breath rushed out at the unexpected sound of Xanthia's gentle voice.

Lovely, this was all his battered ego needed ...

The heat of embarrassment stung his cheeks and made his injuries burn even more. Grabbing a cloth, he wiped at his swollen lips. "Fine." He glanced at her. "You should be resting."

"I wanted to check on you." She swallowed hard. "I'm so sorry you were punished for saving us."

He shrugged. "Yeah, well, I assumed my brothers could fend for themselves. They're gigantic, belligerent assholes. And were armed, to boot. You and your children weren't. Don't know why my solren's so pissed off when he's the one who's always said that if we can't defend ourselves against a bunch of pathetic humans, then we deserve to die. He's drilled us every day of our lives to protect ourselves and fight against them."

"We were taught to live peacefully by their sides. That if we didn't learn to fight, or carry weapons, they'd leave us alone and not cause us harm. We were farmers and shepherds. Not a warrior among us."

"Aye, I know. Davyn's father was furious when his sister went to live with her husband's family. He told her it was a mistake. That the humans would never suffer them to live in their world ... if you lie down with a wolf, expect to get eaten."

"He was right." She took the cloth from his hand and used it to wipe at his brow. "You need to feed in order to heal. Who nurses you?"

"I'm between donors." It wasn't exactly a lie. He just omitted the fact that there weren't any living donors he fed from, but rather bladders in which his father collected the blood he forced his men to give up.

"Then I offer my blood to you."

Stunned by that offer, Urian salivated at the mere thought, but he couldn't do that to her. Not after everything she'd been through. "Xanthia—"

She placed her fingers over his lips to stop his protest. "It's the least I can do after everything you've done for us. My God, Urian ... for the first time in my life, I can see! Please, let me do this for you."

Any thought of further protest vanished as she bared her neck to him. Maybe if he hadn't been starving and emotionally raw he might have been able to find a shred of noble hero inside himself.

But right then and there, he was in too much pain to turn away from the comfort she offered.

He needed this. It was selfish, yet he didn't care. Hurt and aching, he let the demon inside take control and sank his fangs into her flesh before he could find any shred of decency to stop it.

And the moment he did, he growled as an inexplicable pleasure ripped through him unlike anything he'd ever experienced before. Everything became sharper and clearer. He saw color more vibrantly. The scent of her hair awakened a deep-seated hunger that went straight to his groin. Holy gods ...

No wonder Apollites and Daimons lost their minds. He understood that now.

Sucking his breath in sharply, he barely caught himself before he lifted the hem of her peplos and sought to satiate the beast inside him. But given what the humans had done to her, he refused to use her like that. It was enough that she fed his need for blood. He wouldn't take more from her.

Not tonight.

Even *he* wasn't that much of an animal.

Taking her blood was enough trespass. Still, he wanted more from her. She raked her hands through his hair, splaying them against his scalp as she cradled his head in her palms. Moaning deep in her throat, she wrapped her body around his, which really wasn't helping him maintain his restraint.

Urian licked and teased her skin as he tasted the warm blood he needed. It was so much sweeter than the cold, lifeless shit his father had provided for him. And he was all too aware of her soft, sweet body pressed against his. Of the way she rubbed those curves against every inch of him until he was ready to die.

With a deep, starving growl, he pinned her against the wall and ground his hips against hers.

Xanthia gasped, then reached down between their bodies so that she could cup him in her hand.

The moment she touched his cock and began stroking him, he cried out as his body reacted against his will and he released himself into her palm. Mortified, he pulled back to meet her knowing gaze.

But it was too late.

She smiled up at him with a knowing gaze. "You're a virgin?"

If his cheeks heated any more, his head would ignite. He glanced away, too embarrassed to admit the obvious truth.

Smiling, she kissed his lips, then nipped them so that his blood mingled with hers. "Anytime you're hungry, Urian, I'll be more than happy to feed you. Come and find me."

Shocked and amazed, he watched as Xanthia washed her hands in his basin, before she left him alone in his room to try to sort through everything that had happened tonight.

Damn.

Shaken. Dazed, and more confused than he'd ever been about anything in his life, he had no real handle on any of it. But he wanted more of what she'd offered.

No, he *needed* more of this. The taste of her blood was still in his mouth. On his lips. Her scent still lingered in his nostrils and on his skin, making him even hungrier. His body began to stir back to hardness.

Until another thought intruded and took precedence.

He needed to check on one idiot brother and kick the ass of another.

So he washed and redressed quickly, then went to find Telamon, who wasn't quite as near to death as his father had led him to believe. In fact, it looked more like a flesh wound from where Urian now waited at the end of the bastard's bed.

With his legs spread wide, Urian stood, arms akimbo, glaring at Telamon, who lay there staring back at him. "I was expecting you to look more like a corpse, brother."

Telamon grimaced at the sight of Urian's abused face. "Please tell me that I'm not the reason you look like that."

"Nay, Paris is. And when I leave here, he's going to look a lot worse than I do."

Telamon laughed, then groaned in agony. "Don't ever turn your back on a human, Uri. They're treacherous little bastards! Thanatotic bitch was so petrified that someone actually fought back, he dropped his sword and fell over. I thought him dead, so the minute my back was turned, he rose up and I was stabbed with a pitchfork. Couldn't even scramble to get his own sword back. Ah! The indignity. Rather have been pissed on and set fire to."

Urian laughed with his brother, grateful that Telamon wasn't as close to death as his father had led him to believe. "Glad he missed your vitals."

"As am I. Though to be honest, I'm more embarrassed that I owe my life to Archie. Gah! I'll never hear the end of *that*."

Shaking his head, Urian walked over and hugged him. "I'll let you feed and rest. Really, I'm glad you're all right. Hate you, but I'd miss you if you were gone. Wouldn't have anyone to blame for my mistakes, then."

"Aye. Hate you back, you motherless, goat-humping dog."

Urian squeezed him hard, then yanked at his blond hair before he let him go. "Die in your sleep."

"You, too."

Natassa, Telamon's wife, scowled at Urian as he pulled away from his brother. "I will never understand the bizarre relationship you boys have. You're so mean to each other."

Urian grinned. "It's brotherly affection, little sister. End of the night, we know we'd die for one another."

"Provided we don't kill each other first."

Urian nodded at Telly's words. "Exactly."

She shook her head. "My point. I'm so glad I have only sisters."

Telamon snorted. "Shudder that." Then he glanced back to Urian. "Good luck with Paris."

"Don't need it." Urian closed the door and headed down the hallway to leave. In the front room he paused to watch his niece and nephew playing near the fire. Elias was a dead ringer for Telamon. Same golden-blond hair. Same dark brown eyes and chiseled cheeks. Meanwhile, Thesally was a much smaller version of Natassa. She was even dressed in a matching pale green peplos. And her blond hair was coiled around her small head in a similar fashion. Telamon was going to have fun guarding his daughter's virtue in the near future.

So glad I don't have one of those.

Walking over to them, Urian gave them a kiss and a hug before he left. His nieces and nephews were the best parts of his brothers. They reminded him why he loved his siblings, without the repugnant mouths that made him want to knock them through walls. He'd never understand what it was about his siblings that made them so repellent at times. Why couldn't they keep their opinions and fists to themselves?

Their children were precious. Perhaps that would change one day. But so far, he adored *them*.

He prayed it was always so.

Urian drew his cloak tighter as he headed down the street.

Now to wreak mayhem on his twin.

It didn't take him long to reach the small cottage Paris shared with Davyn. Because Davyn hadn't come from the privileged background Paris had, he didn't feel comfortable in their father's larger, more opulent dwelling. And servants made him downright nervous. To Urian's eternal shock and surprise, Paris had actually managed to care enough about another person that he'd given up being pampered and catered to so that he could move in with Davyn and live an extremely modest lifestyle. It still screwed with his head. Altruism was a foreign concept for any of his hedonistic brothers.

Yet Paris was the one brother he had who never cheated on his partner. It said a lot about both of them that they were so committed.

Urian opened the door without knocking. "Paris! Davyn!" He shouted only because he didn't want to walk in on an awkward scene. One thing about his brothers—none of them were particularly circumspect.

Not that he needed to have bothered.

The cottage was empty.

Fine. Little shit must be in the main hall still, bragging over his exploits and battle skills. That was good, then. He could use an audience to witness the beating he planned to give his brother.

With his temper mounting, Urian headed for it.

Sure enough, he found the two of them in the circle of Daimons and Apollites, with Paris bragging as he'd expected. And demonstrating some of his "techniques."

Urian's gaze narrowed. Growling deep in his throat, he ran

forward. The crowd parted as he went straight for Paris. His brother turned. He caught Paris about the waist and raised him up so that he could body-slam him to the ground.

"What the Tartarus, Urian!" Paris punched at his throat.

Urian was too furious to care as he returned the blows with his own counterstrikes.

Paris tried to flip him over his head. Urian wasn't having any of it. All he wanted was his brother's blood.

"You lying sack of scytel!" His need for vengeance mixed with his bloodlust. And it drove him to a new level of anger that his own twin had fed him to their father.

One moment they were slugging it out on the floor.

The next they were hanging in the air.

"What is this madness that has possessed you?" their father demanded, hands on hips where he watched from below.

Urian squirmed in an effort to break his hold. "Ananke and Lyssa!"

His father gave him a droll grimace that said he didn't appreciate Urian's blaming his outburst on the goddesses of compulsion and rage.

"You're not funny, *pido!* And I'm not amused. This is twice tonight that you've sorely tried my patience. Were I you, I wouldn't press me for a third."

Urian had to force himself not to reply to something that would only get him beaten again. But it was hard when sarcasm was his native tongue. And salty barbs were his most favored nutrient.

Worse, with his elevated acute Apollite senses, he could actually hear his father grinding his fangs.

Their father cast his sneer around every Daimon in the room and saved the worst of his censuring for Paris and Urian. "Now will one of you please, in the name of Apollymi, explain this outburst to me?"

"Urian started it, Solren."

His father let out a long, exasperated breath. "Am I insane or is that not the most uttered phrase by my sons?"

Urian scoffed. "What can I say, Solren? I am the grandson of Apollo. I spread sunshine in my wake everywhere I go."

With a deeply vexed growl, his father pressed his fingers to the bridge of his nose as if trying to suppress a massive headache. "By the gods, boy ... Forget Lyssa and Ananke. It's Koros you make sacrifices to, and serve with your every breath. If I didn't know better, I'd swear you were the god of insolence incarnate. Are we sure Hybris didn't swap you out at birth with my real and true son?"

"Perhaps she did. It would explain so much." *Damn it, Uri. Keep your mouth shut!* He didn't know why he had such a hard time riding herd on his tongue.

It was a reckless beast, and traitorous to boot. Worse even than his brothers when it came to getting him into trouble. And even less help when it came to getting him out of it.

If he was smart, he'd cut the thing out before it did any worse damage.

And the look on his father's face said he was about one syllable away from losing a tooth or vital organ.

"Paris ... I think you should take Davyn and retire for the coming day. You've both had a long night. No doubt you can use the rest." He lowered him to the ground.

"Aye, Solren." He saluted their father, gathered Davyn, and left.

Irritated, Urian let out a deep breath and boldly folded his arms over his chest, as if bored by it all.

His father shook his head slowly. He dropped Urian without warning.

Instead of sprawling, Urian caught himself with his powers and landed in a predator's crouch. That caused an audible gasp to go through the crowd around him and his father's jaw fell open.

Head up and alert, in a perfect pose, Urian rose to his feet and swept a challenging stare around the room.

Bring it on, bitches.

All of them underestimated him. They always had. Because of his age, they tended to forget that he was the son of a demigod and a priestess. So while his mother was human, she'd been gifted with her own set of powers by Apollo. For whatever reason, Urian seemed to have inherited more of those abilities than any of his brothers.

So be it.

As his father had noted, he was an insolent bastard who'd suckled venom from the teats of Hybris and the Neikea and had been raised here in this Stygian pit on the knee of Apollymi with demons for friends.

Really? What had he expected? A well-adjusted, happy child? That ship hadn't just sailed, it'd sunk in the harbor, never to be seen again.

"What am I to do with you?"

Urian shrugged. "Take me out and leave me for the dawn?"

"Don't tempt me." A tic started in his jaw.

Of all my sons, you are my greatest pride and the one who scares me most. I pray whatever it is that drives you to such courage and madness doesn't one day drive you to suicidal stupidity.

Urian scowled as he heard his father's voice in his head. "Pardon?"

"What?"

He glanced about the room, unsure if he'd heard what he thought he had. "I ... I thought you said something."

"I'm only debating a punishment that might actually work on you, as I have yet to find anything that curbs your stubborn will." His father grabbed a handful of his hair and jerked him into his arms. He crushed him against his chest in an excruciating embrace. "Don't make me have to mourn you, you worthless son of a bitch." He growled those harsh words in a whisper in Urian's ear so that no one else could hear them. But it wasn't the words Urian heard. It was the emotion beneath them that he felt.

His father loved him. Just as he loved all his sons.

But Stryker was a warrior first and foremost. One raised beneath the iron fist of a cold, uncaring progenitor who'd given him nothing save cruelty and the back of his hand. Unlike them, Stryker had never known the loving embrace of a mother's arms.

Never had her sing to him whenever he'd been ill or had her rock him to sleep at night. She'd never laughed with him or tickled him to bed.

While the others here might curse them for their human mother, Urian knew the truth. They were blessed to have been wrapped in her loving ways. There was nothing about his childhood he would have changed except for the curse their grandfather had placed on them.

Or the hatred that Apollo had put in his father's heart long before any of them had been born. He would give anything to spare his father that misery that tainted his smile.

"*S'agapo para poli, Baba.*" Urian whispered the words he knew his father seldom heard from any of his boys ... *I love you very much, Daddy.*

His father kissed his cheek. "Love you, too. Now off with you." Roughly, he shoved him away in a gesture that would seem rude to any onlooker who hadn't overheard their exchange or been privy to the way his father's hands had trembled with fear while he held him.

Yet for all his father's gruffness, Urian knew the truth. He was cherished and loved.

It wasn't just their blood that bound them as family. It was their loyalty and devotion.

Urian ...

He glanced over his shoulder as he felt his summons.

Careful as always, he teleported to the doors of Apollymi's garden. No one was allowed to flash themselves inside her garden. For that act of blasphemy, the goddess would react violently and blast him into pieces.

So he gently opened the double doors and walked into her garden with a humble gait. Neither of her Charonte moved or acknowledged his presence in any way as they flanked her where she sat on the edge of her marbled pool. The magical black waters were especially bright tonight.

Urian bowed low before her.

Only then did she move. "You fed."

Not a question. A statement that said she knew somehow what he'd done with Xanthia. Though why he was surprised, he didn't know. She was a goddess, after all.

"I did, akra."

Apollymi swirled her hand through the black water. "Have you any idea how much it pains me that I cannot see the future, Urian? It was such a bone of contention with me, that my love made sure that my harbinger ... my son, would have that gift and be my sight for me."

"Apostolos?" he asked.

She didn't speak often of her second-born son, who'd been cursed by the Atlantean gods and murdered by Apollo.

Much like her firstborn, Monakribos, who'd been betrayed by her siblings and murdered years after they'd killed her lover, the pain of Apostolos's death was too raw. So she seldom picked at that wound lest it begin to bleed anew.

"Aye. And it pains me that I don't know how this woman you've been with will impact your life. Does it scare you?"

"Nothing frightens me, akra."

A smile toyed at the edges of her lips. "You know, Urian, in my pantheon bravery—Akeon—and stupidity—Koalemos—were twin gods who walked hand-in-hand everywhere they went. For it was oft said that in order to be brave one must first hold a degree of reckless stupidity." Her gaze and tone darkened. "Be careful where it leads you."

"I will be vigilant, akra."

"Good boy, Urian Kleopas."

He frowned. "Pardon, akra?"

"Haven't you heard? It's what many have begun calling you. At least behind your back. Does it bother you?"

"To be called my father's glory?" Urian paused to consider it. On the one hand, it was a bit irritating. Bad enough his brothers mocked him for being his father's pet.

He didn't exactly relish the thought of others joining in. Yet on the other hand ...

"Nay, akra. I strive to honor my father, in all things. My

only hope is to one day be half the warrior he is, and to live my life as nobly as he has. In service of his people and his family. His goddess."

In the whisper of a breath and without any warning, she materialized directly in front of him so that she could cup his cheek in her icy cold palm. It spread chills over his body. "That is the trick of all life, Urian. Perspective. In all things. For you cannot change what people say about you. Only how you feel and react to their endless gossip. Whether to be offended and hurt or to embrace it and rise. Sage is the one who chooses the latter."

The coldness of her touch began to burn his flesh as those swirling silver eyes darkened to a vibrant red. "Never lose sight of who you really are, *m'gios*. Be true to your own heart. For there is a power inside you far greater than that of your father. One day, you will learn to embrace that side of yourself. That is when childhood really ends. The day we cease to walk in the shadow of our parents' protection and we stand alone to face the full light of our lives, on our own two feet. Most fall and stumble. Some to never rise again. Others will eventually find their standing and relearn to walk. And a small handful ... "

Narrowing her gaze, she smiled at him. "That tiny few will rise up with a blinding fury in their gut to the very heavens. They do not just stand on their own two feet, Urian. They soar on mighty wings. I see your father in you, *pido,* and it scares me."

"Scares you, akra? Why?"

She blinked and released his face. "He was a stubborn bastard."

Her word choice confused him. "Was?"

"Is," she said quickly, clearing her throat. "It's been a long night, *ormourpido*. You need your sleep. For with every dawn that comes, the day will find new ways to try and break you."

Not sure if he should trust that answer, Urian bowed and left, but he didn't return to his father. There was only one place he wanted to be right then. Apollymi was right. It'd been a long, long night.

And he wanted comfort.

There was only one place he ever found that peace.

Making sure no one was paying attention, he carefully made his way to Xyn's bower.

"Sarraxyn?"

She tsked in the darkness. *What am I to . . .* Her voice drifted off. *You're hurt?*

That worried tone never failed to bring a smile to his lips. He didn't know why. Only that it warmed him.

"I was in battle."

Xyn materialized behind him so fast that it was shocking. He'd never understand how a creature so large could maneuver so quickly and silently.

Something brushed against him that felt like hands. *My armor didn't protect you?*

"In ways you can't imagine." He reached up to cup her face and nuzzle her spiny jaw. "Thank you. Sadly, it doesn't cover all of me. And most of this isn't from battle, but rather afterward . . . when my solren found out we were in the human realm without his knowledge."

She pulled back and cocked her dragon's head to frown at him. *Pardon? Your father beat you for fighting?*

He felt the same bitterness her tone betrayed. "Aye. The man makes no sense. He's ridiculous."

Wrapping him in the warmth of her scales, she gave him a deep, rippling caress. *Bathe yourself in the falls so that you can heal.*

"You sure?" If they were caught, she could be executed. No one was allowed near Apollymi's healing waters. Normally, Xyn wouldn't let him so much as look at them unless she knew for a fact where the goddess was.

Xyn nuzzled against his back and nodded. *Aye. Go quickly before I change my mind.*

Urian didn't need more than that. He flashed himself out of his clothes and quickly dove into the water, which was unbelievably soothing. It was so warm and inviting. Like a mother's caress.

Normally their only exposure to the waters came in small

sips that a Charonte might dispense to him or another whenever they were injured and Apollymi approved the water being
brought to them.

To actually bathe in it …

This was Katateros. The Atlantean version of paradise.

Xyn crept toward the edge of the falls so that she could watch
Urian as he frolicked naked in the rainbow pool. If only he had
any idea how much she wanted to join him there …

Damn, he was gorgeous. Perfect in every way and completely
delectable. …

She took one long, lingering look at his lush, muscular body
and the way the water made those ripped muscles glow …

Yeah, it was worth it. And it always made it difficult for her
to remain in her dragon's body whenever she watched him bathe.
It was why she allowed him to do so, even though it would mean
her life if they were caught.

Biting her lip, she felt the heat inside her rise and it wasn't
from her dragon's fire.

For years now, she'd been venturing into the main Apollite
town in the guise of one of them to spy on him from a distance.
Sometimes when he trained. Or whenever they gathered for cel-
ebrations. Always in crowds so that he wouldn't notice her or,
goddess forbid, approach her to talk.

Although there had been a few close calls when she'd been
too caught up with his beauty that she hadn't pulled away
fast enough.

Now …

*You're different tonight, Urian. What else happened that you
haven't told me about?*

Urian had a confidence to him that hadn't been there before.
A peculiar air she couldn't quite place. In spite of his injuries,
she sensed a peace she didn't understand.

Most of all, she wanted to wrap him in her arms and hold
him close so that no one could harm him or threaten his safety
in any way.

He paused in the black water to stare up at her where she

waited on the bank. Floating on his back, he gave her an uninhibited view of his entire perfect body. *Every* inch of it.

Her throat went dry as she felt even more heat rushing through her. All she wanted was the courage to change forms and climb on top of him so that she could take him inside her and claim him as her own.

That would be heaven. And it was the one dream she had that she knew could never be.

Especially when he finally broke the silence with words that shattered her heart.

"I fed tonight."

An unbelievable wave of anger and jealousy tore through her as her happiness splintered at the thought of him having sex with another woman. A wave so fierce and furious that she almost belched fire at him. It made her long to do him harm. More than that, it demanded she find whatever female he'd found and pluck every strand from her head until she was bald and bleeding.

Begging for mercy!

How could he do this?

Then again, how could he not?

The truth stung like a hive of hornets, and it brought tears to her eyes as she forced herself to calm down and face a bitter, harsh truth. He had to have an Apollite to feed him. She could never do that and she knew it. With all her powers and abilities . . .

She could never be what he needed.

Never.

"Xyn?" He swam closer to her. "Are you all right?"

No. How could she be? The man she loved had broken her heart. He'd taken another lover and there was nothing she could do about it.

He was faithless and here she had to stand in silence while he cavorted with someone else and rubbed her very nose in it. While he laughed and went off with another, right in front of her very eyes. How could any woman be all right with *that*?

It was madness for him to even postulate such a question to her.

Yet in spite of the pain. In spite of the travesty, she swallowed hard before she answered in a calm, steady voice that belied her tattered heart. *Of course.*

With a worried frown, he came out of the water, dripping and naked, and headed for her.

Unable to bear the sight of his beauty when she knew she couldn't have any part of him, Sarraxyn got up and flew away, wishing more than ever that she could leave this horrible place and find her own family. Be among her own kind again. At least there she wouldn't be so horribly alone.

Forever. An outcast in a world where there was no one like her. Where no one could love her or see her for what she really was. She was a freak here.

Unwanted. Unneeded.

Judged for things she couldn't help.

And seen for only half of who and what she really was. But one day ...

One day, she'd break free and the world would know her for her real heart and force.

That would be the day they'd all tremble in fear before her.

Even Urian.

June 12, 9511 BC

"Your matera is human!"

Urian froze the moment he entered Xanthia's home and she spat those hate-filled words at him as if they were fiery grenades launched from a parapet and meant to incinerate his entire being. Forcing himself not to react, he took a deep breath. "She is."

Xanthia hissed and bared her fangs at him. "Why did you lie to me?"

His anger pitched and churned at her unwarranted attack. It wouldn't take much for it to explode at this point. Xanthia had no idea how tenuous a ground she tread upon. No one assaulted him for his mother. Hellen of Delphi was sacrosanct to him and he would die defending the woman who birthed him—even against Apollymi herself.

"I didn't lie, Thia. You didn't ask. My mother is Greek. I am not. Now if you'll excuse me ... " He left before she pushed him further and this became the ugly situation that experience had taught him invariably followed such heated exchanges.

You should have told her about your mother.

It would have been the prudent thing to do. No doubt some asshole had run to her with the news, just to spread the gossip of it for no other reason than to wreak havoc with his screwed-up life. He'd never understood that urge that others had. To tell half-truths and pretend to know something when they didn't. To make up whatever bullshit they wanted for whatever sick game they'd contrived for the sake of drama. As if they had some kind of inside information on a given topic when the only ones who knew the truth were those who were the actual participating parties.

The rest were just dumbasses.

"Urian!"

At Xanthia's call, he paused in the middle of the street and turned to wait for her to catch up to him. She'd swept her blond hair up in tiny braids that teased her ears and caressed her neck. A style she knew he found fascinating. Inviting. One that left him hard with longing for those sweet, succulent curves.

Even though she was just barely three years older than he was, and in spite of the fact that Apollites aged quicker, somehow she still managed to appear younger than he did.

His mouth watered for a taste of the blood he could hear rushing through her veins. But the sting of her condemnation was raw and bitter inside his heart. He'd had enough of it in his short lifetime that he wanted no more.

He was already done with this world and the judgment people gave him.

Breathless from having to run to catch up to him, she struggled for composure and licked her plump lips. "I'm sorry. I didn't mean to accuse you or lash out. The news caught me unawares. Given what had happened in my village and how you protected us, I never expected to hear that you were partly human. I assumed you hated their race as much as I did."

A tic started in his jaw. "No one can help where they come from, Thia. Only where they go."

"I know. Can you forgive me?"

His heart softened the moment she batted her lashes and gave him that sweet, beguiling look of hers. Probably because no woman had ever done that before. Unlike his brothers, who were used to being flirted with, he had no defenses against it. He was hopeless where she was concerned.

And horny any time she came near. Damn his hormones. He couldn't control himself. She knew it even more than he did.

"Of course."

Rising up on her toes, she pressed her lips to his. That melted the last of his defenses.

Urian growled at the sweet taste of her tongue sweeping against his and the sensation of her warm curves pressed against his body. It reawakened his hunger instantly.

"Come home with me, Urian. I've sent my children over to my sister's so that I can properly feed you."

That was all she needed to say to finish wrapping him around her pinkie as he imagined peeling her peplos from her body and sliding himself deep inside her while he drank until he was drunk from her blood. The more she fed him, the hungrier he became for her. It was a madness really.

And he was happy for her that she had family here. Her sister had shown up among the survivors of her village. Sadly, Davyn's hadn't.

Before he could speak a word, she took his hand and led him back to her small cottage, which wasn't very far from where Davyn and Paris lived.

With every step that took him closer to her bed, the ardent hunger mounted inside him. He knew from his mother that their cravings were very different from what humans felt whenever they were hungry. Part of the Apollite curse was a ravenous madness unlike anything imaginable, one that required a partner to be on their guard lest the feeding end up a murder scene where one of them ripped the throat out of the other.

No doubt that was Apollo's malicious intent, too. The burning hunger that begged their species to devour each other. To possess and ravage as violently as possible. Maybe the humans were right and they were more akin to animals than sentient beings.

Sometimes he did feel as if the demon inside him were the one in control more than the human. And he hadn't even gone Daimon yet. He could only imagine how much worse he'd be once he converted.

It was a fear that plagued him constantly. That he would become trelos and uncontrollable. What if he lost himself to that madness and never returned?

They lived so close to the edge anyway. Danced with madness on a nightly basis. He knew it wouldn't take much to nudge anyone over the edge of that precipice.

It was terrifying to know what one was capable of. To be born a killer who preyed in order to live. He could deny the monster inside, but only for so long. The day was coming when he'd have to embrace that beast.

And he knew it.

As soon as they were inside her modest cottage, Xanthia shut the door and locked it. There was no light because monsters didn't need it. They could see in pure darkness.

She untied her belt and let it fall to her feet.

Urian's breath rushed out of his body in sweet expectation, then caught as she reached for the fibula on her shoulder. She unfastened it so that her entire gown dropped to the floor.

His throat went dry at the sight of her unadorned beauty. Monster or not, she was perfection. Her pale skin glistened in the darkness and beckoned him with the promise of a lot more than just a succulent meal.

With a gentle smile, she approached him and reached for his baldric and sheath. "So bashful and handsome."

"I don't want to scare you."

That was what came easiest to them.

Laughing, she nipped at his chin while her fingers nimbly worked the leather until she freed him from his armor. Piece by piece, she dropped it to the floor, where it landed with a dull clank. "I never realized how much of this a warrior donned for battle."

All the better to kill with.

She grimaced at his vambrace. "Nor how heavy it was. No wonder you're so muscular."

He smiled as she fumbled with the straps of his hauberk, which was heavier than regular armor. Xyn's scales weren't like forged armor. They were more pliable and stronger. And a lot stronger and more durable. "*That* you won't be able to lift, akra."

She arched her brow at his term of respect. "Oh?"

"Mmm." He pulled it off, over his head, and held it out to her. With a frown, she gripped the shoulder.

Urian only released a portion of the weight to her and yet it was enough to cause her to stumble forward.

"Oh dear gods!"

He grinned as he placed it carefully on the floor. "Told you."

"How in the name of Archon do you walk about in this?"

He shrugged. "I've been wearing armor since I was a boy. I think nothing of it." Besides, he adored Xyn's armor. It reminded him of her and her care for him. He felt invincible in it.

When he moved for his greaves, she knelt down to unbuckle them. Grinding his teeth, Urian growled at the sensuous way she stroked and massaged his leg while she freed him from the scales and leather. Then she nipped his calf with her fangs, dragging her nails down the length of his well-muscled leg.

His head spun. Chills ran up and down his flesh as every nerve ending sprang to life in the wake of her caresses. He'd never felt like this. His powers sizzled and arced. It was as if lightning danced through his body. For the first time, his demon was quelled and quiet.

Tamed.

Urian reached out for the wall to steady himself while she slowly explored his body with her lips and tongue. He'd foolishly thought nothing could feel better than what she'd done to him the other night.

He was wrong.

Those thoughts vanished a moment later when she slid her lips over the tip of his cock.

"Oh dear gods," he breathed.

She laughed, and that vibration shook him to the core of his entire being.

Closing his eyes, he quickly bit his palm so as not to embarrass himself again with her. The throbbing pain brought him back from the edge.

It also distracted Xanthia. As soon as the scent of his blood hit her, she lifted her head.

Urian hated to take her away from her current task, but he cupped her cheek so that she could lick and suckle the blood from his bleeding fingers. She swept her tongue over his flesh, heightening his pleasure all the more. Harder and harder, she sucked at his fingers.

Unable to stand it, he lifted her up and pinned her to the wall. She sank her teeth into his shoulder at the same time he entered her. They both cried out in ecstasy.

"That's it!" Crying out in pleasure, she dug her nails deep into his back and yanked at his hair. "Harder, Urian! Bite me, now!"

He sank his fangs into her throat. She came with an ear-piercing scream that caused her to thrash in his arms. He growled deep in his throat as she thrust her hips against him ever harder, while her body shuddered in his arms.

And when he found his own release, he realized that he'd never again be able to go back to the stale blood his father had been bringing him.

Not after this.

For that matter, he'd never again judge his father for his numerous affairs where his mother was concerned. Now he understood why his father had sought Apollites and Daimons to feed on. There was no way any of their people could take stale blood given the way Apollo had meant for them to eat. This was primal and raw.

More than that, it was divine.

Yet even so, his brothers were another matter. Their wives were Apollites and could feed them. It was unforgivable that they would deprive their wives of *this* while they sought nourishment from another. How dare they betray a true heart. That was cruel beyond measure.

Urian would never understand why his father condoned their behavior. If he could have one person who'd cherish him like that . . .

He'd never break her heart. Never take for granted such kindness. Just as now. Grateful beyond measure to Xanthia for sharing her blood and body with him, Urian cradled her in his arms and tucked her head beneath his chin. "Did you get enough to eat?"

She nodded. "You?"

"Aye . . . for now," he teased.

Laughing, she kissed him. "I have a bath warming. Come and join me."

Weak and at the same time stronger than he'd ever been before, Urian followed after her to a room in back.

He savored the sight of her crawling into the bath first before he joined her in the large bronze tub that glistened in the dim candlelight. The hot water sloshed over the sides as he slid in and sighed in contentment.

Completely sated for the first time in his life, he leaned back against the edge and allowed Xanthia to bathe him.

The one thing about Apollites and Daimons, they didn't bleed after their feedings. Their saliva held a coagulating agent that instantly stopped and healed their wounds. Unless it was a really deep or major injury, they never had to worry about cuts.

She sat back in the gilded tub to stare at him with a perplexed frown. "Are you all right?"

Urian sighed heavily. "I fear I shall never be the same."

"How do you mean?"

Pulling her up so that she lay over his chest like a blanket, he kissed her lips and savored the sensation of her wet body sliding against his. He dipped his fingers down in the water so that he could stroke her and delve deep into her velvety softness.

She sucked her breath in sharply.

"You've shown me Katateros, Thia. How can I ever be content with Kalosis now?"

Her smile was radiant as she gripped the sides of the tub and slid herself onto his cock. His head spinning, Urian let out a deep, satisfied breath as she slowly began to ride him again.

Leaning his head back against the lip of the bronze tub, he watched her through hooded eyes while he toyed with her perfect breasts. Water splashed over her body, and against the sides, more spilling over the edges. But she paid it no heed as she moved even faster against him.

"Warrior you may be, *kyrios,* but tonight I think I'm the one who has conquered you."

Urian wrinkled his nose in denial of something he knew was impossible. "Nay, *m'edera.*" He used her favorite endearment that meant *precious baby.* "Not conquered. Merely tamed me a bit." He nipped at her neck to take a small snack.

Gasping, she clung to him while he fed a bit more.

Until he glanced down and saw something that turned his stomach.

Urian pulled back to frown at the fresh bite marks on her arms that he knew didn't belong to him. Anger flared deep at the sight of them there.

"Thia? Who do these belong to?"

She glanced down, then cast him a taunting grin. "Are you jealous?"

He tightened his grip.

"Urian, you're hurting me and you've no right to even question me on this subject."

He released her immediately. She was right. He didn't. But that didn't stop the brutal sting of betrayal. Nor did it change the fact that he couldn't stand the thought of another man feeding with her. The mere thought of it moved him to homicide.

Glaring at him, she rubbed her arm. "If you must know, it's from my children." She held her arm out. "Look closely and you'll see the sizes are small. *Child*-sized."

With a frown, he fingered them much more gently. Then he felt horrible over his actions and even worse for the malicious thoughts he blamed his brothers for. Because they were faithless, it didn't mean everyone else was. "You're right. I'm an ass."

"Aye, you are."

Kissing her arm, he allowed her to dunk his head beneath the bathwater.

He came up sputtering. "Can you forgive me?"

"Maybe."

Urian wiped the water from his eyes. "Then will you marry me?"

She froze. "Pardon?"

He brushed his hair back from his face to grin at her. "Not the most romantic proposal, granted. But most sincere." He moved closer to her until he had her pinned against the opposite edge.

"I want to be your only source of nourishment, *mi kyria*. Let me protect you and your children."

She bit her lip in indecision. "And what is your intent for the future?"

A most important and dire question for all Apollites given the brevity of their lives and what all of them would have to decide on their twenty-seventh birthday. If one partner went Daimon, then he or she could no longer feed the other. It would force the other spouse to either go Daimon with them or choose infidelity to eat, as to feed from a Daimon would instantly cause an Apollite to turn into one, too.

"I plan to go Daimon before my twenty-seventh birthday. But you are older than I am. So the choice on that falls to you first. For myself . . . better the predator than the prey. Always."

Her features softened. "Then I will marry you, Urian Kleopas. And I shall accept your protection, for myself and my children."

How strange that those words left him with a peculiar hollowness inside. He should be elated. He'd finally found someone who would feed him. A beautiful woman of good reputation who'd allowed him inside her body.

Yet for all the ecstasy and physical pleasure, he felt as if there should be something more.

You don't love her.

He knew it in that instant. This wasn't what the great poets wrote about. It definitely wasn't the insane passion that had driven Paris to give up the luxury of their father's home to live in squalor with Davyn.

It wasn't the friendship he had with Xyn.

And perhaps that was a good thing. Perhaps it was all the cursed grandson of Apollo deserved or could hope for.

Either way, it was a necessity that he no longer had to worry over.

You should be relieved.

Instead, what he felt was more akin to a stomach illness. And he had a peculiar urge to run to Xyn and hide there.

But that was ridiculous. So what if he was settling? At least he had someone who would feed him. He should be grateful beyond measure. It wasn't like women were lining up to offer themselves to him.

Like they'd done for Paris and his other brothers.

No one wants you. They never have.

Not wanting to think about that, Urian cleared his throat. "I should go and let my solren know. He'll need time to prepare our wedding celebration."

"When are you thinking we should marry?"

"We're Apollites. Sooner rather than later, don't you think?"

"Sure."

"A fortnight hence, then?"

Xanthia choked. "You're serious?"

"I'm already quite old for marriage, and your daughter will be nearing a marriageable age before much longer. As the granddaughter of my father, she'll have a far greater standing in our community the longer we're married at the time you begin seeking husbands for her."

"I can't argue with any of that." She smiled. "Very well. A fortnight hence."

Kissing her, Urian climbed from the tub and dressed. Then he went to Apollymi first to tell her of his coming marriage.

Urian hesitated outside her dark garden. Especially since he could hear her light sobs through the doors. He hated whenever she sat alone at her mirror, with her small black pillow in her lap, weeping for her son she could never hold.

He ached for her lonely pain. The goddess of destruction wasn't without a deep-seated misery that the world had carved into her heart. No one should hurt this much. Especially not alone.

Not even a goddess.

She didn't deserve what had been done to her. Not once, but twice. They had taken everything from her. Both her sons—Monakribos and Apostolos. And the only man she'd ever loved. Kissare.

They had duped her into believing Archon was Kissare

reincarnated. A cruel, cruel prank that had crushed her to the core of her being once she learned that it had only been a power play made by Archon so that he could have authority at her expense.

As alone as he felt, it was nothing compared to Apollymi's pain. Her betrayal.

For all she'd given to the world, she truly had nothing and no one.

Not even the Daimons and Apollites she'd saved gave her her due. They quickly forgot the debt they owed this great lady who had spared them the worst fate imaginable. But for her, none of them would be alive now. Or have any hope for the future.

How soon people forgot the kindnesses shown to them, no matter how great they were or the sacrifices made. What they owed to another. Yet they never let go of any grudge, no matter how petty. Nor any wrong ever done them, no matter how inadvertently.

"Akra?" he called lightly through the doors.

She drew a ragged breath and instantly composed herself so that he wouldn't see her misery.

Yet he knew. He always saw what she kept hidden. That was his gift.

And his curse.

"Enter."

He used his powers to open her doors and walked slowly toward her perch. Xedrix narrowed his glowing gaze at Urian, but Sabine ignored him as the Charonte female always did. Yet she watched him with an alertness that said she wouldn't mind adding him to her menu should he do anything that displeased her mistress.

Apollymi placed her red sfora down on the pillow and turned to meet Urian's gaze. "What can I do for you, *ormourpido?*"

"I have a favor I should like to beg of you, akra."

That caused one brow to arch. "If you ask me about freeing that dragon one more time—"

"Nay, akra. It's not that ..." Obviously, he'd aggravated her about Xyn so much that it'd become a sore topic for the goddess.

So he quickly changed the subject to what had caused him to disturb her tonight. "I've asked Xanthia to marry me."

She dropped the sfora.

Xedrix ran to catch it.

Apollymi rose up to float above them all. She wasn't standing; she hovered in the air, over the black waters. "Pardon? Do you love her?"

Unsure of her mood for once, he swallowed hard before he answered her honestly. "Nay, akra. It's . . . a mutual benefit."

"I see." Her eyes began to glow red. "And this favor you would have of me?"

More than a little nervous at her peculiar act, Urian took a deep breath. "Do you remember what I said to you when I was a child?"

"Aye, but you said many things to me when you were young. To which one are you referring now?"

The one that haunted him constantly. The one that weighed on his conscience the heaviest. And it was the one he couldn't go into marriage without addressing first.

"About children, akra. I meant what I said. The last thing I want is to father a babe I have to watch die. Or one I have to stand over when he or she goes Daimon and becomes a soulless killer. Hunted. Hated. Can you please make it so that I will never father any while I'm an Apollite?"

Her jaw dropped at his request. "Do you understand what it is you're asking me, Urian?"

"Aye, akra." His gaze went to the pillow she'd dropped on the ground. "I know the pain that haunts you. The pain that drove *mi solren* to bargain away his very soul. I've killed enough treli here, and seen enough Daimon conversions and Apollite deaths to know well what fate awaits me. I don't want that for my children. It's no way for anyone to live. Please spare me your heartache, akra. I beg you for that mercy."

More tears glistened in her eyes as she lowered herself to stand before him. Reaching out, she drew him into her arms and kissed his forehead. "Then it is done, my precious one. You are sterile."

Strange, he didn't feel any differently. But if she said he was sterile, he would trust in her. "Thank you, akra."

"Don't thank me, Urian. Not for this. Because I've taken from you the single greatest joy I've ever known."

"Nay, akra." He glanced down at the tearstained pillow. "As you said, it's all about how you look at things. What you took from me was the greatest heartache and pain you've ever suffered."

She inclined her head to him. "As you say, *m'gios*. Life is all about perspective."

Xanthia froze as she felt a chill rush down her spine. It was one she was intimate with and the one she hated more than anything. Yet she knew better than to let it show, for that would be a death sentence. Bracing herself, she forced a false smile to her lips.

"My lord." She curtsied before the ancient god.

Disguised as an Apollite, the god of sorcery and the blackest craft glanced around the small room with a sneer. "What a wretched hovel they've given you."

Honestly, it was better than the death sentence his pantheon had bestowed upon her and her children. All things considered, she'd much rather have the cottage.

Besides, experience had taught her that the ancient god didn't want her to speak. So she kept her gaze on the floor and her thoughts to herself while he pranced and preened about in front of her. And she didn't miss the irony that the god of sunshine certainly brought none whatsoever to her life whenever Helios came near. Indeed, she'd be hard-pressed to decide who was gloomier—Helios or Apollo.

He stopped short and turned toward her. "How far have you progressed in my plans?"

"Stryker's son has proposed to me."

"Good girl! Which son?"

"His favorite."

For once he seemed pleased. "Well, aren't you full of surprises . . ." He smiled. "Does he love you?"

"Not yet, but he will."

His gaze intensified. "Excellent. You've proven yourself worthy. So I will give you what you've asked. You want to walk in daylight again . . . help me to remove Apollo from my pantheon. Destroy his bloodline and I'll see to it that you reign at my side as the new queen of the dawn."

"And what of my blood-hunger? How am I to eat if there are no more Apollites?"

"You remove Stryker and his wretched brood from existence, child, and I'll hand-feed you the ambrosia and nectar you need for immortality, myself."

He moved to stand in front of her. "It's a simple exchange. I want that repulsive upstart removed from my pantheon and you want your life back. Give me what I deserve and I'll give you your dreams. All you have to do is remove Apollo's bloodline from this domain where I cannot reach him without causing a war."

Helios smiled coldly. "A simple exchange and we'll both be happy."

X*yn shivered as* she felt a presence she hadn't felt in so long that at first she thought she must be imagining it. Surely, this was some forgotten nightmare.

"I'll be damned, daughter."

Her blood went cold . . . er.

Turning, she was stunned to see her father in the shadows of the falls, where Apollymi would splinter him into oblivion if she caught him invading her domain. "What are you doing here?"

Helios swept an appreciative gaze over her human form. "But for the red hair and green eyes, you are the very vision of your mother . . . before her curse."

"And again, I ask why you're here. You have one heartbeat before I alert my goddess and see you well met for your treachery."

"I doubt that. If Apollymi comes, I'll simply tell her you let me in. How else would I have been able to get through her portal without her knowledge?"

Xyn sucked her breath in sharply at his threat. She'd call him a liar, but it was the type of betrayal he and his kind specialized in. The Greeks were bastards that way, and none more so than the Titans. Hence why Zeus had castrated his own father after his father had murdered his own child.

There was nothing she'd put past them.

"How did you get in?"

"Like I'd tell you my secret?" Helios reached to touch her chin.

She recoiled from his touch as if he were a viper. And indeed, that was how she viewed him. "You've never been a father to me."

"True, but then you've never been useful before."

A chill went down her spine. "How do you mean?"

His gaze went past her to the grove where Apollymi's sacred tree grew. "The ypnsi of the Haxyn tree. There's something I want you to do with it."

She wanted to tell him that she wouldn't help him. But she knew that she didn't have the power. He'd blackmail her into it. So long as it didn't harm Urian, she'd go along with his plans.

And that made her hate herself all the more.

Just please don't let Urian find out about this . . .

June 27, 9511 BC

Urian paused as he caught sight of Apollymi sniffing at the air around him. She even smelled his hair and cloak. "Is something wrong, akra?"

She sniffed twice more at his shoulders. "I swear I smell Greek!"

Perturbed by the way she continued to sniff and paw him as if his body were the odor that offended her, he scowled. "There are a lot of olive vines my solren placed about for the ceremony."

Apollymi gave him a most peeved glare. "I know the difference between a plant and the greasy smell of one of their ilk. It reeks of a god. And this is the repellent odor of . . ." Her voice trailed off as Davyn approached them.

With Urian's mother.

Delighted beyond belief, he gasped at the sight of her. "Mata!"

Smiling, she rushed to hug him and kiss his cheeks. "Oh! Look how beautiful you are!"

"What are you doing here?"

"You didn't think I'd miss your wedding, did you?"

Apollymi scoffed and pressed her hand to her nose.

Urian ignored her as he realized that it was her way of saying that his mother must be the Greek she thought she'd been smelling.

He glanced at the goddess over his mother's head to catch her swirling gaze and rolled his eyes at her meanness.

Xedrix choked at Urian's audacity but quickly caught himself as the goddess turned her haughty gaze toward her favorite blue demon. While she might tolerate insolence from Urian, she'd never take it from her Charonte. Xedrix, she might very well pull his wings off and mount them to the wall.

Urian tucked his mother's hand into the crook of his elbow. "Come, Mata. Let me introduce you to my Thia."

Always perceptive and wary of the number of Daimons who

now called Kalosis home, she followed and stayed closely by his side. "I've missed you, Urian."

Urian tightened his hand over her fingers. "I've missed you too."

She pulled him to a stop. "Please ... I have to know. Did I do something to upset you? Is there a reason why you've stayed away for so long?"

"I know about ... " He choked on the words that burned bitter in his throat. He couldn't bring himself to mention her human lover no matter how happy the man might make her. It galled him too much to think about it.

His mother's eyes bulged as she realized what had him upset. "How do you know about Memnus?"

He ground his teeth as he realized that it was the man he'd met the last time he'd seen her. That was even more galling. "I came to see you one night and overheard the two of you."

The color faded from her cheeks. "Urian—"

He squeezed her hand reassuringly. "It's all right, Mata. I understand. You're entitled to have someone who cares for you, and I harbor no ill will toward either of you." He offered her a sincere smile. "There's nothing I want more than for you to be happy."

Cupping his jaw, she pulled his head down and pressed her cheek to his. *"S'agapo para poli moro mou."*

Those words brought tears to his eyes. He'd forgotten how much he'd missed his mother. What it felt like to be wrapped in the warmth of arms that didn't judge him or expect anything from him at all. This was the only thing missing from his relationship with Xyn. He'd give anything to have her hold him like this and warm him inside and out.

"Baba Urian! Can I go play with Abiron and Kylas?"

He laughed as he pulled back from his mother's warm embrace to see his own son. "Mata ... meet Geras, my new little one." He stepped back so that she could see Xanthia's golden-haired cherub. His short monochiton was already stained from play. No doubt his mother would have a conniption when she saw how dirty he was. But having been that age not so long ago, Urian well understood the boy's rambunctiousness. As well as the fact that his fibula wouldn't stay on his shoulder.

Kneeling, Urian repinned it a bit tighter before Xanthia saw it and fussed at Geras the way his mother used to do with him and his brothers. "Of course you may play with your cousins. Just don't get into trouble or let them lead you too close to the Charonte. They tend to eat little Apollites who venture too close to their domain."

Eyes wide in fear, Geras glanced toward Xedrix and Sabine. The orange-and-yellow-swirled Charonte female looked over as if she'd heard his words. Her eyes flashed.

Geras gasped and ran off.

With a laugh, his mother shook her head. "Fatherhood looks good on you. But then you were always patient with your nieces and nephews."

Though she'd meant it as a compliment, it only saddened and wounded him deep in his heart. In a perfect world, he'd have loved a house full of children. To watch them grow and play.

But not in this world. Not with their curse hanging over their heads.

He and Paris both agreed on that. They refused to do what their other siblings had selfishly done and force their children to face their death sentence. He was all too aware of how close that deadline loomed. Of how precious every night between now and then was.

And how precarious every breath afterward would be. He vowed that he would relish whatever time he had.

Even if it meant being married to a woman he didn't really love for the sake of convenience. After all, he didn't have the luxury of waiting.

"Is he her only child?"

"Nay. She has a daughter." Urian jerked his chin toward Nephele, who was standing off in a small circle of friends. Her purple peplos had been borrowed from Tannis, yet it was extremely fetching on the girl. Too fetching for Urian's comfort, as he wanted to chase away all the young boys Nephele's beauty attracted. While she might not be his natural daughter, he was no less protective of her and he considered her as much his daughter as if he'd sired her. "Her name is Nephele."

"If she looks anything like her mother, then your Xanthia must be a great beauty indeed."

"Thank you."

They turned at the sound of Xanthia's voice to find her behind them.

Urian inclined his head respectfully. "Mata . . . meet my bride."

Gripping one another's forearms, they gracefully kissed each cheek in turn, and then Xanthia curtsied to the human mother she'd cursed Urian for having. He watched them closely, ready to intervene at any second if Xanthia said anything to hurt his mother's feelings.

"It's a pleasure to meet you, *kyria*. Urian has had such wonderful things to say about you. I feel as if we've already met."

"You're too kind, Xanthia. And I'm thrilled to see my boy so well settled, and with such a great beauty no less. I'm sure the goddess will bless you both with even more children."

"I hope so. Nothing would thrill me more." Xanthia's eyes widened. "Please excuse me. . . . Geras! Don't you dare!" She rushed off after Geras, who was trying to light a fire from his posterior.

Urian shook his head at the boy's antics.

"Don't you dare laugh." His mother popped him playfully on his bare arm. "I seem to recall a certain pair of twins doing the same thing at that age."

"Aye, but we were better at it. We actually succeeded."

"And almost set fire to your solren's study."

"And he in turn set fire to our asses," Paris said with a jovial laugh as he joined them. "Greetings, Mata. How are you?"

Smiling, she cupped his chin and kissed him. "Wonderful, now that I've seen my boys. And where's your better half?"

"Ah! I always knew you preferred Davyn to me, and now I have proof." His golden-blond curls dancing, he sobered as the merriment went out of his eyes. "I told him to stay home, if that's all right. He's still mourning the loss of his sister and her family."

Urian winced. "Understood. The last thing I want is to cause him more pain."

"Good. He feared you might think his absence was meant as a disrespect or slight."

Urian was aghast. "Never. I know his heart better than that. I'd never lay such ill intent upon him."

That relaxed his twin instantly. "Such evil's not in him, either. It's why I'm with him over anyone else. While others scheme and plot, he's loyal to a fault."

No one knew that better than Urian, except for probably Paris.

Their mother straightened Paris's cloak. "Then I will make sure and visit with him before I leave. I can't go home without seeing all my boys and letting them know I love them."

Paris smiled. "I've missed you, Mata."

"And I you." She glanced over his shoulder to where one of the Daimons was eyeing her.

Urian glared at the bastard, daring him to even think about coming near them.

"I've got him." Paris left them to go have words with the man who was new to their world and who had no idea that Hellen was off his menu.

Forever.

Even so, she moved a little closer to Urian. "There are a lot more here than there were before."

"Aye. More come here every day to seek refuge from the human world."

"Like your soon-to-be bride."

He nodded.

"Yet you do not love her."

Urian froze at those words.

His mother slid a gimlet stare toward him. "Deny it if I'm wrong."

The problem was, she'd seen a truth he didn't like admitting out loud. A truth he did his best to conceal from everyone.

Even himself.

But she was his mother and she knew his heart better than anyone other than Xyn, who had also commented on a fact he couldn't hide from her either.

His mother's face fell instantly as tears welled in her eyes. "Oh, baby . . . why are you doing this if you don't love her?"

"She feeds me, Mata. No one else will. I have to have blood to live."

Swallowing hard, she squeezed his arm. "I'm so sorry, Urian. You deserve to have a fiery passion. The kind that makes you mindless and—"

"Nay, Mata," he said, cutting her off before someone overheard her words and carried them to Xanthia. "I don't want that. Ever. Our lives are too short. I want control of myself. We have to have that in order to survive."

She scoffed. "My pragmatist. You're too young to be so old. So jaded. What has killed the boy inside you?"

His gaze went to where his father sat alone on his cold, black throne made of the bones of Misos's enemies, and old memories stirred inside him. "That boy died the night I saw my father go Daimon after his own father tried to end his life, and I realized that there is no mercy in this world for any of us. We are all damned from the cradle to the grave. Life isn't for the meek. It's for those too stubborn to give in."

She sucked her breath in sharply. "What have they done to you?"

Simple. He'd been slapped on the ass the moment he'd arrived into this world, covered in someone else's blood, and life had been steadily kicking his ass ever since. Without stopping or hesitating. Honestly, he was punch-drunk from it all.

It seemed as if every time he thought he could stand up and breathe, someone or something else came along with a stunning blow that knocked him to his knees. He could never catch a break.

But he didn't want her to worry. "Nothing, Mata. I merely gave in to the demon inside me sooner than the others. Instead of fighting him, I embraced him as a necessary part of me. Now we snuggle up under the covers as great bedfellows. After all, we are Daimons, aren't we?"

Her eyes saddened over his words. "You're part human, Uri, and you're not a Daimon yet."

But he couldn't afford to be human. Not now. Not ever. That would only get him killed. Just as it had done Davyn's family.

The meek only inherited earth six feet beneath their feet.

And he was about to have his own family to look after.

Time for childhood was over. This world didn't allow for compassion or mercy. It required vigilance and a merciless sword arm.

After tonight, he would be a husband and a father himself. He had much more than just himself to think about now. His gaze went to Nephele and Geras.

To Xanthia.

Much more.

"Urian? You're scaring me." No one could miss the terror in his mother's kind voice.

"Don't be afraid, Mata. I'm the very thing you raised me to be."

She sank her hand into his white-blond hair and forced him to meet her gaze. "Never lose sight of what I taught you, Urian. Honor. Integrity. Loyalty. *Mercy*."

Aye, but only for his own family.

No one else.

After all, he was his father's son, too. And like Stryker, his mercy had a finite limitation. *If I don't feed on it or fuck it, I don't give a shit.* His father's code was a simple one to grasp.

This world was brutal to its core and it cared nothing for them. Therefore, they cared nothing for it. Their only goal was to survive. Whatever it took.

Over, under, around, or through. Those who stood behind you, you protected. Those who stood at your side were worthy allies, and anyone who stood in front of you was a target to be destroyed.

It was a simple code. And it was one that kept them alive.

From this night forward, he would be Urian Kleopas, and they would all rue the night they'd facetiously given him that epithet.

June 30, 9511 BC

"Damn, what's in that woman's blood that it fuels you so?"

Urian laughed at Archie's question as he kicked his brother back and almost beheaded him. "What's the matter, *adelphos*? Can't you keep up?"

"Theo!" Archie cried out for reinforcement.

Urian turned to take both of his brothers on at once. They weren't supposed to use their powers while practicing on the field. It was something their father insisted on, just in case they were ever in some kind of trap or device where their powers were locked or stripped, and they were forced to use nothing except their battle skills.

Tonight, Archie and Theo decided to cheat. Without warning, both unleashed a god-bolt on him that knocked him flat on his ass. Groaning in pain, he rolled and came to his feet. He felt the fury rush through his veins.

Before he could stop himself, he lashed out with his own powers. His blast rolled out and sent them flying.

"Urian!"

At first, he didn't recognize his father's stern voice. Not until Stryker grabbed him and shook him hard.

Slowly, Urian came to and saw what his family did.

Peculiar symbols glowed all over his body, iridescent and beautiful. He'd never seen anything like it.

Blinking, he swallowed. "Solren? What happened?" He had no memory of anything from the last few minutes as he turned a slow circle, trying to get his bearings.

His father let out a deep, sinister growl. "Do you remember anything?"

Shaken by what he saw, he slowly scowled. "Nay."

His father turned to glare at Archie and Theo. "What did you do?"

They gaped.

Then Archie sputtered, "Why's it *our* fault?"

Releasing Urian, his father stalked them like a fierce predator ready to tear them apart. "Because you're the ones who assaulted your brother."

Theo used his sword to gesture at Urian. "That doesn't make us responsible for the fact that he's a freak!"

Paris draped himself against Urian's back. "Hear that, Uri. You're a freak."

"Shut up." Urian shrugged him off.

Laughing, Paris staggered away.

But Paris's amusement and Urian's irritation were cut short as a scream rang out.

"Dear gods, what now?" Stryker sighed heavily.

Until he realized it was Telamon's wife, Natassa, they heard. Then he teleported to their home.

Urian stood paralyzed in their practice arena as he felt pain piercing his chest. It was unlike anything he'd ever experienced before. Without being told, he knew his brother was dead. He didn't know how, but he did.

Rage blinded him as he went running through the dark streets of Kalosis. He was so blinded by it that he didn't even think to use his powers to flash himself to his brother's home.

Instead, he dodged the curious onlookers who were heading toward the screams to see what was happening. By the time he got to Telamon's house, Urian was breathless and panting. Shaking and sweating.

Terrified, he pushed his way through the crowd, into the house to where his family was gathered, in hysterics and tears.

If Urian lived for eternity, he would never forget the sight of his father kneeling on the floor of Telly's room by his brother's side. Holding Telamon's hand, their father wept as if his very soul had been shattered. Urian hadn't even known that his father was capable of such gut-wrenching tears. Never mind the racking sobs that shook a warrior so fierce. So proud.

His father clutched at Telamon's lifeless body as if it were a rag doll. All around him, his brothers were on their knees, every bit as shaken.

Those communal wails rumbled through Urian's body like a second heartbeat and shook him to the core of his foundation. Only Apollites left a corpse to bury. Daimons disintegrated upon death. Were his father to die, there would be nothing left of his body for them to mourn. Within minutes of death, all six feet, eight inches of their father's massively muscled warrior's body would be nothing more than a fine golden powder that would flitter away, forever lost in the breeze.

A faint memory.

But Telamon was still an Apollite.

His body remained intact. And their father refused to release him.

His brother looked as if he were simply sleeping. As if he'd awaken any moment and insult Urian. Or call him out for some imagined slight.

In that instant of his own grief, Urian felt his entire being heating up again. Felt the same electrical charge stirring that had gone through him when his brothers had attacked him earlier. It was bitter and tasted like acid in his mouth. Those peculiar markings on his flesh returned. Only brighter this time. From shoulder to fingertip, his arm glowed.

Before he realized what he was doing, he moved across the floor to where his brother lay in his father's arms and splayed his hand against the center of Telamon's chest.

The instant he touched him, a bright flash shot from his fingertips and into Telamon. Urian felt the jolt charging through his entire body, radiating through his cells and flowing into his brother's chest.

Telamon's back arched. He vibrated all over as if he were being electrocuted. Then after a few minutes, he went stone still.

Everyone turned toward Urian. They glared at him accusingly. His father rose slowly to his feet.

Urian didn't move. Nor did he let go of Telamon's chest or arm. It was as if they were bonded together. As if were he to let go, it would kill him for sure. He didn't know why he thought that, but he did.

Gasping, his brother opened his eyes to stare up at him.

Then cursed Urian.

Their father's jaw fell open. He eyed Urian as if he were Zeus himself, come down from the theocropolis of Olympus to meet them. "What did you do?"

Stunned, Urian shook his head, every bit as dumbfounded as they were. He looked down at his glowing arm and hand. They continued to throb with a power of some primal energy he couldn't even begin to describe or comprehend.

Not until Apollymi appeared in the room in her Destroyer incarnation.

Her black hair whipped out around her while her red eyes swirled. An unseen wind caused her hair and gown to twist about her lithe body like ribbons in a hurricane. "Who dared to summon a Source god into my domain!"

His father moved to shield him so that the Destroyer couldn't see Urian's glowing arm or anything else. "No one, akra."

Those actions only made him love his father more. The fact that he'd seek to protect him was the ultimate act of loyalty, but Urian wasn't a fool.

No one could hide *this* from Apollymi. It would be suicide to try. And she'd kill them both for the lie.

"Something happened to me, akra." Urian held his arm up for her to see it.

Her hair turned white again as she lowered herself to the floor and became the goddess who used to let him gaze into her mirror to see the daylight. She cast her gaze around the room to everyone gathered there. "Come with me, Urian."

Without hesitation, his father stepped forward. "Akra—"

"Stay out of this, Strykerius," she hissed.

His father hesitated.

Urian wanted to reassure his father that he'd be fine, but by her tone, he knew better than to speak. She was not in the mood for *any* kind of argument or another word.

Though to be honest, he wasn't quite sure what this mood of hers was. It hovered between a pique and unadulterated fury.

So instead, he cast what he hoped was an unassuming smile toward his father and followed her from the room, out toward her palace.

As soon as they were alone, Apollymi turned toward him with a glower that he normally received from his father after he punched one of his brothers. "What did you do?" Her tone was sharp and brittle.

Urian shrugged. "My brother was dead, and I touched him and . . . "

She cursed beneath her breath.

Completely baffled, he tried to comprehend why she was so angry at him. "What is it?"

"A power I never foresaw you possessing. Now you must learn to control it or else, like Midas, it will destroy your life. And everyone around you."

Those words chilled him all the way to his soul, especially the way she said them. What could she mean? "I don't understand, akra."

She growled deep in her throat before she answered. "Those markings on your arm are from the most ancient of languages. One of the very first. You hold powers from the goddess Bathymaas."

His jaw went slack at the mention of the first goddess of balance and life. A goddess of divine justice.

Long ago, when the gods had warred with each other, she alone had found a way to protect mankind and the Apollites from them. Until the bitter gods had destroyed her for it.

But it didn't make sense that he'd have been born with her mark. Why?

"How is that possible?"

"You're born of the gods, Urian, you know this. Such creatures are ever a hodgepodge of peculiar gifts. One never knows how they'll align inside their children. Not until it's too late."

He supposed that made sense. Yet Bathymaas was one of the oldest of the goddesses. A primary power.

Enemy of Apollo.

Why would she choose *him* as a vessel to carry a gift of such magnitude when they weren't related and didn't even share a pantheon? It didn't make sense.

Apollymi's expression turned even grimmer. "But the real question is, what will become of that power inside you once you turn Daimon? Therein lies the rub, *pido*, as no one has ever done so before. And it's not something Apollo took into account when he cursed you and your father and brothers."

"What are you saying, akra?"

"That your inherited power from a goddess that powerful could mutate into who knows what." She let out a long, tired breath. Then she turned to stare at him. "Today you saved your brother's life, Urian. Tomorrow, you could kill them all ... and yourself. Because we know nothing of your powers and you don't understand how to wield them. One day, you might even have the ability to rupture the very fabric of the universe. There's just no telling who or what you could become. All we know is that it'll be an exciting day."

She laughed bitterly. "Maybe not a good one for whomever is in your path. But exciting nonetheless."

July 9, 9511 BC

"From leper to god in three heartbeats. It's terrifying. Really." Urian passed a disgusted grimace to Davyn as he dislodged another beautiful woman from his crotch.

This one actually whimpered in protest.

Urian was tempted to do so as well, especially given how irritated he was at the never-ending line of women who were intent on his seduction.

"I'm married," he repeated to her for the third time. Gah! Where had all this attention been when he'd been literally starving and in need?

She pursed her lips at him. "As am I. My husband said he wouldn't mind. That *your* infused blood could fortify us both. He wants me to feed from you. He'll even join us if you want. My sister, too."

Disgusted by that, Urian stood up and moved away as if she were on fire. Last thing he wanted was an orgy from people who only wanted to use him. Forget that!

Davyn quickly stepped between them to provide a block for him. "Sorry, love. If anyone gets an extramarital piece of his scrumptious ass, I've a prior claim to it, as I've been the one begging for it far longer than you." He winked at her.

Her jaw dropped.

As did Urian's. Flashing his fangs in an unrepentant grin, Davyn grabbed his arm possessively and dragged him away. But not before he cast an evil smirk at the woman, then grabbed a handful of Urian's buttocks.

"Hey now!" Urian gasped, stepping away before Davyn got them both clobbered by a jealous Paris.

Or worse, a furious Xanthia. "I can't believe you just said or did that."

Davyn shrugged. "I can't believe she had the nerve to search your private business in such a public manner. Makes me rather jealous I hadn't thought to do so, but I'm not so rude. Or suicidal. Paris would kill me if I dared to sit on your crotch or fondle it."

"So say you. I recall a few rather daring gropes from you in that particular area in the past."

Davyn scoffed. "Name me one!"

"You were drunk, still—"

"Those don't count."

Urian snorted in defiance of his glib tone. "I beg to differ, and so does my private business, as you say."

Davyn laughed. "Aye, well, be that as it may, I don't remember it, so it didn't happen. Besides, I can't believe we're now having to guard you as carefully as we used to have to guard my man-lamb and his hind and front quarters from others. Who'd have thought?"

"Indeed," Urian agreed. "The world's gone madder than normal."

"It's not that." Ophion grabbed Urian away from Davyn and hauled him toward an exit in a different direction.

Once they were on the street, Ophion reached back into the building and pulled Davyn through the door, then slammed it shut and locked it. "Word's out on you, *adelphos*. Everyone knows what you did for Telly. Now they all think you have the powers of a god and can heal them. So if they partake of your semen, they believe they'll become instantly immortal."

Urian's jaw fell again. "I'm not the god Set! Are they insane?"

Ophie raised his arms in surrender. "Don't spear Hermes. Merely passing on the town gossip. They're the ones hailing you as the savior of our people. Sickening, truly, as I know you for the idiot you are. Half of them are proclaiming you as the mystical Day-Walker, prophesied to save us from our curse. They think you're capable of anything, now."

Urian went bug-eyed. "Shite to that! Last thing I need is a bunch of fools tossing me to the daylight like I'm Andromeda to Poseidon's sea monster or something."

"Well, I'd like to feed you to a sea monster, most days, but for other reasons."

Urian shoved at his brother. "You're such a pain."

"Learned it from you."

Growling, Urian rolled his eyes. "Oh, to have had a solren who could have kept his prick to himself for one night. Damn him for all the brothers I trip over constantly. Should have let Hades take the bastard and beat him, rather than save his life and start *this*."

Ophie kissed his cheek. "Ah now, you'd miss us if we weren't here to aggravate you."

Urian scoffed. "Doubt that."

Davyn stopped suddenly and without warning, causing Urian to walk right into him.

"What are you doing?" He rubbed at his forehead, which he'd banged into the back of Davyn's skull.

Davyn didn't speak. He merely gestured at the crowd lined up outside the door of Urian's home.

Ah, bloody hell . . .

He'd never seen the like. It was as if they were giving out alms on a feast day.

Davyn leaned his head back to grin at him over his shoulder. "One well-placed god-bolt could take out about half of them." He flashed his fangs in an evil grin. "What say you?"

Urian grimaced in absolute agony of the thought of what waited there for him. "Don't tempt me." And it *was* tempting. These were the same people who'd had no use for him just a few days ago.

Until he had a power they thought they could make use of.

Funny how that worked.

And it left Urian extremely disenchanted with the lot of them. For he'd seen their true colors at a much earlier age than most saw it. Because he'd been born with the abnormality of blue eyes and not their brown Apollite ones, they hadn't hidden their disdain for him. That made it all the harder for him to hide his resentment of them now.

Especially when they turned to rush him, begging for favors, these Apollites who'd refused to share the most basic sustenance with him when he'd been in need. They'd have seen him dead and in the street without losing a bit of sleep over it.

They were deplorable in their hypocrisy.

"Urian! Remember how close we were when we were boys? We were always together. Inseparable!"

He stared at Theo's friend Iolus, who'd never spoken to him before. This was the same friend who used to tell Theo to make sure he left Urian at home, because he couldn't stand Urian. *"Your brother creeps me out with those freakish eyes of his."*

Aye, Urian remembered him well.

"Enough!" his father roared as he joined them. "Let the boy alone! If you want a miracle, write them down and hand them to Trates. Urian can review them later to see if he wishes to indulge you."

They protested, but luckily his father wouldn't be swayed.

Urian jerked his head as he felt something strange in the air.

His father scowled at him. "You all right?"

"Nay. Did you feel that?"

"Feel what?"

"Something . . ." Urian scanned the dark street around them. But the sensation crawling along his skin only grew worse, not better. "There's a god here."

His father gave him a droll, bored stare. "That would be Apollymi. You can't miss her. Tall, blond, angry goddess. Lives in the big, dark hall on your right."

He snorted at his father's sarcasm. "Nay. This is different. Can't you sense it?"

His father shook his head. "I can only feel Apollymi and her Charonte."

Yet Urian sensed it. Fiercely. There was no denying the powerful sensation of another god in their midst. The sensation crept along his skin. Undeniable.

Unmistakable.

Worse, it was malevolent.

"This is something else, Solren."

His father glanced around the crowd that didn't want to disperse before he lowered his voice to speak to them. "There's something I need to speak to all of you about. I was going to wait until later, but ... "

"What?"

"War's coming. Unlike anything you've seen. The devastation in Xanthia's village wasn't just an isolated attack. We've been blessed that the goddess took us in when she did. Because life on the surface ... " His father visibly winced. "After Apollymi's attack on Atlantis that devastated most of the world, and the loss of the Atlantean pantheon, it's thrown the power balance of the gods into turmoil. And with it, the Chthonians."

Paris scowled. "What do you mean?"

"Just what I said. With the destruction of one pantheon, the Chthonians are at each other's throats on how to restore the balance of the universe and realign the gods and their territories. And while they fight, the gods are vying for power. Our scattered people haven't found their footing and are being systematically slaughtered the instant they are identified."

Urian glanced to his brothers as he digested that news and what it meant for all of them. "Is that why so many Apollites have bartered with all manner of fey and demons? To spawn races in an effort to try to circumvent Apollo's curse?"

His father nodded. "I don't know how that'll play out in the coming years. But knowing the gods as I do, they usually put such races down like rabid beasts. Until we see how this goes, my suggestion is to lie low and give them time to kill each other off."

Ophion bristled at those words. "You speak of cowardice at a time when we should be helping them?"

Their father backhanded Ophion for the insult. "I speak of sanity, idiot! The nail that stands out is hammered down. And I won't see our people fall needlessly to feed anyone's ego."

"What of our mother?" Urian braced himself for an equally violent reaction from his father.

To his surprise, he handed him a small yellow sfora similar

to the red one Stryker used to spy on the human realm. "I'll entrust this to you. I gave her a means to summon us should she be attacked, as well as the option of returning here to live. She chose to stay among her own kind. Hellen made it clear that she doesn't want to return to Kalosis."

Those words stung his heart, but Urian wouldn't fault her for them. It was wrong to make her live in darkness when she didn't have to. His mother deserved to live in the light. "I will watch over her."

Paris took Davyn's hand. "Do we have a Chthonian who protects us, Solren?"

"Nay. They don't care about us. Apollites are on their own as far as the gods are concerned. Apollymi is all we have. She alone cares."

Ophion's eyes darkened. "That's not right."

"Since when is life fair or just?" Urian laughed bitterly at his brother's stupidity.

His father sighed. "Sadly, Urian's right. This isn't about fairness. It's about survival. Fuck my father! I am not burying my sons or daughter because he's an asshole who had to screw a cheap Greek whore. Let the world above burn to the ground and let them tear themselves apart. We're safe here, and here we will stay."

Paris cleared his throat again. Louder this time. "Um ... Solren? There's only one small problem."

"And that is?"

"You're already a Daimon and the rest of us aren't far behind. So how are we to survive locked down here without the human souls we need to keep from becoming dust?"

Urian flinched at a very raw truth that could kill them all. A truth that filled him with absolute terror.

Urian?

He savored the sound of Xyn's voice in his head. It was like a mental caress that never failed to warm him all the way through.

Desperate to see her, he found her next to her falls, near the orchard. "Greetings, my fairest lady." He wrapped his arms around her long, warm neck and breathed in that sweet scent that was uniquely his dragon.

She lifted him up in her clawed hand to cradle him. *What's wrong?*

Laughing, he eyed the razor talon that was only a few inches from his face. "Most would see *this*." He carefully tugged at it. "What kind of fool am I to lie here with *that*, this close, and not have any fear?"

You know I'd never harm you.

"True." Sighing, he tucked his hands behind his head and crossed his ankles while she carried him toward her cave. "I felt a god here earlier. Did you?"

She arched a spiny brow at that. *Apollymi.*

Irritated, he grimaced up at her. "I swear, if one more person says that to me, I will react violently. Not Apollymi. Someone else. Completely different power."

Sarraxyn pressed her lips together as fear spread through her. Somehow, Urian must have sensed her father's earlier visit when he'd dropped in again to press her to act against Apollymi and Urian. She'd told Helios not to come.

He didn't listen. Part of being a god—they thought they knew best and were always up to speed. But if that were true, then Helios wouldn't have been pushed aside so easily by the Olympians.

However, the last time she'd made the mistake of pointing that out to her father, he'd blasted her so hard that her brother Veles had been forced to intervene. Otherwise, she wouldn't have survived the vicious assault.

Closing her eyes, she tried to think of some way to distract Urian from this mess.

How are you adjusting to your wife? Though she hated to ask, and resented Xanthia with a passion, it seemed the safest topic.

At least that was her thought until she felt him go rigid in her palm. Perhaps marriage didn't agree with her little Apollite, after all.

One could hope.

Urian?

He sighed and sat up to make a face. "I should be grateful."

I sense a "but" in that statement.

"But"—he smirked at her—"there's a coldness to her some-times. Is that normal?"

Xyn bit back a scoff at the question. *You're asking me when I've never been around anyone to know?*

He winced visibly. "Sorry. That was cruel of me. I didn't think."

She fell silent as she listened to the rhythm of his heart change. He was so sad that it made her own heart ache for him in sympa-thetic pain. More than that, it made her bold enough to speak a secret that she kept buried deep inside. *What if you had someone who loved you, Uri? But couldn't feed you?*

"What do you mean?"

Like your father. What if you fell in love with a human or someone else? Someone not an Apollite or Daimon. What would you do?

He snorted disdainfully. "That would never happen. I wouldn't let myself."

Xyn felt her heart shrivel with his bitter words. *It's rather small-minded of you, isn't it?*

"Hardly. I'm only being practical. How could I eat if I chose to love another?"

How easy he made it sound—like love was a choice. If it were, she wouldn't be in this kind of pain. And his attitude seriously pissed her off. Her vision darkened as she had a sudden urge to fling him to the ground and crush him. "Being an idiot, you mean!"

His eyes widened as she spoke her words out loud. "Xyn?"

Furious, she set him down on the ground before she gave in to her impulse to harm him. "Go home, Urian. You're not safe here."

"What do you mean?"

When he refused to go, she shot a blast of fire at him.

Urian barely dodged Xyn's incendiary breath. The flames were a lot hotter than a normal fire. As it was, it singed him and burned his skin even though it didn't come near his position.

Holy Katateros! He'd had no idea of her power until then. No idea just how dangerous his dragon actually was.

Blowing cool air over his skin to alleviate the burn, he rushed away from her garden. He was halfway home before he realized what must have angered her.

The question she'd asked before she lost her mind.

But no ... Xyn couldn't care for him. Not like *that*. She was a dragon.

He was an Apollite.

That wasn't even physically possible.

Then again, dragons abducted maidens all the time. Of course, in his mind, he'd always assumed they'd eaten them.

Now he wondered about the outcome ...

Zeus and even his grandfather had supposedly impregnated humans while in the forms of other beasts. Bulls, swans, water ...

Surely Xyn didn't want him to do *that* with her.

Did she?

The thought terrified him. It horrified him. He was married, and even if he weren't, they were friends.

Best friends, and had been for years. Like ...

Paris and Davyn.

Shite.

Urian slowed down as he realized that they were closer than regular friends. The two of them had shared much in their seclusion. More than that, Xyn had taken care of him. She'd been his refuge when the others were more than he could bear.

It can't work, Uri. She's an animal. A dragon.

And he had a wife to care for. There could never be anything between him and Xyn.

Never.

Yet still there was something inside him ... something that scared him even more than his thoughts. A feeling he had that he honestly couldn't deny.

He did love her.

And that would damn them both.

September 7, 9510 BC

Urian drew up short as he entered Apollymi's palace and found the one thing he'd never found before.

A stranger.

"Who are you?"

The tall, exceptionally thin woman turned around. She was breathtaking. And dressed in a most peculiar fashion—a short green chiton similar to what a man might wear, cut just above her shapely knees. A long, brown, finely woven chalmys was carefully draped around her thin shoulders and pinned with an ornate pearl-and-gold fibula that formed a double bow. Her golden-blond hair was intricately braided and coiled around her head in a style befitting a goddess.

By her grace, height, and beauty, Urian might have mistaken her for an Apollite. Except she didn't have fangs. Nor were her eyes brown. Rather, they were a vivid, exceptional green that were more akin to those of his aunt Artemis.

Or at least that was what he'd been told about her.

And now that he thought about it, this woman reeked of Greek divinity. To such an extent that he was surprised Apollymi wasn't out here trying to locate her position with one of the three-headed dogs she used in her palace as guards.

Or a few sniffing Charonte. Normally such a powerful presence in their midst would warrant at least Xedrix out here to investigate it.

So why was this Greek maiden in Apollymi's Stygian palace? Holding a war bow? And wearing running sandals in the garb of a boy?

Nothing about this made a bit of sense to him.

"You haven't answered my question." He used a sharper tone this time to let her know how dire her situation was.

Her brow arched, she raked him with a hostile glare. "Who are *you*, and why are *you* here?"

That audacious growl set off his own temper. "I'm not the one trespassing."

"Neither am I."

Yeah, right. No Greek belonged here and he knew it.

Hissing, he teleported to stand in front of her. "I would beg to differ."

She smirked. "Beg all you want. Your theatrics leave me cold."

Before he could respond, Xedrix appeared beside them. His mottled blue skin seemed darker than normal as he glared down at them and tsked like an irate parent. "Do not try the patience of the Destroyer, children. She's in no mood for your foolery."

He snatched them both by the arm and dragged them down the hall to Apollymi's garden, where the goddess waited in her spot by her mirror.

Urian locked his jaw so as not to protest the harsh grip, and noticed that the girl did the same.

Apollymi gasped as she saw how they were being treated. "Xedrix! Release them!"

He did so immediately. "Forgive me, akra. They were quarreling."

Rising from her seat, she shook her head. "So you beat them?"

The demon shrugged with an unfathomable nonchalance given the anger in Apollymi's eyes. "I wanted to eat them instead, but thought you might take more issue with *that*. This seemed the better option."

She sighed heavily, as if curbing a desire to skin her favorite demon. "Fine." She waved the demon aside with her hand, then came forward to address Urian and the girl. "I suppose it's time the two of you met, as you were bound to cross paths at some point. Urian, this is my Abadonna, Katra. Katra, meet Urian, the son of Stryker—leader of my Spathi army."

Urian's nostrils twitched at the introduction. "She reeks of Artemis." This must have been the stench he'd smelled earlier.

Katra bristled. "I'm one of her servants, and you could use a bath yourself, buddy. How many days have you been sweating in that training armor, anyway? You should make a point of meeting the goddess of hygiene and making friends. Really." She pressed her hand daintily to her nose to emphasize her insult.

He narrowed his gaze dangerously. "Why is she here, akra?"

With an uncharacteristic glint in her pale eyes, Apollymi watched them curiously. "She's a spy for me."

Urian gaped.

The wide-eyed look on Katra's face said that those words were news to her as well, but Urian wasn't dumb enough to contradict a highly volatile goddess.

Even so, Katra cocked her head to study him with the same curiosity someone might use with an insect. "I've never seen an Apollite before." She lifted her hand. "May I?"

Offended that she'd treat him like an experiment, he lifted his chin to protest. "I'm not a freak."

"I know. But you are different from anyone I've ever seen before, so I'm curious."

He glanced toward Apollymi.

"Show Katra what the bastard did to your people. Let her see what an animal does to his own son and grandchildren. Help her understand why she should hate him and never trust Artemis, who has turned her back on you. You are the goddess's nephew, after all. Yet she does nothing for her own blood. Let Katra see how much love the cold bitch has in her heart for her family."

Katra passed a peeved stare at her but didn't speak a word of contradiction.

Opening his mouth, Urian allowed the girl to examine his fangs. Though the term "girl" was probably uncharitable of him. Most likely, she was close to his true age and yet she looked to be a teen, whereas because he was an Apollite, he appeared a full-grown man in his mid-twenties.

She gently fingered the sharp tips of his fangs. "Do they hurt?"

"Nay. I've never had any other kind of teeth."

"And you don't eat food or drink anything other than blood?"

He shook his head.

She fretted. "How awful."

"You don't miss what you don't know."

"Not true. I miss my father every day of my life, yet I've never known him. And I'm forever curious about every detail of him and his life."

That was different, he supposed. Missing a father wasn't the same as being forced to drink blood. He couldn't imagine a life where he didn't know who his father was. Or not seeing him every day.

There was nothing in life more important to him than his family. And in particular, he valued his parents. Both of them.

But all in all, Katra was an odd bit of fluff, with some rather peculiar thoughts. Urian scowled at her. "And I prefer not to torture myself with thoughts over what I don't have or what I'm missing. Life's too willing to do it for me."

"Dark much?"

He snorted at her sarcasm. "Hard to be light and fluffy when you're banished to a hell realm."

Katra paused to consider that. "You've never seen daylight, have you?"

He glanced past her to Apollymi, who watched them with a disturbing intensity. How he wished he could read her thoughts. Or Katra's at the moment. "Only through the goddess's mirror."

"Wow. I'm sorry." Katra appeared to actually mean it.

Urian shrugged before he spoke an absolute truth. "Don't be. I'd rather not see daylight than be stuck serving Artemis."

Katra gaped at his insult. "Ouch! I can tell we're going to get along not at all."

"Fine with me." He turned toward Apollymi and offered her a quick bow. "If you'll excuse me, akra?"

Katra watched Urian leave and shook her head.

"Is something wrong?" Apollymi asked.

"Why didn't you tell him we're cousins?"

"For the same reason no one needs to know you're my grand-daughter, Katra. Of secret things, we are silence. As much as I hate your mother, we have to protect Artemis's reputation in order to protect my son. Therefore, Strykerius is never to know that you're Apollo's niece."

And still there was another matter that disturbed her as Katra stared after the peculiar Apollite who'd left them.

"For goodness' sake, child. What else is on your mind?"

Katra tilted her head. "Why does Urian look so much like my father?"

Apollymi scoffed. "They say Urian is the image of Strykerius."

She scoffed at that explanation. "I've seen Stryker. Aside from his blond hair and carriage, there's only passing similarity between them. But I've seen my mother watching after my father enough to know his *every* feature. While I've never seen Acheron in the flesh, I know the line of his jaw, the shape of his nose and eyes. The fine arch of his brows. And he and Urian could be twins. The only difference is that Urian's skin is a bit darker in tone."

"Because his mother's Egyptian."

The news shocked Katra, who'd had no idea of Urian's real mother. "Pardon?"

Apollymi froze as she realized the unintentional slip she'd made. But it was easy to do. She spent so much time alone that she wasn't used to having to guard her tongue or censor herself. And here she was telling Katra to be careful ...

"Nothing. Just remember what I said. Speak of nothing said here. Keep to yourself."

"Believe me, I'm good at that. I have to be to protect my matisera from the other gods."

Apollymi pulled Katra against her and hugged her. "You should let me kill Artemis. For all our sakes. Cut her throat while she sleeps."

"Yaya! I can't do that! I do love her."

Those words wrested a deep-seated groan from her. "Why?" she groused. "She's completely unlovable."

"Not to me. Besides, there are many who think the same of you and it's completely untrue. And speaking of which, I need to get back before she misses me. She'll die if she ever learns I come here to see you."

"Good! Should I send her a basket to thank her for your visits?"

"Yaya!" Katra huffed, then kissed her cheek. "Take care and I'll see you soon."

Apollymi let her go reluctantly. She still couldn't believe that Katra was real. That her precious son had fathered a child without anyone knowing. Had she not seen the girl with her own eyes and held her in her own arms, she wouldn't have believed it. But there was no denying this truth.

Katra was Apostolos's daughter.

If only Katra would renounce her loyalty to her mother. So long as she remained tied to two pantheons, Katra was a danger to both. She could be used against either side.

Just like Urian's real mother. Had Bethany not inadvertently given her protection over to the Greeks because she loved Prince Styxx, the Atlanteans would have destroyed the Greek army that first day in battle and won their war against Greece before it started.

Then Princess Ryssa wouldn't have been given to Apollo to win his favor, and she and her son wouldn't have died, thus causing the curse for Stryker and his people.

More to the point, had Bethany not had divided loyalties Apostolos wouldn't have been slaughtered. And Atlantis wouldn't have been destroyed.

Divided loyalties could never be trusted. She only trusted Strykerius now because his father had forever severed their bond when he'd cursed Strykerius's children to die. There was no repairing *that* with mere words. Strykerius would never forgive Apollo for his damnation of their innocence.

She would make sure of it . . .

April 17, 9508 BC

"Solren? Please don't get mad ... I was playing with your sfora when I saw *this*."

Urian looked up from where he sat in their front room, polishing his sword, to see Geras holding his crystal sfora in his hand. He smiled gently at the boy. "I'm not angry, *m'gios*." He tried to have patience with his son. "Though you should ask before you get into my things."

Placing the oiled cloth aside, Urian held his hand out for the boy to show him why he was so upset and fretting.

Geras moved closer to hand him the small ball.

Urian took a moment to reassure his nervous son that he wasn't angry. Geras was literally shaking, he was so frightened. He set his kopis aside and pulled Geras into the circle of his arms so that he could stand between his knees and see into the sfora clearly. "So what did you glimpse that has you so upset?"

Biting his lip, Geras held it up in front of the fire to show him.

The flames flickered in the pale crystal. At first there was nothing except the mist that swirled like Apollymi's eyes.

Until Urian saw his mother's home.

And the body of her lover lying in the yard with four arrows protruding from his back.

Cold fear went through him and shook him to the core of his soul. He couldn't breathe or think.

He shot to his feet.

"Solren?"

Too scared to look closer at the house on his own, Urian almost stumbled over his son. "I-I'm not angry, Geras. I'm grateful." Kissing him on the head, he reached for his sword. Before he summoned his brothers to this waking nightmare, he wanted to verify the vision with the goddess.

His heart pounded with denials and any other explanation his mind could conjure.

Maybe it was wrong. Maybe, maybe it was something else.

Please, gods, let it be anything else!

He teleported to her garden.

Too panicked to consider what he was doing, he flashed straight to her pool.

Apollymi rose up instantly and slammed him down with a god-bolt. Unexpected pain exploded through his body as if he'd been hit by a mountain. It was so extreme and violent that for a full minute, he couldn't breathe. He honestly thought that every bone in his body had been shattered. His ears rang with an unparalleled shrillness.

Why didn't I put on Xyn's armor? At least that would have given him *some* form of protection.

As it was, he had nothing. And he wasn't sure if he'd ever walk again.

In fact, it took him a second to realize that Apollymi had pulled him into her arms and was holding him, calling his name as she stroked his cheek. That was how much pain he was in. Just how senseless she'd knocked him.

He struggled to move or have any semblance of a rational thought.

"What were you thinking by barging in here unannounced?"

He hadn't been.

"My mata," he breathed.

She scowled. "What?"

"W-w-wanted to check on my matera."

"You foolish boy!" She looked over to her Charonte. "Xedrix, fetch water from the falls. Fast!"

The demon didn't have to go far. A beautiful priestess was already there in the gardens. One Urian had never seen before. Dressed in a black gown, she had long, curly auburn hair that held tiny braids and ribbons, intricately designed and laced through the dark tendrils. Even though she kept her gaze on the ground and he felt as though he were about to die, he couldn't miss the vibrant beauty of her green eyes as she came closer to hand Apollymi a jewel-encrusted cup.

Apollymi tipped it to his lips. "Drink!"

Urian flinched at the black water as his stomach heaved in revulsion of it.

"Drink!" she insisted.

Bracing himself, he obeyed, praying it didn't taste as bad as it looked.

The moment the black water invaded his mouth and burned his lips and tongue, he choked but somehow managed to swallow it down. Scented with roses, it tasted more like peppermint and some kind of sweetness he'd never known. And it swept through his body like fire, taking with it all his pain.

The priestess laid a gentle hand to his hair, then his shoulder, before she vanished.

Urian glanced from her to Apollymi. "Who is she?"

"Never you mind. Are you all right?"

Still shaken by his near-death experience, Urian frowned. "Pretty sure you knocked out the last three or four bits of my brain cells, akra."

She scoffed at him. "What have I told you about intruding so rudely into my sanctum?"

"A point I shan't ever forget after tonight."

"See that you don't." Glaring pointedly at him, she helped him to his feet. "Now, let us look and see what's going on with your mother."

Urian was still having a bit of trouble seeing straight after her violent assault as they went to the pool. It'd been a long time since he'd last ventured here for this. His days of wanting to see the sun had long passed. He'd learned not to yearn for things he couldn't have. To not torture himself with such pointless endeavors.

But as the waters cleared and he saw the bright light where his mother lived, his breath caught. It hadn't been an illusion. She was under vicious attack. In the mirrored waters, he could see the humans who were ransacking her farm and delighting in the harm they caused.

Urian started to teleport but couldn't. Apollymi had locked him in.

"Are you insane? It's daylight!"

"I don't care!" Frustrated tears filled his eyes as he watched his mother being attacked. "She's my mata!" Hysteria welled inside his heart as he heard his tiny mother screaming for help and mercy. Neither of which came for her.

Rather the humans continued on and on with their brutality.

Apollymi rippled the waters, scattering the images so that he could no longer see or hear them.

Not that it mattered. They were seared into his mind and soul. Forever scarred there.

"Ni!" Urian shouted, rushing back. "You can't leave her. She's alone and unprotected! We have to do something!"

She caught him against her chest while he struggled. "There's nothing we can do."

"Bullshit! You're a goddess. Send your Charonte. A storm! Something! Help her! Please! Please!" Urian sobbed and struggled, desperate to help his mother.

How could they do nothing?

She refused to let him go. Instead, she held him tighter to her breasts. "I know, *pido* ... I know. I couldn't help my son when he needed me. Either of my boys, and it killed me to know how they suffered when there was nothing I could do to stop it. To know that with all the powers I have, I couldn't go into Hades and pull my boy out and restore his life. It tore out my heart and left me this shattered shell you see before you that barely functions here in this hell. I know how bad it hurts. But there is nothing to be done. If you go, you'll die. Plain and simple. You know this. Your mother wouldn't have you harmed for anything. She would rather die a thousand times more than see you hurt. Believe me, I know the heart of a mother. And if you were gone, then who would protect your children and wife from such a fate?"

None of that mattered to him right now. Not when he knew

that his mother was being assaulted and he, a full-grown warrior, couldn't help her. It wasn't right or fair.

Damn them all!

What good was training if he couldn't defend what he loved? Why were they even bothering? What was it for?

Why!

For the first time in his life, he felt completely helpless and he hated it.

He hated himself. Damn the gods! Damn his father!

Damn his own soul!

"Shh," Apollymi whispered as he wept against her shoulder. She held him with a tenderness he would have never attributed to such a violent goddess.

But she wasn't his mother. She could never be the gentle, sweet woman who'd nursed him when he was a child. The one who'd sung him lullabies and had made his entire world right with nothing more than a warm hug and tender smile. No one would ever be able to make him feel that loved again.

And she was being torn apart by brutal hands in a harsh world he hated.

"I failed her."

"Nay, *pido*. You live. That's what she wanted for you. All she ever wanted. Your life and your happiness. So long as you have those two things, you have never failed her. Trust me, I know."

Yet he wanted more than that.

He wanted his mother alive and well. Happy.

Most of all, Urian wanted blood from those who'd desecrated the most sacred lady to ever walk this earth.

And come the sunset, he would have it in spades. May the gods have mercy on them, because Urian would not.

Not now.

Not ever.

It *wasn't often* that as an ancient, primal goddess, Apollymi feared anything. But as she watched the sons of Strykerius gather together, dressed in their armor to lead their first strike against humanity, she feared this.

For she couldn't get the words of her brother out of her head from aeons ago.

Beware the hellhounds of war. Once unleashed they are as quick to eat their master as they are to feast on the throats of their enemies. At the time, she'd thought Jaden was a coward for his sentiment. A pathetic fool.

Now . . .

A deep sense of foreboding went through her. Urian was a chimera unlike any ever conceived. Worse, he'd been lied to from the moment of his birth.

Cursed by the very gods whose blood he shared.

His true father, Styxx, had been a volatile creature, both as a Greek prince and as the Atlantean hero he'd been a lifetime before—Aricles of Didymos. A man who'd been betrayed and slaughtered just as her own husband had been. The gods should have never allowed the great war hero Aricles to be reincarnated as Styxx.

That one warrior had been dangerous enough, but Aricles had held a childlike innocence that Styxx had lacked. And after being betrayed and murdered by Apollo, Aricles had been reborn into a ruthless and cunning prince unlike any other. In the incarnation of Styxx, he had been invincible as he sought to protect what he loved. As if Styxx somehow knew all that Aricles had been through and understood innately the cruelty of this world and the bitter necessity of striking the first killing blow to quell all enemies before they rose up against him.

He'd passed that passion and drive to his only son so that Urian also held an unbelievable skill and birthright. When coupled with the powers of the goddess Bathymaas, who'd been reborn as Bethany . . .

What have I done?

She'd infused the blood of two of the deadliest creatures ever born with Apollo's DNA, and given Urian who knew what additional powers when she'd saved his life as an infant and placed him into the belly of Hellen and allowed his powers to merge with Stryker's.

Well, you wanted to destroy the world, Braith. With this child, you may very well have created the perfect vessel for it.

The only problem was, she wasn't sure she had control of Urian.

As her brother Jaden had noted all those centuries ago with his dire prediction, Urian was just as likely to cut her throat once her hellhound learned of her part in his birth as he was to embrace her for the gift of his powers.

That was what had her scared.

She'd set things in motion that she couldn't see or direct.

And as she watched him and his brothers teleport to his mother's cottage through the dark waters of her mirrored pool, her blood ran colder than ice.

Surrounded by his brothers, he held himself together with a rigid composure that would have done Styxx and Bethany proud. Indeed, Urian was the very image of the Stygian commander as he found his adoptive mother's body and tried to bring her back to life with the powers he'd inherited from his true goddess mother, Bethany.

But Hellen had been dead for too long. There was no hope for her now. And that horror caused Urian to let out a visceral cry that rang through the fabric of time and space. It was the anguished cry of utter agony. A soul-deep misery that shook the walls around her and resonated deep in the halls of the gods.

Apollymi had tried to warn him of what he'd find. Not all dead could be saved. For many reasons. Telamon had returned to life because he hadn't been ready to leave his wife or children. Hellen was another matter. As a human, she'd been tired. Her reasons had nothing to do with Urian or his powers.

And though it was possible to bring the dead back against their will, that was never a good idea.

Her son, Apostolos, was a prime example of what happened when one interfered with the will of another.

As was the Malachai.

Never let your pain make your decisions, my love. For it is in our darkest hours that we make our darkest hells. Kissare had been right. Everyone was the architect of their doom. To this day, she hated him for that.

Apollymi watched in her mirror as Urian realized it, too. In that one instant, the light inside his eyes went out. It was a sight she knew all too well—like one of Hephaestus's automatons that could pass for a living creature at first glance.

Until one realized their eyes were soulless and cold.

The only hint of humanity was when Urian cradled his mother's body briefly in his arms and kissed her cheek. He removed his bright red chalmys and wrapped it around his mother's ravaged body.

Then he'd lifted her in his arms and carried her outside to the pyre that he quickly built with his powers and placed coins upon her eyes.

One by one, his brothers each placed a black mavyllo rose onto their mother's body. Roses Apollymi had plucked from her own garden and sent with Urian as the ultimate sign of respect from the Destroyer. A final mark of honor that she paid to the woman who'd unknowingly carried Bethany's son in her womb and birthed him for Apollymi's vengeance.

"I have made so many mistakes," she whispered as tears filled her eyes.

Some she regretted.

Some she did not. But she did feel terrible for the boy she'd helped to raise. No one deserved the pain Urian felt tonight. To feel so victimized and helpless.

It was a misery that lived inside her heart as a constant companion. No one should feel powerless in their own life.

Ever.

Stryker's sons said a prayer, then lit the funeral fire. And as the pyre burned, Urian looked up and somehow, he met Apollymi's gaze through the mists of the waters where she gazed. How he knew where her vantage point was . . .

It sent another chill over her. His powers were astounding. But then, he was the Stygian heir.

The fire lit the sky and burned bright as Urian used his powers to conjure the identities of the men who'd killed his mother and her servants. Pyromancy wasn't his favorite choice, but the flames licking his mother's body were craving vengeance as much as he was.

Together, they gave him everything he needed to vindicate them both.

The humans had come to her farm for Daimons because of whispered rumors they'd heard. And they'd taken it upon themselves to punish her for harboring Apollites.

Time the humans actually met some.

Be careful what you wish for. You just might get it.

The saddest part of life was when you manifested your own fears by your actions or inactions. Perhaps that was what karma actually was, in the end. Not some great, mystical force that came out of the blue to strike someone down without warning.

Rather a by-product of someone's own stupidity or cruelty where they sought to harm another that boomeranged around to take them down instead.

Because that was what this would be tonight. The humans had feared his kind. Had they not lashed out and attacked his innocent mother needlessly, then he and his brothers would have left them in peace. But because they had attacked in their own vicious stupidity, he and his brothers would slaughter them in a manner far worse than anything they had envisioned or feared.

There would be no quarter.

No mercy.

Only blood and screams.

Theo grabbed Urian's arm to stop him. "Are you sure we should be doing this? It's the last thing Mata would want. She'd be horrified if she knew what we were planning in her name. You know how she felt about violence."

Urian glanced past his shoulder to meet Archie's gaze. For the first time, they were united. "If you don't have the stomach for this, Theo, go home. I'm not leaving this realm until I've tasted the blood of every human who participated in this, and if any of the others get in our way ... fuck them."

He looked back at Theo. "Decide."

Theo swallowed and glanced to his own twin. "Alki?"

Alkimos shook his head. "I'm with them in this, *adelphos*. But you follow your conscience. I won't judge you."

Theo refused to give up as he sought to win more to his cause. "Atreus? Patroclus?"

They both patted his shoulder. "We're going," they said in unison.

Theo sighed heavily. "I can't do this. Killing to survive is one thing. This is vengeance. It won't bring her back. And I can't shame her memory in this manner."

Urian forced himself not to sneer at his brother's newfound religion—Devout Cowardice. "Perhaps, but it will make me feel better, and it is justice. That is what she deserves for what they did to her." And with that, he summoned a portal for his brother. "Go home."

Nodding, Theo stepped through.

Urian glanced to his brothers. "Anyone else?"

United for this blood quest, they stood fast.

"All right." Urian closed the portal home so that no one else would find them until it was over.

More to the point, no one could stop them.

Then he used his powers to locate the place the flames had shown him. A small, sleepy human village where the cowards had run back to, thinking themselves safe and protected. Far away from any Apollite's or Daimon's reach.

As if.

Instead of killing a Spathi, the humans should have learned a few things about them first.

One, they valued family above all. To attack one invited the group to come for you.

Two, you only had one shot. You'd best make it count. Because when they got up, and they would, there would be no stopping them.

The humans had made their strike and withdrawn.

It would be their last mistake. In the end Urian didn't care what his brothers did tonight. He had no intention of policing their actions. It wasn't his place. Right and wrong made no nevermind to him. Not now. Not where his mother was concerned. The humans had forfeited their right to any form of mercy the moment they had failed to police their own. The moment they had set foot on his mother's farm and laid a single cruel hand to her flesh and taken her property.

Just as they had punished his mother for helping her family and shielding them, he felt the same for any human they might happen upon.

They were all guilty by their births to human mothers.

He was Apollo's grandson, after all.

Let there be blood. Let there be chaos.

Most of all, let there be vengeance.

Therefore when Urian kicked open the front door of the first attacker he tracked down and they threw in the torches to burn them out into the street where they waited to kill them, he felt nothing about the screams of that man's family. He heard nothing and saw nothing other than the huge beast of a bastard who had beaten his tiny mother.

That was the brute he seized. The brute he showed his fangs to.

"Daimons!" the man shouted, trying to escape and fend Urian off.

Urian laughed. "You wish. A Daimon would just want your soul."

But he wanted so much more. Blood vengeance. He wanted to make the man suffer long and hard. To listen to him scream and whimper for mercy until his throat was raw and bleeding.

Urian used his powers to snap the human's legs in multiple places. He wanted him to suffer as much as possible and to beg and cry, until the human was sick from it.

He grabbed the man by his hair and pulled him up so that he could bare his fangs. "That's it, human. Cry and beg me. I want to hear your pleas until you're hoarse from our beatings and you choke to death on your own blood and bile."

The man screamed out even louder as his son ran through the streets to escape his brothers. With his powers, Urian trapped him and Archie caught the screaming boy up in his arms.

Urian *froze the* moment he came through the portal to find his father seated on this throne, staring at him with a lethal glower.

Yeah, that could melt arctic stone.

His father didn't move until all of them had arrived through the portal and were standing in the hall in front of him. Then he came off his throne like a lethal predator out of a frightening crouch.

Except Urian wasn't afraid. Not even a little. Honestly, he was still too grief-stricken to care.

In a deadly mood, his father closed the distance between them. Urian felt the blood rolling off his armor. It dripped from the nasal guard of his helm and landed in a bright splatter pattern on the cold tile at his feet.

Still, he didn't move or flinch as he met his father's gaze levelly.

His father stopped in front of him and pulled the helm from his head. He swiped at the guard with his thumb, then placed the blood on his tongue to taste it. Licking it clean, he arched his brow as he realized it was human. "The least you could have done was taken a few Daimons with you to collect the souls."

Urian narrowed his eyes. "I would have gutted anyone who possessed any part of them. So long as my mata lies dead, so do they. No part of them should survive. Not even for a heartbeat."

With respect shining in his eyes, his father inclined his head to him. "Noted."

Archie bowed his head. "Are you angry at us, Solren?"

Their father scanned them in turn. "What do you think?"

One by one, his brothers mumbled an apology.

"I'm sorry."

"Forgive me, Solren."

Until his father locked gazes with Urian. "Have you no apology for your actions?"

Urian shook his head. "I'm not sorry. At all. The humans attacked what was mine and I retaliated with enough force to let them know that we will not tolerate their unprovoked assault on our people anymore. Besides, I would not have my mother's Shade wandering the banks of the Acheron lamenting that her sons didn't love her enough to see her properly avenged. I sent her to the underworld with more than enough coins to pay Charon's fare, and with enough blood to fill the cups of any god who demands it."

His father let out a long, tired sigh, then turned toward his sons. "Go ... get cleaned up and see to your families."

As Urian started to leave, his father stopped him.

"Urian?"

He dreaded the stern lecture he was sure was about to start, but he withheld his reaction from his father and forced himself to appear stoic. "Aye, Solren?"

His father scowled as he studied the bloody helm in his hand. A tic worked furiously in his jaw as he returned it to Urian. "You do me proud, but ... " He shook his head and growled.

Those words and his reaction confused him. What was his father trying to say? "But what?"

His gaze turned dark with warning. "Be careful of the demon that drives you so. I was hoping your Xanthia would help to take the edge from it. Instead, you seem to be even more hostile lately. It concerns me."

Some nights, it did him, too. "I'm fine, Solren."

"Are you?"

He nodded, even though a part of him had doubts.

Taking his helm, Urian headed for his home. But with every step, he shook more from his pent-up rage and grief. Worse? He knew he couldn't go home like this. Not covered in blood and gore. The last thing he wanted was for his son and daughter to have this image of their father.

Or Xanthia.

What he'd done tonight was bad. On that count, Theo hadn't been wrong. He had gloried in their deaths in a way that sickened even him. His wife and children didn't need to know what he was capable of.

Worse, he didn't regret it at all. He'd do it again, without hesitation.

I'm an animal. Theo was right. Their mother would have been ashamed of him.

And yet he wasn't. His need for justice still burned so deep in his bones that he wanted to go back and desecrate them more. There was some innate part of him that he didn't understand. It screamed out for action with a madness he couldn't comprehend.

What is wrong with me?

His brothers didn't feel this same screaming need to right the scales of order that he did. To balance chaos and seek out those who'd done wrong.

Why was he so different from them?

Not wanting to think about it, he craved Xyn's presence more than any other, but he knew better than to seek her out, especially after what had happened when he'd intruded on Apollymi's garden. The last thing he needed was another head injury. So he headed for Paris's home to wash and change clothes.

To his surprise, Paris wasn't there. Davyn answered the door with a shocked expression as he saw the condition Urian was in.

Urian wiped at the blood on his face. "I was wondering if I could wash up here before I went home?"

Davyn sputtered. "Depends ... please tell me none of the guts or gore you're wearing belongs to Paris."

Aghast and offended by the question, he scowled at his friend. "Nay, but if you don't let me in, I might add yours to it."

Stepping back, Davyn made room for him to enter. "Well, you can't blame me for asking, given how you two go at each other sometimes. It's a natural assumption that it would be his, or another of your siblings." He closed the door while Urian set his helm on a cloth atop their table. "Where is Paris, anyway?"

"I don't know. I assumed he'd be heading straight here." Removing his cloak, Urian headed for the washing basin and poured the water while Davyn helped him unbuckle his armor.

He wrinkled his nose in distaste. "What did you get into?"

"Human entrails mostly."

"Ew!" Davyn shuddered. "Remind me never to disembowel them, then. They smell horrible!"

"Indeed. I have to say that it makes me rather happy we have a liquid diet."

Suddenly, someone cleared his throat loudly behind them. "Should I ask why you're stripping the clothes off my brother, Dav?"

Urian glanced over his shoulder to see a clean and neatly polished Paris glaring at them. "Like you, I didn't want to go home bloody and reeking to my wife."

Paris crossed his arms over his chest. "But you don't mind reeking around my husband?"

"Not really. Don't care if I repulse him."

Paris laughed as he finally relaxed. "Fair point." He came over to help Urian strip down so that he could clean up. "It was disgusting. I can't believe I let you talk me into this."

Davyn snorted. "I can't believe you two didn't take me. She was my mother, too."

Paris was instantly contrite. "Oh, honey. I'm sorry. I didn't even think about it. And I didn't want you to feel bad."

Urian quickly finished bathing while they drifted off to their bedroom, dropping garments as they went. "Paris, I'm going to borrow some clothes and let myself out while you apologize for being an ass."

They rumbled a response that was punctuated by some rather eyebrow-raising sounds that made it even more awkward for him.

Wishing he shared that level of passion with his spouse, Urian quickly finished, then picked up his sword and shield and Paris's cloak before heading toward his quiet, secluded home.

Unlike Davyn for Paris, no one waited up for him.

A quick sweep of his cottage found the children nestled in

their beds, fast asleep. As was Xanthia. Which only made the emptiness inside Urian ache all the more. Even at home, he felt like an outsider.

Unwelcome in his own house.

In his own family. He still didn't feel as if he belonged anywhere.

Except with a dragon.

How weird was that?

Sighing, Urian placed his sword in its bracket on the wall and hung up his shield, then stoked the fire for his wife. Xanthia was cold natured, so he always made a point to put new wood on the fire before he went to bed and to get up before her so that the room wouldn't be too chilly whenever she awoke.

As he stood, he realized that she was watching him from the bed. "Sorry. I didn't mean to wake you."

"I heard what you did tonight." Her tone was cold and brittle.

He did his best to play it off, hoping she'd let the matter go. "Oh?"

She glared up at him. Her eyes were bitter in their judgment. "Everyone was talking about it after Theo returned without you and the others, and he told what the lot of you had planned. They say the humans will retaliate now. That they'll come here to find us."

He snorted at her ridiculous fear. As if a human could get through one of Apollymi's bolt-holes, and even if they did, they'd land at his father's feet in the center hall. A bad day for the human, but a good dinner for whatever Daimon happened to be there.

They could use the snack.

So he smirked at his wife. "I doubt that. If anything, they should fear us more." It was the first time any Apollite or Daimon had ever struck back at them.

And it was long past time for such, in his opinion.

Sadly, Xanthia didn't share his point of view. Rather, she curled her lip at him. "You're a monstrous killer, Urian. I'm ashamed of what you've done."

Those words cut him deeply. But not nearly as much as the condemnation in her eyes. That stung soul deep.

"I see." He put the poker down beside the fireplace and headed for the door.

"Where are you going?"

He kept walking, without looking back. "Somewhere I'm wanted. Which obviously isn't here."

Xyn *was still* in her human form when she smelled that warm, sweet scent that was her Urian. For the longest minute, she started not to change. To tell him that she'd been the one who'd handed him the cup earlier after Apollymi blasted him.

That she'd finally felt the silk of his hair with her flesh that had burned from the memory of it ever since.

If only she dared ...

Hating herself for the cowardice, she changed into her dragon body and tucked her black wings down so that she could meet him by the falls.

By the sharpness of his scent, she knew he was furious.

Most of all, she knew he was upset, and emotionally hurt.

What happened?

"We gutted every last one of them."

That made her feel better for him, but his mood confused her all the more. Shouldn't he be happy? *Good.*

Judging by the stunned expression on his face, her comment seemed to catch him off guard. "You're not horrified?"

Should I be?

He gave her a pointed stare. Then spoke slowly, enunciating each word. "I slaughtered them, Xyn."

She nodded slowly. *I got that, Urian. They killed your mother. They deserved whatever it is that you did and then some.* She nuzzled him with her snout to offer him comfort. *I just wish I could have been there to help you.*

He latched onto her and held tight.

Xyn savored his embrace, wishing it were a real hug with their bodies pressed against each other. Why couldn't she find the courage to tell him the truth?

But then, she knew. She was terrified of losing what little contact she had with him. How would he react?

What if he never wanted to see her again?

It was a chance she just couldn't take.

Urian kissed her snout and pulled back. "Did you see Apollymi's priestess today?"

She froze at his unexpected question. *Pardon?*

"A redheaded woman brought me water from your falls earlier. I know how you are about trespassers. So I was wondering how she got it." He stroked her scales. "Her hair matched your coloring."

She swallowed. Hard. Then did her best to keep her voice and tone level and even. *Did it?*

He scowled, then tilted his head to study her eyes. "Aye. It did ... Even her eyes."

Stumbling back, he shook his head as he stared at her in disbelief. "Sarraxyn? Can you take human form?"

Why did he have to ask her that?

Why now?

Fear wedged itself inside her heart. She wanted ... nay, needed to lie to him. She knew it was the prudent thing to do.

If only she could.

Gods, help me.

Bracing herself for whatever would happen, she transformed into her human self so that he could finally see the truth of her.

And waited.

Then waited some more.

Urian stood there, completely stunned and unable to move. Rage and betrayal warred within him. They mixed with grief to such a level that he didn't know what to think. How to react. He'd come here for comfort and now ...

Who and what was she?

"Why didn't you tell me?"

Her long auburn hair shimmered in the dim light. In all honesty, she was exquisite in her fey beauty. Her green eyes practically glowed. She was, indeed, the woman he'd seen earlier. The one who'd touched his hair.

"I was afraid to."

He swept his gaze over her. Dressed in a flowing bronze-colored peplos, she was a goddess. Her lips were perfectly formed and made for kisses.

And her body ...

Urian had a hard time reconciling this woman with the dragon he'd known all these years. At least until he saw her pointed ears. There was something strangely apropos about them.

She stepped toward him.

He moved away.

"Urian—"

"Don't, Xyn." He needed time to accept this. The fact that she'd lied to him all this time.

Well, maybe not lied. Misled or withheld.

Whatever it was, it left an ache inside him.

"Please, understand. I didn't want to hurt you. I know there's nothing for us. You're Apollite and I can't feed you." Tears welled in her eyes and made her lips quiver. "I've loved you all these years."

Urian winced as he realized how much he'd loved her, too.

And there was nothing they could do. Because she was right. This was beyond cruel.

To both of them.

How could they be together when the only way for him to eat would be to take his nourishment from another woman, knowing that the feeding would drive him to have sex with someone else? Or else he'd have to go back to his disgusting bladders of congealed blood ...

That wouldn't be fair to her or him.

She cupped his face in her hands and pressed her forehead to his. "I've snuck off to see you so many times."

Pain burned his throat as he realized how many times he'd glimpsed her among the people of their town. "I know. Now that I see you ... Yours is the face I've seen in the crowd so many times." Fisting his hand in her soft, vibrant hair that stood out among their drab paleness, he kissed her and growled at the bitter sweetness of her mouth.

She was so much to him. His best friend. His touchstone.
His dragon.

And he could never have her.

Never.

His heart breaking, he let her go and stepped away. Tonight, he hadn't just lost his mother. He'd also lost his dragon and best friend.

And probably his wife, too.

April 30, 9508 BC

Ophion ducked as a vase flew past his head and shattered less than an inch from his face. It was even closer to Urian, who didn't move at all.

But then Urian was used to shit flying at him when he least expected it. Too bad it didn't kill him.

His jaw agape, Ophion stared at Urian in utter disbelief, not only at the shattered projectile but at Urian's complete nonreaction to it. "Shite, brother! What have you done to your wife?"

Urian rolled the dice across the table and sighed as he lost another round. Figured. His luck was holding.

Bad to worse.

"I've been taking my meals in other places, and she's rather pissed because of my poor life choices."

Ophion grimaced in sympathetic pain. "What happened?"

Sighing, Urian sat back in his chair. "Let's just say I'd rather starve than take meals that turn my stomach."

His brother glanced through the open doors in the direction Xanthia had gone off with her friends. "What's *she* doing for food, then?"

"Haven't asked and I don't care." No doubt his wife was spreading her legs for someone.

Ophion's eyebrow shot up. "You really mean that?"

Urian nodded. "Unlike you, *adelphos*, I married for convenience and sustenance, not passion. When she ceased being those things ... she can seek her comfort wherever she finds it." He shrugged at a sad, painful truth. He really didn't care whom she screwed or when. "The children, however, are another matter. I'm still caring for them." His father had bred responsibility into them and would be the first to beat them down if they neglected to care for those who couldn't fend for themselves.

As he'd always said, you protected whoever stood at your back. Fought with those who stood by your side, and killed whoever was dumb enough to stand before you.

Never be their enemy.

Trates appeared out of thin air, at their side. "Urian? Your father summons you. Immediately."

That tone was extremely disconcerting. As was his unexpected appearance. It was rare for such a summons to come and even more so to be in such a dire manner.

Exchanging a frown with Ophion, he rose.

His brother remained seated.

At Urian's unspoken question, he laughed bitterly. "I'd come with you, but I don't like the sound of it. In fact, I'm pretty sure my testicles just crawled back into my belly." He smacked Urian on the arm. "Have fun, brother. I'll make a pyre for your funeral games."

"May the gods strike you down, asshole," Urian grumbled as he followed after Trates to see what their father wanted with him now. Though to be honest, he could think of nothing he'd done particularly vexing.

At least not tonight.

Which was actually a record for him, given how most nights went. Normally, he'd be due a good ass-kicking by this time.

For once, and in spite of his wife's anger toward him, he'd been on his better behavior.

He hadn't punched anyone in the face. Started any revolts. Most miraculously of all, he hadn't even brawled with his brothers.

Yet as he entered his father's study and found a group of unfamiliar Daimons there, he drew up short.

This is unexpected. Especially given the fact that every member of the party, including their leader, was a woman. Dressed in a breastplate of white orichalcum, she, like the rest of them, was strikingly gorgeous. Her long blond hair was plaited, and laced with bright red ribbons that matched her cloak. A cloak that contrasted with the studded black leather of her pteruges and tall black war sandals.

Damn …

She and her warriors were the epitome of a teen Apollite fantasy made real. The kind of dream he'd spent a lot of his youth wishing would happen upon him while he was alone in the woods, lost and naked.

The moment their leader met his gaze, he felt an instant jolt of electricity go straight to his groin, which also remembered those countless hours of his misspent imaginings.

At least until she scowled angrily, then turned back toward his father. "He's an Apollite?"

Seated on the smaller version of his bone throne that he kept in their main hall, his father shrugged nonchalantly. "Indeed. I would have warned you, but I didn't think you'd believe me unless you saw it for yourself."

Aghast, she closed the distance between them until she stood in front of Urian so that she could study him, nose to nose. "You're the one who led the raid on the human village?"

"I am."

"*You?*" Could there be any more disdain in that tone? "You killed them all with only a handful of men?"

Crossing his arms over his chest, he nodded. "My brothers."

Her jaw dropped again. "Also Apollites?"

"Of course."

There was a raw, unfettered heat in her dark eyes that sizzled in the air between them as she stared up at him with a tangible hunger. "We came to pay tribute to the Deathbringer. I assumed one of such courage and skill would have to be Daimon."

His father chuckled. "To answer your question, Urian, they're an Amazon tribe of Daimons from the north."

Even more confused by that, Urian glanced past her shoulder, to his father. "Amazons?" He'd never heard of a group of Daimons with that kind of loyalty before.

It defied all logic.

The woman answered for his father. "We were Atlanteans in service to Artemis when the curse came down from the sun god. When the goddess refused to go against her brother to help us, we turned our services and bows to whatever god answered our plea for mercy. Since then, my sisters and I have been on a quest to find others of our kind to help them and to put our war skills to any who get in our way."

Urian related to that. He knew the stories of his own father's panic in his quest to spare them Apollo's wrath. No god had wanted to get involved for fear of what Apollo or Zeus would do to them.

"Who answered your call?" To Urian's knowledge, only Apollymi had shown mercy to their race and dared to defy Apollo.

"The goddess Marzanna."

He glanced to his father. "I've never heard of her."

"She's a northern goddess." His father's lips twisted with wry humor. "An interesting one, I'm told. Sort of a combination of Persephone and Hades, all in one. With the psychosis you would expect from such a mash-up. She's the wife of Koshchei the Deathless."

His father's tone held a strange note that Urian couldn't quite make out. "Have you met them, Solren?"

"Just once. As a boy. They were a peculiar couple who left quite an impression on my young mind."

Urian's scowl deepened. He'd never known his father to be so diplomatic before.

The woman smiled. "We've traveled a long way to meet the Daimon who dared strike back at the human vermin. Your courage impressed us before, but now that we know you're not even a Daimon ... "

Urian flashed her a taunting grin. "You're overwhelmed? Impressed? Would you like to sample the fruit of Apollo?"

She laughed. "You are a cheeky one, aren't you?"

His father let out an exasperated sigh. "Ever my bane. Never could curb or control *that* one. I blame his mother, completely."

She smirked. "Yet I hear the pride in your voice as you say those words, Strykerius. You'd have it no other way." With her hand on her sword hilt, she turned back toward his throne. "So do you accept our bargain?"

His father arched a brow. "To sell you my son?" He met Urian's shocked gaze. "Let me think. Um, no. Never. Cheeky though they all are, I am attached to my sons. *Especially* that one."

Good, because he didn't like the place this conversation was headed.

At all.

"I will give you any price you name."

His father shook his head and chided her. "Bethsheba, you could offer me the throne of Olympus and I would refuse it. I will not put a price on my children. As you said, you came here for a Daimon and my sons are still Apollites. Even if Urian were a Daimon, the answer would still be no."

"But you have a dozen sons, do you not?"

"Ten."

"Surely—"

"One son does not replace another. You obviously haven't any or you'd know that."

Um, yeah. Urian was exceedingly grateful for his father's loyalty at the moment.

As she started back toward him, his father threw out his hand and encased Urian's entire body with a bright blue glow.

"My lady, I said no and that's my final answer. I won't be swayed." Slowly, his father rose from his seat and descended the steps to approach them. "Make no mistake about my sincerity. You fight for your people, as do I. But I would see my people and the entire world burn to the lowest pit of Tartarus to spare my children the loss of one single tear. Therefore, the thought of putting them into slavery to fight for you ... unacceptable."

She tsked. "Why don't we let your son decide? What if I were to win his heart? Would you approve our marriage then?"

Urian gaped at her words. Was she serious?

"My sons are all married."

A scheming light came into her eyes as she swept an appreciative look over his body. He'd feel a little more flattered if she weren't treating him like a side of lamb on a feast day.

She smiled at him. "You're Apollites. You can always take another wife, can you not?"

Technically, she was right. Polygamy wasn't illegal or unknown among their people, especially after Apollo's curse. They merely looked upon it as greedy. But so long as all the participants were agreeable to the arrangement and no one was slighted by it, financially or emotionally, it was legally, if not always socially, acceptable.

His father raked a look over him. "I suppose if he's that stupid . . . "

Thanks, Solren.

"But," his father warned, "he's too young to be made Daimon yet. You are not to convert him."

She smiled. "I don't want to convert him, Strykerius. My tribe isn't the same as your people. As you noted earlier. Nay . . . I want to breed with your son."

Well, this wasn't awkward at all. Discussing sex in front of his father . . .

What he lived for.

More than a little dismayed by their bargaining, Urian met his father's gaze. "Have you nothing to say to *that?*"

His father stared at him blankly. "What? You want me to interfere with your sex life?"

Kind of. Urian was beginning to feel like a piece of livestock being offered up to stud. Especially as every one of them stared at him, and in particular, his crotch, as if they wanted a turn on him like he was their new favorite toy.

Suddenly his youthful fantasy was beginning to take on the sinister appearance of a nightmare—and these Amazons were turning from goddesses into the forms of bacchanalian lamiai.

"Well?" his father prompted at his delay in answering.

"Guess not. You know, being a *breeder* and all." Of course, it would be a little difficult to accommodate her on that particular request to impregnate her, given that he was sterile, but this didn't seem like a convenient time to bring that up.

And she really didn't appear to be in the mood to hear it.

Neither did his father.

So being the sole pork chop in the kennel, he decided to keep his mouth shut.

The pork chop image wasn't helped a few minutes later when Bethsheba came up and grabbed the knot of his girdle to pull him out of the room.

Urian started to pass a look of "help me" toward his father, but given the fact his father had thrown him to the she-wolves, he figured it would be useless. His father seemed to think he should be enjoying the attention.

"Are you planning to diggle me in the street, or do you have a destination in mind?"

She smiled seductively. "Don't you have a home?"

"I do, and it's filled with a wife and two children who would be most upset to have you bang me in front of them."

"You're rather hostile about this. I'm beginning to think you don't want to have sex."

He gave her a droll stare. "You think?"

"You don't?"

Was she serious?

"Not like *this*."

That seemed to stun her into silence. At least she finally let go of the knot over his crotch.

Urian straightened his clothes. "Contrary to what you think you know about men, Bethsheba, we don't like being treated like whores any more than a woman does."

"Is it that, or do you feel threatened by a powerful woman?"

He laughed at her challenge. "Have you met Apollymi, or my wife for that matter? Trust me, you're quite paltry in comparison. Powerful women don't frighten me. I prefer them to weak ones."

"Then why are you so standoffish with me?"

"Because of the way you've treated me. I'm not a bitch to bark at your command."

And speaking of strong women ...

"What is this?" Xanthia materialized so fast by his side that she almost bonded their DNA together. One more heartbeat or step and she would have caused a tragic biological mistake.

"What is what?" he asked drolly.

"A new wife?" she shrieked. "Did I hear that correctly? You're planning to marry someone else?"

Praise Apollymi for their small community. Bad news traveled so much faster than the good.

Sighing, Urian decided it was probably time he introduced the two women. "Xanthia, meet Bethsheba."

"The hades to Kalosis I will!" She shoved Bethsheba back. "You lay one fang to my husband and you will find yourself toothless and bald, bitch!"

Urian quirked a brow at Bethsheba. "What was that you were saying about weak women?"

Xanthia turned toward him with the wrath of the Furies in her eyes. "You don't speak. Maybe never again!"

Strangely pissed and amused by that comment, he held his hands up and decided to stay out of this particular fight since it wasn't one he wanted to be in to begin with. "Aye, my love."

Out of nowhere, Paris appeared at his back and draped himself against Urian's spine. He wrapped his arm around his neck and rested his chin on Urian's bare shoulder. "This looks quite interesting and entertaining. What have you gotten yourself into now, brother?"

"Not sure."

Bethsheba shoved Xanthia back. "Don't you ever dare touch me again without invitation."

"And don't you even think of touching my husband's loins."

Bethsheba sneered at her. "You hardly seem fit for a champion's wife. What hole did he dredge you from to elevate you to such a grand status?"

Shrieking, Xanthia lunged forward, but Urian extracted himself from his brother and caught her before she could attack the warrior queen who would tear her to shreds. While he admired his wife's fire, he wasn't a fool. He'd given Xanthia basic training and nothing more. She'd never really cared for fighting and wasn't any kind of challenge to a warrior of Bethsheba's skills. And though he was presently furious at his wife and wanted to beat her himself for her unwarranted condemnation of him, she was still his wife and he wouldn't have her harmed for anything. He'd sworn his loyalty and troth to her and no matter how much of a monster she might think him, he was at least an honorable monster.

"Let me go!" Xanthia screamed, kicked, and pinched.

Urian ground his teeth against the pain. "Calm down." He regretted those words as soon as they passed his lips. How could he have forgotten that the worst thing to ever say to anyone when they were furious was to calm down?

Invariably, it only pissed them off more.

First lesson he'd learned as a boy when dealing with Archie and Theo. He still had the scar on his left cheek from one of those blatant acts of stupidity.

Bethsheba had the gall to laugh. "You do have your hands full with that shrew."

And that got him one massive heel kick to his thigh. Urian grimaced.

"Do you mind not antagonizing her further?"

Xanthia slammed her head back into his nose.

Urian felt it break instantly. *Sonofabitch!* He almost lost his grip on her as the pain of it split his skull and his eyes watered in protest.

"Enough!" His father's shout finally succeeded in calming his wife down. While she might not fear him, she had a healthy respect for the fact that his father held no love or loyalty to her and wouldn't hesitate to rip out her heart to feast on it.

Urian set her down on her feet so that he could wipe away the blood that was pouring from his nose.

His father's eyes widened in fury the moment he caught sight of his injury.

Xanthia shrank back to stand behind him.

Yeah, wasn't this perfect? *Now* she liked him again. She even clutched at his chalmys for protection.

He passed an irritated grimace at her.

"Are you all right?" his father asked in a concerned tone.

Urian had a moment when he considered telling his father the truth—that his nose felt like shit and that he was done with Xanthia's theatrics. But sadly, her children loved her, and he loved her children. "I'm fine, Solren."

Still, his father's gaze narrowed threateningly on Xanthia. "Go home. Now."

She ran off.

Bethsheba walked toward Urian with a sassy, seductive swagger. She pulled out a piece of soft deerskin cloth so that she could tenderly blot and care for his nose. And as much as he hated to admit it, his body did react to the gentle warmth of her fingers cupping his chin. Especially the way she traced his lower lip with her thumb to soothe the throbbing where Xanthia had busted the center of it. "Your wife should appreciate the care you have for her well-being. And the fact that you saved her life."

"I don't blame her for her fury. She's a good woman. I'm an average husband." Whatever problems they might have, Urian wasn't about to see her reputation tarnished or her character abused by anyone.

Bethsheba snorted at that. "You've raised a remarkable son, Strykerius."

"I know."

Stepping back, Bethsheba removed a tribal emblem necklace that was nestled snugly between her breasts. "For that reason, I shall leave you in peace, good Urian. When you come to your senses and realize that your shrew is unworthy of a man of your caliber, call us. So long as I reign, the Marzanni are forever allies to the Apollymians."

She leaned forward to kiss Urian's cheek and to whisper in his ear. "When you're ready to ride a real woman, my thighs will be wet and open for you."

If those words weren't enough to make him salivate, the sound of her ragged breath and the scent of her blood mixed with his were almost enough to make him grab her right then and embarrass them both. It was all he could do to not accept her invitation on the spot.

Because the truth was, he hadn't been with anyone in days. He'd been starving since his wife had insulted him and he was dying for something to eat.

And after the fight with Xyn, he was hornier than hell. He'd been without any form of compassion or care. He felt so lost and alone.

Adrift. Honestly, he just wanted to feel welcomed somewhere. By someone.

As if she knew his thoughts, she gave him a hot, hungry kiss that left him hard and aching with longing. She ran her tongue across the cut on his bottom lip. "Just put a drop of your blood on the amulet and call my name. I'll hear you and come instantly."

With a wistful sigh, she stepped back and inclined her head to his father. "Take care, Strykerius. May we meet again one night."

"Indeed." His father opened the portal for them so that they could take their leave.

Urian didn't move or speak until after they were gone.

Not until his father approached him and took the deerskin cloth from his hand. "You're a royal fucking idiot. I can't believe you came from my loins."

"I know."

With a disgusted sigh, his father shook his head. "How long have you been sleeping at Tannis's home?"

Urian let out a ragged sigh before he confessed the truth. "Three days."

"Have you fed?"

"Not really. Tanny's tried to feed me some of her blood in a cup, but I haven't felt like taking any of it."

His father grabbed his arm where he had fresh bite marks. "Yet you've been feeding your children." There was no missing the angry condemnation in that tone. "You know you can't keep feeding them if you're not taking anything for yourself."

Urian knew. It was the quickest way to make an Apollite sick. And it could give them a rare disease that would kill them.

"I'm only feeding Geras. He won't go to sleep unless I rock him. He only takes a little right before he drifts off."

A tic started in his father's jaw. "You coddle that boy. He's getting too old for that kind of foolishness."

"Just looking out for my son, as my solren taught me to do."

Disgusted, his father flung his arm away. "The difference being that *I am* your solren."

Urian gave him a chiding frown. "In my heart, Geras is as much mine as if he'd come from my seed."

His father grabbed a fistful of his hair and yanked him closer. "Nay, Urian, there's a difference. I was there when you slid into this world, still covered in your mata's blood. My hands were the first that held you. My face, the first you saw. Even before your mata's. I held you every day of your childhood. I promise you that whatever love you have for that boy pales in comparison to what I feel whenever I look at you and your brothers and sister, knowing it is my blood you carry. Knowing my hands delivered you into this world, and that your welfare falls unto me all the days of my life. That it was my blood that caused you all to be cursed by the gods. You've no idea how much I hate myself for that. How much I hate my father. Not because he cursed me. But for what he did to my children, and theirs. And if your wife does not do right by you, I will see her throat ripped out. For her life is nothing to me, but your happiness is all."

"I will make sure to convey your insanity to her, Solren, forthwith."

His father winced before he kissed Urian's forehead and playfully shoved him away. "You try my patience, *pido*."

"Someone has to, Solren. Otherwise your head will grow too swollen to fit inside your helm. And you need that for battle."

Growling, his father headed off toward the theocropolis. "I blame your mata!"

"She always blamed you."

"And we both overcoddled you when we should have taken a heavy strap to your ass."

"*Now* he figures that out?"

Urian arched a brow at Archie's low tone as his brother stepped out of the shadows behind him. "Dare you to say that louder. And to your solren's face."

"I'm not you, Uri. Me, he'd put through a wall."

Yeah, right. "He's never struck you any harder than he's struck me."

"I would beg to differ. He was a much harsher parent prior to the curse. Ask Theo. There's a reason why we curb our tongues and actions more than you younger assholes. Guilt rides him harder than you know."

That Urian believed.

Archie grabbed him in his huge paw of a hand.

What the hades? When Urian tried to fight him off, he only intensified his fierce hold.

"Stop it, Uri, before I slap you. I want to see how much damage you took from Thia."

"Why?"

"Because you're my little brother and I don't like to see you hurt." Grimacing, he straightened his nose for him.

Urian hissed in pain. "Is it fixed?"

"Aye ... you're as pretty as my sister again." He curled his lip. "That has to be painful."

"Hurt less before you rebroke the bone." Urian gingerly fingered it.

Archie scoffed at his irritable mood. "C'mon. Let me see you home."

"I'm fine, Archie. Besides, your concern frightens me."

"Then we're even. Your stupidity scares me." He slapped him on the arm. "You know where I am if you need me or a place to sleep today."

Well, this night kept getting stranger and stranger. Baffled beyond his ability to cope, Urian decided to head home and check in with Xanthia. It seemed like the right and decent thing to do, given all that had transpired.

At least that was what his thought had been until he opened the door to his home and heard a most distinctive sound ...

And he knew his daughter was far too young to be rutting with a man. Or his son.

His suspicions were foul enough. And he knew before he pushed open the door to his bedroom what he was about to walk in on. So the sight of his wife sprawled naked on top of another man didn't shock him.

The fact that it was his brother-in-law did.

Only had it been Davyn would he have been more stunned. But the moment Erol's blood-drunk gaze met his, he had an even more sickening realization.

This was why Archie had been so *nice*. So concerned about him. Xanthia must have made a pass at his brother earlier, and unlike Erol, Archie wasn't a complete and unethical bastard. No doubt he'd wanted to warn him but hadn't had the heart.

Instead, he'd offered Urian a place to stay.

Comfort for the fact that his wife was a whore . . .

"Wow . . . don't I feel like an asshole. I turned down a queen so that you could screw an unscrupulous bum."

Xanthia sat up and faced him without a bit of remorse in her eyes. Wiping her mouth with the back of her hand, she glared at him. "Is that all you have to say?"

Not really. His head rang with a number of insults. Insults that his tongue begged him to unleash. But his children didn't need to be awakened to such violence against their mother. "Just for you to get your scrawny ass off him so that I can kill him. Not because I give a shit who you spread your legs for, but because he did this to my beloved sister, and I don't want to traumatize our children. So as soon as he's dressed, I'll take care of him . . . oh, and after this night, dear Xanthia, consider us divorced."

June 27, 9506 BC

Urian's head spun while Bethsheba came in his arms with a shrill battle cry. Laughing at her enthusiasm, he sank his fangs into her throat and let her blood invade his mouth so that he could feed on her sweetness. There was something about whenever she climaxed that made her all the tastier to him.

He didn't know if it was something about her adrenaline or if it came from her being a different form of Daimon. Whatever it was, she made his senses reel. Quickening his strokes, he lost himself to her cries and her scent.

"Majesties?"

Urian cursed in frustration.

Sheba went rigid in his arms as her climax was cut in half. First lesson he'd learned when he'd moved in with her—make sure she was done completely with her orgasm before he finished or there would be hell to pay.

She let out a shriek that challenged the elasticity of his eardrums as she flung a heavy gold wine cup at the hapless maid. Fortunately, the girl was used to dodging projectiles from her volatile mistress. "Damn it, Niva! What have I told you about interrupting us?"

Cringing, the petite blonde picked up the cup and deftly policed the wine before it stained the rugs and resulted in a beating for the girl for *her* carelessness. Which would have later caused a fight between Urian and his wife after he defended what Bethsheba viewed as a lowly servant.

"Forgive me, Majesty. But I have visitors for King Urian ... his brothers are waiting for him."

Sheba let out a frustrated breath as Urian gave her an apologetic grin. Stroking her intimately and deftly beneath the covers in an effort to placate her ire, he nuzzled her breast with his whiskers. "Sorry, my love. They have always been my bane."

She yanked at his hair. "Should I have them beheaded?"

Urian laughed. "Tempting . . . but nay. They are my brothers and my solren would demand satisfaction for it. Let me see what they need and I shall spend the rest of the night making this up to you." He pressed a kiss to her bare stomach and breast, then moved to slide over her.

She caught him and wrapped her legs about his waist, holding him between her thighs. "I will be here, naked and waiting for your return. Don't take too long."

"I'll return, posthaste."

With a precious pout, she released him.

Urian slid from the bed, washed quickly, and grabbed his linen shendyt from where his wife had tossed it earlier when she'd attacked him for her "dinner." Raking his hair back from his face, he grabbed a lightweight robe and left their room, which had been carved from the heart of an ancient mountain that Bethsheba's people considered sacred to the goddess they served as devoutly as his father did Apollymi. The dark stone walls were soothing to their eyes that Apollo had cursed them with and it kept the temperature cool.

Quite similar to Kalosis, the only real difference was that humans could actually access this home.

If they climbed high enough.

That being said, Sheba's culture was nothing like the Apollymians'. Which made it hard for him at times whenever he paused to dwell on it. He'd married Bethsheba out of anger, and he was paying for it in ways he'd never imagined.

While she was kinder to him than Xanthia had ever been, he still didn't love her. And he felt every bit as used.

Thia had wanted a protector to keep her safe from the humans and to guarantee her and her children a permanent place in Kalosis. Sheba wanted an attack dog to unleash at her command. One with no will of his own. She expected unquestioning obedience. A loyalty that overrode his conscience.

She'd wanted Urian Deathbringer.

That myth had only lived to avenge his mother. A rabid

hellhound who wasn't as mindless as she'd assumed. What he found out here in the human realm after his temper cooled was that he bore no hatred or grudge whatsoever toward humanity. They were that far beneath him. He was completely ambivalent toward them.

He reserved his hatred solely for the gods who'd cursed his people.

And away from his family and Apollymi, the volcanic heat inside his blood only seemed to arise whenever injustice occurred. Day-to-day, without his brothers around to nettle him for shits and giggles every time they drew near, he was rather mellow.

Frightfully so, in fact.

He'd had no idea just how quiet and introspective he actually was.

Worse than that, he really missed Sarraxyn. More than he'd have ever thought possible. So much so that he no longer even cared that she'd lied to him about her abilities.

Part of him just wanted to see her again—even if it meant apologizing. But he didn't know how after all this time.

In truth, he barely recognized the stranger who resided inside his skin nowadays. He really had lost himself. And that feeling was rammed home hard when he opened the door to the ornate throne room where Archie and Theo waited.

They turned toward him, then gave him their backs so that they could continue their whispered conversation, because neither of them realized he was the one they'd come to visit. They thought him a stranger.

I haven't been away that *long.*

Well, almost a year. But still . . .

They shouldn't haven't forgotten what he looked like. Or failed to recognize their own flesh and blood.

Bitterly amused, Urian glanced around the familiar room. Black marble was veined with gold and dusted so as to awe and impress any who came here, not that it appeared to have any effect on his obtuse brothers.

Sheba was big on intimidation. Hence her two pets she kept

chained to her throne. Agitated at the presence of his brothers' unfamiliar scent, both oversized lions were pacing around and growling at Archie and Theo, straining at their chains as they sought a way to get nearer their intended victims.

He paused to grab them a bit of steak from their larder. "Shh, Nero, Leo ... it's all right." Urian tossed the raw meat onto the golden platters set on the floor next to Sheba's throne.

They immediately pounced on the food.

Archie was the first to gape at Urian's half-naked state. "Damn, Uri. What happened to you?"

Scowling, Theo moved to his side so that he could paw at Urian's hair, which now flowed just past his shoulders. "What's this?"

Urian snatched at the tiny braids Sheba had plaited with care that were interwoven throughout his hair with beads. While it was the fashion of his father's people to keep their hair length just below their ears, Sheba's tribe wore theirs much longer. Urian's now fell past his shoulders. "It's a sign of nobility among their culture. The long silver and gold beads mean that I'm their ruler."

"And the eye makeup and face paint?" Theo fingered the intricate pattern that Niva painted along the left side of Urian's face and hairline every morning and from the tip of his nose to just under his chin.

"It's tradition, moron." Just like the ruby stud in his left ear that said he was a free man and not owned by his wife—which was a rare thing for her tribe. "And also indicative of our rank in their society." Urian scratched at his bare shoulder. "So is there a point to your visit? Or were you two bored and thought, what the hades? We've got nothing better to do, let's go annoy Urian?"

Archie rolled his eyes. "And here we were actually missing you." He glanced over to Theo. "Why again?"

Shrugging, he held his hands up. "I don't know. Maybe because we had something to show him?"

Now that was a scary thought. "What? Did the two of you finally locate a single brain cell between you and you needed someone to show how to use it?"

Archie shoved him.

The moment he did, an arrow went whizzing for his heart.

Urian barely caught it before it landed in the center of his brother's chest. Had he been a breath later, it would have killed his brother instantly.

Eyes wide, Archie went pale. "What the—"

"Halt!" Urian snapped as his wife's guards moved forward to slaughter his siblings. Smirking, he returned the arrow to Birgit, who'd shot it. "I appreciate your protection, but I'd be most upset if you killed my brother for his stupidity."

"Forgive me, Majesty." She cast a warning glare at Archie before withdrawing back to the doorway.

Both of his brothers gaped in shock.

Crossing his arms over his chest, Urian gave them a smug grin. "Not your little brother *here*."

"Apparently." Theo let out a nervous laugh. "Damn, Uri. How are you doing with it all?"

Some days were better than others. But he wasn't the kind to share those thoughts.

So he cleared his throat. "Why are you here again?"

Recovering their earlier mischievousness, they exchanged a grin. Then, they pulled open their tunics to expose their chests to him. More to the point, the Daimon's mark that now rested over their hearts.

Urian's stomach shrank at the sight. For several seconds, he didn't react. He couldn't. Honestly, he didn't know how to respond to their news. While a part of him was glad to know they wouldn't die horribly from Apollo's cold stupidity, another part was sick with the thought of how they'd have to live from this night forward.

That their futures could end in a single heartbeat if they didn't kill on time . . .

As precarious as life was for an Apollite, it was so much more for a Daimon.

Theo sobered. "Aren't you happy?"

"More confused than anything." He scowled at Theo, unable

to understand why he'd convert so soon when he didn't have to. "You still had three years left until you turned twenty-seven."

"I know, but Archie was afraid."

That he understood. They were only a few months away from Archimedes's birthday when he would have to make a choice. But . . .

Archie rubbed at his neck. "I couldn't do it, Uri. I tried so hard . . . I did. Theo had gone with me and I had the human there. Compliant. I had the human's will mesmerized to my own, just as Solren had taught us. More than willing to surrender his soul to me. The human was a bastard dog with no regard for anyone— he abused everyone around him, I figured he deserved to die so that I'd have less guilt killing him. I mean, the world is better off without his ilk. And he was more than willing to give up his soul. But then he started whimpering and begging pathetically, and I . . . I couldn't do it."

Theo nodded. "So I did it for him. I killed the human and took the soul, then shared it with Archie."

Urian flinched. "So what does this mean?" He frowned at Archie. "You're having to live as an Anaimikos?" They were Daimons who fed from other Daimons in order to remain alive— like a baby bird feeding from its mother.

Sheepishly, Archie nodded.

However, that image quickly turned into something much more graphic and horrifying as Urian thought about how Theo would have to "feed" Archie. Surely this wasn't as sexual as when Apollites fed . . .

Was it?

His eyes widened.

They immediately protested as they caught on to where his mind had drifted.

"Oh dear gods!" Archie snapped. "It's not like *that!*" He shuddered violently. "I'd rather *die!*"

"Why would you think something that disgusting?" Theo started to slap Urian's arm, then glanced at the guards and lions before reconsidering. "It's not the same as a feeding! Besides, if I were going to sleep with a man, I'd pick someone a lot better-looking than that oaf! Uh! He's revolting! I'd at least go after Davyn."

Urian scoffed. "Well, how would I know how you share a soul? I'm not a Daimon!"

Theo rolled his eyes. "Soul exchanges are completely different."

"How so?" Urian had always been curious how it worked. It was the one thing no one would ever go into. Rather the best-kept secret of their people.

"You wouldn't believe me if I told you. It's something you have to be shown when you're ready."

Urian moved closer to Theo so that he could study him to see what else might be different about his brother. "So what's it like?"

They both sobered.

"I don't know how to describe it, really." Theo didn't move as Urian fingered his ear. "My powers are heightened now. In ways you can't imagine."

Archie made a face. "For one, the souls are loud."

Theo nodded in agreement. "I now know why the treli go mad. You can hear the human in your head all the time. It's like the worst sort of nagging wife."

"Aye." Archie sighed. "They beg and whine and barter. And you can't escape the sound. It rattles in your brain."

"Is there anything you can do to quiet them?"

They shook their heads. "Solren says it'll get fainter as they weaken and the soul dies. That we have to pay attention as that will tell us when we need to hunt again. So for that reason, we want them to be yelling loud and clear in order to maintain our life."

That was terrifying. His own inner monologue was loud enough at times. He couldn't imagine having something inside him trying to outshout it. "And there's no other way to live?"

They shook their heads.

Archie scowled. "What about your wife's people? How does it work for them?"

"Their goddess bonded them to fire demons to preserve

their lives. I don't recommend it, either." Especially given some of Sheba's more particular vicious mood swings whenever the demon in her acted up.

Archie glanced over to the guards. "So are they Apollites?"

Not anymore. Even their young were different from what Urian was used to. "The Marzanni are a different species ... more akin to Daimons. With some differences."

Theo arched a brow at that. "Such as?"

"They don't age the way we do, but they're not immortal. They can still have children, at any point." Unlike Daimons, who couldn't have children. Once they ceased to be Apollites, they lost their fertility.

"Can they walk in daylight?"

Urian shook his head. "No one has thwarted that part of the curse yet. At least not to my knowledge. Though I've heard of some who've tried."

All had ended in disaster. It seemed Apollo was determined to make sure no one with a drop of Apollite blood would ever again see the light of day.

"Majesty?" Niva nervously cleared her throat from the doorway shadows. "Forgive my interruption, but my lady bid me to remind you of your duties."

Ever his horny mistress. He sighed. "I'll be right there."

She scurried away.

"Duties?" Archie mocked. Then he sobered. "Truth. Are you happy?"

He couldn't honestly call what he had here *happy*. While it wasn't miserable or abusive, he'd only ever been really happy with one person.

Xyn.

And since she wasn't here and he was never able to see her ...

"I'm content."

"That's not happiness, Urian." Theo passed a concerned glance toward Archie.

How he hated the fact that his family could read him so easily. He'd never been able to hide anything from them. No matter how hard he tried. "You two worry like old women. But I would ask one thing before you leave."

"That is?" Archie cocked his head.

"Would you escort my children home to their mother? They've been missing her and I know they'd like to see her."

"Sure."

Urian inclined his head to Archie before he went to ask Niva to gather them for the journey. Nephele in particular had been begging to see her mother. Keeping them away from Xanthia had been the shittiest act of spite he'd ever done in his life, and given some of the things he'd done to his older brothers as a boy, that said a lot.

But the truth was, they'd been the only part of his marriage to Xanthia that he'd enjoyed. And they'd been the one thing that had kept him sane here with Sheba and her people. A balm against his loneliness and his own homesickness.

Especially where Sarraxyn was concerned. He'd needed them as a distraction so that he didn't dwell on how much he missed his friend.

Nay, not friend. The only woman he'd ever loved.

The one woman he could never have.

And the thought of being here without his children ...

Heartsick, Urian sighed. It wasn't fair to Geras and Nephele, and he knew it. They didn't belong here and they were miserable. He was being selfish and it was time for them to be with their mother. Not their stepfather.

"Baba!"

He paused at his bedroom door as he heard Nephele's call from the other end of the hallway. Her voice echoed off the stone as she came running toward him. Even though she tried not to show it, he saw the excitement on her beautiful face as she neared him.

"Are you really taking us home?"

Those words were a fist to his gut. How he wished, but if he went home, he'd never return here either and that would cause a war between their people.

Urian sighed at the tears that choked him. "Nay, love. My brothers are here. They'll take you and Geras back to your mata."

"Oh." Her voice mirrored the same disappointment he felt. "What about you?"

Pain swelled up inside as he fingered her blond braids. "I have to stay here with the Marzanni. But if you wish to stay in Kalosis, I won't force you to return. I shall miss you terribly, though." His voice cracked on that last bit. He would miss them every day.

Tears welled in her eyes as her lips trembled. With a sob, she threw herself against his chest.

Closing his eyes, Urian held her there as he fought against his own tears. He really did love his children. He always would.

Geras came running and threw himself against them so that he could pout over the fact that Urian wouldn't be joining them.

His heart breaking even more, Urian held them until he heard Sheba calling for him to join her from the other side of the door.

Damn it. He shouldn't have to choose between her and his children. But life was never fair.

And it seemed to take a special joy out of racking his balls.

"I have to go and your uncles are waiting." He kissed them each in turn. "Take care. I shall come visit as soon as I can."

"I'll miss you, Baba!" Geras said.

"Miss you already, scamp." Urian chucked him on the chin, then wiped away the tears on Nephele's face. "Be good for me."

"I will. You take care, Baba."

Her words made his heart swell and ache. Every time they called him that, it tore him apart and made him glad that in spite of how it'd ended, he'd married their mother. For them alone, his hell with Thia had been worth it.

He paused to watch as they walked down the hall. Geras glanced back to wave and Nephele to blow him one last kiss.

Urian returned both gestures with a heavy heart. *I hate change.* He always had.

That was the worst part about being an Apollite. Change came fast and furious for them all in their pathetically brief lives.

Twenty-seven years just wasn't long enough for anyone to live and die. They were gone before they had a chance to begin.

Game over. Why? Because his own grandfather was a selfish ass. Why did people have to be so selfish and cold?

What a world it would be if others could look around for three seconds each day and realize that they weren't the only ones in pain. That everyone suffered.

If people would take a breath before lashing out to take into account everyone who was in their line of fire.

Yet they never did. Instead, anger was a double-edged sword that cut in both directions as it swung a wide arc and left a bloody swathe in its wake.

Urian sighed. His personal fate was looming faster than he could keep track of. He had less than five years to that fateful birthday.

Five years . . .

A blink, and he'd either be dead like his mother or a Daimon like his brothers and father. In a way, he envied his brothers for having already made their decisions. It no longer weighed on their minds.

Would he be able to do it? Or would he be like Archie and Davyn, and have to be fed by another Daimon?

While Urian thought himself strong enough to go Daimon, he didn't really know for certain. It was one thing to tear apart the humans who'd hurt his mother. Another to kill those who were innocent.

The gods knew that Archie was the last one he'd have thought would falter in the face of a human. His brother had never spared *him* any conscience.

Or any blow. Physical or mental.

And he'd been the one to rip apart the human children that night . . .

But then the true measure of any warrior was never known until the day they were battle-tested. Only in the heat of that moment would they come to know if they would be shattered from the blows of a superior enemy or rise victorious to overcome all challengers. It was one thing to say what he'd do in the abstract but another to actually do it when that moment came barreling down with crushing brutality.

Stand and fight, or turn and flee.

The irony wasn't lost on him that the brother who'd gone out to avenge their mother and slaughter humans in her name wasn't the brother who'd been able to turn Daimon to save his own life. Yet the one who'd been a coward and run home to hide that night had been the very one to take that soul to save his own.

You just never know who will fight for themselves and who will fight to save another.

Whom you could trust and when. That was the most frightening part of life. It was ever unexpected.

Opening the door, he found Sheba waiting. Just as she'd said.

Even though she was highly agitated, he didn't let it bother him, as that was basically her normal state of being. Rather he undressed and returned to bed. Ever the dutiful pet.

She frowned as soon as she saw the grim expression on his face. "Are you all right?"

"My brothers . . . they went Daimon."

Her jaw dropped. "Did they want you to join them?"

"Not yet. It was merely a courtesy call."

Sheba ran her hand over his chest, raising chills in the wake of her warm caress. She paused over his heart, where a dark Daimon's mark would rest were he to convert as they had. "You know you have a choice, love. I can petition our goddess to make you one of us. You don't have to go Daimon like them."

Her eyes flashed that peculiar shade of amber-orange as she trailed her hand lower to cup him and toy with his sac while she slowly teased his Adam's apple with her tongue. Urian sucked his breath in as his cock hardened in her palm.

It was a tempting offer. To become a different sort of demon. Serve another goddess.

At least he had options.

"Just say the word . . . "

How could he when at the moment he couldn't think straight

while she did that? He was a slave to his hormones whenever she stroked him like this. All he could feel was her.

Suddenly, a jarring scream rang out through the stillness. "Majesties!"

Well, that ruined the mood. And irritated the crap out of him.

More screams were followed by the sounds of clashing steel. Frustrated at another interruption, Urian used his powers to flash himself into the armor that his wife insisted he wear to blend in with her army, and gathered his sword and shield while Sheba scrambled from the bed with a rush of creative expletives.

Worried about her given the escalating violence that was heading for them, he used his powers to dress her in her own armor.

She met his gaze with a grim smile. "Remind me later to tell you that I love you."

He handed her battle helm to her. "Rather remind you of that when I do something that pisses you off."

Laughing, she rose up on her tiptoes to give him a hot kiss. "You are a sexy beast, Urian Deathbringer." Her eyes smoldered as she scraped his chin with her fangs. "I ache for you to fill my belly with your children."

Guilt stung him as she pulled away to grab her own sword and shield. While she never held it against him that he had yet to make her pregnant, he dreaded every month when her flow came and he saw the disappointment in her eyes that she hadn't conceived. That was the only good thing about Apollites. Once they converted to Daimons, their women could no longer carry children and that part of nature's cycle ceased for them. While the transition could be hard on some of the women who mourned their premature loss of fertility, others met it with joy.

Sheba craved children. So much so that she'd been a good stepmother to Thia's. It was why he had yet to tell her the children had left without saying good-bye. He wasn't sure how she'd handle it.

But that could wait.

Placing his helm on his head, he stepped outside and sucked his breath in sharply as he saw the chaos that awaited them.

Never had Urian seen such carnage. While he'd been on raids, those were skirmishes . . . such as the night they'd attacked the human village. The humans had been caught off-guard and asleep.

Likewise, over the last year while he'd lived here, Sheba and her warriors had led small raiding parties against human caravans and small groups of human travelers—which was why he hadn't protested the loss of Xyn's armor overly much. He hadn't really needed it to fight against their lesser skill.

But this wasn't a raiding party.

It was an army. Heavily armed and well trained. Their golden armor shone like the sun in Apollymi's pool all those years ago. It was near to blinding and was marked by a sun emblem. And they were cutting through Sheba's warriors with a bitter ease that left him gaping.

Until he saw his sister-in-law, whom Sheba had made her commander—she was under attack and about to go down. Too late, Urian remembered himself. His powers. Roaring, he summoned the strength of his grandfather Apollo and shot out an invisible sonic blast toward them.

It knocked down the first wave of humans and gave Sheba's warriors time to pull back and regroup. He caught his wife about her waist. "We need to retreat."

Her eyes flared indignantly. "Retreating is for cowards!"

"Sheba! Open your eyes. We're outnumbered twenty to one. Half your people are already dead."

"Never! I will not—" Her words were cut short as an arrow went through her throat.

Stunned, Urian couldn't move for a second as she gurgled on her own blood. Then as Urian went to shield her, two arrows penetrated his armor and sank into his chest.

"Cut their heads off!" the humans cried. "Burn the demons' bodies! Make sure nothing remains!"

Another human was shouting to the soldiers. "Find the kids! Whatever you do! Hunt down all children! Round them up!"

Tears of pain blinded him as more arrows rained down so

thick, he could barely see the walls of their home. He didn't even know where the archers were. All around, their people fell with screams and cries. Some with whimpers. He held on to Sheba and tried to summon his powers, but he was in too much pain.

The best he could manage was to open a portal. If he could get them to Kalosis, his father could help them.

But he was too weak even for that.

The blue shimmering doorway began to fade as soon as he opened it.

"Baba!" Urian gasped, trying to crawl toward it. If he could just make it to that ...

It vanished.

Ni! He felt Sheba's hand in his hair. Turning his head, he met her gaze.

Blood trickled from the corners of her lips as she tried to smile. "My Uri," she breathed. "So fair." Then the light went out of her eyes.

Two more arrows landed in his back and three in her body. She didn't react at all.

His soul screamed out in agony that she was dead.

Furious and aching, he shouted and pulled her closer so that he could shield her. It made no sense and he knew that. She was already gone. Yet he didn't want her hurt any worse than she already was. His Sheba was a vain woman. She would never want her beauty scarred, even in death.

I failed her.

Worse, he'd failed her people.

At least I got my children to safety. He could die in peace knowing they were safe. Thank the gods he'd let them go when he had.

And his brothers.

He heard the humans running toward them. Stabbing and slicing as they came. Beheading any body that was lying on the ground to make sure they were all dead.

"Over there! Get those!"

Urian reached for his dagger, but his numb fingers were too weak to grasp the hilt.

He felt the human grab his hair and lift his head to cut his throat. And there was nothing he could do to stop them. Nothing. He was too weak and numb to even protest.

Suddenly, a light flashed in the hallway, blinding them. With it came a loud, fierce shriek that cut through the stone like thunder. It broke loose pieces of their masonry, bringing down sections of the wall.

The humans ran for cover as a huge red dragon burst through the portal.

Urian fell forward into a pool of his own blood as he felt his father stepping past him to let loose a blast of dragon's breath upon them. Their enemies ran, screaming. More Daimons rushed through the portal to pursue them while his father transformed into his human body so that he could rush to Urian's side.

"What have you done, *pido?*"

Urian blinked up at his father. "I failed her, Baba. I failed you."

A single tear fell down his father's cheek. "Nay, child. You stay with me and you haven't failed me. You hear that? You'll only fail me if you die." He glanced over his shoulder. "Trates! Get Bethsheba and bring her body to Kalosis." Then he picked Urian up and cradled him in his arms the way he'd done when Urian was a boy and he used to fall asleep in his father's lap while he told him stories of the world before they'd been banished from daylight.

Urian hated how much it comforted him to be coddled again. He was a grown man. Far too old for something like this. And yet ... he wanted his father.

More than that, he wanted his mother. For the pain in his heart was so great that he feared it would make it explode. In truth, he wished he were dead. That would be easier than living with the guilt of what had happened tonight.

Knowing that he'd stood right there when Sheba had died and done nothing to protect her. Nothing to stop them from harming her. Why hadn't he seen or heard the arrow in time to stop it? Why?

Dear gods ... how would he ever get that sight of her death out of his mind?

How?

Urian didn't realize he was sobbing until his father had him back in Kalosis and they entered his father's palace where Paris and Davyn were waiting.

"Holy Apollymi, what happened?"

His father didn't answer Paris's question. "I need you to go to Apollymi and tell her Urian's near death. Beg her for assistance. Davyn, help me ready a bed for him."

He rushed to assist them.

Without a word, Paris did as he was ordered.

By the time they reached the bedroom, Urian was barely conscious. But he was still awake enough to know that this wasn't over. "How will I live with this, Solren?"

"The way we all live with tragedy and injustice, *m'gios*. One breath at a time until the day comes when you wake up and realize that the sick lump in your stomach has finally dissolved."

Urian winced at those words, which left him no comfort. "How long will that take?"

His father paused. "I don't know, Uri. I've been choking on mine since the hour I was born."

June 28, 9506 BC

"You shouldn't be here."

Urian swallowed hard at his father's words. "She's my wife, Solren. I owe her this honor."

Yet as he moved forward to light the pyre where Sheba's washed and shrouded body had been placed and her eyes covered with coins, he stumbled. Paris and his father caught him.

Grateful, Urian didn't argue as they assisted him toward the tall structure that Apollymi had used her powers to build in the center courtyard, where the damned had once been tortured under the iron fist of the Atlantean god Misos.

And perhaps they still were. He certainly felt like it tonight as he climbed up to do his final duty for Sheba. For he was emotionally wrecked. Physically weak. Gutted.

Too young to be this tired and defeated.

Tears filled his eyes as he saw the beautiful corpse of a once proud queen. Dressed in her white orichalcum armor, she appeared to be at peace finally.

Dressed in white to honor and mourn her, Urian kissed the mavyllo—Apollymi's sacred black rose—and placed it in Sheba's hands, which held her sword. "You were ever a great and mighty warrior. A beautiful lady and an inspiration to us all. I shall miss your company every day I live without it."

With those words spoken, he climbed down. Then he and Paris and his wife's two remaining bodyguards shot lit arrows up to set fire to her perch. Silent tears of guilt and anger fell as he watched the hungry flames take root and spread over the structure.

His father clapped him on the back and pulled him close. "We shall avenge her."

How? Rumors claimed it was Helios behind the attack. Yet

another god out to end them. Which made sense given the armor he'd seen on their attackers.

The only question was why? Sheba and her people had stayed out of Greek territory for the most part. There'd been no reason for a Greek god to strike against the Marzanni.

It made no sense.

Through his own pain, Urian heard his children crying. Pulling away from his father, he went to Geras and knelt by his side. The boy threw himself into Urian's arms so that he could weep there. Urian closed his eyes and held him.

"It's all right, Geramou."

"What if they'd killed you, Baba!"

He kissed the boy's cheek. "Your baba doesn't go down easy. It'll take more than a Greek god to bring me low."

Nephele didn't speak. She merely fisted her hands in his hair and held on to him as if afraid to let go.

"Goodness, child. Why do you tremble so?"

Still not a single sound from her.

Worried about her, Urian let go of Geras so that he could stand and pull her closer. "Neph?"

Her lips quivered, but she kept them pressed tightly together as she wound her fists in his cloak. Urian held her by his side, assuming she was merely upset like her brother over the fact that he'd been badly injured and that they'd barely escaped the raid.

No one else spoke until after the fire began to burn low. And not until after the pyre had collapsed. Only then did Apollymi's Charonte come in to finish the ceremony where Sheba's remains would be gathered and taken to Apollymi's sacred garden to be scattered in her orchard.

The same garden and orchard where Xyn lived.

He still hadn't seen her and he was hurt that she hadn't come for this. In truth, he'd expected her in the crowd. She'd always shown before whenever he needed her.

Never had she failed him.

Until today.

But as he lost count of how many came up to him to share

their condolences, she wasn't among them. And it hurt so badly that it was almost unfathomable. Indeed, he felt gutted. And the faces of the others and their words were lost to his own grief as he mumbled what he hoped was an appropriate response.

He remembered nothing really. Just the smell of pungent ash that stung his throat and burned his eyes. The hollow ache in his gut. And the deep stinging pain of a friend who couldn't be bothered to put aside their spiteful words to check on him.

"Come on, *m'gios*. You should rest."

This time, Urian didn't protest when his father took him home.

Paris was the first to ask the insensitive question everyone else had avoided around Urian. "Why didn't Sheba decay like we do when we die?"

Theo punched him in the arm. "God, you're an asshole! Have some brains! Your brother's in pain and you'd ask him that? Seriously? What is wrong with you?" He grimaced at Urian. "Say the word and I'll beat his ass."

Urian sighed. "It's okay. Truth is, I don't know why they don't. I think it's because of Koshchei the Deathless. He's a trickster god. Would make sense that he wants to play havoc with Apollo. That's my theory anyway."

He entered his father's home and drew up short at the sight of a group of his wife's guards. A small remnant of those who'd survived their attack. "Small" being the operative word.

So few had been left. A pathetic number, really.

They immediately bowed to him.

Urian frowned. "Why are you here, Kisha?"

The tallest blonde came forward with a blue-tinted bottle. "We have nowhere else to go, Majesty. They've destroyed our home. Annihilated our people. You are still our king. We await your orders."

How weird ... he hadn't considered that they would look to him for leadership and guidance. Especially since Sheba had never treated him as anything more than a favored decoration.

He glanced over to his father. For the first time in a long while, he felt like a child again. Like a lost little boy. A part of him wanted to ask his father what to do, if he should stay or go, but he curbed that petulant child and forced himself to meet his father like an equal.

Urian knew what to do. Most of all, he knew what Sheba's people needed.

"Do I have your permission to bring our survivors here, Solren?"

His father appeared offended by the question.

So be it. Urian took the bottle. "We shall find a place to rebuild."

"Are you insane?" his father snapped. "Of course you can stay here! I glared at you because I couldn't believe you thought you had to ask me for something that was a given. You know that you're always welcomed in my home."

Oh. Now he felt even dumber than he had a moment ago. Shaking his head, Urian glanced back to Kisha. "Send for the others and we'll see them settled."

"Thank you, Majesty." With another bow, she and the others rose and quickly left.

As soon as they were gone, his brothers and father stepped closer to examine his bottle.

"What is it?"

"Did they bring you blood?"

Urian smiled wistfully at their curiosity as he remembered the first time Sheba had served it to him. "Sort of." He uncorked it. "It's blood mead. They also have sanguine wine. And yes, even Apollites can drink this. You'll like it. Trust me." He took a drink directly from the bottle, then passed it over to them.

In the beginning, they were skittish, but once they tasted the wine, they had the same reaction he'd had the first time he'd tried it. Utter delight, followed by gluttony as no Apollite or Daimon had ever known such before. Normally whenever they tried to eat or drink anything other than each other's blood, their bodies rejected it—courtesy of his grandfather Apollo.

Food and drink made them violently ill.

Not this. Somehow, Sheba's brewers had found a way to mix

the right proportions so that their bodies would accept the drink, just as if they'd never been cursed.

It was wonderful to finally have some form of variety to their diets.

All of a sudden, they heard a loud commotion outside, punctuated by angry shouting and a lot of threats of bodily harm to anyone who didn't withdraw immediately. Fury darkened his father's eyes, but Urian recognized the deep cadence of that unmistakable baritone. "Wait!"

Urian teleported outside in time to see the massive beast of a warrior about to take the heads off the three Daimons who were dumb enough to confront him because they assumed this belligerent newcomer was a trelos in their midst.

Not that Urian blamed them. Given his rage and demeanor, it would be a natural assumption.

But this was no trelos.

He was something a whole lot deadlier.

Almost seven feet tall, with golden-blond hair, he made a fierce sight. His muscled shoulders would be wide enough on their own, but covered with armor and war-matted furs, those shoulders promised a crushing blow to anyone who angered this beast of a man. And it was only part of the reason why he'd been termed the Widowmaker.

Well that, and the two massive double-headed axes strapped to his back that he was not only a master of using, but way too quick to make use of.

And usually for no other reason than he was mildly perturbed.

Curling his lips, the Widowmaker headed for the first Daimon who neared him.

"Ruyn!" Urian shouted. "Halt!"

He hesitated as if he still wanted a piece of the one who'd annoyed him, then turned slowly to face Urian. "Where's my sister?"

Urian flinched at the pain-filled question and hated that he had to be the one to gut the man who loved his sister dearly. Choking on his guilt, he closed the distance between them. "I'm sorry."

The agony that haunted those steel-blue eyes was searing. Of all the people in the world, Ruyn had loved Sheba more than anyone. She was all the family he had.

Throwing his head back, he let loose a thunderous, pain-filled roar.

One that caused several of their men to rush forward.

Urian held his hand up to stop them. Then he shook his head. "I should have sent word to you. Again, I'm so sorry."

Before he could respond, they were joined by his father, who eyed Ruyn suspiciously. "Who is this?"

"Sheba's half brother Ruyn." Urian had barely spoken those words before Apollymi appeared in her full Destroyer form. Black on black, with her red eyes glowing. Hurricane-force winds swept through the whole of Kalosis, knocking most of them to the ground and sending bodies flying.

Stryker caught Urian to keep him from being harmed and anchored them to the side of a building with his powers.

But what stunned and shocked Urian most was a sight he'd never seen before. Faster than anyone could blink, Ruyn manifested a long wooden staff that he planted in the ground at his feet. At the top was a silver hand holding an oblong ball that opened to reveal a large green eye.

From an indefinable source, a low-pitched cry built to a shrill war cry that drove the goddess back. More than that, it forced all the Charonte with her to their knees. A bright orange light shot out from the center of the eye, in all directions. It glowed as bright as a sun and it caused the Daimons and Apollites to shrink away in total fear.

Only then did Ruyn lift it over his head so that he could scan them all.

He turned a slow circle, as if looking through the crowd for someone who might attack him. Once he was satisfied that everyone was quelled, he turned back toward Apollymi.

She was once again pale and frigid in her appearance.

"I come in peace, Apollymi."

Urian arched a brow at the strange way he pronounced her

name. It sounded more like "Apple-me," instead of their way, "Uh-PAUL-low-may."

She sneered at him. "Yet you dare to ground my Charonte? What kind of peace is that?"

Ruyn offered her a charming grin. "I'm the son of a demon, am I not?"

Her look turned to ice. "You are indeed. And every bit as worthless and treacherous."

His humor died instantly as hatred settled across his face and turned his features to stone. "There is no need to be insulting. You and my father were allies once."

"And when I needed him most, he turned his back." She spat on the ground at Ruyn's feet. "You're lucky he cares nothing for you. Otherwise I'd send you back to him in pieces."

Urian didn't miss the pain those cruel words caused to flare inside Ruyn's eyes. A deep-seated torment he quickly hid.

"Again, my quarrel is not with you, goddess. I only wanted to pay respects to my sister and her husband."

She flung her hand out and this time her powers lashed across him like a razor whip, cutting deep into his flesh and leaving his clothes split and his body bleeding. "You ever breach my portal again without an invitation or key, dog, and I will send your head home to your father and your heart to your mother."

To his credit, Ruyn barely reacted to the pain of that blow, which had to be agonizing. Rather he stood stalwart before the angry goddess and inclined his head. "Understood."

And then he had the audacity to turn his back on her and walk toward Urian, who didn't miss the white-knuckled grip he had on his staff that said he was barely keeping his temper in check.

Pushing himself away from his father, Urian moved closer to his brother-in-law. "I'm sorry, Ru."

He wiped at the blood on his chest and shrugged. "I can handle physical pain." Glancing back at Apollymi, he curled his lip. "Hers is no better or worse than my own mother's loving touch." Then his gaze turned stormy again. "Did Sheba suffer?"

"Nay. The attack was too quick." Urian removed the necklace

he wore that had belonged to his wife and handed it to Ruyn. A strange blending of her family, the amulet was a design of Thor's hammer with a wolf and raven. "She would want you to have this more than me." Urian tightened his grip in Ruyn's hand. "I'll also cede kingship to you. By all rights, it's more yours than mine and I know she'd much rather see you as the leader of her people."

Tears gathered in Ruyn's eyes. His hand trembled. "Why would you give up a throne?"

He smiled. "I'm Greek. Apollymian. The Marzanni were Sheba's. And I know what *you* did." He projected his thoughts to Ruyn. *Sheba told me the sacrifice you made so that she could live longer in spite of Apollo's curse. What you did to save her tribe.* He tightened his hand on Ruyn's. "As Sheba said, we will always be allies. You and I will always be brothers, and while I may fight with my brothers over trivial things, I will never screw one over. Especially not for something as inconsequential as a throne."

Ruyn yanked him forward into his embrace and held him for a long minute.

Urian felt his hot tears as he silently wept. With a ragged breath, Ruyn pounded Urian twice on his back and stepped away to clear his throat and wipe at his eyes.

Gruffly, he pulled his own necklace off and extended it toward Urian. "That is my mark. You need me, brother, you call and I will come. No matter what. No matter when." He chucked Urian on the arm. "Remember, all roads lead to Ruyn."

Urian snorted at his bad pun.

Then he sobered and cut a dark, serious grimace toward Urian's family. "And let me leave you with one bit of advice, little brother, as I've lived a *lot* longer than both of you. Remember that you serve your goddess today. But loyalty given is seldom returned. Take it from a survivor of the Primus Bellum. At the end of the day, it doesn't matter who we swear our fealty to, we're just a bunch of demons to them. Useless things they will cast off and leave to die without a second thought. Me, Caleb, Dagon, Shadow, Xev … countless others. They thought nothing of us. Yet we sacrificed everything we had to the Kalosum to make sure they'd win—even though we were born to serve the darkness of the Mavromino, we fought for the Kalosum's light. In the end, those who were supposed to be good, who were supposed to reward us for our service and had promised to do so, turned their backs on us and chose not to see us for who and what we really are. Instead of looking into our hearts and seeing what we'd given and lost, they threw us aside like garbage. When all was said and done, they were no better than the ones they'd hated, and for all the reasons they hated the other side. So be careful where you lay your trust, and twice as careful who you serve. It's not so much don't bite the hand that feeds you as to make sure you sever your master's hand before it has a chance to strike you down for no reason other than they judge you unworthy of breathing their air."

Ruyn sighed as he settled Sheba's necklace over his heart. "It is ever the saddest indictment against humanity that they cannot live in peace. Too many believe the path to happiness can only be achieved by walking over those around them. When the truth is so much simpler."

"If you can't be happy alone, you'll never be happy in a crowd." Urian said the words before Ruyn had a chance, as they were something Sheba had often spoken to him. It was the philosophy their mother had raised them on.

Ruyn nodded. "If you can't stand yourself, why should you expect anyone else to? And if you seek to cause harm to others, it will always return to cause harm to you."

He was right about that.

"Take care of yourself, little brother. I hope we meet again." And with that, he was gone.

While everyone slowly and nervously dispersed, Apollymi made her way toward Urian.

"How is your son, Strykerius?"

His father rubbed his back. "As well as can be expected."

"He looks as if he needs to feed."

Urian felt his face heat up at those words, given their personal nature. At least that was the one good thing to come out of his two marriages ...

No one feared feeding him anymore. He now had women lining up to give him their blood.

Men, too.

And not just Davyn. It was actually quite disconcerting how many wanted a piece of him.

"I'm fine, akra."

"If you have a moment, then, I should like to ask you about your attack."

His father opened his mouth to protest, but Urian interrupted. "I'll be fine, Solren. Just a moment."

"Are you sure?"

He nodded.

His father reluctantly allowed Urian to follow Apollymi back to her palace.

She didn't speak until they were alone inside the marbled walls and out of the sight of prying eyes. Then she turned to face him with a probing stare. "Was it Helios, as they claim?"

"It could have been. But in all honestly, the attack was swift and fierce. I barely saw it before I was down."

She cursed under her breath. "Keep your eyes peeled, Urian. There is much danger around us. Already, I've found one traitor and killed them."

"For Helios?"

She nodded. "He's after your grandfather and Rezar."

He scowled at her words. While he understood why the Titan sun god would want to kill Apollo, who'd replaced him—there was no one alive who didn't understand and know about that grudge match—Rezar was different. One of the oldest primal gods, he should have the powers to destroy Helios. Why would the Titan be so stupid as to pick a fight he couldn't win? "I don't understand."

"And it's good that you don't. That will keep you alive. Just know that if you hear anything more about Helios, bring it to me."

"Always, akra."

"Good. Now go."

Urian started away, then hesitated. "Before I go, may I ask one thing?"

She arched a brow at that.

"The dragon who guards your garden?"

Her eyes flashed red. "You needn't worry over her anymore. She's no longer here." And with that, she vanished.

Those clipped words hit him like daggers through his flesh. They were a staggering blow that caused him to step back as he reeled from pain.

Gone?

How could Xyn be gone?

Urian stood without moving as he tried to come to grips with what Apollymi had just told him. A million questions ran through his head.

Had she died? Been killed?

What the hell did Apollymi mean she was no longer there?

Unable to accept that, he teleported to Sarraxyn's cave so that he could see for himself what was going on. And to make sure it was the truth. Because honestly, he couldn't accept it. He refused to accept it.

Until he saw the truth with his own eyes.

Her cave was empty.

She was gone and there was no trace left of his once beautiful dragon. Not a scale. Not a scuff on the floor. It was as if she'd never been.

And that tore his heart asunder. It bled pain through every molecule of his body. How could this have happened? Tears blinded him as his memories slammed into him and he cursed himself for not coming home sooner to see her.

For not ever apologizing.

She was human and I treated her like shit.

Hurt and wounded, he felt so guilty for everything he'd ever said or done. How could he have let them part like this? She'd been so important to him. Why hadn't he told her that?

Just once?

I am an asshole.

Regret burned so deep inside him for everything that had gone unsaid. He'd hurt her and now there was no way to make amends.

Never harm a heart that loves you, for there are too many in this world that are out to cause you pain. His mother's words haunted him now. She'd been right.

He'd wounded Xyn and for what? His own vanity?

My own stupidity.

For that, he deserved to be alone. Because in his heart, he knew he'd never have anyone else who could come close to his dragon. How could he? It wasn't every day a guy met a woman who had those kinds of skills.

A woman who made him feel like he could fly. Whose smile made his heart sing.

How could he have given that up for anything?

Cold and alone, he'd started to leave when he caught a strange glimmer in the corner. Scowling, he headed toward it to see what it was.

How odd ... Embedded in the wall of the cave was the small necklace Xyn always wore. She'd called it her dragon's tear.

And in a small leather bag was a folded note. His hands shook as he unfolded it and then began to read the sweet, flowing script.

My dearest Urian,

While you are gone, my brother has secured my freedom. I don't know if you'll ever come back here or even think of me. You've no idea how many times I've regretted what happened between us.

That last night I saw you.

I miss my best friend in so many ways. There's not a day that has passed without you in it when I haven't carried your face in my heart, and I will do so until the day I die.

Wherever you are, I hope you're happy, and I hope your wife knows how very lucky she is to have you as her own. That is the one thing I wish I could have called you. Just once. Please take care of yourself and if you do think of me, I hope you'll forgive my words that were spoken in anger. And that one day, maybe, you can think of me and smile again.

Just remember that I will always love you.

Ever yours,
Xyn

Unable to bear the guilt and pain, Urian closed his eyes and choked on his tears. He sank to his knees and cursed himself for having left in anger.

What have I done?

How could I have been so stupid?

She was a dragon. There was no way he'd ever be able to find her again.

July 1, 9506 BC

"So you live."

Urian let out a tired sigh as he heard Xanthia's sharp, shrill tone. Reclining in his chair, he was grateful his back was against the wall. Otherwise, she might very well have driven a dagger through his spine.

He looked from Ophion and Atreus, who sat across from him while they played a game of dice in the main hall, to his wife, who stood beside an Apollite he didn't know, and smirked. "Much to your dismay, apparently."

Her gaze narrowed on him, then softened. "You did manage to save the lives of my children. So for that, I might be able to find a degree of forgiveness for you."

Somehow, he doubted that. And he wondered what point she had to this visit.

Sighing, Urian reached for the cup at his elbow that held the wine he'd taught his father's people to brew from their blood. "How are the kids?"

"Geras misses you."

He was stunned she admitted that. Normally, she only berated and cursed him during their exchanges. "I miss him, too." Urian reached for the dice.

And still she stood there. Eyeing him in awkward silence.

He rolled his turn and lost. Apparently, she was sucking out all his luck as well as his good humor. "Is there something else you need, Thia?"

"I was curious if you'd found a place to stay since your return."

His brothers snorted in unison.

Urian gave them both a droll stare as he wondered why she'd bother to ask him that, given the way they'd last parted company. Surely she wasn't offering herself to him now. Was she mad?

He glared at his brothers. "What are you laughing at, you hyenas?"

Atreus blinked at him with giant goo-goo eyes. "Take me home, you big strapping stud, and feed me! I'm starving for you!" He started panting and pawing at Urian.

That was bad enough.

Worse? Ophion joined in on it. He even went as far as to plant a sloppy kiss on Urian's lips.

Disgusted, Urian shoved at them. "I swear to the gods, Solren should have sacrificed you both to Eunomia to spare me this madness!"

Xanthia rolled her eyes at his brothers, then turned her attention to Urian. "Should I leave my door unlocked?"

Holy shit, she wasn't joking. She'd actually been making a play for him. Helios was riding icicles now.

And Urian would be crying them before he ever repeated the mistake of returning to Xanthia's bed.

Smirking, he cut his eyes to his brothers. "How could I leave a home where I'm so wanted?" He leaned back against his brothers so that they could grope him more openly.

She screwed her face up in distaste. "You're all degenerates!"

"We are?" Urian asked with a laugh. "You're the one I caught fucking Erol! At least my brothers aren't diseased."

Shrieking in outrage, she rushed through the crowded hall to flee their presence as quickly as possible, while calling him every name she could think of.

Ophion sucked his breath in sharply as he moved away. "Damn, Uri, that was cold."

Unrepentant, he sat up with a grimace and straightened his clothes. "Not as cold as I'd like to be. Besides, I didn't do it in front of the kids and I have yet to kill *her*." Tannis still wasn't speaking to him over the fact that she was a widow after Urian had dispensed with her first husband.

Though to be honest, his sister should be grateful. Her second husband was much kinder to her than that ass had ever been. Especially whenever Urian was around, as he didn't want to meet the same fate as Erol.

All marriages should have one good disembowelment in them. It set the tone for proper respect.

Atreus fell silent as they resumed their game.

Ophion wasn't so kind. "So what are you going to do for food?"

Urian glanced over to where one of the xōrōn was soliciting a client while both of them eyed him like he was the sweetmeat of choice. Finding someone to feed him these days wasn't the problem. "I'm done with marriage."

"For now, you mean?"

His gut clenched at his brother's question as remorse and guilt speared him. He touched Xyn's necklace, which was concealed beneath his chiton, and tried his best not to think of the one and only woman he'd ever met who'd understood him completely. She alone had known his soul.

And she was lost to him.

"Forever."

March 22, 9503 BC

"Urian!"

Sucking his breath in, Urian groaned at the sharp hysterical tone. At first, he thought it was his sister's screeching howl. Surely, no one but Tannis could hit *that* particularly heinous note.

But as it continued and grew even louder and shriller, he realized it was Xanthia.

And it took on a whole new level as she crashed into his room and found him entwined in furs on the floor with three naked women who were draped over and under him. Not that he liked the floor. Simply, it'd been the only option as the bed wouldn't accommodate all of them and the bacchanalian orgy they'd been having the night before.

"What is this?"

He would assume it was fairly obvious given that his pillow was an extremely large bosom, and there was really no doubt given where his hand was buried. And he knew from having walked in on his ex-wife's antics that she was by no means a woman of pristine virtue.

"Keep your tone down," he snapped, then cursed himself as even his whispered tone cut through his head like a dagger. "What's wrong with you now?" He yawned and carefully extracted his hand so as not to harm his sleeping companion whose name he couldn't quite remember.

"It's Nephele! For spite, she's run off with that ... that ... piece of nothing I forbid her to marry!"

Rubbing at his head, he lay back down and snuggled up to the nicely rounded, warm bosom on his right. To his deepest chagrin, he couldn't recall the name of its owner either. But then to be fair, she hadn't asked his. "I'm sure she's at Daphne's or Idora's."

Xanthia moved to squat beside his pallet and dared to tug the covers off him. "You're not listening to me, Urian!" She rudely shoved something in his face. "She's left Kalosis!"

He blinked to clear his vision and took the note she was waving in front of his nose. After a couple of seconds, he was able to focus on the words.

And with each one he read, his blood ran cold.

"Damn it, woman! Where were you when she did this?" He rose to his feet.

Xanthia's nostrils flared. "Certainly not trapped between the thighs of a whore!"

He glared at her. "I wouldn't tilt at that dragon were I you." He ground his teeth and reread the letter. "I can't believe she went to the human realm."

"That's what I was trying to tell you." She gestured at the letter. "You have to do something. Find her!"

Scratching his head, he nodded. "Okay. Go home and watch Geras. I'll get her back." At least he was fully sober now.

As fast as he could, he washed, then used his powers to dress.

He went straight to Apollymi's palace and sought out their goddess in her garden. Her mirror was the only thing he knew that had any chance of locating his daughter. He prayed he could talk the goddess into letting him use it for such a purpose.

But the moment he asked, she didn't appear pleased.

Sitting on her perch while her two ever-present Charonte watched on, Apollymi arched a withering brow. "You know the answer, Urian. When it comes to such things, the mirror shows what it wants."

Hence why he had no idea where Xyn was, even though he'd asked it repeatedly. The damn thing would never tell him where she was located. And he had no idea why. Maybe he kept it from working.

Or *she* did. He wouldn't put much of anything past Apollymi, especially when she got into one of her moods.

Not wanting to think about that, he went over to the edge and froze as he caught sight of himself in the black water. Normally, Apollites couldn't cast a reflection. And that had driven Sheba to utter madness as she'd endlessly asked him how she looked. As if such a great beauty could ever have a day where she didn't look amazing.

Yet never once had she ever believed him when he told her that. Women ... he'd never understand that about them.

Personally, Urian had never thought much about it.

Until now. For the first time, given that his kind couldn't cast reflections, he saw himself and understood why the other Apollites and Daimons treated him the way they did.

I am a freak.

His eyes were even more horrific than they'd led him to believe with their ridicule. While his father's were the swirling silver of their goddess's—which, granted, were off-putting—his were an unnatural shade of vibrant blue. They practically glowed. Unlike any color he'd ever seen before on any person.

And while he'd removed the beads and ribbons of Sheba's tribe, he'd kept his ghostly white hair long.

Though he'd never shared a great passion with his second wife, he had cared for her and he felt that he should honor her memory and their time together.

He owed her that much. For she had changed him. She'd taken a boy and shown him that he could function without his family, and made him a confident man. Independent in a way he wouldn't have been had she not come into his life and taken him away from Kalosis.

For that he would always be grateful.

But the one thing he couldn't do was wear Xyn's armor. Even if it meant his death. *That,* he'd packed away in a chest and laid a spell upon it to keep it safe from harm. Because it was all he had left of her.

Plus the pain of bearing her love without her here ...

That stinging bite was more than he could handle. So he was dressed in the black Spathi armor of the rest of the Apollymians. And yet he looked nothing like them. Not really. He stood out as deadlier and toxic.

Urian Deathbringer.

Sheba would be proud. Releasing a tired breath, he forced his thoughts to the matter at hand. He had a little girl to find. One who thought herself a woman and had no idea how complicated her young life was about to get if he didn't locate her and drag her home to her mother.

At first the stubborn waters refused to show him anything. They swirled and remained frustratingly blank.

Urian was about to give up and go searching on his own, when they finally began to swirl very slowly. Then they picked up speed.

Suddenly he saw that sassy little blond head he knew so well. She was in a large hall with other Apollites. Relief coursed through him that she was all right.

Until one of the men present grabbed her. She cried out in alarm.

The man in front of them curled his lip and unsheathed his sword. "We might as well kill her. If she's not his blood daughter, she's no good to us. And serves no purpose. Besides, why would he care? I heard he divorced her mother, long ago."

"He still dotes on her. She can bring him to us." The Apollite tightened his grip on Nephele's arm and turned his hate-filled glare toward her. "Call for Urian to open the portal."

She shook her head. "I will not betray my solren."

He backhanded her so hard that she hit the floor.

With a deep growl, Urian teleported without a second thought. And realized too late that he should have probably looked around at how many men were actually in this hall before he acted.

Then waited for at least one more Apollite to join him on this venture.

Probably more.

Yeah, this was a bad idea, as he was severely outnumbered. Glancing around while trying to act nonchalant, he saw at least one hundred Apollites and Daimons in the hall.

With him.

And Nephele.

Damn, I should have taught her to fight better. Though he'd tried, she'd never been interested in it and had always ended up spending more time arguing with him about going into the ring than actually learning to defend herself. Which had been completely counterproductive, so he'd given up out of frustration.

Note to self—I failed at parenting.

Then again, given the huge number of warriors in the hall, it wouldn't have mattered with just the two of them.

They were doomed.

Doing his best not to show his true feelings on the subject, Urian cleared his throat and arched a brow at the men surrounding him. There was only one thing to be done.

Bluff and swagger.

He crossed his arms over his chest and glared at the one in front of him. "I suggest you remove your hands from my daughter or lose them."

Sounded tough enough. He could almost believe it.

The Apollite had the nerve to laugh. That lasted for about three seconds until Urian blasted him with his powers and rendered the hyena a smoldering pile of ash on the floor. Before the others could recover from their shock, Urian grabbed Nephele and summoned a portal. He sent her through it and was about to go after her when the others rushed him.

He closed it instantly to protect his family and Kalosis. Which meant he was on the wrong side of things.

Damn it.

Forcing himself to remain calm, he blinked slowly as he scanned the men. "Now that my daughter's safe . . . " He reached up toward his necklace. It was his last line of defense.

Might not work. Might even get him killed faster. Honestly, he couldn't blame Ruyn if he chose not to answer. Or kill him on arrival. But Urian was really out of options.

He pricked his finger and hoped the blood was enough to summon his brother-in-law while they closed in.

"Kill the bastard of Apollo!"

Urian scoffed at those words. For one thing, he wasn't a bastard, he was quite legitimate. Second . . . "Why?" he snarled, unsheathing his sword. "Not like I love him, either."

Their answer came as a mass attack.

Bloody wonderful. Kill him for a piece-of-crap grandparent he hated. That was just all kinds of wrong.

Summoning his powers, he really regretted not wearing Xyn's armor right now. He should have gotten over his feelings and remembered that he was a warrior and it was enchanted.

And that he liked having his balls attached to his body.

A light flashed beside him. He turned to attack, intending to kill whatever it was that had decided to join their party. Then he hesitated and pulled back as he saw Ruyn manifesting there.

Thank the gods, he finally had some reinforcement.

It took Ruyn less than a minute to assess the situation.

And Urian's stupidity that had caused it. With a sardonic grin, he shook his head. "Brother, it appears to me that you seriously picked the wrong day to carpe your diem."

"Better than allowing my diem to get carped. So are you going to stand there, admiring my posterior, or lend us a hand with it?"

"Rather it should be a certain finger I lend you, mate." Growling, Ruyn hefted the two axes off his back and angled them at the ready. "It's a good thing I like you. Anyone else would be my first victim."

Urian snorted. "Too bad you don't like a few more. Am thinking some friends with you wouldn't have been a bad thing." He used a god-bolt to blast the Apollite closest to him and swung with a sword at the next. Times like this, he wished he had his father's or Xyn's ability to transform into a dragon. They could use the firepower right about now.

Sadly, those powers were beyond his scope.

Ruyn scoffed at his words. "Bah, friends. Who needs them? They just drink your beer and ruin a perfectly good rotten mood by trying to cheer it." He took the heads off three Apollites with one stroke.

Urian was impressed. He had to slaughter his enemies the old-fashioned way. With his hands and magick.

The worst part was that he still didn't know why this group was after him or what they wanted. What had he done?

Normally, he only drove his brothers to homicide. And that was on purpose.

Ducking as he struck an artery and blood sprayed across his face, Urian licked his lips. At least he was getting fed. Ruyn was not so happy about that part of this. Unlike Urian, Ruyn wasn't an Apollite. He and Sheba had shared a mother, not Apollo's blood or the curse.

So Ruyn kicked and twisted his way through them. Urian held his own better than he'd have thought, given their number. Until a barrage of arrows flew at them.

Ruyn deflected the ones aimed at him with his axes.

Urian wasn't so skilled. While he could catch a single one, he couldn't catch more than that without dropping his sword. Had he been more experienced, he might have been able to use his telekinesis to deflect them or some other trick.

Sadly, he wasn't his father.

And three of them embedded in his chest.

With a staggering amount of pain that brought back a fierce round of déjà vu, he fell to one knee. *Get up, damn it!*

He couldn't. The best he could manage was to pant.

One of them kicked him to his back. Urian rolled toward him as he went to stab him, knocking the bastard off balance and tripping him. That only drove the arrows in deeper and caused more pain to rip through his body. Groaning out loud, he thought for a moment that he might pass out from the agony of it.

Somehow he managed to rise. The man in front of him was a Daimon who had the nerve to laugh at his pain.

Pain he knew wouldn't last much longer. Any heartbeat and he'd black out.

Turning toward Ruyn, he saw his brother trying to make his way closer to help him.

But there was only one way to make it through this. And he wasn't about to let some slimy, crappy Daimon get the better of him. Not like this. *I won't die on my knees ...*

With an evil grin, Urian turned back toward the Daimon. Then he sank his fangs into the bastard's throat and ripped it open.

The moment he tasted that blood, he understood what his brothers had tried to tell him. The shot of adrenaline to his system was unnerving. It literally felt as if he'd gone to sleep and been jolted back awake by something fierce and frightening.

Only now he was more alive. More alert. In tune with the very universe itself.

He heard more. Saw more.

Felt more.

Including a whine in his skull that was deafening. For a moment, he thought he might go insane from the intensity of it. Like a high-pitched squeal embedded deep in the center of his brain that only he could hear.

"He's a Daimon!"

Those words rang and echoed in his ears loud enough to cause him to flinch. More than that, their attackers instantly stood down. They literally stepped away and withdrew.

Why?

Ruyn scowled at him. "Now while I like to think I'm an awe-inspiring beast whose battle skills are such that it causes my enemies to tremble and flee at the very mention of my name, that's just a story I tell women to get myself laid." He gestured at the now-behaving group with his bloody axes. "That shit is surreal and just doesn't happen except in braggart tales and old men's fantasies. What'd you do, Urian?"

He sputtered. "I don't know."

The one who'd first called for Urian's head spat blood on the floor. "There's no need to kill him. He's dead now."

Ruyn made an impressively foul face. "While his stench might suggest a dead body, he's always smelled that way. Bastard looks live enough to me."

The man rolled his eyes. "He's a Daimon. We're out to end the line of Apollo. Once the last of his Apollite brood is dead, our curse is lifted."

Now it was Urian's turn to frown. What the hades did he mean by *that?*

"That true?" Ruyn asked him.

"Not that I know of." Urian glared at the leader. "Where'd you hear that stupidity?"

"From the oracle of Helios. She swore to us that it was the truth. When the last of his Apollite children are dead, then there won't be a curse left on us."

Urian curled his lip at that. Since when had the oracle ever once in the history of oracles spoken that plainly? *When the sun rises in the east, the sun will have risen in the morning* or *after the battle a mighty kingdom will fall*, nay—shit was all anyone could ever get from an oracle. They spoke in useless riddles that would be true no matter what so that they hedged their bets, and you interpreted them into whichever you wanted it to be the truth.

He'd never understood why anyone would listen to an oracle.

The Apollite on his right jerked his chin at Urian. "Hey? Can't *he* take us to the rest of his family so that we can finish them?"

Urian groaned at another stupid epiphany. Especially as all the others realized he was right.

"Shite," he and Ruyn mumbled under their breaths at the same time.

"I got the asshole on the left," Ruyn said.

"Better yet, I got a portal." Urian opened it fast and grabbed him.

Only instead of landing in Kalosis, Urian hit the ground on the precipice of a mountain unlike anything he'd ever seen before. And no sooner did he land on it than the bottom collapsed out from beneath his feet.

Urian felt himself falling fast and furious. What the hades was this?

Convinced he was dead, he didn't even have time to pray. There was nothing to grab onto.

Until he slammed into the cold, jagged ground so hard it jarred his teeth. Rattled and momentarily dazed, he dangled over what had to be a thousand-foot drop. His heart hammered so hard, he was amazed it didn't rip out of his chest. He latched onto the only thing that kept him from falling.

One massive trunk of an arm.

"Thank you," he breathed as he looked up into Ruyn's eyes.

"Don't thank me yet. I still might come to my senses and let go. 'Cause the gods know you're more trouble than you're worth."

"You know you'd miss me if I were gone."

Ruyn scoffed as he struggled to pull him up and over the jagged ledge without losing his grip, or harming either of them. Grunting and panting, he cursed Urian the whole time. "Lose weight, man! Never seen anyone on a liquid diet weigh so damn much! Shite, already! Usually whenever someone gives me this much trouble, I at least get a blow job for my efforts."

With one last massive grimace, he succeeded in hauling Urian over and rolling with him until they were tucked underneath a small ledge.

Urian let out a bitter laugh. "You can cuddle me all you want, you brute. But you have to buy me dinner and a ring before you think about kissing me, and any other oral activities are strictly off the table until marriage. I'm not a cheap whore you picked up, you know?"

Laughing, Ruyn shoved at him. "You're all kinds of wrong, Greek. No idea what my sister saw in you." He shook his head, then frowned and gripped Urian's chin so that he could examine his face. "Are you all right?"

"You just said I wasn't."

"I know what I said. But you've gone kind of green."

Urian snorted irritably. "My head hurts."

"Well, if I had a head like yours, it'd hurt, too."

Grimacing at the oversized oaf, Urian groaned again. "In retrospect, I think I would have rather they killed me."

Ruyn hugged him before he got up and helped Urian to his feet. "Do you believe any of what they said?"

"About ending the curse?"

He nodded.

Urian considered it as he continued to rub his throbbing temples. "I don't know. It's the gods. Anything's possible, especially when it comes to screwing us."

"Well, if it is ... will your father be able to kill his own children to save his people?"

That was an easy answer. "Nay. Never. But I don't think it would matter."

"Why not?"

Urian laughed bitterly. "Given the number of women my father and brothers screwed before they turned Daimon? There's no telling how many children they could have fathered between them. The only two in my family I know haven't spawned are me and Paris."

"You sure?"

He nodded even though it felt like his brain was slamming against his skull. "I'm sterile. It's why Sheba and I never had children."

"And your brother?"

"Doesn't sleep with women."

Ruyn let out a heavy sigh as he cleaned his axes off on his vambraces, then returned them to their sheaths. "So are you going to tell your father about the prophecy?"

"No idea. Not sure he'd even believe it. He doesn't put a lot of faith in the gods ... other than Apollymi." Urian glanced around the barren, windy precipice where they stood. "Not that it matters right now. We might never get out of here."

"How do you mean?"

"Not sure where we are and for some reason, my portal isn't opening. You and I could be here for a while."

Ruyn let out a long, drawn-out sigh. "Awesome. Trapped here with you. No wine. No beer." He scanned him with a look. "And you can't even shapeshift into a woman. Damn, I pissed off the wrong god last night."

"Excuse me?"

"I would, but there's really no excuse for this level of incompetence. So I'm going to take a nap. Wake me up if you ever figure out how to open a portal or something else decides to eat you. If I'm bored enough, I might lend another axe."

Urian snorted at the irritable ass. He didn't know why he

liked him as much as he did. On his brothers, that attitude was intolerable. For some reason, Ruyn made it charming and funny.

Though at the moment, he was more than a little tempted to kick him.

Still, he wondered about Helios's prophecy. Could there be any truth to it?

Was there a way to ever free them from Apollo's curse? Or was it simply another lie from the gods? After all, that was what hope really was. The worst of all the curses Zeus had laid at the bottom of Pandora's box so that when she opened it, she would release into the world that one stupid thing that would make sure humanity carried on and kept going no matter what despair, degradation, and nightmare the gods heaped on them.

So long as they had hope, they suffered.

How he hated that bitch. She was the worst of all plagues ever concocted by the gods and the cruelest joke they'd ever played on any sentient being—hence the real reason it was inside Pandora's box. But for his own hope that he might find Xyn again, he wouldn't be here now.

And that was why he hated Elpis more than any other goddess on Olympus. Because she hid her true purpose behind the guise of lies and treachery. She wasn't there to comfort. She was there to punish and to prolong the torment of man.

No more. Urian was done with her.

Helios *glared at* the Daimons and Apollites around him. "You were supposed to kill the children of Apollo. Not let them go."

"He's a Daimon, my lord. He can't have children."

Helios sent a god-bolt through him that splintered him into pieces. Then he glared at the others. "Anyone else want to voice a stupid opinion?"

They quickly backed down.

Feeling the fire ripple up his arms and over his skin, he turned his blazing gaze toward each of them in turn. "When next I give an order, you will do as I say, without question or fail. I want the death of Apollo's children and grandchildren. Bring me their hearts or I will have yours in their stead!"

He was through with this game, and tired of watching Zeus and the other Olympian upstarts feeding him table scraps.

War had been declared and he intended to win it.

June 30, 9501 BC

"You know what today is."

Urian flinched at his father's question as he came into the study where he'd been summoned. "Of course I know."

"Did you talk to her like I asked?"

"I tried. She wouldn't listen."

"Did you get her children to talk to her?"

Urian arched a brow at that question. "Didn't you?"

"Of course I did!" His father paced back and forth. And then he saw it. The tears that glistened in his father's swirling silver eyes as he choked on the sobs he was doing his best to hold back. "She's going to die, Urimou."

He barely heard those words and the nickname his father hadn't used for him since he was a child.

"My precious girl. And there's nothing I can do to stop it. I even tried to trick her. To bespell her. Damn her for her stubbornness!"

Choking on his own grief, he went to his father and pulled him into his arms. "I'm sorry."

Urian was unprepared for the ferocity of his father's hug. While he'd known his father was a powerful man, he hadn't realized just how much until those arms wrapped around him with the strength of a Titan. Burying his face in the crook of his neck, his father wept with soul-racking sobs the likes of which Urian would never have imagined him capable of making. They made the ones he'd shed for his brother pale in comparison. He fisted his hands in Urian's chalmys and held him there as if terrified of letting him go.

He had no idea what to say or how to comfort him. So he merely stood there, holding his father and rubbing his back while his own tears fell.

When his father finally pulled back, he buried his hand in Urian's hair in each side of his face and glared at him. "A father isn't supposed to bury his children. We live to protect them, and we die first so that we can be there to welcome them on the other side. This is so wrong, Uri."

"I know, Baba. I know."

His lips trembling, his father wiped at the tears on Urian's face, then kissed his cheeks. "I love you, *pido*." With a ragged breath, he released him and headed for the door. "Let me go and sit with your sister."

Urian couldn't move as he heard him walking away. He was paralyzed by his own grief and anger. This was so wrong. And he felt horrible for his father. Furious for his sister who had to leave her own children.

And madder than hell that he would be forced to watch her agony on this day.

Not like they all hadn't seen it before.

Countless times.

They even had a term for it. The Thanatogori—deathwatch, or daylong vigil—whenever one of their species turned twenty-seven and decided not to turn Daimon.

Already his sister would have begun the painful process of dying. Urian had seen enough of his friends die like that. He'd never watched family perish.

Dreading this, he knew he had to go sit with his father. So he left and headed to her house, where all of his family was already gathered.

Even Geras and Nephele, along with Nephele's husband, were there. The only one missing was Xanthia. But then she hadn't really spoken to him much since the night he'd returned Nephele to Kalosis. He wasn't sure why, and since she refused to speak, he didn't press it.

Besides, her psychosis wasn't really his problem, especially now that she was remarried. Though it was ironic that Geras and Nephele still considered him their father. And that was fine by him.

He continued to think of them as his children.

Paris and Davyn greeted him first at the door. Both had swollen eyes.

"I can't believe she's doing this." Paris wiped at his cheeks while Davyn held him.

"Me either. She'd always seemed more levelheaded than this." Trying to distract himself, he glanced over to the table, where a strange urn had been set. "What's that?"

Davyn winced. "Tobias made it. He wants to put his mother's dust in it so that he can keep her with him after ... " His voice broke off as his tears began to flow.

Urian understood. Tobias was Tannis's youngest and her only son. He was the one who was closest to his mother. "Where is she?"

Paris drew a ragged breath. "On her bed. He won't leave her side."

"Let me go see them, then." Urian headed to the back and had to finagle his way through the crowd. By the time he reached Tannis's room, he barely recognized his own sister. She was so much older already.

Her two daughters lay on each side while her son was at her feet on the bed. His father knelt on the floor, holding Tannis's infant granddaughter, Marcella, whom her eldest daughter had birthed only two weeks ago.

Helena, who'd been named for their mother, clung to Tannis, but her other daughter, Rhoda, launched herself at Urian as soon as she saw him. "Uncle Uri! Make her stop this!"

"I wish I could, stormy. I tried all day yesterday. All I got for it was insults." He kissed his niece's head.

Rhoda wailed in the shrillest of tones. "I'll never die like this. So help me, I'll eat every human alive first!"

"Good girl," his father snarled with pride. "Make sure you pass that fire on to your children."

"Baba!" Tannis snapped. "Don't you dare encourage her to such things."

Someone took Urian's hand. He glanced down at first, thinking it would be a niece or nephew.

It was Archie.

"Think if one of us bit her, it would keep her from dying?"

Urian considered it. "Might. But then she might kick our asses for the effort. Feel free to try."

He snorted.

And so their day went, with insufferable slowness as they listened to her screaming in agony and watched her dying. Urian had never felt so helpless. Nor had he hated so much.

By the time dawn came to end her suffering, they were all scarred so deeply that none of them could speak as their father slowly gathered her dust to place in Tobias's jar.

Tobias cradled it with the tenderest care and placed it on the mantel before he and his sisters went to hold their silent vigil. Urian's brothers began to disperse with their families. Theo spoke in a quiet whisper to his father while Paris and Davyn came up to Urian.

Paris glanced over to their father. "Davyn and I are going Daimon tonight."

Urian arched a brow at that. "Pardon?"

A tic started in his twin's jaw. "After this ... I'm not waiting another day or night. Davyn only has a few more months. We decided not to push our luck. You've been one for two years now, yeah?"

He nodded.

"It's not so bad, is it?"

Urian scratched at the back of his neck. "Honestly? It's not the best. Especially in the beginning. I spent a lot of those first months sick with it. Tricking a human into granting permission to take their soul isn't as easy as you think. Picking a human with a strong soul is even harder. They're corrupt little bastards. And the constant whining will drive you to insanity."

"Then how do you cope?"

Urian gave them an evil grin. "I live on venom."

"I could do that."

He snorted. "You're too much in love. But I'm here to help. If you need anything, you let me know."

Nodding, they left him alone. Urian waited on his father since they were the only two who didn't have anyone else.

"You worried about me?"

He heard the stern note in his father's tone. "A little."

"Don't. I'm not that fragile."

Perhaps. But unlike his brothers, Urian never forgot the fact that his father really wasn't that much older than they were. He'd been a teen when Archie and Theo and Tannis were born. Barely twenty when Urian and Paris had come along. Too young to have been thrust into the decisions that Apollo had forced onto him.

Too young to be cursed to die.

His father met his gaze. "So are you."

"Pardon?"

"I can hear your thoughts, Urian. And you're too young to have been put through so much." His father picked up Tannis's pillow from the bed and pressed it to his face so that he could breathe her scent in. Then he cradled it to his chest like an infant and closed the distance between them. "I don't want to bury another child. Help me protect your brothers."

"I intend to."

"Good. And I've been thinking about what you said."

"About Helios's prophecy?"

He nodded. "Apollo had another Apollite mistress. We'll start with that line before we worry about ours. I want you in charge of hunting down every last one of them and cutting their throats. Let's see if there's any truth to this."

"You sure?"

Tears welled in his eyes as he stroked Tannis's pillow. "Kill them for me, Urian. Every last fucking one of them."

He winced at the agony in his father's voice. It mirrored his own. "I will see it done, Baba."

Urian *sat by* Xyn's pool, with his feet dangling in the water, seeking some form of comfort, even though there was none to be had for his vacant and damned soul. *I am too young to feel this old and defeated.*

Because today, he felt ancient. Indeed, the weight of his soul and grief was so heavy that if he were to throw himself into the water, he had no doubt it would drag him to the bottom of those black waters and drown him. He'd have no ability to swim with it wrapped around him like this.

How did his father manage? If he hadn't respected the man before, he definitely did now. Because this shit sucked the very breath out of his lungs and made him want to just surrender to the pain and end it all. It was a struggle to come up with one single reason why he should bother to find another soul and not just allow the one that was currently screaming in his brain to take him to the grave and end it all.

Unlike the rest of his family, he was completely alone. Even his father had a girlfriend or wife or whatever Nelea was.

Urian wasn't really sure what her true role was, other than a convenient meal. As much as she stayed at their home, he was rather sure she lived there and nowhere else. But neither she nor his father had made a firm declaration of their relationship, and Urian wasn't certain if he wanted to know whether he had a new mother. So he didn't ask, and they didn't say.

He simply remained cordial with her, and passed brief, polite conversation with her whenever their paths crossed.

Sitting up, he rubbed at his head. For some reason, the human soul inside him was screaming louder than normal. He didn't know if that was because of his grief or perhaps the human had been whinier than most.

Whatever it was, it only added to his misery. He should probably go to the hall and find someone to feed with. It might help alleviate some of the internal screaming. But he wasn't hungry. What he wanted was real comfort. Too bad there was no one to make him feel better.

"Urian?"

His heart stopped as he heard a voice he'd never thought to hear again.

Nay, it couldn't be. Stunned and unable to believe it, he turned, then stood up slowly. "Xyn?"

In human form and dressed in bronze armor over a red chiton, she walked slowly toward him. Her vibrant Titian hair was braided and coiled around her head, exposing her pointed ears. "I felt as if something was wrong." She glanced about nervously. "If Apollymi finds me here, she'll have a fit, but I had to come and see if you were all right. I can't explain it. I just had to check on you."

His throat was so tight from the sudden rush of happiness and grief that he couldn't speak. Cupping her face with his hands, he did the one thing he'd always wanted to do.

He kissed her.

Xyn gasped as she breathed Urian in and melted against him. He smelled so intoxicating. Of leather and haxyn, and sweet rowan. No one smelled quite the way her Apollite did. They never had. And she shuddered as his tongue swept against hers. Fisting her hand in the linen of his chalmys, she felt his muscles bunching beneath her fingers.

When he finally pulled away to stare down at her, she smiled impishly up into those beautiful blue eyes. "I take it you missed me?"

He laughed at her question. "More than you can imagine." A stricken expression darkened his eyes. "I found your letter. And I'm sorry for everything."

She toyed with his soft hair. "So am I. But I can't stay."

The agony in his eyes tore at her heart and made her ache for him. She brushed his hair from his eyes. "What's wrong?"

His lips trembled. "Tannis died today."

"Oh, sweetie, I'm so sorry."

A single tear fell down his cheek. "I'll be fine." He cleared his throat and fell into that staunch, tough leader role of his. "You should go before you get into trouble."

How could she leave now, knowing what had happened? Knowing what his sister had meant to him? "Do you have anyone with you?"

When he hesitated, she scowled. "Where's your wife?"

He sighed. "Sheba was killed."

Xyn felt sick to her stomach. "When?"

"A few years ago."

Years? He'd been alone all this time? She couldn't believe it. "You haven't remarried?"

He snorted with a hostility that set her back. "Why would I?"

Companionship would be the normal reason, but he had one that made a lot more sense. "To eat?"

"I have women willing to feed me now. No need to rush into *that* again when I don't have to."

She barely caught herself before she rolled her eyes. He sounded so much like her brother Veles that it was frightening. "So you're alone?"

"Aren't you?"

Well ... aye. But she didn't want to think about that. She was a dragon. It wasn't quite the same thing. They were used to being alone. It was in their DNA. In all her life, his was the only company she'd ever craved.

And crave him, she did. More than had ever made sense.

Burying her hands in his hair, she tugged playfully at it. "My poor Uri. You've ever been my aggravation."

He arched a brow at her.

"It's true."

With a tender light in his eyes, he buried his hand in her braids so he could toy with them. "I'm so happy that I got to see you again. But how did you get in without being detected?"

"I have friends among the Charonte. You'd be amazed what they'll do for a taste of honey cake."

"I'll have to remember that in the event I ever get locked out of here."

She smiled. "Well, I should be going."

The sadness returned to his eyes. "I'm sure your husband misses you."

"I don't have a husband."

When he opened his mouth to speak, she caught his jaw to

keep him from speaking. "I've already told you. There's only one person I love, Uri, but as much as I love you, I can't stand by and watch you feed on the blood of another woman, knowing you'll be cheating on me."

His eyes turned dark and stormy. "I hate my grandfather."

"So do I."

He hesitated. "But what if I could find a way to break the curse?"

For a moment, she couldn't breathe. Could it be so simple? "What do you mean?"

"We think we might have a way out from under the death sentence."

"You know my answer. I want to be with you, Urian, I do. But I can't share you. That's not fair to me."

She saw Urian's happiness return. "Then I have twice the reason to end this curse, twice as fast." And this time when he took her into his arms, his kiss was possessive and filled with a deep promise. His lips tasted of passion.

Wanting something she knew she might never have another shot at, Xyn unpinned his chalmys and let it fall to the ground. When he didn't complain, she made sure his chiton followed it down to their feet, exposing his chest to her hands. He sucked his breath between his teeth as she touched his hard, hot body.

Gingerly, she traced a line over the healing wounds on his chest. "What happened?"

He smirked. "Apparently, you're not the only one I annoy."

"I don't find you amusing at all."

"That hand you have on my cock says differently." His voice was deep as he cupped her fingers with his palm so that he could show her how to stroke him.

"You better be glad that I can't harm you."

Heat stung her cheeks as he cupped her face in his hand and looked at her fiercely. "At this moment, my lady, I'll take your attention any way I can get it."

Xyn smiled, until her gaze went to the Daimon mark over his heart. "When did this happen?"

"Does it matter?"

"My conscience says that it should." Biting her lip, she wanted to pull away and leave him where he stood and not look back. If only it were so simple.

Or easy.

"You live by killing others. Obliterating their souls for all eternity."

"I do what I have to."

Her heart broke with those words. He didn't even seem remorseful about the lives he took.

His eyes darkened. "What do you want from me, Xyn? To lie down and die, or to fight and live?"

She wanted him to be human. Whole. To live without preying on the souls of humanity.

The hurt in his celestial gaze tore through her and made her stomach ache. She knew that look. It was what had caused him to divorce Xanthia. "I'm not judging you."

"Aye, you are. Don't lie to yourself. And don't lie to me."

She caught him as he started to leave. "Urian ... " She used her powers to remove her armor.

The moment she was naked, the anger evaporated from his eyes. Never before had she been more grateful to her brothers for their candor about how to immobilize a man or to catch his attention.

It worked.

Urian's gaze darted all over her naked body and with every part of her those eyes licked, the hunger in their depths darkened. The air between them became charged.

"I will always love you, Urian. Nothing you do will ever change that."

Closing the distance between them, Urian curled his hand against her cheek, then buried his lips against her throat. A thousand ribbons of pleasure tore through her as he nibbled a trail around her neck, his warm breath tickling as his tongue gently licked her skin.

Xyn shivered as she ran her hand down his naked spine and pulled him closer.

Urian shuddered in ecstasy. Never in his life had he felt this way. Never had he been with a woman and felt so welcome and wanted. All he could taste was this moment, and all he could feel was her love. Her warm acceptance. Even though she didn't approve of his Daimon lifestyle, she still loved *him*.

That was a miracle.

He trembled from the force of it and from the need he had to possess this woman who was the closest thing to Katateros he would ever know.

He pulled back and stared into her vibrant green, passion-dulled eyes. "You are beautiful," he whispered.

She answered his words with another kiss that left his lips tingling. And he had to remind himself to be careful with his fangs. She wasn't an Apollite.

Xyn was a dragon. And her boldness amazed and thrilled him. He pulled back slightly as she placed her lips to his jaw so that she could gently tongue her way down the line of it, teasing his whiskers. Urian closed his eyes as a thousand chills went through him.

Her breath electrified every part of him and made him harder than he'd ever been in his life. He nipped playfully at her earlobe and smiled as he felt the chills spring up along the length of her body beneath his hands. Her nipples tightened to rigid peaks that beckoned him to taste them.

Xyn sucked her breath in sharply as Urian dipped his head. Her senses reeling, she'd never felt anything like it. But then, she'd never been with a man before.

Because she'd been sequestered here so young, there hadn't been anyone she'd wanted. And once free . . .

Her heart had stayed with Urian.

There was no need to find another when she knew it wouldn't satisfy her. She wanted this . . . Daimon. Good or bad, he was the only one who made her heart race and made it weak and strong at the same time.

And when he picked her up to carry her to their cave, she laid her head on his shoulder, unable to believe it was real. How many times had she dreamed of this?

She gasped as they entered it. "You've kept it up?"

His eyes sparkled in the darkness. "It was all I had of you."

Tears filled her eyes as she realized he'd turned it into a shrine. Everything was exactly as she'd left it. "You still come here?"

Laying her down on her pallet, he gave her a sheepish smile. "Only when I miss you."

"It looks like you miss me a lot."

"Of course I do."

Her head swam as he laid his body over hers and his naked flesh collided with hers. The hard planes of his chest pressed against her breasts, which hardened ever more as they brushed against his muscled pecs.

Urian moaned against her lips as his hands pressed her hips closer to his. He could feel the soft curls at the juncture of her thighs against his swollen shaft as she ran her hands down his back.

Damn . . .

He was torn between ravaging her and taking his time. The two urges were killing him. He reached out and cupped her breasts in his hands, then skimmed his hand over her stomach toward her dark auburn curls. "Your skin is so flawless."

"The beauty of being a dragon. The skin doesn't take much damage."

He smiled at that. Then dipped his head down to toy with her right breast.

Xyn hissed as tendrils of pleasure shot through her. He trailed kisses to her other breast. She moaned, marveling at the mixture of pleasure and desire he stoked.

He returned to her lips as his hands ran the length of her body, stroking and exploring everywhere they went. She craved his touch with a blinding need.

Honestly, she didn't think anything could feel better until he ran his hand down her stomach and touched the center of her body. Xyn curled her fingers into his hair and arched her back against the intensity of *that* pleasure. Never had she felt anything like it as all the heat in her body pooled to the point where her legs met.

Suddenly, she felt Urian's entire body stiffen as he pulled away from her with a curse.

"Did I do something wrong?"

His jaw slack, he stared at her in utter disbelief. "You're a virgin?"

She blushed at his question. "I didn't realize you'd be able to tell."

He gaped even more. "Little bit, um, aye. You really weren't going to tell me?"

"Why are you so angry?"

"I'm not angry."

She gave him a mocking, pointed stare. "Really? Then what would you call that tone? Where I live, it's not happy."

"Confused."

"Not even close."

He snorted. "You're being impossible. I'm upset that you'd hold back something so ... so ... "

"Personal?"

"Aye."

"My business?"

He visibly cringed. "Now you're making me feel bad."

"Good. You should feel bad." She tweaked the edge of his nose with her fingertip. "Actually, that's not true, you should feel special that I want you."

He took her hand in his and led it to his cheek and then his lips so that he could kiss her palm and then hold her hand against his heart so that he could stare into her eyes. "I'm just angry at myself. I wish I were as pure for you, Xyn. You deserve that."

Those words touched her so deeply that for a moment she feared she might cry. Loving him more than she would have ever thought possible, she wrapped her legs around him and pulled him closer so that she could kiss him with everything she felt.

Growling, Urian rose up on his knees between her thighs. The expression on his face was one of utter desperation. "I'm sorry, Xyn. I can't wait for you," he whispered. "I want you too badly."

She didn't understand his words as her gaze ran down his muscled chest and lingered over the dark mark that covered his heart.

He kissed her, then gently entered her body.

Xyn cried out at the feeling of him deep and hard inside her as his muscled thighs pressed against hers. For a full minute, she couldn't breathe. This was unlike anything she'd imagined. He was humongous! And it burned a lot more than she'd have ever thought.

"Are you all right?"

"Um-hmm."

"The bleeding death grip on my back refutes those words."

Sucking her breath in, she realized he was right and immediately withdrew her claws from his flesh. "Sorry."

"It's fine, says the one who's been flayed." He glanced back at his side. "Is there a lot of blood loss?"

Xyn wrinkled her nose playfully. "Minimal."

With a laugh, he leaned down to capture her lips before he began to slowly thrust against her hips.

Her body on fire, Xyn held her breath.

Urian buried his lips against her throat and made sure not to harm her with his fangs. He hated the way she remained tense. "Relax," he breathed in her ear.

But she didn't. If anything his words seemed to distress her more.

He cursed himself for not knowing what to do to alleviate her discomfort, but he'd never been with a virgin before. Wanting to make it better for her, he breathed in her ear and then ran his tongue over her lobe.

She immediately moaned in pleasure and ran her hands over his ribs. He could feel her supple form against him as she surrendered herself to his touch. His body burned with need, but he forced himself to move slowly so that he didn't hurt her.

Xyn whimpered when Urian left her lips to nibble a trail down her cheek to her neck, and up to her ear. She writhed in pleasure as her body shook in response to his tongue while he swirled it around the outside, and then darted it inside the tender, sensitive flesh. Holy Olympus, she'd never imagined anything like this!

Forget dragons ... she couldn't imagine anything better!

His warm laugh echoed again. "Like that, do you?"

"'Deed I do."

He moved lower with his kisses. To her breasts, her stomach. His warm breath tickled her while his whiskers gently scraped her skin as he licked her all over.

Xyn closed her eyes and savored the feel of his warm skin against hers while he rolled his body against hers in the most delectable strokes and nibbled her in time to them.

She buried her hands in his hair and lifted her hips to draw him in ever deeper. And this was why she knew she would never be able to share him with another woman. She felt too close to him right now.

This wasn't simply sex. Not with him.

He was hers.

As a dragon, that meant something. For they were a jealous breed and they shared nothing.

But Urian would have to eat, and sex was part of that for his species. How she hated Apollo for what he'd done to Urian and his people. Damn him and all the gods of Olympus.

Staring up into those blue eyes, she knew that she'd never want anyone else. Not like this. He was her best friend. The only one she felt truly comfortable with.

In all things.

A strange light came into Urian's eyes a moment before he stopped moving.

"Is something wrong?"

The most wicked of grins spread across his face before he slid out of her and shifted his body. Xyn wasn't sure what he intended as he moved lower down her body. Not until he gently parted her tender folds and took her into his mouth.

Her head spinning, she cried out as pleasure ripped through her. Never had she felt anything more incredulous than the sensation of his tongue doing the most wicked things imaginable to her body.

Relentlessly, he teased her, making her body hotter and hotter. Her pleasure greater and greater.

Her ecstasy mounted until she was sure she'd die from it. And then, just as it became a very real possibility, her body exploded with pleasure far greater than anything she had ever experienced.

Throwing her head back, she screamed out in release as her entire body convulsed from a force unimaginable.

Urian took her hand into his and slid back inside her while her body was still in the throes of her orgasm.

She cried out even deeper in her throat, then pounded the ground with her fist.

"Are you all right?"

"Aye," she breathed, wrapping her body around his with a dragon death roll.

Laughing, Urian closed his eyes to better savor the feel of her surrounding him. If he could, he'd stay like this forever. How he wished he could. That there were some way to convince her to stay.

But it wouldn't be fair and he knew it. If only he could leave with her.

Yet sooner or later, he'd have to feed. While he could go back to blood donors, it was such a disgusting way to feed that he couldn't bring himself to contemplate it.

Not really.

Why can't I find a spell or a god who could lift this from me?
But there was really no hope.

Trying not to think about it, he moved slowly against her hips. Her sighs of mounting pleasure delighted him, especially when she began to move her hips so that she could meet his strokes.

And when his release came, he thought he'd go blind from it.

Xyn smiled as she felt him shuddering. Then he collapsed and gently laid himself over her like a blanket. She savored the sensation of his skin against hers. The feeling of him still inside her.

For the longest time he didn't move but simply stayed there until she feared he'd fallen asleep.

Or worse, had died.

"Urian?"

"I'm here. Just thinking."

"About?"

"The fact that when I get up, you'll leave. And that when you do, my heart will go with you." He lifted himself up on his arms. "Promise me something?"

"What?"

"That you'll meet me at least once a year."

"Uri—"

"It doesn't have to be here, Xyn. I'll meet you in the human world. Or wherever you pick. That way you don't have to know about my meals, or even think about them. We'll meet for one night. If you find someone who makes you happy, then we never have to meet again. You don't even have to tell me. Just don't show and I'll know."

"And if you find someone?"

He scoffed. "I swear that I won't."

Leaning up, Xyn kissed him. "All right. I'll meet you. And if you ever stand me up for another woman, Urian Deathbringer, I'll kill you both."

October 30, 7383 BC

Urian was starving as he sat at a table in an inn with his brother Theo and a friend. They'd entered the human realm from a portal not that long ago, and made their way into the city to find this out-of-the-way place where humans gathered to eat and find companionship and news after dark.

How he adored this new modern age.

Women had looser morals. So did the men.

It was so much easier to find prey. These days, they gathered together for them. All they had to do was order drinks and pretend to be human for a bit. Although he'd heard of some Apollites who were beginning to open places like this that catered to their people to make it easier on them to find meals, both Apollite and Daimon.

He hadn't found one yet, but he was hopeful, especially as he was supposed to meet up with Xyn for their annual rendezvous.

Theo laughed beside him with his friend Manades. The two of them had gotten into Urian's last batch of bloodwyne and were passing it around quite liberally.

That had become a lucrative product in their world. Thanks to Ruyn.

And Sheba. After all these centuries, Urian still thought about her from time to time, and wondered what it would have been like had she lived.

Xanthia ... she'd died a few centuries back when she failed to renew her soul on time.

That was a delicate matter for them. One they had to be careful about, as it was as much guesswork as science. Each soul was different, and how long it would keep them alive was completely dependent on the person it belonged to.

No two were ever the same. Some souls could last for a

few months and some for only a few hours. Until a Daimon claimed the soul, he never knew its endurance. The exterior of a person was no guarantee. A tiny human could have a remarkable soul that wouldn't be defeated, while the most arrogant giant could have a shriveled-up, cowardly soul that was good for nothing.

When Theo went to guzzle the wine, Urian snatched it from his brother's hand to take a swig. "Wish you would sober up. I need you both to pay attention."

"Sorry." Theo snickered, which led him to believe that the apology wasn't sincere.

Urian rolled his eyes. Until he spotted a possible victim off to the right. It was a huge brute of a bastard and he was groping a tiny serving wench. She looked as if she'd rather be anywhere else, while the man laughed at her misery. When she tried to pull away, he backhanded her so hard that it was a wonder he hadn't broken her neck.

Yet no one lifted a finger to help her or even looked in her direction.

Urian slapped at his brother's arm and jerked his chin to let Theo know he'd found his prey.

Yeah, that bastard needed to be removed from the gene pool. He wouldn't mind listening to a soul that cruel beg for mercy for a while.

They had to wait until the human decided to take a piss before they got up to follow him out back. Urian was already salivating for his soul, especially when he overheard his words to the girl asking her if she had a younger sister he could plow.

Disgusted, he could barely refrain from murdering him.

Instead, Urian paused to hand the girl his purse.

She was so skittish that she actually flinched.

"It's your tip," he assured her. "Please, take it."

Her hand trembled, but not as much as her voice. "Thank you, my lord."

He narrowed his eyes on Theo. "And that's why I don't want Nephele in the human realm."

"I know, *adelphos*. I have two daughters. You think I ever sleep?"

Manades snorted. "Try having six. I haven't slept since the day the first one was born, and it hasn't gotten any better as they've aged."

Not wanting to think about that, Urian drew up short as they left the building and a tall, dark-haired man cut them off on their way to kill their prey.

"Excuse us." Aggravated, Urian tried to step around him.

He intentionally moved to stand in their way.

Urian arched his brow. "Did you not hear my apology?"

"I heard, Daimon. Just don't care."

That sobered him quickly, as it'd been a long, long time since anyone in the human realm had known who or what they really were. Their breed had been lost long ago to myths and legends. "Who are you, stranger?"

"The who isn't important. I'm a Dark-Hunter."

Urian scowled. "You hunt the dark? Isn't that a little futile?"

As expected, he had no sense of humor. Rather he glared at Urian as if he could cut his throat. "A warrior of Artemis. Charged with putting an end to your kind."

"Isn't that a little harsh? Brother, I just met you. Shouldn't you get to know me before you want to kill me?"

Baring fangs, he lunged at them and stabbed Manades right through his Daimon's mark. Poor Manades didn't even have time to scream.

He burst apart into a shower of gold dust.

Theo turned pale as Urian's humor evaporated.

"Did you know we did that?" Theo breathed.

Urian opened a portal as the Dark-Hunter moved to engage them. He blocked him from Theo and shoved his brother through so that he could return home.

Or at least he tried to. Stubborn bastard wouldn't go, and Urian didn't have time to argue as the Dark-Hunter pulled out a kopis and made ready to carve him like a roast.

Using his powers, he manifested his own. But before he got a chance to parry, Theo bit into the Dark-Hunter's neck. They both screamed out. However, the Dark-Hunter's cry turned into cruel laughter.

"Didn't anyone tell you, Daimon? Dark-Hunter blood is poisonous to your kind."

Urian blasted the bastard with a god-bolt, then used his powers to fry him with everything he had. He didn't wait around to see if it killed the Dark-Hunter. Instead, he seized his brother and carried him into the portal.

By the time they landed in Kalosis, Theo was barely breathing.

His father shot to his feet and came down from his throne as Urian laid Theo on the floor. "What is this?"

Theo gasped and choked as he shook from head to toe. "He's been poisoned. By a Dark-Hunter."

"A what?"

Urian met his father's gaze. "A Dark-Hunter. Apparently Aunt Artemis has been busy. She's created something to hunt and kill us."

"Apollymi!" his father called.

Urian felt his arm begin to glow, but he wasn't sure if his powers would work on this. He'd never tried to use them on a Daimon. "Theo? Look at me!"

Theo was barely coherent.

"Don't you dare die!" Urian choked on his tears.

Apollymi appeared at his brother's feet, then froze. "Xedrix! Fetch the sap!"

Her Charonte flew off to obey.

She immediately rushed to Theo's side and knelt down to touch his forehead. Urian didn't miss the tears in her own eyes as she met his gaze. "I didn't know about these creatures."

His father glared at her. "When were they created?"

She glanced toward his father. "I don't know. But I will find out, and I promise if they have a weakness, I will learn it for you."

"Uri?" Theo reached up and grabbed his chiton.

"Aye?"

"Be a father to my children for me. Tell Prax—" He burst apart into nothing.

Urian couldn't breathe as he stared at the golden dust that had been his brother. Stunned disbelief kept him paralyzed. How could this be?

How?

Theo couldn't be dead. Not like this.

Nay ... He looked up to meet his father's equally shocked gaze. Fury descended over his features as he summoned his armor.

"Trates!" he roared. "Give me six men. Now!"

Urian stood up.

His father blasted him with a god-bolt that sent him reeling and crashing into the far wall. "I will not lose another son tonight! Damn it to the farthest pit, boy, you will stay here if I have to feed you to the Charonte!"

And with that, his father and Trates, along with their team, were gone.

Embarrassed and in pain, Urian pushed himself to his feet. Apollymi came over to him with a sympathetic smile. "I'm so sorry, Urian."

"For which part?"

"All of it, but mostly for your brother."

He felt the tears stinging his eyes. "We were blindsided. The Dark-Hunter stabbed Manades in his mark and he burst apart. Did you know that about us?"

She shook her head.

"Then Theo bit him and he told us that their blood was poison to us."

She cupped his cheek in her hand. "Artemis has always been a treacherous whore. If she's created an army, you know it was for selfish reasons."

That didn't change the fact that he now had to go to Praxia and tell her that her husband wasn't coming home. That he'd have to tell his other brothers about this. His stomach tightened so much that for a moment, he thought he might be sick.

A sob broke, but Urian caught it with a ragged breath.

Unexpectedly, Apollymi pulled him against her and held him in her arms. "Just breathe, child. Life is loss. It's harsh and it's pain. There are days when it seeks to drive us to our knees. When we're left asking ourselves why we shouldn't just slit the wrist and be done with it all."

"I've been feeling a lot of that lately."

"I know." She kissed his brow. "But it also surprises us. Fills us with warmth and happiness, and those moments when we know there's something more. Something wonderful."

He scoffed at her words. "I haven't felt that in a long, long time, akra. All I have inside me is an aching hollowness that wakes every night, seeking some reason as to why I should bother finding another soul to elongate my useless life."

"I'll tell you why, Urian. Don't let the bastards win."

"Pardon?"

"You want a reason to live? That's one good reason, there. It pisses off your enemies. If you can't live for those who love you, then live to spite those who hate your guts. Every breath you take is a spit in their eye. Savor it as such, knowing they begrudge you every intake that feeds your starving lungs."

He actually gave a bitter laugh at that. "Spoken like a true goddess of destruction."

"Absolutely. Sometimes it's not a matter of being the best. You just have to be the last man standing."

"Is that what you are?"

"Nay, good Urian. I'm the most dangerous enemy of all. I'm the patient one. I lie in wait, letting them think that they have me quelled when the truth is far different. I'm watching and learning. After all, the tiger lies low not from fear, but for aim."

"It doesn't matter if you strike the first blow, but you better make sure you strike the last one." That was what his father had always said.

Apollymi nodded. "Exactly."

Sighing, he wiped at his eyes. "Thank you, akra."

She rubbed his back. "You know where I am if you need me."

Urian didn't move until she'd left him alone. His mind was still reeling with the events of the night and the fact that he needed a soul.

Artemis had changed the rules on them. A part of him wondered if it had anything to do with the fact that they'd been hunting and killing Apollo's other lineage. But then, he couldn't imagine that Artemis would care.

As Apollymi had noted, she was too selfish for that.

Paris and Davyn entered the hall, looking for his father. Urian flinched as he realized they had no idea what had happened. Unable to tell them about Theo, he opened a portal and for the first time in his life, he ran.

Which was a stupid thing since he didn't know where the portal would drop him. Fortunately, it didn't drop him in daylight.

It took him a full minute to realize that this was the ruins of Sheba's capitol. He was standing in what had once been the hallway where she'd died.

Haunted by the ghosts of his past, he tried to remember that night. But time had dulled his memories. It was so long ago now. He could barely remember what she looked like. Even the fact that he'd been married seemed more like a dream than reality.

And still the human souls in his head screamed. The only time they gave him peace was whenever Xyn was with him. For some reason, he didn't hear them with her around. He didn't know if he was so occupied by her presence that he just didn't pay attention or if there was something about her that blotted them out.

Whatever it was, her presence gave him a precious reprieve from the madness.

As Urian was thinking about Xyn, he caught a peculiar flash buried in the rubble. Scowling, he walked over to it. At first, he thought it was some bit of trash. Until he got closer and picked it up.

It was a piece of armor that had broken off. Not just any armor.

This was a symbol he knew and had seen. Many times. His heart hammering, he took it and returned to Kalosis.

Without a word to anyone, he teleported to Apollymi's palace and headed for her garden.

As always, she was sitting at her mirror, watching the world.

But when she felt his approach, she came to her feet. "Has something else happened?"

He bowed to her, then held the armor piece out toward her. "What is this emblem?"

She took one look at it and her eyes flashed red. "Where did this come from?"

"From Sheba's palace. It's part of the armor our attackers were wearing that night."

The piece burst apart as her black dress fluttered. "It appears we have a most potent enemy. Helios went after you, along with my sister Azura."

"Why?"

"You are the children of Apollo. My guess is, he wants to eradicate all of you and retake his godhood."

"But we hate Apollo."

She laughed bitterly. "That doesn't matter, Urian. When you carry the blood of a god, you carry a death sentence. For we are petty creatures. Far more so than mankind. And our grudges and power plays take on far worse consequences than anything mankind can conceive."

Apollymi took his hand and pulled him toward her mirror. "Look into the water."

As he did so, she stood behind him with one hand on his shoulder and the other at his waist. The top of her head barely reached his shoulder. Strange how she seemed so much larger and more fierce until now.

But really, she was a tiny thing physically compared to him. Her frame was delicately boned and almost fragile in appearance. Meanwhile, he might not be as well muscled as his father, but he still wasn't slight of frame by any means. His physique was honed and lethal from all his battles and practice. Scarred from war, and even from play.

She danced her fingertips lightly over his collarbone and as she did so, his arm illuminated. The scroll pattern became luminescent and vibrant as if it had a life of its own. And the color shot all the way to his eyes.

"You are a creature of great beauty," she whispered in his ear. "Like me, a weapon of absolute death and yet you can give life."

"I couldn't save my brother or sister." He choked on his tears.

"That is our tragedy and heart fires that forge us into who and what we are. We hate them for it, but they mold us against our wills. And we have a choice; we either allow those tragedies to bend us into the weapon we're meant to be so that we can continue to fight the battles we must, or we shatter under the weight of them to become useless things. I will never be a useless thing to lie on the floor and bemoan what has happened to me. Rather I will strike back and strike down all those who've tried to break me. For that is what a weapon forged by fire does."

She moved her arms so that she held him in a mother's embrace. "I know you don't feel like a weapon tonight. You're shaken by the blows you've taken, and you feel as if one more will break you. But I know you, Urian. You are the phoenix on your shield. You will rise from these ashes, a stronger, greater warrior, and you will tear down your enemies."

He leaned back against her and nodded. "Thank you, akra."

She nodded grimly. "While you were gone, I found out about your Dark-Hunters."

He turned to face her. "Why did she create them?"

"For control. No other reason. It's a power play against her brother."

"With no care for our lives?"

"If she cared for you lives, Urian, she'd have helped all of you when you were cursed."

She was right and he knew it. Though Artemis was his aunt, he'd never met her or seen her. She was a goddess and she could have saved them, yet she'd done nothing to intervene on their behalf.

"But I do know their weaknesses."

His heart skipped a beat with that. "What are they?"

"Mostly the same as yours. They cannot go out in the daylight. Though they are immortal and don't have to feed on blood, they can be killed. Beheading. Daylight. Total dismemberment.

And they have human helpers—shield-bearers who watch over them while they sleep. They do have to eat, so they are out and about, and they live in the human world, which makes them vulnerable. They can't harm any Apollite or human. They can only slay Daimons."

"If they break that code?"

"They will be killed."

"So we can use humans against them?"

She inclined her head to him.

"Good . . . then it's war."

Apollymi smiled in approval. "And I designate you as my primary general."

September 3, 7382 BC

Urian felt the power of an ancient being roll through the room like a tidal wave three seconds before the door to the inn opened. No one else seemed to notice, but it made every nerve ending on his body stand up.

And how could it not?

This creature, for lack of a better term, stood every bit as tall as his father, at six feet eight inches. With long jet-black hair that flowed past his shoulders, he was dressed as a barbarian in furs and black flowing robes and trousers. But what caught Urian's attention even more than his godlike essence was the staff he carried.

The twisted wood was topped with Apollymi's sun symbol, which was pierced by three lightning bolts.

Even Paris, who stood beside him, scowled as soon as he saw the emblem. "Is that ... "

"It is." Urian felt his arm heating up to an unbearable level. Especially when the man-creature turned a pair of swirling silver eyes toward him.

Paris sucked his breath in sharply.

"You should go."

His brother hesitated. "What about you?"

"I won't be far behind."

Still Paris didn't move.

Irritated, Urian pushed him toward Davyn. He projected his thoughts to both of them. *Take your husband and get out of here. Now! Through the back door.*

"Acheron?"

The creature turned toward a Greek soldier while Urian shielded his brother's exit. He wanted to make sure nothing happened to either Paris or Davyn. Not tonight.

Yet he felt a peculiar pull toward Acheron. There was some kind of familiarity. As if he should know him. He couldn't explain it. Like something inside him knew this man, or that he should who he was.

He'd never felt anything like it.

Still his arm throbbed. Thank the gods he had it completely covered with a leather pauldron, bracer, and glove, and his chalmys.

Suddenly, the voices in his head grew louder.

Not just the human souls he'd taken. There were more now.

Disoriented, Urian moved to leave only to find Acheron in his way. Up close, he appeared physically younger than Urian. Not by much, maybe a couple of years. And they were about the same build. Yet it annoyed him that the bastard had a couple of inches on his height.

Acheron narrowed his gaze on him. "Do I know you?"

Urian shook his head and without a word, he quickly brushed past him and left.

Acheron gasped as he felt the light touch like a physical blow to his body. More like a sledgehammer to his chest. Indeed, he could barely breathe. It was so severe that it activated his Charonte protector on his arm.

"Shh, Simi," he breathed, stroking her with his hand to calm her so that she didn't peel herself off his skin in front of the humans gathered in the tavern and frighten them with her sudden demonic appearance.

He wasn't harmed. At least not physically. But he was concerned.

Heading back toward the table, he sat down across from the hardened warlord he'd come here to meet. With dark blond hair and frigid green eyes that gave the illusion they glowed, he had a scar across his collarbone where it appeared someone had once tried to cut his throat. Given the violence Thorn was capable of, Acheron was certain that person hadn't survived their stupidity. Indeed, in this din of warriors, Thorn stood out as one not to be trifled with. He had an air of death and cruelty.

But Acheron knew better. He wasn't cruel to anyone who didn't have it coming. Thorn was a champion for humanity. Centuries ago, he'd taken it upon himself to police the demons who preyed upon them and send them back to their dimensions so that they couldn't harm innocents. It was a thankless task, yet Thorn never complained.

Well ... "never" was a bit of a stretch.

And while Acheron was the newly designated leader of the Dark-Hunters Artemis had created, he knew nothing of leading others.

Thorn, on the other hand, had been born to lead an army. From the minute he'd been old enough to sit on his own, his stepfather had taught him to ride. Back then, he'd assumed he would one day be heir. Little had he known, he had a much larger destiny.

One in which he wouldn't lead that man's empire, but rather an army of Hellchasers who fought demons and drove them back to their respective hells.

If anyone had leadership advice on how to wrangle the snarly bastards Acheron was now charged with keeping alive and intact, he couldn't think of anyone better than Akantheus Leucious Forneus of the Brakadians, or the Death Collector as he was best known.

And he definitely looked the part. Dressed in a mad ensemble of furs and leather that was covered with an assortment of metal plates sewn on to resemble dragon scales over chain mail, he looked as if he were part man, part beast. His long, unbound hair didn't help. Nor his beard that was neither long nor short. It merely appeared that he couldn't make up his mind whether he wanted to have one or be clean-shaven. But then that was Thorn. He lived by no one's dictates but his own.

Even his weaponry was that way. While most carried swords, his weapons of choice were a whip, a sling bow, and a long dagger, and one clawed glove that resembled the hand of a falcon.

Acheron gave him a head tilt. "Did you see that blond warrior who was just here?"

Thorn squinted toward the door where he'd exited. "What of him?"

"Was he a Daimon?"

"With blue eyes?"

He had a point, but ... "What was he?"

Thorn's brow shot north at Acheron's question as he reached to refill his cup. "You don't know?"

"No." There was no missing the shocked disbelief in his tone. As an Atlantean god, it wasn't often Acheron didn't know everything about everyone the moment he met them. The only time he didn't was if they impacted his future some way, or if they were a friend or family.

Yet he'd never met that person before.

Thorn snorted, then smirked and took a long drink of the mead. "Love that look on your face, Akipoo."

He gave him a droll stare. "Don't make me stab you."

"You can try."

And that was why Leucious went by Thorn—as in he was a thorn in everyone's arse. Especially that of his father, the source of all evil.

"Do you, or do you not, know anything about the man who was just here?"

Thorn scratched at his neck. "I know he wasn't human. Whatever is setting off the hairs on your ass is making mine stand up too. But what he was ... I don't know."

"Animal, vegetable, or mineral."

Thorn laughed. "Demon or Daimon."

"You said he wasn't a Daimon."

Thorn shrugged. "I say a lot of things. Usually no one listens."

Acheron shook his head.

"So ... tell me again about these Dark-Hunters. Their job is to hunt down Daimons and free the human souls inside them before the souls perish completely?"

He nodded. "That's the theory. According to Artemis, the moment a Daimon coerces a human soul into their body, it begins dying. If we can get to them in time, we can pierce the mark and release the soul back into the universe where it can return to its source."

Thorn let out a low whistle. "How do they get the souls?"

Acheron shrugged. "Damned if I know."

"Well, I don't envy you this task."

"Why?"

Thorn sat forward. "I just return demons. You're talking about training warriors to kill them. My experience, things that have psychic powers and are related to a god don't die easy. And when they do, they try to take you with them."

September 8, 7382 BC

Urian stared at the human in front of him. His eyes were glazed from the spell Apollymi had taught them to use to drain a human down to a dangerous level where they hovered close to death. "Do you surrender to me?"

He nodded as his head lolled back.

Forcing his head up, Urian slapped him to an alert state. "Focus ... I want your soul. Will you give it to me?"

"Aye," he breathed.

Urian sank his fangs into the man's throat and ripped out his jugular. He'd feel bad, but for the fact that it was better he should die than Urian. And as he drank, he felt the man's fear. That was the worst part about feeding on humanity.

Their emotions tangled together. They shared their memories.

It was why a lot of Daimons didn't like to prey on criminals even though they were a lot more powerful than the others, as a rule. What he did took a lot of control and discipline. Because of their corrupt souls and inhumanity, they could easily poison him, too. He could slide right into their cruelty.

If he were weak.

But while he had to do this to survive, he wasn't the same breed of animal they were. This was forced on him. It wasn't a choice.

Big difference.

Urian pulled back as he felt the man's death rattle. He held him against his chest as he waited for that critical moment. Pinching the man's nose, he tightened his grip on his chest and began to hum the summoning spell.

It was a tricky thing to lure a soul. Trickier still to absorb one into his body. When he'd first started doing this, he'd had several escape because he hadn't been able to detect that moment when they left the human body. Now, his sight was well honed.

He could even smell them.

Like now. Urian sucked his breath in as the soul rushed toward him and slammed into his body, merging with his physical being. The shock of it was always exhilarating.

Shaking and light-headed, he let go so that the man's body could slide to the street.

Where am I? What happened? Hello!

Urian flinched at the shouting in his skull. Rubbing at his forehead, he sighed heavily. *That,* he hated. It was like a migraine that had a baby run over by an elephant that had been struck by a hurricane in the middle of a volcano erupting.

And he wished he were exaggerating.

All of a sudden, someone brushed their hand through his hair. He tensed and started to strike until the scent of the woman hit his nostrils.

Urian relaxed instantly. "Xyn." Her name left his lips like a prayer.

"I would ask about the body at your feet, but the blood on your lips gives me a pretty good idea."

Opening his eyes, he wiped away the blood with his knuckle as he met her beautiful gaze. Until he saw the bruises and scratches on her forehead and cheek. Anger cut through him. "What of you?"

"War."

His gaze darkened.

She cupped his face in her soft hands and rose up on her tiptoes to place a gentle kiss to his lips. "Calm down, my angry Daimon. I'm fine. In battle you tend to get knocked about."

"Doesn't mean I like it."

"I know." She nipped at his bottom lip. "How are you?"

At the moment?

"Hungry." But not for blood. He was starving for something a little more exotic . . .

Urian pulled her closer to savor her curves against his body, though to be honest, he'd rather they were both naked and not covered in armor.

She curled her arm around his neck and held him tight as he pressed her against the wall. "I couldn't believe it when I saw you. What are you doing here?"

"Came out to feed. You?"

"Someone stole my brother's egg."

"Egg?" Urian was aghast that anyone would dare go after a dragon's child.

"Not what you're thinking." She teased. "It's something we use to heal with."

"Ah."

Xyn gasped as she felt Urian's hand sliding down inside her armor so that his fingers could delve deep into her body. Her heart began to pound. "What are you doing?"

"I think you know."

She glanced around the deserted alley. "We're in public!"

"Then you'd best take me somewhere private. I fear I'm a bit soul-drunk and between that and the smell of you, I'm rather feral at the moment."

Indeed. She'd never seen him like this before. There was an edge to him that wasn't normally there. While she'd always known he was lethal, this was different. He was . . .

She didn't know how to describe it.

Using her powers, she teleported them to her bower. Urian shrank back with a hiss.

"Nay! It's all right!" She grabbed his arm and pulled him back toward the light. "It's not the sun. The brightness is from fey fire."

His breathing ragged, he still appeared terrified from it. He had the wildest look in his eyes.

"Shh," she reassured him, stroking his back.

Urian stared up at the brightest light he'd ever seen in his life. It was unlike anything imaginable. How could that not be sunlight?

Squinting, he stared up at it.

Xyn smiled. "See, you're not bursting into flames."

"Easy for you to say. You've got immunity."

"True." She nuzzled at his neck while she stripped him to the waist.

Urian could barely breathe while her hands worked their magick on his body. Gods, how he'd missed her.

"Lean your head forward."

His mind was dulled by his rampant lust and the blood he'd drunk along with the new soul. He obliged her without question. She brushed her hands through his hair and gently massaged his scalp. It felt so good that he had to grind his teeth to keep from moaning aloud.

Her fingers slid around the contours of his skull, tugging ever so gently on his hair, stroking and teasing until the pleasure was almost blinding with its intensity.

Then she moved her hands lower to his neck and shoulders. His abdomen. In that moment, he swore his body became liquid. "What are you doing to me?" he asked, his voice thick.

Xyn kneaded her fingers into his rigid muscles, easing them. "Making you mine."

"I was already yours," he breathed as her hands pleasured him all the more. Her touch was forceful yet so tender that it caused no pain, only joy.

"Come and lie down on my bed." Xyn pressed her lips together to keep from smiling at how quickly he complied.

He moved so fast that but for the fact he didn't know where her room was, he'd have beaten her to it. As it was, she had to rush to get in front of him to lead the way to where her large round bed was set in the center of an oversized bower. White silk was draped from the ceiling, shielding the bed from drafts.

Tossing away pieces of armor as he neared it, Urian lay down dutifully as if he craved her touch like a starving man at a banquet.

She laughed as she crawled up beside him and rested on her knees. "Put your hands under your head." She sat forward so that she could gently knead the muscles of his scarred back. How she hated to see how many more scars had been added since the last time they'd been together. That was always the worst part about their absences.

Cataloguing his injuries. Seeing the additional pain in his eyes that seemed to worsen. While he didn't physically age, the mental toll was ever evident in those beautiful baby blues that seemed to turn a bit duller as the years went by. And that made her ache for him. Every time she saw him, she wanted to ask how many of his friends and family had been lost while they'd been apart, but she didn't dare.

For one thing, she didn't want that pain in her heart, and for another, she didn't want to pick at his own festering wounds that haunted him.

So she pushed those thoughts aside and savored the fact that he was still here with her this year. For now, he was safe and they were together. That was all that mattered.

Urian let out a deep breath as utter ecstasy washed over him and her tender hands eased his sore, strained muscles, soothing him in a way nothing ever had before. There was truly no one else like his precious dragon.

It was why he loved her so. Why he wanted to stay with her.

If only he could . . .

But the pain of his past and the difference in their worlds would never allow it. He still hadn't found all of Apollo's other bloodline. The curse remained.

And yet something about Sarraxyn completely erased the pain of his past. Just looking into her eyes was enough to make him feel better.

Until he had to leave her. Every time he left her side, he was terrified he'd never see her again. Because he knew that everyone, even dragons, died. He'd lived the whole of his life stalked by Hades and his minions, and he never wanted to lose another person who meant anything to him.

It hurt too much.

The thought of losing her gutted him.

Xyn felt him tensing. "Shh, Urian," she whispered in his ear, moving her hands back to his head, to stroke his scalp and temple. "Put your ill thoughts aside and think of nothing but happiness while I'm with you."

That was certainly easy enough to do. She even began humming in an effort to help him.

Grateful to be with her tonight, Urian closed his eyes as her gentle voice soothed him as much as her hands did. He felt so incredibly calm. Peaceful. At no time in his life had he ever experienced anything close to this.

It was perfection.

And he owed it all to his beautiful dragon who made his entire body burn with nothing more than a sweet, shy smile.

Xyn kissed his back as all the tension left him. She gently dug her thumbs under his shoulder blades, then moved her hands down his spine until she reached the small of his back.

She traced one of the scars there. One of them was deep and angry as it ran from his hip down across his left buttock. She wasn't sure if it had been caused by a sword or some other injury. Either way, the wound must have been excruciating when he received it.

So much pain . . .

Before she could stop herself, she leaned forward and placed her lips to that spot. Urian hissed in pleasure, but he didn't pull away from her or try to roll over.

Encouraged by that, she slowly trailed her lips up his spine to his muscled shoulders. Even with all the scars over his caramel flesh, his back was perfect to her. Beautiful. And she wanted to taste every inch of him. To lick him from head to toe until he begged her for mercy.

Urian felt himself growing hard as she gently laved the scars on his skin. It was strange to feel so much pleasure over something that had given him so much pain. But then that was his dragon lady. It was what she excelled at.

Making his agony vanish.

Rolling over, he caught her before she pulled away. He cupped her face in his hand, then brought her near up to his lips to kiss her. He could taste the desire on her lips, feel the heat of her body.

And he wanted more.

Every day they had been apart had been pure torture. Being so close to her now and not inside her already ...

His resistance melted under the onslaught of her presence. He was too tired to fight, too weary to deny himself her comfort. Whether he liked it or not, he needed her touch. She was the air he breathed.

The heartbeat he needed to survive.

Xyn closed her eyes and let the masculine scent and feel of Urian wash over her. He tasted of decadence and power. Of lethal masculinity. His kiss was fierce and passionate, filled with promise.

Love me, Urian. Hold me tonight and never let me go!

The words were a prayer deep in her soul. He was all she'd ever wanted in her life. How strange to have every comfort and luxury her position as a dragon could afford her and to still want the dream of her golden Daimon champion.

Even though he was the son of an evil demon, he was also the symbol of all things good to her. For he was love. Nobility. Honor. Passion. She couldn't imagine being with anyone else.

Not like *this*.

She trembled as he left her lips to trail his kisses down her throat to her neck. His hot hand cupped her breast, spreading chills over her. His grip tightening, he pulled her beneath him so that his weight was pleasant yet crushing.

His caresses weren't slow and playful as they normally were. Tonight he was bold and hungry, as if he couldn't get enough of her. As if he wanted to touch every part of her body at once.

And she was every bit as hungry for him. Her body thrummed with fervent need that was stoked by his own urgency.

To her utter shock, his eyes flashed a vibrant red before he used his powers to strip her clothes from her body so that the lower half of her body lay bare to him.

"What have you done to me, my lady dragon?" Urian whispered in her ear before he licked her lobe and sent white-hot chills exploding through her. "I crave you more than I've ever craved anything."

"Show me how much you crave me, Urian," she said, her voice thick and deep from her own wanton passion. "I want to feel you inside me."

Urian's cock jerked at her brazen words. And then it grew even more as her hand slid down between their bodies to cup him in her palm. He rubbed himself against her touch, delighting in the coolness of her skin on his fevered flesh.

"How do I feel inside you?" He was desperate to hear her describe it.

Her smile turned wicked as her eyes flashed. "Full and warm. It's as if I can feel the tip of you all the way to my navel."

He growled as she cupped him and gave a light squeeze. Hissing, he rolled over until she was on top of him. "Show me what you like, my dragon. Our passion is in your hands."

Urian held his breath as she sat up on her haunches and surveyed his body. She trailed a blinding circle around his nipple before she spread her thighs and straddled his body.

His heart thundering, he reached to touch the part of her that was now opened for his delight. He watched the ecstasy on her face as he gently stroked her with his thumb until she was thoroughly wet for him.

Wanting and needing more, he lifted her up slightly and buried himself deep inside her body.

Xyn gave a small cry at the perfect feel of her Daimon. He lifted his hips, driving himself even deeper into her. He held her hips as she rode him slow and easy. It was glorious.

His beautiful eyes were hooded and warm as he watched her. "That's it, love. Have your way with me."

She smiled as she quickened her strokes. Urian arched his back as complete pleasure glowed in those magical eyes. He sat up beneath her to ravish her mouth so thoroughly that it actually made her dizzy. She loved the sensation of his breath mingled with hers, of his tongue darting through her mouth in time to her strokes. Xyn ran her hand down his muscled arm as it began to glow, delighting in the steely feel of it.

Urian laid his head against her shoulder as he watched her

body giving pleasure to his. Her sleek wetness was a haven to him as tenderness for her exploded through him.

For the first time ever, he regretted being sterile. He would love nothing more than to have children with Xyn. To be normal for her.

That was his one true regret.

If he could have one wish in life, it would be to have met her as another dragon or even a simple human. Anything other than the monster he was. To be whatever hero she would accept and to be whole for her.

All he wanted was to possess her with a ferocity that wouldn't be denied.

Their bodies still entwined, he lifted her up until he could lay her back against the mattress so that he could take control of their union. Dear gods, he needed this woman more than he needed breath to live. He was no longer in the mood to be easy and playful.

The demon inside him was in control now and it wanted only to possess her. To bury himself in her over and over again until he was at last sated and content.

Xyn bit her lip as Urian rode her fast and hard. His strokes echoed through her, sending pleasurable tremors the length and breadth of her body.

Her head spun as she came in his arms.

He bared his fangs as he smiled and gently cupped her face before he kissed her in satisfaction. Then Urian nibbled her mouth as he drove her climax on. She dug her nails into his shoulder as his name was torn from her lips.

Two heartbeats later, he joined her there in that moment of perfect bliss.

When his body was finally drained and sated, he collapsed on top of her, panting hard in her ear. He laid his head against her breast so that he could hear her heartbeat pounding beneath his cheek.

She played lightly with his damp, long, white-blond hair while she cradled his body with hers.

Neither of them spoke in the still quietness of her secluded home. Urian merely let her touch soothe him until he fell asleep, skin to skin, his body still resting inside hers.

Xyn kissed his brow as she felt him relax fully against her as he fell asleep in her arms. Never before had he done such a thing. It was the most blissful moment of her life as she realized the trust it'd taken for her Daimon to do such a thing.

And Urian trusted no one like that. It just wasn't in him. Cradling his body, she closed her eyes and tried to imagine what it would be like to have a normal life with her Daimon. One where they could live together as husband and wife.

Perhaps it was a stupid dream. But it was the only one she had. Her brothers would laugh at her if they knew she had it. Dragons weren't supposed to think of such things. They were born to be solitary. They weren't supposed to have lovers or to crave spouses. This was a most unnatural thing.

Yet she couldn't help what she felt.

Urian was her heart.

And they could never be together.

Urian came awake to the scent of his precious dragon on his skin. Even before he opened his eyes, he felt her hand in his hair, her thigh resting between his. Her buttocks pressed against his loins.

It fired his lust immediately. Still groggy from his sleep, his only thought was to feel even more of her warm, supple body.

Xyn awoke to the sensation of Urian deep and hard inside her. Gasping, she realized that he had one of her legs bent up as he entered her from behind and thrust against her hips.

"Good morning," he whispered against her ear before he tenderly kissed her cheek.

She drew her breath in sharply as he went particularly deep inside her. "Morning, Daimon. It appears you've made yourself at home."

"You want me to leave?"

Hissing sharply, she pulled his hand down to the center of her body. "Hardly," she said breathlessly as she met his deep strokes. "But I do expect you to please me."

His laughter warmed her as he took care to tenderly stroke her in time to his thrusts. He dipped his head so that he could run his tongue around her ear. Xyn shook from the force of the chills that went through her.

Urian inhaled the scent of his dragon as he reached up to smooth her vibrant red hair. In that moment, he never wanted to leave her body or her side.

He wrapped his arms around her and let her feminine scent wash over him as he thrust himself in and out of her body until he felt her spasm. She cried out and dug her nails into his glowing arm.

His breathing ragged, Urian quickened his strokes until he happily joined her. He ground his teeth as his own orgasm swept through him and he growled deep in his throat. The force of it left him weak and sated, and at the same time he was invigorated.

Closing his eyes, he lay entwined with her, never wanting to leave. This was his Katateros. His heaven.

If only he could he stay.

Urian!

He jumped as he heard his father's summons.

Xyn turned her head to look at him over her shoulder. "Are you all right?"

"My father's calling for me."

The disappointment in her eyes stung him.

"Sorry."

"It's all right. I know I can't keep you."

Rolling her over, he laid himself over her and held her close. "You know I don't want to leave."

"I know."

Urian! Where are you!

He winced.

"Still calling?"

Urian nodded.

"You'd best go, then."

"Take care, my love."

She kissed him. "And you."

His stomach tight, Urian nodded as he got up and dressed. He returned for one last, lingering kiss before he teleported back to Kalosis.

The moment he landed in the great hall, he found his father on his throne, surrounded by Daimons. The dire look on his face would have chilled anyone, but something sinister had happened.

"Where have you been!"

"I went out for a psuché." The psuché or psuché-sullambano was what they called the act of seeking a human soul. It was very different from the ichoraima, which was the act of feeding on Apollite blood. "Why? What's happened?"

"Jason, Abiron, and Melissa were all killed last night."

That news hit him like a crippling blow. Archie and Hagne must be reeling. That was three of their four children. "How?"

"A Dark-Hunter."

Urian couldn't breathe. The pain was so great and so overwhelming it was if his body and mind couldn't react, so it shut down. He just stood there, stunned. Trying to process the fact that in one fell swoop, Archie had lost the majority of his children.

I have to go to him.

Urian teleported to his brother's home. Without knocking, he opened the door to find the house strangely empty. He used his powers to sense where they might be. As he neared the bedroom, he found his brothers and sisters-in-law comforting Hagne, who was in bed, curled in a ball, unable to cope with her loss. She was completely catatonic.

Archie was nowhere to be seen.

Terrified of what that meant, Urian went to find him. For a few minutes, there was no sign of his brother anywhere.

Not until he had a peculiar thought. Acting on instinct, Urian went to the small garden where the kids used to play.

Sure enough, he found Archie sitting alone, underneath the

tree where Abiron had carved his name. As he drew closer, he realized that his brother held one of Melissa's dolls in his trembling hands.

"Archie?"

He didn't speak.

Urian knelt by his side and placed his arm around his shoulders.

Then his huge brute of a brother looked up at him and burst into tears. Clinging to him, he sobbed in a way Urian had never heard him do before. Not when they'd lost their mother. Or their sister or brother. Never once had anything broken the mighty Archimedes.

Until today.

"I'm so sorry."

Archie tightened his hold on Urian. "I should have been with them. Why wasn't I there? How could I have let them go alone? I was their father, Uri. It was my job to protect them."

"Shh, Archie, you didn't know."

"I left them alone ... "

"You did nothing wrong."

"Nay, but I did. I left them to fend for themselves when I shouldn't have. I should have been there!"

Suddenly, Urian felt a powerful grip in his hair. Looking up, he saw his father. Without a word, he pulled Urian back and then cradled Archie in his arms to rock him. Then with his other arm, he pulled Urian against his chest to hold him like he'd done when they were boys.

His hold was brutal and crushing, and yet it was strangely comforting.

"We won't be broken. Not by this. The gods can try, but we are stronger than they know. And we are mighty. Do you hear me, my sons?"

He wiped at the tears on Urian's face and then Archie's. "Look at me, both of you." He waited until they complied. "We will rise up and strike back. We are not the only ones to lose in this and we will not allow them to take it all from us. Not without a fight. Blood for blood. Life for life. We all have a choice. You either cave to the blows of your enemies ... "

"Or you mount their heads to the wall," Urian finished for him.

His father nodded. "Thánatago." Deathbringer.

And after this, he would forge his own Thánati. A team of Spathi to hunt and prey on their predators. If the gods and Dark-Hunters wanted a war, Urian was willing to bring it to them.

July 18, 2945 BC

Urian was getting ready to leave with a strike team when a bright light flashed in the main hall of Kalosis. Grimacing, he stepped back, expecting another Apollite or Daimon. That was what normally came through their bolt-hole.

Although over the last few thousand years, they'd had the occasional Dark-Hunter or demon be stupid enough to try, and that had been highly entertaining.

But this ... this was something else.

Everyone in the room froze.

His father came off his throne. Tall and muscular, the man held the aura and smell of an Apollite or Daimon, yet his dark hair said he was definitely not one of them.

Not that a Daimon couldn't have dark hair. Their father and Archie dyed theirs. But this man's skin tone suggested that his hair might actually be naturally that shade. That, and the fact that he smelled of an animal scent.

Like Xyn.

As if he were a hybrid being of some sort.

"Who are you?" his father demanded.

Screw that. Urian wanted to know *what* he was.

"Nicander, son of Simonides." He glanced around at them with a scowl as they circled him, trying to determine if they should welcome him, restrain him, or kill him. "What is this place?"

His father didn't miss a beat. "It depends on your intent and species. What exactly are you?"

"I'm a Katagari Tsakali."

Urian was the first to snort. "You say that as if we should have a clue as to what it means."

He cast a disdainful smirk toward him. "Means I'm a shape-shifter. You don't get out much, do you?"

"Enough to kill what annoys me." Urian raked him with a sneer. "And to skin enough animals to make a new pair of boots whenever I need them."

When Nicander started for him, the Daimons between them grabbed him and held him back.

"I wouldn't do that," Trates warned him. "He might look young, but Urian's one of our strongest warriors. Trust me, you don't want to tangle with him."

Curling his lip, Nicander backed down, then turned toward his father. "King Lycaon—"

"Who?"

"Lycantes of Arcadia. He was crowned Lycaon VI of Arcadia. Stupid bastard had the unfortunate luck of falling in love and marrying an Apollite bride without knowing it. Somehow, she kept it a secret from her husband until her twenty-seventh birthday. When Queen Mysene died, Lycaon realized that their sons would fall prey to the same fate."

Crossing his arms over his chest, Urian cringed at the sad reality of their mixed marriages. The gods had given them no reprieve even with that.

"Lucky him, his sister was the goddess Shala."

Urian let out a low whistle. As the daughter of Erebus and Nyx, Shala was literally born of Night and Darkness. But more than that, her husband was the god Dagon, and his mother, Hekate, was the daughter of the Titan sun god, Helios. *That* was quite a family tree. No wonder Mysene had wanted to marry into it. As an Apollite, that was a wise decision if one wanted to save her children.

"I take it the king decided to invoke some family intercession?" Urian asked.

Nicander nodded. "Dagon came to their aid and used his magick to splice animal DNA to Apollite biology."

Now he had Urian's full attention. "How'd that work out for you?"

Spreading his arms wide, Nicander turned a small circle for all of them to see. "Better than anyone could ever imagine. There are two breeds of our species now. Arcadians, who have human hearts, and thus that is their primary form."

The hairs on the back of Urian's neck stood up. "Meaning what?"

"They're born human and live their lives primarily as human beings. At puberty, they are able to shift into whatever their alternate animal form is."

His father narrowed his gaze on him. "And the Katagari?"

"Katagaria is the plural form. Katagari is singular. We are born as animals and have an animal heart. Therefore our base form is that of whatever animal we were born as. In my case, I'm a jackal. Which means I sleep in that form, and if I'm injured or I die, I revert to it. It's my strongest form."

"That's so fucked up," Archie said.

Urian concurred.

And apparently so did Nicander. "I didn't choose this anymore than you chose to be Apollite. We were rounded up and experimented on against our wills. This was forced on us. But the upside is that we don't die at twenty-seven and we don't have to feed on blood anymore to live."

Now *that* got everyone's attention.

"Beg pardon?" His father stood up.

Nicander nodded. "You heard me. We live hundreds of years. With our magick intact."

"Sign me up!"

Urian cast a droll look at his son. "Don't be so quick, Geras. The gods are never so bountiful. There's always a drawback."

"He's right." Nicander sighed. "As soon as Zeus found out, he demanded that we be put down. When the king refused, we were cursed."

Urian gave his son an I-told-you-so stare.

"What's the curse entail?" his father asked.

"The Arcadians and Katagaria are to war against each other and never know peace until the last of us are dead. We cannot choose our mates. They're chosen for us by the Fates. If we don't accept who they choose, our males are rendered impotent for the rest of our lives."

Geras's eyes bulged in horror as he cupped himself.

Urian smirked. "Take it you changed your mind, *m'gios?*"

He nodded vigorously.

Nicander sighed again. "Like the animals we are, we're hunted continuously. Our mates even more so. And when they're pregnant, they can't shift forms or use their magick. That's how I ended up here. I was leading a tessera—a team of four of them—away from my pregnant mate. I'd gotten them clear of her, but couldn't shake them from my trail. When the portal opened, I didn't care where it took me, so long as it was away from my enemies."

Nephele scowled at him. "How do you know when your mates are chosen?"

He held up his hand to show her an intricate pattern that appeared to be branded into his palm. "A matching mark appears on each of our palms to let us know. Once it's there, we have three weeks to cement the union or we're screwed. A woman will never be able to have children, and as I said, a man is left impotent."

"So glad I'm an Apollite," Geras whispered in Urian's ear.

Urian elbowed him. "So do the Dark-Hunters hunt you, too?"

He shook his head. "They're not allowed. Not even if we're trelos, slayers, or marked."

His father arched a brow at that. "You still go trelos?"

"Not for the same reasons a Daimon does, but aye. Something about our hormones at puberty causes a similar madness in our species. A slayer is the same thing, only that's the term they use when it affects a Katagari Were-Hunter ... the term given to cover both our branches."

"And marked?" Urian asked.

"When our council has gotten together and, with Savitar's approval, determines that someone needs to be put down because he or she is a danger to us all. Once the Omegrion decides, we're marked for termination and hunted."

"And they call us cold." Paris shook his head. "So glad I live *here.*"

Urian didn't comment on that. "Who's Savitar?"

Apollymi answered that one. "A rank, arrogant Chthonian bastard. Surly as hell. Pray to the gods you never have to deal with *him*."

Urian was shocked by the venom in her tone. That was the type of hatred usually only reserved for Apollo or Artemis and in the back of his mind, he seemed to recall her speaking of him before, now that he thought it. But it'd been years ago.

They all bowed to their goddess.

The Were-Hunter hesitated, then realized it was probably a good idea to follow suit.

Apollymi walked over to Nicander to examine him a little closer. "So you're Savitar's current *pet* project. Why?"

"No idea, my lady."

She narrowed her gaze speculatively. "He doesn't come off that island lightly. Nor does he meddle in the affairs of the gods without a damn good reason. Did the Dark-Hunter Acheron ask him to?"

"I don't know anyone by that name."

But Urian did. He immediately remembered the creature he'd met whose eyes matched hers. Were they related?

"Who leads the Were-Hunters?"

"You mean the Omegrion?"

"Not that. Who are the founders of it? The first blood children?"

"The Kattalakis princes. Dragons and wolves."

That still didn't seem to pacify her.

She cut a gimlet stare toward his father and then him. "I leave it up to you, Strykerius, if you want to allow the Were-Hunters a haven here. They are cousins to you, after all. Their blood ... and souls should feed you, being that they are hybrids."

There was something Urian hadn't thought about. But the goddess was right. They were chimeras and since she'd pointed it out, he could detect the soul within them.

That baby was ripe for the plucking, and he wasn't the only one to know it. Several of his men around him were now salivating.

But his father quickly put a stop to that. "So long as they hold to Eirini Law, so will we."

Damn those peace laws.

Nicander inclined his head respectfully. "Thank you. And know that my people are setting up limanis with Savitar's approval and his oversight. Not even a Dark-Hunter can breach their sanctity without suffering his wrath. It's a place where Daimon, Apollite, and Were-Hunter can gather in the human realm in peace."

"And if the humans attack?"

A slow smile spread across Nicander's face at Urian's question. "Come in peace or leave in pieces." He turned back toward Apollymi. "We're slowly learning to live among humans. Although a lot of Apollites have done what you have. They've moved to underground communes. We're setting up networks, with signs that will subtly alert our kind without the humans knowing."

"About time," Archie growled.

Paris rubbed his back, but he shrugged off his sympathetic touch. Not that Urian blamed him. He'd now lost all of his children and his wife to Dark-Hunters, and three grandchildren. They were sick of their predators.

Right now, they were losing this war. Not even their aunt Satara was able to help them with the information she gleaned from spying on Artemis and Apollo while she attended Artemis as one of her handmaidens in her temple on Olympus.

There had to be more they could do.

And Urian was done with this. He motioned for his team and headed for the door.

"Where are you going?" his father asked.

He smirked. "Same as what I always do, Solren. Going out and getting even."

"What does he mean by that?" Nicander asked as they stepped through the portal and vanished.

Apollymi laughed. "Those are my Stygian Thánati. They hunt and slay the Dark-Hunters who prey on Daimons."

Stryker smiled as he pointed to the ornate display of weapons on the far wall. "Those are their trophies, taken from every Hunter they've slain."

"Are they rewarded for it?"

Stryker's eyes flashed red at the stupidity of that question. "Of course they are. Satisfaction in the destruction of your enemy is its own reward. No one understands that better than their commander."

"And who is their leader?"

"My son, Urian."

Urian *froze as* they came up against a familiar power.

Eleni was the first to step toward it, but he caught her arm and shook his head. "You need to return. Every one of you."

All six members of his guard turned in unison to gape at him, as those were never the orders he gave.

His second-in-command, Spawn, in particular, had rebellion in his eyes.

Urian tightened his grip on his shield. "I mean it. Spawn, take my son and the others and lead them back."

He saw that same rebellion in his son's eyes, but he knew better than to question him.

As did Spawn. They'd fought together too many times for him to start questioning him now. "Aye, *kyrios.*"

Urian stayed behind to cover their retreat. They had barely vanished when he was hit with a blast so hard it staggered him, but somehow he managed to remain standing.

"Why do you carry the shield of Styxx of Didymos?"

"I don't."

Another blast almost tore his arm off. "You think I don't recognize that symbol!" The fury in that tone almost shattered his eardrums.

Urian sent his own blast toward his attacker. Though he couldn't see him, he hoped he was close to the mark.

It was then he saw Acheron. He planted his staff in the ground and used it as leverage so that he could kick him back with both of his feet.

Urian stumbled back and landed on his ass. He scrambled to rise and used his powers to gather his kopis back into his hand.

"Who are you?"

He lifted his chin with pride. "Urian Strykeros."

That took the anger out of him. "The one they call Thánatago."

"You've heard of me?"

Before he could blink, Acheron was in front of him. No longer human in appearance, he was in a full Charonte form. Horns, wings, and mottled blue skin.

Stunned, Urian couldn't breathe. He'd always been told that no Charonte existed outside those that served Apollymi. What the hell was this bastard?

"You insult me with that shield and by killing my soldiers," Acheron growled.

"Your Dark-Hunters insult me by murdering my family."

"Boy, you don't want to make an enemy of me."

He laughed at Acheron's threat. "We were born enemies the minute you set your soldiers after my people."

Growling, Acheron blasted him.

Urian caught it with his glowing arm and returned the blast. The shock on Acheron's face was priceless. With a battle cry, Urian charged his sword with his powers and went in to attack. Just as he would have struck, a portal opened and grabbed him, sucking him back to Kalosis.

He was slammed unceremoniously to the ground at his father's feet so hard that for a full minute he thought he'd shattered every bone in his body.

Gaping, his father stood, then rushed to his side. He pulled Urian's helmet from his head and quickly checked him for injuries as Apollymi appeared in one of her finer rages.

Typhoon winds whipped through the hall, tearing at the Apollites and Daimons gathered there and sending anything not tied down flying. Her white hair spiraled around her body as she glared at the two of them.

"You. Don't. Ever. Attack. The. Elekti!" Those short, clipped words reverberated through the hall.

Since his father hadn't been there, he had no idea what she was talking about. "What?"

She pointed out Urian. "He attacked that which is never to be touched. If you ever dare strike the Elekti again, I will have you flayed until there is nothing left of you but the marrow of your bones. Understood?"

Given the amount of pain he was in? "Understood, akra." Urian panted, trying to get his lungs to work again.

Still in a huff, she vanished.

His father cupped his cheek. "What happened?"

Urian cradled his arm to his chest. It was definitely broken. "I don't know. He's the leader of the Dark-Hunters. Acheron. I think he's part Charonte, or part god. He had powers unlike any I've ever seen or felt."

Hugging him, his father kissed his forehead. "All right. Let's see you tended. And make sure you cut him a wide berth. In the future, I want you and the others to stay low and out of Acheron's sight. Nothing is worth losing one of you."

Urian agreed out loud, but inside, he was seething. There was something wrong about this. All the way around.

And he wanted to know what.

February 18, 1650 BC

Urian scowled as he heard a woman crying. That was not something he was expecting. Grimacing, he got up slowly from his bed and forced himself to stand in spite of his wounds and headed for where she seemed to be.

From the opening of Xyn's old cave in Kalosis, he saw Katra sitting alone near the falls, weeping.

At first, he started to return to bed and leave her there. It wasn't his business. She definitely didn't concern him.

But those sobs were gut-wrenching. Sighing, he headed for her even while he called himself all kinds of stupid for it.

"Here."

Kat looked up with a sharp gasp.

Urian wiggled the handkerchief in front of her face.

She took it and wiped her eyes. "Thank you."

"Any time. Are you all right?"

She blew her nose loudly, then skimmed his half-naked body, which was bruised and covered with healing injuries. "Better than you, obviously."

He wouldn't argue that. He'd almost been gutted by a Dark-Hunter who'd been working with demons for helpers. Bastards. The worst was a massive cut across his chest. Half an inch closer and they would have had his mark and killed him.

By the expression on Kat's face, she realized it, too. She wiped her nose.

"What happened to you?" he asked.

With a ragged sigh, she shook her head. "Ever done something you're really ashamed of?"

A number of times, but one stood out above the others. "Broke my mother's favorite dish when I was a boy and blamed my twin brother. Then let him take the beating for it."

"You're such an asshole."

Urian shrugged. "That's what my brothers tell me." He'd have felt worse had Paris not done his own share of blaming him for things Paris had done. "Anyway, you were saying?"

Katra pressed her hand to her forehead. "I did something . . . a favor for my mother. Now . . . it was wrong and I feel terrible and I think I really screwed up and I-I have no one to talk to about it."

Carefully, he sat down by her side. "Yeah, we've all been there. Well, maybe not there"—he gestured to where she was sitting—"but you get the idea."

She snorted. "I just don't know how to fix this."

"What exactly did you do?"

"I stole the powers of a god."

His eyebrows shot north as he fought the urge to step away from her. "You can do that?"

She nodded.

"Well, I'm not going to lie. That was pretty harsh."

"I know!" She started sobbing again.

Urian felt terrible. "There, there." He patted her awkwardly.

She threw herself against his chest, which only made it all the more awkward since the only bit of clothing he had on was a shendyt.

After a few minutes, she finally got hold of herself and pulled away. "Thank you, Urian."

"Not sure I did anything."

"You listened." She wiped at her eyes with the heels of her hands. "It's more than most people do. And where I come from, there wasn't anyone who would do that much. So thank you."

"No problem." He pushed himself up and groaned as pain cut through him.

Kat frowned. "Why are you here by yourself?"

Shrugging, Urian didn't want to tell her the truth. He didn't feel comfortable with his own family. He never really had. Paris had Davyn. His father was shacked up with three women he could barely tolerate. Archie had gone psychotic after the deaths of his family and stayed in an orgy most of the time. The rest just pitied him for being alone.

And the one woman he wanted lived in the human realm and was banned from here. So he tended to stay as close to Xyn as he could. Which meant sleeping in her bed if he couldn't sleep with her.

At least here, he didn't have to worry about waking up with one of his father's leftover meals groping on him.

Kat scowled as she studied his unbound hair. "Gah, it freaks me out to look at you."

"Gee, thanks," he said sarcastically. "Way to bolster my ego."

"Sorry. You just remind me a lot of someone else."

Whatever. Urian started back for his cave. But he didn't get far before Katra called out to him.

"Hey, Uri?"

He paused to look back at her.

"The Dark-Hunters have one more weakness you don't know about."

"And that is?"

"If you put two of them together to fight, they weaken each other."

Stunned, he stared at her. "Why are you telling me this?"

"Because they were created as pawns to manipulate and control someone very dear to me. And I don't think it's fair that he has to suffer because of them. While I don't want to see the Dark-Hunters killed, I hate the fact that he's been hurt over them even more. As much as I want to stop it, I can't. But if you do ... "

Urian frowned at her words. There was more to it than that. He knew it with every instinct he had. Why would she tell him that now.

Unless ...

Unless it had something to do with her guilt. "You're the reason, aren't you?"

"What do you mean?"

Urian was incredulous as he put the pieces together in his mind. "Those powers that allowed you to drain a god ...

somehow they're the same ones that created the Dark-Hunters, aren't they?"

She didn't have to answer. The horrified expression on her face confirmed it. The guilt in her eyes.

"You didn't mean to do that either."

Tears filled her eyes. "We all make mistakes, Urian. Can you imagine what an incredible world this would be if we didn't have to spend the rest of our lives paying for them?"

Those words bit to the core of his soul and struck the mark she wanted them to. "Welcome to adulthood, princess. The time in our lives when we no longer have parents to scare the monsters out from under our beds. Rather, we realize that we're the monsters who live under everyone else's."

June 1, AD 780

"Xyn!" Urian was nearly hysterical as he searched for his dragon.

There was no sign of her. He'd waited all night at their rendezvous, and she'd never shown. So he'd done what he wasn't supposed to . . .

Come to her bower.

By the looks of it, she hadn't been here in a long, long time. A thick layer of dust covered everything. Even the bed. And that wasn't like her. She was a meticulous housekeeper.

This time, there were no notes. No gifts.

Nothing.

She was gone without a trace.

Without a word.

It was as if she'd never existed.

Tears blurred his vision. Sarraxyn wouldn't do this to him. She wouldn't.

Of all the creatures in the universe, she knew how much he needed her. That she was the one thing he relied on. His only tenderness. And if she wasn't here and this place was in this condition, it could mean only one thing.

She was dead.

His knees buckled. Urian hit the floor as he choked on a sob. Of all the deaths, and there had been so many in his lifetime, this one was the hardest to bear. He pressed his fist to his mouth and sank his fangs into it. How could she be gone?

In that moment, he wanted to join her. Truly, he couldn't think of a single reason not to. What was he fighting for at this point?

They had no hope of breaking this curse. Of seeing daylight. His father was a fool for even thinking it. Damned and cursed. Forever banished to darkness.

Closing his eyes, he tried not to think of the night he'd watched

Geras die by the hands of a Dark-Hunter. The pain-filled look on his son's face when he'd been unable to reach him in time. That panic and fear an instant before he'd shattered into dust.

Or Nephele, who'd gone too long without a soul.

She'd been sitting right beside him when she'd just burst apart. To this day, Urian didn't know if she'd simply been inattentive to the signs that she needed to replenish, or if it'd been a form of suicide. If it had, she wasn't the only Daimon to do so. It was so common, they even had a name for it—suntribó.

That moment when they just became too tired to continue. When the voices wore them down and the deaths of those around them were more than they could contend with.

When they felt just like he did right now. Life was too harsh and they just gave up.

Lifting his knees, Urian cradled his head with his arms and wept. Not for himself, but for those he loved. Gods, it hurt so much. So deep.

And he was so tired of it.

How could he hope now? The last bit of his kindness and goodness was gone.

Without her, he had nothing. He was nothing.

His body shaking, he stared with blurry vision at the *dakruon* that were tattooed along his hand and forearm in an intricate pattern. Black teardrops to mark the deaths of everyone he loved. There were so goddamn many.

Now there would be one more.

He drew a ragged breath as his gaze went to the phoenix on his shield. He bore that same mark on his biceps.

His totem animal. *From this too, I will rise.* Though he didn't know how. He couldn't imagine how. But he would. Xyn would be the first to kick his ass.

We are warriors.

And his dragon wouldn't have given her heart to anything but the strongest of the strong. "You cannot break me," he whispered. "I'm already shattered."

October 3, AD 801

Spawn, Paris, and Davyn sat across from Urian as they watched the intriguing crowd around them. The Varangians in particular held their interest, as they were known to have some of the strongest souls of the bunch.

"I thought the Rus were supposed to rape and pillage," Spawn muttered irritably as he watched them carouse and revel in friendly comradery.

Paris snorted. "You can always go Kassandrian. I won't tell." Kassandrians were the branch of Daimons who lacked all semblance of decency or ethics. They didn't care who or what they preyed upon. Even children and pregnant women were fair game. And they were a pariah to all the rest of them.

Which meant Paris was joking.

No one could stand a Kassandrian. To prey on a pregnant woman or child was forbidden to them. They were exiled and turned out immediately. Much like a trelos. The only difference being that a trelos couldn't control their behavior. A Kassandrian knew exactly what they were doing. They just didn't care. Nothing mattered except their own petty selfishness.

Truly, they were disgusting creatures.

And because of the way they fed, they smelled bad, too.

Urian wore many hats in their world. As a warrior, he was considered a Spathi, and since he led groups into battle, he was a Rigas. Because they targeted primarily Dark-Hunters and the Squires who served them, that made him and his soldiers Dikisi Daimons.

But the two titles that would make anyone other than the three Daimons at the table with him scorn him if they knew were that of Anaimikos and Akelos. Akelos were Daimons who only preyed on human souls that were corrupt. The very kind that often led them into turning their species into trelos Daimons. And Anaimikos were those like Davyn who fed from Paris. Daimons who fed other Daimons. Those who didn't kill at all. They split the souls with their partners.

It was actually very sweet what his brother had with Davyn. While Davyn couldn't kill to eat, he would kill to protect Paris. Without hesitation and with extreme prejudice.

And speaking of which . . .

Urian didn't mind killing to live. He felt his powers surge as the Apollites they were seeking came in.

The other line of Apollo. Two sons. One was already a Daimon, but the other was on their list.

He passed a knowing look to Spawn. "How are you?"

"I could stand a charge."

"Then you can have the Daimon."

As they started to rise, a Norseman approached them. "Leaving?"

Urian nodded.

The large, burly, dark-haired man grinned. "Hey, Wulf! Over here!"

Another huge Norseman inclined his head to Urian as he brushed past. "Enough, Erik Tryggvason! By the gods, you're too loud, brother."

Ignoring them, Urian headed after their prey.

October 7, 1988

Urian's head pounded from the voices that screamed louder and louder. It drummed to the point that he felt as if he were about to go insane and turn mad. Standing on the edge of a rooftop, he pressed his fingertips to his temple, tempted to step over the edge and end his suffering.

Nights like this . . .

It'd be real easy.

Especially the way the frigid wind whipped through his sweater and long leather coat.

Blinking fast, he shook his head and forced himself to focus. With a sigh, he jumped down the fire escape and was about to case the building when all of a sudden he almost landed on top of one of his targets.

With a startled gasp, the woman looked up, shielding her face.

Well, this wasn't supposed to happen . . .

Stunned, he wasn't sure what to say or do as he stared into a pair of dark brown eyes set into a perfectly sculpted face. Her golden-blond hair was stylishly cut and framed her features in a way that made them appear strangely elvish.

Up close, she was tiny and frail in appearance. Much younger than he'd have thought, but still a woman full grown.

And she blushed.

"Sorry! I thought I was the only one sneaking out."

Urian scowled. "What?"

Wrinkling her nose in the most adorable fashion, she gestured up at the windows, then leaned forward to whisper. "I'm sneaking out past curfew to meet friends. Are you running from a boyfriend or husband who came home early?"

He laughed at her presumption. "Neither."

"Oh, please don't tell me you're a pervert or burglar."

"Hardly!" Although ... he was here to stalk her. Now that he thought about it, it was kind of pervy. Maybe he'd spoken too soon.

"Then why are you on the fire escape?"

Shit ... he needed a viable excuse. "Um. I'm testing it."

"Testing it?"

"Yeah. I work for the city. And uh ... we're conducting a safety check to make sure they're in working order. You know? Can't have them faulty."

She laughed. "You're so full of shit!"

"What makes you think that?"

"Midnight and you're dressed like a Bond villain." She let out an evil cackle.

Urian wanted to hate her. He'd been sent here to kill her and her family.

All of them.

She and her sisters and mother were the very last of Apollo's living line. After all these centuries of hunting and killing, they'd finally done it. Finally tracked them down to the last few.

And this one ...

"I'm Phoebe Peters, by the way." She held her hand out to him.

For the love of God, don't tell me your name! That was just wrong when he was here to kill her. "Urian." He even shook her hand like an idiot.

Gah, I'm a moron. Because the moment he touched that tiny little hand, he realized just how soft it was. How delicate.

How good she smelled. How much he wanted to taste a piece of this most forbidden fruit. Especially when she looked up at him with an adorable grin.

I'm so doomed.

And he was. Especially when she bit her lip and he saw the tiniest flash of fang.

She's your enemy.

Yet it didn't feel that way. And his body wasn't reacting to her like she was his enemy. In fact, he was harder than he'd ever been in his life.

"Well, nice meeting you, Urian." She rose up on her tiptoes, kissed him, and vanished as if she had no clue how lethal he was.

Dismissed him! Completely stunned, he tried to get an idea where she'd gone, but his clever little bunny had gone to ground with resounding skills.

Damn. Just damn.

He certainly couldn't report *this*. His father would put him through a wall.

October 31, 1988

Urian was trailing after Phoebe and her sister, Nia. He wasn't sure where they were headed. The London street wasn't too busy tonight. The faint strains of music could be heard blending in with traffic.

It was so different from the old world he'd been born to.

The women had just turned a corner when a shadow moved out in front of them.

"Hey there, give us your purses!"

Two more shadows, armed with knives, stepped in behind them. Terrified, Phoebe and Nia were trying to obey, but they were shaking so severely that they could barely comply. Which caused their attacker to lose patience.

He slapped Phoebe.

Furious, Urian rushed in before he could stop himself. He disarmed the first one he reached. Kicked the second one into the wall, yet the one who'd slapped Phoebe had the audacity to actually stab him.

Stab him!

Hissing as his rage mounted, Urian yanked the knife from his side, turned, and grabbed the man by his throat. He slung him into the wall and would have ripped out his jugular had Nia not screeched and reminded him that they were in a public place and this might not be a good idea.

Phoebe rushed forward. "Urian, right?"

"Yeah."

"Oh my God! Thank you!"

Similar in looks, but not quite as pretty, Nia gaped at them. "You know him?"

"I met him a couple of weeks ago." She cast him a devilish grin. "We just kind of randomly ran into each other."

"Well, I'm definitely glad you ran into him tonight."

"Yeah, me, too." Her smile turned luminescent and did awkward things to his body in spite of the pain he was in. "You're my hero, Urian!"

And before he realized what she intended, she kissed him. This wasn't just any kiss. It set him on fire.

For reasons he couldn't even begin to explain, she tasted like home. Pulling back, he stared down at her.

Until he heard the police sirens.

Shite! "I have to go."

Nia gaped. "You're wounded."

It didn't matter. Urian stepped back into the darkness, taking a second to take one last, lingering look at Phoebe. In the moonlight, she was exquisite.

Until then, he hadn't realized how numb he'd become without Xyn around to remind him how precious life was. How good things could be.

Forget the soul exchange he had to have with humans. Her kiss was the psuché—the breath of life.

Damn shame I'm going to have to kill her.

November 15, 1988

"Okay, now this is getting creepy. Are you stalking me? Should I think about getting a restraining order?"

Urian froze as Phoebe grabbed him from behind as he stood in the alley near her building. Her humor and nerve amazed him. No one was ever this forward where he was concerned. Most wet their pants if he so much as glanced in their direction. "Are you not afraid of me?"

"Should I be? I mean ... I was joking about the restraining order, but should I call a lawyer?"

He laughed. "You do know that I'm a Daimon, right?"

That finally seemed to catch her off guard. She even took a step back. "Are you?"

He opened his mouth to show her his fangs. Like an intrepid child, she reached up to touch them.

"Mine aren't that large. You think it's because my father's human?"

Wow ... he couldn't believe her grit. "You're really not afraid of me at all, are you?"

She shrugged. "I like people. Even Daimons."

That shocked him most of all. "Met a lot of us, have you?"

"Not really. Most of the ones I've met have tried to kill me. But you saved my life, so I'm assuming you're not one of *those*. You're not one of those, are you?"

He was definitely one of those, and yet something about her innocence reached out and wrapped itself around a heart he'd thought was long dead.

Worse, it made him strangely protective of her.

In a weird way, she reminded him of Nephele and his niece that he'd inherited after Theo's death. One he'd carefully watched over and take care of, until she'd been slaughtered by Acheron's bastard Hunters. "I'm definitely something that goes bump in the night."

She laughed at his bad double entendre. "You know, lines like that will get you friend-zoned."

He gave her his most charming grin. "Will they?"

"Big-time!"

Don't tease her! She's an infant!

He was thousands of years old. In comparison to his ancient age, she'd only been alive for five minutes. A gross exaggeration, but not really. It was a fair comparison, all things considered.

And still neither his heart nor his body listened.

They were asking for the impossible.

Her.

You're an idiot!

There was no arguing that. Especially when she reached for him. Terrified of what he might do, he did the one thing he'd never done in his life.

He turned and ran.

Phoebe scowled at the sight of the man rushing off. Again. It was the darnedest thing. On the one hand, he seemed to always be interested and then on the other, he was as skittish as a brand-new colt.

Men! She'd never understand them. They were all so weird. Her sisters were right. It was something with that broken Y chromosome.

Shaking her head, she sighed and went into the condo where they were temporarily staying. Then again, that was all they ever did. She couldn't really remember ever having a real home.

Because she and her sisters were the last of Apollo's line, they had been hunted since birth. By all kinds of Daimons and demons who thought that if they killed them off, it would end the Apollite curse.

How stupid was that?

A part of her was tempted to tell her mother about the Daimon. In the past, she would have done so without hesitation. But Phoebe knew exactly what it would mean.

Leaving immediately. They wouldn't even take time to pack. Her mother and father were so incredibly paranoid. All they did was tighten the noose around her neck.

All their necks.

What if he's one of the ones hunting you?

But then why would he have saved them?

No. She didn't believe that. There was something about him that seemed kind and sweet. She didn't know what, but Phoebe saw something different whenever she looked at him.

He wasn't a monster.

Urian was ...

She couldn't find words. But she wanted to see him again.

Urian sighed as he met his father's gaze while Stryker sat on his throne in a disgruntled pique. "They're not as easy to get to as you'd think. They're under a lot of security."

His father's nostrils twitched. "Take more men! I want them dead!"

"I'd rather keep a lower profile at the moment. It's just a matter of time."

His father actually growled at him. "Don't fail me, Urian. We've come too far and we're too close."

He pushed down the urge to bristle under his father's swirling silver gaze. "I won't fail."

Besides, their enemies were closer than ever before. Helios was still trying to take down Apollo, even though he and his siblings and all their children were considered dead now since they were Daimons.

Urian didn't know why, other than perhaps spite. But he was growing tired of the fighting and the games. Bowing to his father, he left and headed home.

Davyn met him outside the great hall, on the street. "Are you all right?"

No, but he didn't want to confide in his friend right now. "Fine."

"You don't look fine."

Davyn would know.

Urian gave him a droll stare. "Why are you annoying me?"

"I like to annoy you. Besides, I know the look on your face."

"What look?"

"The one that says you have someone."

Urian stopped dead in his tracks as horror pounded through him. This was one secret he couldn't afford to let anyone know. Not even Davyn. "Pardon?"

"You heard me. Who is she?"

Urian shook his head. "You're wrong. I have no one."

Davyn caught his arm and held him in place. "Don't, Urian. This is me you're talking to. Just like when Paris was afraid to tell your father about us because he didn't know how he'd react. Just like when you were afraid to tell anyone about Xyn. I know you better than anyone. Who is she?"

Damn it to hell.

Davyn was a little ferret and whenever he had something like this, he was fixated. Either Urian told him, or he'd have no peace.

Glancing about, Urian drew in a sharp breath. "*That,* I can't tell anyone. Not even you."

"Does she make you happy?"

He laughed bitterly. "I don't know. I've barely spoken to her. But then, I guess the question is if anything in life ever makes anyone truly happy."

"No, Uri, that's not the question. The question is, can you live without her?"

Urian glanced down to all the teardrops on his arm and hand that marked all the people he'd loved and lost over the centuries. Including his twin. Of all the losses, Paris's had hurt the most. He still couldn't bear to think of it.

And he knew how hard that death had been for Davyn. To this night, Davyn had never been able to take another husband. Had never even tried to find someone else.

Because no one could replace Paris.

Each death had been a gut wound. Each one a laceration to his heart that Urian had never thought to survive.

Yet here he was.

Numb and not.

Damn you, life. Damn you straight to hell.

"You really want to make that comment to me?"

Davyn placed his hand over Urian's tattoos and gave a hard squeeze. "How about this then, Urian? Surely after all you've sacrificed and done for your people, after all you've lost in your lifetime, don't you think you deserve for the heavens to send down an angel to finally save you?"

November 29, 1988

At midnight, Urian tapped on Phoebe's bedroom window.

Dressed in a pink dorm shirt and thick yellow bathrobe, she pulled back the curtains to see him there. Her eyes widened. Then she immediately let out a squeak and ran to a mirror to check her hair.

While he waited outside.

Baffled, he watched her quickly brush her hair, remove a retainer, and then sniff daintily at her armpits. Then, remembering that he could see her, she covered her face with her hands and appeared mortified.

He laughed at her antics. Though why he found them so funny, he had no idea. Not to mention, he was surprised that she could see her reflection while he and his kind couldn't. It must be because she was part human that she didn't have that part of their Apollite curse.

Slowly, she made her way back to the window and opened it. "Tell me that you didn't see what I just did."

Urian laughed again. "No worries. I didn't see you sniff anything."

"Oh my God!" She began repeating that in an endless loop.

He scowled at her. "Did I break you? Are you stuck like that? Should I thump you out of that rut?"

She stopped and turned back to face him. "What?"

"At least *that* worked."

Cocking her head, she stared at him. "Why are you still hovering on the fire escape?"

"I have no choice. You haven't invited me in."

"Oh." Then her eyes widened even more as she remembered he was a Daimon. She glanced around her room for a second as if debating whether she should break protocol. Finally, she bit her lip and whispered, "Come in."

Urian slowly entered her bedroom. It'd been a long time since he'd been inside the home of anyone else. As a Daimon, he didn't get to randomly venture into many places. Only those that were public domain, or homes of friends and family.

This one was very different from anything he'd been in before. Decorated in tans and pinks, it was very . . .

Feminine.

Right down to the posters of boy bands that littered the walls. "Interesting wallpaper. Duran Duran?"

"'New Moon on Monday' is my all-time favorite song. Do you like them?"

Not really. "More of a Krokus 'Screaming in the Night' or 'Eat the Rich' or a Sex Pistols 'Anarchy in the UK' kind of guy."

She nodded. "Ah, that makes sense. Being a Daimon and all."

A sharp knock sounded on her door. "Pheebs?"

She motioned him to silence. "Yeah, Mom?"

"Who are you talking to?"

She ran to her door and cracked it open. "Myself. Sorry. I'll go to bed. Didn't mean to keep you up. Love you." She kissed her mom's cheek, then closed and locked the door.

After taking a small detour to turn on her radio, she returned to Urian and pulled him as far away from the door as she could.

His heart pounded to be this close to her while she wore so little. And he couldn't help wondering if she had on anything beneath her dorm shirt . . .

There in the dim light they stood. Not touching with barely a hand's breadth of distance between them. Urian kept his hands to his sides and yet he could feel every inch of her body with his. Her presence was so vibrant that it was like an all-over caress.

Her dark eyes sparkled as she looked up at him with wonder and excitement. How strange that he who had lived for so long and had done so much evil in the name of his father felt suddenly reborn in those eyes.

Felt recast as something other than what he was.

A monster who killed innocent people in order to live.

Yet Phoebe didn't see a Daimon to be feared or a demon to be hated.

Phoebe saw a man.

A hero.

God, how he wanted to be that. To see the good in others, even though he knew them for the evil they were. To be anything other than the shattered, unfeeling shell who'd been walking this earth for so long, hurting and aching and lost. Wanting to feel something more than abandoned and forgotten.

Wanting to be part of someone.

To be loved and claimed.

It'd been so long since anyone had really cared.

Unable to resist her or the part of him that was still human, he reached for his last lifeline and pulled her against his chest for the one true psuché.

Phoebe closed her eyes as she tasted a passion the likes of which she'd never imagined. This was what she'd read about in those books Nia kept hidden from their mother. What the poets went mad trying to capture on paper. The passion that Hollywood never quite got right.

Savoring the taste and smell of her beautiful Daimon, she reached up and freed his white-blond hair so that it fell loose about his shoulders. Then she buried her hands in it.

Holy heaven! He was gorgeous beyond compare! Every part of her was on fire as she felt that hard, honed body flexing around hers.

He buried his lips against her throat as he picked her up and pressed her back against the wall.

Phoebe lifted her legs from the floor and wrapped them about his waist as chills ran up and down her entire body.

She was on fire. Until he sank his fangs into her neck. The moment he did that, her body exploded with pleasure the likes of which was indescribable. She shook from the force of her very first orgasm.

Urian growled as he tasted her pleasure. Wanting more of that sweetness, he slid his hand down under her shirt and beneath the elastic band of her panties to the sweet moisture so the he could stroke her and let her ride his fingers while he fed.

Phoebe groaned as he worked magic on her. Wanting more, she moved to bite him.

Urian immediately withdrew. "No!"

Panting and shaking, he stepped to the other side of the room. Every bit as disoriented, she scowled at him. "Why did you stop?"

"If you bite me, you'll become a Daimon." He wiped at the sweat on his brow. "You can feed me, but I can't feed you."

"That's not fair."

"Welcome to Kalosis," he said bitterly. "That's where I live." He headed for the window.

"Urian, wait!"

"No, Phoebe." He glanced to her door. "This is a mistake. Everything I touch, I destroy. And I don't want to destroy you."

Not anymore. Not even if his father killed him for it.

And he would.

March 4, 1989

Stryker paced his office furiously. His commanders were gathered there as he reamed them all.

Including Urian.

"They're mortal. Mere Apollites. How in the name of Hades can they continue to elude my best strike teams? You are Illuminati, are you not?"

Allegra and Trates turned away.

Urian met his gaze without flinching. Mostly because he was the reason. He'd personally killed two of the Daimons his father had sent after Phoebe. But he wasn't about to tell him that.

His father would gut him on the spot.

He curled his lips at them. "Get out of my sight!"

Urian headed out the doors, but not before Trates took his arm.

"Why are they failing?"

Urian shrugged as he gave Trates a reason other than the truth—that he'd killed them. "Jefferson Peters has a lot of resources. He's spending them all to protect his daughters."

Trates shook his head. "It doesn't make sense."

"Life seldom does." And that was an understatement. Especially here lately. Nothing about his life made any kind of sense at all. He was living all kinds of lies and having to hide from everyone around him.

Apollymi. His father.

Even Davyn.

Whenever he was away from Phoebe, he began to doubt his sanity for throwing his life into this kind of chaos. And for what?

They hadn't even slept together.

Then just when he had himself convinced that he would sever the ties and break it off, he'd see her and all rationale fled. One smile. One frown.

He was undone.

And her tears absolutely devastated him.

I'm so screwed.

Sighing, he stepped into the portal and headed to Zurich. Phoebe had sent over a Vax note with her new address a short time ago. Her parents would kill her if they knew what she was doing.

That she was sending their updated addresses to the very leader of the group out to kill them all.

But it was a risk they were both willing to take.

Urian straightened his jacket the minute he was out of the portal and in Zurich. He checked the time.

"Here, you little inkblot."

A tic started in his jaw as he heard that lovely little insult some jack-off Dark-Hunter had come up with for them, thinking it was cute. It stemmed from the dark mark over their heart from the souls.

Pursing his lips, Urian crossed his arms and turned toward the tall, muscular beast and let out a bored sigh. "What? Did you burn out your last remaining brain cell coming up with that one?"

The Dark-Hunter flicked his wrist to release a spring-loaded dagger. "And here I thought I'd have a long patrol tonight. Where are your friends?"

"Got bored. Ate them. Decided I'd troll for bottom feeders, and I found you—lowest of the low. Lucky me."

The Dark-Hunter lunged at him.

Urian tsked. "What? Are you rusty or new?"

Shrieking in rage, he countered with an upward cut. Urian blocked it with his hands and used his toes to release the dagger in his boot. He scissor-kicked the Dark-Hunter and slashed him across the chest.

He hissed in pain and staggered back.

"You might want to call your Squire and let him know you won't be coming home."

The Dark-Hunter rushed him.

Urian released his razor wire from his vambrace and caught him around the neck. With one twist and a sidestep, he snapped the Dark-Hunter's head from his body.

Luckily, they tended to decay almost as fast as a Daimon. They just left a bigger pile of dust that quickly blew away.

"Sorry." Urian sighed as he knelt down to collect the Hunter's weapon and ID. He always made sure to notify the Squire's Council that oversaw Dark-Hunter care whenever they killed one so that they'd know who died.

It was an odd thing to do, but he felt like he owed it to them. While Dark-Hunters didn't have families per se, they did have Squires and other Hunters who were attached to them.

The worst thing in the world was to not know what happened to someone you loved. To be left waiting for them to come home again.

His stomach grew tight as he thought about Xyn. Even after all these centuries, he still missed her and wondered what had happened. If maybe, by some miracle, one day he'd pass her on the street.

It was stupid, but he couldn't help it. The not knowing was its own form of hell. And that endless, miserable hope.

Yeah, he couldn't do that to someone else. So he always made sure to let them know they had a Hunter KIA. As a soldier, he considered it an act of mutual respect for a comrade-in-arms. While they might be enemies, they were both fighting for what they thought was right.

Both protecting what they loved.

Urian looked at the Hunter's license to see his grim smile. Cuthbert Ruriksen. Yeah, he looked like a Viking bastard from back in the day.

Remembering how they'd been in more primitive times, he slid the license and sword into his pocket and drifted back into the darkness.

By the time he finally found Phoebe's new apartment, it was late. He'd expected to have to try to find a way to get her attention.

Instead, she was on the street and almost ran into him in her mindless rush to nowhere particular.

"Hey! What's going on?"

She threw herself against him. "Take me home with you! Now!"

Urian held her against his chest and scowled. "Um, okay. Sure. My father would probably eat you alive, but sure. I could do that for you if suicide is really what you're going for."

She hit his chest with her fist. Not hard enough to hurt, but just out of frustration. "I don't want to stay here, Uri. I'm done!"

Seriously concerned, he cupped her face in his hands. "What's going on?"

With a ragged sigh, she gestured back toward the apartment building she'd been fleeing. "You don't know what it's like to have so many rules and dictates. All the time! I live under a microscope! I can't change my mind without permission!"

"Yeah, no idea what that's like. At all." His voice dripped sarcasm.

She glared at him. "Not the same."

He arched a smug brow at her.

"Don't look so gorgeous at me. I'm not in the mood. Be angry on my behalf."

He bared his fangs.

She laughed and hugged him.

Closing his eyes as he sighed in contentment, Urian cuddled her close and rested his chin against her head. "Is it really *that* bad?"

"Yes. They want me to wear body armor."

"*I* want you to wear body armor."

"Not funny."

"Dead serious."

He could actually feel Phoebe rolling her eyes against his chest. "So where were you heading just now?"

She pulled back to glare up at him. "You're not really going to lecture me, too, are you?"

"Of course I am."

"Don't make me rack you. I'm a lot closer to your balls right now, buddy."

"Well, if that's what it takes to get you to touch them ... "

She gaped at him. "You did not just go there while we're arguing."

"I'm a man. Of course I went there. And it's not my fault, anyway. You're the one who brought my balls into it first."

She wrinkled her nose. "I did, didn't I?"

"Yeah." His voice dropped an octave. Not that it was his fault. Unlike him, she could eat real food and take transfusions for her blood cravings.

Since they'd started seeing each other, he'd stopped feeding from anyone other than Phoebe. And since he couldn't see her every day, it meant that when he did get to see her, he was starving.

Like now.

Phoebe bit her lip. "I have bad news, by the way."

"What?"

"I have to share a room with my sister in the new apartment. It's tiny."

That was bad news.

"But ... " She jerked her chin down the street in the direction she'd been headed. "I found a hotel nearby."

"So you did have a destination."

"Of course. I'm not *completely* stupid. I am a Peters, you know? Armed with a credit card and ready to charge like a demon." She winked. "Checked in earlier today." She pulled the key out of her pocket and handed it to him. "Room 1452."

"All right. I still worry about you."

"Good, 'cause I worry about you."

When he went to drape his arm around her shoulders, she gasped. "Is that blood?"

Too late, Urian realized he'd left a little Dark-Hunter DNA on his sleeve. "Um ... maybe."

"Yours?"

He started to lie, but she was the one person he didn't want to lie to. "No."

Her eyes flared with fury. "Who was she? Huh?" She shoved him back.

Now there was a place he hadn't expected her mind to go. Stunned, he gaped at her accusation that reminded him a lot of one of Xanthia's irrational rants. "She was a he, and he tried to kill me on my way over." He pulled the ID out of his pocket to show it to her. Now he was twice as grateful he'd gone to the trouble of getting it. "A huge Dark-Hunter bastard."

"Was he really six foot nine? Three hundred pounds?"

"Sounds about right. Though that was muscle weight. He had arms like tree trunks."

"He could have crushed you!"

"Trust me, I know. I had a brother about his size. Ophie used to sit on me for hours just to piss me off when we were kids. Him and Archie both would take turns slinging me around the yard like a rag doll."

Reaching up, she pulled his lips to hers. "I'm sorry, baby. I didn't mean to get so angry. I just can't stand the thought of you with another woman."

"I would never do that to you."

With a smile, she nibbled his lips. "Take me to the room."

Urian was tempted to use his powers, but since he'd never been in the hotel before, that was a bad idea. His luck, he'd land them inside a wall or something a lot worse.

So he had to pretend he was "human." Gah, the horror of that!

But at least she'd chosen an elegant hotel. Victorian in style, it was quaint and lush.

Urian expected Phoebe to lead him to a regular room. Instead, she'd booked the penthouse suite. While it was true that he'd grown up in a palace and a temple, they were rather cold and austere.

He'd never seen anything like the luxuries in this place. Nor lights so bright. He held his hand up to shield his eyes as they watered in protest of the giant crystal chandelier.

"Sorry!" Phoebe immediately began turning lights down or off. "I forgot how sensitive your eyes are."

Urian rubbed his eyes as he walked around. "What is that?"

She scowled at him. "The couch?"

"Yeah. Is it a bed?"

Phoebe was stunned until she realized something. "You don't ever stay out in my world, do you?"

"What do you mean?"

"Just what I said. You visit here to nab a soul and then immediately leave, don't you? You've never watched TV or really taken time to experience any real part of it."

He shook his head.

Her heart broke for him. All the history he'd lived through but not experienced. Heartbroken, she reached for the remote and turned the television on.

To that, he gave her an irritated glare. "I know about TV, Pheebs. Not an idiot. They have those everywhere. Even bars."

"Oh." Yeah, that would be the one place he'd have spent a lot of time. Der. She should have thought of that. She felt like a fool now.

Until she thought of one thing she knew they didn't have in a bar . . .

"Bet you've never had a Jacuzzi bath."

"A what?"

"Yeah . . . a what!" Crooking her finger, she motioned for him to follow her.

She also watched the way his gorgeous blues darted around the moldings and art, as well as the wall decorations. He ran his finger down the gold flocked wallpaper to the marble bathroom, where he gasped. "Yeah, indoor plumbing."

He cast her another droll stare.

"Okay, so you've probably visited a men's room, too."

"A few times, yeah."

"But not this!" She plugged the tub and began to run water from the ornate faucet shaped like a swan. While it ran, she turned on music through the intercom and began to slowly peel her clothes off.

If she lived to be a thousand years old, she'd never forget the look on his face as he stood in the doorway, completely catatonic. Laughing, she approached him and hooked her fingers in the belt loops of his jeans. "Charonte got your tongue?"

Urian had no response as she slowly unzipped his pants. Her pace was excruciating. And when she dipped her hand down low to cup him, he thought he'd die on the spot. He couldn't remember the last time a woman had touched him so intimately—decades? Centuries? He knew this was all kinds of wrong. But one look in those innocent eyes and he was lost.

Laughing, she rose up to kiss him.

He cupped her face and then trailed his hands down her shoulders and over her soft skin, to her back and buttocks to press her closer to him so that he could feel her curves meld to his body. He leaned his head back as she peeled his coat off, then pulled his shirt off over his head.

Phoebe hesitated as she saw the scars that marred the perfection of Urian's chest. She'd never seen him unclothed before. Because he'd always visited her in her room, they hadn't dared.

But damn. While she'd known he was battle hardened, seeing it was a different story. There were fresh and healing bruises as well as scratches, all over him. Her heart wrenched at the sight. Biting her lip, she traced them with her fingertips, until she got to the Daimon mark at the center of his chest, over his heart. "Does it hurt?"

"No."

It looked like a big bruise. One that was larger than her hand. No wonder it was so easy for a Dark-Hunter to kill them. "Do they have to pierce it in the center or just nick it anywhere?"

He tilted his head to look down at her hand. "You know, I've never really thought about that. Thanks, Phee, for giving me something else to worry about in a fight."

She laughed. "Well, you do have to think about it, you know?"

"Hmmm."

Kissing his mark, she tongued her way across his chest to his peculiar phoenix-dragon tattoo. "What's this for?"

"My Spathi unit that I lead. The Stygian Thánati."

"Ooo, that sounds so impressive."

"Glad you think so." He glanced past her to the tub. "Is it supposed to do that?"

"Do wha—" She gasped as she realized it was spilling over the edge. "Ah, crap! You distracted me!" She ran to turn the water off and grab towels to mop up the overflow.

Urian took a moment to admire the view of her bare bottom as she bent over to clean the mess. Damn, that woman had the one of the nicest asses ...

Trying not to think about it, he went to help her mop up some of the water. But that was as useless as trying to resist her. The moment he was near her and his hand accidentally brushed hers, he was lost and he knew it.

But then that had happened the moment he'd first seen her, when his father had sent him in to slaughter her and her sisters.

Just like now—one second they were cleaning water off the floor, the next Urian was in the tub, naked and holding her as he fed and cradled her in his arms in the warm water. He didn't know what it was about Phoebe, but she held magick over him.

Sighing in contentment, Urian savored the sensation of her fingers playing in his wet hair while she held him nestled between her bare thighs and breasts.

"Urian?"

Blood-drunk, he could barely recognize the sound of his own name on her lips. "Hmmm?"

"Would you let me make love to you tonight?"

Urian licked her neck as he struggled for sense and control. He wanted to deny her. They were playing a dangerous game that would blow up in both their faces. He knew it.

It wasn't fair to either of them.

His father would kill him. But his gaze drifted over her glistening body—down her damp, golden hair that curled around her impish face. Her creamy, bare shoulders where droplets of water caught and glittered like jewels on her alabaster skin. And those breasts that begged for a lover's touch ...

He was damned and he knew it.

"Phoebe," he breathed. "What if—"

"Shh." She kissed him to cut off his words. "Not another

word." She raked him with a ravenous hunger in her eyes. "I promise you, I won't change my mind."

Maybe not, but Urian knew this was a profoundly bad idea. In every sense of the word. If he had an ounce of decency in him, he'd get up and leave.

But then, he wasn't sure if he'd ever been noble or decent. If he had, those traits had died a long time ago.

And before he could find some semblance of decency inside him, she became treacherous to his cause and reached down to run her hand over his chest, across his own taut nipple, dragging her nails ever so gently over his flesh. A thousand chills erupted in the wake of her caress, burning him from the inside out.

She moved her hand from his lips, then dipped her head to where she could draw his nipple into her mouth and suckle it ever so tenderly.

And by that, he was undone.

Urian moaned from the pleasure she gave him. Especially when she dipped her hand beneath the water and cupped him there with gentle fingers that danced and played with the tenderest part of his body.

Dizzy and on fire, he was past the point of rational thought. All he could think about was finally sating the deep hunger that had gnawed at him incessantly since the moment he had first seen her on that fire escape and she primly left him there.

Cupping her face in his hands, he tilted her head up so that he could claim her lips with his own. Brushing his fangs with her tongue, Phoebe moaned into his mouth as she continued to stroke his swollen cock with her hand.

She feared she might faint as her head swam from the taste of her dangerous Daimon, from the silken feel of his rigidness under her fingers. Never had she imagined what a man would feel like. He was so strangely soft and hard at the same time. Like velvet stretched over steel.

"You had this all planned, didn't you?" he asked with a light, humorous note in his voice.

She nodded.

"What if I had turned you away?"

"I wouldn't let you," she whispered, then wrapped her arms around his neck and pulled his head to hers for another long, deep, and satisfying kiss.

Urian didn't disappoint her as he deepened his passion and kissed her until she lost her breath from it. She sighed in contentment and ran her hands down his lean, hard back.

Oh, but the man felt good and he tasted even better.

He left her lips and trailed a scorching kiss to her neck, where he suckled and teased her flesh with his fangs and tongue. Phoebe arched her back, writhing in pleasure as his hands skimmed over her body. Down her arms, over her waist to where he cupped her hips in his hands.

As he moved toward her breasts, she stopped him. He looked up with a frown.

"This is my fantasy," Phoebe said with a smile. Then she forced him to the opposite end of the oversized tub and straddled his waist.

Stunned and excited, Urian stared up in awe of her as he felt her hairs gently teasing the flesh of his belly. "And just what does this so-called fantasy of yours include? Hot wax? Whips? Handcuffs?"

Blushing at his suggestions, she dipped her head toward his and instead of giving him the kiss he expected, she lowered her mouth on his throat.

Urian tensed as he felt her fangs scraping his skin. "Don't bite me, love."

"I know. Relax. I promise I won't break the skin."

Forcing himself to trust her, Urian groaned at the heat of her mouth as she slowly explored his body with her lips. Her tongue darted over the stubble of his neck, teasing and tormenting him with wave after wave of pleasure.

She leaned forward until her breasts were flattened against his chest. Then she moved lower. Slowly, thoroughly, she covered his chest and arms with her scorching kisses.

Phoebe savored the sounds of Urian's pleasure. She should

probably be worried about her actions, given that he was a Daimon, but she had made her mind up. Her life had a ticking time bomb on it. Unlike her sisters, she didn't want to get married and have kids to give them this miserable life that had been theirs.

Running scared. Dreading every day and night. Always looking over their shoulders as they were uprooted and relocated because someone or something was trying to kill them. In spite of all their father's money, their life had been misery and fear, and she'd hated every fucking minute of it.

Until Urian.

For the first time in her life, she had happiness. Someone she loved, who loved her. With him, she felt like she belonged. And when they were apart, all she did was count down the heartbeats until she saw him again.

She didn't live when he was gone. She endured.

And she was over it.

No, Urian was what she wanted and she was going to do this. Completely and without reservations. Before this night ended, she wanted to know him from the top of his head all the way down to the bottom of his Daimon toes.

That thought foremost in her mind, she began draining the water so that she could dip her mouth to the flesh of his hip bone. Urian sucked his breath in sharply between his teeth as he quivered beneath her. Phoebe laughed as she continued her relentless exploration of him.

She was going to claim him tonight. And she made a vow to herself that when he left here after this, he would forever be hers and no one else's.

And it must have been working since a second later his eyes flashed red and he transported them from the tub to the bed.

Phoebe looked up with a startled gasp. "How do you do that?"

He shrugged. "A lot of practice and a little prayer that I don't fuck it up."

Laughing, she returned to nibbling that succulent hip bone and exploring a six-pack of defined abs she didn't think a man could have unless they were airbrushed in by an artist.

Urian buried his hand in Phoebe's hair as he fought the urge to take control. He wanted to be inside her so badly that he could barely stand it. It was an overwhelming craving. But he refused to take this from her, especially because it was her first time and he wanted it to be as special as she was. She meant so much more to him than his base urges. So he would hold back, even if it killed him.

And the way he felt, right now, it damn well might. Because this was hard. And getting harder by the minute.

Along with a certain piece of his anatomy ...

Curious and sweet, she moved her hand again to cup him as she explored his body with the inquisitiveness that was part science experiment and passion. He'd never had a lover be so strangely attentive to his body. Almost as if she wanted to commit it to memory.

And then to his utter amazement, she moved her head and took him fully into her mouth.

With a fierce, deep growl, Urian shook all over as her tongue toyed with him. *Oh dear gods!* Panting and weak, he stared in awe of her golden head buried between his thighs.

To hell with this, he couldn't take it anymore.

Phoebe looked up in surprise as Urian shifted his body. What was he doing?

With a devilish grin, he stretched out beside her and positioned his hips even with her head. She was completely baffled by what he was doing and what he intended.

His blue eyes turned warm and wicked. "Don't stop, love." Before she could respond, he nudged her thighs apart and buried his lips against her.

With a cry of supreme pleasure, she closed her eyes as he slid his tongue deep inside her. Dear God in heaven! It was incredulous. Never had she experienced anything like this! Forget the crap her sister read and kept shoving in her face! Nia was an idiot! Cassandra an even bigger one! They didn't know anything about men! And she'd never listen to them again.

Her head spinning from it, she opened her legs wider. He took her invitation. Wanting to return the favor for him, she dipped her head and went back to what she'd been doing because if this felt half as good to him ...

Yeah, she wanted to keep him happy and make sure he never belonged to any woman but her again.

Urian's head spun as he again felt her mouth and tongue close around him. He cupped her hips to him as he ran his tongue over her and felt her quiver in his arms. His little angel was incredible. And to think he'd actually considered killing her.

You were an idiot!

Yeah, he was. But then he'd never had a lot of brains to begin with. For so long now, he'd been running on empty. Just doing whatever his father told him. A mindless tool that killed on command.

He'd become the very thing Sheba had wanted him to be.

An attack dog.

Urian Deathbringer. Thánatago.

But with Phoebe Peters, he was something more. Something better.

For the first time since Xyn's death, he felt alive again. He found a reason to breathe. To get up in the evening and to let himself feel real emotions.

He wasn't sure if he should be grateful or curse her for it.

Phoebe couldn't believe what was happening to her. Where she found the courage to do these things with a cold-blooded Daimon, she didn't know. She'd been told her entire life to run from creatures like Urian. That they would kill her and her family.

Yet she'd never felt safer.

More wanted or beautiful.

The heat of his mouth seared her as he teased and suckled. And even more incredible was the feel of his fingers plunging inside her. In and out and around. Her body quivered and jerked as her head reeled from the sensations.

She closed her eyes. It was too much for her. And just as she was sure she would die from it, her body exploded with more pleasure than she would have thought anyone could ever feel.

Throwing her head back, she screamed out in release as the entire world spun around. Never, never had she experienced such a thing.

And still his tongue tormented her and made it even more intense and incredible. "Oh God, Urian!" she gasped.

He let out an evil laugh as he kissed her thigh. "Don't think for one minute that I'm done with you, *agapi mou*."

"Agah who?"

He laughed. "Uh-gah-pay moo. My love."

Closing her eyes, she savored every syllable. "I love your accent so much. You speak and I melt!"

He rose up between her legs and positioned his body over her. Phoebe reached up and buried her hands in his hair as he used his knees to spread her legs wider.

Cupping her face with his hand, Urian kissed her tenderly, then gently plunged himself deep inside.

Phoebe froze as pain overrode her pleasure. "Uri?"

"Shh, *agapi mou*," he whispered against her lips. "Give it a second."

He leaned back ever so slightly and reached his hand down between their bodies so that he could stroke her and help her focus on something else.

Phoebe bit her lip as she quickly forgot the pain while he gently toyed with her body, building her pleasure again.

Instinctively, she rubbed herself against him, impaling herself even more deeply than before.

Urian sighed in pleasure as she began moving against him. "That's it," he breathed, closing his eyes to savor the warm, tight heat of her body around his.

His breathing ragged, he let her take control of the moment as she milked his body with hers.

Opening his eyes, he watched the wonder play out on her face. Yeah, she liked being in charge. Probably because she'd had so little control over anything else in her life. Her parents never let her have any decision. About anything. Even her foods were tasted before they trusted her to eat them.

She'd lived her entire life in a vacuum, and under scrutiny.

So he let her have this one. Smiling, Urian rolled over without withdrawing from her.

In awe of this new vantage point, Phoebe groaned as she found herself on top of him. She wiggled her hips at the strange sensation of his body inside hers and between her legs.

His eyes dark and gentle, he reached up and cupped her breasts in his hands. Smiling even wider, she covered his hands with her own, then lifted her body up, drawing herself down his cock.

And then his hand returned to cup her between her legs as she rode him hard and fast.

And this time when she came, he joined her with a deep guttural growl that left her a little scared for a second. But after a second, she realized that he wasn't going to harm her and she relaxed again.

Sated and exhausted, Phoebe stretched out on his chest and simply enjoyed the feel of his arms around her as his breath stirred her hair.

Urian leaned his head back, shaken by what had occurred between them. Her passion humbled him. But worse, he was far from sated. If anything, he wanted her more than he ever had before. Because now that he'd tasted the Katateros that was Phoebe, he knew she truly had no equal.

And that scared the Kalosis out of him.

Phoebe lifted her head up to look down at him. "Is something wrong?" she asked, her brows drawn together into a deep V.

Shaking his head, he ran his hands over her back. It wasn't really a lie.

In truth, things had never been more right.

And likewise, they had never, ever been more wrong. Because in the back of his mind, he couldn't stop thinking about the fact that if his father ever learned about this, he would kill them both.

August 8, 1990

They were going to kill Phoebe. Urian was frantic to get to her and warn her. He'd been trying to call her, but some asshole was on the phone and wouldn't get off the line. He'd tried to have the operator break through it and whoever it was had rudely refused.

"It's not an emergency. Tell my sister's boyfriend he can wait."

When he got his hands on Cassandra, he was going to beat the hell out of her.

And since he was trapped until nightfall, there was nothing he could do. He didn't dare go to Apollymi or try to use her mirror for fear of her telling his father, either.

Damn it. This had been the longest day of his life. By the time the sun set and he could leave, he felt as if he'd been flayed alive.

He headed straight to her apartment. Normally, he'd never approach her door. He called from a pay phone with a prede-signed ring code and she'd come out to meet him.

But he was too scared to wait.

As he ran down her street, a car passed him and someone inside it waved at him.

Too late, he realized it was Phoebe.

Panting and terrified, he stopped dead in his tracks. *Phoebe!* he projected with his thoughts. *Stop the car! Get ou—*The car exploded in a bright burst of light, raining shrapnel through the neighborhood and knocking him from his feet.

Temporarily blinded, and with his ears ringing, Urian lay on the sidewalk stunned.

No ... No! That didn't just happen. It couldn't have.

His heart pounded so fast and furiously that he couldn't breathe. Pain and grief racked him. They left him paralyzed and shredded.

Until he heard the tiniest whimpering sound.

Phoebe?

He wiped at his tears and teleported to the wreckage, not giving a fuck who saw him. His stomach heaved at the sight of the mangled bodies. *Please don't be my Phoebe . . .*

"Uri . . . "

He turned to find her a few feet away. His world stopped as he realized that the blast had thrown her from the car, into a nearby pole. He ran to her side and knelt down to pull her into his arms. She was bleeding profusely.

While it might not have killed her on detonation, it was killing her slowly. There was no way she'd survive. There was too much damage. Every Daimon instinct he had told him that. He could hear her vitals slowing. It was what allowed him to know the precise moment when he could take over a soul to feed on it.

"Phoebe?"

She was so weak, she could barely focus on his face.

"Marry me?"

With the tiniest laugh, she nodded and gasped.

Knowing she was too weak to bite him on her own, Urian used his fangs to rip into his own wrist and held it to her lips. He lifted her up so that she could drink his blood.

At first, he thought he'd lost her. That he'd waited too long or not gotten there in time.

But after a few seconds, he felt her grip tighten. Felt her lips strengthen as she sucked and licked harder. His arm began to glow. Too late, he remembered that he'd had the power to save her life without resorting to this.

Damn it! Why hadn't he thought of that? But he hadn't used those powers in centuries. So used to hiding what he could do because of the way the others reacted, he'd all but forgotten them. *I'm so sorry, Phoebe . . .*

In that moment, he hated himself. He'd turned her into a monster for no reason.

"Urian?"

Heartbroken, he brushed the blood from her lips with his thumb. "I'm right here."

"Where's my mother and sister?"

He shielded her eyes from their bodies. "They didn't make it, sweetie."

Tears welled in her eyes. Sirens began to wail and too late, Urian realized the size of the crowd around them. All staring. The prudent thing would be to try a spell or ...

Fuck it. Let the human mind rationalize it as space aliens or whatever psychosis they wanted to name it. Mass hysteria. Hallucination. They had more excuses than stars in the heavens. It wasn't his concern.

Phoebe was. His only concern was making sure she didn't get taken to a hospital where they wouldn't understand her now Daimon blood.

So with that thought, he used his powers to teleport her to the one place he knew she'd be safe. The only place where his father couldn't find her or hurt her.

Elysia.

The minute they made an appearance inside the secure underground facility, alarms went off. Urian cringed at the piercing shriek that threatened to shatter his already abused eardrums. Phoebe covered her ears and cringed against his shoulder.

Braden, along with two dozen guards, came running with weapons drawn to surround him.

Urian took their panic in stride. "Well, I'd put my hands up, but I don't think Phoebe would appreciate it."

Braden rolled his eyes. "Sheez, Uri, what are you doing here?"

"I've come to ask a favor and I need a doctor."

Braden's gaze went to Phoebe. "You know our laws."

"And I know what you owe me. *You* know what you owe me. I need this from you. Don't make me beg. Worse, don't make me angry."

Braden only hesitated for three heartbeats before he nodded, then motioned for the guards to lay aside their weapons. "Follow me."

Urian glanced down at Phoebe as she began whimpering in pain. "Stay with me, *agapi mou*."

"My head hurts so much." She twisted her fist in his shirt.

"I know. It's the soul. Just breathe through it."

Once they reached the infirmary, Urian followed Braden into a room in the back and laid her down on the hospital bed. He stepped back as a stern-looking female doctor came in. "We don't treat Daimons."

Braden snorted. "You *will* treat this one."

"Why's he so special?"

"He built the facility you're standing in."

Her jaw went slack. "Excuse me?"

Hands on hips, Urian smirked. "You heard him. And I'll kick your ass if you don't."

She gaped.

"Yeah, you heard me. I bought into equal rights. You're an Apollite. Means you're more than capable of fighting back. And my fiancée's life means a lot more to me than yours does. Save it or lose your own."

Irritated at him, she reached for a pair of latex gloves and made a grand show of putting them on before she went to tend to Phoebe. "Is he always that big a dick?"

"No," Phoebe said, panting and weak. "Sometimes he's worse."

That succeeded in making the doctor laugh. Shaking her head, she forgot about Urian as she began tending to Phoebe's injuries. Which was more than fine with him.

Satisfied that the doctor wouldn't hurt her, he left them alone and stepped outside the room to speak with Braden.

Tall and blond, he was almost even in height with Urian. Like almost all Apollites. Since they were direct descendants of Apollo, the blond hair was almost always a staple. Though through the centuries some of them, such as Phoebe's family, had married humans or other creatures. So it wasn't unheard of to meet an Apollite with reddish hair or even a brunette. Still, it wasn't considered normal for an Apollite to be anything other than blond. And they were almost always tall and brown-eyed.

Braden and his kinsmen had been civic leaders here in Elysia since Urian and Davyn had helped them establish the huge underground bunker back in the early days of America. Back when Theo's daughter had fallen in love with an Apollite who had wanted a safe haven for his family to hide. Because they were Cult of Pollux followers, Urian had known better than to ask his father about bringing them into Kalosis.

Since the night they'd mourned Tannis, the CoP had been banned from their domain and if anyone mentioned it to Stryker, they came up short a pair of fangs.

And testicles.

Because he and Davyn had helped them establish their city, and were quick to come if they had any kind of trouble with Daimons who didn't abide by their laws, they were given special privileges.

Like being able to come here even though Daimons were banned.

Urian arched a brow at him. "Aren't you going to ask what you're going to ask?"

"What do you mean?"

"I know you heard what Phoebe is to me. Aren't you curious?"

Braden nodded. "That and why you brought her here."

"Because if I take her home, my father will kill her." Urian let out a tired breath. "In all these centuries I've never asked for anything or any kind of payment. I'm asking now."

"You know it's forbidden."

"So is my helping you. Yet here I am." He gave Braden a pointed stare.

At least he had the good sense to look shame-faced.

"C'mon, Braden. I know you have the ability to bend some of the rules. Phoebe's harmless. She's never taken a soul and she never will, I swear to you. She's half human. More a babe than the infants here. She's not even tasted blood to live on. Not until tonight when I forced her to drink mine to save her life."

His eyes widened. "Half human?"

He nodded. "Another reason I don't dare take her near Kalosis."

Braden didn't say a word—he headed straight into the room. Urian went after him.

The doctor had Phoebe covered by a sheet. She was still pale, but some of her wounds were beginning to heal. However, the doctor held a peculiar expression on her face.

"Millicent—"

"She's part human," she blurted out, cutting him off. She met Urian's gaze with an incredulous gape. "*You* saved the life of a half-human Apollite?"

"I love her."

"That's what she said. And I told her you were a bastard. Then she quickly informed me that I didn't know you at all."

He didn't know why, but those words sent a warmth through him the likes of which he'd never known before. "Is she going to be okay?"

"She shouldn't be. I don't know what's in your blood, boy, but yeah, I think she'll pull through."

Braden crossed his arms over his chest. "Do you think she's dangerous?"

Millicent didn't hesitate with her answer. "No. Not at all. She strikes me as the kind of person who picks a spider up on a napkin and releases it out the back door instead of killing it." She jerked her chin toward Urian. "He's the one who's lethal."

She was right about that. "Only when crossed. Or annoyed."

Which was probably most of the time, and easily done, but that was another matter.

Braden let out a tired sigh. "All right, then. So long as she only feeds from you, Urian, she can stay. But she can't leave here."

"I'll make sure that she knows that."

"Very well then. We'll make sure she's taken care of and given a place to stay."

"Thank you, and Davyn and I will make sure you have extra protection."

"You better, because I'm holding you both personally responsible for everything she does."

August 23, 1990

Urian took a deep breath as he waited in the small Apollite temple for Phoebe. Dressed in a kilt with his long hair worn loose about his shoulders, he felt *so* ridiculous. He even had what was tantamount to a furry purse hanging over his junk, and making him nervous as hell that it was going to accidentally pop him too hard and put him out of commission. But this was what Phoebe wanted him to wear for their wedding. So here he was.

Looking like an idiot to make her happy.

Gah, what part of you're marrying a Greek Daimon and not a Scottish Highlander did you miss, woman?

If he ever met her sister Cassandra he was going to beat the holy hell out of her for her sick romance novel fetish that had put this idea in Phoebe's head.

But as the doors opened slowly to show Phoebe on the other side dressed in a shimmering gown of flowing white silk that hugged her lithe body to perfection, all complaints scattered. Mostly because all the blood drained from his brain and pooled to the center of his body.

Um, yeah. For her, he'd set himself on fire.

Especially when her gaze met his over the single white rose wrapped in red and white ribbons that she carried, and she gave him that sweet, shy smile.

His heart pounded as she headed toward him with Braden at her side to be her sponsor for their union. How weird that after all the times he'd been married, he was actually nervous.

Phoebe couldn't believe her eyes as she stared at the sexiest man alive. He was completely gorgeous. Tall, lethal.

He was hers.

The only thing that could make the day better would be to

have her family with her. For a moment, her eyes teared, but she refused to be sad. Not tonight.

She wouldn't regret what she'd lost. For weeks now, she'd been crying. There was nothing to be done about that. It still burned and hurt and ached. Worse, was knowing that her father and Cassandra were still alive, and that they both thought her dead. But the truth that she was a Daimon would be even more cruel.

So she was learning to live her new life.

With Urian.

And tonight, they would be united.

With a ragged breath, she took his hand. Braden pulled the ribbons from her rose and wrapped them around their combined hands to join them together. Then he moved to stand in front of them to act as their officiant for the ceremony.

Phoebe licked her dry lips as she stared up at her gorgeous Daimon.

His blue eyes glowed with warmth and love as Braden began their ceremony. "It is through the light that we are born and through the night that we travel. The light is the love of our parents who greet us and welcome us into this world, and it is with the love of our partner that we leave it.

"Urian and Phoebe have chosen to be with each other, to ease their remaining journey and to comfort one another in the coming nights. And when the final night is upon us, we vow to stand together and ease the one who travels first.

"Soul to soul we have breathed. Flesh to flesh we have touched. And it is alone that we must leave this existence, until the night comes that the Fates decree we are reunited in Ouranlie."

Ouranlie was the highest point of Katateros where only the purest of souls could reach. It was considered the highest point of Atlantean heaven. Reserved for saints, heroes, and soul mates.

Braden moved to the sacred font where they kept an elaborate gold cup housed. Engraved with an image of the three Fates, it was reserved for weddings and special feasts. He took it to Phoebe first.

Urian held the cup while Braden pulled out a small knife and cut a tiny incision on her wrist so that he could place some of her blood in the cup. Then he did the same with Urian.

Once they had an equal amount of blood in the cup, Braden swirled it around three times clockwise and then counterclockwise. He whispered a prayer beneath his breath.

Braden handed the cup to Phoebe for the first drink, and then she handed it to Urian, who drank from the same spot she did. He handed the cup to Braden, and as was their custom, Urian leaned down to kiss his wife and mingle their blood while it was still on his lips.

Braden returned the cup to the pedestal, then came back to stand in front of them. "Now we present, Phoebe Jane Peters. She is unique in this world. Her beauty, grace, and charms are the legacy of those who have come before her and will be gifted to those who are born through her.

"This man who has chosen to unite with her, Urian Thánatago, on the other hand, stands before us a product of honor and integrity. A paragon of his parents, he sheds his house to unite with his wife and become Urian Peters. It is your similarities that brought you together and your differences that add variety and spark to your life. May the gods bless and protect your union and may you be blessed with fertility and happiness. And may the two of you enjoy every minute left to you."

With those words spoken, Braden tied the ribbons into a double knot. Hopefully, the ribbons would last for seven days. At the end of which, they'd be cut and buried for luck.

"Congratulations." Braden clapped Urian on the arm before he left them alone.

It was only then Phoebe realized how alone they were. "I'm sorry, Urian."

"For what?"

"That you don't have any of your family here."

He shrugged. "It's all good. I have you and that's all that matters to me. Besides, I'm grateful that none of my family are here to see me dressed like this. My father would shit his pants."

She laughed. "You're terrible! And I don't want to hear

it. Especially since it's not like you didn't wear a toga back in the day."

Sputtering, he clutched at his chest. "Ah! You wound me. It was a chiton, woman! Hello? Not a Roman."

"Oh whatever, like anyone knows the difference or cares!"

"I care!"

She rolled her eyes at him. "Only *you* would."

Suddenly, Urian had a strange feeling.

"Something wrong?"

He glanced around the room as his skin crawled. "You feel that?"

"Feel what?"

"Like we're being spied on."

Phoebe shook her head. "You're being paranoid. How could they?"

Maybe, but it was tangible. His flesh literally shivered with it. Unmistakable.

Something wicked danced on his spine. Like Acheron on steroids.

Unmistakable. And malevolent as hell.

June 15, 1996

Urian had barely taken out two of their own who'd been chasing his sister-in-law when he rounded a corner and ran into the last creature he'd ever expected to see.

The god Helios.

And judging by his expression, he wasn't happy. In fact, if looks alone could kill, Urian would be splintered.

"What's up, sunshine?"

That had the intended effect. The Titan hurled a god-bolt at him.

But instead of harming him, it hit his arm and caused it to light up and deflected. The moment it did, the ancient god's eyes widened. He blasted Urian again.

And again, nothing happened.

His nostrils flared.

"Losing your touch?"

"Don't you dare taunt me." Helios narrowed his gaze. "So you're the one whose been slaughtering my soldiers."

Urian shrugged with a nonchalance he didn't feel, because he knew he was dancing with the devil. "Returning the favor."

"Says the boy playing with fire?"

Urian's blood ran cold. "What do you mean?"

A slow, evil smile crept across his face. "When you keep a lot of secrets, they *will* creep out. There's only so long you can keep the lid on a boiling pot. And you know what you've done."

Helios vanished.

Panic filled Urian as he considered those words and the fact that Helios must know what he'd been doing to protect Phoebe.

The god was right. Every night Urian woke up, he felt like he was balancing on a razor blade. To keep his wife happy, he was lying to his father, protecting her last sister with everything he had—even killing his own people to do it.

To protect his own ass and marriage, he lived in terror of Phoebe finding out that he'd been the one who'd led the strike team that had taken out her eldest sister and her grandparents. That he'd been personally responsible for about half of her childhood traumas and those of her mother.

He was the bogeyman that caused her to wake up in the middle of the day, shaking.

What have I done?

His happiness had been bought on a lie. Sooner or later, it would unravel. He knew that. It had to.

All things built on a lie would always come crumbling down, sooner or later. The truth about Cassandra was going to come out. They would all learn it and it would destroy her. People didn't like being lied to, and they always turned on the liar and dragged them to beat them twice as hard for the betrayal. It was the worst thing anyone could ever do.

Suddenly, he felt a presence behind him. Urian turned, ready to fight.

Then he smirked at the last person he expected to see.

Ruyn Widowmaker.

And he wasn't alone. He was traveling with a demon Urian had only come across a few times over the centuries, but he was one he knew better than to get tangled up with.

Shadow. His allegiance was always questionable at best. One never really knew where his loyalties lay. Not even with himself. He could be a spiteful bastard. And when he saw Urian, the expression on his face said he had about as much trust for Urian as Urian had for him.

That they'd rather set each other on fire than pass pleasantries.

"Should I ask what trouble you two are getting into?"

Ruyn smiled. "Mostly mayhem. You?"

"Same." Urian jerked his chin at Shadow. "I see you're hanging out with a whole new level of loser."

Shadow made a face at that. "I'd be insulted, but for the fact that coming from you and your class of demon, that's a compliment."

"How you figure?"

"My boy could be hanging out with a lot worse. He could be with a Daimon."

Urian snorted. "Touché."

And as he studied them, he realized that their timing here was a bit suspicious. "You two looking for Helios?"

"No."

"Yes," Shadow said at the same time. He glared at Ruyn. "Why are you lying?"

"Why are you being honest?"

"I didn't get the lie memo." Shadow smirked. "You have to keep me up to speed on these things. Otherwise, expect absolute honesty."

"Really? Thought you were Prince of Shadows?"

Shadow grimaced. "What's that supposed to mean?"

"Dubious? Nebulous? Questionable character?"

"You have me confused with your mother."

Urian let out a low whistle at that. "Hey, now, no need to invoke that dig. That's seriously going low, Shadow. I'm flagging that play. And on that note, I need to get back."

As he started to leave, Ruyn stopped him.

When he looked back at his former brother-in-law, Ruyn laid a verbal bomb on him. "There's something weird going on in the Nether Realm. Something has kicked the proverbial hornets' nest and they're going crazy. Watch your back, brother. The gods are crazy, and we're in their way. Which means they're going to be coming for us."

February 15, 2004

Urian pulled out his cell phone and masked his number to appear to be that of a Dark-Hunter's Squire. He called their senior dispatch and made sure to disguise his thick Greek accent. "Uh, yeah, I was at Dante's Inferno and I just saw a couple Daimons in there cruising for vics. You might want to wake a Hunter and send one in before they kill somebody."

"Thanks, Squire. Could you give us your ID?"

He hung up, knowing they'd comply. They always did. Back in the day, he'd call in the reports like that from pay phones to lure Dark-Hunters out to kill them.

Never, ever in those days would he have dreamed he'd be using this tactic to protect Apollo's heiress.

Hades is sitting on icicles.

Worse? One of Davyn's friends, Jensen, was on the strike team. He'd tried to get the moron to stay home.

He hadn't listened.

At least he'd been able to get Davyn to stay out of it.

Standing on the rooftop of the building next to the club, Urian watched the alleys as people came and went. His phone rang. He glanced down to see Phoebe's number.

He answered immediately. "Hey, *zoi mou.*"

"Don't call me 'your life' right now. I hear that and it makes me afraid you have bad news."

"God, no, Phee. Your sister's fine. I don't have eyes on her, but the guys aren't here yet so she's safe."

"You're sure?"

"Positive. I can feel Kat inside. There's no mistaking her power. And it's calm. No fire-bolts are flying. No one's calling the cops."

"Okay. Love you."

"Eimai trellos gia sena."

"You know that's just Greek to me, right?"

He laughed at her teasing tone. "I'm crazy for you."

"Ah ... well hurry up. Save my sister and get your hulking sexy ass home. You know whenever you speak Greek to me you make me horny."

And those words made him instantly hard. "That was mean."

"I know. Get here soon."

"Yes, ma'am." He hung up the phone and sobered as he saw his friends arriving.

Crap! If the Dark-Hunter didn't arrive, he was going to have to go into that club, and ruffle some Were-Hunter fur to protect Cassandra himself.

That would go over like a Charonte in Artemis's temple.

Shit ...

Urian had just reconciled himself to that miserable fate when he finally saw the huge hulking predator swaggering toward the door. Yeah, there was no missing that kind of arrogant stride.

Dark-Hunter.

Thank the gods.

Saluting the bastard in silence, Urian stepped back into the shadows. Now he was off to get laid and put this shitty night to rest. He'd deal with his father later.

And deal he would.

Because there would be hell to pay. But the smile on Phoebe's face when he told her that Cassandra was safe would be worth it.

His wife would definitely return the favor and show him her gratitude.

Yet as he opened the portal to take him to Elysia, he couldn't help thinking he was living on borrowed time and that everything was about to come crashing down.

He could feel it in his bones.

Death was coming. And the bastard already had him marked.

February 16, 2004

Urian entered his father's study with the pride and grace of a lethal predator. Looking neither left nor right, he made his way straight to where his father stood in front of his desk to report his findings from the Inferno, where he'd gone earlier to speak to the owner Dante Pontis's brother, Sal. A smarmy little panther.

After that encounter, he still felt the need to shower and he'd barely spent fifteen minutes talking to the were-beast.

His father narrowed his gaze on him. "Any word?"

Urian shook his head. "Not yet. The Were-Hunter said he'd lost her scent, but that he will pick her up again."

His father clapped him on the back. "I want at least twenty standing by. There's no way she'll escape us all."

Effing awesome. Make this as hard on me as you can. Outwardly, Urian showed no emotion whatsoever. "I'll summon the Illuminati."

His father inclined his head to him. "Good. And this time, I'll go with you."

That was a whole lot of disconcerting. His father never went on these runs with them. For that matter, Urian couldn't remember the last time his father had even left Kalosis.

Normally Trates brought the meals here for his father to suck the souls of humans out in their main hall.

Damn, the world really was coming to an end. And he had a front-row seat for it.

A part of him wanted to warn his father that the human realm was extremely different than it'd been the last time he'd ventured out, but experience had taught him to never do such a thing. His father tended to view "advice" as condescension. And *that* never went well for the person giving it.

Not even his sons.

So Urian bit his tongue and summoned his soldiers for their raid on Cassandra's apartment. But in the back of his mind was the question of how to safely get her out of there now that his father was going with him. It'd never been easy in the past.

This was going to be a hell of a lot harder.

Yet there was no way he could let her die. Phoebe would never forgive him for it.

Shit. This was about to get ugly.

Urian *was still* trying to come up with a plausible escape plan for Cassandra, but damn it, every one of their people was right on top of him. He couldn't take a breath that one of them didn't exhale.

It was ridiculous. He was about to feign a heart attack. If only a Daimon could have one.

Frustrated, he had no choice but to watch as his father knocked on the front door of Cassandra's apartment and pretended to be a deliveryman.

Using his powers, he listened carefully to see if Kat was in there with her.

"Kat?" He heard Cassandra calling.

No one answered.

"Kat?" she tried again.

His father knocked again, more demanding this time.

Urian heard the sounds of rushing feet, as if his sister-in-law were searching the rooms for something. He could taste her fear as she headed to the back of the apartment.

His father vanished, no doubt intending to meet her there.

Cassandra stopped moving. "Kat, is that you?"

"Yeah, let me in."

Urian flinched as he realized that wasn't Katra's voice, but his father pretending to be her. Crap! He'd heard the kori speaking enough to recognize the difference in cadence.

He's going to kill her ...

Cassandra laughed nervously as she opened the door and

Urian flashed himself to the back to run interference, and hopefully save her life.

Sadly, he misjudged the distance and ended up landing *inside* her apartment, a few feet behind her. *Good going, dumbass.*

Lucky for him, she was too mesmerized by his father to notice that she had company inside her home, and his father was too busy taunting her to care that he'd screwed up. That was bad enough. Worse? Another Daimon popped in beside him.

Seriously? He couldn't catch a break tonight with them. Leave it to him to get stuck with an overachiever.

"Did you miss me, princess?" his father taunted from outside her back door in a voice identical to Kat's.

Cassandra stood there, gaping. "What are you, the friggin' Terminator?"

His father smirked. "No. I'm the Harbinger who is merely preparing the way for the Destroyer." He reached for her.

Cassandra stepped back and almost *into* Urian, who also had to take a step away from her to keep from being a rude awakening that she had an uninvited guest—courtesy of a loophole she didn't realize about apartment buildings. He also had to shove his companion out of her way.

Still unaware of them, she pulled out a dagger from her waist and sliced his father's arm.

His eyes turning red, his father hissed.

Then she spun about and realized they were in the apartment with her. Awesome. With a piercing scream, she caught his friend in the chest with her dagger.

He evaporated into a golden-black cloud before Urian could pull him to safety. Grinding his teeth, he cursed himself for not being quicker.

Spinning around, Cassandra kicked his father back, but he didn't go completely out the door. Instead, he only blocked it more. Which prevented her from escaping.

"You're quick." He healed his arm, causing her to gasp at his powers. "I'll give you that."

Cassandra lifted her chin defiantly, reminding him of a

gesture Phoebe used whenever Urian pissed her off. "You don't know the half of it."

She kneed the next one of their guys who reached her and fought Urian's second-in-command. His father stayed back, watching her carefully so that he could learn her techniques and use them against her.

Urian knew if he didn't get her out of here, or shield her movements, his father was about to attack her any second and end her existence.

It was now or never.

Determined, he rushed her.

To his shock, she didn't run away. Rather, she caught him under the arm and flipped him over. Urian hit the ground with a loud grunt that left him reeling. Just as she went to stab him, his father came out of nowhere and grabbed her arm before she could pierce his Daimon's mark.

"No one attacks Urian!"

She shrieked as he wrenched the dagger from her hand. Then she made the fatal move as so many had before her.

Cassandra met his father's eyes that swirled like mercury silver. Those eyes were hypnotic. They danced and held everyone spellbound. Turned their thoughts to oatmeal.

Urian literally watched as all the fight inside her vanished. A sly, seductive smile curved his father's lips. "See how easy it is when you don't fight?"

He tilted her head to the side to give him access to her carotid artery. His father met Urian's gaze and let laughter rumble deep in his throat a moment before he sank his teeth into her neck.

"Am I interrupting?"

Urian bared his fangs as he recognized that deep baritone. This was the one he affectionately called the Muppet Dark-Hunter because his accent reminded him of the Swedish Chef.

The huge bastard jerked his father away from Cassandra. Which was good, but . . .

Urian ran to check on him while the Dark-Hunter whisked his sister-in-law up into his arms and ran with her. "Get them!" he shouted at his team, knowing they'd never catch up. So it gave them a chance to get away, and Urian an excuse to let them.

Or so he thought.

No sooner did he touch his father's shoulder than his father's eyes turned red and he sprang to life. Worse, he shifted into his dragon form and launched into flight.

Cursing, Urian went running to catch them.

He manifested a motorcycle just so that he could chase after Wulf's dark green Expedition.

Cassandra and crew had just locked the doors when his father struck the roof in his large black dragon form.

"Let her out and you can live," the dragon said in Stryker's voice.

Wulf answered by putting his SUV in reverse and gunning it. He turned the wheel and sent the beast flying.

The dragon shrieked and blew a blast of fire at them. The Dark-Hunter kept going, without slowing. The dragon took flight and dove at them, then arced up, high into the sky, before it vanished into a shimmery cloud of gold.

"What the hell was that?" Wulf asked.

"He's Apostolos," Cassandra murmured as she struggled to snap herself out of her daze. "The son of the Atlantean Destroyer and a god in his own right. We're so screwed."

Wulf let out a disgusted sound. "Yeah well, I don't let anyone screw me until they kiss me and since there's not even a snowball's chance in hell of me kissing that bastard, we're not screwed."

But as his Expedition was suddenly surrounded by eight Daimons on motorcycles, he reconsidered that.

For three seconds at least.

Wulf laughed. "You know the beauty of driving one of these?"

"No."

He swerved his Expedition into three of the bikes and knocked them from the road. "You can swat a Daimon like a mosquito."

"Well, since they're both bloodsucking insects, I say go for it."

Urian wasn't amused as he heard their conversation. And definitely not when Wulf almost clipped him. Braking, he motioned for the other four Daimons with him to let them go.

Not just because it was Phoebe's sister, but because he didn't want to see anyone else die tonight.

He swerved his Hayabusa and went back to check the three Illuminati who'd been wrecked to see if they needed medical attention to get home.

March 9, 2004

Stryker paced the floor of the dimly lit banquet hall, wanting blood and not from one of their own. For three weeks now they hadn't been able to find a single trace of the Dark-Hunter Wulf Tryggvason or the Apollite heiress Cassandra Peters, who was the final key to eliminating their curse for once and for all and getting Helios off their backs!

How could they go into hiding so effectively? It didn't make any sense!

He had Urian working on it now, but it seemed useless. "How hard can it be to find where a Dark-Hunter lives?"

"They are crafty, *kyrios*," Zolan said from his right.

Zolan was his third-in-command and one of Stryker's most trusted soldiers, after Urian and Trates. He'd been promoted through the Spathi ranks for his ability to murder ruthlessly and to never show mercy to anyone.

Like Stryker, he chose to dye his hair black and wore the Spathi symbol of a yellow sun with a dragon in its center—the emblem of Apollymi the Destroyer.

"If they weren't," Zolan continued, "we'd be able to track and kill them through our servants while they slept."

Stryker turned on Zolan with a glare so malevolent that the Daimon shrank away from him. Only his son held enough courage to not flinch from his anger. Urian's bravery knew no equal.

Out of nowhere, Xedrix appeared before him in the hall. Unlike the Daimons, Xedrix didn't bow or acknowledge Stryker's elevated stature in their world. Most of the time, Xedrix treated him as more of a servant than a master, which pissed him off to no uncertain end.

No doubt the demon thought Apollymi would always protect him, but Stryker knew the truth. His mother loved *him* absolutely and no one else.

"Her Benevolent Grace wishes a word with you," the demon said in a low, even tone.

Benevolent Grace. As if! Every time Stryker heard that title for Apollymi, he wanted to laugh but knew better. His mother didn't really have a sense of humor.

Without delay, he willed himself to her palace and walked through the double door that led out to her private gardens where she was waiting for him.

As usual, Apollymi leaned over her pool where black water flowed backward up a glittering pipe from this world into the human realm. There was a fine, rainbow mist and vapors around the water. It was here the goddess could scry so that she knew what was happening on earth. Past. Present. Future.

"She is pregnant," the goddess announced without turning around.

Stryker knew the *she* that the goddess referred to was Cassandra.

"How can that be?"

The goddess lifted her hands up and drew a circle in the air. Water from the mirror formed like a crystal ball. Even though nothing but air held it, it swirled about until it held an image of the woman they both wanted dead. There was nothing in the ball to give him any indication of how to find Cassandra.

Apollymi dragged one fingernail through the image, causing it to shake and distort. "Artemis is interfering with us."

"There's still time to kill both mother and child."

She smiled at that. "Yes, there is." She opened her hands and the water arced from the ball, back into her pool. "Now is the time to strike. The Elekti is being held by Artemis. He can't stop you. He won't even know that you attack."

Stryker flinched at the mention of the Elekti. Like the Abadonna, Stryker was forbidden to attack him.

He hated restrictions.

"We don't know where to attack," he told his mother. "We've been searching—"

"Take one of the ceredons. My pets can find them."

"I thought they were forbidden to leave this realm."

A cruel half smile curved her lips. "Artemis broke the rules, so shall I. Now go, *m'gios,* and do me proud."

Stryker nodded and turned about sharply. He took three steps before the Destroyer's voice gave him pause.

"Remember, Strykerius, kill the heiress before the Elekti returns. You are not to engage him. Ever."

He stopped but didn't look back. "Why have I always been forbidden to touch him?"

"Ours is not to question why. Ours is but to live or to die."

He ground his teeth as she gave him the human quote.

When she spoke again, the coldness in her tone only angered him more. "The answer to that is how much do you value your life, Strykerius. I have kept you close all these centuries and I have no desire to see you dead."

"The Elekti can't kill me. I'm a god."

"And greater gods than you have fallen. Many of them to my wrath. Heed my words, boy. Heed them well."

Irritated by that, Stryker continued on his way, pausing only long enough to unleash Kyklonas, whose name meant "tornado." Once unleashed, the ceredon, like him and Urian, was a deadly menace.

"Keep hitting them with everything!"

Urian cringed at his father's orders. They were blasting Wulf's mansion like the final round of *Call of Duty*. It was a wonder someone hadn't called in the National Guard on them.

This is ridiculous!

But he didn't dare speak reason to his father when he was in this mood. It would be the same as trying to reason with King Leonides, and he had no desire to be kicked into a spiked pit or fed to lions.

And he was equally shocked when Kat appeared in the guardhouse with them. She winced as her gaze went to the two dead men on the floor that his father had slaughtered on arrival. Not to mention the dozen Daimons his father had on the lawn preparing for another round of attacks.

Only four Daimons were inside the guardhouse. Him, his father, Icarus, and Trates.

Trates looked up from the monitors and went pale at the appearance of the one person none of them could harm.

"How did you get in here?" Kat demanded.

Urian gave her a droll stare. "We walked."

Stryker turned slowly, methodically around to face her with a sardonic grin. There was no fear in him, only wry amusement. Unlike Urian, he wasn't quite as sarcastic. "The guards came outside when we ate the pizza deliveryman and tried to stop us. We dragged them inside after they were dead."

"You are so evil."

Urian snorted. "Judgmental much?"

Ignoring his comment, his father took pride in Kat's insults. "Thank you, love, I pride myself on that."

Kat opened the portal back to Kalosis. "It's time for you to all go home."

Stryker looked at the opening, then laughed. "'Fraid not, sweetie. Mama likes me better at the moment. So you can shove that portal up your very attractive ass. Me and my boys have work to do. Either join us or leave."

Urian didn't miss the light of fear in Kat's eyes that those words wrought. He couldn't blame her. His father was terrifying. "You *have* to go. Those are the rules. The portal opens and you have to walk through it."

Stryker came forward, his eyes sinister and cold. "No, we don't."

The portal closed.

She gasped. The Destroyer had given him a key too and placed him in control.

Stryker cupped her face with his hand. "It's a pity she protects you so. Otherwise I would have had a taste of you centuries ago."

She glared her fury at him. "Get your hand off me or lose it."

To her surprise, he obeyed, but not before he kissed her rudely.

Kat shrieked and slapped him.

He laughed. "Go home, little girl. If you stay here, you might get hurt."

Her body shaking, Kat flashed back into the house.

Urian shook his head. "You shouldn't treat her like that." The words came out before he could stop himself.

His father passed a disbelieving stare toward him. "Pardon?"

"You taught us better and if we'd ever grabbed a woman or spoken to one like you just did, you'd have torn our asses up."

"I know. There's just something about her that makes me insane."

Not wanting to argue, Urian went back to watching the monitors.

A few minutes later, he saw a bright flash and heard his father's violent curse.

"Careful," his father warned his men as they fired another round at the house. "Not that it's likely, but give them a chance to come out before you blow the house apart."

"Why?" Trates asked. "I thought the objective was to kill the heiress."

Urian gave the man an irritated stare that said, *Are you totally stupid?* "Yes, but if we hurt the Abadonna in the process, we're going to find out what it feels like to be turned inside out. Literally. Like most beings, I actually like the fact that my skin is *outside* my body."

"She's immortal," Trates argued. "What's a bomb to her?"

"Immortal like us, bonehead." Urian snatched the rocket launcher from Trates's hand and handed it off to Icarus. "Blow her body apart and she *will* die. None of you want to know what the Destroyer would do to us if that happens."

Icarus aimed more carefully.

Stryker nodded his approval to his son, then projected his thoughts to the rest of his team. "Watch the exits. I know the Dark-Hunter will have a back way out of this place. When they run, you'd better catch them. Stand ready."

Stryker studied the security cameras closely. He knew the heiress and her guards wouldn't stay inside much longer. His men had already blown up the entire garage and were now slowly shooting into the house, section by section. There was a lot of exterior damage, but he couldn't really tell how much was being done internally.

Not that it mattered. If this didn't work, they'd burn it down. He already had the flamethrowers on standby.

Anyone worth his salt would have exit tunnels. And Wulf was certainly worth his salt.

Urian had found several exits so far.

His son just had to make sure they had found them all *before* their prey left the premises.

Urian? He projected his thoughts out to his son. *Are you in position?*

Yes. We have all of the exits covered.

Where are you?

The back lawn. Why? Is something going wrong?
No, I just want to make sure we can get to them.
They're ours, Solren. Relax.
I will after *she's dead.*

Urian *cursed at* the madness in his skull that was giving him a migraine. It was bad enough to have the human souls in his head screaming at him all the time. Now his father was a raging lunatic while he silently shouted orders at everyone as he sought to micromanage every single nanobit of this night.

Not to mention, Trates was so terrified of making a mistake that his current adrenaline level was running at scared Chihuahua on steroids with double espresso shots every ten and a half seconds.

Factor in all the other Daimons on the property who were shitting their pants and ...

No wonder he kept getting nosebleeds.

"Are you all right, baby?"

He melted as Phoebe placed her soft hand to his forehead. "No. I'm a dumb sonofabitch for letting you talk me into this."

She rose up on her tiptoes to kiss his lips. "It's the only way. My sister would never trust you without me. And I don't want to risk a Dark-Hunter killing you."

Funny, he didn't want to risk *her,* at all. "He lays one hand on you and so help me—"

"Shh—" She placed her fingers over his lips to silence his protests. "We have to hurry, right?"

He hated whenever she used his words against him. Phoebe was the most potent weapon the universe had ever devised to lay him low. And honestly? He was hoping to delay long enough that they might screw up and capture her sister, kill the bitch, and he wouldn't have to risk his wife. *That* would suit him fine.

Better Cassandra die than Phoebe, and if the curse ended in the process ...

Even fucking better.

"Urian," Phoebe said calmly, "we're not moving forward."

He growled low in his throat. "All right." Hating himself for the fact that this had disaster written all over it and he was actually participating in something he knew was stupid, risky, and against every survival instinct he possessed, he took her to the one place he hadn't told his father about.

The boathouse.

Of all the exits for the house that he'd found, Urian figured this was the most likely escape route. For four people, it would have the most cover and be the quietest means to get past an enemy without being seen. Especially one who kept carpet bombing them.

Besides, who would expect a boat? And what were the odds that your enemy would just happen to have a boat on them to pursue you with?

Yeah, a boat escape made the most sense. Plus the bastard was a Viking. Taking off on water would be his first thought. Not the thought of a normal well-adjusted modern person, but for a Viking raider ...

Boat.

So here they were.

Urian pressed Phoebe back into the shadows. "You wait here and don't move. Let me secure the perimeter."

"Aye, sir." She gave him a mock salute.

Rolling his eyes, he headed for the back door.

Phoebe pressed her lips together as she admired the sweetest ass and deadliest walk any man had ever had in the history of mankind. Really, no one could surpass Urian's. Even Davyn agreed and he'd been married to the man's twin brother.

That said a lot.

Though there were times when she wondered if she should be jealous that Davyn was so preoccupied by her husband's hindquarters. Or even worried, given the way Davyn joked.

Thankfully, she knew her husband was loyal to a fault. Otherwise, she would be a little nervous given how much time they were forced to spend apart. It took a lot of trust to let a man that hot live away from her for the majority of their marriage. Likewise, it took a lot of trust for Urian to leave her alone, too. Because the loneliness was hard to bear.

Not wanting to think about that, Phoebe glanced around the humongous building she was in. It was larger and more elegant than most houses, and given the extreme wealth she'd known growing up, it took a lot to impress her.

This place did that in spades. All around her was an impressive collection of high-end, high-tech boats that even her dad would have drooled over. You could tell the Dark-Hunter who owned this place had been a Viking in his mortal life. He obviously was still drawn to the sea and all things nautical.

Earlier, she'd gone exploring through the second floor, which had four bedrooms, a kitchen, and living, dining, and game rooms. Which was weird that he'd have it set up that way given how huge his main house was . . . or had been before Stryker had bombed half of it into oblivion trying to kill her sister.

Urian hadn't been kidding about his father. That man was insane. He truly wouldn't stop at anything to kill them. The car bomb he'd used on her and her sister and mother should have told her that, but she barely remembered that night. It was as if her mind had been unable to handle it and so she'd blocked it out.

All she really recalled was Urian waving as they drove by, and then waking up in Elysia, with him telling her everything would be okay.

She didn't know what she'd do without him. How she could cope.

But damn, his father was a special level of hell that made no sense whatsoever. How could Urian have come from that whackadoodle?

And speaking of that . . .

Urian appeared with not one but two bodies.

Phoebe gasped at the sight and the irritated look on his face. She knew they couldn't be Daimons because they were actual bodies. "What happened?"

"Two of our men got in the way."

"Those aren't Daimons."

"Worse ... Apollites. But I couldn't risk them telling my father about the boathouse." He placed them on the floor, near the rear of the building. With a disgusted look he wiped at his nose. "Stay here. Let me make sure there's not any more. Be right back."

Phoebe covered her face, as she felt terrible for having caused this. Though Urian didn't say anything, she knew the hell she was putting him through. All these centuries, he'd fought and risked his life for the Apollymians. They *were* his family.

And she'd pitted him against them.

Pitted him against the father he adored. For her.

I suck as a human being.

She hated that it came to this. That she was forcing him to compromise everything he held dear to be with her and risk his life. It was so unfair.

Yet he never said a word.

She looked at the bodies and cringed. How could he not hate her? That was her worst fear. That one day he'd wake up and realize she wasn't worth *this*.

In that moment, Phoebe was truly humbled by what she had. It was rare to find anyone in life who would be loyal to you. Brother. Sister. Parent. Friend. Even a spouse or child. Betrayal was a natural part of life.

To find someone who would actually kill to protect you? Who would risk and sacrifice their life every single day to keep you safe, without question, and without asking anything in return, and to never, ever throw it in your face? Not even on those days when she was bitchy for no reason ...

She wasn't worthy of a love so pure, and in her heart she knew that. As much as she loved him, she didn't know if she could do what he did with the courage he showed.

Damn.

Suddenly, she heard whispering and the sound of feet shuffling in the darkness.

Terrified it might be her psycho father-in-law, she darted into a small closet to hide. Thus proving to herself just what a coward she was and why if anything ever happened to Urian, she'd be lost.

Worse? She'd be dead.

Slowly, she heard something scraping and moving around like some kind of giant sewer rat that brought up images of *Willard* in her head. For that matter, every horror movie with giant rodents she'd ever seen. So help her God, if anything furry with whiskers came scurrying out, she was going to scream like a B movie actress and cause an avalanche! She'd break the sound barrier. She would!

There better not be rats in this place ...

Then all of a sudden, there was no more motion or sound.

Still panicking, Phoebe held her breath. Was it a trick? Had the little bastards frozen to death? It was cold out here.

Or maybe it was a trap to lure her out? Stryker could be treacherous that way. She'd heard all kinds of stories from Urian about things his father had done to people over the centuries. She wouldn't put anything past him.

Still there was no motion in the room. No sound of someone or something walking about. She bit her nails in nervousness as she scanned the shadows with her sharp Daimon eyes, trying to detect anything at all.

Yet the only thing she could hear was the creaking of the ice and the howling wind outside the building. And of course, the stupid human voice in her head whining about being trapped there. *That* made her want to scream! But she was kind of used to that going on.

Just as she was about to leave her closet to find Urian, she heard someone moving just in front of her again.

Oh holy crap, they were coming up through the floor only a few feet from where she was hiding!

If that was Stryker or one of his Illuminati, she was dead!

Terrified, she tried to think of what to do, but unlike Urian, she didn't know how to teleport. Crap, crap, crap! Trying to control her breathing, she pressed herself as far back into the shadows as she could and prayed they didn't see her.

To her absolute horror, the hole opened and sure enough something furry and whiskered came out. Only this bastard was six and a half feet tall. Well muscled. And he was the mortal enemy of her people. Christ almighty! He looked like Sasquatch!

Phoebe felt her eyes bugging out of her head at the lumbering sight of him. Scared and furious, she looked around for a harpoon gun to spear the whale. Just as she was about to grab a flare, she realized he was pulling her sister up to stand beside him.

Joy replaced her fear as tears blinded her and froze in her eyelashes. She hadn't seen Cassie in years. She was so fixated on her that she barely registered the other two people who came up behind her sister. She was tempted to rush forward, but the giant with Cassie terrified her.

"Okay," Sasquatch whispered. "It looks good so far. I want you"—he said to Cassandra—"and Chris to stay back. If anything happens, you two dodge back into the tunnels and press the red button to lock the door behind you."

"What about you and Kat?" Cassandra indicated Sasquatch and the tall blond woman who'd climbed out with them.

"We'll take care of ourselves. You and Chris are the important things."

Phoebe frowned. So this was the Muppet Dark-Hunter. Now that she heard his accent, Urian's nickname for him totally made sense.

He gestured at the boats that were trapped in chains, suspended over the ice. "It'll take a couple of minutes to lower the airboat from its harness down to the ice." He glanced around. "Let's hope the Daimons don't hear it."

Cassandra nodded and kissed him lightly. "Be careful."

Phoebe gaped at her sister's lack of taste. Sure, Muppet was cute and all, but seriously?

He was a Dark-Hunter! How disgusting was *that*? What kind of Apollite could even think of crawling into bed with one of those animals who'd been hunting and stalking their race for thousands and thousands of years? One who'd been heartlessly slaughtering them for generations!

Gah! Her sister was an idiot! If their mother were still alive, she'd be the first to beat her!

Wulf hugged her sister gently, then opened the door. He took a step out, then acted weird.

Ah, crap, he must have found the bodies Urian had dumped there. Which meant he'd panic and do something stupid. Because that was what Dark-Hunters did.

Something stupid that got her kind killed.

I have to do something. And quick before he exposed them and caused Urian to be harmed.

She was running through her options when he pulled his retractable sword from his boot. *Now or never, Pheebs . . .*

With a deep breath for courage, she came out of the shadows and moved toward him. He prepared to attack.

"It's okay," Phoebe said quickly, praying he didn't stab her. "I'm a friend."

The look on his face said he wasn't buying it at all.

But thankfully, Cassie recognized her. Gasping, she stared at her in utter disbelief.

Time stopped as Phoebe took in her sister's long strawberry-blond hair and those features that were way too close to their mother's. She'd missed her family so much!

"Phoebe?" Cassie breathed. "It's really you?"

Tears blurred her vision as she choked on her tears. "It's me, Cassie. I'm here to help you."

Her sister stepped back and collided with the much smaller dark-haired guy who stood behind her. He was eyeing Phoebe with all kinds of malice. And so was the tall blond woman who looked like she ought to be on an island somewhere shooting the bikini issue of *Sports Illustrated* rather than locked in a boathouse being chased by Daimons.

But it was the doubt in Cassandra's eyes that stung. "You're supposed to be dead."

"I *am* dead," Phoebe whispered.

"You're a Daimon." There was no missing the accusation and judgment in the Dark-Hunter's tone.

Phoebe nodded.

"Oh, Phoebe ... " Cassandra's voice was thick with disappointment. "How could you?"

Seriously? Her, too? Like she had *any* room to talk given the company she was in? At least Phoebe hadn't turned traitor. "Don't judge me. I had my reasons. Now we have to get *you* to safety."

Cassandra gaped. "Like I'm going to trust *you*?" She actually bowed up on her and acted as if she'd attack. "I remember Uncle Demos."

So did she. There was no forgetting a trelos when they turned and came after you with that kind of fury. It was terrifying and now that she had the demons in her head, she understood. But still ... "I'm not Uncle Demos and I have no intention of turning you into me."

Phoebe took a step toward her, but that hulking, irritating Dark-Hunter prevented her from getting any closer to Cassandra.

Phoebe glared at him for his interference. She was family. He was not! Desperate, she looked at her sister. "Please, Cassie, you have to believe me. I would never, ever harm you. I swear it on Mom's soul."

She'd barely finished speaking when Urian came through the door from outside. Phoebe cringed at his bad timing. Urian wasn't known for his peacekeeping techniques. More for whenever someone was ready for nuclear fallout.

The blond with her sister gasped.

"Hurry, Phee," he whispered. "I can't keep this covered much longer." Ever defiant, he met the Dark-Hunter's gaze without flinching.

There was no missing the anger and hatred of the two men as they barely restrained their urge to go at it. It sizzled in the air and made every Daimon instinct in her body rabid.

"Why are *you* helping us?" the Dark-Hunter demanded.

Urian sneered at him. "Like I give a rat's ass about you, Dark-Hunter. I'm only here to help my wife protect her sister."

The blond woman gaped. "Urian has a heart? Who knew?"

Urian passed an equally repugnant stare toward her. "Shut up, Abadonna."

Now it was Phoebe's turn to gape. That bombshell was Katra? That was the Kat Urian had told her about so many times over the years? Funny how he'd forgotten a few details.

Like the fact that she was fucking stunning! And inhumanly gorgeous.

She barely suppressed her anger as a wave of jealousy flew through her. What else had he left out?

He better not *know* know her, or else one or both of them were going to be bald later.

But that thought scattered as he ignored the blonde and neared her and kissed her cheek. Phoebe smiled at him. "Urian's the one who saved me when Mom died. He pulled me from the car after the bomb exploded and hid me. He tried to save Mom and Nia too but couldn't get to them in time."

By her sister's face, she could tell Cassandra didn't know what to think about that. And she couldn't blame her. It didn't make sense that a Daimon, let alone one related to Stryker, would help them when all their lives they had been pursued by Urian's kind. "Why?"

"There's no time for this," Urian hissed. "My father isn't a stupid man. He'll catch on quickly when he doesn't hear from the two dead Apollites."

Phoebe nodded, then turned back to Cassandra. "I'm asking you to trust me, Cassie. I swear you won't regret it."

Cassandra exchanged frowns with the Dark-Hunter and Kat. "I think we can trust her."

Sasquatch glanced to Urian, then to Kat. "You said they were sadistic. Any chance they're playing with our heads?"

Urian gave a low, bitter laugh at that. "You have no idea."

Phoebe smacked her husband in the stomach. "Behave, Uri. You're not making this any easier."

Scowling at her, he rubbed his stomach where she'd hit him but didn't say anything else.

"Go for it," Kat said. "If he's lying, I now know how to hurt him." Her gaze went meaningfully to Phoebe.

Urian went ramrod stiff. "Destroyer or no, you *ever* touch her and I will kill you, Katra."

Sasquatch made some kind of Wookiee noise. She half-expected him to raise a rifle over his Bantha and *grr* at her. Okay, that was a Tusken Raider, but still ... "Then we understand each other. Because if anything happens to Cassandra, Kat is the least of your problems."

And of course his being so macho and overbearing only notched her own alpha's testosterone levels into overdrive. So naturally Urian stepped forward intending to beat the utter crap out of him. Which was the last thing they needed. With a grimace, Phoebe caught her teddy bear and forced him back. "You said we have to hurry," she reminded him. She made sure to swipe her finger over his nipple several times to get his attention on something other than murder and mayhem.

Lucky for the Sasquatch, it worked.

Urian's rigid features softened as he looked down at her and nodded. Without another word, he led them toward a black air-boat that was already on the ice, waiting for them.

The human male climbed on board first, followed by Kat.

Cassandra followed suit. "Is this the same boat the Canadian Mounties use for search and rescue?"

The Dark-Hunter stiffened as if the question offended him. "Same company makes both, but I'd like to think mine is a bit nicer."

Phoebe passed a look to Urian and rolled her eyes.

He laughed silently at her.

Though to be honest as she climbed on board the boat, she had to admit that he wasn't really lying. That boat was exceptional. Plush to the extreme, right down to the padded chairs.

"Yeah," Chris said as he took a seat and strapped himself in. "Dudley Do-Right is us."

Phoebe scowled as it dawned on her that Urian was still on the dock and didn't appear to have any plans to join them. Surely, he wasn't going to stay. Not after *this* ... "Come with us, Uri," she begged, reaching up to take his hand into hers. "They'll slaughter you if they find out about this."

The pain on Urian's face as he stared longingly at her made her want to cry. His grip trembled as he held her hand. "I can't, baby, you know I can't. I have to stay and cover your tracks, but I promise I'll be in touch as soon as I'm able." He kissed Phoebe passionately, then kissed her hand and let her go. "Be safe."

"You, too."

He nodded, then removed the last bit of harness rigging. "Take care of my wife, Dark-Hunter."

Wulf glanced at Phoebe and nodded. "Thanks, Daimon."

Urian snorted. "Bet you never thought you'd utter those words."

Urian raised the doors to the dock at the same time a group of Daimons broke into the boathouse.

Phoebe gasped and ran toward him. She couldn't leave while he was in danger. Oh God no! But the weaselly little human pulled her back as the Dark-Hunter gunned the engine and flew north over the ice. Luckily, the wind was with them and they accelerated quickly.

"No. No!" Phoebe shrieked as they sped across the lake. Her heart hammered in denial as terror shredded her. "We can't leave him."

Though his face was sympathetic, she wasn't fooled for a minute. Like a human or a Dark-Hunter would ever care what happened to their kind.

"We have no choice," the human said. "I'm sorry."

Yeah, right.

Even though her heart was broken, Phoebe didn't cry. Urian had taught her better than that. He was a warrior, battle born and battle hardened. As his wife, she would honor his courage and show the same strength he did. So she breathed through her pain and forced herself to stand at the rear of the boat, staring desperately where he'd been, hoping to glimpse some sign of his fate.

You better be okay. I won't forgive you if you die saving me.

Cassandra held on tightly to her seat belt. "Hey, Chris? How fast are we going?"

"Over a hundred at least. These things can move as fast as one hundred forty with the wind, but only about forty against it."

The blonde moved to stand beside her. "He'll be okay, Phoebe. His father wouldn't really hurt him. Stryker may be psychotic, but he loves Urian."

She didn't believe that for an instant, and Kat was a fool if she did. Damn her husband for his protective ways.

And damn her for asking him to do this.

Hating herself, she glared at Cassandra, hoping that she didn't live to regret this action. Then she turned to the Dark-Hunter. "Keep going north. We have a safe place where we can hide all of you."

Two seconds after those words were spoken, a horrendous shriek sounded above the boat engine, winds, and cracking ice. It was followed by the distinct sound of wings flapping.

Plugging her sensitive ears, Phoebe looked up and gaped. Holy Katateros, it was a dragon!

And not just any dragon. That would be Urian's psycho dad after them.

You better not have eaten my husband . . .

"Oh my . . . " Cassandra didn't finish her sentence. She stood there as catatonic as Phoebe felt.

Kat threw herself over Cassandra.

Stryker shrieked louder as if frustrated by her actions. Fire blew across the prow of the boat, making Phoebe duck. The Dark-Hunter didn't slow down at all. He pulled his gun out and fired up at the beast.

Still in dragon form, Stryker dove straight for them, screaming as he came. When the bullets struck him, the dragon recoiled. Yet those wounds didn't faze his animal form at all.

Stryker continued toward them with a single-minded determination.

Closer.

Closer . . .

If anything, it just seemed to piss the creature off.

The Dark-Hunter reloaded his clip and fired more rounds.

Then just as Phoebe was sure they'd be toast, Stryker vanished.

For a full ten seconds, no one moved.

Chris popped his head up like a scared meerkat. "What happened?"

"He must have been recalled," Kat answered. "It's the only thing that could have stopped him like that."

The Dark-Hunter finally slowed a degree. "Recalled by whom?"

"The Destroyer," Phoebe said. "She won't let him hurt Kat." For reasons no one knew, she was more sacred to Apollymi than anyone.

"And just why is that, Kat?" the Dark-Hunter asked.

Kat appeared uncomfortable with that question. "Like Stryker, I'm one of her servants."

Cassie frowned. "I thought you served Artemis."

"I serve them both."

Phoebe scoffed at that. No one could serve two pantheons. She knew better.

Cassandra tilted her head. "Question? What happens when you have a conflict of interest? Which one of them will you follow then, Kat?"

D*awn was coming.* Since neither Phoebe nor her enemy was immune to the sun, they had switched the boat for a custom-built, heavily modified Land Rover that Urian had left for them to use. Chris was asleep in the backseat, sitting between her and Kat with his head on Kat's shoulder, while Kat looked out the window.

They had left the boat behind well over an hour ago and were now racing for Elysia.

How weird to be in this stupid car without Uri. She'd always thought it odd that he wanted it. He'd never bothered with the human world at all.

Until her.

But since they'd been married, he'd tried to make himself a bit more "human" to placate her. And though Braden had insisted she never leave the compound, Shanus had relaxed those orders once he'd taken over as their leader.

So six years ago, Urian had bought this silly car so that the two of them could go on "dates" because she'd made him watch a couple of John Hughes movies with her and had told him that the only thing she really missed about her old life was "dating."

They'd actually fought over the car.

"*Uri, it's stupid!*"

"*No, Phee. I've been doing research. It's not a date unless you drive somewhere.*"

She'd snorted at the very thought. "*What? You learned to drive?*"

"*Yeah, kind of. Don't you trust me?*"

"*With driving? Hell, no!*"

"*C'mon, I paid a lot of money for a fake license. Took lessons and everything. Besides it's more a tank than a car. Nothing can hurt you in it. It's shielded and everything. I made sure of it. I promise you'll have fun. It'll be your best birthday ever.*"

And it had been. God, she loved that man more than her life. If anything happened to him because of her . . .

She was sick with worry. There was no telling what was going on right now in Kalosis. The anger and fury Stryker would have over failing this mission. And Urian as his prime commander would bear the brunt of his wrath.

Had she chosen her sister's life for her husband's? Had she repaid Urian's kindness in saving her life by demanding his own?

All he'd ever known from women was betrayal. Now she might have just given him the worst one yet.

Cassandra turned around in the front seat to look at her. "How much longer?"

"Not much farther." She hoped.

Cassie had to the nerve to take Sasquatch's hand. "Will we make it before sunrise?"

Phoebe looked away before she slapped them both, which

would be a suicidal thing to do since Sasquatch was driving. "It's going to be close." Then under her breath, she mumbled, "Real close."

Then, when her sister started making goo-goo eyes at Sasquatch, she really feared she might hurl.

Luckily, they were nearing the next turn, so she took the opportunity to sit forward in the seat and break that shit up. Wedging herself between them, she pointed to the small trail where there was no road. "Turn right there."

Sasquatch didn't question it. She'd give him bonus points for that.

They crashed through the woods with relative ease, which was something Urian always loved to do. As he so often said about his SUV—*Drive it like you stole it.* The armor plating made it relatively easy to plow straight through smaller trees and travel over the snow, ice, and debris. The only thing missing was her gorgeous Daimon's laughter and that wicked grin as he blasted some obnoxious metal music while he slung them all over the woods.

Gah, the weird things her husband did for fun.

She sat back and buckled herself in as Sasquatch cut the lights off so that he could see better. While she trusted Urian's driving, she didn't trust Sasquatch at all. The Land Rover bounced over the uneven terrain like a bucking bronco.

Chris came awake with a curse. "Is Stryker back?"

"No," Kat snorted. "We had to leave the road."

Sasquatch slowed a bit so as not to throw one of the tank tracks that replaced the SUV's tires. They were a lot sturdier in this climate but were still a fair cry from being infallible, and the last thing they needed was to be stranded out in the open with daylight so close.

Just as the sun peeked over the mountains, they broke through the trees and came to the concealed entrance for Elysia. Phoebe let out a relieved breath as she saw Shanus and two counselors standing outside it. Waiting.

Cassandra hissed and released his hand.

"It's okay." Phoebe opened her door and ran over to them. She lifted the hood on her jacket to protect herself from the rising sun.

Tall and blond, Shanus stood in the shadows with his companions. "Cutting it close, aren't you?"

"Don't even. It's been a rough night."

"Where's Urian?"

She bit back her tears. "He's not with us."

"He let someone else drive his truck?"

"'Let' is a word for it." She gestured at the SUV. "He'll die when he finds out it's a Dark-Hunter."

Shanus's eyes bugged out, along with those of the two men with him. "Are you out of your fucking mind? You can't bring one of *them* here! You know better!"

"We have to let him in."

"No! And I mean no! No, no, no! All kinds of no!"

"Shanus—"

"No, Phoebe, no!"

"I'll tell Urian. You don't want me to make that call."

A tic started in his jaw. "You're making it really hard to like you right now."

"I know, and I swear if he does anything wrong you can kill him. Urian will help."

He let out an exasperated sigh. "Fine, but only because it's dawn and I don't want to burst into flames." He glared at her. "Damn you!"

"Believe me, I know."

Of all the crappy timing, Sasquatch and Kat picked then to get out of the SUV and head for them. If that weren't bad enough, Sasquatch had his hand on his sword as if *they* were the problem here.

Yeah, right. Gah ... Dark-Hunters and their arrogance!

Phoebe glared at Sasquatch. "Do you mind, Dark-Hunter?" She gestured at the sun. "We're running out of time. Don't need your attitude right now. But if you hand over your weapons instead of preening like a peacock, it sure would help facilitate things and go a long way in helping me convince my guys that you're not here to kill anyone. And it would allow Cassandra to get to the Apollite doctor who's inside waiting, and one who actually knows how to tend an expectant mother in her unique condition."

Sasquatch looked over his shoulder at her sister before he gave a subtle nod. His face unreadable, he finally handed over all his weapons without protesting.

Grateful to the gods, Phoebe finally let out a relieved breath. "Thank you!"

"You're not welcome."

Ignoring Sasquatch's dig, Phoebe clapped Shanus on the arm while the two councilmen led him inside. Then she and Kat went to get her sister and Chris.

The expression on Cassandra's face said that her sister wanted to claw out her eyes for letting them take her large hairy boyfriend. "What's going on?"

Kat let out a tired breath. "They're taking Wulf into custody to make sure he doesn't hurt any of them. Come on, they have a doctor inside waiting for you."

Cassandra hesitated as she looked in the direction where they'd vanished. "Do you really trust them?"

"I don't know. Do you?"

"I trust Phoebe. I think."

Kat laughed at that.

Phoebe didn't find it funny at all.

Cassandra scooted out of the truck and let Kat lead her and Chris into the cave while Phoebe stewed over her sister's response, especially given the fact that it was her husband who'd just put his life on the line to save them all. How dare they!

Ungrateful bastards all!

But she managed to be a little compassionate. After all, her sister was pregnant and she was the last surviving member of her family. "Don't be afraid, Cassie. We all know how important you and your baby are. No one here will hurt either of you. I swear it."

"Who are *we?*"

"This is an Apollite community." Phoebe led them deeper into the cave, past the hired human contract mercenaries who guarded the entrance during the daylight hours. "One of the older ones in North America."

Making sure everyone was inside and it was safe, Phoebe placed her hand against the Coil Stone, where a spring release opened the elevator door.

Chris gave an exaggerated gape. "Holy hand grenade, Batman, it's a bat cave!"

Phoebe smirked at the college-aged guy with dark hair who looked like the Dark-Hunter's much smaller kid brother. He was actually really cute in a very wholesome, innocent kind of way. Oddly enough, he was growing on Phoebe.

Had he not been a Squire to her enemy, and if they'd met under another set of circumstances, she could have seen them being friends. He was likable and friendly. Even funny at times.

Sasquatch, on the other hand, she wanted to stab every time she glanced in his direction. And it took everything she had not to cut his head off.

Gah, Cassandra! Just ... damn!

"Oh, come on!" Chris glanced around their group like an exuberant kid. "Someone other than me has to see the humor in this?" He looked around their unamused three faces, then deflated. "Guess not."

Cassandra entered the elevator first. "What about the men I saw outside? Who are they?"

Phoebe tried her best not to think about the group who'd met them. "Those are our ruling council. Nothing can be done here without their direct approval."

Kat and Chris joined them. The door to the elevator closed.

"Are there any Daimons here?" Chris asked as Phoebe pressed a button to start the elevator on its long descent to the facility where she lived.

"The only Daimon in this community is me. They allow me to live here because they owe Urian for his help. So long as I don't

draw attention to myself or their existence, I'm allowed to stay."
She waited for one of them to make a nasty comment about that,
but wisely, they kept their mouths shut.

However, she knew her sister well enough to see the mistrust
in Cassandra's eyes. Her sister was afraid of her.

So be it. She'd risked everything for Cassie. Everything.

And she hadn't even had the decency to say, *Thank you. You
and your husband might be Daimons, but how kind and generous
of you to risk your lives, for your husband to kill people he con-
siders family, and for you to hand your throats over so that I and
my baby and idiot Dark-Hunter Sasquatch can survive tonight.*
Really, was that too much to ask? A basic, simple thank-you?

Figured, right? Phoebe had forgotten how selfish her sister
could be.

When the doors opened, Cassie gasped at something Phoebe
had gotten used to long ago. But she remembered the first time
Urian had brought her here in 1990. It did look like something
out of some science fiction movie. Everything was fashioned like
some Isaac Asimov or Larry Niven future city. Made of steel and
concrete, the walls were painted with brilliant murals of bright
landscapes awash in sunshine that their kind had never seen
except in pictures.

Urian spent a lot of time when he was here staring at this one
piece in particular. And going through her old photos of her with
her family, asking her what sunshine felt like.

That was when it hurt most.

Because she was part human, up until she'd become a Daimon,
she had some tolerance to sunshine. She couldn't sunbathe
or swim. But she could take a few minutes outside without
becoming dust.

Urian couldn't. And so Phoebe had done her best to make
him understand what used to piss her off because she'd never
realized how lucky she had it. Not until she met the boy who
had never seen daylight at all. To this day, his story about trying
to see a glimpse of the sun with his brother Paris brought tears
to her eyes.

Damn her sister if anything had happened to him.

Wiping at her eyes, Phoebe stepped out of the elevator, into the central area that was roughly the size of a football field. From the center atrium, there were corridors that led to the other areas and centers of the facility.

This main part was the hub of Elysia and held most of their shops and vendors, with the exception of restaurants. Being Apollites, they didn't need any.

"The city is named Elysia." Without slowing her gait, Phoebe led them through a handful of residents who had paused to stare at them. "Most of the Apollites here live their entire lives below ground. They've no desire to go topside and see the humans and their violence. Nor do they wish to see their kind hunted."

Once they'd passed through her people, Chris cleared his throat to get her attention. "What do they do with the Daimons?"

"No Daimons are tolerated here since they require a steady diet of human or Apollite souls. If an Apollite decides to go Daimon, they're allowed to leave, but they can never return here. Ever."

Kat arched a brow at that. "Yet you live here. Why?"

"I told you, Urian protects them. He was the one who showed them how to build this place."

"Why?" Kat pressed.

Phoebe stopped and turned to give Kat a measuring stare as she fought the urge to slap her and Cassandra both for their continued mistrust, which was ridiculous at this point. What more did she have to do to prove herself to them? Light herself on fire? "In spite of what you might think of him, my husband is a good man. He only wants what's best for his people." Phoebe's gaze went to Cassandra. "Urian was the first child to ever be born a cursed Apollite."

Technically second, since his twin was the firstborn, but close enough. And as psycho as Stryker was, it was a fact that he'd tried his best to keep from Urian for years. He'd even lied to both of his sons about when they were really born so that they wouldn't know.

Until their brother Archie had cruelly told him the truth one day when they'd been fighting as boys. *At least I wasn't the first one born cursed, Uri! That tells you how bad even our own grandfather must hate you!*

The news had hit Urian like a sledgehammer and he'd never told a soul that he knew the truth.

Not until Phoebe. He'd only shared his shame with her.

Cassandra gasped. "That would make him—"

"Over eleven thousand years old." Phoebe finished the sentence for her. "Yes. Most of the warriors who travel with him are that old. They go back to the very beginning of our history."

Chris whistled low. "How is that possible?"

"The Destroyer protects them," Kat said. "Just as the Dark-Hunters serve Artemis, the true Spathis serve her." She sighed as if the conflict pained her just as deeply. "Artemis and Apollymi have been at war since day one. The Destroyer is in captivity because Artemis tricked her into it, and she spends all her time plotting Artemis's torture and death. If she ever gets out, Apollymi will destroy her."

Cassandra frowned. "Why does the Destroyer hate Artemis?"

"Love. Why else?" Kat said simply. "Love, hatred, and revenge are the most powerful emotions on earth. Apollymi wants revenge on Artemis for killing the one thing she loved most in the universe."

"And that is?"

"I would never betray either one by saying it."

"Would you write it down?" Chris asked.

Kat rolled her eyes.

Cassandra and Phoebe shook their heads.

Chris scoffed at their reaction. "Oh yeah, like the two of you weren't thinking the same thing."

No, but Kat's words made her think of Urian's snarky pessimism whenever she made him watch a romcom instead of the horror movies he preferred—*Love doesn't conquer all. Only a quick sword does that.*

And with that thought in mind, Phoebe took them to the

residential area. "These are apartments. You'll be given a large unit with four bedrooms. Mine is down a separate hallway. I would have liked to have you closer, but this was the only one available that was big enough to accommodate all of you."

The last thing Shanus and the others wanted, or would agree to, was the four of them spread out. Not only would it make them harder to guard, it made them harder to watch. This was much easier and safer all the way around.

Cassandra hesitated at the door. "Is Wulf already there?"

"No. He was taken to a holding cell."

Aghast, then angry, her sister gaped. "Excuse me?"

Phoebe had to ride herd on her own temper. She really wasn't in the mood right then. She would have liked to go and verify the safety of her own husband, who was in a much, much worse situation at the moment than Sasquatch was. "He's our enemy, Cassie. What would you expect us to do?"

"I expect you to release him. Now!"

"I can't."

Cassandra stopped dead in her tracks. "Then show me the door out of here."

Was she fucking kidding? After everything Urian had gone through for her? After everything they'd risked to save her life? Never had Phoebe wanted to hurt someone any more than she wanted to slap her sister right then and there. Cass better be grateful she was pregnant. "What?"

"You heard me. I will not stay here unless he's welcomed. He has risked his life for me. His home was destroyed because of me and I will not live comfortably while the father of my baby is treated like a convict."

Someone behind them started clapping.

Phoebe looked past her sister to see that Shanus had joined them.

Standing at almost seven feet in height, he was gorgeous and lithe. Very graceful, and fast approaching the age when he'd need to find his replacement because he would be decaying into dust courtesy of Apollo.

He smirked at Cassandra. "Nice speech, princess. It changes nothing."

She narrowed her gaze on him. "Then how about a good ass-kicking?"

He laughed at the threat. "You're pregnant."

"Not *that* pregnant." She shot one of the daggers from her wrist at the man. It embedded in the wall just past his head.

His face lost all humor and Phoebe couldn't blame him. She was mortified and embarrassed by her sister's lack of gratitude.

"The next one goes into your heart."

"Cassie, stop!" Phoebe commanded, grabbing her arm.

Cassandra shrugged her hold off. "No. I've spent the whole of my adulthood putting any Daimon or Apollite who made the mistake of coming after me out of his misery. If you think for one minute Kat and I can't tear down this place to free Wulf, then you need to think again."

"And if you die?" the man asked.

"Then we all lose."

He gazed at her thoughtfully. "You're bluffing."

Cassandra exchanged a determined look with Kat.

"You know I'm always itching for a good fight." Kat pulled her fighting staff out of her coat pocket and extended it.

The man's nostrils flared as he saw them preparing to engage him. "This is how you repay my kindness for sheltering you?"

Cassandra lifted her chin like the spoiled, ungrateful little bitch their father had made her. "No, this is how I repay the man who protects me. I won't see Wulf kept like this after all he's done."

Shanus stepped back and bowed his head respectfully toward her. "She does have the courage of a Spathi."

No, she had all the spunk of a brat wanting a cookie, with no care about how it affected anyone else around her. And Phoebe felt her face heat up with her embarrassment. She'd warned them that Cass could be difficult whenever she didn't get her way, so in an effort to be diplomatic, she inclined her head. "I told you so."

Shanus offered them a slight smile. "Go inside with Phoebe, princess, and I will have your Dark-Hunter brought to you."

Even then, Cassandra eyed him suspiciously. "Promise?"

"Yes."

Still skeptical, Cassandra looked at Phoebe, who at this point was about at her end with her. "Can I put any faith in that?"

Hold me back . . . Counting to three, she smiled through her anger. "You can. Shanus is our Supreme Counselor. He never lies."

"Phoebe, look at me."

Don't take that tone with me, bitch. I'm about to slap you!

"Tell me the truth. Are we safe here?"

With them? "Yes, I swear it by everything I hold dear—even Urian's life. You are here because Stryker will never think to look in an Apollite commune for you. Every one of us here knows that if your baby dies, so does our world. And our lives, such as they are, are still precious to us. Twenty-seven years to the people here is better than none at all."

But if you don't shut your hole and get in that room so that I can check on my husband, I'm going to beat your ass.

Finally, Cassandra took a deep breath and nodded. "Okay."

Passing an annoyed look behind her back to Shanus, Phoebe opened the door.

Shanus choked on a laugh and excused himself.

Furious, Phoebe followed them into their new home. Like all the units here, the main living room was about five hundred square feet and had everything a regular human home had. An oversized, stuffed sofa and love seat, and an entertainment center complete with television, stereo, and DVD player.

Chris headed straight for the entertainment center. "Does that stuff work?"

"Yes. We have relays and uplinks that can bring the human world down to us."

Kat opened the doors to the bedrooms and bathroom, which were off the main living area. "Where's the kitchen?"

Phoebe gave her a droll stare for the stupidity of that question.

"We don't have kitchens," she reminded her. "But the counselors are working on getting a microwave and refrigerator brought in for you since you do actually eat. Along with groceries. There should be something here very soon for all of you."

Since they didn't have phones, Phoebe showed them the small dark green box on an end table. "If you need anything, the intercom is here. Just press the button and one of the operators will help you. If you want to buzz me, tell them you need Urian's wife and they'll know which Phoebe to put you through to."

A knock sounded on the door.

Phoebe went to answer it while Cassandra stood back with Kat and Chris. "What do you guys think?"

Chris shrugged. "It seems okay. I'm not picking up any evil vibes, what about you two?"

Kat looked around. "I agree with Chris. But there's still a part of me that doesn't trust them. No offense, Cass, but Apollites aren't known for being honest."

"Tell me about it."

Phoebe snorted at *that* comment, especially given the track record of human honesty. Um, yeah ... Last article she read said the average person lied thirty times an hour. *Average human.* Thirty times an hour. Didn't speak well for what a pathological or "unaverage" human did, did it? And they dared to call Apollites dishonest?

Yeah ...

Irritated to the extreme, Phoebe exchanged a peeved smirk with Dr. Lakis, who was even in height to her and dressed in a light pink sweater and jeans. Since she was on duty, she had her shoulder-length blond hair pulled up into a loose bun.

Lucky for her sister, Dr. Lakis was better at hiding her irritation. "Cassandra?"

She waited for Cass to look at her.

"I'm Dr. Lakis." She extended her hand to Cassandra. "If you don't mind, I would like to examine you and see how the baby is doing."

The two of them headed off.

Phoebe took a moment to check in with Kat and Chris. "You two need anything?"

Katra cocked her head at her. "Stryker's not going to hurt Urian. Why are you so worried?"

Phoebe let out a bitter laugh. "You don't know him at all, do you?"

"I've known them both a lot longer than you have."

"Then you should know how violent Stryker gets and how often he lashes out."

Kat passed a smug look to Chris. "But not against Urian."

"Really? On the night Urian left his brother, who was a trained soldier, to save the life of a blind Apollite woman and her children, his father almost beat him to death. But for Apollymi's intervention, he probably would have."

Kat gaped. "He told you this?"

"No, a friend of his did as a warning to me to never make the mistake of putting him in the crosshairs of his father's wrath. He wanted to stress to me that while Urian constantly assures me that he's okay and that everything will be all right, Urian is not okay and he's playing an extremely stupid game with his life. For me."

D*amn it! How* did they get to that boat?"

With his arms crossed over his chest, Urian stood in the council room stoically and listened to his father's tirade. Which had to be a record for the longest rant ever. He would yawn, but in the mood his father was in, he'd probably cut his throat.

"Urian!"

He snapped his head up. "Sir?"

"How did they get past you?"

"No idea. I was in the boathouse. Checked on Jason and Bryan. They were fine at the time. Went outside because they said they heard something. Then Trates was calling for assistance around front, so I headed that way. Next thing I knew, you were screaming that they were in a boat."

"You didn't sense anything?"

"I couldn't pick up any smells because of the gunpowder residue. My hearing was shot from the explosions. Same for my vision. My ears are still ringing."

His father curled his lip. "I'm disgusted by all of you! Get out of my sight!"

Relieved to have an end to *that* and still be in one piece, Urian exchanged a sideways glance with Davyn. But neither of them dared to speak until they were clear of his father's hearing.

Davyn let out a long, slow breath. "Damn, Uri."

"I know."

"Hold me?"

Urian laughed before he pulled Davyn into his arms and gave him a hug. "Better?"

"No! You scared the shit out of me! Between that and your father ... I don't think I'll ever be the same."

"Yeah, well, I appreciate you, brother."

"Glad someone does."

Urian kissed his cheek before he released him. "Did everything go okay?"

"Not really. But I made do. How about on your end?"

"Not really. But I made do." His gaze fell to the necklace around Davyn's neck. Paris's.

Davyn looked down at it and touched it. "I still can't believe he's gone."

"I know. Seems like yesterday. Not seventy years."

He nodded. "He'd kick your ass if he knew you helped a Dark-Hunter."

"Yeah, he would. Stab me himself."

Davyn snorted. "I should do it for him."

"I should probably help you. If I had any sense I would."

"Urian!" his father shouted.

Now there was a tone to make even Ares drop a load.

Davyn turned a shade paler. "Glad I'm not you," he whispered before he headed off down the hall.

Resigned to whatever ass-crawling was about to manifest, Urian headed back toward his father's office and opened the door. "You rang, my lord and tormentor?"

"Don't get cheeky with me, *pido*, I'm not in the mood. Come in and shut the door behind you."

Urian obeyed.

"I think we have a traitor in our midst."

Those words sent a slice of fear down his spine. "Why?"

"I keep running over everything that's happened. It's the only explanation for how the heiress keeps eluding us. Someone has to be helping her."

Urian kept himself completely still as the hair on the back of his neck began to crawl with guilt. "What do you want me to do, Solren?"

"You know what I want! The head of the traitor. I want you find whoever it is and gut them!"

Urian sighed. "Solren, have you ever considered that the words of the oracle could have been a game sent by the gods to make you destroy yourself? Like Oedipus? It was by trying to avert his fate that King Laius caused his own death. And the same for Oedipus. Had either king not tried to stop their fate, they wouldn't have taken the very actions that caused it."

"You're not making any sense."

"Sure I am. Solren, think about it. We are our own worst enemies. It's by our own actions we're destroyed."

"And by the sword the knot was undone."

"Pardon?"

"The Gordian knot? Even the most complex and unsolvable problem can have a simple solution if you apply enough brute force to it."

"Um, I don't think that's what that means, Solren."

"Of course it is. Don't you dare argue with me!"

Urian held his hands up in surrender. He wasn't about to argue philosophy when his father was in a mood this foul and armed. "When was the last time you took a soul, Solren?"

"Why are you asking?"

"Thinking you're a little peckish. You might want to feed soon. Take the edge off."

"Fine! Bring me the heiress and I'll be thrilled to feed on her and her unborn child."

Urian snapped his fingers. "I will see about that pronto. Anything else I can do for you?"

He growled like a lion.

Urian left immediately. And almost collided with Sabine, Apollymi's favored Charonte since Xedrix had gone missing a few weeks back.

"The goddess summons you."

Weird that she'd send her demon. Normally she just screamed in his head.

Scowling, he followed the orange-fleshed demon back to Apollymi's garden, where the goddess was not at the pool but out in the orchard where the rowan trees and black roses grew.

Seriously concerned now, Urian approached with a great deal of caution. "You summoned me, akra?"

She handed the rose she'd just cut to the demon beside her so that he could add it to the basket in his hands. "You should be honest with your father, Urian."

"Beg pardon?"

"You heard me. Lies are unbecoming for one such as you. And I've allowed yours to go on for way too long now. I kept thinking that you'd come clean with him. It bothers me to see Strykerius so upset. He's gutted three innocent men tonight in his rage."

Urian glanced to the demon behind her, not quite sure what to say to that.

Apollymi turned toward him with a biting stare. "Just like when you visited with Sarraxyn, and she violated my sacred pact to keep her cove private from all."

"Akra—"

"Not a word, Urian. The bitterest truth is better than the sweetest lie. Your father deserves to hear it from you and not another. Sooner or later, the truth will come out. It always does. No matter how hard you strive to keep it hidden. It will crawl its way to the surface and those who have been lied to will turn on you with a vengeance unimaginable. Because with it comes a righteous fury fueled by betrayal. They trusted you, and trust is a sacred thing not to be abused. Of all people, you know this. And those so abused will demand an accounting, and they will rise up and demand blood for appeasement. Then you won't be able to lie your way out. It will be too late for words to save you. Do you understand?"

He understood, but it wasn't that simple. His father would demand Phoebe's life and that of Cassandra.

How could he choose between them?

"Have you ever had to choose between two things you loved most, akra?"

A deep, dark, and bitter sadness burned in her eyes. It was so heart-wrenching that in that moment, he knew that she was well aware of what she was asking from him. "I have."

"Do you regret the decision you made?"

"Every day of my life."

March 12, 2004

Phoebe was in tears. She'd been trying to be strong and hide them, but this silence was shredding her.

Closing the door to her apartment, she felt someone standing right behind her.

"What's wrong, *agapi mou*? Did the Muppet offend you? I'll rip out his tongue if he did."

Her breath left her with a rush as she recognized Urian's thick accent and then realized that he'd already lit candles for them all around her room. Turning, she threw herself against him and rained kisses all over his face and neck. "I thought you were dead!"

He tsked at her. "You know me better than that. I just had to wait for it to calm a little."

She was already peeling his clothes off his body.

Laughing, he helped her with his powers. "Take it you're hungry?"

"Starving, and not just for blood and soul. *Se hriazome!*"

Urian's eyes widened as she said "I need you" in Greek. In all this time, she'd only picked up a word here or there. Never had she ever said a whole phrase before. "You must have missed me."

"More than you can imagine." She sank her fangs into his neck and sent him reeling.

Urian barely made it to the couch with her. She was absolutely wild tonight. So much so that she immediately slid herself onto him and took control with wanton abandon.

She ravaged his neck and tore at his arms and chest with her nails as she rode him with fury. There was a strange kind of pleasure with the pain, while his head spun from her insistent hunger. Her emotions overrode his until he lost himself completely.

He lost all sense of time as her body milked his and all he felt was Phoebe. He didn't care about anything or anyone else. His life began and ended with her.

Suddenly, the door slid open.

Phoebe jerked up, clutching at Urian, who was too weak to even turn his head to see who was there.

The door closed again.

Panting and weak, Urian tried to focus his gaze. "Who was that?"

"My sister," she hissed, climbing off him to rush to the bathroom.

Urian attempted to get up and go after her, but he fell back onto the sofa. "I'm going to wait here."

If Phoebe heard, she didn't pause or say anything. She merely ran out of the apartment to catch up to her sister.

After a few seconds she came back in and sat down primly by his side.

"You okay?"

"That was embarrassing."

"Let me guess? Your sister and Muppet had a little PMS meltdown over what they saw?"

"I call him Sasquatch, but yes. Yes, they did."

He laughed. "Remind me later to kill him ... and I won't be calling him Sasquatch."

"Why? I think it's quite fitting."

Urian scoffed. "Not really. That implies he's intimidating and scary. Trust me, he's not."

"Maybe not to your hulking, almost-seven-foot-tall ass he isn't, but from my vantage point, he's terrifying."

He snorted. "Trust me, don't feed Muppet's ego. If it gets any bigger, we're going to have to put in for a larger apartment for them. I think it's why his mansion was so big. They needed it just to house his inflated self-image."

Phoebe laughed. Until they heard a loud commotion from outside.

"Ah shit ... " Urian used his powers to summon clothes.

Without being told, he knew Wulf had pissed off the natives and trouble was brewing. Because that out there was the sound of hell's wrath, and only a Dark-Hunter in the middle of an Apollite commune could cause that much ruckus.

Teleporting into the middle of it, Urian took one second to get the lay of the drama before he grabbed Wulf and inserted himself between the Dark-Hunter and the Apollite who wanted his head. Still weak from Phoebe's feeding, he kept one hand on each of them to make sure they kept a safe distance from each other.

"Enough!" Urian roared at the two of them.

Wulf frowned at him. "Are you all right?"

Not really. He felt rather queasy and he definitely didn't need this shit.

Urian released both men. The Apollite was taken off by some of Shanus's watchmen, but he cast a parting malevolent glare at them.

Grateful it was over, he wiped a hand over his sweat-covered brow. "You need to stay out of sight, Dark-Hunter."

"You really don't look good. Do you need something?"

Urian shook his head to clear it. "I just need to rest for a while." He curled his lip at Wulf. "Can you stay out of trouble long enough for that?"

"Uri?" Phoebe came up behind him and placed her hand on his forehead. "Did I take too much, baby?"

Wanting to reassure her, Urian pulled her against his side and kissed her cheek. "No, love. I'm just tired. I'll be fine."

He pulled away and had just started back for their apartment when his legs buckled.

"Bullshit!"

Much to Urian's absolute horror, the Muppet came up and slung his arm over his shoulder to help him back to Wulf's apartment.

"What are you doing?" Urian asked angrily.

"I'm taking you to Kat before you pass out."

Urian hissed at the very thought of being with her. "Why?

She hates me." Artemis's handmaiden was more likely to gut him than help him.

"So do I, but we both owe you."

Chris and Kat sat on the floor playing cards when they entered.

Kat shot to her feet as soon as she saw Urian's condition. "Oh jeez, what happened?"

Phoebe rushed in behind them. "I think I took too much blood from him."

Wulf laid Urian down on the couch. "Can you help him, Kat?"

Kat pushed Wulf out of the way. She held up two fingers in front of Urian's face. "How many fingers do you see?"

"Six."

She popped him on the side. "Stop that. This is serious."

Urian widened his eyes and tried to focus his gaze on her hand. "Three ... I think."

Kat shook her head. "We'll be back."

Cassandra watched in awe as Kat flashed them out of the room.

"Now why didn't she do that when we were being chased by Stryker?" Chris asked.

Phoebe scoffed at the clueless human. "She's taking him to Kalosis, Chris. I doubt any of you want to go into a realm ruled by nothing but Spathi Daimons and one really pissed-off ancient goddess who is bent on destroying the entire world."

He nodded like a clucking chicken. "You know, I really like it here. Not to mention, I can now look at Kat's hand." He picked up her cards and cursed. "I should have known she wasn't bluffing."

Her face turning bright pink, Cassandra moved closer to her. "I'm so sorry I interrupted you two."

"Please don't be. I mean, don't make it a habit, mind you, but if you hadn't come in, I might have killed him. He has a bad tendency to not tell me when I've taken too much blood. It scares me sometimes." Actually, it scared her a lot, as she wondered if Urian didn't have a death wish.

There was something about him. A darkness inside that she'd catch a glimpse of from time to time that never quite went away.

Whenever she asked about it, he'd tell her that she was imagining things. But she knew what she saw.

He'd lived a long time and lost a lot of people he cared about. That kind of tragedy left its mark.

Whether he owned up to it or not, her husband was very shattered.

Wulf crossed his arms over his chest. "So Daimons can die from blood loss?"

Phoebe gave him an arched stare. "Are you planning on using that against us?"

Wulf shook his head. "I'd rather die myself than suck on another man's neck. That's disgusting. Besides, didn't you tell me that's how Apollites can be changed to Daimons? It begs the question of whether a Dark-Hunter could be made a Daimon, too."

"Yeah, but DH blood is poisonous to them." Chris shuffled the deck of cards. "Isn't the point of that so that no Daimon can feed off or convert you guys?"

"Perhaps . . . " Phoebe watched Chris cut the deck again. "But then disembodied souls can possess a Dark-Hunter and since Uri and I share souls, it makes you wonder if perhaps a Daimon and Dark-Hunter could share one too."

"Let's hope we never find that one out." Wulf moved to sit on the couch in front of Chris.

Phoebe turned back toward Cassandra. "So what did you want when you came to see me?"

"I've been putting together a memory box for the baby. Notes and pictures from me. Little mementoes to tell him about our people and family after I'm gone, and I was wondering if you would mind putting something in there from you."

"Why do you need something like that when we'll be more than happy to tell him anything he wants to know?"

Cassandra hesitated as if there were something she didn't want to tell her. She glanced to Sasquatch before she answered. "He can't grow up here, Phee. He'll have to be with Wulf in the human world."

Phoebe ground her teeth at that. Of course. Leave it to Cassie to be prejudiced against her own people. "Why can't he grow up here? We can protect him just as well as Wulf. Probably more so." At least *they* wouldn't hate him for being part Apollite.

Wulf glanced up as Chris dealt him a hand of cards. "What if he's more human than even Cassandra is? Would he be safe here?"

Phoebe hesitated. He should be, but ... There were some Apollites who had a lot of problems with humans. Even as long as she'd been here, she still had trouble with a few once they learned her father was human.

And she was grateful that at least they didn't tie each other to stakes anymore and set fire to them.

At least not often.

Wulf gave Phoebe a meaningful stare. "I can protect him and his children a lot easier than you can. I think the temptation of having a human soul here would be way too much for some of your people to handle. Especially given how much they hate Dark-Hunters. What a coup—kill my son, get a human soul, and get revenge on the very thing all of you despise most."

Phoebe nodded. "I suppose you're right." She took Cassandra's hand. "Yes, I would like to add some things to the box for him."

And Phoebe knew *exactly* what she wanted her nephew to have.

So after she wrote her note, she excused herself and went to get her present for Cassandra's box.

She returned to her sister's apartment a short time later with the book.

Cassandra looked up with a frown as Phoebe slid it into the keepsake box Cassie still had out on the couch next to her. "What's this?"

Phoebe gave her a wicked grin. "It's a book of Apollite fairy tales. Remember the one Mom used to read to us when we were kids? Donita sells them in her shop, so I went just now and bought one for the baby."

With suspicious eyes, Wulf picked the book up and flipped through it. "Hey, Chris?" He handed it to his Squire. "You read Greek, right?"

"Yeah."

"What's in here?"

Chris started reading silently, then burst out laughing. Hard. "I don't know if you want the baby to see this if you're the one raising him."

"Let me guess?" Wulf glared at Phoebe. "He'll have nightmares that Daddy is going to hunt him down and rip his head off?"

"Pretty much. I'm particularly fond of the one called 'Acheron the Great Evil.'" Chris paused as he turned to another story. "Oh wait ... You'll love this one. They've got the story of the nasty Nordic Dark-Hunter. Remember the story with the witch and the oven? This one features you with a furnace."

"Phoebe!" Sasquatch's glare turned to murder.

She blinked innocently. "What? That's our heritage. It's not like you guys don't swap stories on Andy the Evil Apollite or Daniel the Killer Daimon. You know I see human movies and read their books too. They're not exactly nice to my people."

Wulf scoffed. "Yeah well, *your* people happen to be soul-sucking demons."

Crossing her arms over her chest, Phoebe cocked her head with attitude. "You ever met a banker or a lawyer? Tell me who's worse, my Urian or one of them? At least we need the food. They do it just for profit margins."

Cassandra laughed at their bantering, then took the book from Chris's hands. "I appreciate the thought, Phee, but could we find a book that doesn't paint the Dark-Hunters as Satan?"

"I don't think one exists. Or if it does, I've never seen it."

"Great." Sasquatch picked up another card. "Just great. My poor son's going to have nightmares all of his childhood."

"Trust me," Chris said as he upped his bet against Wulf. "That book's going to be the least of your kid's problems with you as his father."

Cassie frowned. "What do you mean?"

Chris put his cards down and met her gaze. "You do know that as a small child, they actually carried me around on a pillow? I had a custom-made helmet that I had to wear until I was four."

Sasquatch scratched at his beard. "That's because you banged your head every time you got angry. I was afraid you were going to get brain damage from it."

Chris snorted. "The brain is fine. It's my ego and social life that's in the toilet. I shudder at what you're going to do to that poor kid." He dropped his voice and imitated Wulf's lilting Norse accent. "Don't move, you might get bruised. Oops, a sneeze, better call in specialists from Belgium. Headache? Odin forbid, it might be a tumor. Quick, rush him for a CAT scan."

Wulf shoved his shoulder playfully. "And yet you live."

"Ever the better to procreate for you." Chris met Cassandra's gaze. "It's a hell of a life." Then Chris dropped his gaze as if he was thinking about that for a minute. "But there are worse ones out there."

He was right about that. Phoebe sighed as she wondered about Urian and what he was doing.

Katra waited outside Urian's bedroom until Davyn came outside to meet her. "Is he all right?"

"He will be, but that was *very* close."

She let out a long sigh. "Yeah, I've never seen him like that. Didn't know he could get weak."

"Me neither."

She glanced to the closed door. "Do I want to know what you did to fix him?"

With grim expression, Davyn shook his head. "You wouldn't approve."

"Pardon the pun. Sucks to be a Daimon."

"You have no idea. Believe me, it's not something we enjoy. There's not a one of us who wouldn't give our souls to change it."

Kat saw the truth in his dark eyes. And oddly enough, she saw Davyn's gentle soul, and his guilt. "I'm sorry."

"No, Kat. That's an empty sentiment. You really don't get what your uncle did to us."

"Pardon?"

"I know who and what you are. Urian doesn't."

Panic filled her. "How?"

Davyn laughed. "I see and hear a lot more than anyone credits me with. And I'm not as dumb as everyone thinks. I've seen Artemis. You look just like her. Right down to the eye color. Given that, I figure you have to be related to Apollymi's son in order for her to tolerate you to live. Never mind come and go here, whenever you like."

Katra's jaw dropped. "You've never told him?"

"Of secret things I am silence."

"The *Bhagavad Gita?*"

Davyn shrugged. "I read a lot of things."

The door behind him opened to show Urian looking a lot better. His deep tawny skin had a healthy glow. His eyes were bright and for once he wore his long blond hair down around his shoulders. She would give Phoebe credit. Her husband was extremely gorgeous.

Dressed black on black, there wasn't much difference between Urian and a Dark-Hunter.

"You look like you ate someone who agreed with you."

Urian wasn't amused with her joke. "Ha, ha, Katra. Do you have any real reason to be here? Or are you just wanting to piss me off?"

"I was making sure you lived. Sorry I cared."

"I'm not sorry you cared. I am sorry you feel the need to nettle." Sighing, he met Davyn's gaze. "Thank you, brother."

"You know I love you."

"You, too."

"Aw!" Kat threw herself against them both and hugged them close. "It's a Daimon love fest!"

Urian screwed his face up. "Gah! I'm getting Olympian cooties. Someone call an exterminator! Better yet, a Charonte!"

Snorting, Kat pulled away. "Fine. I'm heading back. See you later."

Urian took a minute to talk to Davyn. "I got rid of the body."

"Thanks."

When he started to leave, Davyn stopped him. "Uri ... it's none of my business, but you know that's not normal, right?"

"It wasn't her fault. I picked a particularly nasty asshole to feed on and it affected her. You were lucky—Paris was particular about the souls he took. To keep you safe, he preyed on gentle ones so that you wouldn't have to listen to them screaming as much."

Davyn looked away, shame-faced at a secret they'd all kept from him. Paris had been the only one of them who had taken the lives of women and weaker humans so as not to risk Davyn going trelos. "Yeah, I know. I didn't realize that until he was gone and I had to pick my own meals."

And it made a big difference. Urian was used to feeding himself only. Because he'd been doing it for so long, the voices had become a part of him. He could ignore them most of the time. Phoebe was still adjusting. And when they were dying, they were louder and worse. Especially the strong ones.

She was still getting used to all that.

He'd considered going after a weaker human. But he just couldn't make himself do it. His warrior's code was too strong. It wasn't in him to prey on someone weaker. There was no honor in that.

He smiled at Davyn. "I'll be more careful with her in the future."

"What if she goes trelos?"

"She won't. She's part human."

"A human who almost killed you tonight!"

Urian shook his head. "My stupidity almost killed me tonight, not Phoebe. I've got this."

Davyn scoffed as Urian headed off. And the last words he heard him say were ominous indeed. "Strange. Those were the last words Paris said."

It *was just* after midnight when Urian returned to the Muppet's apartment to collect his wife. Phoebe smiled as he neared her.

Wulf didn't. In fact, the tension between the two of them was fierce.

"What's the matter, Dark-Hunter?" Urian couldn't resist taunting as he draped his arm around Phoebe's shoulders. "You were hoping I'd succumb?"

"No, I was just wondering who you killed to reclaim your health."

Urian snorted. "I'm sure the cows you eat aren't exactly thrilled by their slaughter either."

"They're not people."

"In case you haven't noticed, Dark-Hunter, there are a lot of people out there who aren't human either."

Taking Phoebe's hand, Urian led her toward the door. "C'mon, Phee, I don't have much time before I have to return to Kalosis and I don't want to spend it with my enemies."

He took her back to their apartment.

Phoebe watched him carefully. "Are you sure you're all right?"

"Other than hacked off? Yeah. I'm good." Urian turned toward her. "What about you?"

"I have a headache, but other than that, I'm fine."

A headache ... that didn't bode well. Urian tried not to let Davyn's words infect his mind and panic him. Phoebe was fine. She was. She wasn't going trelos. His father wasn't going nuts and he wasn't playing with fire.

Everything would be fine.

Yeah, he didn't believe it either.

March 19, 2004

Since Urian was supposed to be the sponsor for this godfor-saken event, he opened the door to collect his sister-in-law. At the request of his wife and Cassandra, he'd worn his long blond hair down around his shoulders and he was dressed in an elegant black silk tuxedo. He didn't know what it was about women that they liked his hair down, but ... whatever.

If it made Phoebe happy and got him laid, he'd oblige her.

"Are you ready?" he asked Cassandra.

Standing in the bedroom, she was dressed in her wedding gown, with her long strawberry-blond hair down around her shoulders. She wore a silver crown intertwined with fresh flowers.

She fidgeted with her hem. "Is Wulf ready?"

He nodded. "He and Chris are waiting for you in the main complex."

Kat handed her the single white rose that was wrapped with red and white ribbons.

Cassandra took the rose.

Phoebe and Kat took their places in front and led the way. Urian came into the room to offer Cassandra his arm so that they could walk behind them.

For some odd reason, Cass had wanted the wedding out-side, but after much laughter and refusal, they'd finally rented the open merchant area. Shanus and several council members had gone out of their way to bring hydroponic plants and flowers to simulate a garden center. They'd even constructed a small fountain.

Cassandra hesitated as they entered the complex. Urian arched a brow at that. Given how pregnant she was, he hoped she wasn't getting cold feet.

"I'll take it from here."

Urian inclined his head to his father-in-law, whom he had yet to meet, but Phoebe had warned him he'd be here for the event.

Cassandra gasped. "Daddy?"

"You didn't really think I'd miss my baby getting married, did you?"

"But how?"

He indicated Wulf with a nod. "Wulf came to the house last night and brought me here. He said it wouldn't be a wedding for you unless I came, and he told me about Phoebe. I spent last night in her apartment with her so that we could catch up and then surprise you." His eyes teared up as he stared at her stomach. "You look beautiful, baby."

She threw herself into his arms, or at least as close to that as she could given her distended belly, and held him tight. "Should we call the wedding off before you drown us in tears?" Kat asked.

"No!" Cassandra pulled herself together with a sniff. "I'm fine. Really."

Her father kissed her cheek, tucked her hand into the crook of his arm, and led her to Wulf. Kat and Phoebe moved to stand behind Chris while Urian took his place by Phoebe's side. The only other person present was Shanus, who stood back but watched them with a friendly expression that said he was more than happy to bear witness to the event.

Urian kissed Phoebe's hand as he remembered marrying her, and he hated that she hadn't had her father present for their wedding. To her credit she didn't say a word about it as her father wrapped the ribbons around Cassandra's and Wulf's hands.

Once he was done, their father began speaking the words to bind them together. "It is through the night that we are—"

"Light," Urian whispered loudly, interrupting him.

Her father's face flushed a bit. "I'm sorry. I had to learn this rather hastily." He cleared his throat and began again. "It is through the light that we are born and through ... through ... " Her father hesitated.

Amused by the fact that their human father was completely clueless, Urian came forward to whisper in his ear.

"Thank you," Mr. Peters said. "This ceremony is nothing like ours."

Urian inclined his head and stepped back, but not before he gave Cassandra a wink to let her know he had her back.

"It is through the light that we are born and through the night that we travel. The light is the love of our parents who greet us and welcome us into this world, and it is with the love of our partner that we leave it.

"Wulf and Cassandra have chosen to be with each other, to ease their remaining journey and to comfort one another in the coming nights. And when the final night is upon them . . . " Her father stopped as he teared up again.

Ah, good grief. If this kept up, Cassandra's baby would be born and graduate before they got to the end of it.

"I can't," he said quietly.

"Daddy?"

Her father stepped back as a tear fell down his cheek.

Phoebe rushed forward and wrapped her arms around him.

Cassandra started for him, but Phoebe stopped her. "Finish it, please, Uri."

Phoebe escorted their father off to the side.

Great . . . he'd rather be denutted. Sighing, Urian moved to stand with them and marry his worst enemy to his wife's sister. *Someone kill me now.* "When the final night is upon us, we vow to stand together and ease the one who travels first.

"Soul to soul we have breathed. Flesh to flesh we have touched. And it is alone that we must leave this existence, until the night comes that the Fates decree we are reunited in Ouranlie."

Great, now Cassandra was starting to cry.

Urian stepped to the pedestal that had the same gold cup he'd used to marry Phoebe. He brought it over to Cassandra. "Normally this would be the blood of both of you combined, but since neither one of you is particularly gung ho for that, it's wine."

He handed the cup to Cassandra, who took a sip and then gave it to Wulf, who followed suit. Wulf handed the cup to Urian.

As was the Apollite custom, Wulf bent down and kissed her so that the taste of wine was mingled with them.

Urian returned the cup to the pedestal and finished the ceremony. "Here stands the bride, Cassandra. She is unique in this world. Her beauty, grace, and charms are the legacy of those who have come before her and will be gifted to those who are born through her.

"This man, Wulf, on the other hand, stands before us a product of ... " Frowning, Urian paused. "Well, he's the product of a bitch who can't stand the thought of Apollo's children ruling the earth."

"Urian, behave!" Phoebe snapped.

He bristled at her command. "Considering the fact that I just bound a member of my family to one of the people I have sworn to annihilate, I think I'm being remarkably good."

Phoebe cast him a glare that loudly proclaimed he'd be sleeping alone for at least a week.

Maybe longer.

Urian curled his lip at Wulf. *You utter Muppet bastard.* "Fine. I'm glad I didn't say what I really thought," he muttered under his breath.

Louder, Urian returned to the ceremony. "It is your similarities that brought you together and your differences that add variety and spark to your life. May the gods bless and protect your union and may you be ... " He paused again. "Well, you already are blessed with fertility so we'll skip that."

Phoebe growled low in her throat.

Urian cast another murderous glare at Wulf. "May the two of you enjoy every minute left to you."

Then Urian tied the ribbons into a double knot, although he would rather have knotted them around Muppet's throat.

Chris and Kat led the way back to the apartment.

As soon as they could, Urian and Phoebe left with her father in tow.

Which made for an awkward silence as her father treated him more like a bad lab experiment. It didn't matter that he'd saved both of Jefferson's daughters. The man just continued to treat him like shit.

"I don't bite."

"Sorry. It's just I've heard so much about Daimons from my wife and daughters. But you're the first one I've ever met."

"It's okay. I get it. Kind of like human kindness and compassion. I've heard of such mythical beasts, but I have yet to encounter them personally. Keep hoping to, though."

Urian decided to leave Phoebe alone with her father and let them catch up. But as he walked around the underground city, he kept having the strangest premonition.

He saw himself in the past. Alone. And he heard someone weeping, but he didn't know who.

It was so strange. But not as strange as him being here tonight, the son of Stryker who had been tagged to annihilate Phoebe and her bloodline. Now being the very one who'd married Cassandra to Wulf, his enemy, so that they could safeguard that bloodline for all time.

Apollymi was right. It was the ultimate betrayal. He was his father's right hand. The only one Stryker trusted.

And tonight, he'd just stabbed his father in the heart.

May 24, 2004

"Your father has lost his mind."

That was an understatement. Ever since Cassandra had birthed her son, Erik, his father had been spiraling out of control with an insane need to kill the two of them.

Raking his hands through his hair, Urian was at a loss on how to deal with the man. In all these centuries past, he'd never seen him quite like *this*. "I don't know, Dav ... has he gone trelos?"

"I was about to ask *you* that."

That would be his best guess. It would make the most sense. He was definitely acting like an utter lunatic.

"Urian!"

Davyn sighed. "I am *so* glad I'm not his son."

"Way to have my back."

"Yeah, well. I'd rather have your ass."

"Not funny."

Davyn held his hand up with his fingers pinched together. "I'm a little funny."

"Urian!"

He teleported into his father's office. "You rang down the temple?"

His father gave him a cold, murderous glare. "Don't even. Are you aware that the bastard Dante Pontis killed our informant?"

Urian gaped. "Dante murdered his own brother? Damn, that's cold even for a Katagari Were."

"Do we have anyone else in his club we can call on?"

Urian scratched at his neck as he considered his sources. "Not really and probably not after that kind of tantrum. Pretty sure anyone who might be bought would have a serious sphincter clinch after that."

His father moved to stand in his face. "I want a spy, Urian. Find me one."

"Yes, sir." Urian stepped back and spun on his heel to put as much distance as he could between him and crazy. Because as much as he loved his father ...

That was nuts and in case it was contagious, he didn't want it to jump on him.

Letting out a deep breath, he left the hall and tried to think of whom he could call in to try to get information. The Weres as a rule were always a bit shaky. They had to tread a fine line between Daimons and Dark-Hunters. And because of that, their loyalty couldn't always be trusted or relied upon. Some had been known to hand them over without a second thought, if they thought it could buy them favor with Acheron or Savitar.

Urian racked his three brain cells.

A shadow moved to his right as a couple of Daimons headed toward their home for a feeding.

Strangely, that gave him an idea ...

Teleporting to the nebulous no-man's-land that hovered between the realms, he went to find the one creature who could walk just about any place he wanted to.

"Shadow?"

"No."

Urian snorted at the gruff, disembodied voice. "No, what?"

"Whatever it is you're selling, I don't want it. Take your ass and go."

"C'mon, don't be that way."

Winds whistled in his ears. The shadows beside him solidified into a man who eyed him with malice as he crossed his arms over his chest and tsked. Just above average height and well built, Shadow had eyes of steel. And like his very soul, his shoulder-length hair that he wore pulled back into a short ponytail was neither light nor dark, but strands of varying shades that were trapped squarely between his two dueling natures.

The demon was fearless as a rule, hence his personal motto that he feared no evil, for he was the most evil thing that stalked the darkness and called the deadliest night home.

"Good to see you, Shay."

"No, it isn't, and I'm not your fucking date. What do you want, asshole?"

Urian smirked. "Really? Do we need all the profanity?"

"What you call an overuse of profanity, I call sentence enhancers."

"Of course you do." Urian shook his head. "I lost my spy at the Inferno and I could really use someone else."

He burst out laughing. "Are you fucking crazy? 'Hey, Shadow, long time no see . . . got a dude killed. Could you go replace him? 'Cause I don't like you at all, which is why we haven't talked in a few centuries. So if you die, I really don't give a shit.'" He pursed his lips. "Gee, thanks, Daimon."

Urian had forgotten just how sarcastic Shadow could be. "The reason I'm here is because you have a unique skill set."

"Yeah, I keep out of other people's shit. You know, no soweth of the discord among the brethren. My feet do not head to mischief. They're quite happy here at home."

"Shay . . ."

"Uri . . . " he mocked. "No."

"Please?"

"That only works if you're a grown female. Naked. And in my bed or writhing on top of me. And brother, you're none of those."

"You really won't help me?"

A tic started in Shadow's jaw. "Maybe, but only if I get bored with reruns, have no more belly lint to pick, and something causes me even more brain damage than I already have, maybe, just maybe I might—might—do it. So what is it?"

Closing his eyes, Shadow lifted his crossed fingers and said under his breath, "Please let it be to spy on a hot woman in her underwear."

Urian slapped him in the chest. "You're such a fucking pervert!"

"The hell I am! You know, I could do that any time I wanted, and notice that I never have. That makes me a saint."

Urian rolled his eyes. "Find out what Wulf Tryggvason is up to for me."

"That burly Viking Dark-Hunter bastard?"

"Yeah."

He screwed his face up. "Couldn't even give me Corbin. Effing figures."

As he started to disintegrate, Urian called out to him. "Thank you, Shadow!"

"You can thank me by not getting me killed, too, Daimon. Really, that's all the favor I need."

Oddly enough, Urian would settle for that himself because as he headed back to Kalosis, he couldn't shake the feeling that something horrible was about to happen.

That feeling only intensified as soon as he returned home and his cell phone lit up with Wulf's and then Phoebe's number. The Muppet could wait. He called Phoebe first, but for some reason, he couldn't get through.

Weird. So he tried Wulf.

Again, no signal. Frustrated, he went through his messages. The first one was Phoebe's hysterical screaming, "Your father has mine! He wants Erik! What the hell have you done, Urian! What the hell! You better call me as soon as you get this! Oh my God!"

Um, yeah. What the hell was right.

He listened to the next one, which was Wulf.

"You motherfucking, worthless Daimon bastard! So help me, Thor, when I lay hands on you there won't be enough left to flush, you hear me? You shitstain! You better call me back! Right now!"

Well, that was certainly not the way to motivate someone to want to dial you back, buddy. In fact, Urian had the urge to lose his phone.

And change his number.

Yeah . . .

Damn, Solren, what have you done? Gone for five minutes and what? You summoned the Furies? And their brats?

Disgusted, he headed for his father's office, but Trates caught him in the hallway. "I wouldn't do that."

"What's going on?"

Trates let out a tired sigh. "He's on a rampage."

"He's been on one for days." *Ever since Erik's birth.*

"Yeah, but he's all out of sorts at the moment. He had a conference with Apollymi. I don't know what the goddess said, but he is fit to be tied. We're all lying low for a bit."

Rubbing his forehead as he listened to furniture hitting the walls, Urian grimaced. "Did he kidnap Jefferson Peters?"

"Who?"

"The heiress's father."

Trates shrugged. "If he did, I wasn't in on it."

"Is that Urian?"

"Run," Trates whispered. "Just stay low till he cools off. I'll cover for you."

Thanks, Urian mouthed before he vanished. While he wasn't a coward, he just wasn't in the mood for anyone else to shout at him tonight.

His head throbbing, he strangely found himself in Xyn's cave. Sighing, he sat down on her bed and hung his head in his hands as he remembered simpler times.

God, how he missed it. Those nights of lying here with her. Of stretching back on her scales while she heated them to keep him warm. In all his life, she was the only one who'd ever really taken care of *him*.

While he loved Phoebe to distraction, it wasn't the same. She was his responsibility. He was forever worried about her. Sighing, he forced himself not to think about things that were long gone. This was the present.

If only he could see some kind of future. But with every heartbeat, that was getting darker and darker. And less likely as a possibility.

U*rian had done* everything he could to get word to Phoebe and Cassandra not to panic. Jefferson was safe. He'd made sure of it. Shadow was guarding him.

But his father was in such a state that he didn't dare try a more direct line of communication. Not the way Daimons were dropping. Right now, Stryker was taking a shot at anyone who looked at him cockeyed.

And even a few who didn't.

His phone vibrated again. Urian glanced at it. This time it was Shanus.

What were they doing? Swapping his number around for shits and giggles? They were about to get him killed if they didn't stop. This was the fifth time Shanus had called.

Not the time or the day . . .

Eyes wide, he exchanged an annoyed stare with Davyn, who rubbed his back comfortingly.

Until his father neared them. The kill-them-all-and-let-Zeus-sort-them-out expression on his face caused Davyn to shrink away.

"You ready, *pido?*"

"Always."

His father nodded, but something in his eyes made Urian's blood run cold. What had happened? He glanced over to Davyn, who looked as freaked out as he felt. For the merest second he had the thought to go exchange his black jeans and shirt for the armor Xyn had made for him centuries ago.

And to get his shield, too.

With no choice, they followed his father into the portal that was to take them into Dante's Inferno, where Wulf would be waiting with who knew how many Were-Hunters and Dark-Hunters. While Wulf had been told to come alone, none of them were dumb enough to believe for one yoctosecond that he would. Not while Acheron was alive. He would protect his Hunters at all costs. Since Dante Pontis owned the club, they knew the panther Were-Hunter would be there, along with his large number of brothers and cousins.

The rest was anyone's guess.

Urian took a deep breath and stepped in. Sure enough, as they appeared inside the nightclub, it was loaded for Daimon. Hunters abounded. Urian saw Wulf immediately and made sure to keep his expression stone and unresponsive, or else they'd both pay for it. He immediately moved over to the side so that in case that was his infant son Erik Wulf had strapped to him, he could help protect the baby.

His father looked around with an evil, gloating smile. "How nice ... you brought dinner for my men. If only everyone could be so considerate."

Several of the Daimons laughed. Urian wasn't one of them.

But one of the Dark-Hunters laughed. A tall, dark-haired one who looked about as crazed as his father had been acting lately. "You know, I almost like this guy, Acheron. Pity we have to kill him."

His father slid a sideways glare to the Dark-Hunter before his gaze went to Acheron. The two of them stared at each other without a word or emotion.

Urian, however, lost his composure as he realized how many times he'd seen Acheron over the years. More than that, he had a sudden epiphany of who and what he really was.

And why Katra visited them.

Holy shit!

Acheron was Apollymi's real son!

How had he missed it all these years? His father thought of himself as Apollymi's son, but he wasn't. He was just her adopted child. That was her full-blooded Apostolos. The child she mourned for.

Acheron was why she sat by the mirror all the time. She was watching over him!

Everything was so clear now.

Why they'd been called back. The no-touch laws ...

Everything.

Urian had to let him know. "Father?"

"It's all right, Urian. I know all about the Atlantean. Don't I, Acheron?"

"No. You just think you do, Strykerius. I, on the other hand, know your every flaw, right down to the one that enables you to believe in the Destroyer while she toys with you."

Urian gave the Dark-Hunter leader credit. Bastard just laid it all out on the table better than he could.

"You lie."

And his father chose not to believe it. Damn ... what could he do? How could people be so blind? Urian didn't understand it. He never would.

How, when given all the true, absolute facts, people would still blatantly choose to ignore them all.

"Perhaps. But perhaps not."

Stryker turned to Wulf and dropped his gaze to the baby. He cocked his head. "How sweet. You went to so much trouble, didn't you? All of you did. I should feel flattered."

A bad feeling went through Urian. His father was acting really, really peculiar. He glanced over to Davyn, who appeared equally concerned. Meanwhile his phone was vibrating again. He reached to silence it as his father headed toward him.

'Cause that wasn't unnerving at all.

To his instant chagrin, his father draped an arm over his shoulders and kissed him on the cheek.

What the fuck was this? While it wasn't unusual for his father to be affectionate, he'd never done it right before battle and in such a public manner. Urian scowled even more at the action and grew rigid as he waited for some shit to go down.

"Children are the very thing we live for, aren't they?" His father played with the leather laces that held his blond braid. "They bring us joy. Sometimes they bring us pain."

Was he blood-high?

"Of course, you'll never understand the pain I mean, Wulf. Your son won't live long enough to betray you."

Urian opened his mouth to explain, but before he could, his father slashed open his throat with his dragon claw. Then he shoved him away.

Stunned and unable to speak, Urian fell to the floor gasping, holding his hands against his neck to stanch the blood flow. But it was useless. It ran through his fingers and spread over the floor.

"You didn't really think I was stupid enough to fall for this trick, did you?" His father's gaze bored into Wulf. "I knew you would never bring me the baby. I just needed to get the guardians away from Elysia for a while."

Wulf cursed at his words as he moved to attack.

His father vanished into a black cloud of smoke while the Daimons attacked.

"Ak'ritah tah!" Acheron shouted.

The portal opened.

One of the Daimons laughed. "We don't have to go through—" Before he could finish the sentence, the Daimon was violently sucked through the opening.

The others quickly followed.

Meanwhile Urian lay there, blinded by his tears as he tried to breathe. He had to get to Phoebe. He couldn't die like this.

Ash ran across the floor and knelt by his side. "Shh." He covered Urian's hands with his own. "Breathe."

Warmth spread from Acheron's hand through Urian's body as the Dark-Hunters moved to surround them. With each heartbeat, Urian's breathing became easier and the pain receded.

Until it was gone.

Urian took a deep breath as he realized that for reasons unknown, Acheron had healed him. "Why?"

"I'll explain later." Acheron stood up and lifted the hem of his shirt until his stomach was exposed. "Simi, return to me."

The baby shot out of Wulf's hands immediately. She turned from an infant into a tiny dragon, then laid herself over Acheron's skin until she became a tattoo.

A blond Dark-Hunter snorted. "I always wondered how your tattoo moved."

Ash didn't speak. Instead, he raised his hands.

One second they were in the Inferno. The next they were in the middle of Elysia.

Urian shot to his feet as he ran to find his wife. Horrific screams and pleas for mercy rent the air. Bodies of Apollite men, women, and children lay everywhere. He hadn't seen anything like this in centuries. Not since the days when humans used to raid their villages.

"Phoebe!" Urian headed straight for his apartment. Fear tore him apart as every instinct he possessed told him what he'd find. And he was terrified of being right.

Why hadn't he answered his phone? Why?

And the moment the door opened, and he saw the destruction in his apartment, he knew.

He knew.

Everything had been torn apart. Their furniture was overturned. The stereo had been ripped from the wall and Phoebe's records, tapes, and CDs were littered everywhere, as if his father had wanted to punish them for trying to have a life without him.

Urian choked on his tears as he tried to come to terms with this moment.

With this reality.

Life with no Phoebe.

It was like the day he'd lost Xyn. Sinking to his knees, he threw his head back and cried out in fury. How many times in his life was he going to lose everything? Why? Was it too much to ask to be loved? To have one person he could keep in his heart?

One person for himself?

Was that really so selfish?

Damn you, Acheron!

The bastard should have let him die! Why couldn't he have left him where he was?

This was so much worse. Phoebe was dead and it was all his fault! He'd done this to her. Caused it.

Blinded by tears, he heard the others outside who shared his grief. That, too, was his fault. He'd failed them all.

Shaking and heartbroken, he paused as his gaze fell to something glittering amid the wreckage on the floor. At first he thought it was a reflection caused by his tears until he realized it was something else.

Something metallic.

Phoebe's necklace!

Incredulous, he scooped it up and let it dangle from his fingers. This was all he had of her. Such a paltry trinket for a life so vibrant. And yet it was worth more than the Taj Mahal. More than all the gold and diamonds of the earth. Because it had belonged to her and it was all he had left.

He would kill anyone who ever laid a finger to it. That was how dear and precious this worthless trinket now was. Because it was Phoebe's.

And he wished himself dead to be with her. Not here and now to feel this pain wrought by her absence.

I can't do this without you, Pheebs. He didn't even want to try. Because honestly, he was too old and too tired to have one more fresh start in him. He was done with this life.

Done with trying.

Honestly? He just wanted to die and be done with it all.

Ash found Urian on his knees in the center of the trashed living room. There was a small gold locket in his hands as the man wept silently.

"Urian?" Ash said in a low, steady tone.

"Go away!" he snarled. "Just leave me alone."

"You can't stay here. The Apollites will turn on you."

"Like I care." He looked up and the empathetic pain Ash felt from Urian made him take a step back. It had been a long time since Ash had come into direct contact with so much hopeless grief. He remembered a time, long ago, when he'd felt the same way, and it staggered him for a moment. "Why didn't you let me die too? Why did you save me?"

Ash took a deep breath as he grappled with a past that had once brutalized him and left him a hollowed-out shell. If he could, he would save Urian from that additional misery. "Because if I hadn't, you would have sold your soul to Artemis over this and killed your father."

"You think I'm not going to kill him over this?" He turned

on Ash with a growl. "There's nothing left of her. Nothing! I don't even have anything to bury. I . . . " His words broke off as he sobbed.

Ash placed his hand on Urian's shoulder. "I know."

"You don't know!"

God, how he wished that were the truth. Ash gripped his chin and lifted it until their gazes locked. "Yes, Urian, I *do* know." In ways this Daimon couldn't imagine.

Urian struggled to breathe as he saw images flickering through Ash's swirling silver eyes that were identical to Apollymi's. There was so much pain there, so much agony and wisdom.

It was hard to maintain eye contact with him.

"I don't want to live without my Phoebe." His voice broke on the words.

"I know. For that reason, I'm giving you a choice. I can't lock onto your father to monitor him. I need *you* to do that. Because sooner or later, he'll be back after Apollo's lineage."

So what! Urian curled his lip. "Why would I protect them now? Phoebe died because of them!"

"Phoebe lived because of them, Urian. Remember? You and your father were responsible for killing her entire family. Did you ever tell Phoebe it was you? You. Who killed her grandmother? Or her sisters?"

Urian looked away shamefaced as that guilt tore through him. "No. I would never have hurt her."

"Yet you did. Every time you, your father, or one of your Spathis killed one of her family, she felt the pain you feel now. Her mother's and sisters' deaths tore her apart. Isn't that why you saved Cassandra to begin with?"

Of course it was. One tear from Phoebe's eyes had always shattered him. "Yes."

Acheron stepped away from him while Urian pulled himself together as best he could.

"You said I had a choice?"

Acheron drew a ragged breath. "The other is that I will erase your memories of everything. You'll be free of all of this. All your pain. The past, the present. You can live as if none of this had ever happened to you."

A blank slate. Thousands of years gone. It sounded so easy, but Urian didn't believe even Acheron had those powers. He knew the gods better than that.

Besides, he was tired of it all. Life meant pain. It was brutal and it gutted everyone to their knees. And he was so sick of this. "Will you kill me if I ask it?"

"Do you want me to?"

At the moment, it was all he wanted. How ironic was that? He who'd taken so many lives in an effort to live one more day, to breathe one more breath, just wanted to finally expel his last and be done with it all.

But in this, his weakest, darkest moment, how strange that it was Xyn's voice he heard.

Remember the precious cost ...

Damn his dragon for making him see truth even now.

Weaker than he'd ever been in his life, he met Acheron's gaze. And damn this son of Apollymi for making him into what he'd become, because he knew that by saving his life, Acheron had turned him into something else entirely. But he had no idea what he was now. "I'm no longer a Daimon, am I?"

"No. Nor are you an Apollite, exactly."

"Then what am I?"

Acheron took a deep breath before he spoke again. "You are unique in this world."

Unique. Wonderful. Just what he'd never wanted to be. All he'd ever wanted was to fit in, and now he stood out even more.

"How much longer will I live?"

Acheron shrugged. "You're immortal, barring death."

Urian curled his lips at what had to be the dumbest answer ever. "That doesn't make sense."

"Most of life doesn't."

He wouldn't argue that. The gods knew that he'd never been able to figure it out. Urian sniffed and wiped at his eyes. "Can I walk in daylight?"

"If you want, I can make it so. If you choose amnesia, I will make you fully human."

Urian arched a brow at the most shocking thought of all. "You can do that?"

Ash nodded.

Yeah, only one born of a primal power could do that. Born of the light *and* dark. Not even Apollymi had the powers Acheron had.

Damn.

Urian laughed bitterly as he raked a cold look over Ash's body and in particular where the tattoo dragon had gone. He knew exactly what that was. And what it meant. "You know, Acheron, I'm not stupid, nor am I as blind as Stryker. Does he know of the demon you carry on your body?"

"No, and Simi isn't a demon, she's part of me."

With Simi being a Charonte demon, that was an understatement, since they bonded to their master and became a symbiotic life form. Acheron was full of surprises. No wonder Urian hadn't been able to get a reading on him when they'd crossed paths in the past.

Urian's gaze bored into his. "That I find most interesting of all. Poor Stryker, he's so screwed and he doesn't even know it."

He moved to stand closer to Acheron. "I know who and what you are, Acheron Parthenopaeus."

"Then you know if you ever pass your knowledge along I'll make sure you regret it. Eternally."

Yeah, he just bet Acheron would at that. Urian nodded. "But I don't understand why you hide."

Acheron shrugged. "I'm not hiding. The knowledge you carry can't help anyone. It can only destroy and harm."

Perhaps there was truth to that. Just like his powers of healing. Whenever people knew about them, they went crazy for them and there were limitations to what he could do. And when they failed, it got ugly fast. So like Acheron, he kept his powers hidden. For his own well-being as much as for others.

Urian winced as he thought back to all the lives of the people he'd loved who were lost to him. His children. His mother. His wives. Brothers and sisters. The humans and Daimons he'd killed for the right to continue living. "I'm through being a destroyer."

"Then what are you?"

Urian let his thoughts wander through the events of this night. He thought about the aching pain inside him that screamed over the loss of his wife. It was so tempting to let Acheron erase it all, but with that he would lose all the good memories he carried, too.

Though he and Phoebe had only had a few years together, she had loved him in ways no one ever had. Touched a heart he had thought was long dead.

No, it hurt to live without her, but he didn't want to lose all connection with her.

He fastened her locket around his neck as he realized that for the first time since he was a boy, his head was quiet. The only voice in it now was his own.

"I'm your man, Acheron. But I warn you now. If I'm ever given a chance to kill Stryker, I will take it. Consequences be damned."

. . .

Stryker snarled in outrage as he found himself in the Destroyer's throne room. "I was so close to killing them. Why did you stop me? How could you have pulled me back here?"

Still the demon, Sabine, held him back from Apollymi's throne.

For once Xedrix wasn't in the room with his mother, but Stryker didn't have time to ponder the demon's whereabouts. His thoughts were too consumed by hatred and vexation.

His mother sat on her chaise completely poised, as if she were holding court and hadn't just destroyed all their years of careful planning.

"Do not raise your voice to me, Strykerius. I will not take your insubordination."

He forced himself to level his voice even while his blood simmered in fury. "Why did you interfere?"

She pulled her black pillow into her lap and toyed with a corner of it. "You cannot win against the Elekti. I told you that."

"I could have beaten him," Stryker insisted. No one could stop him. He was sure of it.

"No, you couldn't." She dropped her gaze again and ran her hand elegantly over the black satin. "There is no pain worse than a son who betrays your cause, is there, Strykerius? You give them everything and do they listen? No. Do they respect you? No. Instead they shred your heart and spit on the kindness you would show to them."

Stryker clenched his eyes shut as she voiced the very thoughts inside his heart. He'd given Urian everything. And how had his son repaid him? With a betrayal so profound that it had taken him days to come to grips with it.

Part of him hated Apollymi for telling him the truth. The other part thanked her. He'd never been the kind of man to welcome a snake to his bosom.

He still couldn't get over the fact that Urian hadn't trusted him, his own father. That his son honestly thought, after all these years, he couldn't tell him the simple truth.

He'd remarried.

And now what had those actions done? Urian's wife had gone trelos and attacked her own commune. Because she was human and couldn't handle it. His son's lies had forced him to commit even bigger ones to protect Urian.

You killed him for his betrayal. That was the lie Stryker would live with. Not the truth. That he'd done it to spare Urian from finding out that Phoebe had gone insane. Because that would kill Urian's heart. He knew his son too well. And he'd never be able to watch what that would have done to his boy.

The anguish and self-hatred.

Stryker was already hated and loathed. Better he remain the monster they all thought him to be, than watch his son die slowly from his own recriminations.

Urian died for betrayal. Betrayal to the community and to him.

And Stryker would never do that to his mother. "I will listen to you, akra."

Sighing, she cradled the pillow to her breast. "Good."

"So what do we do now?"

She gazed at him with a small, beautiful smile. When she spoke, her words were simple, but her tone was purely evil. "We wait."

Urian *really didn't* feel like being here. In fact, *this* was the absolute last place he wanted to be.

Muppet's house.

But he had nowhere to go. How pathetic was that? Eleven thousand years old and he was homeless. Friendless.

And the only family he had was this Viking piece of shit.

Glorious. Just glorious.

Even better, he could hear Chris grumbling as he came to open the door to let him and Acheron into the house.

Wulf rose to his feet as they entered. He also gasped. Not that Urian blamed him. He knew he looked bad. He was pale, his clothes still covered in blood. And he was madder than ten liters of hell saturated by demon piss and poured down the throats of a starving Charonte. No doubt all of that radiated in his body language and eyes.

The blond Armani-wearing Dark-Hunter who was seated on their right was the first to recover himself and speak. "We were getting worried about you, Ash."

The surly dark-haired bastard from the club who had a goatee snorted. "I wasn't. But now that you're here, do you need me for anything else?"

"No, Z," Ash said quietly. "Thanks for coming."

He inclined his head. "Any time you want me to help rip something apart, just give me call. But in the future, could you pick somewhere warmer to do it?" He flashed out of the room before anyone could respond.

The biker blond covered with Celtic tattoos smirked. "You know, it really pisses me off that he's a god now."

"Just make sure you don't piss *him* off," Acheron said in warning. "Or he might turn you into a toad."

The Celt blustered. "He wouldn't dare."

Armani snorted. "We are talking about Zarek, right?"

"Oh yeah," the Celt said. "Never mind."

Armani stood up with a groan. "Well, since I'm one of the few nonimmortals in the room, I think I'm going to head to bed and rest."

The Celt flexed his bandaged arm. "Sleep sounds like a plan to me."

Chris threw the medical supplies back into a plastic box. "C'mon, guys, and I'll show you where you can crash."

Cassandra stood up with Erik in her arms, intending to follow after them. "I guess I should—"

"Wait," Urian said, stopping her. "Can I hold him?"

She hesitated with a worried frown that he knew he'd earned. He'd barely looked at Erik before this. He hadn't wanted to.

Part of it had been jealousy. Phoebe had wanted a baby desperately, and it had been the one thing he'd never been able to give her. Another had been pure, unadulterated grief. Because when he saw children, it took him back to his youth. Back to the days when his nieces and nephews had been born, and they'd been hopeful of finding an end to their curse.

Before there had been so many deaths. He hadn't wanted to think about all the times he'd held Geras and Nephele when they were young.

But now . . .

Cassandra glanced to Ash, who nodded.

Her features reluctant, she handed Erik over to him.

Damn, it'd been so long since he last held a baby that he almost dropped the little squirmy thing. She actually had to show him how to hold one again.

How could he forget something so important as to hold the baby's head and neck? But then it had literally been hundreds of years. Lucky for them both, it didn't take long for it to come back to him. And the smell . . .

That he definitely remembered. That newborn baby smell. Before the world came and tainted them. Scarred them with its brutality and ugliness. Taught them to hate and to hurt. Taught their hearts to bleed.

He would give anything to spare this child the nightmares that were ahead for him. The harsh lessons that would come in the future and bring him to his knees.

"You're so fragile," Urian breathed at the tiny boy who eyed him so cluelessly about the misery this world was getting ready to unleash on him. "And yet you're still alive while my Phoebe isn't."

Wulf took a step forward.

Acheron held him back. "Will you stay and guard your family?"

Urian snarled at Acheron for a reminder he despised him for. "My family is dead." Thanks to Acheron and his mother.

Acheron's gaze turned sympathetic as he glanced down at the infant in his arms. "No, Urian, it's not. Phoebe's blood is in that baby. Erik carries her immortality with him."

Urian hated him for that reminder that made him feel again. Made him care when he didn't want to. In his mind, he saw how excited she was every time she talked about Erik and his imminent arrival.

"She loved this baby," he whispered. "I could tell how much she wanted her own whenever she spoke of him. I only wish I could have given her one."

"You gave her everything else, Urian." Cassandra's eyes filled with tears as she spoke of her sister. "She knew that, and she loved you for it."

Those words broke him in a way nothing else had. And for the first time, he actually liked his sister-in-law.

Acheron was right. She was his family.

So was this baby.

And that stupid Muppet asshole.

Urian wrapped an arm around Cassandra and pulled her close. He laid his head down on her shoulder and finally gave in to the tears that had been choking him. Clutching him tight, Cassandra sobbed against his shoulder.

After a time, Urian let go and handed her Erik. "I won't let your baby die, Cassandra. I swear it. No one will ever hurt him. Not as long as I live."

Cassandra kissed him on the cheek. "Thank you."

His throat tight, Urian nodded and withdrew from her. He drew a ragged breath and wiped his tears off on the sleeve of his jacket.

"What an alliance, huh?" Wulf asked after Cassandra had left them. "A Dark-Hunter and a Spathi united to guard an Apollite. Who would have ever imagined?"

Acheron snorted. "Love makes strange bedfellows."

Muppet scowled. "I thought that was politics."

"It's both," Acheron said with a grin.

Urian folded his arms over his chest. "Would you mind if I slept in the boathouse?"

Wulf nodded. "Sure. Consider it yours for as long as you want it."

Urian inclined his head to him and headed out, trying his best not to think about the last time he was here.

With Phoebe.

For Phoebe.

He'd barely reached it when he felt a strange presence behind him. It was one he knew all too well. He felt his arm heating up as he prepared to hurl a bolt at it.

"Oh now, akri-Daimon, don't be doing that! You smack the Simi, and the Simi be sad. She not coming to hurt you. I just wanted to come bring you some barbecue chips and make you smiley 'cause you gots the hurts. Now put your arm away."

What the hell? "Who are you?"

Tall and thin, she stepped from the shadows. Unlike the Charonte he was used to, she didn't have wings or horns, or mottled skin. Rather she appeared human. Dressed in a short Goth skirt, with striped leggings and a corset top, she was adorable. Right down to her coffin pocketbook and tall, stacked heels. Her black hair had the same odd red stripe in it that Acheron's did. Only she wore her hair up in pigtails.

Flouncing over to him, she took his arm and led him upstairs. "You are a Charonte, right?"

"'Course I am. All the demons are."

"Then why aren't you in Kalosis?"

She made an adorably cute face. "Mostly 'cause the Simi's not visiting akra-goddess. That's why, silly!" She opened the door with her powers and led him in.

"I am so confused."

She grinned. "Knows whatcha mean. The Simi stays confuzzled most the times. Face it. The world's just a confuzzling kind of place."

Suddenly, Urian felt like an idiot as he realized who and what the demon was. "You're Acheron's tattoo? From the club."

She gave him a look that said he was a complete and utter moron. "Well, yeah. You don't think the Simi would let some ole other Charonte come and lay down on her akri and not eat its head, do you?"

From what he knew about Charonte, no. They weren't exactly into sharing.

She made him sit on the floor in front of the TV. Then she opened her purse and pulled out two surprisingly large bags of potato chips. "Red meat? White meat?"

"Pardon?"

She cocked her head. "Red meat?" She wagged the bag of barbecue chips in front of his face. "Or white meat?" She rattled a bag of sour cream and onion chips.

"I've never eaten either."

Simi sucked her breath in as if that were the worst thing she'd ever heard. "That's right. You eats the blood! Except you don't no more." Fanning her face, she danced around excitedly, then handed him both bags. "Open them! Open them!"

He obliged her.

"Now eats!"

Urian wasn't sure about this. Cringing, he held one up to his nose.

Simi made a rude noise and popped his hand. "Would you

stop! You done been eating on the people! Stop being all finicky. Eat the dang chip! Unlike the people, which don't be getting the Simi wrong, 'cause they's mighty tasty, them's chips is good! Eat it!"

He laughed at the demonic tone that somehow managed to be childlike. "Yes, ma'am." He bit into it and gasped. "Holy shit, that's good."

"Told you! Eat more!" She held up the bag for him. Then she made an adorable noise and dropped it so that she could run to another room.

After a few minutes, she came back with several drinks. "Fruitsie juicies! You gots so much catching up, akri-Daimon!"

Simi scooted in beside him and started pulling more snacks out of that tiny purse, then turned the TV on to something called QVC, where she educated him on modern shopping.

"Why are you doing this, Simi?"

She lay beside him on the floor with her feet up on the couch— he didn't know why, but most Charonte slept and relaxed like that. Cocking her head, she scowled at him. "Don't you know, akri-Daimon?"

"No idea."

She reached up and touched his chest where his mark used to be. "You gots the heart sadness. Friends don't leave friends alone when they heart-sad."

"I didn't know we were friends."

She snorted at him again. "Of course we are. That's how you make friends. You see somebody when they heart-sad and you walk over and say, it'll be okies and you hug them and share your chips. Then you're friends."

She took his hand into hers and held it. "See. Friends. The Simi don't bite you. You don't bite the Simi. We friends."

"I guess it is that simple, huh?"

Nodding, she tilted her head back to watch more TV.

She was still there a few hours later when Acheron came to see him. Only Simi was asleep, which was easy to tell as the little demon came with a giant snore.

Cocking his head, Acheron actually lifted his sunglasses up to rest on top of his head as he studied his sleeping demon. "I wondered where she'd gone off to. This was the last place I'd have looked for her."

"She's quite the chatterbox."

Acheron laughed. "You've no idea."

"Oh, you would be wrong there. Got a pretty good earful tonight."

Still laughing, he nodded. "I can imagine." Clearing his throat, he sobered. "How are you doing?"

"Been better." Urian tucked the blanket he'd draped over Simi higher around her chin. "But she helped a lot."

"Yeah, she has a way of doing that." Acheron jerked his chin toward the door. "You got a minute?"

"Why?"

"There's something I think you want to see."

"Unless it's my father's head on a platter, not really."

Acheron lowered his sunglasses to cover those screwed-up eyes. "I wouldn't take that bet. C'mon."

Taking care to not disturb Simi, he got up to follow Acheron toward the back door. Acheron used his powers to open it so that Urian could see the dawn that was breaking over the water.

Out of habit, he hissed and headed for the shadows.

Acheron caught his arm. "It won't hurt you. I swear."

His breathing ragged, Urian looked up at him in disbelief. "Really?"

"I swear," he repeated. "I know you want to see it." He manifested a pair of sunglasses for Urian and held them out to him. "You'll need these."

Urian put them on and then slowly, carefully made his way to the door and then to the deck outside. It was a chilly morning. Biting, in fact. But he didn't care.

His gaze was held captive by the amber rays breaking through the darkness, setting the landscape aglow.

In all honesty, he had no idea how long he stood there. A million thoughts spun through his head. A billion memories. But the one that kept playing loudest was the one of him and Paris. Tears choked him as he looked over to Acheron. "I wish my brother could have seen it."

"I know."

He shook his head. "You don't know what it's like to be born with a twin, Acheron. To come into the world with someone."

"Actually, I do."

He gaped at that. "Pardon?"

"Not something I share. With anyone. Unlike you and Paris, my brother and I were enemies. He was a selfish bastard who conspired against me. But life takes us to places we don't always want to go, and in directions we never think it will."

Urian laughed bitterly as he considered the understatement of *that*, given that he was a Daimon currently living in the guesthouse of a Dark-Hunter.

"But," Acheron continued, "we all have a choice. Toss the oar and let the current take us wherever. Or grab the oar with both hands and fight the current with everything we have. In the end, we all determine what fate we embrace. For we are either pawns or players. The final decision is always ours."

"Don't worry. I've no intention of being a pawn. There's too much piss and vinegar in me for that. You may have taken my fangs from me, Acheron, but at my core, I remain a demon. Forever. Venom was the milk I drank from my mother's breast, and I won't rest until I bathe in the blood of my father."

His father hadn't quelled him with his actions.

He'd fueled him.

October 1, 2008

Urian was aghast at what he found in the temple housed next to Acheron's in Katateros. When he'd heard a noise, he'd expected one of the souls to have escaped out of one of the other areas. But this was no Shade.

This was a man.

Swimming in the wrong place. At the wrong time.

"Who are you?"

Yet as he turned around in the pool, Urian felt as if someone had slapped him. Hard. For there was no doubt who he had to be.

Acheron's despised twin brother. Holy shit ... They *were* identical. Same height. Same build. Sculpted features. Virtually indistinguishable, except where Acheron had those freaky swirling silver eyes, Styxx had a pair of vibrant blue ones. Eyes that were the closest shade to Urian's he'd ever seen on another person.

Weird.

And while Ash preferred to keep his hair long and dyed black, the evil anti-Ash held to their natural blond shade and wore his cut short. He was also scarred abysmally.

And still the defiant bastard had yet to speak.

"I asked you a question," Urian snarled. "Do you not understand me?"

"I heard you."

"And?"

With a slowness Urian was sure was just to piss him off, he climbed out of the pool and reached for a towel. He dried himself off, then wrapped it around his hips before he closed the distance between them. "Ask me when you find a new tone. One with respect in it."

Oh yeah, this guy was a douche on steroids. Now all the

stories he'd heard about the infamous brother made *total* sense. "You must be Styxx."

"So you're not as stupid as you look."

Urian would have made an equally nasty comeback, but he couldn't get over how many scars Styxx had on his body. While Urian had more than his fair share, they paled in comparison to the number this man carried.

Apparently, Styxx pissed off everyone he'd ever come into contact with.

Urian grimaced at that road map of pain. "Damn, you're scarred up."

"Aren't we all?"

He didn't comment on that, especially not with *his* past. "I was told you'd been put on one of the other islands."

"I was."

"Then why are you here?"

Styxx picked up another towel to dry his hair. "I liked this one better."

Wow, his arrogance was quite a special thing. "Are you always this big an asshole?"

"Are you?"

That was a loaded question and then some. Urian flashed a grin. "Basically, yes. However, I thought I'd tempered it for you. Guess I'm an even bigger ass than I knew."

Styxx laughed. "Then I'd hate to see you on a bad day if this is a good one."

"Yeah, well, according to Ash I pretty much get on his nerves every ten minutes."

"It takes you an entire ten minutes? I'm impressed. All I have to do is enter his line of sight to wreck his whole year."

Urian smiled. It wasn't often he met someone who could match his sarcasm. He'd love to put this guy in a match with Shadow.

He indicated Styxx's scars with a tilt of his head. "You must have been a soldier who saw a lot of combat for those."

"I was ... and I did."

"Cavalry?"

"Protostratelates."

Urian's eyes bugged at such a prestigious role. Especially for someone so young, that was almost unheard of. In fact he only knew of one who'd done that. "At your ... ? Oh wait, wait a minute. Styxx ... Styxx of Didymos, Styxx?"

He nodded.

No! No! What were the odds? Seriously? Urian sputtered at something that was too surreal to be reality. "How stupid do I feel? I never put the two names together before. Mostly because I assumed the protostratelates who damn near defeated Atlantis was an old man. Oh wow ... " he breathed. "You were a legend. When I was a kid, I extensively studied your surviving war notes, and reports, and everything written about you. Your tactics fascinated me, but there was so much you left out."

"I didn't want someone to use my strategies against me."

"As I said, brilliant, and if you knew me, you'd know I gush over no one." Stunned and thrilled to meet his hero, Urian held his arm out. "This is really an honor."

Styxx hesitated, then shook it. "So how old are you ... really?"

"I was born a few weeks before you and Acheron died. And before you condemn me, I mostly lived on people who deserved to die."

"Mostly?"

Urian shrugged. "Sometimes you can't be picky. But I never fed from a human woman or a child. Or anyone who couldn't fight back."

Styxx held his hands up. "I'm in no position to judge anyone for how they survive."

A deep scowl furrowed Urian's brow. "It's strange, though."

"What is?"

"How much you and Acheron favor each other not to be related at all."

Sighing, Styxx dropped his second towel, then finger-combed his short blond hair. "Trick of his mother's to throw off the gods looking for him."

Urian snorted. "She did well. I had a fraternal twin brother myself."

"Had?"

"He was killed a long time ago by a Dark-Hunter."

"Oh, I'm very sorry."

Urian inclined his head to him as that old wound opened and bled. "Thanks. Me, too. It's hard to lose a brother, and twice as hard when you're born together. Kind of like losing a limb."

Styxx snorted. "In my case, more like losing a sphincter."

Laughing, Urian shook his head. "What happened between you? I mean, damn, Acheron forgave me, and I definitely didn't deserve a second chance. You don't seem like an outright bastard, and you definitely didn't battle like one. Things you did ... you protected your enemy against your own troops. And you were barbecued for it by Greek historians and commanders."

"I was barbecued for it by many people."

Now that he knew who he really was, Urian followed him from the pool into the bedroom. He had so many questions to ask. Things he'd always wondered about that no one had documented. Really, how often did someone get to interview their hero? "So how old were you when you first went into battle? Five?"

"Sixteen." Styxx picked his clothes up and went behind a screen to dress.

"Damn, that was harsh. My father refused to let us near battle until we were past our majority." For Apollites anyway. "He waited so long, it was actually embarrassing." Urian didn't want to think about the times his father literally picked them up and threw them down to keep them from battle.

He took a step back and gestured toward the door. "Would you like to come up to the main hall with me? Dinner should be about ready."

Styxx shook his head as he came around the screen. "I'm not welcome there. Acheron would have a fit to find me in his temple."

Urian had forgotten about that small fact. It would be the same as inviting his father to dinner. Yeah ... real bad idea.

Acheron hated his twin with a special kind of vim. "Don't worry. I won't tell the bossman you're here. Stay as long as you want."

"Thanks, Urian." Styxx went to hang his towels up to dry.

"Hey," Urian called. "Would you like me to bring you some dinner?"

"Gods, yes, I'd kill for some." Embarrassed by the emotion he'd betrayed, he cleared his throat. "Yes, please. I'd appreciate it."

Urian suppressed a smile at Styxx's enthusiasm. "I'll be back as soon as I can."

Though to be honest, Urian hated leaving him there. Alone. If there was one thing he understood, it was loneliness. Isolation. And Styxx had had more than his fair share of it.

Before, when he'd assumed him to be Acheron's villain brother with no conscience, Urian hadn't cared what happened to him.

Now he had a face and a history.

It made a lot of difference. Perspective. Life was all about perspective. If anyone should appreciate that, a former Daimon should. After all, his people had been misjudged by everyone.

And they still were. It was why Spawn was one of his few friends among the Dark-Hunters. He was a former Daimon, and one who'd served under his command; they understood each other. And both were ostracized by the rest of Acheron's army.

They were the brotherhood of misfits.

Styxx was their newest recruit.

Welcome to my madness.

And that was what it was. That raw, biting loneliness that never left him. The bitter gut punch that ached through and through. He'd lost both the women he'd loved most.

Xyn and Phoebe.

Life was so bitterly unfair.

Why couldn't it have taken him instead?

Trying not to think about it, Urian snuck into Acheron's temple where he lived and did his best to act nonchalant. He shared the temple with Acheron, Simi, and Acheron's steward Alexion, who was one of the first Dark-Hunters ever created, and sadly the first to have been killed. And Alexion's wife, another

Dark-Hunter who'd died in the line of duty, Danger. And of course, Alexion's own Charonte, Simi's sister, Xirena.

They, and a few peculiar pets, made up Acheron's happy home. Aside from the collection of statues in the basement no one ever talked about.

And Urian meant *no one*. As that topic quickly sent his boss into a fit of anger.

"You okay, Uri?" Danger asked as soon as she saw him skulking about.

Urian dropped the banana he'd been trying to smuggle out. "Um. Yeah. You?"

"Always."

"Good." Crap ... why did she have to be so nosy?

Hours went by before Urian was able to head back to where he'd left Styxx. Though what the man was doing, Urian didn't want to know, as it appeared he was pulling out some kind of nasty seafood grossness to eat. Pushing that aside, Urian set his backpack on the table beside Styxx.

He frowned at Styxx's dinner. "What is *that?*"

Styxx shrugged, then returned the unidentifiable ick to the urn on the table.

Urian's scowl deepened as he tipped the chipped clay cup to see the coconut milk in it. "Ew! Really? You were really going to drink this shit?"

"Anánkai d'oudè theoì mákhontai," Styxx said simply.

Urian laughed. "'Not even the gods fight necessity' ... nice. You said that to your men right before the battle for Ena."

"Did I?"

"You don't remember? I used to use that for my own men to motivate them. It got me stabbed once. Apparently, what works for Greeks doesn't work for Spathi Daimons."

"Honestly, no, I don't remember. And it got me stabbed a time or two, too. Besides, I can't really take credit for it. It was something my mentor used to say to me all the time."

"And what would he say about this?" Urian held up a bottle of wine.

"*Brôma theôn.*" *Food of the gods.*

Urian handed it to him, then dug out the opener and two glasses. "I'm going to hazard a wild guess that you're a little short on supplies. Would you like me to bring you something?"

"I can make do, but some fresh water would be nice. It doesn't rain here, and it doesn't get quite hot enough to make a lot of condensation. It's been difficult to desalinate the river water, which I can't figure out why it's salty ... "

Urian scowled at something he hadn't known about the island. Or Styxx, for that matter. "Why didn't you stay where your supplies were?"

Styxx dug a fork out of the backpack and sat down to eat. "I haven't received any."

Urian was aghast at the last thing he expected to come out of Styxx's mouth. "What have you been living on?"

Closing his eyes, Styxx savored the unfamiliar taste. He swallowed and wiped his mouth before he answered. "Clams mostly ... whenever I can find them. Coconuts. Some greens I found out back." He took a drink of wine, then sighed in appreciation. "What?"

"Nothing." Urian grabbed the backpack up. "I'll be back in a few minutes, okay?"

Styxx nodded as he kept eating. "Urian? What's this called?"

It took Urian a second to realize that Styxx was as innocent about the world as he'd been when he was first made human. Damn, that was pathetic. "Spaghetti."

"It's really good. Thank you."

"*Parakaló.*"

Urian hated leaving Styxx alone. But once again, he found himself hiding a massive secret from those around him. Weird that this seemed to be some recurrent theme in his life and he didn't know why. He'd done so much to avoid drama, yet that bitch kept hunting him down just to put stress on him he didn't want.

So here he was again.

But what else was he to do? He couldn't let the poor guy starve. Styxx needed help and it wasn't in him ...

Yeah, okay, so maybe it was in him to turn his back on people and not care. Urian was a bastard that way. Yet there was something about Styxx that was so familiar. A kinship he couldn't deny. Maybe because he looked so much like Acheron and he owed Acheron so much.

Whatever it was, he found himself back in the temple where Styxx sat at the pool with his feet dangling into the water while he stared off into space, at nothing in particular.

"Is this what you do at night?" Urian asked him.

Styxx got up and pulled his jeans down. "There's nothing else to do, really. Sometimes I go outside and stare at the moon."

"You must get a lot of sleep."

"Not really."

Urian couldn't imagine living like this. And he'd always thought his life was lonely. "How are you not crazy?"

Styxx snorted. "Who says I'm not?"

Touché. Perhaps they all were. "I couldn't take three days of this boredom without being stark-raving mad."

"As far as prisons go, trust me, this isn't so bad. No one's sticking hot brands on me or beating me, and I'm not chained to anything or drugged. Best of all, I don't have to bend myself in half to lie down."

Urian cringed at what he was describing in a monotone, yet the scars on his body said that he spoke from absolute experience. "When were you a prisoner?"

Styxx laughed bitterly. "Honestly? In the whole of my extremely long life, I've only spent roughly a high grand total of fourteen years where I wasn't imprisoned for one reason or another."

That number staggered his mind and left him reeling. More than that, it left him furious on Styxx's behalf. What the hell? "Imprisoned for what?"

"Being born Acheron's brother ... well, except for when Apollo and the Atlanteans held me here. That was entirely my fault. Turns out, gods don't like it when humans defeat them and invade their homelands. Who knew?"

Urian had to sit down for a second on that one, especially when he remembered Apollymi's reaction the day she'd seen his shield. And Styxx would have been just a kid . . .

Where the hell were his parents?

"Didn't anyone love you?" He looked up at him.

Styxx let out a bitter laugh and ignored his question. Instead, he swung his arm around the room. "Did you know this temple belonged to Bet'anya Agriosa . . . the Atlantean goddess of misery and wrath? The next temple on the right belonged to Epithymia, their goddess of desire. She was a royal fucking bitch. Vicious. Cold. Lived to hurt others. It always made me wonder if Aphrodite was anything like her." He paused as he caught the pained expression on Urian's face as he grappled with trying to reconcile the horror of Styxx's life in his mind. And kept failing to do so. He just couldn't imagine what this man had been through. "Sorry. I'm not used to having anyone to talk to."

Honestly, Urian wasn't sure what to make of Styxx. From what Acheron had said of his brother, he'd expected some arrogant, demanding prick who looked at the people around him like they were dirt.

The man in front of him was definitely *not* what Acheron had described. There was no arrogance in him, at all. If anything, given that he'd been born a prince to one of the richest kingdoms in the ancient world, and had been a young commander of one of the most successful armies, the bastard was exceedingly humble. He had a very quiet, suspicious nature more akin to Urian's. He reminded Urian more of the gators that called the swamps home in Louisiana.

Styxx kept his eyes on everything around him, assessing each corner and shadow as a possible threat. Though he seemed to be at ease, there was no doubt he could launch himself at someone's throat and roll them under for the kill before they even saw him move.

Yeah, Urian could easily see in Styxx the legendary general he'd read about. The one who didn't complain over anything and who had sacrificed and sold his own personal effects to buy supplies for his men. Just the physical scars on his body alone made a mockery of the person Acheron thought him to be.

This was not some pampered prince who'd been waited on hand and foot, and who expected the entire world to bow down to him. In over eleven thousand years, Urian had never seen any man more scarred. Even Styxx's fingers and the backs of his hands said he'd lived a hard and harsh life. For that matter, Styxx barely had the use of his right hand. Two of his fingers, the pinkie and ring fingers, stayed permanently curled against his palm. And the other two didn't fully extend.

More remarkably still, there were just four scars on his face. And one of them was only noticeable if you paid close attention. He had a faint scar beneath his left eye. One that ran along his hairline across his forehead that was covered by his hair most of the time. One that slashed across his right eyebrow, and the one in the center of his upper lip where it'd been forcefully busted open so many times that it'd left a permanent divot and thick vertical line.

The awful condition of Styxx's body verified what he'd said about captivity. As did his knowledge of the temples. As with Kalosis, there was nothing left inside any of the buildings here to say whom they'd belonged to, and not even Acheron knew.

But Styxx did.

And what really screwed with Urian's head was the fact that Styxx had been imprisoned for more than eleven thousand years. The duration of Urian's long, long life. So he could easily appreciate exactly how many mind-blowing years that was.

Alone.

He would call the man a liar for that, but again, the scars and his calm acceptance of Acheron dumping him here and forgetting about him testified to the fact that Styxx was more than used to isolation and neglect. More than used to scrounging for scraps to eat.

And all Styxx had asked him for was untainted drinking water. . . .

Buddy, you get the prize bonus in my book. Urian still couldn't believe how humble a request that was.

"I brought you more food," Urian said, trying to break the suddenly awkward silence.

"It wasn't necessary."

"Having seen the shit you had on your plate when I brought in the spaghetti, I'm going to respectfully disagree." Urian headed back to the other room and, as a trained warrior himself, didn't miss the fact that Styxx kept a lot of empty space between them. He also walked at an angle so that he could see if Urian was reaching for a weapon.

The way Styxx did it, it was hardwired into him. That, too, made a mockery of the pampered-prince bullshit.

At least until he saw what Urian had brought in a large plastic box, and then Styxx relaxed his protocol and rushed forward.

"Bread?" he whispered.

"Yeah, that's the white stuff in the plastic bag."

His expression said he hadn't had bread in a long time. Urian imagined he must have looked like that the first time he saw daylight.

He stepped back so that Styxx would look through the box and see what else it contained. The minute he was clear, Styxx rooted through the contents like Erik breaking into his presents on Christmas morning.

"Thank you."

"You're welcome." Urian picked up another box that he'd set on the floor. "I have your water and more wine in this one. And I put candles and a lighter in here, too."

Styxx placed the lid on top of the box. "Thank you, but I won't need those."

Urian glanced around the cave dubiously, and that was from a former Daimon who'd once called Kalosis home. "You sure? It's really dark in here."

Styxx shrugged. "I'm used to it. Besides, if Acheron sees a

light, there's no telling how he'll react, and I don't want to fight with him. Most of all, I don't want him to take away what little freedom I have."

Damn. For that, Urian wanted to beat Acheron's ass. What kind of bad history did they have?

But then, having fought off-and-on with his own brothers, and even his sister, he understood. It didn't make his brothers or sister bad people, it just made them family. "Okay. I'll ... um ... I'll bring more food after tomorrow."

Styxx smiled at Urian. "Careful, you keep this up and I won't have anything to occupy myself with."

Urian's phone rang with Cassandra's ring tone, though it could be Erik calling since he'd started using it to update him on his daily routines.

Excusing himself, he pulled it out and turned it on to answer. Unfortunately, it wasn't the cuter of the two on the other end. "Hey, Cass, is everything all right?"

"It's fine. Wulf and I had our babysitter crap out on us and Chris's wife is sick. You know what that means. Big guy doesn't want the kids near her for fear they might come down with something fatal. And I really would like to have one last night out before the little ones outnumber us."

Urian laughed. Neither their son Erik nor their daughter Phoebe had ever had a cold in their lives. And baby three, soon to be named Tyr, was due any second now, which was why he'd panicked when he answered. His first thought was that she'd gone into labor early. "Sure. I don't mind babysitting. You know that. I love your rugrats."

"They love their Uncle Uri." She'd no more said that than he heard Erik in the background begin chanting, "Uncle Uri's coming!" Then his nephew started a happy war cry that warmed Urian's heart and simultaneously saddened it to a level Cassandra would never understand, as it reminded him of all the other nieces and nephews he'd never see again.

"I've got to go run that one down, Uri. He's off the chain. Love you! See you soon."

"Yeah, see you soon. Love you, too." He hung up and slid the phone back in his pocket.

"Your wife?" Styxx asked.

"My wife's sister."

"Ah. So does your wife live in the main temple with you?"

Well, that question sucked every last bit of joy and humor out of his year. His stomach tight, Urian reached to touch Phoebe's necklace. "No. She died."

"I am extremely sorry. I know how hard that is."

While Urian had no doubt Styxx had seen his share of pain and then some, the guilt he felt over that night was its own special form of eternal hell that he could never reconcile. No matter how hard he tried. No matter what he did. It all came down to one harsh, bitter truth ... "I appreciate it, but I had a very special bond with my Phoebe, and she was killed when I should have been there to protect her."

Styxx drew a ragged breath. "I do know your pain, Urian. My wife was murdered by Acheron's mother while she was pregnant with our first child. And I have absolutely nothing left of them, except my memories."

Wincing at the nightmare Styxx carried, Urian dropped his gaze to his arm, where Styxx had carved two names into his own flesh. It didn't take a genius to figure out who they were or why Styxx had done it. And how much pain that man held in his heart to have inflicted that much harm on himself because of it. "Bethany and Galen?"

He nodded. "I had no other way to honor them. I never even got to see their bodies." He cleared his throat. "You need to go to your family. Don't keep them waiting."

Yeah, if anyone ever understood his pain where Phoebe was concerned, Urian had found him. In that, they were joined in a very sad and pathetic brotherhood of misery. "What about you?"

Styxx laughed. "I assure you, I'll be here when you get back."

Yeah, he guessed he would at that.

Urian gave him an ancient salute that Styxx quickly returned, and then Urian left to head up the hill. But with every step he took, he had a strange feeling. Like he knew Styxx from some-where. The man was so familiar to him.

He's Acheron's twin, dumbass. . . .

There was that.

And it wasn't like you didn't obsess over him as a kid or anything. He laughed as he remembered his father banning him from even saying Styxx's name in his presence.

"If I hear you speak of that Didymosian bastard one more time, Urian, I will beat you until you can't sit down. And stop dressing like him! He was an enemy to Atlantis and Apollymi."

For that matter, Urian had Styxx's phoenix emblem tattooed on his biceps. Best not to ever let Styxx see that, though. It might freak him out. But then Urian was used to keeping it covered. It'd been another thing that had enraged his father.

Much like his shield.

I just excel at pissing off everybody.

Urian paused to look back at the dark temple. Had he not been out for a walk earlier and heard the faint splashing, he'd have never known Styxx was in there. And he'd almost ignored it and kept going. Only his centuries of honed senses and incessant need to check and lock down his perimeter had caused him to investigate the foreign noise.

Wow. As he resumed the path to the main temple, he couldn't understand Acheron's reasoning where Styxx was concerned. Having lost all his brothers, he'd give anything to see one of them again. Even Archimedes, who'd bullied and shoved him to the point where Urian had wanted to rip his heart out, more times than not. The two of them could barely be in a room and not walk out bruised from the unfortunate event.

Still he'd welcome that asshole back if he could.

Dang, Ash. Who in their right mind throws out a perfectly good brother?

October 24, 2008

With his arms crossed over his chest, Urian frowned at Ash while Ash sat on his throne in Katateros and played his shiny black Warlock guitar.

A few feet away from them, Simi lay on her stomach, watching QVC as she devoured a tub of barbecue-flavored popcorn. Dressed in black tights and a short plaid skirt with a pink-and-black peasant top and corset, she had her feathered wings draped around her and her tail kept drifting over to poke at her sister during the commercial breaks.

Because apparently annoying your sibling wasn't just something humans did.

Ignoring the demons, Urian moved to where Alexion stood off to the side, with the same exact expression on his face that Urian had. The one that said Ash was the supervillain who'd been dropped in a vat of acid and they were waiting for his anti-hero powers to manifest and destroy the world.

'Cause face it, for thousands of years, Alexion had been the only person Ash had allowed in his home besides Simi. Of course, that had been out of profound guilt since Alexion had been one of the first Dark-Hunters Artemis created. And when Ash had tried to make Alexion human again to return him to his family, Ash had royally fucked it up.

To spare Alexion an eternity of extreme pain and torture, the best Acheron could do for him was an eternity spent in a quasi-ghost existence by using his own blood to bind Alexion here.

Too bad Savitar hadn't explained those powers to Ash sooner. It would have saved both of them a lot of grief.

But at least Alexion wasn't in constant pain and misery. And now he had Danger here for company.

Yet that wasn't what Urian found disturbing.

Oh no ... Not by a long shot.

In all the centuries he had lived, the most terrifying thing ever was the fact that the leader of the Dark-Hunters—the head badass, son of the Destroyer, was sitting there playing ...

"'Push'?" By Matchbox Twenty? Seriously?

Urian stared aghast at Alexion. "What's the deal with the bossman?"

Alexion shrugged. "I don't know. He came in last night with a book, went to his room to read, I suppose, and then he came out here this morning and has been playing ... *those* songs ever since."

Urian was stunned. *Those* songs were ballads, which Acheron *never* played.

Godsmack, Sex Pistols, T.S.O.L., Judas Priest, but not ...

"Is that ... " Urian physically cringed before he spat out the name, "Julio Iglesias?"

"Enrique."

Urian grimaced in horror. Both at the fact that Acheron was playing it and that Alexion knew it. "I didn't even know he knew any mellow shit. Dear gods ... is he ill?" Was the world coming to an end?

'Cause if it was, he had some stuff he needed to pack and e-mails and Internet history to delete.

"I don't know. In nine thousand years, I've never seen him like this before."

Urian shuddered. "I'm beginning to get scared. This has to be a sign of the apocalypse. If he breaks out into Air Supply, I say we sneak up on him, drag him outside, and beat the holy shit out of him."

Alexion snorted. "I'll let you and the demons do that. I personally like my semiliving state too much to jeopardize it."

Ash looked up and pierced them both with a malevolent glare. "Don't you two girls have something better to do, like pick toe lint?"

Urian gave him a taunting grin. "Not really."

Ash growled a low warning, and just as he appeared ready to

tear into them, his phone rang. Leaning his head back, he sighed in frustration.

Urian smirked at Alexion. "Five dollars it's Artemis."

Alexei checked his watch. "This time of day, it's a Hunter. You're on."

Urian frowned as they watched him closely. "Well, he's not getting pissed, so it's definitely not Aunt Artie."

"Yeah, and the tic hasn't started in his jaw, so I don't think it's a Hunter ... what the hell?"

Acheron ignored them. "What time?"

They both exchanged an exaggerated gape at his unorthodox question.

"Say what?" Urian asked.

"I'll be there." Acheron hung up, started to slide the phone into his pocket, and then pulled it out again and dialed it. "I just realized I don't have your address."

Now, Urian really was floored. He turned back to Alexion. "Oh yeah, total Armageddon coming. We better duck and cover."

"I shall see you later then." Acheron hung up and glared at both of them. "Mind your own business." Then he vanished.

Alexion let out a nervous laugh. "You know, I would say that Acheron has a girlfriend, but that makes my sphincter clinch."

"Hey, anything's possible."

He laughed nervously. "No, Urian. It's not. And this definitely isn't. Trust me. No one wants Acheron dating."

Maybe, but if Acheron was happy, then maybe he could reconcile him with Styxx and get Acheron to stop paying attention long enough for him to kill his father. Because a morose Ash was a focused Ash. If Urian had learned anything over the last few years, it was that he couldn't get anything past that bastard. Acheron seemed to be everywhere.

And he watched Urian like a hawk.

But love made men and gods stupid.

It was what had gotten Urian's entire race cursed. If Ash had a girlfriend, then Urian had a chance for vengeance.

November 1, 2008

Urian woke up to the most glorious smell of bacon. Now that alone almost made living worthwhile. At least it made the fact he was no longer a Daimon worthwhile.

Getting up, he quickly dressed and headed for the kitchen, where Danger and Alexion were in the middle of some heated discussion over something.

"What are we talking about?" Urian asked as he joined them. "Do I smell bacon?"

She sighed irritably. "Teach a Daimon to eat real food and he's impossible." She went to make more for him. "We were talking about your houseguest you didn't mention feeding."

Urian's eyes widened as he realized he'd been caught. "Um ... "

"Don't worry. You're not in trouble. I was just telling Alexion that I think there's a lot more to him than we've been told."

Grateful that she was being reasonable where Styxx was concerned, Urian nodded. "No shit, right? You know who he is?" he asked Alexion.

He gave Urian a droll stare. "Acheron's brother."

Urian returned the stare full force. "You ever heard of the Stygian Omada?"

"I'm Groesian. Of course I've heard of them. Who hasn't?"

Danger looked up from the frying bacon. "Well, I'm French and confused. What's the Stygian Armada—"

"Stygian *Omada*," Urian repeated.

"They were a legendary army that waged war against Atlantis," Alexion explained. "In all of Greek history, it was the only army that ever fought on Atlantean soil and won. They were practically on the main steps of the palace when they were called back to Greece for peace talks."

"Yeah." Urian jerked his chin in the direction of the temple where Styxx was staying. "And brother Styxx was their general the army was named for."

"Bullshit!" Alexion roared in denial.

"No. Real. I saw the battle scars on him myself. Ash has always said he was from Atlantis. He's never mentioned the Greek city-state he was born in so I didn't know. ... But Styxx is Styxx of Didymos."

Alexion gaped. "You're shitting me."

Urian shook his head sarcastically.

"Again, French Revolution here. *Les Mis,* I get. This ... " She wagged the spatula. "My extent of Greek history is *Troy* with Brad Pitt and"—she looked over at Alexion—"Mr. Luscious in his armor."

Alexion went bug-eyed. "Please don't call me that in front of Urian."

Urian laughed, then sobered and explained it to her. "Didymos was the Athens of its day, and Athens was not much more than a big village back then. The largest and strongest of the Greek city-states, Didymos was two border islands that buffered the rest of Greece from Atlantis. And Styxx was the greatest, most successful general in their long and prestigious military history. His battle tactics and the way he ran his army were studied extensively by the soldiers of my time. We all wanted to grow up and be him. In fact, the way he trained and the principles his mentor taught him were the foundation of the Spartans and their military ethics. That's how good he was. But in all my readings about Didymos and Styxx, I never saw more than one prince mentioned. ... Him. And nothing of a princess in anything, not that that was unusual." He held his hand up to Danger to stop her before she spoke. "And don't lecture me on ancient stupidity and their treatment of women. ... I am not personally responsible for misogynistic ancient writers just because I happen to be male."

He looked back at Alexion and resumed their discussion. "Because of that, and the fact that he and Ash were babies when they died, I never made the connection that Acheron's brother Styxx was the leader of the famed Stygian League." But now that he thought about it, he should have realized that Styxx's sister was Ryssa. That had been really dense on his part not to put that together.

Alexion snorted. "That explains his arrogance."

"But he's not arrogant," Urian and Danger said simultaneously.

"Yeah," Urian said, grabbing a slice of bacon, "what she said."

She put more bacon on a plate for Urian. "He's sweet, Alexion. Really sweet."

Swallowing his bacon, Urian laughed. "I would not use *that* word myself for him. He's lethal and you can't miss it, but I'll be honest. I'd call Ash arrogant before I would Styxx."

Alexion sucked his breath in sharply. "Don't let Acheron hear you say that."

"I know. Believe me." Urian sighed heavily. "Man, I don't know what happened between them, but it's a damn shame. Can you imagine having Styxx of Didymos train you to fight?"

"Be like taking lessons from Achilles or Alexander the Great."

"That settles it then," Danger said as she put the uncooked bacon back in the refrigerator.

"What?" Urian asked.

"We've got to reconcile them."

Alexion burst out laughing. "That is a pipe dream, honey. I've known Acheron for over nine thousand years. And it will be freezing on the equator before Acheron forgives Styxx for what he did."

She shrugged. "Well, you know what they say—"

Urian passed a knowing stare to Alexion. "We who are about to die salute you?"

She rolled her eyes. "No. Over, under, around, or through, there's always a way."

Urian snorted at her optimism. "Unless the rock falls on you while you're trying to go under it. Then you're toast."

Alexion laughed. "Well, she is French."

Urian brushed his hands off as he left them to plot. Personally, he didn't want to know. Last time he'd been embroiled in something like this ...

He'd lost Phoebe in the worst sort of way. And in the back of his mind, he kept seeing the huge sun emblem on Styxx's back. Given how much that man hated Apollo, he couldn't imagine he'd put it there.

A mark like that reminded him of the Dark-Hunter bow that Artemis placed on all of her Dark-Hunters. Or the Spathi marks that he and his brethren had from Apollymi. Ownership brands from the gods.

Marks those bastards had worn when they'd attacked Sheba's tribe.

For thousands of years, they'd been fighting this war with the gods. Against Apollo and Helios. Artemis and Apollymi. While they all wanted to pretend they were something more than pawns, Urian was beginning to doubt if they were anything but.

Was there ever such a thing as free will?

His mind went back to what he'd told his father about Oedipus. He was no longer sure if he had the right answer. Did they bring about their own downfall?

Or were the gods just that damn determined to ruin them that even if they hadn't taken the steps necessary for their own destruction, the gods would have found some other means to wreak their havoc upon them?

It certainly felt that way right now. That none of them had control of anything. Not even the gods.

And in the middle of their petty feuds stood mankind and the Apollites, both of whom were getting their asses kicked.

Urian sighed.

November 4, 2008

"Who the fuck let *him* out?"

Urian snorted at Acheron's unwarranted hostile tone over his casual mention that Styxx was outside the throne room, waiting to see him. In fact, the poor man had been out there for hours, waiting.

Yeah, Ash was definitely Apollymi's son. He saw the resemblance right now in this little tantrum over something trivial. All they needed was a herd of angry Charonte spiraling about, devouring Daimons, and the picture would be perfect.

Bitterly amused, Urian smirked. "The girl ghost who wants the two of you to kiss and make up."

"I'd rather be hit in the head with the tack hammer Tory threw at me."

"Tory?" Urian asked.

"Long story." Acheron let out a tired sigh. "Thanks for the warning. I'll go deal with him."

Deal with him ... yeah. Nice. Urian shook his head at his irritable boss, as he felt really sorry for his friend. But at least he now had a name to go with the woman Ash had been seeing.

And an explanation for Acheron's fluctuating moods.

The doors behind Urian flew open in a staunch show of power that Ash only used whenever he was in an Apollymi-style mood. Dressed in an Atlantean formesta that bore Acheron's sun symbol and a pair of black leather pants, he walked toward Styxx like a predator.

Urian was so glad he wasn't the one that bitter scowl was directed toward, but he hated the fact that Styxx had the unfortunate luck.

"I'm really not in the mood to deal with you, Styxx. What little patience I have was eaten alive about two minutes ago."

To Styxx's credit, he didn't flinch at all. Nor did he get angry. He stood there calm and strangely tranquil. "I know. I can sense your moods ... it was a *gift*—" Yeah, okay, Urian detected a bit of sarcasm in those words. "From Artemis when she threw me into Tartarus. I'm only here to ask you one favor."

Acheron sneered at him. "*You* would dare ask another favor of me?"

Styxx's countenance broke to say that he was baffled by Ash's accusation. Apparently he didn't remember ever asking anything from his brother.

Urian wisely chose to stay out of this. He'd been thrown into enough walls in his lifetime already.

A tic started in Styxx's cheek before he took a deep breath and then spoke in a well-measured tone. "I ask as your brother and as a supplicant to a god."

"As a supplicant, what sacrifice do you offer for this favor?"

Urian gaped. While Ash, like anyone else, could have moments of irritability, he'd never once seen him be a total asshole to anyone before.

Not even to his father, and Stryker had deserved it.

Wow, this was a side of Ash he hadn't known existed. But then again, Archie and Theo had often brought out the worst beast in him, too. So he wouldn't judge Ash.

Family was hard. No one could bleed you more or cut you deeper than blood relatives.

And the rigidity of Styxx's body language and the fact that he didn't pop Ash one said it all. Whatever was between them was bad.

When Styxx finally spoke, his words confirmed it. "My heart."

Acheron scowled. "I don't understand."

Styxx took a deep, ragged breath. "I offered you my loyalty and it wasn't enough. So in this, I offer my heart to you. If I lie or betray you, you can rip it out over and over again. Chain me next to Prometheus on his rock."

Damn. Yeah, it must really be bad and then some.

"And what favor do you ask?"

"Let me go." Styxx's voice broke slightly on those words, and they brought a lump to Urian's throat. "I can't live here anymore, isolated from people. I just want to have some kind of peace that neither of us ever had a chance to experience." He looked past Ash to Urian.

I feel you, brother. And he did. Better than anyone. But unlike Styxx, Urian had never really lived in the world of man. He didn't feel at home there. It was too wide. Too open. Too effing bright.

He'd tried to live in the boathouse and it hadn't lasted six months. Lucky for him, Acheron had taken mercy and allowed him to live here with Alexion. Otherwise, Urian would have gone insane.

Finally Ash answered Styxx's request. "Fine. You'll have everything you need to start over."

Before Styxx could finish expelling a relieved breath, he was sucked out of the throne room.

Acheron turned around to glare at him.

"Where did you send him?"

"None of your business," he growled.

"Okay then. Love our chats, boss."

Ash didn't say a word.

Alexion shook his head. "You know, Urian, I can't decide if you're the bravest person I know or the dumbest to taunt him the way you do."

Urian snorted. "Neither, Lex. The answer to that puzzle is a lot simpler. I'm suicidal. Just don't give a shit if he kills me or not. In the immortal words of Janis Joplin, 'Freedom's just another word for nothing left to lose.'"

And the one thing that Urian never talked about to anyone, not even Acheron, was the fact that his father hadn't killed him mercifully.

He thought about that a lot. His father prided himself on the fact that he didn't like to torture those he deemed worthy. Those he respected.

Worthy opponents, he put down quickly.

He only tortured those he thought of as weak and vile.

Which raised the question of why he'd chosen to slice open Urian's throat as opposed to stabbing him in his Daimon's mark. That would have been a quick and painless death. So fast, Urian wouldn't have even felt it. He'd have been gone and Acheron wouldn't have been able to put him back together.

Which meant either his father knew that Acheron would save him, and he would live out eternity, isolated from his friends, family, and home, agonizing over the loss of Phoebe, or his father intended for Urian to bleed out slowly, in agony, knowing his father had killed him.

Either way, his father was a cold, mean son of a whore.

And Urian had yet to find some way to settle the score between them.

November 8, 2008

"Are you sure about this, Urian?"

Urian scoffed at Acheron's doubt when he'd told him what was going on, as he waited for Spawn and Davyn to join him in the restaurant where he was meeting them. Like he would have wasted Ash's time on a rumor ...

"Absolutely—it pays to have friends on the dark side. Stryker's sending out scouts even as I speak to find that journal, at any and all costs."

Come to find out Ash's little girlfriend was an archaeologist who'd been busy digging up "dirt" Urian's father wanted in the worst way.

Now his father had a hit on them.

"He wants to take down Artemis and Apollo and absorb their powers. He's also hoping there's something in the journal she found to hurt *you,* which now has your mom going apeshit and sending out her demons to look for it too." Urian laughed evilly. "Welcome to Armageddon, buddy. Looks like they're starting without you."

"Thanks for the warning. Let me know if you hear anything else."

"Will do." Urian hung up the phone as Spawn finally showed up for their meeting and slid into the booth seat across from him.

Dressed black on black, in jeans, a turtleneck, and a motorcycle jacket, he reached over for one of Urian's fries.

Urian popped his hand for the affront. "Did I say you could do that?"

"Really? You'd deprive one of your best men basic sustenance?"

"Yeah, well, we're not Daimons anymore. Get your own order."

"Fine, irritable asshole." Spawn grabbed a menu from the table to look at it. "So why am I here, anyway?"

Because Urian was homesick and he couldn't admit that out loud.

To anyone.

"Figured you needed an outing and you make more money than I do."

Spawn rolled his eyes. "Awesome." He paused as the waitress came over and he ordered a shake and burger ... with his own fries.

Urian tried not to stare at his old friend. Like him, he had white-blond hair, only Lucian's was cropped short, but longer on top and in front. He also bore the same blue eyes that had made Urian an outcast as a boy among their people.

For similar reasons. Spawn's father had been a Dream-Hunter, which was why he had heightened powers most Apollites didn't.

Damn, it was good to see his old friend. They really didn't get to do this much. Spawn was lucky that like Urian, he hadn't been killed by being staked through the heart. He'd been bled out. Otherwise, he wouldn't have been able to come back as a Dark-Hunter.

Well, "lucky" wasn't the right word given that he'd died trying to save his Apollite wife and children from humans who'd cornered them and thought it would be fun to expose them to daylight. Urian was the only one who knew Lucian had actually been a Daimon before his death. Or that he'd served in their elite guard.

As bad as the Dark-Hunters hated him, thinking he was an Apollite, they both knew it would be a lot worse if the Dark-Hunters ever learned the truth.

"So you're homesick."

Urian laughed. "Tuck the telepathy and get out of my thoughts."

"You know I can't. You're too close to me."

He growled, then sighed. "What the hell? Read away."

Before Spawn could say anything, Davyn walked in and took a seat beside Urian. "Man, whatever you or Acheron did ... Stryker is pissed off." He slid a small packet toward Urian.

"What's this?"

"My ass."

Spawn arched a brow at that. "Your ass fits into an envelope that size? I'm impressed. Mine barely fit into my jeans tonight. And after I eat everything I ordered, I doubt it'll fit into them tomorrow."

Snorting at his screwed-up sense of humor, Urian opened the envelope. Then gasped. "Is this right?"

Davyn nodded grimly. "Yeah. They're planning to take down Acheron and stab at his mother."

Urian had been trying to tell Acheron what he'd learned from Davyn, but his boss wasn't in the mood to listen. Even Simi was staying clear of him. And that said it all.

She hadn't even asked for Acheron's black Amex.

Doors had been slamming. Glass had shattered. Danger was in hiding. Not even Alexion would show himself.

If Urian had a lick of sense, he'd run for the hills, too.

But his sense had taken a hike a long time ago and left him sadly wanting. So here he was, grateful he was suicidal as he knocked on the big guy's door. The thundering AC/DC riff stopped immediately. Well, at least Ash was back to playing his usual ear-splintering repertoire.

"Yeah?"

That was not a friendly sound. More like a bear clearing its throat to make more room for the prey it was about to shred to pieces and shove into its hungry jowls.

Preparing himself for the possibility of death, Urian pushed open the door to find Ash sitting on his black tester bed with his guitar in his lap and his cell phone lying on his thigh. "You're really not right, are you?"

Ash narrowed his gaze. "I hope you mean that the way I'm going to take it. Otherwise, in the mood I'm in, you might get your ass kicked."

Urian laughed. "Yeah, I do." He entered the dark room, which was lit only by flickering red candles, and shut the door. Then he moved to stand by the bed so that he could finally tell Acheron what'd been on his mind. "Look, I heard you when you came in. Not what you said, but what was underneath it. I know it's in my best interest to stay out of it. However, you saved my life once, even though I didn't want you to at the time, and I feel like maybe I should return the favor."

The look on Ash's face said that Urian was one syllable away from searching the cold marble floor for his teeth. But after a moment, his expression softened. "I shouldn't have interfered with that, Urian, and I'm sorry for the pain you live with because of it."

"You know, it's all right. If I'd died, Phoebe would have followed me to the grave, anyway. She wasn't capable of taking a human life, even if the human deserved to die. The only way she could have continued living would have been to feed from another Daimon, and that she wouldn't have done either. So you didn't really change her fate by saving me. My father was going to kill her regardless."

The only thing that would have changed was the years he'd missed of helping Davyn and Spawn.

And the biggest gift of all . . .

"Besides, if I'd died that night, my niece and nephews wouldn't have someone to threaten their dad when he's over-protective of them." Muppet was much worse with his own flesh and blood than he'd ever been with Chris. Poor Erik, Tyr, and little Phoebe. Urian was the only thing that stood between them and sanity. "I'm the only uncle they have. Kids need an uncle, you know?"

That priceless expression on Acheron's face said that he heartily disagreed, and made Urian wonder what was in his past to cause *that* look. And his instincts were verified by Ash's next words. "So why the sudden girlspeak, Urian? Neither one of us is really into discussing our feelings . . . and no offense, I like the fact that we don't."

Urian couldn't agree more. There were some things he really didn't want to know about his boss. "I do too most times, and I'm truly grateful you don't pry. But as a man who defied everything he once valued in this world, and one who sacrificed the love of a father he worshiped ... even though it ended badly, the days I had with Phoebe were worth *every* wound I've suffered."

He moved closer to Ash. "I know what it's like to be torn between a love so pure it burns you deep down in a place you didn't know someone could touch you and between your oath and duties. Between the love of a father you've always known and one you know you can depend on forever versus a love that's new and untested. But you know what I learned? It's a lot easier to live without my father's love than it is to live without Phoebe's. I just thought you ought to know that."

"There's a lot more at stake. You know? Like the survival of the entire world."

"There always is, and my father is sending everything he has after Tory. Who, given the way you're acting, I would say *is* your entire world. I stayed away from Phoebe because I thought she was safer that way. In the end, Ash, I should have been there, fighting for her, by her side. 'Cause I can tell you one thing beyond a shadow of doubt. The greatest regret isn't what you did, it's what you should have done."

"I hate you, Daimon."

"Only because you know I'm right." And with that, Urian left him to ruminate on it, as he felt his phone vibrating in the unique pattern that meant either Styxx or Cassandra needed him.

With Cass, he had the fear that something might be wrong with Tyr since he was only a few days old, and with Styxx ...

He didn't have anyone else who gave a damn about him. Ash had dumped him alone in the middle of New York City, and the poor guy was trying to figure out modern existence.

Speaking of which ...

"Hey. What's up?"

"Jumbo shrimp?" Styxx had the baffled tone he always got whenever he tried to shop for food. "How? Is this some trick of Lyssa's or Poseidon's?"

Urian laughed. "Neither. It's a trick of marketing, to make you buy it."

"Ah. Is that why it looks so strange?"

"No, that's because the store already prepared it for you. You can take it home, wash it, and eat it."

Suddenly, Styxx was real quiet.

"Hey, you there? Did I lose you?"

"Um, yeah. Urian ... they have worms in alcohol that you drink. My God, man, what is wrong with you people?"

He laughed at the serious tone Styxx used. "It's tequila. You're fine."

"That's all kinds of wrong."

Like Styxx had any room to talk given what his people had eaten back in the day? "Cobra hearts? Blood soup? Bitter vetch?"

Styxx blustered. "I only ate those during war, and because it was that or starve. And they were disgusting ... and speaking of? Casu marzu? Is this what I think it is?"

"Yeah, maggot cheese. Stay away."

Styxx made a loud sound of disapproval. "That's it. I'm getting Pop-Tarts and I'm going home."

Urian laughed at his horror. "Can you identify them? Or do you need me to come and help?"

"Little blue box. I've got this. And I know what milk looks like. Get a jug from the back. I remember what you said."

"All right. I'll be there tomorrow to help you shop for groceries."

"Thank you. Sorry to be such a pain in your ass. I'm slowly learning."

"It's all good, brother. Think nothing of it. See you tomorrow." Urian hung up, feeling bad for him.

That was the worst part of what Ash had inadvertently done. He'd forgotten the small fact that while Styxx could speak English, he couldn't read it. Unlike Acheron, he wasn't a god who was fluent in all languages, nor was he like Urian and the other Hunters who'd been exposed to modern culture throughout history. He'd been imprisoned away from everything and everyone.

Styxx's native tongue was ancient Greek. He couldn't even read the modern Greek version. Nor did he understand modern currency. He knew nothing at all about the modern world or how to navigate it.

So when Ash had literally dumped him in his apartment without any kind of orientation, Styxx had been at a loss on how to do anything, such as write a check or use a credit card.

He'd never used a phone or computer. Had Urian not tracked him down, he'd have starved to death.

But to be fair to Acheron, Styxx had asked to leave at a bad time. That very day, Acheron had been in a near-fatal accident and had almost lost Tory. Normally, Acheron would never have been quite that cold.

Even to Styxx.

But his mind had been on other things and other concerns. As the old saying went, bad times made for bad people. And these times were making for some of the worst. So in anger, Acheron had lashed out, and sadly Styxx had been in the line of fire to catch the fury that should have gone toward the ones who hurt Tory.

They were all under threat, and the most insidious part of their enemies was that the darkness was trying to drive a wedge between them. To isolate them.

And it was working.

Divided we fall. It was much easier to take down an enemy when they were fighting among themselves than it was one united against you.

But what Urian couldn't figure out was how to unite two brothers who were determined to destroy each other, any more than he could figure out how to stop his father and get his own vengeance.

November 20, 2008

Urian went to Styxx's apartment to find him sitting at his bedroom desk, playing the New Atlantis campaign for *Age of Mythology* on his PC. Okay ... that just messed with his head on a multitude of levels.

The irony of the Stygian commander reliving his past. And for an ancient warlord to be playing a conquest game on a modern PC.

Yeah ...

Suddenly, Styxx jumped out of his chair and turned on Urian as if he were about to take off his head.

Holding his hands up, Urian made sure to let him know he wasn't a threat. Especially since he was here to ask something he knew would piss the man off.

Styxx immediately curled his lip. "What does he think I've done now?"

Urian scowled. "Huh?"

"Acheron. Is he not the one who sent you for me?"

Urian shook his head. "He actually didn't send me. I came to ask a favor."

That appeared to shock him. "What do you need?"

"Acheron's woman, Tory, has been kidnapped and taken into Kalosis, where his mother is. Ash is ready and willing to go get her." Which would free his mother from her prison and end the world.

Styxx took that news with complete stoicism. As if he didn't care at all.

Not until he asked one simple question. "Is Tory immortal?"

Urian shook his head. "Completely human. She's being held by my aunt Satara, who is unstable at best. Viciously brutal at worst."

The daughter of Apollo, that bitch was about as crazy as anyone Urian had ever known. And given some of the stellar loons his father kept for company ...

Said it all.

That familiar tic started in Styxx's jaw. "You're going in with him, aren't you?"

Urian nodded. "You did it once to help an enemy. Would you do it again to help a friend?"

Styxx laughed bitterly. "How would I know? I've only had two friends in my life and both were brutally murdered."

That stung the shit out of Urian. Especially given everything they'd been through together. "You don't consider me a friend?"

"No, I consider you a hemorrhoid."

Well, that was fair enough, he supposed. Urian grinned. "Ah now, that's just mean."

"Yeah, yeah ... Fine. But I am doing this for you and the innocent woman, not Acheron."

"Well, on behalf of myself and Tory, I can't thank you enough. By the way, how are your battle skills?"

Styxx snorted. "According to my father, I never had any. I shoved my men out in front of me and hid behind their fallen bodies for cover."

Scowling, Urian didn't comment as he teleported Styxx to a small room where everyone had gathered to plot out what they wanted to do.

Ash was already there with Savitar. Every bit as tall as they were, Savitar had dark hair and a perfect goatee. His eyes were an iridescent lavender. He hadn't changed much since the last time Urian had seen him.

His jaw slack, Savitar looked back and forth between Acheron and Styxx. "Holy Were-shit. This messes with my head."

Acheron glared at Styxx, then Urian. "What is *he* doing here?"

Urian shrugged unapologetically. "You can't go in. Styxx can."

"No." Acheron was emphatic.

"Stop," Savitar snapped. "The kid has a point. Think about it. You can get Tory out of there and not end the world. Win-win."

The hatred in Acheron's eyes was searing. "I'm not leaving him alone with Tory. I don't trust him with her."

Styxx was aghast. "What do you think I'm going to do?"

"Rape her, kill her ... with you there's no telling."

Urian's jaw dropped at the severity of *that* particular allegation. Where the hell had *that* come from? Yet the vim of it said it was deep rooted.

"With *me*? Really?" He shoved Acheron.

Acheron ran at Styxx, but Savitar caught him and pushed him back a step. "Stop thinking with your emotions. Calm down." Then Savitar turned to glare at Styxx. "And you, punk, lay off him or I'll fry your greasy ass where it stands. I know I can kill you and not kill Acheron. So don't push me."

Styxx snorted in derision. "That is not the way to motivate me to leave him alone, Chthonian. But it's a hell of a way to make me attack." He met Acheron's swirling silver gaze.

Instead, he snatched his sleeve back to show his brother his forearm. "I know what it's like to lose the only thing you love, and to be forced to live without her for eternity. As bad as I want to cut your throat and watch you bleed out at my feet for the insult you just dealt me, I won't see your woman dead for it. Unlike your fucking whore mother, I don't kill innocents."

Both Savitar and Acheron blasted him for that comment. Styxx hit the wall behind him so hard, he broke through part of it.

Stunned, Urian teleported to him.

This was bullshit! Furious at them for their unwarranted and unreasonable attack, Urian glared at them both. "What are you doing? I asked him here to help you and you kill him? Good job. Both of you. Congrats, you stupid assholes!"

"He insulted my mother," Acheron roared.

Urian scoffed. "No offense, boss, your mother killed his wife and his son. Instead of putting him through a wall, I want you both to take one second and imagine his loss. I have buried almost every member of my family. And the one thing that truly tore my heart out was losing Phoebe. You mourn your sister, Ash? So did I. Trust me, it ain't shit till you lose your wife, especially when you know you should have been at home protecting her, and not leaving her to die brutally by the hand of your enemies." He turned and helped Styxx extricate himself from the wall.

In that moment, he actually hated Acheron.

And he didn't think much more of Savitar. What kind of Chthonian could do this?

Styxx had come here to help them. To hell with it.

"I'm sorry," Urian said. "I shouldn't have asked you to come."

Styxx spat the blood in his mouth on the floor, then wiped his hand over his lips. "Trust me, they're pussies compared to the real Atlanteans I fought."

They went to blast him again.

Holding his arms out, Urian shielded Styxx with his body.

Styxx stepped around Urian, then patted him on the shoulder. "I'm not afraid of them. Hits, I can take. After all, I was slapped on the ass the minute I was born, and not a damn thing has changed since."

Acheron curled his lip. "Don't listen to him, Urian. He's a liar and a thief. He was never married. He was only engaged, and he didn't have a son."

The pain in Styxx's eyes refuted those words and left no doubt in Urian's mind. His pain was too real to be faked. "You know nothing about me, brother. After all, I'm just a liar and a thief to you."

Styxx swallowed. "By the way, tell Artie thanks for the memories. 'Cause now I not only know everything about what really happened to you, I know what you really think of me. I would say that one day I would love to return the favor, but honestly the only person I hate that much is your putrid mother."

Styxx wiped his hand across his face. "Now either use me or send me home. I'm in no mood to play."

Urian winced at the tremor in his friend's voice.

Savitar took a deep breath as he faced Acheron. "Urian's right. Styxx is the best shot we have at getting her out alive. We don't know what going into Kalosis will do to you, Ash. It could rip out your human soul and leave you nothing but your mother's tool for destruction. If that happens, you're as likely to kill Tory as they are."

Acheron shook his head. "It'll never work. His voice is hoarser than mine. And no one's going to believe I cut my hair off and bleached it blond."

Savitar snapped his fingers. Instantly, Styxx's hair was an exact copy of Acheron's. He even had fangs and matching clothes. "I can't mess with his voice. But they can assume you've been screaming insults at them. It would account for the difference."

Urian ran his gaze up and down Styxx's body and then Acheron's. "That is creepy. *Really* creepy."

"He still doesn't move like me."

Styxx scoffed. "People aren't that observant. As you saw in New Orleans."

He was right about that. Urian remembered when Styxx had easily passed himself off as Acheron. And that had been to Acheron's fellow Dark-Hunters, who should have known better.

Savitar inclined his head to Urian and Styxx. "Let's do this, ladies. And Styxx ... for the record, you let anything happen to Tory and I will hand-deliver you to Apollymi for her eternal enjoyment."

Styxx laughed out loud at the impotent threat, which made both Acheron and Savitar scowl at him. "What's she going to do, Savitar? Drag me out into an arena butt-ass naked, make me fight elite Atlantean champions until I can barely stand, set her starving dogs or leopards on me, and then have me publicly fucked for her entertainment? Or better yet, gut me on the floor ... or how about this ... murder my wife and child, and make me live with that for eternity in a dark hole by myself? Sure ... threaten me. Go ahead and make me live in total fear and terror." Flipping Savitar off, he turned to Urian. "Get me out of here."

Urian scowled at him as he digested details that were a little too specific to not be real. Yeah ... holy shit. None of that had been listed in a history book, and it explained a lot about Styxx's personality.

"You're really not sane, are you?"

"No, Urian. I'm not. A sane man would have told you to go to hell and meant it."

Sick to his stomach that he'd even asked him to join them for this when he should have left him alone and at peace, Urian opened the portal to Kalosis. *I've got your back, brother.* Because obviously, no one else ever had.

With a sharp nod to his friend, he made a promise to himself that no one was going to hurt Styxx again. "Walk this way." Urian stepped into it and vanished.

Without so much as glancing at Savitar or Acheron, Styxx followed.

When they finally stopped falling, they were inside a main room that was filled with Daimons and demons.

Beautiful ...

Styxx let out a severely annoyed groan. "Great location, Uri," he said under his breath. "Think one of them is willing to sell us a summer home here?"

Urian grinned at him. "You can always ask."

Every demon and Daimon was frozen into place by their sudden appearance in the middle of the hall where Urian had grown up. Ah, it was good to be back.

Styxx cut a sideways glance to Urian. "What are they waiting for?"

Urian winked at him because he knew exactly why they were nervous. Every Daimon here had been told that if Acheron ever stepped foot into their domain, Kalosis would splinter. That Apollymi would be free and the worlds would tear themselves apart.

"Armageddon," he said drily.

Styxx narrowed his eyes on Stryker.

Stryker glared at his son with an expression that was best defined as pained hatred. "You dare to stand with my enemy?"

"Against you, Solren, I'd stand with Mickey Mouse."

Stryker curled his lip. "You worthless son of a bitch. You should have never been anything more than a cum stain."

Urian scoffed. "I could definitely say the same thing about you. It would have saved the world and all of us a lot of misery now, wouldn't it?"

Styxx and Urian braced themselves to fight as the Daimons started forward, but they were thrown back by some unseen force.

Not sure what had happened, Styxx turned to Stryker and growled. "Enough of the family reunion bullshit. Where is Soteria?"

Out of nowhere, Apollymi appeared a few feet from them.

She indicated a door behind him with an imperious jerk of her chin.

Urian went still as he watched her, cautiously. There was something strange about her that he didn't quite understand. An odd undercurrent between her and Styxx.

"She's over there." Then she crossed the short distance to embrace his friend.

What the hell?

Styxx's breathing turned ragged at her touch. He clenched his fists tight.

"At last, *m'gios*." Atlantean for *my son*. "You've come to set me free." She placed a kiss on his cheek and then whispered in his ear words that Urian barely heard. They were harsh and cold and made him suck his breath in sharply. "For my son's sake, you better embrace me, Greek whoreson. If I can touch something as vile and repugnant as you, you can touch divinity."

Urian knew his friend well enough to read the fury in his body language as he forced himself to hug her. Nodding to her, Styxx stepped back, then headed for the door.

Before Styxx reached it, a tall, thin woman with brown hair and very pretty features came running out of the room. She wore a black jacket that was much too large for her and clutched it over her shirt, which had been torn open.

Oh shit. Urian cringed as dread went through him. If anyone had done to her what he feared, Acheron would tear this place down.

And the world would end.

All of a sudden, she threw herself into Styxx's arms and kissed him. Then she stiffened and pulled back slowly to stare up at him suspiciously.

Double shit.

Urian passed a panicked stare to Davyn as they both waited for everyone to realize that he wasn't Acheron.

And they probably would have, had Nick Gautier not chosen that moment to walk out of his father's study.

Unholy crap . . .

There was something you didn't see every day. A Malachai sporting a Dark-Hunter bow-and-arrow mark on his left cheek that made it look like Artemis had bitch-slapped him when she marked him. His eyes dark with rage and madness, Nick ran at Styxx as if he intended to kill him. But before he could reach him, Urian grabbed Nick and shoved him back into the room where they'd been.

Styxx pulled Tory in after them.

And Urian realized just how fucked they all were as he saw his aunt's dead body on the floor.

This just gets better and better.

Panicked, he looked at Styxx and Tory. "We have to go." Then he looked at Nick. "And you need to come with us."

Nick curled his lip in obvious hatred. "I'm not going anywhere with *him*. I'd rather be dead."

Urian forced Nick to look down at Satara's body. "I'm going to make the wildly founded assumption that Satara's dead by your hand and not Tory's."

Gripping Nick's chin, Urian forced him to meet his gaze. "Now, stay with me on this, Cajun. My father slit my throat and murdered my wife because he thought I'd betrayed him by getting married. Before that, he loved me more than his life, and I was his last surviving child. His second-in-command. Now what do you think he's going to do to you once he sees her body? I can assure you, it won't be a fun-filled trip to Chuck E. Cheese. For all their animosity toward each other, Satara is his sister and she's served him well over the centuries. If you really want to stay here and have some fun with Stryker, I won't stop you. But I really wouldn't recommend it."

'Cause Stryker would gut him just for the shoelaces.

That finally seemed to get through to Nick. Sanity returned to his eyes. "Fine. I'll go with you."

While they argued, Styxx cracked the door to check on their restless enemies. "Urian," he said between clenched teeth. "I think they're catching on."

"Catching on to what?" Nick asked.

Tory rolled her eyes at Nick. "That this isn't Ash."

The words had barely left her lips before they faded out of the room.

Zolan, *Stryker's third-in-command* and the leader of his personal Illuminati attack force, cleared his throat in the silent room. "Um ... boss, I don't mean this disrespectfully, but why are we still here? I mean, if Acheron has come to free Apollymi, shouldn't there be an explosion or something?"

The Daimons and demons looked around as if waiting for an opening to the outer world to appear or for Apollymi to burst into song and dance, or for something else unnatural to happen.

Meanwhile, Apollymi just stood there completely stoic, appearing almost angelic and sweet, as she watched Stryker closely.

Davyn scratched the back of his neck nervously as he waited for a sign from Urian that they were clear. "I agree, *kyrios*. It doesn't feel like the end of the world."

Stryker turned a cold sneer to Apollymi. "No, it doesn't, does it?"

Apollymi arched a taunting brow. "How does the song go, 'It's the end of the world as we know it, and I feel fine'?"

In that moment, Stryker knew exactly what had happened. Launching himself from his throne, he ran to the room just as Urian, Tory, Nick, and what had to be Ash's twin brother Styxx vanished.

His anger over the obvious trick mounted until he saw Satara lying on the floor in a pool of blood. Fear washed away his rage as he ran to her only to find her dead. Her eyes were glazed and her skin tinged with blue.

His heart shattered as he pulled her into his arms and held her close, fighting against the tears of grief and pain. "You stupid psychotic bitch," he growled against Satara's cold cheek. "What have you done now?"

Apollymi stood in the doorway, aching for Strykerius as he rocked his dead sister in his arms, reminding her of the day she'd found her precious Acheron's cold and lifeless body dumped on the cliffs of Didymos after Apollo had gutted him.

Like he was garbage.

She had died that day, and every day since that she'd been forced to live without him.

Sympathy and a newfound respect for Stryker tore through her.

The fact that he could love someone as broken as Satara had been said much for him. Yes, he could be cold-blooded, but he wasn't heartless. Closing her eyes, she remembered him the day they'd first met. Stryker had been young and bitter over his father's curse.

"I gave up everything I ever cared about for him and this is how he repays my loyalty? I'm to die in agony in only six years? My young children are now banished from the sun and are cursed to drink blood from each other instead of eating food, and to die in pain at only twenty-seven? For what? For the death of a Greek whore killed by soldiers I've never even seen? Where's the justice in that?"

Understanding his agony and wanting to exact her own revenge on Apollo, Apollymi had pulled Stryker into her ranks and taught him how to circumvent his father's curse by absorbing human souls into his body to lengthen his life. She'd given him and his children shelter in a realm where the humans couldn't harm them and where there was no danger of his children accidentally dying by sunlight. Then she'd allowed him to convert others and bring them here to live.

In the beginning, she'd pitied him and she'd even loved him as a son.

But he wasn't her Apostolos, and the more he was around her, the more she wanted to have her own child with her no matter the cost. She admitted it was her own fault that she'd put a wall between her and Strykerius. And the two of them had used each other to get back at the people they hated.

Now it all had come to this. . . .

The death of his beloved sister.

"I'm so sorry, Strykerius."

He looked up at her, his silver eyes swirling in pain. "Are you? Or are you gloating?"

"I never gloat over death. I may relish it, from time to time, when it's justified. But I never gloat."

"And I don't let challenges like this go unanswered. There will be payback."

"But you owe it to Styxx and Nick, not my Apostolos or his Soteria. Remember that."

Urian *sighed as* they made it back to the Sanctuary bar in New Orleans that was owned by the Peltier Were-Hunter bear clan.

Acheron launched himself at Soteria and gathered her into his arms. Urian remembered when Phoebe used to run to him like that in Elysia. How they'd savor every minute.

Gods, how he missed her . . .

"Are you all right?" Acheron asked Tory.

"I'm fine. Really."

"But we're not," Urian said drily from the other side of the room. "Nick killed Satara while they held Tory."

"He did it to protect me," Tory interjected.

Urian snorted. "We'll put that on the headstone for you. In the meantime Stryker's going to want blood for this. A lot of blood."

Nick scoffed at his dire tone. "No offense, but your father doesn't scare me, especially given how bad I want a piece of his hide. Come get some."

Urian looked less than impressed. "I know you think you

share powers with him, Nick, but trust me, he didn't give you anything but the leftovers. Not to mention one small thing. No one gets a piece of him until after I do."

Acheron let out a shrill whistle. "Down, children. We have more things to do than just save your machismo."

Acheron leveled his glare at Nick. "We have a battle to prepare for. I'm not letting Stryker take Nick."

Nick laughed bitterly. "I don't need your fucking help. I can fight on my own."

Acheron didn't flinch at the hatred in his tone. "I know why you hate me, Nick. I get it. But your mother wouldn't want you to kill yourself again. Hate me tomorrow. Tonight, tolerate me as a necessary evil."

Nick shoved Acheron away from him. "This doesn't make us friends."

Acheron held his hands up. "I know." He turned back to Tory and took her hand in a tight grip. Indecision hung there before he spoke and shocked Styxx to the core of his being. "Styxx, take her out of here. Keep her safe."

Tory gaped as she skimmed Styxx with a horrified expression.

Stryker came through a portal and his gaze went straight to Urian. "You've betrayed me for the last time." Flicking his wrist, he sent a leaf-shaped dagger right at Urian's heart.

Before it could reach its target, Acheron caught it in his hand. "Take your girls, scream, and run away now, Stryker. It'll save you time later. Believe me, you don't want a taste of me in the mood I'm in."

Stryker took that with flippant disregard. He ran his tongue over his fangs as if he were savoring the idea of feeding on Acheron. "There's nothing I crave more than the taste of blood." He looked around at the men who stood with Acheron and laughed in derision. "Tonight we feast, Spathi. Attack!"

More than ready to battle, Urian pulled Tory behind their group as the Daimons swarmed them.

"Stab them in the heart," Urian said to Styxx before he demonstrated how to kill the Daimons.

Another blast of light in the room left them with a huge group of enemy reinforcements.

Styxx stabbed the first one to reach him. Only he didn't explode into dust like the Daimon had. "Urian? A little instruction, please."

"Demons ... eyes." Urian stabbed a demon between the eyes to show him what he meant, before he turned and ducked the fangs of a Daimon. "And whatever you do, don't let the demons bite you or they can control you."

Styxx disarmed a Daimon who held a sword, then spun around and caught him with his dagger. The Daimon exploded all over Styxx.

Stryker went for Nick, but Acheron caught him and the two of them went to the ground, punching with a fury Styxx knew all too well. *Glad I'm not the only one you hate that much.*

More men arrived. Since they were neither Daimons nor demons, Styxx pulled back until he could determine if they were friends or foes.

A demon launched itself at Soteria. She tried to kick him back but failed epically. Just as it would have reached her, Julian of Macedon, a longtime friend of Acheron's, was there with a xiphos. He severed the demon's head with one well-placed swing. Balancing the leaf-shaped blade on his shoulder, Julian turned to face her. "Can you handle a sword?"

"Yes."

"Kyrian!" Julian shouted to his best friend, another blond Greek. "My kingdom for a sword."

Kyrian tossed what appeared to be only a hilt. In one fluid move, Julian caught it and pressed a button on the cross hilt. The blade shot out to just under three feet in length. He handed it over to Soteria. "Daimons have to be stabbed through their hearts. Demons between their eyes, and if you cut the heads off any of us, we all die."

"How do I tell the difference?"

"Most of the Daimons are blond and they explode into dust when you pierce their hearts. Hit the heart and if that doesn't work, try the eyes. If you stab someone who whimpers, then hits the ground, you attacked a good guy. Just FYI."

One of the demons made for Urian's back. Styxx pulled a smaller knife out of the demon body closest to him and used it to pin the new demon between his eyes.

Urian turned to fight as the demon fell to his feet. He met Styxx's gaze and inclined his head to him.

Styxx whirled and, forgetting he didn't have a hoplon, raised his arm to catch a sword down across it. Hissing, he stumbled back, then lunged with the sword in his right hand. His opponent spun, then came back immediately with another blow. Styxx narrowly jerked his head away in time.

Urian tried to reach him to help, but he was swarmed with his own Daimons and couldn't get to him at all.

Then Urian saw Stryker, and the expression on his face was one of controlled fury. He was locked on his target, and in his hand was the one weapon that could kill Acheron.

An Atlantean dagger imbued with the blood of Apollymi and with poisonous ypnsi sap from the darkest trees grown in the forests of Kalosis.

For a moment Styxx didn't react. If Stryker killed Acheron, it was over. All of it.

He would finally have peace.

But then he made the fatal mistake of looking at Soteria, who saw what he did.

Acheron's imminent death.

The horrified agony on her face and the tears in her eyes undid him. Love like that didn't deserve to be separated. There was no worse hell than being one half of an eternally separated whole.

No one knew that better than Urian did.

Twice in his life, he'd been dealt that blow. First with Xyn and then with Phoebe. He wouldn't let that kind of hatred crush Tory.

He went to stop it, but before he could get there, Styxx ran at Stryker. He caught the Daimon lord right before he reached Acheron, who had stupidly closed his eyes while he fought.

Because Styxx still wore sunglasses, Stryker lost focus on Acheron and mistook him for his brother.

Stryker laughed in satisfaction as he buried the knife deep into Styxx's stomach.

Urian felt that blow as if he'd taken it himself.

Styxx stumbled back and fell into someone. His sunglasses went flying.

Time hung still as they all watched him fall against Acheron and his brother stepped aside to let him go down hard on the floor.

Growling at the fact he'd missed Acheron, Stryker reached for the dagger in Styxx's stomach. Styxx held it inside him with one hand while he tried to beat Stryker back with his other. But his blood made the hilt too slippery and the pain and scar weakened his grasp. Against his best effort, Stryker yanked the dagger out.

Styxx gasped. "Acheron!" he shouted, warning his brother.

Turning in time, Acheron caught the Daimon overlord with the blunt end of his staff and shoved him back. "Flee or die," he snarled.

Stryker curled his lip. "Fuck you."

Narrowing his gaze on Stryker, Acheron shoved him back, then slammed the staff to the ground. A wave of raw, unfettered power shot out from it to the demons and Daimons around them. Every one of them turned to dust.

And it knocked Urian to his knees.

Except for Stryker. He hovered above the ground in a dragon's form, snarling and flapping. Bellowing in rage, Stryker spewed fire at Acheron.

Acheron lifted his arm, barely in time to keep it from burning him. He shot another god-bolt at Stryker, who dodged it.

"This isn't over, Acheron. Next time you won't be able to use your powers."

With another blast of fire, Stryker vanished.

Urian rushed to Styxx's side at the same time Ash did.

Opening his eyes, Styxx panted in sheer agony. "You know, brother, you're never supposed to close your eyes in battle."

Ash laughed. "I wasn't the one training to be a general."

Styxx sighed. "Perhaps. But you do a much better job of lead-ing than I ever did. I definitely think Father trained the wrong one of us."

Without a word, Acheron placed his hand over Styxx's wound. Styxx hissed. "Fine, then, you're a stupid fucking asshole. Get your hands off me," he snarled through gritted teeth.

Still Acheron held him down until Styxx was ready to whim-per. Only then did Acheron pull away.

Urian held his hand to give him comfort.

"Am I dead yet?" Styxx asked sarcastically.

"Not yet. You still have a few years left to seriously piss me off."

Styxx snorted. "I look forward to it."

He inclined his head to Styxx. "You did a good job for me. Thank you."

"Yeah, well, next time you need someone to descend into a Daimon sanctuary, pick one of your other assholes to do it. I don't have the powers of a god when they come at me, and it puts me at a definite disadvantage."

Then Acheron left him and went to be with his men.

Urian helped him to his feet. "You want me to take you home?"

Styxx nodded at Urian. "Thanks."

"No problem." Feeling horrible for what he'd gotten him into, Urian teleported him home. Styxx started for the couch, and then his knees buckled.

Urian caught him against his side and helped him to his bed. "Are you still wounded?"

"It's the poison from the dagger. Acheron healed the wound, but he didn't draw the poison out."

"How do you get it out?"

"You draw it out before you stitch the wound closed." Styxx looked down at the sealed scar. "Oops, too late." He started shaking again as sweat beaded on his forehead.

"Do you want me to call Ash?"

"I'll be fine."

"Not like I can die. I just need to rest." Styxx had barely slurred those words before he passed out.

December 1, 2008

Urian watched as Ash checked the blades in his boots to make sure they were working. Suddenly, he turned his head as if he knew Urian was there.

Furious, he glared at his boss. "You're helping my father?"

"We have to stop War." That dry, flat tone did nothing to improve Urian's mood or need to beat Ash's ass.

"Stryker murdered my wife," Urian snarled.

"I know."

Oh well, he was so glad they got *that* cleared up. "How could you help something like him?"

Ash growled at him. "Get off the cross, brother. Someone needs the wood. You helped your father for centuries. Need I remind you of how many lives you took under his command? Lives of people who were related to you—you killed Phoebe's mother and her sister."

He flinched at a truth he didn't want to hear. Ash was right. He should have stopped their deaths. It was all his fault. He'd been the one who tracked them down. Stryker would never have known where they were had he not found them. He led the assassins straight to their location. "I loved my wife. I never meant to hurt her."

"Changes nothing. You took your wife from the very people she loved more than her life. For too many centuries, you and your brothers were a tool Stryker used most effectively."

"Times change."

"Yes, they do ... And you should know that you have another sister."

Stunned, Urian stared at him as he tried to digest the impossible. "What?"

Ash met his gaze levelly and kept his expression completely

stoic. "It's the life of your other sister we're going to protect. Not your father's."

No ... not possible. "My sister died eleven thousand years ago."

"Medea is a half sister."

Medea? How was that possible?

But in the end, it didn't matter. "And I should care, why?"

Ash held his hands up in surrender. "You're right. You shouldn't care at all. She's nothing to you, which is why I haven't invited you to join us." Ash started past him.

Urian pulled him to a stop as the need to beat him flared to an all-time high. "How would you feel if my father had killed Tory?"

Ash answered without hesitation. "I would feel soulless. Lost and hurt beyond repair."

Urian looked away. "Then you understand me. And why I want him dead."

Ash pulled Urian's hand off his arm. "He knows that, too. But have you ever considered that he might regret what he did to you?"

Yeah, right. "My father? Get real. The bastard has never regretted a single thing in his entire life."

"We all have regrets, Urian. Nothing that lives is immune from that nasty emotion."

The problem was, his father was dead. "So what? You want me to go kiss and make up?"

"Hardly. But I want you to set aside your own hurt and anger to see clearly for a minute. This isn't about you and your father any more than it's about me and Nick hating each other over something we can't change. This is about saving the lives of a million innocent people. People like Phoebe who don't deserve to be hunted and killed. If I can stand at the side of my enemies for the greater good, so can you."

Urian scoffed. "Well I guess I'm just not as special as you are."

"No one knows their true mettle until it's been tested. This is yours. Whether you pass or fail at being human or a hero is entirely up to you. I can't tell you what to do, but I know where I'll be tonight ... fighting beside my enemies to save the lives of those who can't fight what we have to." He hesitated before he asked the most important question. "So what do you choose?"

"Gory death."

Ash shook his head. "You stubborn bastard. Take it from someone who knows firsthand, there's a lot to be said for forgiveness. Grudges seldom hurt anyone except the one bearing them."

"And there's a lot to be said for knocking enemies upside their heads and cracking their skulls wide open."

Ash felt a tic start in his jaw over Urian's obdurate nature. "To everything there is a season, and tonight ours is to stand together or lose everything. I'm not fighting for Stryker or to save your sister. I'm fighting to protect the ones *I* love. The ones who will suffer most if war isn't stopped ... children like Erik, Tyr, little Phoebe, and—"

"Low fucking blows," he snapped at the mention of his nephews and niece.

"Do you?"

Urian's gaze hardened. "I will be there, but once our enemies are put down—"

"We fight each other again. Understood."

Urian nodded. "I want the honest truth about something. Could you really fight with someone who did as much damage to you as my father has done to me?"

Ash met his gaze without blinking. "I subjugated myself to the goddess who drugged me to the point where I couldn't protect my sister and nephew the night they were brutally slaughtered, and they were the only two people in the universe who'd ever given two shits about me. Later that same day, she stood back and let her twin brother butcher me on the floor like an animal to protect humanity, yet within hours after that I sold myself to her to protect mankind. For the sake of the Dark-Hunters, I subjected myself to her cruel whims for eleven thousand years. So yeah, Urian, I think I could manage to suck it up for an hour to protect the rest of the world."

Urian let out a slow breath as Ash put his own pettiness in brutal perspective. He was being a spoiled brat and Ash was right. "You know you're the only man alive I'd ever follow after what I've been through. You're also the only one I respect, and who could talk to me the way you do and not get slapped for it."

"And you're one of the extremely few I trust."

Urian held his hand up to him. "Brothers?"

"Brothers to the end," Ash said, taking his hand and clutching it tight. "Now before we break into tears, get your ass upstairs and prepare for what's coming."

"Don't worry. I always have your back."

"Yeah, but this time, we're up against the god of war."

Which meant all the backup in the world might not be enough.

January 19, 2009

Urian ground his teeth as he led Savitar into Styxx's bedroom in New York where he'd been holding a silent vigil on and off since they got back from Kalosis with Tory and Acheron, and Styxx had collapsed on the floor.

He was terrified about Styxx's condition. And he was at a loss about who else to call. Who else would know how to fix a sick immortal, other than Apollymi, and given their current relationship, he figured it was best not to try that venue, as the goddess was likely to splinter him into pieces.

"He's been like *that*."

Savitar gave Urian an arch stare.

"I know, right? It's like his whole body has shut down. He hasn't eaten or drunk or even moved. Every now and again, he whispers in ancient Greek, Arabic, or ancient Egyptian, but I can't make it out."

Frowning, Savitar pulled the blanket back to examine the wound Acheron had sealed. But the moment he saw Styxx's extensive scarring he gaped in horror. "What the hell?"

Urian more than understood his reaction. He'd had the same one himself the first time he'd seen it. "Aside from being a war hero who fought in dozens of battles, he spent a year as a POW in Atlantis. He never really says much about it other than it sucked, but from the scars I'd say they tortured him the whole time he was there."

Savitar expelled a heavy breath. "I had no idea. Does Acheron know about this?"

If he did, he didn't care. Obviously. Nor had he bothered to check on them or even ask. While Urian had cut him a lot of slack because of Tory being threatened, he was getting a little pissed about it at this point.

"I don't know. From his hatred of Styxx, though, I'd say he doesn't care. He'd probably say Styxx deserved it."

Savitar felt Styxx's forehead. "How long has his fever been this high?"

"Since the fight with Stryker. He had it when I brought him home and it hasn't broken or gone down at all."

Savitar placed his hand to Styxx's throat. "He barely has a pulse."

No shit, Sherlock.

Savitar gave him a pissed look that said he might have heard that.

Clearing his throat, Urian reminded himself to rein his thoughts in around the omniscient, irritable one. "Yeah. I didn't know what to do. Not like I can call a doctor. When I tried to call Ash, he said Styxx was probably faking it for attention. He told me Styxx couldn't die and would be fine. Not to concern myself with it. But he doesn't look fine. He looks like a corpse."

And since Ash had sounded distracted and hung up without saying good-bye, Urian had taken the hint.

Whatever had gone down between him and Styxx had left them as strangers. Ash didn't want anything to do with his brother.

Period.

Damn, Styxx, What'd you do? Piss on his favorite toy and make him eat it?

"All right. Stand back. I'm going to shock him out of this."

Urian moved to stand in the doorway as Savitar placed his hand over Styxx's chest. A slight hum filled his ears a few seconds before what appeared to be a sledgehammer-like bolt shot from Savitar's hand into Styxx's chest.

Styxx's eyes flew open. Panting, he frowned at Savitar and then Urian as if he didn't recognize them at first. As soon as he did, his eyes filled with panic and tears.

"No!" Styxx breathed raggedly, sweeping the room with his gaze. "Beth! Galen!"

Well, that wasn't the reaction Urian had expected. Nor was

the next one, where he flung himself out of bed and frantically searched his condo room to room. Stunned, he exchanged a wide-eyed stare with Savitar that turned into a gape when Styxx fell to his knees and bellowed. "Why did you bring me back here? Why? I was with them and we were happy! I was with them. . . . "

Styxx curled up into a ball and wept as if his entire world had shattered. "Beth, don't leave me again . . . please . . . please come back to me . . . I can't live without you anymore."

Urian choked at the sight of a profound agony he knew better than anyone. For a long time, he'd hated Ash for bringing him back to life. Even now, every day he lived without Phoebe was a day he despised with fury.

Why didn't I leave him alone?

Had he known Styxx was in a coma with his family, he'd have left him there forever.

What the fuck have I done? How selfish could I be?

His heart breaking for his newfound friend, Urian knelt down by Styxx's head and gathered him into his arms. "I'm sorry, Styxx. We didn't know."

Savitar came up to them and placed his hand on Styxx's shoulder, knocking him out again. "Unfortunately, he won't stay that way."

"Help me put him back in bed."

Instead of helping, Savitar picked Styxx up as if he weighed nothing and carried him to the bedroom. There was something weird about how Savitar was acting now. But Urian didn't know him well enough to even hazard a guess about his thoughts.

"It's disturbing, isn't it?" Savitar asked him as Urian entered the bedroom.

"What?"

"How much he favors Ash."

Urian shrugged. "They're identical twins. I had two sets of brothers who were, too. But while they may share looks and some tendencies, they are usually very different people."

Savitar swept his gaze around the room, then opened the closet where Styxx had two pairs of jeans folded neatly on the top shelf. One sweater, a jacket, two long-sleeved button-downs, and three short-sleeved shirts. One pair of shoes. Frowning, Savitar continued searching all six rooms of the condo.

Curious, Urian followed him around. "What are you looking for?"

"What's your impression of this place?"

Urian answered with the first word that popped into his head. "Spartan."

Savitar nodded. "Not exactly the kind of place a spoiled prince would be happy in, is it?" He handed a bankbook to Urian. "Acheron gave him plenty of money. And you can tell by the lack of dishes, he doesn't do much, if any, entertaining. The only thing he appears to have splurged on is the computer."

"Only because I ordered it for him. He didn't know anything about them and asked my advice." He'd even come up here and set it up for him.

Savitar picked up Styxx's phone, looked at it, then handed it to Urian. "Yours is the only number he has, and it's the only one he's called."

And not that often, and even then not for very long. Their longest conversation had been about the computer and that had probably been no more than twenty minutes, tops.

Urian sighed. "I was hoping he had other people he hung out with."

"Has he said anything to you about being alone?"

"He really doesn't talk much. Mostly asks questions about modern things he can't figure out. Or customs and phrases he's unfamiliar with."

Savitar scowled. "Does he ever mention Ash or their sister?"

"Only if I bring them up, and then he quickly deflects the conversation to another topic. Tonight notwithstanding, or when he and Ash went at each other, he's usually quiet and reserved. Unassuming. But he does have a wicked sense of humor."

"How so?"

Urian smiled at the memories of their brief conversations. "One of my personal faves ... he made a snarky comment on something, and then apologized by saying that he was so allergic to stupidity that it caused him to break out into rampant sarcasm. Another time, he made the comment that he was a leader and not a follower. Unless it was a dark place with loud growls, then fuck that shit, he'd gladly follow me in to investigate it."

Savitar laughed.

Urian continued, "He also wanted to know why sour cream, buttermilk, and blue cheese have expiration dates. Why boxing rings are always square. Why buildings burn up as they're burning down." He paused to laugh. "And my two favorites, he asked why we have doctors now and not physicians."

Savitar screwed his face up. "They're the same."

"That's what I said, but then he pointed out to me that back in the so-called barbarian days, we didn't have doctors who practiced medicine, but rather physicians who healed you ... or killed you, just like now. He asked me how modern man could trust someone with so little knowledge of their field that they told you right up front that they were still in the learning process."

Savitar snorted. "I never thought of it that way."

"Yeah, and a few months ago, he was in a grocery store and wanted to know why lemon juice was artificially flavored, but dishwashing soap contained real lemons. And what did modern people have against turkeys? He could find turkey masquerading as bacon, steak, and burgers, but no plain turkeys. Needless to say, I never thought about any of that, either. Probably because the only time I was ever in a grocery store, I was shopping for humans."

Savitar ignored those last comments. "It must be hard for him to adjust."

"He doesn't complain. He just tries to understand modern mind-sets, such as how can he be a chauvinist pig if he opens a door for a woman and then he's an insensitive pig if he doesn't."

"The day he figures that one out, tell him to write a book and we'll all be rich."

"He already has. He stays back until she goes in and then he runs for it before another one comes along."

Savitar laughed, then sobered. "Tell me honestly, Urian. What do you think of him?"

"I like him, and it's not because I idolized him as a military hero when I was a kid. He was a fierce old fart to me then. Kind of like you."

Savitar arched a censuring brow, then smiled and hehed.

"You know me, Chthonian; I don't play well with others, and I basically hate everyone, all the time, but I would actually cross the street to have a conversation with him. ... In fact, I have."

"Coming from you, that's the highest endorsement I can think of."

Urian shrugged. "I just don't understand their mutual hatred. I mean, I get not liking your brother. Had more than my fair share I couldn't stand to be around for more than five minutes. But I didn't really hate them. We were just different. While I might deck one from time to time, I never really tried to kill one."

Savitar glanced around at the sparse, humble furnishings. "I understand why Acheron hates him, and it is justified. Believe me. Apollymi herself has told me about their bad blood, and I know she's not lying. I'm just having a hard time reconciling the stories I've been told with the man who lives in this apartment. Of course, eleven thousand years can change someone. ... I don't know." Savitar sighed. "Keep an eye on him and let me know if he slips back into another coma."

And with that, he was gone.

Urian started to leave, too, but given how distraught Styxx had been, he didn't want Styxx to be alone when he woke up.

That was the last thing anyone this lonely needed.

Besides, it wasn't like he had anywhere else to go or anyone else waiting for him.

Loneliness he got as much as he understood wanting to pound on a brother who wore out the nerves. And having been left alone to struggle to pull his life back together twice already, he wouldn't do that to Styxx. So he glanced around for something to occupy himself with.

His gaze fell to a sketchbook on the end table. Curious about what it contained, he walked over to it and flipped it open.

His jaw went slack at what he found inside. The majority of the book was filled with drawings of an absolutely stunning woman who must be the Bethany Styxx talked about. Damn, no wonder he was obsessed. She was gorgeous.

Some of the pictures of her were so real, she looked like she could step off the page and touch him. But the ones that were truly haunting were drawings of Styxx and her. He'd perfectly captured their smiles and laughs, but most of all he caught the anguish and love on his own features as he held her.

There were also pictures of Bethany with a son, and of the boy by himself. A boy Styxx had never met. It wrung Urian's heart. Because these weren't just images of memories.

These were memories Styxx had wanted to have. They were longings of a broken promise the gods had stolen from him.

There was nothing crueler than to steal someone's dreams. To take a future. And he should know. It was what he grappled with every day of his own life.

His tomorrow had become his yesterday. There were no more left to look forward to. And that was the moment when you knew you wanted to die and you began every day with a breath and a whisper that searched for a reason to get up out of bed, because really? What was the use?

Life just became rote.

In that, he and Styxx were bonded brothers.

The one difference being that Styxx was talented in a way Urian would never have guessed.

And what he found most telling about his friend was that while a couple of Bethany's drawings showed her seductively clad in Greek gowns, none of them were of her naked. Even though Styxx had never intended for anyone else to see this, he'd kept his wife's honor sacred and respected her. That said it all about how much he loved that woman.

Urian stopped on the next page as he found the image of

a toddler boy dressed in a hoplite's Corinthian helm. It was hilarious and adorable. Beside it, Styxx had written the name "Galen" in Greek. ... He also had a few of an adult Galen, one of a woman named Tig, a horse and a dog, and a few scenes from what must have been his native Didymos.

The pages went on and on. Including a large number of Acheron in his modern Goth wear and long black hair, as well as pictures of them together with a bolt of lightning coming down between them.

When Urian turned to the next page, his heart stopped as he stared at a face he'd never thought to see again.

It staggered him so much that he had to sit.

Styxx had drawn him with Phoebe. Even though the bastard had never seen her, he'd penned her perfect likeness from Urian's descriptions. It was absolutely eerie that he could do that, and it showed him just how true to life his drawings of Bethany must be if Styxx could do this just based off words.

Incredible.

And in that moment, the pain that rifled through Urian was crippling. It merged with the same agony and madness that had driven Styxx to fill this book with image after image of his wife and longed-for son. Since Styxx had nothing left of her to hold on to, he must have created this. And it was like looking into Styxx's soul.

Unable to cope with it, Urian set the sketchbook back right where he'd found it. Honestly, what disturbed him the most about that book ...

He saw his own future. Phoebe had only been dead a handful of years and it still burned inside him like a raging furnace. For Styxx, it'd been eleven thousand years and he still ached as much now as he had then.

That did not bode well for Urian. Because he knew the other truth.

He still missed Xyn. Just as much today as he had the day she'd vanished.

That pain never ended and he knew it.

Maybe that was why he was so drawn to Styxx. They were bound by similar tragedies and had been born virtual contemporaries in ancient Greece. Well, not quite. Styxx was the same age as his father, but close enough.

Urian glanced back at the sketchbook and cringed. *So that's what I have to look forward to. Bitter insanity.*

So awesome.

Just after midnight, Styxx woke up covered in sweat. Urian wanted to weep for him. He was so cold, his teeth chattered. Feeling for his grieving friend, he pulled another blanket over Styxx's shoulder, then stepped into his field of vision. "How are you?"

His expression said clearly that he was broken.

When he didn't respond, Urian squatted down next to the bed until their gazes were level.

"I know," he whispered. "I still wake up and expect to find Phoebe beside me." Xyn too on the really bad days. "I haven't even deactivated her cell phone. I keep it so that I can call and hear her voice on those hours when I feel like I can't take it anymore. It's not fair that we're forced to live without them while the world goes on, oblivious to the fact that it's missing the most vital part of it."

He let out a bitter laugh to try to clear the pain that was choking him and making him want to scream out from the injustice of it. "It's why I'm here with your hairy ass. I don't want to see Tory and Ash. Not because I hate him like you do, but because they remind me of what I no longer have. And while I don't begrudge them their happiness, it makes my loneliness burn even deeper."

Styxx finally blinked. "Why do you talk to me, Urian?"

"I don't know. You're entertaining when you're not catatonic or in a coma. Or in a homicidal rage. Why do you talk to me?"

"Because I can't hear your thoughts."

Urian scowled at the last thing he'd expected him to say. "Excuse me?"

Styxx sighed. "It's something I've been able to do from birth. With a tiny handful of exceptions, one of whom is you, I hear every thought in someone's head."

So he shared that talent with Spawn. Wow, that was not something he envied. "That has to suck."

"It does indeed. That was what made me so lethal on the battlefield. I knew what my enemies were going to do and I could cut them off."

"Yeah, okay, that would not suck." Urian had meant to make him laugh, but if anything it darkened Styxx's mood, so he changed the subject. "You think you could eat something?"

"I don't know."

Urian handed him a bottle of water. "You need to sip this. While I know you can't die from hunger or thirst, you still feel both. I'll go recon the fridge while you take a shower." He rose to his feet, then left the room so that Styxx could have some privacy.

Though he was a little worried that he might do something drastic. Hoping for the best, he went into the kitchen to make them both sandwiches. It was one of the few things he knew Styxx really liked.

That and spaghetti, but sadly Urian couldn't cook. He needed Danger for those skills.

Without a word, Styxx came over to get his sandwich from the counter.

Urian swallowed his bite and wiped his chin as he watched Styxx dig in with gusto. "You know, food still tastes weird to me. It's hard to get used to eating when I lived on blood for eleven thousand years."

Styxx frowned at him. "I'm surprised you haven't filed down your fangs."

"Hadn't really thought about it. But I've never seen myself without them. Too old to change now. Might throw off my bite and I have enough trouble chewing as it is. You probably don't realize chewing is a skill. And the first time I bit my tongue ... be glad you weren't there for it."

Well, so much for his humor. That, too, had fallen flat.

Without so much as cracking a smile, Styxx sat down to eat his ham sandwich. "What made you decide to go Daimon?"

Urian paused at a most personal question that he hated

answering. Because the truth … not for public consumption. Last thing he wanted was to relive the day that had set them on the course of hunting down Phoebe's family.

Not to mention, he'd been a fool to get caught like that.

So as much as he loved Styxx as a friend, he didn't want to share a story of that much rampant stupidity. At least not tonight. Instead, he defaulted to a partial truth that was kind of right … ish. "Rage, mostly." That was true … "My best friend was a couple of years older than me and he refused to fight the curse. So I watched him age to an old man in less than twenty-four hours, screaming in utter agony the entire day until he decayed into nothing but dust."

While he hadn't seen Darius actually die, he'd witnessed plenty of others do it, so it wasn't entirely bullshit. "All I could think about was that he'd never harmed anyone. Never even been in a fistfight, and all because of my own grandfather over something that happened before I could walk. It pissed me off. But after losing Phoebe, I can understand why Apollo was so upset and cursed us. I'd have done as much, if not more, if they'd murdered my son and beloved mistress, too."

Styxx released a painful sigh. "He didn't love Ryssa."

Urian arched a brow. "What?"

"She was a possession. Nothing more. Most of the time, he bitched about her whining and complaining … which she did all the time, about everything."

"That's not what Ash says."

"He and I had two entirely different sisters. She coddled him and hated me."

"Why?"

Styxx swallowed his bite of food. "What can I say? I'm an asshole. As for Acheron, she felt sorry for him. In her mind, she was convinced that I stole our father's throne and his love from my brother."

"Is that why he calls you a thief?"

Styxx shrugged. "I don't know. Ironically, I didn't even want the throne. I just wanted a family that didn't hate me."

He could understand that, given the fact his father had killed his wife and cut his throat.

Urian finished off his sandwich. "I'd have gladly given you some brothers. Man, there was so much testosterone in that house, I don't know how my mother and sister stood us. But we were mostly happy. Although my older brothers said that my father was a very different man after Apollo cursed us."

"How so?"

Urian shrugged. "He was happier and much more easygoing." He picked up the pickle from his plate. "The only thing I really hated was not seeing sunlight." He laughed bitterly. "My father used to get so mad at me when I was a kid. I'd sneak out, trying to catch a glimpse of the sunrise. And he'd start screaming that if I wanted to burst into flames, then he was willing to begin the process by setting my ass on fire if I didn't get to safety."

Styxx laughed. "He loved you."

"Yeah, to the day he cut my throat. I've never understood it. After Darius died, I adopted his son and daughter." They had come along after Nephele and Geras had both died. "When Ida and Mylinus died, it about killed me. I can't imagine ever getting so mad at them that I'd do something like that, and they weren't technically mine." Just as he'd been with Neph and Geras. So long as he lived, he'd never understand his father's motivation. "How do you cut your own son's throat?"

"I don't know, Uri. I've never understood it, either. When I was just a boy, my own mother tried to kill me for giving her a birthday present. She stabbed me I don't know how many times."

Urian's eyes widened with incredulity. Was he kidding? "Your mother?"

He nodded. "Ryssa, too."

"Stabbed you?" Urian couldn't wrap his head around what he was telling him.

Styxx took a drink of his milk before he responded. "Ryssa gutted me the day before she died."

He gaped at that. While his brothers and sister had threatened that on a near daily basis, none had actually ever attempted it.

And he could think of a few times when it might have been warranted. "What'd you do?"

"She attacked me over your grandfather."

"Apollo? Why?"

Styxx scoffed. "Would you believe jealousy? She stupidly thought I was trying to seduce him as a lover to take his attention from her."

"Ew!" He couldn't think of anything more revolting. Not because Apollo was a man. But because he was so lacking in anything remotely resembling a decent human trait.

"Believe me, I couldn't agree more. No offense, but I hate your grandfather with every part of me. Just being in a room with him makes my skin crawl and my stomach turn."

"Don't worry. I'm not going to defend him. I personally think he's a rank, sorry, selfish son of a whore." Urian's phone rang. He looked down and checked the ID to see that it was Davyn. "Excuse me, I need to take this."

He went outside onto the terrace. "Hey—"

"What do you know about Cratus?"

"The video game character?"

"Seriously? Don't make me slap you."

Urian snorted. "Fine. God of warcraft. Nasty Titan bastard. Why?"

"If you can, you might want to head back. There's a situation brewing."

Oh, how he hated whenever Davyn said that to him. "Okay. Thanks."

So, his dad had lost his mind and unleashed absolute evil again. Oh goody!

Disgusted, he headed in to find Styxx cleaning up. "I have to head out. *AOM* later?"

"Sure."

"Don't forget, your brother's wedding is this afternoon."

"Is it?"

"Yeah. It's why I came to get you."

Styxx looked as thrilled to attend it as Urian did. While they were both happy Acheron had Tory, neither was looking forward to a wedding given what they'd lost.

"Hey, we'll go in. Get it done. Get drunk and get out."

Styxx snorted. "I like your plan of attack."

He winked at him. "I learned strategy from the master." He lifted his sleeve to show him his tribute to the Stygian Omada.

As he'd predicted, Styxx made a face of distaste. "That's creepy."

"But in a good way."

"We'll pretend so, if it makes *you* feel better." In spite of those words, Urian heard the teasing note beneath them. A part of Styxx was touched by it.

Glad that he'd shown the tattoo to him, Urian held his hand out. When Styxx took it, he pulled him into a brotherly embrace with their hands between their chests.

Without another word, Urian vanished.

Urian sighed as he handed Styxx a longneck beer and they hung out in the back of the reception hall. "Damn, how many people are in Tory's family?"

"I don't know." Styxx scratched at the collar of his tuxedo. "I swear I've been in countries with smaller populations."

He nodded.

Alexion walked over to them. "Don't you two look a little green around your gills. You okay? Or should I get a bucket to catch your vomit?"

Urian was definitely choking on bile. "There's an awful lot of Hunters in this place."

"Mostly former."

"When you're a Daimon, same difference."

"Ex-Daimon," Alexion reminded him.

Urian scoffed. "Same difference."

Styxx screwed his face up as Tory went down a line of relatives, chatting with each one of them. "How does she keep them all straight?"

"It's her superpower." Kat came up behind him, laughing. "Impressive, right? I spent a summer on a boat with her and her cousin Geary when Tory was a kid. She's a pistol."

Urian was baffled by it all. "How are you handling it?"

"What? That Ash is my father? Or that Tory's my stepmom?"

"Yeah, *that*."

Katra laughed. "You two need more alcohol."

"Kat? Mia's hungry."

Urian grew quiet as Sin, Kat's husband, handed her their infant daughter so that she could take her off to breast-feed her. Sin was probably the only one here who hated Artemis more than Styxx, Acheron, or Urian.

And only because he was the god Kat had stolen the powers from all those centuries ago when she'd cried on Urian's shoulder from the guilt over it.

Weird how life turned out. Had she not done that, she wouldn't have gotten together with Sin centuries later and had that beautiful daughter ...

Urian glanced to Ash and Tory, who had a similar eerie encounter in that Acheron had saved Tory's grandfather as a boy and brought him on a ship to America after he'd been orphaned. Had Ash not brought Theo to New York, Tory's father wouldn't have been born and Theo wouldn't have told him the stories of Atlantis that led to Tory's birth and her quest that led her to Ash.

By your actions you will be saved. Savitar's prophecy for Acheron.

Styxx frowned at him. "That's a peculiar look on your face, Urian. What thought is in your head?"

He shook it off. "Irony." Smiling, he smirked at Sin. "How you and Yaya getting along these days?"

Sin laughed. "Artemis hates it when I call her that, which is why I do it ... often."

The laugh from Styxx was so evil that it actually sent a chill over Urian, and it caused Sin to excuse himself.

"Are you okay?"

"Why are we still here?"

Urian shrugged as he looked around the oddball group. Simi was plowing her way through the desserts with her sister. The Peltier bears were dancing to the Howlers who were playing a polka for Tory's aunts who were dancing with a group of wereleopards. Dev Peltier danced with his niece on his feet. Tabitha and Valerius Magnus were in a corner with Kyrian and Amanda Hunter and their children.

The Kattalakis lycanthropes were huddled in a corner ... but he felt the same thing that Styxx did.

Out of place. Out of time and sync.

End of the day, no one here would notice if they left. They'd done their duty. Put in their appearances. Bought the right presents.

Yeah ...

Styxx might share blood with Acheron, but they weren't really family. And Urian wasn't anything to any of them. A barnacle to Acheron and babysitter for Simi didn't really count.

Urian set his beer aside. "I'm ready if you are."

"Brother, I was ready as soon as the ceremony ended."

Snorting, Urian inclined his head and transported them back to Styxx's apartment.

Styxx let out a long sigh and immediately began peeling off his tux. "Thank the gods."

He resembled that remark. Urian pulled his tie off and opened his collar, then decided to just use his powers and change it out for a black T-shirt and jeans.

Styxx snorted. "I envy you those powers."

"Yeah, they can be handy."

Awkward silence filled the room. "Well," Urian finally said to break it. "Guess I'll head back, unless you need something?"

Styxx shook his head. "All good."

Urian didn't leave, though. He paused to ask the one question that had been bothering him. "Have you tried to date while you've been here?"

Styxx let out a light laugh. "I had perfection. Anything else would be settling."

"Yeah, but the loneliness ... "

"Is hard. But you never know how strong you can be until you have no other choice." Styxx clapped him on the shoulder. "That's *my* path, Uri. You're not me. If you're lonely, go find a beautiful woman. You deserve to be loved."

"What if you're right?"

"What if I'm wrong?"

Urian laughed.

Styxx jerked his chin toward the door. "Go on, Urian. Find your happiness. Or at least a good drink."

"All right. I'll talk to you soon."

Styxx inclined his head to him. "Take care."

But as Urian left, he had a bad, bad feeling that he might not see Styxx again.

That was utter foolishness. He'd just about convinced himself of that when he reached Sanctuary in New Orleans and teleported into the third floor, which was reserved for such activities. Because the club was owned by a family of Were-Hunter bears, they took a lot of precautions when it came to catering to their "special" clientele.

Of all the limanis located throughout the world, none was more famous or legendary than Sanctuary. The Peltier bears had seen to that. Its reputation for fairness and hospitality set it apart.

Urian came here because he knew his father had a spy among their happy family.

He just didn't know who. Sadly, neither did Davyn. They'd both been trying to find out, and that had been one piece of trivia that kept eluding them.

Since the staff tonight would be minimal, Urian thought that maybe he might get a better handle on who to look for. So with a nod to the guard on the "landing pad," he headed for the stairs so that he could walk to the bottom floor and not spook any humans in the bar and grill.

It was weird to be here with so few Were-Hunters. Most of them were still at Ash's wedding. Urian headed to the bar, where Tony, one of the few humans who worked here, was bartending and ordered another beer.

He'd just gotten it when he had that unique sensation at the base of his neck that alerted him a Daimon was near.

Urian turned to skim the bar . . .

No one was there. Now *that* was weird. Disturbed, he walked all the way through both levels. Because he still had the sensation. It was unmistakable.

There was a Daimon here.

He couldn't find them.

And that had never happened before.

What the hell was going on?

Urian tried calling Styxx again, and again it rolled to voice mail. Afraid Styxx might have slipped into another coma, Urian flashed himself to Styxx's condo.

He knew the minute he materialized that something wasn't right. Everything about the condo felt off. But glancing around, he saw nothing out of place.

"Styxx?"

No one answered.

He quickly searched the condo to find it empty. This time when he went into Styxx's bedroom, he saw that Styxx had pulled out the sketchbook page of him and Phoebe and left it on top of his desk with a folded note. Fear cinched his gut as he opened it and read.

> *Urian,*
>
> *You're the only one who will notice that I'm not here. Don't worry, I'm not doing anything particularly stupid. I just don't want to live in a world I don't understand anymore.*
>
> *When I find my place and the peace I need to function, I'll be in touch. Until then, take care, my brother. And thank you for being my friend.*
>
> *S*

Grinding his teeth, Urian wanted to find Styxx and beat the shit out of him for the pain he felt right now, and he didn't know why he felt it. Why should he care? He barely knew Styxx.

It must be that they were kindred spirits. Styxx was the only one who really understood about Phoebe. After almost six years, everyone else had lost patience with his unwillingness to move on and find someone new to love.

But it wasn't that easy. Not when you had a past that was so hard to share with another person. One that left you bleeding and vulnerable. It was difficult to open up to anyone because the moment you did, you knew you ran the risk of being hurt worse, and humiliated should they ever tell your secrets, and when you'd been hurt all your life by others ...

There was only so much bravery in any given soul. And while Urian was more than willing to risk his life, he'd never again risk his heart. He was done with that shit.

Not even sex was worth the possibility of getting emotionally attached. He'd rather take things into his own hands than risk going through one more bout of Xanthia-style psychodrama, or worse, Xyn or Phoebe heartbreak.

At his age, it just wasn't worth it.

That level of burn was unending.

To finally find the courage to trust and to dare lay your heart in the hands of another and then to lose them was the ultimate cruelty. And it was not something you ever got over. Ever.

Six years was just a blink of the eye. And apparently so was eleven thousand. As he well knew. 'Cause not a day went by where he didn't think about Xyn.

If he closed his eyes right now, he could still see the red of her hair in his hands. Feel her lips tickling his skin. Smell her scent on a stray breeze. She was every bit as deeply embedded in his soul as Phoebe.

They had left him changed. Had left him marked.

And in the end, they had left him abandoned.

Lost.

He couldn't go through it again. He'd rather be dead.

Urian cleared his throat. "Good luck, brother. I hope when you find a way to sleep through the night and breathe again, you'll share the secret with me."

Because right now, he still wasn't sleeping. Some days and nights, he barely functioned.

July 4, 2009

Urian cocked his head as he watched Xirena and Simi arguing. "Um, demons? What exactly are you doing?" 'Cause from his vantage point as he entered the room, it sounded like they were attempting to decide what flavor of barbecue went best on a baby to eat it.

The two of them were in the throne room of Katateros, which Ash had turned into a giant living room, with four boxes of Burberry layettes for an infant girl and were about to come to blows in their argument.

Simi got up from her furry purple bean bag chair. Dressed in a short black ruffled skirt and crop top, she pursed her lips. "Akri-Uri, tell the Simi's idiot sister that the hickory sweet sauce is better with the pink baby! 'Cause it more tasty and sweet!"

Xirena actually let out a burst of flames. "No, Xiamara! For baby, you must have more spice for the digestion. You need it!"

Yeah, no, that sounded like they planned to eat someone's baby.

At a loss, Urian glanced back and forth between them, unsure how best to handle this situation, because he didn't want to be on either of their menus.

Crossing her arms over her chest, Simi cocked her hip and looked at him. "Wells?"

"Uh ... what baby are you going to eat?"

Simi froze, then became extremely happy. "Can we?"

"No!" He rushed to correct that, if that wasn't where they were going with this weirdness. "You aren't planning to eat a baby?"

Simi shook her head. "But if the Simi can, she will. Cans she?"

"No," he repeated. "What are you doing?"

"Now the Simi sad she can't eat a baby 'cause they's so tender." She pouted.

Xirena sighed. "I know, sissy. So sad." She shook her head as she folded up the layette. "The nice pirate man and his wife had their baby. So we were sending this for them."

"Oh." Urian had forgotten about that. "Rafael Santiago and Celena."

Simi nodded enthusiastically. "Baby Ephani!" She held up the bottles. "Which flavor do you think Baby Ephani would like?"

Urian bit back his laughter. "Why not both? Let the baby decide?"

She gasped. "Good idea!" She dropped the bottles into the box, then ran forward to hug him.

Only she hit him so hard, it was more like a tackle. Urian smiled, especially when her wings fluttered and feathers went flying. That was the strangest part of all about the Charonte. When they were happy, they had feathered wings. When you pissed one off, their wings turned fleshy and leatherlike, complete with spiked tips on the ends of them.

Simi pulled back to scowl at him. "Why you so sad, akri-Uri?"

"I'm okay, Simi."

She put her hand over his head. "No, you're not. You gots a lot of heart-hurt." Her lips quivered. "Simi sorry. It's not fun being one-of-a-kind. Believe me, the Simi knows."

That she did. The reason she spoke the way that she did was that Apollymi had sent her to live with Ash when she was a toddler. With no other Charonte in the human world, she'd grown up with no one to teach her anything about them. It was only after her sister and brother had managed to escape, thousands of years later, that she'd finally had another Charonte with her.

"I'm not as cute and precious as you are, Simikee."

She smiled so wide, her fangs showed. "You gots the blue eyes. They's very beautiful, just like you are." Taking his hand, she turned back toward her sister. "We should make akri-Uri an honorary Charonte, what do you think, Xixi?"

Screwing her face up, Xirena narrowed her gaze as she stared at him. "He could look cute with horns."

Urian's eyes widened at the thought of them putting horns on his head. The image of them drilling them into his skull was horrifying. Charonte were known to do things like that.

Luckily, Xirena got up with a pair of stuffed red ones that attached with clips. Making herself taller, she handed one to Simi and each one clipped a horn to his head.

They stepped back to stare at him, then high-fived each other. "Charonte!" they said in unison.

Simi gave a firm nod. "You's a perfect, beautiful Charonte now!" She grinned. "Can you look in a mirror or are you still too Daimon for that?"

He laughed. "I can look in mirrors now." That was one of the things Ash had fixed about him that still freaked him out whenever he happened to see his reflection.

"Goody!" Simi used her powers to conjure a crystal-encrusted, Hello Kitty hand mirror that she held up for him so that he could see the horns.

Urian grinned at the silliness of it. "Perfect."

"Charonte!" She held her hand up for him to high-five her.

"Charonte!" he said, and gently touched her palm with his.

Alexion picked that moment to come in and burst into laughter. "Should I even ask?"

Urian glared at him. "Not if you want to live."

Simi snorted. "Akri-Uri is a Charonte now. We's adoptive him. He our baby now so if you make our baby cry, we make you cry."

Urian's grin turned to straight shit-eating. "I like that a lot." Crossing his arms over his chest, he dared Alexion. "I've got Charonte mamas now. Go ahead, insult me."

Alexion sputtered as he looked back and forth between the two demons, who were now very alert. "The only Danger I flirt with is my wife. Who I'm going to find right now. But word to the wise about your adoption, Uri ... they feed their babies habanero sauce straight up from the bottle, and good luck with the burping." Then he vanished.

"Hey! That a joke?" he shouted after him.

No answer.

A bad, sick feeling went through Urian. He turned toward the demons. Both of whom were now on their feet and coming closer with purpose.

Oh shit . . .

"We have a problem."

"You'd have had a bigger one had you arrived a minute earlier before I pulled my pants on," Acheron said drily as Urian materialized directly in front of him as he stood in the kitchen of the New Orleans home he shared with Tory. He'd been scooping ice cream when Urian made an unannounced appearance. "Were you raised in a barn?"

A loud knock sounded on the back door.

Acheron rolled his eyes at Urian's sarcasm when it was obvious Urian had thrown the sound as a "screw you" to him. The expression on Ash's face said, *Lucky for you, I just had great sex with my wife that put me in such a happy place that not even your assholishness can disturb it.* Otherwise Urian was sure he would have been a flaming stain on the wall. "What's up?"

"Dev's not on crack." Dev Peltier being the Were-bear from Sanctuary who normally stood guard at their front door, which let out onto the street. Apparently, the bear had claimed that he saw Daimons out in daylight, walking around with tourists. Since everyone knew Daimons couldn't do that ... the natural assumption was that the bear was on crack.

Acheron licked the back of the spoon before he set it in the sink. "Never thought he was. ... Ketamine maybe, but never crack. Why, did you?"

Urian watched Ash return the ice cream carton to the freezer. "I just came away from a chat with one of my old friends." Which really just meant Davyn as he had no other friends on the Dark Side. "He told me that the Daimons are able to take gallu demon souls into their bodies and that Stryker is converting his army with their blood."

Just as Urian had done when Davyn told him what his father was up to, Acheron froze at those words. The Sumerian gallu powers were intense. The ultimate in evil, one of them in a Daimon's body was a nightmare of biblical proportions.

More than that, gallu bites turned their victims into mindless drones. Like a zombie on steroids. One could make thousands.

A Daimon would now be able to make more of their kind. Lots more.

While the great Acheron could take one down without breaking a sweat, a normal Dark-Hunter ...

Good luck with that.

"What's Stryker planning?"

Urian gave him a droll stare. "What he's always wanted. To kill my grandfather and subjugate the humans while staying beyond Helios's reach."

Ash returned his "duh" expression. "I didn't ask for the goal, Urian. I've known that. What I need is the game plan. Why is he converting his people?" Ash's phone rang. He started to ignore it until he saw the ID.

Sighing, Acheron looked at the bowl of melting ice cream on the counter. He refroze it, then flashed it away.

With an aggravated expression, he flipped open his phone.

"Nick is working with the Daimons." Urian couldn't identify the voice on the other end, but he heard those words plainly.

"Nice hearing from you too, Spartan. Care to tell me why you think this?"

"'Cause the little shit tried to kidnap Sam out of Sanctuary. He was there in all his glory, offering her up to our enemies."

Urian tried to make sense of that. Nick was the current Malachai after the death of his father, Adarian. And after they'd rescued Tory and Nick had killed Satara, they'd discovered that Stryker had somehow tied Nick's life force to his own.

Ash hung up the phone and met Urian's curious gaze.

"Get over to the Charonte club and ride herd on Dev and Sam. Anything comes at her, I don't care who or what, you protect her."

Great. Protect another Dark-Hunter. Just what he wanted to be assigned. Especially Samia, who'd once been an Amazon who had taken out a large number of his people and who was related to the gods who'd cursed and abandoned them. "Okay. What's going on?"

"Just do it."

That tone always flew over Urian and made him want to punch Acheron when he used it. It also made him want to feed Sam to the Daimons.

But the gallu were a whole other matter. They were as big a threat to the Daimons as they were to mankind.

What the hell was his father thinking now?

October 24, 2010

Urian was supposed to meet Davyn at Sanctuary so that he could gather more information about Stryker's plan. He and Davyn had always tried to pick spots where there was no chance of any of the Apollymians seeing them together. If Stryker ever learned that Urian still talked to his old friend, he'd kill Davyn immediately.

And it wouldn't be quick. Last thing he wanted was to cause any harm to befall Davyn. He'd sooner cut his own throat.

Instinctively, he rubbed the scar left by Stryker's attack on him the night Phoebe died. The bitter memory of that night was never far from the surface, and it was carved in blood on his heart.

He'd worshiped his father his entire life—had committed all manner of atrocities to please him.

And for what?

So the bastard could kill Urian's wife and then cut his throat the first time he displeased him? *One day I will have my vengeance.*

If it was the last thing he did, he would kill Stryker for what he'd taken from him.

"C'mon, Davyn, have something good for me." Urian went over to the bar to order a beer while he waited.

Colt Theodorakolpolis—one of the bears who lived and worked here—handed it off to him.

Without a word, Urian drifted around the game area. He checked his watch. Davyn was late. Highly unusual for him.

Fear tightened his gut. Had Stryker found out? The mere thought made his blood run cold.

Suddenly a familiar tingle went down his spine and danced along his neck, alerting him that there was a Daimon on the premises.

Urian scanned the semicrowded bar, looking for his friend.

He saw a flash of white-blond hair in the far corner and headed for it.

It wasn't until he was within sight that he realized it wasn't Davyn. This was a woman and when she turned toward him, he felt like someone had sucker-punched him.

No, it couldn't . . .

It wasn't possible.

"Tannis?"

The woman frowned at him as if the name and his face meant nothing to her.

But to him that name had meant everything.

Time froze as he was taken back to the day his *little* sister had died. Little not because she was younger, but because compared to them, she was so tiny and fragile. One to be protected at all cost.

Unlike him and his brothers, she'd been too gentle and kind to take a human life in order to live.

And so she'd withered away into dust on her twenty-seventh birthday. The pain of her decay had caused her to scream until her throat had bled. And still she'd had no peace. No mercy. It had been the most agonizing death imaginable.

One given to her by her own grandfather's curse. After they'd scooped up her remains and buried them years later, they never spoke her name out loud again.

But Urian remembered. How could he ever forget the tiny woman he'd protected and championed? The one he'd killed to protect?

But this wasn't Tannis.

She's dead. He'd seen her decay into dust with his own eyes. Yet this woman was a complete physical copy of her, except for the way she moved. While Tannis had been hesitant and dainty, this woman was sure and determined. Fluid. She moved like a warrior ready to kill. She had a self-assurance his own sister had lacked.

Before he could think better of it, he closed the distance between them.

Medea turned as a shadow fell over her. Expecting it to be her informant, she was stunned when she looked into the face of her father.

But this man was different. Instead of her father's short dyed black hair, his was long and snow white, pulled back into a ponytail.

Still, there was no denying the similarity of their features. This was her father's doppelganger.

"Who are you?" they asked simultaneously.

Medea hesitated when he didn't answer right away. Why was he being reserved when it was obvious he was a relative she hadn't met? Maybe a cousin even her father didn't know about?

Curiosity got the better of her so she answered first.

"I'm Medea."

"Medea ... " He seemed perplexed by her name. "I'm Urian."

Urian.

She gasped at the name of her mysterious half brother, whom she'd heard about but never expected to meet. He was now a servant of Acheron. Enemy to all of them after he'd betrayed her father.

"Filthy traitor!" she spat.

He didn't take that well as he gripped her arm and yanked her toward him. "Who are you?"

She wanted to see the shock on his face when she delivered the truth. "*Your* sister."

Urian blinked twice as that news sank in. He'd only had one sister. There was no way he could have another and not know it. "How?"

"Stryker married my mother, then divorced her to marry yours. She was pregnant with me at the time and he never knew."

His jaw went slack. Why hadn't Davyn told him about this? Davyn had told him about Stryker's first wife returning, but a sister ...

A living, real sister. Why would Davyn have kept *that* secret? Ah, shit! Suddenly he remembered Acheron telling him. ...

I wouldn't have forgotten something like that. Ever! Yet he had. *Yeah, I did.*

After the fight when Ash had gone around tampering with memories ... The bastard must have removed that one, too. Why would Ash have done that? Had it been intentional or a mistake? When it came to things like that with emotions and brains, Ash didn't always have the best control with his powers, so until he talked to him, he'd give him the benefit of the doubt.

But if he'd done this on purpose ...

He could kick his ass.

And with that thought came a really bad feeling.

"What are you doing here?"

"Sightseeing."

He knew better, especially with someone sired by his father. "You're spying for Stryker."

She jerked her arm out of his hold. "Don't take that tone with me, little boy. You served him too and for many more centuries."

The thought made him ill. "And I paid the ultimate price for that blind stupidity. Trust me."

She scanned his body. "I don't know. You look pretty healthy and happy to me."

Those looks were definitely deceiving! "Yeah, right. Let me tell you something, *little girl*—I was his favorite. His pride and joy above all others. For *thousands* of years I served at his side, doing everything he asked me to. *Everything*. Without question or hesitation. And in the blink of an eye, because I dared to marry without his permission, he cut my throat. Literally."

"He cut your throat because you married his enemy."

Yeah, right. It had nothing to do with whom he'd married and everything to do with his father's ego. Stryker couldn't stand the thought of anyone questioning his authority. Not even his own son.

"I married a kind, gentle woman who never hurt a soul a day in her life. She wasn't a warrior. She was an innocent bystander whose only mistake was falling in love with a monster." And making him human. Making him care for someone other than himself, and he would sell his soul if he could have one more moment with her. "Don't delude yourself for one minute. Stryker will turn on you, just as he turned on me."

"You're wrong about that."

"For your sake, sister, I hope to the gods that I am." But the bad thing was, he knew better. It was just a matter of time before their father went after her, too.

God help her, then.

And with the gallu on the loose ... they were all about to get screwed.

January 16, 2011

"This ... seriously sucks."

Styxx laughed as he and his giant brown dog came out of their tent to greet Urian in the middle of a godforsaken desert. "Depends on your vantage point, little brother."

Arms akimbo, Urian turned in a circle as he surveyed Styxx's small black tent and the vast desert that surrounded them as far as the eye could see in all directions. "From mine ... you found hell, buddy, except I doubt hell is this hot."

Still laughing, Styxx closed the distance between them. "It's not hot. This is winter. Come back in July or August."

"Yeah, no thanks." Urian hugged him, then stood back with a severe frown. "Damn, you've gone native. But for the blue eyes, I'd have no idea it was you."

Styxx lowered the black veil from his face. "Better?"

"Not really. Weirds me out more." He shook his head. "When you called last week and told me you'd been living in the desert for the last two years, I thought you meant Morocco or another city. But you really live out in the middle of Nowhere, Sahara."

Styxx shrugged. "This place makes sense to me."

"You might like it, but it's bringing back bad childhood memories. Life before toilet paper was not worth living."

"Again, a matter of perspective."

Urian shivered in revulsion. Styxx was definitely having some kind of midlife crisis. "You look good, by the way. Healthy."

"Thanks." Styxx held the flap open so that Urian could go inside, where he had nothing but his bedroll and saddlebags of necessary supplies. "I feel better than I have in a very long time."

The big brown dog came bounding in and curled up on Styxx's bedroll to chew his rawhide bone. Urian arched a brow. "What's his name?"

"Skylos."

He scowled at Styxx for a name that just seemed cruel. "You named your dog ... Dog? Seriously?"

Again, Styxx shrugged. "He doesn't seem to mind."

"Probably because he doesn't speak Greek."

Grinning, Styxx pulled out a bottle of wine and the only two cups he had and poured drinks for them.

Urian sat down beside the dog and took a sip. "So what do you call the horse and camel? Alogo and Kamila?"

Styxx rolled his eyes. "No, they had names when I bought them. Jabar and Wasima. The dog just started following after me one day."

Urian sighed heavily. "I'd go insane here. How do you cope with the solitude?"

"That was what I had to make peace with. All my life, I hated being alone. After we freed Soteria, it dawned on me that I had to make a choice. Either be part of the modern world or not."

"You chose poorly, my friend."

"No, this I understand. It's the existence I willingly chose on my own. No one incarcerated or dropped me here against my will. Not to mention, I really like not having solid walls that confine me."

That Urian could understand. Part of what he'd hated about Kalosis had been the claustrophobia. While it had been expansive, he'd known there was a much larger world to be had and so he'd often felt confined there. Boxed in.

Especially with the daylight ban.

But this was too much daylight.

Styxx sat down next to him. "What about you? How have you been?"

Urian reached for the can of cashews. "Same old, same old. Someone's always trying to take over the world or end it. Really not looking forward to dealing with 2012 and the crap that's coming out to play with us." He laughed as he skimmed Styxx from the top of his agal-wrapped black keffiyeh to his desert boots. "It's really messing with my head how natural you look dressed like a Bedouin. The scimitar and dagger just add to the whole cosplay, *Assassin's Creed* thing you got going."

Styxx laughed. "I also have a handgun tucked at my back, and a rifle." He inclined his head over to where it rested near his bedroll. "But the sword doesn't run out of bullets when bandits attack."

"Another thing I tend to forget. You're human."

"There are many who would argue that."

Urian didn't respond, especially given the shit he had to take from the rabble, given former Daimon status.

Instead, he opened the backpack he'd brought and handed a dark blue box to Styxx. "I got you something I thought you might like."

Styxx set his cup aside to take it and open it. A slow smile curled his lips as he saw four new sketchbooks and a pencil set. "Thank you, very much."

He figured his friend could always use more and had he known where and how he was living, he'd have brought a whole lot more. "Hey, someone with your talent should never be without. That picture you drew of me and Phoebe ... incredible. You nailed her looks and you've never even seen her, and I can't thank you enough for leaving that for me. The only pictures I had of her were the ones in my head. Is that why you started drawing?"

He carefully tucked his gift away. "I actually started as a kid. It was one of my favorite things to do until Ryssa saw me and thought I was copying her journals. She had one of her more legendary hissy fits and then when she opened it and saw my feeble attempts at drawing, she laughed and ridiculed them, and ran straight to my father to tell him I'd been wasting my study time and precious parchment on stupidity. He didn't take it well. He made me burn my sketches and had me whipped. Then he made me earn back all the money I'd squandered on wasting good parchment for foolishness. After that wonderful experience, I had such an aversion to art, I didn't even want to look at figured pottery."

Urian cringed at the thought, given how popular such pottery was in their day. "Then how did you learn to draw like that?"

"Vanishing Isle. I didn't have paper or pencil, but I did have a lot of sticks and a lot of wet sand, and a shit-ton of time. You think I can draw? You should see my sand cities."

"You mean sand castles?"

"Nah, anyone can build a sand castle. I do entire cities, complete with armies and aqueducts."

Urian laughed even harder. "I hate to admit it, but I have missed your twisted sense of humor. And I'm stunned you get cell reception out here."

"I don't. I was in a town a week ago buying supplies when I called."

"Ah." Urian looked around and realized that Styxx was also lacking any form of power. "So how do you charge the phone?"

"Bribe a store clerk to use their outlet for an hour while I shop."

"You've thought of everything."

Styxx leaned over to his backpack and pulled out a roll of toilet paper, then chucked it at Urian. "I try."

Laughing, he shook his head. "Dude, that's so messed up." Sobering, Urian cleared his throat. "You haven't asked me about Acheron."

His expression turned to stone and made Urian regret that he'd brought it up. "I assume he's doing fine. The world hasn't ended and I'm not dead."

"He's expecting a baby in April."

Styxx snorted. "That should make medical news then, and I'm sure Soteria is grateful she doesn't have to go through labor."

"Wha ... ?" It took Urian a second to figure out what he meant and then he felt like an idiot. "Ah, gah. Yeah. You knew what I meant."

He gave him a sarcastic nod. "Do they know what it is?"

"Boy."

Yeah, that was another somber expression on Styxx's face that made Urian want to cut out his own tongue. He really needed to change the topic. Obviously, he was stabbing at some deep scars and ripping them open.

Styxx smiled, but it didn't quite reach his eyes. "I'm happy for them. I'm sure his son will be handsome and strong."

He cleared his throat. "So how's Davyn?"

Urian breathed in relief to finally be on a safe topic. "Insane. I seem to attract that personality type for some reason."

Styxx smirked. *"Aeì koloiòs parà koloiôi hizánei."*

Urian scowled at the old Greek saying as he tried to figure out what Styxx was implying. "A jackdaw is always with a jackdaw?"

"Birds of a feather."

Urian laughed. "Hey now, I resemble that remark."

Styxx leaned back so that he could peep through the crack in the tent flap. He set his cup aside. "If you really want to know why I love it here, follow me."

He was definitely curious, because he couldn't imagine *anything* that would make this worthwhile.

Skylos lifted his head, but since Styxx didn't call him outside with them, he went back to sleep.

As soon as they were out of the tent, Styxx looked up at the sky and started opening the sides of the tent so that they could take advantage of the much cooler night air. "You don't have a view like that in New York."

Urian gaped at the sight of the vivid night sky. Styxx was right, he hadn't seen anything like that in a long, long time. "I'd forgotten how beautiful and bright they are."

"Yeah. When I was a kid, I'd sit out on my balcony for hours staring at them. Most of the time, I don't pitch the tent. I sleep out here on the sands, watching them. It was one of the things I missed over the centuries. They don't exist on the Vanishing Isle or Katateros."

"Kalosis either. And I never think about the fact that Katateros only has a moon. Alexion said the stars faded when Apollymi killed Astors, I think his name was?"

"Asteros."

Urian cocked a brow at his answer. "I'm amazed you remember any of their names."

Again that expression that said he'd stumbled across another brutal memory. Urian kicked himself. He'd come here to make Styxx feel better, but apparently, he was just being an inadvertent asshole.

"Are you hungry?" Styxx asked. "I have dried scorpion, nuts, figs, dates, and apples."

"And you dared to mock jumbo shrimp?" Urian twisted his face up in distaste. "I really hope the scorpion offer is just to screw with me."

"No, it's actually quite good. Tastes like chicken."

"Ar, ar, ar." Urian feigned laughter over what he used to default to whenever Styxx would quiz him on what things tasted like in New York. "I'd rather live on blood . . . or my shoes."

Styxx tsked. "I might have some beef jerky left."

"That I could be talked into."

Grinning, Styxx went back inside. "It's good to have you here, Urian. I'd forgotten what it was like to actually carry on a real conversation with someone outside my head."

"Well, now that I know where you are, I might occasionally bother you. As long as you don't feed me grasshoppers, ants, scorpions, or other nasty multilegged things the gods never intended us to eat."

"Stop being a baby. Eat your meat or you can't have any pudding. How can you have any pudding if you don't eat your meat?"

Urian laughed. "I am stunned you know Pink Floyd."

Styxx shrugged as he opened Skylos's dinner first and poured it into a small metal bowl. "Modern music is the only thing I miss about your world."

"Next time I come, I'll bring you a solar battery charger for your phone. Not like you don't have an abundant supply of sunlight here."

"That I do have. Definitely." Styxx paused as his gaze fell to a small chest near his rifle. He went over to it and opened it, then pulled out an oiled cloth and handed it to Urian. "My gift to you, little brother."

Urian frowned. "Thank you." He unwrapped the cloth to find Styxx's black-and-bronze vambraces. "Wow ... how old are these?"

"They were mine back in the day. My mentor, Galen, gave them to me, and I wore them into every battle I fought."

Urian's jaw went slack as he realized exactly how old and valuable these were. These were a piece of history. And a treasured piece of Styxx's past. They needed to go to a son or a museum, not to someone like him. He shook his head. "I can't take these."

Styxx pushed them back toward him. "I have no use for them anymore. They're just something else I have to pack and carry, or worry about losing."

Urian let out a long, appreciative breath. "These are incredible. I can't believe how pristine they are. Thank you. I'll cherish them always."

His gratitude made Styxx extremely uncomfortable. "I know how much you like to collect antiques. And they don't get much older than those." He went to start the campfire so that he could cook their dinner.

Urian carefully wrapped the vambraces back into their cloth and tucked them into his backpack as he watched Styxx. His heart broke for his friend who'd felt so out of place in the world that he'd had to come to the remotest place on it to find some sense of belonging. Urian hadn't been joking when he said that he'd go insane with this kind of isolation. This was truly a desolate, hard way to live.

But sadly, it was all Styxx knew.

All he'd ever known.

And as sad as it was, at least Styxx had found a place where he belonged. Urian was still looking. He envied Styxx his mental health here. Because the truth was, he didn't have it.

Not even as a boy. Never in his life had he felt completely at home the way Styxx appeared. The closest he'd come had been in Phoebe's arms.

Without her ...

I'm nothing.

When surrounded by a crowd, he was forever alone. And the apocalypse was coming. If he was smart, he'd just roll with it and let it end his suffering, once and for all. Better to go out a hero, fighting.

Yeah. That would be the perfect ending. At least then, he'd finally be with the women he'd loved. Maybe then, he'd finally have the elusive place called home.

June 23, 2012

Acheron sighed in aggravation as he surveyed the empty condo he'd provided for Styxx after his brother had asked to leave Katateros. He'd been trying to catch the bastard for weeks now, but every time he "popped" in, Styxx was gone.

If he didn't know better, he'd think Styxx had moved out. But the bankbook was still in a kitchen drawer, along with Styxx's license and credit cards. He couldn't have gone far without money or ID.

"Ryssa was right. You are always annoying."

Then again, it was their birthday. Maybe Styxx was out celebrating with friends.

Ash paused at the thought. Did Styxx have any friends? Sadly, he had no idea. As Ryssa's journals that Tory had uncovered during her excavations had shown him, there was a lot he didn't know about his own twin brother. And the more he read, the more he was desperate to talk to Styxx.

To find the real truth.

Mentally, Ash flogged himself for not cornering Styxx when he'd been in Katateros. But he'd been too angry then to listen. Too hurt to care about Styxx's side of anything.

Now ...

Closing his eyes, he tried to pinpoint Styxx's location. Yet all he got out of that was a migraine. New York was too big a city, with too many people in it. *I should have stuck his ass on another deserted island. At least then I'd know where he is.*

Even more agitated, he glanced to the bookshelves that were lined with ancient Greek books ...

Written in ancient Greek. Ash held his hand up and used his powers to pull one from the shelf.

Glancing around the room, he realized then that Styxx had

only written in Greek. And not just any Greek. Proto-Greek. The oldest of all the Greek variants. All his notes. Everything. That was Styxx's native tongue.

Oh shit . . .

Can Styxx read English? That was something he hadn't considered before he'd sent his brother out into the modern world. Since Styxx had been imprisoned for more than eleven thousand years, there was a good possibility that Styxx would have no idea how to read any modern language. At all. It would explain the checkbook, cards, and ID. Styxx might not have even known what those were.

You're an effing idiot!

Replacing the book, Ash winced at his own blind stupidity and hoped that he wasn't as big a bastard as he feared he was. Of all people, he knew how bad illiteracy sucked. Having been illiterate as a human slave, he knew that better than anyone. He couldn't imagine trying to navigate the modern world without at least a rudimentary understanding of the English alphabet.

And with that thought, against his will, his mind went to the past—to the days before their uncle Estes had ripped him from the home he'd shared with Ryssa and Styxx.

While Ryssa would spend most of her mornings visiting with her mother, Ash would sit in her room and listen to Styxx's tutors mercilessly grill him on all manner of subjects. As the heir to Didymos, Styxx had been required to study hard and learn as much as he could, as fast as he could. For hours every day, Styxx had been sequestered without breaks or relief. If he dared to ask for one, his tutors would report him to his father, who considered such actions as Styxx's attempt to avoid responsibility. Something the king did not take lightly. *"You're to be a king, boy, not some sniveling wastrel!"* Xerxes had been merciless with his mandates and expectations.

No wonder Styxx had been plagued with migraines.

His free time had been seriously limited. Even so, Styxx had worked around his father as best he could. And in his mind, Ash could see Styxx as a boy smiling at him while he placed a small box in Ash's hand and sat down next to him on his bed.

"What's this?" Ash had asked him.

"Open it and see."

Instead, he'd reached out to brush Styxx's blond hair back from a vicious black eye. And that hadn't been the only damage. A bit of blood still crusted his nose and mouth. "What happened?"

Ashamed, Styxx had looked away. "As a birthday present, Father decided it was time I began my war training. Today was the first lesson, but I fear I have no talent for it. Selinius said that he's never seen anyone more inept than me."

Acheron felt terrible for the pain that eye must have caused him. Styxx cringed every time he blinked but said nothing about how awful it must be.

"What did Father say?"

Styxx sighed. "That I embarrassed him. He told Selinius to take no mercy. It is imperative that I learn to fight as a man and not rely on others to protect me."

Yet Styxx was only a five-year-old child and Selinius a war hero.

Styxx nudged the box in Ash's hands. "Open it already!"

More worried about Styxx and his fate at the hands of another tutor who hated him, Ash had obeyed. As soon as he saw the small wooden soldier, his breath caught. It was exquisite.

"Do you like it?"

Ash smiled. "I love it! Thank you!" Without thinking, he grabbed Styxx into a hug and discovered that his face wasn't the only part of him his war tutor had bruised. "I'm sorry."

His breathing ragged, Styxx shrugged it off. "It's fine." He fingered the soldier in Ash's hand. "I hope I bought the right one. The vendor said that you'd admired it when Ryssa purchased you the horse."

"I did, but Ryssa didn't have the coin for both." Ash scooted off the bed to place the soldier on the horse in his window. "What did Ryssa get you?"

"Did you know the soldier's arms move?" Styxx joined him at the window to show him.

Ash frowned again as he noted the sadness that tainted his brother's smile. "Did Ryssa not get you a horse, too?"

As before, Styxx didn't respond to his question. "I'm so glad I got the right one. I was worried that the vendor might have forgotten or wasn't being truthful with me."

"Styxx," Ash said sternly, "what did you get for your birthday?"

His hand falling away from the soldier, he sighed heavily and stepped back. "A *hoplomachos*."

A drill instructor who had beaten him ... "Is that it?"

All the happiness faded from his vivid blue eyes. "Father also gave me the honor of observing court sessions when he holds them."

"What does that mean?"

"Every morning, I have to sit with him while he settles disputes for the people so that I can see what will be required of me as king. And so that I can witness Father's wisdom and learn from it."

Ash gaped at the boring horror he described. "But mornings are your free time." The only free time Styxx had at all—the rest was taken up with tutors, work, and temple obligations. Those mornings were when Styxx would sneak off to play with him until Styxx's lessons began after lunch.

"Father says I'm too old now for play. He's not raising a boy, but a king, and kings don't play with toys. I have to assume my royal duties and stop being selfish and thoughtless all the time."

Ash looked at his soldier that he knew Styxx would have bought with his own coin that, unlike Ryssa, he'd had to work for. "You're not selfish or thoughtless."

Styxx didn't comment. "I better go. The last time I was late for Master Karpos, he told Father. Father's already angry enough that I asked for a toy today when I'm too old for such. I've no wish to aggravate him further." Without another word, Styxx left.

Closing his eyes to blot out the past, Ash winced as he mentally pushed those memories back into the darkest recesses of his mind.

He and Styxx had been so close when they were young.

Brothers, forever and always. It sickened him that Estes and the others had put such a wedge between them.

That *they* had put a wedge between them. Harsh words and even harsher actions.

On *both* their parts.

For centuries, he'd kept all those happy memories of Styxx bottled up. Kept anyone from knowing he had a brother, at all. And while he'd gone on with his life, he'd abandoned Styxx to absolute solitude.

To Artemis's "tender" care.

Guilt and pain stabbed him hard over his own thoughtless callousness.

Tonight, Tory had a huge surprise party planned for him. Urian was supposed to keep him occupied with his son while Tory and the others decked out Sanctuary and finished the preparations. He wasn't supposed to know anything about it, but her best friend Pam stunk at keeping secrets and had accidentally told him two days ago.

Never in his life had he been happier.

And Ash owed it all to Styxx and Urian for the sacrifice they'd made in rescuing Tory out of Kalosis. Had his brother not stepped in to help Urian save Tory's life, Ash wouldn't have a precious son to hold.

Or a beautiful woman who was his entire world.

He glanced around the stark condo that showed no sign of life and wished Styxx were here so that he could say thank you one more time. So that he could wish him a happy birthday for the first time since they were little boys, bonded as twin brothers.

But then what the hell? He hadn't spent a birthday with Styxx in over eleven thousand years. What difference would one more make?

Still ...

"Wherever you are, brother, I hope you're surrounded by friends."

June 25, 2012

"Where the hell's my brother?"

Urian paused his game that he was playing against his nephews and muted the mic to stare blankly at Acheron. "You need to modulate that unwarranted ire, buddy. I'm not your ho and you ain't my pimp."

A tic started in Acheron's jaw. "Sorry." But his tone contradicted that apology. "Do you happen to know where Styxx is?"

Of course he did. However, he was too pissed to answer. So Urian took a swig of his beer. "Am I your brother's keeper?"

"You gave Tory his e-mail. I assume that means you're keeping tabs on him."

Urian clicked back into play and had to bite his tongue to stop his causticity from saying something that would cause Ash to blast him through a wall. "Your point?"

"I've been to his condo three times this month and he's not there. As far as I can tell he hasn't been there for quite some time."

Nice powers of observation, Atlantean god. It only took you what? Three and a half years to realize your brother had moved out?

For that alone, he wanted to punch Ash.

Refraining from that particular level of stupid, Urian cleared his throat. "Maybe we should put his face on a milk carton, see if anyone has information on his location." He frowned. "Do they still have milk cartons? Now that I think about it, I haven't seen one in a while."

"I'm serious, Urian."

"I can hear that," he said, taking his anger out on his online opponent as opposed to his boss. "I mean, damn, how dare my eleven-thousand-year-old brother not be right where I put him three and a half years ago after he did me a huge favor and saved my life and that of my wife. Rank filthy bastard. Inconsiderate dog! Maybe we should take him out back and beat the shit out of him for worrying you so."

"What is your problem?"

Time to kiss the wall ...

Urian sighed and clicked the mic on for a second. "Hey, Tyr, Erik? Can we pick this back up later, little buddies? Uncle Ash needs me for a little bit."

"Is something wrong?" Wulf asked.

"Nah, I'll be back in a few. Don't let the little guys kill me off yet." Urian signed off and removed his headset.

Picking up his beer, he faced Acheron. "You know I'd die for you. I put my ass on the line for you all the time without fail or hesitation. Hell, sometimes I'm even grateful you saved my life. But you're not perfect, Ash. None of us are, and when it comes to your brother, you're a fucking prick."

Rage mottled Acheron's cheeks as his eyes darkened. "You don't know my brother like I do."

"Really?" His voice dripped with sarcasm. "When was the last time you sat down and had an actual conversation with Styxx? Oh wait ... "

Urian feigned a laugh as he slapped his thigh. "I know this one." He sobered and those blue eyes pierced Ash with contempt. "You were seven years old at the time. So that's what? You're the same age as my dad ... so that would make you older than shit and shit's great-grandfather ... it would have been only about eleven thousand five hundred and fifty-three years ago, give or take a few hours ... Yeah, you're right, that makes you one hell of an expert on everything to do with Styxx, since my last conversation was last week when I spent two nights with him. But hey, why did I even question it? Stupid me."

Ash's cheeks mottled with even more color. "Don't you dare judge me on something you know *nothing* about."

"Why not? You judge Styxx all the time on things you know nothing about."

"I'm warning you, Urian ... "

He scoffed at *that* empty threat. "And I'm suicidal, boss. Fear factor really doesn't play in with a man who doesn't give a shit about life. But . . . you know your brother, you say? Fine, expert, then answer me one basic, easy question about him."

Urian paused for effect. "What was the name of his wife? You know, the one you didn't even know he had? He had a five-year committed relationship with her before he died, while you lived in the same house with him and gained all your expertise where he was concerned . . . and you know him so well. She's the only woman he has ever loved. Not knowing her name is like claiming to know me and not knowing Phoebe's. For that matter, it's not like he didn't carve her name and that of his son into his arm eleven thousand five hundred and thirty-six years ago. Swear to the gods, you cannot miss seeing her name. So if you know him at all, you have to know her name."

Ash's eyes turned vibrant red. "He tried to kill me," he growled.

"Yeah, I know, because I do talk to him. About a decade ago in New Orleans. Surrounded by Dark-Hunters, you were wide awake and an Atlantean god with all his powers available to him when Styxx attacked you out of desperation to escape the eternal hell he was damned to. Not quite the same as being a human boy in bed, sound asleep when someone plunges a dagger through your heart and leaves you in a pool of your own blood to die alone. That was you who did that to *him*, right?"

"He was trying to kill his own father. Did he tell you that? Plotting a conspiracy against him and blaming *me* for it."

"Was he? 'Cause you know, people never lie about shit like that. Ever."

Ash stiffened. "Yes, they do lie, Urian. So why are you believing Styxx when I know what a liar he is?"

Glaring his rage, Urian set his beer aside. "How do you know? You still haven't answered the easiest question on the planet about him . . . if you know nothing else about your brother, you should know his wife's name."

Acheron glanced away.

Urian shook his head. When he spoke, his tone was low and chiding. "All those powers you hold and you can't answer it. It was Bethany, just so you know. They were going to name their son Galen, after his mentor who died in his arms when he was a kid. A mentor who gave his life to save Styxx's when someone other than you tried to assassinate him while he was buying his wife's wedding ring. Now let me tell you about the man I know . . . "

Ash ground his teeth. "I don't want to hear it. And for your information, I'm not the only one who hated him. You have no idea how many people wanted him dead in his human lifetime." His eyes glowed with fury. "Did Styxx ever tell you that he had no friends . . . because no one could stand the arrogant bastard?"

Urian was aghast. "Arrogant? My God, Ash, you are blind. Have you ever, ever once spoken to him?"

"I'm out of here," Ash growled.

Urian stepped forward to pin him with a merciless glare. "You leave, and I'll have Tory hold you down to hear what I have to say. Things you need to know."

"You wouldn't dare."

"Try me . . . Because tonight when you lie down in your bed and your wife snuggles up to you and you smile with happiness, I want you to take a minute and imagine in the morning when you wake up in that same bed and reach for her warmth, it's gone. Forever. That you'll never know another minute of having her limbs tangled with yours. Never wake up and feel her body pressed against you. Then imagine going into Bas's room and finding it empty, too. All the plans you had for him, gone forever. Then I want you to take a minute and imagine the kind of love and decency it took for Styxx to go with me into Kalosis and embrace the woman who murdered them. For *you*, Acheron. The brother who hates his guts."

Urian paused to let those words sink in. "Now I admit I'm not as big a man as you are, Ash. But I can tell you right now, I wouldn't piss on my father to save the world, never mind hug him to keep my brother from sharing the pain I have every time

I think of Phoebe ... which is every other heartbeat. I'm a vindictive son of a bitch. Because after the fit you pitched where you blasted him through the wall just moments before we went down to Kalosis, I would have gutted your mother for what she took from me. And here's another thing you don't know. She whispered something to him before he hugged her, and it was fucking cold and brutal."

Snorting, Urian shook his head. "And then, after he went down there to save your wife. To keep you from spending the rest of eternity in hell, he took a blade for you from my father. I was there, Acheron. I saw it. No lies. Truth. Yeah, you healed him, and then you turned around and put the man who had just saved your life, and your wife's, completely out of your mind. You turned your fucking back on him. I was the one who took him home that night and you never once asked about him again until today."

Urian sarcastically bit his lip. "Oh and by the way, you forgot to pull the poison out of him when you healed his wound. For two months he lay in a coma, burning with fever and delirium, and I had to get Savitar to come in and help him because when I asked you, you told me he was doing it for attention. So while I love you like a brother, I consider Styxx my family, too, and unlike you, Styxx has no one else in this world. Poor bastard got stuck with me alone. Can you imagine *that* nightmare?"

Drawing a ragged breath, Urian curled his lip in disgust. "He left that apartment a couple of days after Savitar brought him out of his coma, over three years ago. He saved your life and Tory's, and it took you three and a half years to realize he'd left." He applauded sarcastically. "Good job, brother. Good job."

Ash wanted to hold on to his hatred for Styxx. He needed it. But right now ...

"And you know what I've always found fascinating, Ash? You never once asked me how I met your brother."

Ash looked away as shame filled him.

"It was in Katateros, just so you know. I went out for a walk on the beach and heard something in the temple down the hill from yours. I found him inside, alone in the dark, with scraps to eat, and when I asked him if there was anything I could bring him, do you know what your arrogant bastard brother asked me for?"

Ash shook his head.

"Fresh water. That's all Mr. Selfish wanted. He was having a hard time desalinating the river seawater to drink. Now I know you don't like to eat, but the next time you're home, I want you to take Tory and walk around your island and have her point out the edible foods she finds there, because there aren't many."

"I assumed one of you was taking food to him."

"You've assumed a lot of things about him that aren't true. Such as telling me that he was in the Elysian Fields for eleven thousand years. He wasn't. Artemis put him on a Vanishing Isle completely alone. No one to talk to, and again with no supplies whatsoever. Not even a hammer."

"That's not what she told me."

"Because Auntie Artemis never lies. Ever. About anything . . . such as having an eleven-thousand-year relationship with you that resulted in the birth of a daughter my age she never told you about until a handful of years ago. Artemis is the fountain of absolute truth, especially where you're concerned. Her kind, benevolent care for all those centuries was why Styxx didn't complain when you dropped him in Katateros. It was how he knew how to survive there with nothing. But the real question is why did he leave?"

"I assumed he got bored."

"There you go again with the assumptions." Urian dropped his gaze down to the tattoo on Ash's body where his Charonte daughter slept. "Our precious little Simi demon attacked him unprovoked and . . . well, she did kill him. But he didn't stay dead, obviously. Now before you call him a liar for that, too, I want you to know he never told me that story. Ever. I overheard it from Simi when she was bragging to her sister about ripping apart the bad copy of you who tried to hurt her akri. In fact, Styxx never says a word against you. Ever."

"He told you I stabbed him."

"Yeah, one night when he was really tore up and drunk and

I was asking him about some of the scars on his body. As many and as bad as most of them are, the huge jagged one in the center of his chest directly over his heart tends to stand out."

Ash frowned at his words. "What scars?"

"Dear gods, Ash ... have you never looked at your brother? They're all over him. Even his face."

No, he'd never seen scars on Styxx. But as Urian pointed out, he never really looked at him.

Only through him.

"Where is he?"

Urian narrowed his gaze. "Why? So you can hurt him again? Forget it. He's gone someplace safe so that you won't have to worry about him darkening your doorstep ever again."

"Yeah, he's so altruistic with his billion-dollar bank account."

"If you're talking about the money you set up for him when you dumped him off without a second thought? He transferred that back to your account before he left New York. That, too, has been closed for three years."

Sick of this game, Ash ground his teeth. "You know, I can find him without you."

"You hurt him, Acheron, and I swear to the gods I loathe that I will beat you down for it. For once in your lives, can you not think of him and just leave him alone? It's all he wants. You've already forgotten him for three years. What's another three hundred?"

Those words were harsh. But harsher still was the truth behind them.

Ash swallowed. "I want to talk to my brother."

Urian sighed. "Fine. He's in the Sahara. Literally. Living like a Bedouin. I had dinner with him and haven't heard anything since. That's all I know."

Inclining his head, Ash left Urian and went to locate Styxx.

Careful to stay invisible, Ash watched Styxx feed his horse and camel. Urian hadn't exaggerated the horrors of Styxx's meager existence in the least. But for the vivid blue eyes that were ringed in kohl, Styxx would easily pass for a Bedouin. Dressed all in black, he had his keffiyeh pulled over his mouth and nose, concealing his hair and features completely. The only color on his body was the brown sheath for his scimitar and the red agal wrapped around his black keffiyeh. And the two brown leather arm sheaths for the throwing knives they contained.

The horse nipped at the black leather pouch on Styxx's hip.

Styxx laughed. "Ah, you caught me." He scratched the horse's ears and patted her neck. "Yes, they're for you." He opened the pouch and pulled out apple slices that he fed by hand to his horse. "Good, right?" His horse actually nodded and snorted.

The camel made a sound of annoyance. "Don't worry, Wasima. I haven't forgotten you." Styxx went to share some with his other mount.

Once the animals were fed and secured, and after he'd washed off his hands in the small oasis, Styxx headed into a tiny black tent.

Ash followed him in and was stunned at what he found. The "prince" had a modest bedroll on top of a worn-out Persian rug where a big brown dog lay sleeping beside metal bowls of half-eaten dog food and water. Next to the bedroll was an iPhone on the ground hooked to a small speaker that was playing Disturbed's "Criminal" low enough to be heard in the tent, but not so loud as to drown out the sound of someone approaching outside. A backpack, saddlebags, four medium-sized solar lanterns, one rifle, and nothing else.

Unaware of Ash's presence, Styxx stripped down to his akarbey.

Damn, Urian wasn't kidding. The scars on Styxx's body were horrifying to look at. When, where, and how had Styxx gotten those? And when Styxx squatted in the corner to search his backpack, Ash's breath caught in his throat as he saw Apollo's sun symbol that spanned the entire width of Styxx's shoulders.

As a god, Ash knew exactly what a mark like that meant and all the horrors it entailed. . . .

Fierce ownership.

It was a warning to any god who saw it that Apollo would fight hard to keep Styxx as his slave. And Apollo didn't do that lightly. The Olympian god had never marked Ryssa as his property. He hadn't cared enough about her to do it. For that matter, Artemis had never officially marked Acheron, and they'd been together thousands of years before Tory had freed him.

And as Ash stared at the mark, Ryssa's last day, with her screams of how Styxx had seduced Apollo, took on an ominous tone. While Ash might have been wrong about many things to do with his brother, the one thing he knew for a fact was that Styxx was completely and staunchly heterosexual.

But Apollo wasn't. And if Styxx had fought his ownership, Apollo would have retaliated with a vengeance. Look what the bastard had done to his own people. . . .

His own son.

Acheron himself.

Tory's words about the gods in human form rang with a frightening possibility. He'd always wondered how Styxx could be so vicious to him. How his own twin brother could essentially assault himself whenever he attacked Acheron.

Apollo castrating him made a lot more sense than Styxx doing so. The Olympian would have wanted vengeance on Ash for having slept with Artemis and "defiling" her. The savagery of that attack over Artemis made a lot more sense than Styxx attacking him for a woman he couldn't have cared less about.

Putting an apple in his mouth and holding it there with his teeth, Styxx stood up with two bottles of warm water and a sketchbook and pencils. He sat down on the bedroll without disturbing the dog, then opened the water to sip at it. While he ate the apple, he turned to a page in the book where there was a sketch of a woman who sat in a beautiful meadow, holding an infant in her arms. The baby's hand was on her lips as she smiled down at him. Even though it was only a drawing, the love in her expression was haunting.

Ash's gaze went to Styxx's left hand, which held his apple,

and then down to the names of his wife and son that Styxx had meticulously carved into his own flesh.

An ultimate tribute. Not something a man would have done lightly.

The full magnitude of what Styxx had lost and how much his brother had loved his family slammed into him with such force that for a moment he thought he'd be sick.

Styxx set the apple aside and wiped his hand against his thigh, then leaned over so that he could draw. Ash winced as he watched the way Styxx had to use his left hand to wedge the pencil into the grip of his damaged right hand so that he could use it. The way Styxx did it said that he was so used to making accommodations for his partially paralyzed hand that he didn't even think about it anymore.

Tears misted in Styxx's blue eyes as he lovingly brushed his fiercely scarred right hand across the page. "Miss you, Beth," he breathed before he began filling in more details. He pushed the book back a bit as he worked, and it was only then Ash realized why.

He was protecting it.

Every so often, a random tear would fall as Styxx worked. Silent and focused, he would wipe it away on his shoulder and keep drawing.

Awed by his brother's heart and talent, Ash sank to his knees to watch Styxx's precise, expert strokes. He'd had no idea that his brother could do such.

Once it was finished, Styxx sniffed back his quiet tears and flipped through the book that was filled with pictures of the same woman and the baby boy at various ages that ranged from newborn to adulthood. It was as if Styxx had created the memories of his wife and child that he'd wanted to have.

Memories that had been stolen from him.

By Acheron's mother.

But what tore out Ash's heart was how much the boy looked like Bas. And when Styxx paused on a drawing of Styxx holding his wife and child, Acheron had to leave.

Sobs tore through him as Urian's words came home to roost and he thought about trying to live without Tory and Bas for even one day. Never mind centuries.

How could I have asked him to save my wife's life and embrace the killer of his own?

Urian was right. He was a fucking prick. And he knew nothing about his brother.

Pressing the heels of his hands to his eyes, Ash fought for control as he saw the drawing Styxx had made of the boy holding a teddy bear. If he didn't know better, he'd swear his brother had met his son.

Now that he thought about it, even their wives favored each other enough to be related.

Was it possible that he'd allowed his hatred for Estes and Ryssa's jealousy toward Styxx to infect him so completely and color his own opinions? Surely he wouldn't have been so easily swayed.

Would he?

All his life he'd preached to others that there were always three sides to every event—yours, theirs, and the truth that lay somewhere in the middle.

Yet when it came to his brother ...

Emotions don't have brains. Ash knew that better than anyone. He'd said it to every Dark-Hunter he'd ever trained.

And as he stood on the solitary dune, looking out at a hot, vast desert, he remembered how much Styxx had hated being alone as a child. How many times he'd sneak into Acheron's room and be beaten for it. But Styxx hadn't cared. He'd come to Acheron regardless.

Brothers. Forever and always.

Styxx had tried to make amends so many times. He'd reached out and Acheron had slapped him away. Repeatedly. Worse, Ash had walked away from Styxx for centuries and hadn't even given him a single passing thought.

Not once.

It's amazing the damage we do to ourselves and others when all we're trying to do is protect ourselves from being hurt. How many times had he said that to a Dark-Hunter?

But then advice was always easier to give than to follow.

Needing to set this right, Ash returned to the tent. He stood outside for several minutes, debating the sanity of this.

But he wasn't a coward.

With a deep breath for courage, Acheron opened the tent flap. "Styxx?"

The dog crouched low and growled at him.

His brother was now sitting forward, holding a blood-soaked cloth to his pinched nose while he calmed the dog beside him. "I didn't fucking do it."

Baffled, Ash frowned. "Do what?"

"Whatever it is you're here to accuse me of. I am not a god. I cannot travel from here to wherever you live in the blink of an eye. It would take me a solid week to reach even a modest village." The anger and hatred seared him.

And Ash knew he deserved it. "I came to thank you for the present you sent to Sebastos."

"An e-mail would have sufficed."

"Would you have gotten it?"

"Eventually."

Ash shook his head as he saw the other two blood-soaked cloths on the ground. "You still get headaches, too?"

"Yes, and the biggest one of all just traipsed through my door." Styxx pulled the rag back to check the bleeding, which was still pouring. He folded the cloth and returned it to his nose. "What do you want?"

Forgiveness. Yet he had no right to ask this man for it. Urian had been right. Styxx had tried to kill him, but Styxx had come at him openly. Hell, he'd even warned him he was gunning for him.

He, on the other hand, had gone at Styxx's back. And both had struck for the same reason. They'd just wanted an end to their suffering.

"Can I ask you something?"

"Yes," Styxx snarled, "you're an asshole and I'm a bastard.

What the fuck is wrong with the men of my family that they always want to interrogate me when I'm in pain and bleeding?"

Ash dropped his gaze to the row of brand scars that ran the length of Styxx's side. They started in his armpit where no hair could grow because of the burn-damaged flesh and vanished beneath his waistline. Even his nipple was severely disfigured. Those unique scars tweaked Ash's memory and brought out a long-suppressed act of stupidity on Ash's part. He cringed as he remembered when he'd seen the scars that covered his brother's groin and thighs in Atlantis.

What did you do? Masturbate with a hot poker?

Instead of punching him as he should have, Styxx had curled into a ball and said nothing. He'd just stared at the wall.

Ash ground his teeth, wishing he could go back in time and slap himself for that cruelty. It was obvious someone had tortured the hell out of his brother.

And he would have had them as a kid. ...

Before he went into battle. Only back then, Ash hadn't cared. Lost in his own misery, he hadn't spared three seconds to consider Styxx's.

Just because you have it bad, Acheron, it doesn't mean I have it good. No wonder Styxx had snarled that at him.

Repeatedly. But the scar that really racked him was the one right over his heart. The one Ash had given his own brother ... out of pain.

Because he'd wanted it all to just stop hurting.

"Why are you still here?" Styxx asked. "You wanted me out of your life. I'm out. I'm sorry I sent that damn horse that I didn't want to look at anymore. I won't ever bother any of you again. Just go!"

"Why did you send it?"

A tic worked in Styxx's jaw. "Because I promised you that I wouldn't let anything happen to it, and contrary to what you think of me, I don't break the promises I make."

Ash closed his eyes as pain overwhelmed him. *Why didn't I talk to you when you were in Katateros like you'd asked me to?*

Because he'd been angry. Hurt.

Mostly angry.

"I just wanted to say I'm sorry, Styxx."

Styxx gave him an astonished glare. "Oh, okay." His tone dripped with sarcasm. "Glad you got it all off your chest. Ta ta!"

You are an asshole.

So what if it was justified?

Ash sighed. "Before I go, would you like to see a picture of Sebastos with your gift?"

When those searing blue eyes met his, the raw anguish in them hit Ash like a groin kick. "You think you know pain? You don't. Trust me. I lived your fucking life, remember? I know every single detail of it. And since Artemis had me locked in that hell and I saw why you hate me for no reason and for things I had no part in, it has taken everything I have to not hate you for it, and for what your mother did to me. For everything she stole from me. But if you show me a picture of your perfect, healthy son, I will not be responsible for what I do to you. And before you go Ryssa on me, and tell me how selfish I really am ... I do not begrudge you your happiness or your family. I don't have room in my thoughts for it as I'm too busy grieving for mine. Now go!"

Nodding, Ash backed out of the tent.

He heard Styxx's anguished bellow of unleashed rage. It was the same sound of injustice that rang out whenever a Dark-Hunter died as a human. It was the sound that summoned Artemis down from Olympus to ask them if they would like to sell their soul to her for an act of vengeance against the person or persons who'd wronged them.

Acheron had never once thought someone would make it because of his actions against them.

And never would he have dreamed it would come from the throat of his own brother. He'd been so wrapped up in his own pain and anger that he'd never once considered Styxx's. From the outside, Styxx's life had looked so perfect.

Beloved prince. Hero of Didymos. Heir to a vast empire.

But a house could look new on the outside and be riddled with termites that ate away at its foundations until it crumbled from the strain of trying to hold itself up under their brutal assault.

And a single smile could hide profound pain.

"I am sorry, Styxx." And this time, he really meant it.

Needing his own sense of peace, Acheron headed for Savitar's island home. Since it was dusk there, he found his old mentor and friend in a black wet suit sitting in the surf beside his surfboard, watching the sunset over the ocean. Leaning back on his arms, he had his legs stretched out and crossed at the ankles.

Savitar groaned the minute he saw him. "Grom coming to disturb my mellow. What up, my brother?"

Ash transformed his clothes into a wet suit so that he could join Savitar in the surf. He sat down. Bending his knees and wrapping his arms around his legs, he sighed heavily. "Urian said that you had to pull Styxx out of a coma?"

Savitar nodded.

"What do you know about his past?"

The ancient Chthonian shrugged nonchalantly. "You were his brother. You should know."

"Don't play with me, Sav. Not in the mood."

He glanced over at Ash. "I truly don't know more than a handful of details."

"Such as?"

With a heavy sigh, he stretched out on the board and raked a hand through his hair. "You know I was the Chthonian for Atlantis so I only know what happened there. Not anything else."

Sav was lying his ass off, but Ash wouldn't call him on it right now. "And?"

"I know what you do ... that Styxx led his army to Atlantean shores and kicked the utter shit out of them. So much so that their gods were forced to make a pact with Apollo in order to stop Styxx and his army while the Atlanteans still had a country to call their own."

Ash frowned at that. "It wasn't the gods who made the pact, though. It was the Greek kings. They offered to give Apollo my sister."

He turned his head on the board to give him an are-you-stupid stare. "Not exactly."

Ash hated whenever Savitar used those words. It was never a good thing. "What do you mean?"

"It was never your sister Apollo wanted. Not really. While she was attractive, Styxx had the same unearthly beauty and sexual allure, courtesy of Epithymia"—she'd been the Atlantean goddess of desire who'd touched Acheron at birth and cursed him to be pursued by anyone who looked at him—"that you did. And Apollo was enamored with Styxx from the moment he first saw him ... like you and Artemis. The Atlantean gods had to get Styxx off their shores before he overthrew them. And Apollo wanted Styxx back in Greece as much as the Atlantean gods did. But they all knew the Didymos king would never agree to publicly give his heir up to be Apollo's mister-ess. So Apollo used Ryssa as a ruse to get to and control Styxx."

Sadly, that explained so much about their childhood and past.

And it made Ash's stomach burn with guilt and pain. "Since you were the Atlantean Chthonian, do you know about the other time Styxx came to Atlantis?"

Savitar gave him a blank, cold stare. "Your brother was in Atlantis four times in his lifetime."

Ash gaped. No, it wasn't possible. ... "Four?"

Savitar nodded. "The first was as a boy to free you from your uncle. Estes caught him and took him into custody."

"And you didn't stop it?"

"Didn't know about that one when it happened."

How could he not? "What do you mean?"

His gaze tormented, Savitar used both hands to rub at his forehead as if he had a throbbing headache. "Because she was so afraid of anyone learning where you were, your mother had my powers shielded when you were young so that I couldn't see you or your twin. I didn't know he'd tried to free you until I yanked him out of his coma in New York."

"What made you look, then?"

"I saw the word 'whore' in ancient Greek and the Atlantean

'*tsoulus*' along with your uncle's slave mark branded into his groin. I foolishly wanted to know how he'd gotten them. Let that be a lesson about looking into an abyss. It sucked me in and bitch-slapped me with a reality I wish to the gods I'd never seen."

Ash closed his eyes as pain slammed into him so hard, he could barely think straight. "Please ... tell me you're lying."

"You know better. That was why Styxx assaulted Atlantis like he had a grudge match against them. He did. Your uncle had kept him and sold him, just like he did you. He even pierced Styxx's tongue ... as did Apollo. He wanted to burn the whole continent to the ground not only for himself, but for you, too."

Ash's breath left him in a bitter wave of sympathy. "Since you looked, how did my uncle capture him?"

"Do not ask questions you do not want the answers to."

But Ash didn't listen. He was desperate for answers. "I want to know." He needed to know.

Savitar cut a harsh look toward him. "You should know already, Acheron. You were there when it happened."

"Bullshit!" Ash paused as he tried to remember, but he had no details. It was total darkness. "Show me."

Savitar shook his head. "There are some memories no one needs."

Still, Ash didn't listen. "Artemis punished Styxx with my memories. She forced him to live my life and instead of it making him forgive me, it's fueled his hatred to an all-time high, and I want to know why. Please, Savitar. I need to see how he got taken."

"And I refuse to show you," he said harshly ... in a bitter tone he'd never used with Ash before. "Suffice it to say, he would have gotten away had you not dragged your feet and called out to your uncle to tell him where you were. You could have voluntarily escaped with Styxx but were too afraid to try. Worse, while Estes held him, you laughed and gloated over what they did to Styxx. Constantly. You threw it in his face the whole time he was in Atlantis with you. You even held him down while he was branded."

No . . .

No! Ash panted as that unbelievable reality slapped him. He choked on denial. "I didn't do that."

"Yes, you did."

Ash shook his head. "I'm not that kind of person, Savitar. I'm not. I would never do that to another person. Especially not my brother."

"Every man, woman, and child is capable of extreme and utter prejudice and cruelty when they feel justified in their hatred. Right or wrong. Even against their own brother. We are all capable of lashing out when we're in pain. No one, not even you or I, is immune from that. As the old saying goes, be kind to everyone you meet for we are all fighting difficult battles. And yes, you thought it was funny to have the beloved prince heir branded a whore and a slave and sold just as you were. In your defense, you were young, drugged, and lost in your own hell."

"That's no excuse." Ash blinked back his tears as he choked hard on guilt he wanted to continue to deny.

"No, it's not an excuse. It's just harsh, biting reality." Savitar let out a bitter laugh. "Ever wonder why the gods created man, Grom? I personally think that we're the original reality show. They were so effing bored that they created us just so that they could feel better about themselves."

"You're not funny."

Savitar sighed. "No. Tragedy never is. Our lives are marked and shaped by our regrets. Things we all want to take back and can't. In a perfect world, we would never hurt the ones we love or cause hurt to befall them. But the world isn't perfect, and sadly neither are we."

Still, Ash couldn't forgive himself for the way he'd treated Styxx all these centuries. "I'm almost afraid to ask about Styxx's second visit."

"You were there for that one, too."

"When they threw me out . . ." And after he'd purposefully baited and mocked Styxx.

No wonder his brother hated him. Urian was right. He'd earned it.

And he owed Urian an apology.

More than that, he owed one to his brother.

But how could he ever make it up to either of them? He was so disappointed in himself. This was not the person he thought he was. The person he wanted to be.

Savitar sat up and drew a ragged breath. "Acheron, look at me."

Heartsick, he did.

"Never look back. You can't change what you've done. You can only change what you're going to do. Pain is always all around us. It's easy to become blind to it. But imagine all the times in your life when you were hurting and going through shit, if just one person had looked over at you and instead of kicking you while you were down, had said, 'It's okay. You're not a bad person. It's just a bad turn of the cards. You'll get through it.' Can you imagine what an incredible world this would be?"

October 12, 2012

"Now there's a sight I never thought I'd live to see."

Urian opened his eyes to find Cassandra standing over him with an amused smile.

She tsked. "Two mighty Daimons cuddling babies, asleep while watching *Toy Story*. Oh, how the mighty have fallen."

Rubbing his eyes, Urian scoffed. "What are you talking about? What kind of mom lets their kids watch this movie? Woody's a psycho bastard, homicidal loon. And Sid? Holy shit. I so relate to him, which means no kid should be watching this for entertainment. I picked up pointers from both of them. Again, not a child-friendly show."

Davyn laughed as he woke up on the floor. "Good thing they weren't here for your earlier diatribe. Or they'd never let you watch their kids again."

Wulf shook his head as he checked on Tyr and Phoebe, who were curled up on each side of Davyn while Jeff was asleep on Urian's chest and Erik was tucked in at his feet on the couch.

Cassandra scowled. "When was Jeff's last feeding?"

"I don't know. 'Bout eight?"

She gaped. "He's never slept this long. You need to stay over more often." Taking the infant, she carried Jeff upstairs.

Wulf sat down in his chair. "Are you two staying the night?"

"Nah, we'll head out." Urian carefully extracted his feet from his nephew's hold while Davyn got up without waking his two charges.

While Davyn gathered his things, Urian pulled a small box out of his backpack and handed it to Wulf. "I got that for you the other day."

Wulf opened the antique box to find an old medallion that glowed a peculiar shade of burgundy. "What is this?"

"Your soul medallion."

He gaped. "What?"

"Since you didn't have yours, I did a little horse-trading with Loki and got it back for you."

"Horse-trading, how?"

"Don't worry about it." When he started to leave, Wulf grabbed his wrist to hold him there. "Why did you—"

"For the kids. I didn't want anyone else owning a piece of you." And seeing the god mark on Styxx's back and some of the stories he knew about it had gotten his mind going into dangerous places. So long as Loki held that soul . . .

This was safer for everyone. Especially with what was coming for them.

No one needed their souls in the wrong hands. First rule of life. *Be careful with your soul. It's the only one you have. And once you sell it, it's hard to get it back.*

"I feel like a thank-you is so inadequate. What can I do for you in return?"

Urian snorted. "Don't lose it again. And remember that Helios is on the move. I don't know what he's planning, but keep Cassandra and the kids on lockdown."

"I always do."

That was true.

Inclining his head, Urian and Davyn left. But Urian still couldn't shake the bad feeling in his stomach. The gods were stirring for war again.

And they were in the center of it.

December 21, 2012

"Simi ... are you sure this is a good idea?"

"Absolutely!" Simi grinned at her sister Xirena as they entered the basement of her akri's temple on Katateros. "Now where's a light switch?"

"There's not one." Xirena breathed fire onto an old spiderweb-covered torch. As soon as one lit, it spread light to all the others in the dark marble room. The flames danced along the wall, adding creepy shadows to the already creepy environment.

Simi stepped back at the number of statues that were housed here. While she'd known her akri had putted them here centuries and centuries ago, she'd never actually visited them, especially since they made her akri very unhappy. "The Simi didn't remember there being so many ... Akra had broked bad on all these nonquality peoples."

"I remember." Xirena's tone was low and breathless. "It was not a pretty day."

Simi arched a brow. "You were there, Big sissy?"

Xirena nodded. "Xedrix, too." Xedrix was their brother who'd been Apollymi's most favored Charonte after their mother's death. But Xed had deflected ... no, defected when akri-Styxx opened the portal in New Orleans and let him out. Now he owned a club in New Orleans where the Simi got to eats lots of good seafood.

"Ooo, so what happened, Big sissy?"

"The bitch-goddess Apollymi was furious. They all died screaming. Excepted for two."

"Who two?"

"Dikastis and Bet'anya. She tried to keep the bitch-goddess from killing her baby, but the bitch-goddess didn't listen. She yanked it right out of her belly, and then turned her into one of these."

Simi touched her own stomach in sympathetic pain. "Why was Akra so mean?"

Xirena shrugged. "The bitch-goddess was always mean. She only likes you and her son ... and Kat and Mia."

Simi climbed up on the woman closest to her and poked at her stone eyeball. "Which one is thisest she?"

Xirena spat on the ground at the statue's feet. "Epithymia. She an even bigger bitch-goddess. She used to pull the wings off Charonte who made her mad."

Simi cringed, then poked harder in the goddess's eye, hoping she could feel it. "Who the one who losted her akri-Styxx's baby? She's the one the Simi needs."

Xirena walked around them, looking at them, up and down, until she found one in the back. "This is Bet'anya."

Simi headed over, then gasped. "She look just likes akri-Styxx's drawings. She the one he loved so much." Biting her lip, she met her sister's gaze. "Was she nice?"

Nodding, Xirena touched Bet'anya's hand. "She was always very sad, though. Even when she was happy, she looked so sad. Like something wasn't quite right in her heart. Chara goddess used to say it's because they took something from her long ago they shouldn't have."

Simi gave her sister a knowing look. "That's 'cause she don't gots her akri-Styxx. He loves her and so this is the Simi's Christmas present to him. The Simi tolds him on his birthday that wishes come true, and his wish is for his akra to come home to him."

"Yeah, but Xiamara, this ... it's bad." Xirena shook her head. "I don't think we should."

"We gots to, Big sissy. This the only time them portals things open. If we don't do it now, akri-Styxx will have to wait a long, long time and he already waited a long, long time. The Simi don't like to see him so sad. He don't get prezzies and the Simi wants to get him the best prezzie ever."

The ground beneath their feet rumbled. Simi's eyes widened. "What's that?"

Bug-eyed, Xirena shrugged.

Simi's watch tingled, letting her know it was time. She had less than one minute to free the goddess. Using her wings, she hovered and placed the sacred anti-aima to the goddess's lips. When her akri had been frozen that time in New Orleans, she and akra-Kat had used this to free him, so she was hoping it would work on Styxx's akra, too.

Hmmm. . . .

Another rumble went through the room. Something akin to a dark shadow shot out and flew past Simi's head.

Suddenly the other bitch-goddess Xirena didn't like opened her eyes. And so did Archon . . .

Uh-oh.

Simi ran to her sister. "Go get help. The Simi will hold them off!"

"Don't be a stupid Charonte!" Xirena grabbed her arm and hauled her upstairs.

Alexion was just walking back from the kitchen when he almost collided with two screaming Charonte.

"They's alive!" Shrieking, they jumped up and down, around him.

"Who's alive?"

"Them gods in the basement bottom!"

Alexion had no idea what they were talking about. But suddenly the floor beneath his feet rumbled and shook. The glass rattled in the panes.

Danger appeared at his side. "What did you do?"

He gave his wife a blank stare. "Why do I get the blame?"

"I know I didn't do it, Alexei, so that clears me." Hands on hips, she tapped her foot in irritation.

He pointed to the demons.

Simi grinned nervously.

"Them gods alive!" Xirena repeated between clenched teeth.

Well, that didn't sound good. Especially combined with Richter scale activity going on under their feet.

"I think the demons woke something that was sleeping in the basement. Any idea what Ash might have hidden down there?"

Simi glared at him. "It's not the book dragon. She's sleeping on her island! I told you, it's them unquality Atlantean gods!"

Cursing under his breath, he nodded. "Sim, go to Apollymi and tell her what's happened. Xirena, find Acheron and tell him that we need him immediately."

Danger staggered as the floor buckled again. "What's down there?"

"Acheron's relatives."

"Pardon?"

Alexion turned pale. "Remember when you asked me what happened to all the Atlantean gods?"

"Yeah."

Alexion sighed. "Apparently, they're all downstairs ... turned to stone by Apollymi, which is the part I knew. I just wasn't sure of their exact location."

Xirena pointed to her sister. "Now set free by Xiamara."

Oh yeah ... this was bad indeed. Alexion knew he had to do something. Fast.

"Where are you going?" Danger called as he started to leave.

Alexion gave her a droll stare. "To get Savitar. We're going to need all hands on deck for this disaster."

She frowned. "Well, how many gods are down there?"

"About a hundred."

"Great," Danger said with a hysterical note in her voice. "Love your calm demeanor, hon. And it's a good thing I'm already a ghost." 'Cause their chances of living through this?

About as good as surviving a brunch where you cut in front of a Charonte in the all-you-can-eat barbecue line.

"Yeah, yeah. Just call Urian in Minnesota!"

Savitar paused as he watched Styxx, silhouetted by the setting sun, on top of a small dune. He'd stripped down to nothing but his loose pants and boots while he played Frisbee with his dog. Over and over, Styxx would laughingly take the Frisbee, praise the animal, then wait for the dog to run out again so that he could toss it for the dog to jump, catch it, and return.

It was the first time he'd ever seen Styxx at ease. Unguarded. For that matter, it was the only time he'd known the prince to play.

Or laugh.

And as he watched Styxx with the dog, he didn't see the feral military commander who'd terrified a pantheon and nation, or the rigid prince who had to ooze decorum at all times. He didn't even see a man. He saw the boy who had never been given a chance to live. One who'd been cut down in his youth and deprived of a normal, mortal life.

Because of the way Styxx and Acheron acted, the maturity, responsibility, and pain they held that went far beyond their years, it was easy to forget how young they'd been when they died. But Savitar saw it now.

And the injustice of it burned inside his heart.

I have no right to ask this of him.

None of them did. Guilt gutted him as he felt for the childhood and life Styxx would have had, had the gods not interfered. Styxx would have been that beloved, cherished prince that everyone thought he was. His destiny would have been something else entirely.

And Styxx would have been a Chthonian ...

To save and protect Acheron from those who hunted him and wanted him dead as a child, they all had taken a turn at ruining Styxx.

Savitar knew he should go and leave the boy in peace. Styxx wanted only to be alone, and he'd certainly earned the right to it.

But he couldn't. Acheron was too important to the world.

Most of all, he was too important to Savitar personally.

Savitar waited until Styxx had poured water into a bowl for the dog before he appeared beside him.

Faster than he could blink, Styxx had a knife in one hand and a gun in the other. Both angled at Savitar's head.

"Impressive." Savitar hadn't even known Styxx was armed.

Gone was any hint of the boy who'd been playing with his dog just moments before. This was the rigid general who had led armies and fought gods and gladiators in an arena with such strength and cunning that his enemies had been forced to resort to tricks and traps to defeat him.

As the old saying went, never say "why me." Rather say, "try me." That was Styxx in a nutshell.

Styxx glared his hatred. "What do you want?"

"You to point those somewhere else."

He lowered them to Savitar's groin.

"Cute."

Smirking, Styxx tucked the gun into the holster at his back and returned the knife to the sheath on his forearm. "Whatever it is you want, it has nothing to do with me."

"Some of the Atlantean gods have returned."

"As I said, it has nothing to do with me."

"They want vengeance."

Styxx bent down to pull his water out from under his aba. "So?"

"On Acheron."

Styxx took a swig of his bottled water before he capped it. "Nothing to do with me."

"So that's it, then? You're just going to let your brother die? And he will. . . . There's no way for him to survive this."

Styxx swallowed the pain inside him. "Are you deaf? The gods know, Acheron has said it enough. I don't have a brother."

"The world as you know it will end."

He laughed at that. "The world as I knew it ended the moment my wife and son were killed. And anything remotely related to the life I once lived ended while I was held prisoner for over eleven thousand years. I know nothing of this place and I have no dog in this fight. It has nothing to do with me," he repeated. He headed toward his horse and camel.

"Tory's pregnant again."

Styxx froze as those words cut him to the quick. "Good for her ... and Acheron."

"Are you really going to condemn an innocent woman and her two children to live without their husband and father?"

"That's not fair!" he growled, glowering at the Chthonian he wanted to shoot.

"Life, like war, isn't fair. It just is. Isn't that what Galen taught you?"

Styxx winced at the reminder of all he'd lost ... because of his brother and the gods he'd hated since the moment of his birth. "You're not helping your case by reminding me of Apollo's treachery, Chthonian."

"Fine, then. Stay here in your desert. At least you'll have the comfort of knowing Acheron's widow and orphaned children will be able to commiserate with your pain."

Whirling about in fury, Styxx threw the water bottle at him.

Savitar ducked. Had it hit him, it would have counted.

"I hate all of you!" Styxx growled deep in his throat. A throat that was still damaged because of Acheron and the gods who could never leave him alone.

Damn it all ...

No, damn *them* all.

None of them had ever taken pity on him. He was thrown aside and forgotten like garbage.

Until they needed him.

All he'd ever wanted was a family. One person who treated him like he mattered to them. And all he'd gotten was disappointment.

From all of them. It'd taken him centuries to come to terms with that one single fact.

What the fuck does it matter? Really? He didn't have a life. He never had.

And he damn sure didn't have his wife or his child ...

Never mind *two* kids.

Go ahead and die already. There was no one to mourn his passing.

Angry, hurt, and aching over a fact he'd never been able to change, Styxx pulled his aba on, then jerked his backpack up from the ground. His breathing ragged, he glared his hatred at Savitar. "Can you make sure my animals and gear go to someone who needs them and that my dog doesn't get eaten by his new caretaker?"

Savitar was stunned. "You agree?"

Styxx averted his gaze as a thousand emotions pile-drived him to the point where he didn't really know what he felt. Other than hurt and alone.

But that was nothing new for him.

He met Savitar's stoic lavender gaze. "I've never been quite the bastard all of you labeled me. You knew I couldn't let him die, otherwise you wouldn't have come here."

"Thank you, Styxx."

"For what?"

"Being the man I knew you were."

"Go fuck yourself, Savitar. Just take me wherever I need to go and stop with the sentimental bullshit you don't mean before I give in to my desire to punch the shit out of you."

U*rian stood beside* Davyn, listening to Sin and Katra review their plans for fighting against the Atlantean gods. It was all well and good, except for one thing.

"Am I reading this wrong? Or in every play does Styxx end up dead?"

Acheron sighed. "I know. I'm trying, Urian. I don't want him dead, either, but I can't think of anything else. Really, I'm open to any suggestion. I guess if there's any consolation, it is what Styxx wants."

Well, he was glad his boss was feeling so cavalier about his brother's life. However ...

"Not really what I want for him, seeing how he's my best friend."

"Excuse me?" Davyn gave him an offended glare.

"You're my brother. Shut up." Urian kissed his cheek and ruffled his hair.

"Rather be a friend. Your friends, you don't abuse."

"Stop your whining."

Ash rolled his eyes. "Anyway, I agree with you, Urian. I'd really rather not do Styxx any more harm either. I've racked my brains every which I can, but—"

"I think I know the problem."

Ash arched a brow at Urian. "Please illuminate me."

"We're missing our star quarterback."

W*ait!" Urian shouted* as he teleported in and saw that Savitar was about to haul Styxx off to fight. Damn, that was close. Another few seconds, and it would have been too late to stop them.

Panting from his mad dash to get there with Davyn in tow, he doubled over to catch his breath.

Savitar growled. "We don't have time for this."

Urian snorted nonchalantly. "Take it up with the bossman. He's the one who sent me in with a time-out. Acheron has called a team huddle before we make our final play."

Shaking his head, Savitar let out an exasperated sigh. "Remind me to cancel your ESPN subscription ... " He glanced to Styxx with an odd glimmer in his lavender eyes. "Fine."

The next thing Urian knew, the four of them were back on Savitar's island with Acheron and Tory, who was feeding crackers to their son. Danger and Alexion were trying to ride herd on Simi and Xirena as they plotted to take Bas's crackers. And Katra and Sin finished off their cozy little End of the World club.

"They're not going to wait all day on us," Savitar warned Acheron. "You know the gods are marching and not waiting."

"I know, but as I was reviewing the situation with everyone and trying to come up with an alternate plan that didn't cost Styxx his life, Urian reminded me that we were missing a most vital member of the team." Acheron pinned his gaze on Styxx. "The quarterback who actually went up against the Atlantean gods and beat the shit out of them."

Styxx scowled as all heads turned to him. "Since no one has bothered to tell me what I'm heading into, I've got nothing."

Ash looked at Simi, who blushed and grinned sheepishly.

"Well, see, akri-Styxx, it all started when the Simi decided she was gonna give you the promise for your birthday for Christmas. See?"

"Clear as a two-hundred-mile-an-hour sandstorm."

Ash gave a low, sinister laugh. "Simi decided to wake up the Atlantean gods for you. Wasn't that considerate?"

Urian bit back a laugh. Ash better be glad Simi was slow to catch that sarcasm or else akri or not, he could have ended up as Charonte barbecue.

Styxx frowned. "Why?"

With an adorable pout, Simi sighed heavily. "Well yous sees, it wan't s'pposed to be all them gods. Is only s'pposed to be the one. But she won't get up. Lots of them others gots up and gots ugly, fast. And I means theys as ugly as a gullu in the morning with no barbecue sauce. And the Simi still don't know why's the only one I tries to wakes keeps sleeping when it's so important she gets ups and talks. It's so confusing."

Yes, yes, it was. And she was there when it happened.

Sin turned to Savitar. "Hey, I have two gods and a demigod requesting permission to enter your home and join our powwow."

Yeah, there was a look on the mighty Savitar's face that said the Sumerian god was about to end up on *his* menu. "Who?"

"My brother, Seth, and your least favorite god of all time."

"Noir?"

"Second least favorite," Sin quickly amended.

Savitar growled low and deep in his stomach—like he was

about to give birth to a space alien. "I thought that bastard was dead."

"Apparently not."

A tic started in Savitar's jaw. "Why?"

"Why is he not dead?" Urian asked sarcastically.

Savitar glared at him. "Why are they here?"

Ignoring Urian's question, Sin shrugged. "They say they can help with this."

Hands on his hips, Savitar glared at Acheron and then Kat. "Apollymi owes me. Big. And so do you." Then he looked back at Sin and gave a curt nod.

Urian heard Davyn gasp as he saw Zakar, Sin's twin brother, appear next to him. But at least they were easy to tell apart since Zakar had longer hair.

The Egyptian god Set had always been a peculiar beast, far different from the rest of his pantheon. One thing being, his dark red hair. Which made sense, Urian supposed, as red was the color that represented evil for them, and Set was the god of evil, darkness, and chaos.

All that bad shit, really.

Tall and muscular, he had an aura of power around him that set Urian's nerves on edge.

Yet the oddest part was when Zakar nudged Set to look at Styxx. "Now there's a photo-op expression if ever there was one."

Urian glanced to the baffled look on Styxx's face.

They weren't wrong.

For whatever reason, Set and Zakar transformed into an odd-looking couple, then quickly returned to their immortal appearances.

Okay, then ...

Obviously there was some weird inside joke the rest of them weren't in on.

Set glanced around at them. "Over four thousand years ago, Apollo and his whore mother used my son Seth"—he indicated the red-haired man at his side who had a mop of curls—"to trap me in the desert without his knowledge of what was being done to him and why, and restricted my powers so that the Greeks could take over my pantheon and hand my son over to my bitterest enemy."

Ah ...

Damn, his grandfather just screwed over everyone he came into contact with. Urian passed a disgusted sneer to Davyn. Really, was there any person who didn't want to jack-slap Apollo into oblivion at this point?

Set clapped his hand on Styxx's shoulder. "But for Styxx, I'd still be there, chained in the desert, fighting off vultures." He glanced to his son and his gaze softened instantly. "And my son would still be hating me for something I tried my best to spare him."

Styxx's scowl deepened. "Why didn't you tell me it was you when I freed you?"

"You were in enough pain over Bet. I didn't want to make it worse on you when I didn't think I could do anything to fix it or help you. After you did me such a massive favor, the last thing I wanted was to repay you with more pain."

Set inclined his head to Sin's brother. "Zakar and I were allies back in the day, which was why I had you take me to his place to recuperate. Since you left, we've been trying to find a way to revive my daughter without awakening the other Atlanteans. Ironic as hell that they woke up and she didn't."

Styxx scowled. "But Bethany was Egyptian, not Atlantean."

"From me, yes. Her mother's Symfora."

Bug-eyed, Urian exchanged a gaping stare with Davyn at a name they both knew. Symfora was the Atlantean goddess of death, sorrow, and woe.

Styxx let out a long tired breath. "Bethany's Bet'anya Agriosa?"

Set nodded. "For an obvious reason, she was scared to tell you the truth."

"I wouldn't have cared."

"Good. Because if you want her back, you're going to have to bleed Apollo and battle the worst of the Atlantean gods for her."

"And you're not going to fight without *us*." Maahes and Ma'at flashed into the room, next to Savitar. Called the lord of the massacre, Maahes was the protector of innocents. A massively muscled brute, he had a lot in common with Urian's brother Archie, except he was much better tempered. And his huge size was a bitter contrast to Ma'at's exceptionally tiny stature. The goddess of justice and truth barely came up to their waists.

But he much preferred looking at her, as she was gorgeous. Her red-and-gold dress set her dark skin off to perfection. And her Nubian locks were held back from her sharp, chiseled features by a dark scarlet scarf.

Eyes flaring with rage, Savitar growled. "Anyone else you want to bring to the party?"

Maahes grinned insolently. "Mother, may I?"

The look on Savitar's face said that Maahes was barely one step away from becoming a lion throw rug on Savitar's floor.

Ma'at stood up on her tiptoes to place a kiss on Savitar's cheek. "Remember, you like me."

"I don't like anyone who barges into my home uninvited, Mennie."

"You'll get over it." She turned her attention to the group. "All right, children. Where are we?"

"Screwed, from what I'm hearing." Styxx crossed his arms over his chest as he considered everything they'd told him. "I'm going to be dense for a moment because I'm having trouble wrapping my head around this. ... Bethany can be brought back? Yes?"

Ma'at and Set nodded.

Styxx turned an interesting shade of green and Urian could actually feel the waves of grief, pain, and rage fight for control of his friend. Honestly, he wanted to help the man gut them for all the needless centuries Styxx had spent alone. He glared his fury at Acheron. "Why didn't anyone tell me this before?"

Ash held his hands up in surrender. "I had no idea your Bethany was Bet'anya or that she was housed in my basement garden of statues. That's the truth. I was a little distraught and disoriented eleven thousand years ago when my mother took me to Katateros the first time. After I teleported those grisly statues to the basement, I locked the door and never went near that area again."

Urian couldn't blame him for that. Those were the gods who'd ordered a hit on him as an infant.

Even so, he wouldn't hold it against Styxx if he sucker-punched Ash where he stood. 'Cause if that had been Phoebe or Xyn in the basement, and Paris standing there, they'd be blood on the floor right now.

Styxx looked at Set and Ma'at. "Why didn't you tell me?"

"Sugar, every one of us thought she was dead," Ma'at said gently. "Believe me, had we known she was frozen in Katateros, we'd have freed her for all of our sakes."

"Well, we would have tried." Set sighed. "Probably would have failed. It was the alignment on the twenty-first that made this possible . . . that and the demon." He turned his gaze to Simi.

Simi flashed a happy smile. "I told you wishes can come true, and not just at Disney World. The real world does a good job, too, sometimes."

Acheron scowled at Simi's familiarity with his brother. "When did you two become friends?"

She wrinkled her nose. "On your birthday, akri. Did you know akri-Styxx don't gots no one to spend his special day with? He all alone on it and so the Simi went to apologize and make him her friend, too, so he won't be alone on his special days. But he done broke my heart so now he my other akri-baby like Baby Bas and akra-Kat. The Simi has officially adapted him . . . no . . . adopted him." She grinned so wide, her fangs flashed.

Instead of being angry, Acheron laughed and kissed her cheek.

Urian cleared his throat and leaned forward to whisper in Styxx's ear. "Dude, trust me, if she tries to burp you? Run fast. Run far. Run like the hounds of hell are on your heels, because they are."

Styxx smacked him on the stomach.

Rolling his eyes, Ash shook his head. "All right, Styxx. Your show. How do we do this?"

Styxx glanced around at the gods and demons. And Urian and Davyn. "Still the sole human in the room. I don't know what we're up against or who we're fighting. I need more details."

Acheron spread his hands out and a schematic of his temple on Katateros appeared on the wall that showed the basement and the statues housed there. As he spoke, the animation illustrated his words. "A dozen gods woke up while Simi was in the basement with Xirena, looking for Bet'anya. Since I was in Vegas with Sin and Katra, and Tory was with my mother in Kalosis, the two demons were alone to create well-intentioned mischief. As soon as the gods began to stir, Xirena ran to tell Alexion and Danger that they were back. The three of them grabbed Simi, and escaped here to Savitar to let him know what had happened."

"That's when they called me in Minnesota," Urian said. "And told me not to come home for a few days as we had ancient interlopers in Katateros who most likely would not host me a welcome-back party. Who knew? Hope they've left my PlayStation alone, as that will seriously piss me off."

Ignoring that comment, Acheron sighed. "We're also flying blind." He motioned to his wall decoration. "We have that based on Simi's recollection—which is flawless. But a little dated since Archon and the others have blocked out our sforas. None of us can see where they are or anything inside the main temple."

"I tried to send in Davyn, but he's a chickenshit."

Davyn shoved at Urian. "No one stopped *you* from going."

"That's 'cause *I'm* a chickenshit."

Styxx completely ignored them. "Do we know who we're up against?"

Acheron glanced to Simi before he answered. "We're not one hundred percent sure, because Simi was an infant when they ruled. As a result, she's a little iffy on some of their identities. Best we can figure, it's ..." He again turned to the images that Simi had created—one that looked more like Wreck-It Ralph than an actual god ... go, Simi. "Dikastis, Ilos, Isorro, Asteros, Epithymia, Diafonia, Nyktos, Paidi, Teros, Phanen,

Demonbrean, and we know for a fact Archon is with them as he's the one we've been talking to. And of course everyone's favorite dickhead, Apollo."

"Beautiful." Styxx looked as if he were about to hurl, and Urian could taste a bit of his own bile. "My ideal guest list ... for a fete in hell."

Urian couldn't agree more. With that cast of Gothamesque villains, the gods were definitely mocking them all today. All he needed was Helios in that mix and he'd have the full list of assholes he wanted a piece of.

Styxx went over them so that they'd all know who and what they were fighting, since most of them had never gone up against them before. "Apollo's not a problem. He's an effing idiot when it comes to things like this. And he's a bully with no courage who will back down to someone more powerful.

"He won't be leading a charge but will stay back until he can land a punch from safety. Unfortunately, Archon isn't any of that. He's sharp and deadly. Vindictive as hell. Brutal. But out of the list, Epithymia and Asteros"—he highlighted them—"are the two we have to neutralize *immediately*. Do not underestimate them, especially Epithymia. The bitch-goddess is crazy and meaner than shit. Show her no mercy or hesitation, because she won't show it to you."

He swept his gaze around the room's occupants. "And whatever you do, do *not* let that bitch touch you ... Demonbrean is even dumber than Apollo, but he's also the size of an effing house. His skin is armored and he lives to crush things. Treat him like a python and don't let him get his arms around you. If he does ... you're fucked. Dikastis will hang back to get the lay of the situation and might not fight us at all. He is all about justice and what's right. If the fight isn't about honor or truth, he won't participate in it. The rest are followers. Lethal, but pawns nonetheless. They are servants for Misos in war, and only do what they're told to do. You take out Archon and they will stand down. ... Now what do we know of their demands?"

Savitar let out a bitter growl. "Because I was their Chthonian, Archon contacted me, not knowing my relationship with the Grom. They want Acheron as a sacrifice so that they can use his blood and heart to bring back the rest of their merry little band of asswipes, except for Bethany. Archon blames her for this, as if he wasn't the one who caused Acheron to be cursed ... what were you telling me about his intelligence?"

"Steadfast denial is not the same as intelligence." Styxx rubbed at his eyebrow as he digested the little gold nugget no one had bothered to tell him about when they'd asked him to pretend to be Acheron. "Just out of curiosity, what was the game plan you had once you sent me in to die and they discovered that my blood and heart couldn't bring back their dead?"

Savitar shrugged nonchalantly. "Buy us time to gather enough Chthonians to take them down."

Styxx scowled. "'Cause what? The Chthonians are such known people-pleasers? Um, yeah? When was that last time you fucks worked together? Last time I checked, your official motto was 'Does Not Play Well with Others. Do Not Mix with General Population or People. Period.'

"'And whatever you do, don't feed them after midnight or any other time of the day as they would take the hand feeding them and shove it in an uncomfortable place on your body.'"

Styxx shook his head. "I'd be tempted to laugh if I weren't so pissed. Thank the gods none of you were among my military advisors. We'd have had our asses handed to us," he mumbled under his breath. Then louder, "Are they at full strength?"

Acheron shrugged. "No idea."

Styxx passed an irritated glare to Urian, who held his hands up in surrender.

I feel you, brother. Urian sent his thoughts to him. Because he truly did. This was exactly why he'd refused to allow them to send Styxx in the way they'd been planning to do. He wasn't about to stand by and watch his friend get slaughtered for their stupidity.

Styxx let out a tired sigh. "Let's assume yes ... So our numbers are basically even. The weakest link in our group is me. ... What are our strengths?"

Simi opened her bag and pulled out her barbecue sauce. "Demons ready to eat, Sir akri-Styxx! Gimme!"

Laughing at Simi's enthusiasm, Acheron jerked his chin toward his other daughter. "I don't want Katra in harm's way, but she's a siphon."

Kat passed a peeved glare to her father. "I'm also a trained soldier, Pops." Kat glanced at her husband, Sin, and warned him with her gaze not to say a word. She turned toward Styxx. "I was my mother's primary kori, and unlike my seriously overprotective father and husband, she—"

"Put her ass in harm's way all the damn time, with a blatant disregard for her safety that still pisses me off," Sin growled.

Kat smiled and cupped his cheek. "Yes, baby, but had she not been so careless, I wouldn't have you. Now would I?"

He grumbled under his breath.

And Kat was born of the two pantheons they were up against. A definite plus.

Styxx nodded. "What else do we have that they won't know about?"

Urian indicated him and Davyn. "Daimon and an ex-Daimon." Though that probably wasn't much.

Set folded his arms over his chest. "For thousands of years, my son was the High Guardian for Noir in Azmodea."

Yeah, they definitely weren't as good as that.

Seth nodded. "I'm used to battling angry gods. I can also get us a bird's-eye view of anything you need. What I use, they can't block."

But they did have one thing the others didn't ... "Thanks to Davyn, we have this." Urian held up the necklace they'd bartered dearly with his parents for.

However, Set's eyes widened with recognition. "How did you get *that*?"

Urian snorted. "My enemy's enemy is my best damn friend.

Davyn borrowed it from my father, who was more than happy to lend it and wants us to tie it in a bow around Apollo's neck."

"What is it?" Styxx asked.

Set laughed, low and evil, and made no moves to touch it. "The Eye of Verlyn. That will deplete the powers of any god it comes into direct contact with."

Which was why every god in the room was currently taking a step back from it.

Styxx looked at it with a new respect. "For how long?"

Urian grinned. "As soon as it touches them, they're wiped. Then it depends on how long it's on their body and how strong they are. Too long, it'll kill them."

Styxx smiled and inclined his head to them. "Does it work on just full-bloods or any other species?"

Set shrugged. "I don't know."

Before anyone could react, Simi grabbed her sister and put her hand on it.

"Hey!" Xirena snapped at her sister.

"You still gots power, Sissy?"

Xirena shot a blast of fire at her.

Grinning and ducking, Simi looked at Styxx and let go of Xirena. "It don't work on us."

Urian laughed. "I helped him carry it over, so ... I'm only a quarter demigod, and it doesn't seem to affect me."

"I think I'm the only true demi then." Seth bravely took it into his hand and waited. After a couple of minutes, he shook his head. "No effect on me, either."

"Since my powers are borrowed from Apollymi, I'm not chancing it. We'll assume I need to stay clear of it. Urian, we'll leave it in your custody." Styxx hesitated as another thought occurred to him. "Can the stone be broken apart or duplicated?"

Set shook his head. "Not without destroying it."

Styxx scowled at Acheron, who was an unknown in all of this. "Would the stone just suck out your god powers and leave the rest intact?"

"That's what usually happens. Why? You thinking of giving me an early Christmas present?"

Urian laughed involuntarily.

"Don't distract or tempt me." Styxx ran over the rest of their arsenal and the layout of Acheron's temple. They'd definitely use Seth's powers to get a peek at what they were going into.

But first . . .

"My most important question of all . . . Where's my Bethany?"

Urian *and Davyn* were behind the demons, Kat, and Styxx as they headed first toward Bethany. The plan was to get her first and then deal with the others.

As Styxx reached for the doorknob, Katra placed her hand on his arm. "I know this is the first time we've met, Styxx, but I'd rather you not go in there alone. Someone should be with you."

"How are you Artemis's daughter?"

Kat smiled. "She's not as bad as you think. . . . Apollo, however, is probably worse."

Simi stood on his other side and leaned in to whisper in his ear. "We'll be super quiet. Akri-Styxx won't even know we're there."

Urian put his hand on Styxx's shoulder. "Don't worry. What happens happens, and we won't think anything about it. We'll just be here for you if you need us."

Tears welled in his eyes and the emotions there said that he wasn't used to anyone standing with him. Urian knew that feeling, all too well. It was what he missed most about his brothers and why he treasured Styxx the way he did.

"Thank you."

Urian tightened his grip before he let go.

Taking a deep breath, Styxx opened the bedroom door. The floor-to-ceiling windows were open, letting in the soft ocean breeze. But it was the huge canopied bed in the center of the room that held their attention. White linen drapes were pulled back with gold cords, obscuring most of the bed's contents.

Urian's gaze was drawn to the bump beneath the stark white

covers. Right before the Atlanteans had attacked on Katateros, Simi had carried Bethany's body out and brought her here for safekeeping until they found some way to wake her.

Urian kept his attention divided between Styxx as he crept closer to the bed and watching out for any unwanted visitors who might sneak up on them.

And as soon as Styxx saw Bethany, he froze solid.

Urian did the same.

Damn, she was beautiful. Perfect. Just as she'd looked in those meticulous drawings Styxx had made. Her dark skin was flawless. Even though she wasn't moving, he could imagine the fluid grace of her movements. Could hear the soft cadent lilt of her voice.

Strangely, Urian felt as if he knew her somehow. As if they'd met in a dream somewhere.

Styxx's hand trembled as he pulled the covers back to expose the blood that was still on her gown from where Apollymi had assaulted her. Throwing his head back, he roared in anger and pain, then gathered her body into his arms so that he could hold her.

"Beth?" he breathed against her cheek as he cradled her head to his shoulder. "Please come back to me. Please. I need you so. . . . " Tears fell down his cheeks.

Urian choked as he felt for his friend's agony. Unable to bear it, he looked away. In his mind, he saw himself the night he'd lost Phoebe. Xyn. He heard his own anguished screams that still hadn't stopped the nights his heart had shattered.

Davyn reached out and pulled him into his arms. Urian tried his best to stand strong. As he always did.

But the truth was, he was never that strong. He'd never been. True love didn't conquer anything. All it did was destroy.

"I've got you, brother," Davyn whispered in his ear as he silently wept, and Acheron joined them in the room to go to Styxx.

Urian pulled away from Davyn just as Styxx let go of Bethany and bellowed in fury. He turned on Acheron with a wide punch.

Acheron blocked it and yanked him into his arms. Styxx tried to fight, but Acheron held him close against him in an iron grip.

"It's all right, Styxx. I know it hurts."

But Acheron didn't know. Even Urian knew that. The Dark-Hunter had no idea of the pain he and Styxx shared. His children were all alive and well. Tory was healthy. . . .

No one was going to kill her baby and leave her frozen and alone like this.

Coated in her own blood.

Urian hoped that Acheron never knew the darkness that lived inside them. Because the Stygian madness that festered there was a devouring agony unlike anything imaginable. Grief for his wife was a hunger that fed on all happiness. It devoured smiles and stole pieces of his soul every single day until he feared he would never see light again.

Like Styxx, Urian had been so lost for so long now that though he walked in daylight, he didn't see it. Nor did he feel any form of warmth in the vast winter lands that swallowed him whole. The sun couldn't chase away the lingering shadows of pain and remorse. The staggering darkness of what could have been.

That profound sense of loss that came the moment you woke up and knew for certain that all your hopes and dreams for tomorrow had become your yesterday.

That was the hell they called home.

And Acheron knew nothing of it.

Lucky bastard.

"I fucking hate you," Styxx growled in Acheron's ear.

"I know, brother . . . I know." And still Acheron held him the way Urian used to hold on to his own twin. Back in the days when they'd been innocent boys, before the world had crashed down on them and made them bitter men, scarred by war and tragedy. Separated by death and heartache. "I wish more than anything that I could take it all back. Everything," Acheron breathed. "That I'd listened to and followed the advice I gave others. I hurt you and I abandoned you and it was wrong. I was wrong and I am so incredibly sorry."

Their sadness choked Urian as he watched them. He felt for both men who'd been divided by hatred and a world that wouldn't let them live in peace.

Styxx glared at his twin. "Why can't I just hate you?"

Acheron's arms tightened around him. "Because you're a better man than I am. You always were." He pulled back and placed his forehead to Styxx's, then gently fisted his hand in the hair at the nape of Styxx's neck. "I will never turn my back on you again, brother. I—"

Styxx covered his mouth with his hand, cutting off his words. "Don't make a promise you might not keep."

It would kill him if he did. That was the curse of the Atlantean gods.

He wiped at the tears on Acheron's face. "Gah, we look like two old women." Styxx balled his fists in Acheron's hair, which no longer fell down his back. "But at least you finally got a decent haircut."

Acheron laughed.

Urian wiped at his own eyes as he remembered his own shock when Ash and Tory had cut their long hair and donated it to charity in honor of Sebastos's first birthday.

With a ragged breath, Acheron released him. "You've no idea how much I missed you when Estes took me away, Styxx. I couldn't stand it."

Styxx snorted. "I do know your pain. I have not only my memories, but yours, too."

Acheron gave him a fierce, stern look. "And now I have yours." Tears welled in his eyes again. "Boy, don't I feel stupid. Honestly, I don't know how you could ever talk to me again. And if it makes you feel better, Styxx, I would have chosen her over me, too. At least she's prettier to look at."

Urian took Davyn's hand as he felt his brother's pain reaching out toward him. They all understood that misery. Love was too rare a gift to ever squander. If you were lucky enough to find the one person strong enough to stand by your side, you held on to them with everything you had and you never let them go.

Because if you lost them, it was an unimaginable hell that cut through you every day of your life.

Acheron gave him a grim smile. "You weren't wrong to protect her. And we will get her back for you. I swear it."

Urian choked on his own grief as he felt Davyn's hand trembling in his. They both would sell their souls to have Paris and Phoebe or Xyn back. Just for one heartbeat.

Damn it, why hadn't he cherished them more when he had them? The only regret Urian had was not spending more time in their arms. He should never have left them. Styxx was right. You climbed into the chariot, hell or high water, and you stayed by their side, consequences be damned.

Styxx wiped at his eyes. "Just promise me one thing. If this doesn't work, you'll finally kill me."

Urian flinched at those words. *Damn me, if I don't understand that.* He'd made the same request. And he hated every day he lived without the women he loved. It wasn't fair to be here when they weren't. They were the better half. How unkind was fate to spare the animal that was him and to take the beauty of their souls in his place? What kind of justice was that? How could that be considered right?

What the fuck was wrong with the balance of the universe that it would do such a thing to humanity? He was the one who should have been killed. Phoebe had never harmed a soul. And Xyn ... she was a guardian. A lady of such beauty and grace.

He was a monster who should have been put down like a rabid dog.

Yet here he lived on for eternity while they were gone.

It wasn't right and every time he thought about it, he wanted to rip the throats from the very gods themselves for their cruelty. For their lack of regard for humanity and leaving him behind because obviously they didn't give a shit about what was right and what was fair.

Life was selfish and it was cold. Just like his barren soul. Why did life have to be like this? Why did the gods show you a glimpse of heaven only to rip it from your grasp the moment you dared to reach for it?

There was no need of an eternal hell. Life was punishment enough. No one deserved it.

Especially not the innocent babes born to this world who came in naked and unprepared for its brutality.

"Is that really what you want?"

Urian snorted at Acheron's question that said it all about his naivete. Ash had never really loved and lost or he'd know that answer. No one wanted to live after having been gutted.

Time didn't heal those wounds.

It didn't cover the scars. The best you could hope for were momentary lapses in pain where it didn't sting quite as bad. And if you were really lucky, those lapses might grow a bit longer in between.

That was it.

Styxx took Bethany's hand into his and nodded as he spun her wedding ring around on her finger. "She was so happy when I put this on her hand. I can still see her smiling. ... " He flinched in agony. "Gods, Beth, why didn't I go with you when you left? I should have climbed on that chariot and never left your side."

Urian clenched his eyes shut as Styxx repeated the words he'd heard him say so many times.

Acheron put his hand on Styxx's shoulder. "It wouldn't have mattered. Had she taken her serum, my mother still would have killed her. At least this way, we have a chance to bring her back."

Urian wished he shared Ash's optimism. His had been slaughtered on the altar of reality a long time ago. That bitch took mercy on no one.

Suddenly, something bright red and furious flashed in the room. Urian's temper flared as he saw his aunt Artemis in all her vibrant redheaded glory. When he took a step toward her in anger, Davyn caught him.

"Don't," he whispered.

Urian's heart pounded as it demanded he beat her until his

need for vengeance against her and Apollo was sated. But Davyn was right. It wouldn't change anything.

However, it might make him feel better.

Artemis drew up short with a severe scowl and a strange noise as she saw Ash and Styxx standing together. If he didn't know better, Urian would think she was scared of them.

Styxx leaned his head back to speak to Acheron. "I think we startled her more than she startled us."

Acheron sighed. "What are you doing here, Artie?"

She started to speak, then closed the distance between them so that she could poke each of them on the shoulder. "That's just . . . not right. Say something else so I know which of you is Acheron."

"What, Artemis?"

She made a face of distaste. "There's that irritated tone I loathe." She turned her back to Acheron so that she could speak to Styxx. "I have brought you presents."

That sent a shiver down Urian's spine. His aunt never sent presents.

To anyone.

Beware a Greek bearing gifts, especially when it was a bitch-goddess renowned for her selfishness.

"Why?" Styxx asked.

"You're going up against my brother and the rest of those animals. . . . I want you to win, and make him bleed. A lot. Buckets and buckets full until it gushes and fills the entire hall."

Urian smirked at Davyn. Wow, Apollo was making friends everywhere he went. Nice to know his twin sister hated him as much as everyone else.

Styxx met Acheron's gaze over her shoulder. "Should I be afraid of the bloodlust?"

"I'm terrified." Acheron's frown deepened. "What did Apollo do now?"

"He attacked my Nicholas while he was weakened. I will not have it. Since I'm not powerful enough to harm Apollo on my own, I want you two to kick his leg."

Acheron rolled his eyes. "You mean ass, Artie?"

"Ass. Leg. Whatever body part pleases you. You can't kill him, but you can make him suffer. Long. Hard. Pitifully. I gave Savitar an assortment of weapons I dipped in the River Styx. It will weaken Apollo to the point he'll be as a mortal." She glared her hatred for Apollo at Styxx. "If I were you, I'd castrate him slowly and with a great deal of—"

"Grammy! Grammy!"

Urian snorted at the sight of Mia popping into the room while dressed as some kind of woodland fairy creature. That little dark-haired toddler was part bloodhound when it came to her grandparents. Unaware of the fact that her grandmother was a nightmare bitch, she immediately leapt into Artemis's arms so that she could wrap her pudgy arms around her with a squeal and give her a big hug and kiss.

Her rant instantly forgotten, Artemis returned the affection. "Mia Bella! How is my precious today?"

The girl squealed even louder as she bounced in her arms. "Gamma, Gamma, Gamma, guess what? Guess what! The Simi gonna put hornays on my head like hers and Pappas's. And she said that I could pick any color I want and that they'd be on all the time and they can glow in the dark, too."

Bug-eyed, Artemis appeared as horrified by the idea as Urian had the first time Simi tried to do it to him.

Acheron laughed and rubbed Mia's back. "How about if Simi makes you a pair that can come off?"

Mia wrinkled her nose at him. "Pappas! No! I want real ones. Like you and Simi and Xireni."

Artemis blew out a burst of air. "You know Pappas only has those when he's mad, right?"

Mia's eyes widened. "Really?"

They both nodded.

Urian waved at Mia as she giggled and waved at him. He had to admit his cousin was adorable. And he still couldn't wrap his head around the fact that he and Katra were related. Or that Apollymi had kept it from him. But then she was the only person he'd ever met who was better at keeping secrets than Acheron.

Mia's attention finally went to Styxx. Her eyes widened. "Who cloned Pappas?" she whispered.

Acheron smiled. "He's my brother ... your uncle Styxx."

Excited, she launched herself into his arms and kissed him.

"You look just like my pappas." Then she put her hands on his cheeks and rubbed noses with him. "That's how Charonte say hello. But only if they like you. Otherwise they eat you with ketchup or barbecue sauce, or if they're like my uncle Xed, jalapeños, which are really hot, too."

"Don't scare your uncle the first time you meet him, silly belle." Artemis pulled her back into her arms and tickled her.

The door opened. Kat and Sin came into the room making irritated yet relieved parental sounds.

"Sorry." Kat took her daughter from Artemis. "She escaped the chain when we took our eyes off her for three seconds. She must have sensed you were here." Hugging her mother, she gave her a kiss on the cheek as Sin took his daughter from Kat.

Urian was always amazed how they passed that kid around like a hot potato and yet she never cared. His nieces and nephews wouldn't have stood for that. But his cousin was a whole other crazy egg. Which, given her parents ...

Well, he understood.

Mia made an adorable face at her father. "Am I in trouble, Daddy?"

Sin had the same reaction Urian did whenever little Phoebe turned her charms toward him. He melted and grinned. "No, baby girl. But you shouldn't vanish like that without telling us where you're going."

Urian laughed. It was hysterical to see a man as rugged and stern as Sin holding such a bright delicate fairy princess. The top of her dress bulged with pink and white cloth flowers, some of which were sewn on the long poofy yellow tulle skirt. Her legs were covered with matching pink leggings and pink patent leather shoes. She was even wearing a pair of miniature pink tulle wings. "You do have to go back to Aunt Tory and Aunt Danger and Uncle Kish and stay with them for a bit, okay?"

She pouted adorably and nodded.

Artemis stopped Sin before he could leave with Mia. "Grammy will be by in a little bit to read her baby belle a story, okay?"

Mia grinned and bounced. "Can we ride in your deer chariot, too?"

"Only if Mommy and Daddy say it's okay ... and you'll have to put on a sweater." Artemis gave her a big hug and kiss. "I'll be there as soon as I can."

She nodded, then went rigid in Sin's arms. "Wait! Wait! Pappas!"

Smiling, Acheron gave her a tight squeeze. "I, too, will be back as soon as I can."

"Then we'll watch *Megamind?*"

"Sure, baby."

"Bye-byes, Uri and Davys!" she shouted at them with a cherub grin.

Then she planted a loud, wet kiss on Acheron's cheek.

Sighting, Kat took her back from Sin. "I'll return her to her closet and lock her in with some kind of baby Kryptonite."

Sin kissed the top of Mia's head before he turned back to them. "Really sorry for the intrusion." He followed after his wife and daughter.

Acheron met Styxx's gaze. "Are you all right?"

"You have a beautiful granddaughter and I truly don't begrudge you your family, Acheron." He glanced to Bethany. "I just want mine."

"That's not going to be easy."

They frowned at Artemis for her comment. The way she said that told them she knew something they didn't.

"What do you mean?" Styxx asked.

"You do know my brother was in love with her, right?"

Urian wasn't sure who in the room was most shocked by that declaration.

"Bethany?" Urian asked.

"Bathymaas," Artemis amended. "He and my mother are the ones who moused you out."

"Ratted ... you out," Acheron corrected in a pain-filled tone.

She sighed. "Whatever. I just don't understand modern idiots."

Moused? Davyn mouthed the word to Urian, who shrugged and then made the hand gesture to remind him that Artemis was a bit crazy.

Acheron cleared his throat. "I think she means idioms."

She turned a peeved glare at Acheron. "No, this time, I got it right. Modern idiots. Anyway, my mother hated her because she coveted Bathymaas's powers and because Bathymaas didn't stop Hera from being such a bitch to us and leaving us with the blood-sucking curse ... "

Yeah, how nice of his grandfather, who hated the fact that he was damned to drink blood from his sister, to put that off on them.

Effing bastard.

For that alone, Urian wanted to cut off his head and deliver him up to Helios.

But Artemis continued her explanation. "So when Apollo fell in love with Bathymaas and she refused to have anything to do with him, he was furious. When he found out she was not only in love with the Atlantean Aricles but sleeping with him, he went crackers."

"Nuts."

"What. Ever." She growled at Acheron and his continued corrections. "Apollo's the one who tricked her into killing you," she said to Styxx, "just like he did me with Orion. Bastard bitch that he is. It destroyed her. But you swore to her if it took you ten thousand lifetimes, you'd find your way back. And I'm glad you did, but Apollo won't be so happy once he realizes you're you."

Urian was confused. "Wait. Bethany isn't Bathymaas. Bathymaas was born of the primal source. Bethany wasn't."

"Yes, she is. She's born of Set."

"Set?" Urian still didn't see the connection.

Artemis nodded. "She went"—she passed an evil grimace toward Acheron—"insane. Rather similar to what Apollymi did when Apollo killed Acheron. But her off knob—"

"Button or switch?" Acheron really didn't seem capable of

stopping himself from correcting her. Urian was beginning to think his boss did it just to get underneath her skin.

She wrinkled her nose at him and kept talking. "Off switch was a lot harder to find than Apollymi's. The only way to stop Bathymaas was to have her reborn without the memory of her life and love with Aricles. It's why her mother was Symfora—the goddess of sorrow—and why Bethany wouldn't marry or really dabble much with men until Aricles was reborn. But weirdly, she'd always go fishing where the two of them used to meet all those centuries before. Like she was waiting for Aricles to come back, even though she didn't remember you or him."

Urian let out a heavy sigh. *Fate will out.* It was what his father had always told him. No matter what you do, some things couldn't be changed. Urian got that.

"And that's why I didn't throw a fit the day I met you that first time."

Urian turned toward Set as he joined them in the room.

"As soon as I laid eyes on you, I knew you were Aricles. That somehow, you'd managed to keep your word and find her again, and I'm pretty sure it's what drew Apollo to you, too. Why he was so hell-bent on making you suffer."

"No." Artemis let out a bitter laugh. "That was my idiot other brother who pointed Styxx out to him. I always hated Dionysus. You give Apollo too much credit. He's like a spoiled toddler ... pretty ... shiny ... gimme. Kind of like Acheron's demon."

She met Styxx's gaze. "Bathymaas was my brother's first love and her rejection emotionally crushed him—at least that's what he claims. Because of that, my mother cursed the two of you to never be together."

"Is that why Bethany can't wake up?"

"In part," Set said with a heavy sigh. "But mostly it's because she only has half her heart. To bring her back and allow her to be sane and not the soul of vengeance she became after the death of Aricles, I had to remove the part of her heart that had you in it and wipe all knowledge of you from her memory."

Acheron frowned. "That's biologically impossible."

"No. You forget, boy, we're gods. Bath isn't human in any way, nor was she born of a mother's womb. She was a gift to me from the Source to teach me compassion for others. As the Mavromino allowed the birth of the first Malachai to calm your mother, the Kalosum created her to keep me from turning my back on what I'd been born to do. It's why she was never supposed to know the love of any man. Her duty was to stay pure and remain the order to my chaos. She was justice. Cold and unyielding, without any personal interests or the ability to play favorites. Aricles changed all that. When her heart broke in half over his death, her tears are what transformed her into ruthless, uncaring vengeance. She lost all balance and nothing mattered except to make the world pay for the wrong it'd done her and Aricles. Ironically, it was that more than anything that showed me why I needed to keep a handle on my own powers. As bad as she was, I would be much worse should I ever let the Mavromino control me."

Styxx glanced back to Bethany. "So how do I wake her?"

"You have to return her heart to her."

"And that is where?"

Set sighed. "Last I heard it was given to Epithymia. The ugly side of desire is covetous jealousy. Epithymia wanted Apollo and thought that if she stole that part of the Bet he once loved, it would help her to seduce him."

Artemis scoffed. "Didn't work. She was too big a slut for my brother. He does have *some* standards."

Not that Urian had ever heard of. Apollo was about as fickle as they came. He cared for no one and nothing.

"Then she's the one we use the necklace on first." After kissing Bethany's hand, Styxx pulled the covers up over her. He stepped back and swept them with a determined grimace. "Let's do this."

Urian nodded. They'd all suffered enough. It was time to take back their lives and make the gods pay.

Y*ou know this* isn't going to work, right?" Styxx asked Acheron as they teleported to Ash's bedroom in Katateros.

"I've had worse odds."

"So have I, but most didn't work out well for me."

Urian didn't comment on that. He'd been there too many times himself. Most of which, lately, had come from Ash throwing his ass to the wolves, gallu, dragons, and just about every other demonic entity the gods had ever created.

So it was a good thing he was suicidal.

Bitterly amused, Urian glanced around the room that had changed about as much over the years as he had. Before Acheron's marriage, the room had been sparsely decorated in black and brown. Now it was powder-puff blue with dancing circus animals on the walls and a canopied crib within easy reach of the large bed ... a holdover from Acheron's paranoia and guilt about his nephew Apollodorus, who'd been killed by the soldiers Urian's grandmother had unleashed on him, thus causing the original curse against all Apollites.

Acheron's son, Sebastos, was never left to sleep alone. The baby had been almost a year old before Acheron had allowed him to sleep anywhere other than his father's chest.

But Urian couldn't fault him for that. He'd been almost as bad with his own children.

Can you hear me?

He frowned as Acheron's thoughts intruded on his, then nodded.

Good. I think it best if we communicate like this for a while.

Styxx nodded again.

Ash turned toward Urian. *You hang back.*

He saluted him to let him know he'd heard him.

Styxx went to the door and listened for the others. Seth's "bird" spirit had shown them that the gods were all gathered in the throne room, where they bragged about what they intended to do once they had Apostolos or Ash, rather, in their custody.

None of it was pretty and it made Urian glad he wasn't his boss and even gladder that they'd reconsidered sending Styxx in as his double.

Acheron joined Styxx at the door while Urian stayed by the windows. *They've sensed our powers.*

Something they wanted the Atlanteans to do since it would throw them off.

Ready? Styxx asked.

Absolutely not.

Urian bit back a snort at Acheron's sick humor.

Locking gazes, Acheron held his hand up in offering to Styxx. Styxx glanced to the crib and Urian could only imagine the thoughts in his mind. The two of them had been through so much betrayal. Ash was as likely to throw him to his enemies as he was to fight for him.

But this was his friend's best chance to get Bethany back. Like it or not, he had to trust Acheron. Urian inclined his head to him to let him know it'd be okay. He was here and he wasn't about to let anything happen on his watch.

With a deep breath for strength, Styxx took Acheron's hand and let his brother teleport them into the throne room.

Urian went to the door so that he could listen and watch through the crack.

Styxx let go of Acheron and took position at his back. He faced Archon, Apollo, and Epithymia while Acheron faced the rest.

Archon rose to his feet. "Well, isn't this unexpected." He smirked at Apollo. "We don't have to play chase for your pet after all. How kind of them to save us time." He glared at Styxx. "Which of you is Apostolos?"

"I am," they said simultaneously.

Urian grinned at something that had to piss off the old god. *Choke on that, old man.*

Archon growled low in his throat.

"Their eyes," Apollo said quickly. "Styxx's are blue."

Leave it to the weasel to out them. Gah, he hoped Apollo got his due one day.

Acheron turned to stand beside his brother. When they spoke, it was as one. "Not anymore."

Archon narrowed his gaze on them. "Then we'll kill you both."

"No," Apollo snarled. "That wasn't the agreement."

Epithymia made a sound of supreme disgust. "Stand down, both of you. There's an easy way to get to the truth."

Urian didn't like the sound of that. He moved to open the portal to let the others through.

His heart stopped. The portal wouldn't open. Closing his eyes, he used all his strength to try to breach the realms.

Seriously? Nothing was happening. How could this be?

Yet nothing. Not even a spark.

What the hell?

Epithymia pulled at the black cord around her neck to show them a small crystal vial. She pulled it over her head and placed it on the arm of Archon's chair, then manifested a hammer. "This is the heart of Bathymaas. If the real Styxx doesn't step forward, I'll destroy her. Forever."

Urian fought harder to open the portal. *Come on!*

"So you don't love her?" She hovered the hammer over the vial. "Really?"

Urian tried even harder.

Nothing! Damn it!

What was going on? How could he be locked down so tightly?

Styxx spoke in Acheron's voice. "You do that and you lose all leverage over both of us. Her life is the only thing keeping you alive right now."

A light flashed suddenly.

Urian knew they were expecting him with the others, but that wasn't him ...

Instead, Artemis flashed in beside Apollo. "Oh my!" she exclaimed as she looked at them. "Am I interrupting?"

Apollo seized her arm. "What are you doing here?"

"I came to see Acheron. This is his house where he lives. I'm allowed to visit."

Urian almost burst out laughing at that lie, and he was amazed Acheron withheld his. Artemis was the first person he'd banned from here. He'd have sooner awakened Archon than let her come into his home.

Archon bellowed in outrage. "This is *not* his home!"

Acheron and Styxx exchanged a puzzled frown. Neither of them had a clue what Artemis was doing here. She was not part of the plan.

But she'd found Archon's underbelly. Too bad he hadn't learned the first rule of warfare that Stryker had branded into Urian's psyche.

Never, ever expose your underbelly.

Blinking her eyes, Artemis gave the older Atlantean an innocent look. "No? Then why are you sitting on *his* throne? That's not yours, you know. I was with Acheron when he picked it out and brought it here."

No, she wasn't.

That mental shout was so loud, Urian was amazed everyone hadn't heard it. Yeah, Ash wasn't real fond of his ex.

Go, Artemis. Apparently, she was here to whip their emotions and frazzle them. And judging by the mottled color on Archon's face, she was doing an excellent job.

"Why is she here, Apollo?" Archon asked through clenched teeth.

"I have no idea."

Epithymia went rigid. "Something's not right ... "

"That's because she's not my daughter."

Urian went cold at those words. *What?*

Styxx and Acheron turned to see Leto, the mother of Apollo and Artemis, entering from a side door. Urian's stomach hit the floor.

If that wasn't Artemis ...

Ah, shit, it would be Kat.

"Mom," Apollo said irritably. "What are *you* doing?"

Ignoring Apollo's question, Leto smirked as she approached them. "Really, Katra? I'm so disappointed in you. But that's all right." She looked at Archon. "We don't need the twins now. Katra is the daughter of Artemis and Acheron. She has the Destroyer's bloodline and is actually stronger than her parents." She grabbed Kat and held a dagger to her throat. "So, Acheron, whom do we kill? You or your daughter?"

Urian tried to blast open the doors to save her.

They didn't budge.

What the ...

He hit them. Still they held.

Furious, he tried everything to get through them to join the fight. This was bullshit! He couldn't stay in here and let Kat be harmed.

Suddenly, a sonic blast went through the room. One so fierce, it knocked everyone off their feet and slammed Leto against the wall.

Even Urian was knocked down in the bedroom.

Artemis appeared instantly and pulled Kat to safety. *"How dare you."* She enunciated each word slowly as she faced her mother. "No one threatens my baby ever! You cow!" She attacked her mother so ferociously, Kat had to pull Artemis away to keep her from killing Leto.

Acheron took advantage of the distraction to use his powers to jerk the vial from Epithymia's hand.

He sent it to Styxx as Urian continued to fight against the doors.

With a mutual nod, they attacked the Atlanteans closest to them. And Acheron quickly learned why pantheons didn't like to war within themselves. Since all of them pulled their powers from a mutual source, they were fighting in a weakened position and their powers weren't working properly.

"Katra!" Styxx called as Epithymia went for her back.

Urian's arm turned blue as he tried to send his own powers to them to bolster theirs.

Kat turned. Instead of backing away, Kat pulled the goddess close and sucked her powers into her own body. "You won't be needing those, bitch."

Urian laughed. She must have gotten over her guilt about leaving gods powerless.

But something weird happened as she pulled Epithymia's powers into her body. Her teeth elongated and her eyes turned that same demonic red that Apollymi's did at times. Her skin began to swirl like Acheron's.

"Acheron!" Artemis screamed. "The demon's taking over Katra. Help!"

His face turning white, Acheron met Styxx's gaze.

"She's more important than I am. Get her out of here." Covertly, he handed Acheron the vial with Bethany's heart. *Free Beth even if I don't make it back.*

Urian saw the hesitation in Acheron's eyes as he debated whether to leave him to fight without Acheron's help. But in the end, he knew he had no choice.

He ran to his daughter to get her to safety.

Styxx manifested his shield and used it to deflect their god-bolts as he covered Acheron's and Katra's retreat.

They teleported out with Artemis, leaving him alone to face the others.

A thousand nightmares ripped through Urian as he remembered the times in battle when he'd watched his brothers die. Screaming out, he blasted the doors and blasted them again. He couldn't watch someone else he love die.

Damn it!

A slow, lecherous smile curled Archon's lips. "It's like old times, isn't it, Prince? And I have to say you're looking mighty tasty."

"Don't kill him," Apollo growled.

"Oh, we're not going to kill our pet. Have no fear. But we are going to have our fun with him again."

Styxx manifested his armor and sword. Lowering his chin, he smiled at them. "Come get some, bitches."

Furious, Urian teleported to the only place he could.

Acheron *handed his* unconscious daughter off to Sin. "Something from the demon bite interacted with Epithymia's powers," he explained. "I drained her, but she needs to feed."

Sin nodded grimly as he took her and vanished.

Acheron was aghast at the others who were supposed to have been there to help them fight. "What happened?"

Set growled. "We're locked out. If you're not Greek or Atlantean, forget it. Only Katra had the ability to get to you."

Urian glared as he joined them. "I couldn't get in either. I tried everything I could. You're all he's got. And they're beating the hell out of him. You can't leave him there."

"Simi, return to me."

She immediately laid herself over Acheron's heart as a dragon-shaped tattoo.

Xirena bit her lip. "Me, too, akri?"

"Absolutely."

That would get the demons in. Urian's arm was neon now as his heart pounded furiously. He couldn't stand the thoughts of what they might be doing to Styxx.

Acheron glanced around. "I'm weakened and the weapons Artemis brought might work on Apollo, but they're shite on the Atlanteans. Who wants to try to go in with me?"

They all stepped forward.

"All right. Here goes nothing." Closing his eyes, Acheron summoned everything he could and teleported them back to Katateros.

It didn't work.

Not until Urian closed his eyes and wrapped his arm around Acheron's waist. He felt the surge through his own body an instant before he shot his own powers into Acheron.

Only then were they able to break through whatever Archon had done to shield the temple.

Unprepared for the sight that awaited them, Urian staggered away from Acheron. Blood was everywhere. It looked like some kind of zombie movie. Yet what terrified him the most was the fact that Styxx's phoenix shield lay twisted and bent out of shape in the middle of the largest pool of blood. Blood that was smeared to the doors as if a body had been dragged out, through them.

Demonbrean and Ilios lay moaning on the ground near Apollo.

Dikastis, true to Styxx's prediction, hadn't joined in with the others. He was standing calmly in the shadows of the hall as if he couldn't believe what he'd witnessed.

Urian wanted his throat.

He started for him, but Acheron reached him first.

"Where's my brother?"

Raw anger flared in the old god's eyes. "They took him to the temple arena."

Urian curled his lip. "Why aren't you with them?"

"I'm a god of justice. I will not participate in something that's so wrong and undeserved."

That alone saved his ass from Urian's wrath.

Acheron inclined his head to the god. "Will you fight with us?"

Dikastis nodded without hesitation.

H*is breathing ragged,* Styxx was so battered and bruised at this point, he wasn't sure why he was still conscious. He'd managed to knock out three of them and weaken the rest, but in the end, he'd been outnumbered and was no match for a dozen gods.

Archon and Asteros had dragged him to the temple Acheron had confined him in years ago . . . to the arena where they'd once made his life utter hell. Against his best efforts, they'd secured him to the rack they'd used for his beatings and other things he didn't want to think about.

Damn them.

Laughing, Archon fisted his hand in Styxx's hair and jerked his head back. "You're not defeated so soon, are you, Prince?"

"Fuck you."

"How I wish, but unfortunately, we're making you a sacrifice." Archon gagged him, then looked over to Leto. "Summon our lady vengeance."

Leto laughed as she neared Styxx. "You didn't really think Epithymia had Bathymaas's heart, did you? Trust me, I kept that for myself. Now I'm going to finish what I started fourteen thousand years ago."

And when I'm done destroying what's left of the Greeks, I'm going to tear apart the Atlanteans as I did the Sumerians and Egyptians.

Styxx's eyes widened as he heard her thoughts loud and clear.

Leto pulled out a knife and sliced open Styxx's cheek so that she could fill a vial with his blood. She mumbled words he didn't understand as she blended his blood with another compound. And as she did so, his head began to spin.

Suddenly, he remembered being Aricles . . .

He saw Bethany at his side as she held on to his biceps. Only she wasn't Bethany. She was Bathymaas. "Do not fight Apollo for my honor. It's not worth a single drop of your blood. Run with me, Ari. Let's leave all this behind and never look back."

"I can't, and neither can you, my goddess. We have too many responsibilities. Too many to protect. We cannot leave this world in their hands."

"I no longer care about them. You're all that matters to me."

His blood racing with fury and pain, Aricles had pressed his head to hers and held her close. "And you're all that matters to me. I won't have your reputation tarnished by that pig. You've done nothing wrong and I will beat that bastard down for you. Have no fear."

She buried her hand in his hair. "I can't live without you, Ari. You are the heart they claim I was born without. It's why I can't be the soul of justice anymore. Because of you, I feel for the first time in my life. You've changed me forever . . . You can't leave me now. Not like this."

He kissed her forehead. "Let me win your honor and then we can leave and never look back."

"Swear it to me."

"On my eternal soul. I will always be with you, Bathymaas. Nothing will take me from you, ever. Not even the gods." He lifted the Egyptian ieb amulet from her chest and kissed it, then tucked it back between her breasts.

Styxx gasped as he fully understood what Set had told him. Bathymaas had been created by the Source, not born of a mother . . .

The Egyptian jug-shaped amulet was the heart Set had given her as a girl when she'd asked her father why she didn't have a heartbeat like others.

"This holds my love for you, child, and while you can't understand it, know that so long as you wear it, you carry a piece of me with you. My heart has great power and it will keep you safe and warm in my absence."

That was how Leto had destroyed the Egyptian pantheon and trapped Set in the desert. She had weakened him with that half of Bathymaas's heart that held her father's DNA and Seth's blood to trap the primal god.

Lifting his head, he saw the broken ieb shard on Leto's wrist that matched the one Bethany had worn as a bracelet. It was so obvious now, but unless you knew what an Egyptian heart looked like, you'd never guess its origins.

Or its significance.

Leto poured the blood from the vial onto her fingers and waved the ieb over it. Then she wiped it down his other cheek. "History always repeats itself. Poor you to die twice by the hands of the woman you love. And once you're dead, she'll destroy the gods for me." Stepping back, she let out a sharp, piercing ololuge . . . a sound used in his time to summon a god's presence when a sacrifice was being offered to them.

All of a sudden, a fierce wind came tearing through the arena. It blew open doors and ripped at his body. Leto stumbled against it.

A baleful howl sounded an instant before a swirling specter joined them. Inhumanly large, it floated on the wind wearing a white cloak. And when it neared Styxx, he realized this was the vengeful spirit of Bethany.

With his gag in place, he couldn't say a word to her.

Leto pointed to him as she spoke to Bethany. "Behold the bastard son of your enemy who cost your prince his life and existence. Take your vengeance on them both! Rip out the heart of Apostolos!"

Bethany screamed in furious agony.

Styxx's eyes widened as he realized she was going to kill him and there was nothing he could do to stop her.

Urian *paused as* he recognized this temple. It was the same one Acheron had confined Styxx to when he'd first brought him here to Katateros to live. The one Styxx had left behind so that he could sneak into the temple next door to Acheron's where he'd been living the night Urian had first met him.

It was beautiful in a cold, sterile way.

"What is this place?" Acheron asked. Since none of the gods had been around to identify the buildings, he hadn't known the names of them.

Now that Dikastis, the Atlantean god of justice, was fighting on their team, they were able to get a few answers.

"This is the arena where we held games and competitions. It's where we brought those who needed to be punished and taught humility."

Urian cut a vicious glare to Ash. *And this was where you put Styxx to rot. Good job, boss.* In that moment, Urian could have slapped him for his callousness.

With a guilty glimmer in his silver eyes, Ash swept his gaze over Urian, Davyn, Dikastis, Seth, Set, Maahes, Ma'at, Zakar, and the demons who were with them to fight. "I don't know what we're about to walk into, but let's move forward with Styxx's original plan. And whatever we do, save my brother."

Yeah, no shit. Urian had lost enough people in his life he cared about. He had no intention of losing anyone else. Not today. And not in the name of Apollo.

Over and over, he couldn't get the sight of Styxx going up against them out of his mind. That couldn't be the last image he had of his friend. It couldn't.

Not after all the other nightmares that haunted him.

So help him, he intended to nail Apollo's head to the temple walls. And yes, that was plural, because he wanted to cleave it into pieces first.

The others nodded in agreement, except Dikastis.

"What do you want from me?" the god of justice asked.

"Help us any way you can."

That was all well and good, but what Urian found odd was that none of the Atlanteans had come out to challenge them for being in Katateros. They had to know they were here. It wasn't like they were, you know ... gods, or anything.

So why were they so quiet while they had this many foreign gods in their domain?

The silence was eerie and wrong.

His heart pounding in fear of what they'd find, Urian entered the building behind Ash. Inside the dark hall, a feral wind howled and plastered their clothes against their bodies. He kept his sword at the ready, watchful of where and when an attack might come.

It took them several minutes to make it to the arena, and to fight the wind so that they could see what was happening. The Atlanteans were all pinned down.

What the .. ?

Then Urian saw what was going on and his stomach drew tight. A ghostly image was wrapped around Styxx, holding a dagger over his heart.

"Bathymaas! No!" Set shouted.

It was too late. She sank the dagger deep into Styxx's chest, all the way to the hilt, then threw her head back and roared in satisfaction. When she spoke, she used Atlantean only. "Take your bastard back, Apollymi. Now come and face me, you wretched bitch, so that I can bathe in your putrid blood!"

Horrified, Urian looked to Set, whose expression was every bit as pain-filled as his own.

They were too late.

In that moment, Urian felt as useless and helpless as he had the day Phoebe died. When Sheba had gone down beside him.

When Xyn hadn't shown up.

What good am I?

Suddenly, Apollymi appeared. It was the same ethereal

shade form she used whenever she was angry. "What have you done?"

Bathymaas ran at her and then through her. "Are you afraid to face me?"

Apollymi shook her head. "You did not kill my Apostolos." Tears filled her eyes as she looked at Styxx's body. "I am still trapped in Kalosis. The man you killed is Styxx of Didymos."

"No," Bathymaas breathed. Disbelief widened her eyes as she turned back toward Styxx and paled. "You lie!"

Blood dripped from the wound Bathymaas had given him and as it did so, it drained Apollymi's powers out of Styxx. His hair returned to blond, his skin darkened, and the scars that had been hidden reappeared on his body.

Urian felt his eyes water as pain racked him. Another friend gone. For no good reason.

Leto's laughter filled the room. "Poor Bathymaas ... you are damned again by your own hand." She materialized behind Bathymaas and ripped the necklace from her throat.

Set ran for them, but before he could close the distance, Leto put the two pieces together.

"Now I will be the soul of justice and you'll ..." Leto frowned as the amulet refused to reunite. "What? Why isn't this working?"

Ash met Urian's gaze and jerked his chin toward the pinned gods.

Because of the pain, it took Urian a second to catch on. Then he nodded in understanding and made his way toward them with Davyn in tow.

Ash had just started for Styxx when all of a sudden, Styxx gasped and arched his back as if something possessed him.

Urian froze with a frown.

The knife Bathymaas had buried in his chest shot through the air and landed harmlessly on the ground. Light streamed out of the wound, sealing it closed. In the next heartbeat, a shock wave went through the room, knocking everyone off their feet, except Ash.

A slow smile spread across his face.

The chains that held Styxx in place shattered, sending shrapnel out in all directions. Urian drove for Davyn to protect him. Styxx rose to hover over the floor as all the gods were pinned down.

"What's happening?" Archon roared.

No one answered as lightning bolts shot through Styxx's body, blowing out the windows and ripping the doors from their hinges. Bolts of light pierced Styxx's eyes and mouth. They shot through his body.

Simi started to go to Styxx, but Ash held her back.

"No, Sim. He might kill you." Ash teleported himself to where Styxx hovered.

The moment Bathymaas saw him, her nostrils flared with anger. "You!"

When she moved to attack him, Ash caught her with his powers. "Kill me and Styxx dies, too. Is that what you want?"

"Kill them both!" Leto shouted, still trying to put the two halves of the heart together.

Urian would laugh if it weren't so pathetic. He let go of Davyn.

Bethany rose up as if she'd obey Leto, but then her gaze went to Styxx and she calmed instantly. "What do I do to save him?"

"You have to ground him. Make him aware of who and what he really is outside of his powers."

"How?"

Ash shook his head. "Damned if I know. I'll try to hold him, but you have got to reach him or those powers will rip him apart and destroy all of us."

Nodding, she stepped back and cleared the way for Ash to launch himself at Styxx. When his brother went to hit him, Ash embraced him with everything he had.

Styxx bellowed furiously as he tried to break free.

In her Bethany form, his wife appeared in front of Styxx and cupped his face in her hands. "Styxx? Can you hear me?"

Another blast went through the room as something like a hurricane swept through it. Ash held on to Styxx and Bethany.

Urian tried to anchor himself and protect Davyn.

Styxx shoved Acheron away and turned on her with a murderous glint in his blue eyes.

Urian saw the fear and uncertainty in Bethany's eyes. Then she did the most unexpected thing of all.

She kissed him.

Styxx froze for a full minute. Urian held his breath, terrified it wouldn't work.

Then Styxx pulled back. "Beth?"

She smiled at him. "Are you with me, *akribos?*"

"I'm not sure. Am I dead?"

She laughed. "I don't know. Am I?"

"No!" Leto screamed as she ran for them.

Without hesitating, Ash intercepted her. But as soon as he neared her, she stabbed him through his stomach with an Atlantean dagger laced with ypnsi sap. While the poison was fatal to mortal beings, it was a potent toxin for the gods, and it was what Apollymi had used on her family to lock them in limbo when she'd confronted them over her son's death.

Ash staggered back and fell to his knees.

Styxx ran to him. "Acheron?"

"Simi!" he called, ignoring his brother.

"Simi on it, akri!" She vanished.

Acheron's body was quickly turning gray as the poison spread from the wound to the rest of him. His eyes flared red as he cupped Styxx's cheek and pulled him closer.

Before anyone realized what Acheron intended, Ash sank his fangs into Styxx's neck and handed over his powers for Styxx's use. He pulled back and locked gazes with Styxx. "Kick their fucking asses, brother."

Urian applauded him, then moved to finish off Phanen.

"With pleasure."

He was just finishing off Phanen and reaching for another god when he heard Styxx's sharp cry. "Urian, on deck."

Urian flashed over, then cursed as he saw Acheron's condition. He hadn't realized how bad it was.

"Watch and protect him."

He inclined his head to Styxx. "Will do."

"Styxx?" Bethany called.

"I'm fine," Styxx assured her.

Urian wasn't so sure about that. All around them, the gods were battling.

Leto came at them with the dagger raised. Styxx stepped in front of Bethany as Leto stabbed at him. The force of her attack unbalanced her. He jerked her forward and disarmed her with a single twist to her wrist.

Leto laughed as she realized he wouldn't strike her.

Until Bethany came around him with a grim, determined glint in her eyes. "I've got this bitch."

Styxx stepped back and let her take fourteen thousand years of vengeance out on the goddess they both hated.

"Zakar?" Styxx shouted.

The god looked past Archon, then fell back as Styxx moved in to engage the Atlantean god in Zakar's place.

Archon laughed. "Really? You think borrowed powers scare me? I've wiped my ass on higher beings and better warriors than you."

Urian arched his brow at those arrogant words.

And so did Styxx. "I'll concede the higher beings, but you should remember, Archon, there were no better warriors than me ... in either of my lifetimes. It's why you helped Apollo and Leto cheat in order to kill Aricles. You knew that I'd be coming for you."

Urian paused to watch his hero battle.

Scoffing, Archon brought his axe down across Styxx's shield, which he manifested along with his sword. Styxx lunged at his feet with his sword. The older god danced away as Styxx twirled with an uppercut that nicked his arm.

Urian cringed. Damn, that hurt.

Archon screamed out in pain.

Styxx drove him back as Archon struggled to keep up with his blows.

"Go ahead," Archon taunted, "put me back to sleep. I will get free again. And when I do, I'm coming for both of you. There's nothing you can do to stop me. I will return."

"No," Styxx said firmly. "You won't." He feinted right and when Archon moved to defend, he shot back with a well-practiced swing that severed the god's head in one final stroke.

Urian's eyes widened at that bold move.

Everyone in the room froze as they realized what Styxx had done. And more to the point, they became aware of what he really was.

A Chthonian god-killer. They alone had the power to destroy a god and send his or her power back to the Source. And while killing a god weakened them, they were still the baddest asses in the Nether Realm.

The only things that could kill one of them was the Source, one of its servants, or another Chthonian.

And judging by the heat in Urian's arm, his powers didn't like it at all. But that was okay, he was impressed.

Apparently, so were the Atlanteans, as they dropped their weapons immediately and stood down.

Except Bethany and Leto, who continued to battle like champions.

Nonchalant about it, Urian walked over to Styxx. "Should we break them up?"

Before he could answer, Set intervened by grabbing Leto in a fierce sleeper hold. As soon as she passed out, he tossed her over his shoulder. "While I respect your need to beat her, daughter, I'm the one with a much larger grudge against this bitch. Not just for what she did to you, but for what she did to your brother." He leaned forward to kiss Bethany's cheek. "I will be back very soon and never fear ... while I would never strike a lady, this bitch is open season." He paused to glance at Zakar, who smiled wickedly.

Then the three of them were gone.

Urian cringed, grateful to the gods that he wasn't his great-grandmother. That batch was burnt.

"Brother?" Bethany whispered as she turned to Styxx. "I have a brother?"

He pointed to Seth, who stood back from them. "Seth was born long after Apollymi had frozen you in Katateros."

Bethany went to meet him for the first time while Styxx knelt beside Acheron, who was stone gray from head to toe. He frowned at Urian. "What is this?"

"Aima," Dikastis answered, kneeling by their side.

Styxx started for Dikastis to finish him off, but Urian held him back so that he couldn't hurt him.

"Easy, god-killer," Urian said with a laugh. "He's on our side."

Styxx narrowed his gaze. "You sure?"

"He stabbed that one." Urian pointed to Teros. "And saved my ass."

Maahes joined Seth and Bethany to help with their introductions, while Ma'at came over to Styxx's side.

She rubbed Styxx's back reassuringly. "Acheron will be fine. As soon as Simi brings the antidote, he'll wake up."

Styxx appeared doubtful. "Are you sure?"

She nodded. "Otherwise, Apollymi wouldn't be so quiet."

Urian realized she was quiet . . .

Even when Simi returned with three leaves from the Tree of Life that only grew in the Destroyer's temple in Kalosis, Apollymi remained extremely reserved and dubiously silent.

That cannot be good. Urian had never seen her like that before. What fresh menace was this? Every hair on the back of his neck was standing on end.

"What do I do with these?" Styxx asked Simi.

"Twist them until they're moist," Apollymi said. "Then drip nine drops into Apostolos's mouth."

Styxx hesitated. "What happens if I do ten by mistake?"

Urian snorted sarcastically. "Let's not find out."

Bethany returned to his side as he carefully counted.

As soon as the ninth one hit Acheron's lips, the color slowly returned to the whole of his body.

Groaning, Acheron opened his eyes, then grimaced. "Next time, add peppermint flavoring, somebody. That is the nastiest-tasting crap on the planet."

Styxx snorted. "You're not seriously complaining that I brought you back. Are you?"

"Yes, and no. Taste it yourself and you'll understand."

Having had a dose a few times, Urian agreed. That was some nasty crap.

Shaking his head, Styxx held his hand out to his brother. Acheron took it and allowed him to pull him to his feet, then hugged him close. After a few seconds, he stepped back to leave him to Bethany.

Styxx turned and wrapped his arms around her. He leaned his head against hers. "I told you I'd come back for you, my goddess. That nothing would stop me."

"Yes, but did you have to drag your feet?"

He laughed. "I'm afraid you're going to have to get used to living with me right here. I will never again let you go. Just consider me a large exterior growth on your body."

Urian felt the tears in his own throat as he more than understood that sentiment. God, if he could only have Phoebe back ...

Her lips trembling, Bethany smiled up at him as her own tears flowed. "I just wish we had our son with us."

"I know, precious," he breathed.

"Um ... about that."

Styxx looked up at Apollymi's trepidatious voice, which she had suddenly found again. "What?"

Urian was amazed he'd bark that word at the goddess of destruction.

"Remember my promise to you, Styxx?"

"Yes?"

Urian frowned as Apollymi began acting even stranger and more skittish.

"I didn't kill your son. I wanted to. Desperately. But as I looked down at that tiny, beautiful baby, I saw Apostolos and I couldn't bring myself to hurt him."

Bethany gasped. "Where is he?"

Apollymi's gaze went to Urian.

Okay ... Dumbfounded by that, he turned around to look behind him.

No one was there.

What the hell?

Styxx's jaw dropped. "Urian is Galen?"

Um, no ... Not even. Was it? Urian shook his head. "It's not possible. I was born before they died."

"No, you weren't." Apollymi smiled sadly. "Your father told you that because he didn't want you to know that you and your brother were the first Apollites born cursed. And that was my fault. I intentionally chose Strykerius's wife because I thought it would be the perfect revenge that Apollo should look after Styxx's child given what he'd done to him. I had no idea he would curse all of you. Like Apostolos and Styxx, your blood mingled with that of Strykerius's real son, and that made you a part of Strykerius, too." She drew a ragged breath. "But yes. You, child, are the only being alive who is part human, Atlantean, Egyptian, and Apollite ... and you are born with the blood of three pantheons, and gods inside you."

Aghast, Urian still couldn't wrap his head around this. "Did Stryker ever know?"

"In a way. I told him long ago, after you were grown and he wondered about some of your heightened abilities, such as your arm. That you were very special to this world, but not who your real parents were. Your unique bloodline was why the evil souls you once lived on didn't turn you trelos. Why you could go longer between feedings than others of your kind, and how your blood sustained Phoebe while she lived. It's also why Strykerius cut your throat instead of stabbing you in the heart. Unlike other Daimons, you wouldn't have died from a heart wound. Only blood loss can kill *you*."

Staggered by her words, Urian looked at Acheron. "Did you know this?"

"I knew it was odd that Stryker cut your throat, but no. I had no clue you were my nephew. My mother"—he passed a peeved glare at her—"never mentioned it to me."

Urian scowled as he grappled with this new reality he'd never imagined. "Man, I'm messed up right now. My best friend is my father? The man I idolized as a kid ... whose tattoo is on my arm ... And he's younger than me. Yeah, I don't think I can handle this. Mind-wipe me, somebody ... please! Where's that dragon from Sanctuary? Simi, go get Max. I need him."

Biting her lip, Bethany approached Urian tentatively.

Urian choked as he realized that he still had a mother ...

She placed a gentle hand on his cheek as she stared up at him. "I see your father in you. My baby's beautiful. Just like I knew you'd be." She pulled him into her arms and held him tight. "I hate that I missed seeing you grow, but I do love you ... my Urian."

Urian felt the connection to her. It rose up in a splash of warmth from inside him. In one instant, it reduced him back to the boy who'd watched his mother die. To the child who'd wanted nothing more than to feel that unique love that only came from a mother's heart. The kind of love that never asked for anything in return. It didn't judge. Or hate or hurt.

It just gave.

He pulled her into his arms and held her as if he'd been hers from birth. Styxx wrapped his arms around both of them.

His eyes warm with pride, Styxx cupped Urian's face in his hand. "My son."

Urian laughed. "Is it just me, or is that creepy?"

Laughing, Styxx kissed his cheek. "Your poor mother has no idea how odd and quirky a child we have. But I can't wait for her to know you."

Urian tightened his hand on hers. "Neither can I."

December 24, 2012

Urian pulled back from his parents to realize that everyone had left the arena.

Except Apollymi. Her crystal tears glistened against her pale cheeks as she watched them. "What I did to all of you was inexcusable. I lashed out in anger and pain, and what I thought was vengeance was nothing more than selfish envy. Because I knew I'd never be able to hold my baby, I took that pleasure from you, and for that, I am truly, truly sorry. But your son is why I saved the Apollites. Once my anger cooled, and I realized how wrong I was, I kept him safe for you both."

Urian looked at his parents. "In all fairness, she did."

A tic worked in Styxx's jaw. "I can't even begin to put into words how infuriated I am that I was alive and imprisoned, and missed seeing my son grow up—"

Apollymi nodded. "I know, Styxx."

Urian tugged at his father's arm. "And I can testify to that. I've witnessed her pain firsthand."

Nodding, Styxx met Apollymi's gaze levelly. "Oddly enough, Apollymi, I can't find any hatred for you right now. I'm too grateful to have them with me to waste one minute thinking about anything else."

Bethany took his hand and Urian's. "I will probably hate you in the morning, Pol. But tonight, I'm with Styxx. I just want to be with my boys for a while."

Apollymi inclined her head to them. "The others quietly made their way back to the main temple and left the three of you to your privacy. Know that if you ever need anything ... I will be here for you." Her shade returned to Kalosis.

Styxx turned toward Urian and his mother. "All I want to do is spend the night talking to both of you. But ... "

"Shit to do," Urian said for him.

Bethany tsked at Urian. "Who taught you how to speak?"

Urian grinned unabashedly. "She's going to be in for a rude awakening with all the modern changes and gadgets, isn't she?"

That deepened her frown. "How long have I been gone?"

Styxx checked his watch. "Eleven thousand five hundred and thirty-nine years, one hundred eighty-three days, and roughly ten hours, give or take a few minutes."

Bethany gaped. "You really did count the heartbeats."

Styxx slid the sleeve back on his arm to show her where he'd carved her name. "You have no idea."

Urian's stomach sank as he realized that it was his name there, too.

Damn. All the times he'd seen it.

This is my solren. He was the baby in those drawings that Styxx had labored over. It was so humbling to know exactly how much his father had wanted him.

Until his mother kissed his name on his father's arm, then lifted her lips to his.

Urian whistled low. "You know, this would be awkward if you *weren't* my parents. The parental designation ups the ick factor exponentially."

Yeah, it was probably immature, but he really couldn't help it. There was something biological going on with his body, but yeah.

Laughing, Bethany pulled away to frown at him. "I am desperate to know you." She looked back at Styxx. "And you and I have a lot to talk about. But . . . "

Styxx sighed. "We have gods to attend to."

She nodded. "I want to make sure they never threaten us again."

"I couldn't agree more," Urian concurred.

Bethany took their hands and teleported them to the main temple. As soon as she saw the signs of battle and the amount of blood on the walls and floor, she sucked her breath in sharply. Horrified, she met Styxx's sheepish gaze. "Please tell me that's not yours."

"Some is, but a lot of it was Demonbrean. That bastard bleeds like a slaughtered pig."

When she started forward, Styxx refused to let go of her hand. She turned back with a frown.

The agonized fear in his eyes made Urian wince. "I let go of your hand once when I didn't want to, and it was the biggest mistake of my life. One I never intend to make again."

She laced her fingers with his and pulled him toward Acheron, who sat on his black throne, surrounded by the others. Urian hung back and moved to stand with Davyn, who held an ice pack to his head.

"You all right?"

Davyn nodded. "Sure. Good to be hit in the head from time to time."

He shook his head at the sarcasm.

Rolling his eyes, Urian took stock of who was remaining among their numbers. Most of the gods were gone. The only ones left were Ma'at, Sin, Artemis, Simi, Apollo, and Xirena.

Bethany moved to stand near the throne. Styxx pressed himself against her back and wrapped his arms around her waist, then rested his chin on top of her head as if he were afraid to let her go for even an instant.

Acheron looked at them.

"Catch us up?" Styxx asked.

Simi blew an irritated breath out. "Akri won't let me eat any of them nasty gods. What's the world coming to when a demon gots to beg for tidbits ... not even a finger sandwich. Tragic. Terribly tragic."

Urian laughed.

Styxx whispered in Bethany's ear. "I'll explain Simi later."

Acheron let out a "heh" sound over Simi's words. "Well, after the way you took Archon's head, the rest are more than happy to be returned to stasis. But I was thinking of allowing a couple of them to be siphoned off by Kat and transitioned into the human world."

By Styxx's expression, Urian could tell he wasn't thrilled

with the idea. But to his credit, he didn't dismiss it out of turn. "Which ones?"

"I wasn't going to make the offer without conferring with you first. I know they were less than kind to you while you were here, and if you want to gut them, I'm going to help you."

Bethany looked up at Styxx with a frown. "When did you two become friends?"

Styxx kissed the tip of her nose. "About five minutes before you woke up."

Her scowl deepened.

"Dikastis," Acheron continued, "I was going to leave alone . . . as long as you agree. He seems to be decent enough."

Bethany nodded. "He is extremely trustworthy and loyal so long as no rules are broken."

Urian didn't have a problem with that.

"Will Epithymia get her powers back?" Styxx asked.

Sin laughed uproariously. "Hell to the no. Trust me. When Kat removes your powers, they stay gone. Technically, in theory, Kat could give them back. And I hate speaking for my wife while she's not here, but I'm pretty sure Epi is going to learn to be without."

Urian laughed under his breath. Yeah, Sin would definitely be the expert on that. He could imagine the fights the two of them must have at home.

"Leto is with Set and I'm not about to step in on that. Especially given what Seth and Artemis have told me about her and what she's done to all of you."

Artemis lifted her chin proudly. "Yes, we threw her over the trolley."

Acheron groaned. "Under . . . bus, Artemis. You throw people under a bus."

"Whatever. My mother threatened my baby, and my loyalty is to Katra and Mia and no one else . . . until Katra has more children, and they have babies. But that's it!" She pursed her lips. "Oh wait, there is one more, but that really is all and it's not the bitch who hurt my girl. Either of them. I want Epithymia for my personal collection."

Acheron met Styxx's gaze. "If anyone can make someone's life a living hell, I can personally attest to Artemis's expertise."

Urian choked on that comment and especially the murderous look Artemis gave him.

Styxx nodded. "I'm in accord."

"Me, too," Ma'at agreed.

"Which leaves us with Apollo." Acheron paused to sweep his gaze around the room. "Most of us have an equal claim against him, so I have no idea how to be fair about his fate."

Artemis sighed. "Even though I'd love it, you can't kill him."

All of a sudden, Styxx started laughing in an evil tone that sent a chill down Urian's spine as he couldn't imagine what it meant.

Bethany frowned. "Why does that scare me?"

"Because I have the perfect gift for someone. Even Simi will approve."

A*pollo shouted in* outrage around his gag as he fought against Artemis's diktyon net that held him tighter than a fly in a spiderweb. If he had his regular powers, he'd be able to escape. But Urian's present—Verlyn's necklace—kept them drained.

Urian chuckled like a bad cartoon villain. "Remind me to never, ever piss off my father. And I don't mean Stryker. Damn, Pops. This is soooo cold."

Artemis smiled. "Yes, well, payback's a cat!"

Acheron sighed and shook his head. "I absolutely give up."

"All right," Styxx said, hauling Apollo to his feet. "One special delivery." He kissed Bethany before he looked at Acheron. "Take care of my girl. I'll be right back." He turned to Urian. "You ready?"

For this shit? Oh yeah. Artemis was right. Payback was a cat. And he was ready to meow.

"After you, Solren."

To Urian's shock, Styxx teleported them directly into Apollymi's garden, where she sat, gazing into her mirror.

Gasping in indignation, she rose to her feet. "What is this?"

Urian covered his father, in case she blasted him. Ever fearless, Styxx forced Apollo to kneel before her. Totally naked and bound, Apollo had no choice but to obey. Urian would feel sorry for the Olympian had the bastard ever shown his people an ounce of mercy or compassion.

But really, he wanted to see him cry.

Styxx saluted Apollymi. "I come bearing gifts, my lady."

Inclining his head to them both, Urian removed the necklace from Apollo. "I'll return this to Davyn and be right back."

Urian teleported to the home Davyn once shared with Paris. Davyn was waiting for him.

The relief on his face was tangible. He pulled Urian against him and held him close. "You ever scare me like that and I will gut you."

"I know. Sorry."

Swallowing hard, Davyn let him go. "You know you're all I have, right?"

"I know. We've been through a lot." Urian glanced around the sparse cottage that hadn't changed in all the centuries he'd known him. "Have you thought about my offer?"

For the last four years, Davyn had been able to walk in daylight. There was no reason for him to live here anymore. The Apollymians were free to leave. They weren't locked here.

Most stayed out of loyalty to Apollymi, who couldn't leave.

But Urian and Acheron had offered sanctuary to Davyn for all the years of service he'd given them.

Davyn's eyes turned bright with unshed tears. "I can't leave, Uri. This is all I have of Paris. All my memories are here."

"You can't move on, either."

"Who says I want to?"

Urian could respect that. Pulling him closer, he kissed him on the forehead. "You know where I am if you need me."

"I know. Love you."

"You, too, brother."

Yet walking away from him was always hard. Davyn had

always been the one constant in his life. If anything ever happened to him, Urian wouldn't be able to cope.

Not wanting to think about it, he headed back to Apollymi's palace, where he'd left Styxx ... his birth father.

Styxx looked at him, then smiled at Apollymi, who was salivating over her gift. "Enjoy."

Together, they teleported back to Bethany, who was holding Sebastos while talking to Tory and Ma'at.

Urian had a surreal moment when it slammed into him again that she was his mother. Especially when she glanced over at them and smiled. "There he is. Bas, say hi to Uncle Styxx."

"Hi, Unkie Six!" he said, laughing and bouncing in Bethany's arms.

She tickled his belly until he squealed and kissed her. His little hand tangled in her long hair.

"Are you all right?" Acheron asked as he came up behind Styxx.

Styxx met Urian's gaze and nodded. "I am."

He took Styxx's hand and squeezed it, then went to Bethany. He brushed his hand over Sebastos's curls. "Hi, Bas."

"You want to hold him?" Tory asked.

Styxx shook his head. "I might break him and piss off Acheron."

Urian laughed.

"You can't break him, sweetie," Bethany said.

"I don't know. The last time I held a child that age, I must have broken it 'cause it leaked all over me."

Bethany laughed so hard, she had to give Bas back to his mother before she dropped him.

Tory kissed Bas's head. "You're right, Bethany. He's hilarious."

"And now that he's back," Ma'at said, "we need to finish something. Will all of you excuse us?"

Urian frowned. "Should I be worried?"

Ash took his son from his wife. "Nah. They're going to finish the ceremony to reunite Bethany's heart. It's all good."

"Ah."

"Don't look so worried, Urian. They'll be fine."

Ash said that, but something wasn't right. Urian could feel it. His family was reunited. He should feel whole again, and a part of him did.

Yet . . .

He glanced around the room and he still had that vacuous ache that defied explanation.

Alexion and Danger were sitting with Xirena and Simi, laughing. Tory and Ash and all seemed okay.

But something wasn't right. Something cosmically was out of order. Every Daimon and demigod sense he possessed knew it.

Closing his eyes, he swore he could see the atoms of the universe realigning. Hear the aether whispering. *This isn't good.* The winds of change were coming and they were bringing with them the scythe of upheaval.

Nothing was ever going to be the same again.

October 23, 2017

"Falcyn!" Urian barked as he caught sight of the massive Were-Hunter bastard in Sanctuary coming way too close to his sister.

He hated that bastard for many, many reasons. Not the least of which was having removed Xyn from Kalosis all those centuries before.

Damn him!

Worse? He knew that look. And no man or beast gave his sister that look without getting an ass-beating from him.

Falcyn tsked at Urian. "Do you really think to make me heel at your command, lapdog?"

Unperturbed by that insult and wanting to drink dragon blood, Urian narrowed his eyes while he rapidly closed the distance between them. He kept his attention keenly focused on Falcyn, watching his every twitch.

He didn't trust the Drakos bastard at all. This was one of Xyn's brothers, which meant that Urian knew exactly how treacherous Falcyn could be.

Stepping between them, Urian gave Medea a bit of breathing room. "I would caution you to remember you're in a Were-Hunter sanctuary."

Falcyn snorted. "As if I give two shits for Savitar's laws." He raked a bitter stare over Urian. "Or *you*, for that matter. And even less for your boss. So don't even think of dragging Acheron's name into this as protection from my wrath. I dare him to say a single word to me ... on *any* matter."

Urian scowled at his words and bravado given the fact that Acheron was the final Fate of all. To defy him while knowing his real place in the universe was a special level of stupid and bravery that most lacked. "Is there nothing you fear?"

Falcyn's gaze went past Urian's shoulder to something in the crowd.

"Aye, but sadly she's not here."

Urian turned his head at the sound of the deep voice behind him. Blaise du Fey. There was a bastard he hadn't seen in a long, long time. Another of Xyn's dubious kin.

But at least he was a little better natured than Falcyn. With hair as pale as Urian's and eyes a peculiar lavender shade, Blaise was a fierce and reliable warrior.

And like Xyn, his ears held a bit of a point to them. Something that always hit Urian hard in the gut whenever he saw Blaise or any of the Adoni as it reminded him of the way he used to nibble and toy affectionately with Xyn's. Those ears had always been a source of fascination for him.

Stop, Uri! You make me self-conscious! I feel enough like a freak because of them.

Don't say that. I adore your ears. They're as beautiful as the rest of you. And the fact that they're not like everyone else's makes them as special as you are. You should never cover them. Rather flaunt them to the world. Let them see the unique beauty that is you.

God, how he missed her. And instead of having her precious kindness, he was stuck with her two asshole brothers to deal with.

Awesome.

Falcyn tsked at him. "Now, Blaise, why would you go and bring Xyn into this? Especially given what a sore topic that is?"

Blaise let loose a charming grin. "Felt the need to rankle my big brother. Besides, everyone else fears you so. You need me to even you out." Blaise kept his hand raised and out so that he could feel his way through them. Because of his albinism, he was blind in his human body. "And if you're through scaring the natives, I've got something I need to speak to you about."

Falcyn sneered. "Rather spend time scaring the natives than listening to your petulant whine."

"Ah, now, you're going to hurt my feelings."

"You don't have any feelings."

"Not true. I had a lot of them, until you, Kerrigan, and Illarion shriveled them into oblivion. But I think I managed to salvage one or two. Please, try not to kill those last two off. I might need them one day."

Urian shook his head at Medea, who was so lucky that she'd been raised as an only child. He envied her that.

Falcyn made a rude noise of dismissal. "Those are called hunger pangs."

Blaise laughed. "Hungry for a kind word, you mean."

"Well, you won't be getting it here." Falcyn gestured toward the stairs as if his brother could see his movements. "So off with you."

Blaise sighed heavily. "'Fraid not. Must intrude. Can't wait."

Urian pulled Medea away from the fighting dragons. "Well, then. We'll leave you to your argument. Come, big sis. Let's get out of here before Godzilla and Mothra go at it and we're caught in the crossfire."

She screwed her face up at him. "Before who and what?"

Urian groaned under his breath. How could he forget that she knew next to nothing about pop culture? It was actually painful how few of his quotes she understood. "One day we've got to do an all-day movie marathon to catch you up on my references." And with that, he pulled her toward the stairs.

"What are they?" she asked him as he led her upstairs to the less crowded area of the bar.

"Blaise is a mandrake. Falcyn . . . hell if I know. He's one of the dragon breeds, but not a Were-Hunter." Even though Urian usually called him that just to piss him off because it was fun to listen to the irritable bowel symptom noises Falcyn made in protest.

"If they're brothers, he'd be a mandrake, too. Right?"

One would think. But he'd learned centuries ago from Xyn that it didn't work that way. "I don't think they're really related. The dragons have an even more peculiar idea of what constitutes family than we do."

"But if he's a dragon and he's not a mandrake or Were-Hunter, how can he be human? Aren't they the only two kinds of pure-blooded dragons who can take human form?"

Urian paused to look from her to the two dragons in the crowd below. "*That,* Medea, is the question we've all asked and no one will answer. All we know is that he's a bloodthirsty beast who's best avoided."

Urian scowled at Medea as they talked inside the small private room in Sanctuary that was reserved for whenever the preternatural clientele became rowdy and needed a time-out away from human witnesses who might not react well to the reality of what they shared their world with. Barely more than a closet, their quarters were cramped, but it allowed them to not be overheard by any of the humans outside.

Or the Were-Hunters, who as a rule had *very* sensitive hearing.

And given the fact that his sister had just told him about a mysterious plague that was about to destroy her people, he was glad no one could overhear them.

"Why are you telling me this? I'm no longer a Daimon." He hadn't been one in years.

Medea crossed her arms over her chest. "Yeah, but for all you know, this plague that Apollo's sent could infect you, too. Whatever it is that Apollo unleashed on us is taking an awful toll. I know you hate our father, but—"

"Stryker's *not* my father!" he reminded her coldly. Thank the gods for that favor.

"Biologically, true. However, he did raise you as his own. His wife birthed you."

"After I was ripped from the stomach of my real mother by that bitch you serve ... and shoved into her womb without anyone's knowledge or consent!" And Medea reminding him of how the gods had screwed him over wasn't warming him to her cause.

At all.

Honestly, he'd had enough of being their bastard stepchild they kicked whenever they became bored.

"*That* bitch is also the mother of your current boss and the beloved protector of your real father and mother, don't forget!"

Urian hissed at her less-than-subtle reminder about Apollymi's position in his world. And the fact that he'd once loved her like a second mother most of his life. But he felt doubly betrayed by her for not telling him the truth, when she'd known it all those centuries. He was so angry at Apollymi for what she'd done that he had yet to even speak to her again after finding out the truth.

When he looked back and thought about all the years—no, *centuries*—he could have had with his real father ... he wanted to kill her for it. How could she have done it?

"You have some nerve to come here and ask me to help Stryker or Apollymi given what they've both taken from me."

It was cruel beyond cruel, even for them.

"I know that. Which tells you how desperate I am." She swallowed hard. "They're not the only ones who are sick, Uri. Davyn has it, too. He'll die if you don't help us."

That news staggered him. Davyn was the one person he couldn't bear the thought of losing. He'd kill himself first.

"Please, Urian. I lost my husband and only child because my grandfather—*the grandfather of* your *birth twin*—was a bastard. Watched them both be slaughtered in front of my own eyes by the human vermin you protect. For no reason other than they feared us when we'd done nothing to cause their suspicions. We were innocent and harmless, minding our own business when they attacked us. So don't think for one minute you own some kind of market share on pain. Because trust me, brother, you're a novice. You've no idea what I went through in my mortal life or this one. I'm sorry for what Stryker did to your Phoebe. I am, but I've lost too many to sit back and watch the rest die and not do something to at least try to help them. That's not who I am."

It wasn't who he was either, and she was wrong about her pain. He'd lost more children than she had. He knew exactly the pain of her loss. While he might not have birthed them, they were his children all the same.

A single tear slid down her cheek as her eyes turned haunted.

"Praxis was five years old, Uri. Five. And he died in agony at the merciless hands of those human bastards, screaming for me to help him while they . . . " She choked on her words. "Tell me, Urian, how am I even sane, given what they violently stole from me? No amount of time can dull a pain that sharp!"

Urian knew her pain. Firsthand. And he hated that anyone had to go through it. He pulled her against him. "I'm so sorry, Dee."

Her breathing ragged, she pushed him away from her. "I don't need your pity. It's worthless. You can keep it, especially if you're not going to help me."

Urian caught her arm as she started to leave. "Wait!" He wanted to deny her this request. In truth, he wanted Stryker to go down in flames and to laugh as he watched it happen.

But Medea was right. He couldn't allow the rest of what had once been his family and friends to die and do nothing.

Not if he could help it.

"There is one thing that might be able to save them."

"What?"

He hesitated. Not because he didn't want to help them, but because he didn't know what Stryker might do with the cure. In his hands, it could prove most lethal.

No good deed goes unpunished.

Somehow this was going to come back on him. He knew it. Such things always did, and they left him bleeding and cursing. Yet even so, he couldn't allow Medea to be hurt any worse than she already had been. She was right. She'd been through enough and at the end of the day, they were family. Maybe not in the conventional sense, but he felt a kinship with her all the same. And he had grown up thinking himself as one of Stryker's sons. Thinking of Stryker's daughter as his own sister.

Every time he looked at Medea, he saw Tannis's beloved face. Remembered their time as children. They'd all been innocent victims of a fetid power game between the ancient gods. All of them had paid a high cost to continue living, just to spite those who would see them fall for no reason whatsoever.

For better or worse, Medea was every bit as much his sister

as Tannis had been. And because he loved her, he refused to add to her pain.

"I don't know if it'll work or not."

Medea chafed at his hedging. "Oh for goodness' sake, just say it, already!"

"A dragonstone." The one thing Xyn had told him about so very long ago. They were incredibly powerful and could curse just about anything.

Pulling back, she scowled at him. "A what?"

Urian hedged as he sought a way to explain it. But it wasn't as easy as it should be. "For lack of a better term, it's an enchanted rock the dragons have. Supposedly, it can cure anything. Even death."

"Where do you get one?"

That was the easy part.

And the hardest thing imaginable, as there were so few left. "As luck would have it, there's one here."

Joy returned to her dark eyes. "Where?"

He visibly cringed at the last place either of them wanted to venture. Because asking for help there was all kinds of rampant stupid. If only Xyn were still alive. She'd have shared hers in a heartbeat. "That would be the stickler, as it belongs to Falcyn." The bastard he hated almost as much as Apollo.

"That surly beast I met earlier?"

He nodded. "To my knowledge, that's the last one in existence. The rest were all destroyed or have gone missing."

Medea groaned out loud. "Great. So how do I go about getting this thing?"

"Word of advice? Ask nicely."

U*rian and Medea* entered the room where they'd been told Falcyn had gone to see Blaise.

Problem was, they weren't alone. And the fey Adoni with them didn't seem happy. Indeed, this appeared about the same as walking into the middle of a bank robbery.

With all the robbers wrapped in C-4.

Falcyn drew up short at the sight of them. "Here to help or to hinder? Declare yourself."

Urian didn't hesitate with his answer. "Whichever choice ends with me on your good side."

"Grab the bitch."

That better not be his sister Falcyn was talking about.

But before anyone could move, a bright light pulsed inside the room, blinding everyone except Blaise, who couldn't see anyway.

Falcyn cursed. "Urian?"

Hissing from the pain, Urian held his hand up in a useless effort to try to see someone past the large white blob. "Blind as a bat!" he snapped in response to Falcyn's call. "Dee?"

"Can't see shit."

"It's demons in the room." Blaise moved to cover them. "Gallu."

Ah, that's just great. At least they weren't Charonte.

"Who invited the assholes to our party?" Falcyn snarled.

They were one of the few breeds that could infect a victim and turn them into mindless slaves. Or killing machines. Neither of which appealed to Urian.

He only killed on command or when threatened. As the old Daimon saying went—*you protect those who stand behind you. Respect those who stand by your side. And defeat or kill whoever stands against you.*

Suddenly, something grabbed them and they were falling.

"Blaise? What are you doing?" Falcyn snarled.

"Hang on! Everyone stay calm!"

Falcyn scoffed. "Then why do you sound panicked and why am I still blind?"

Urian hit the ground hard enough to knock the breath from his lungs. A few feet away, Falcyn and Medea landed in an entwined heap.

"Hey, hey, love! You only touch the no-zone if you intend to make it happy."

Medea grimaced. "There's not enough beer in the universe for me to touch your no-zone, dragonfly. Don't flatter yourself."

"Says the Daimon crawling all over it."

"Jumping off it, you mean, before I catch something I'm sure antibiotics won't cure."

Urian laughed. One thing he loved about his sister—she had a mean sense of humor.

Falcyn scoffed at her insult. "Not what it feels like from where I'm lying and you're still on top of—umph!" He growled as she elbowed the air out of his lungs.

With a fierce scowl, he rubbed the abused area and pushed himself to his feet. "Blaise, what did you do?"

Another thing Urian agreed with. They appeared to be out in middle-of-nowhere Alaska, Nebraska, or some remote end-of-the-world apocalyptic location.

Blaise turned around slowly in a way that said he was using his dragon-sight to feel the aether. "Well, this wasn't what I had planned."

"What?" Urian's voice dripped with sarcasm. "You weren't wanting a trip to Halloween Town? I'm so disappointed, Blaise. Was hoping to get my Jack Skellington underwear signed."

Falcyn scratched at his whiskered cheek. "So how'd we get here?"

"Not sure. I was aiming for the parlor of the Peltier house." Blaise screwed his face up. "Epic fail. Not even sure where we are."

Urian let out a long, tired breath as he surveyed the twisted landscape. "I think I know. But you're not going to like it. I sure as hell don't."

Medea pursed her lips. "Try us."

Urian glanced around at a place where he hadn't been since his marriage to Sheba. Gods, he hoped he was wrong. But yeah, this looked like the realm Ruyn used to party in for shits and giggles. "Myrkheim."

Blaise made an expression of exaggerated happiness. "Oh goody! The borderlands where heathens go to rot! Just where I wanted to build my vacation home! Where's a lease? Sign my scaly ass up!"

Medea rolled her eyes. "What's Myrkheim?"

Falcyn laughed bitterly. "Guess the Daimons don't spend a lot of time here as it's not really part of *your* mythology. It's a nether realm. A holding ground if you will, between the land of light and dark where the fey can practice their magick."

"*Whose* feyfolk?" she pressed.

Legitimate question, Urian supposed, as there was a lot of fey in the world to go around.

Falcyn sighed. "At one time, everyone's. But nowadays, it's mostly reserved for Morgen's rejects. And some other IBS-suffering bastards."

"Yeah, okay ... So what's the—" Before she could finish her sentence a bolt of light shot between them, narrowly missing her.

In fact, it only missed her because Falcyn deflected it. "Stray magick. You have to keep your head up for it. If it hits you, there's no telling what it might do. Could vaporize you. Turn you into a toad. Or just ruin your chances for children."

Which was why Ruyn liked to play here. Bastard lived to play dangerously.

Medea's eyes widened as she watched it explode and morph a tree not far from them into a chicken that screeched, then dove under the ground to burrow like a frightened rabbit. "That happen a lot?"

Falcyn nodded. "'Round here? Good bit."

"Great. Anything else I should watch out for?"

"Yeah," he said bitterly. "Everything."

Blinking, she met Urian's gaze. "Joke?"

"Falcyn has no measurable sense of humor. At least none that we've identified to date."

Blaise braided his long white hair and secured it with a leather tie he'd unwound from his wrist. "Well, Max said that Falcyn wasn't always the pain in the ass we know him as. But I can only speak about the last few hundred years. And he hasn't changed as long as I've known him."

"Not helping, Blaise," Urian said drily.

He spread his arms wide to indicate their surroundings. "In

case you haven't noticed, I'm not real good at that. Tend to fuck up all things whenever I try to help."

"And Merlin chose you for a Grail knight. What the hell was she thinking?"

Blaise hissed. "We don't talk about that out loud, Falcyn! Sheez! What? You trying to get me killed?"

Falcyn shot a blast of fire at the sky. "Still trying to figure out how we got here ... and why. 'Cause let's face it, we didn't get sent here for anything good."

"Was hoping you wouldn't notice that." Blaise cleared his throat. "Way to harsh my zen, dude."

Falcyn rolled his eyes at Blaise. "You need to stop hanging out with Savitar. I hate that bastard."

"You hate everyone," Blaise reminded him.

"That surfboard-wielding bastard I hate most of all."

Blaise arched an inquisitive brow. "More than brother Max?"

Falcyn growled. "Are we going to argue inconsequentials or look for a way home? 'Cause I just tried my powers and they didn't do shit for getting us out of here."

Cringing, Blaise rubbed nervously at his neck. "Mine either, and I was hoping to keep you distracted so that you wouldn't beat my ass over this situation."

Falcyn glanced to Urian. "What about you, Princess Pea? You got anything?"

"Besides a throbbing migraine? No. My teleportation isn't cooperating either."

They all looked at Medea.

"Really? If mine were working do you think I'd be here, listening to the lot of you? Promise, I'd have vanished long ago."

Blaise sighed. "I think I saw this movie once. It didn't go well for the people as they turned on each other and it involved chain saws ... and a whole lot of blood."

"But was there silence? That's the real question."

Urian snorted at Falcyn's irritable comment.

Worse?

There *was* sudden silence. It echoed around them with that

eerie kind of stillness that set every nerve ending on edge. The kind that radiated with malevolence because it was a portent.

The men drew together to stand with their backs to each other so that they could face and fight whatever threat was coming for them.

Suddenly, a bright light flashed near them. One that momentarily blinded Urian with its intensity. The mist solidified into a tall, lanky male with brown hair and red eyes.

You've got to be fucking kidding me ...

"Don't you ever die?" Urian asked as he saw the demon Kessar.

How many times were they going to kill this bastard and have him come back?

Raking a sneer over the demon dressed in black-on-black designer snobbery, Falcyn glanced to Urian. "So, Slim, who is *this* designer asshole?"

The demon quirked a grin at Falcyn's question. "That's Mr. Asshole to you, dragon."

"Sure, punkin. Whatever floats your shit."

Medea poked Falcyn on the shoulder before she rose up on her toes to whisper in his ear. "You might not want to antagonize him."

"Says the woman who knows me not at all. Trust me. I've pissed down the throats of monsters that make this posh-boy look even lamer than what he is. On my scared-o-meter, he doesn't even move the needle."

Kessar smiled grudgingly. "Which is why you've held your dragonstone longer than any other dragon in history. Now be a good boy, hand it over."

Falcyn snorted derisively as he raked a less-than-impressed stare over him. "Uh ... hell to the no."

A slow smile spread over Kessar's chiseled features but didn't quite reach his red eyes. "Give us the stone and I'll tell you how to save your sister."

Urian froze at those words. While it was true that the dragons had dozens of siblings, there was only one sister he knew they actually cared about.

The same one he did.

"My sister's dead. And if you pull a Narishka on me, I swear, demon, I'll eat your heart for lunch and burp it for dessert."

"I don't know what Narishka did, but your sister was turned to stone. So while she's not technically living, she's not exactly dead, either."

"Blaise? Did you know about this?"

"No. I was told she went down fighting against Morgen."

Urian listened intently. Were they or were they not talking about Xyn?

Medea placed her hand on Falcyn's forearm in a comforting gesture before she leaned against his back. "Kessar is a treacherous bastard. Don't trust him. He wouldn't know the truth if it bit his furry little ass off."

She was right about that. It could be a trick.

Urian held his breath.

Falcyn curled his lip. "So posh-boy's the gallu leader the Sumerian gods turned against. Bet that ruined your day, huh?"

Kessar sneered. "You should know, son of Lilith."

Blaise sucked his breath in sharply between his teeth. "Never, ever . . . *ever* bring his mother into things. That's just a good way to get your ass kicked, as he tends to madly lash out whenever you mention she-who-should-never-be-named."

Falcyn gave the demon a wry grin. "You should listen to my brother, demon. At least I know my mother's name. Which is more than you do." He swept a grimace over Kessar. "And if you know that much about me, then you know who and what fathered me. So if I were you, I'd run before I decide to pull the wings off you for fun and pin you to a wall somewhere to throw darts at whenever I'm drunk."

Unperturbed, Kessar examined his claws. "Fine. I take it you've no interest in learning where they sent your sister?"

A slow, insidious smile spread over Falcyn's face. "Oh, I'll find her. As soon as I eat your brains and absorb the information."

Before Urian knew what he intended, Falcyn was on Kessar, tearing at his flesh. With an unholy growl, he snatched the demon's head back and would have ripped out his throat had Kessar not vanished.

Blood dripped from Falcyn's hands and chin as he sneered up at the dismal sky. "What? Was it something I said? Come back here, you pussy bastard! What kind of demon runs like a bitch over a small bite?"

Urian crossed his arms over his chest as he met Medea's shocked stare. "And now you know why I had my reservations about seeking out our not-so-friendly dragon for conversation. You just can't take him out in public. Or private either."

Falcyn licked the blood from his fingers.

Medea curled her lips in distaste. "They have these things called napkins, you know? Been around for thousands of years now. You should try one."

Wiping the blood from his lips with his knuckle, Falcyn grinned at her. "A squeamish Daimon? Seriously? Besides, I like the taste of my enemy's blood. It soothes me. Blood of my friends is even better, but they tend to get a little testy whenever I partake of my favorite delicacy."

Blaise sighed. "Really, we tried home training. He failed miserably. But he's awesome when you need someone killed and you don't have a place to hide a body. He eats all traces of it. Better than a pet Charonte demon."

With one last lick to his middle finger, Falcyn turned back to Blaise. "Can you transform?"

"Haven't tried. Why?"

"I can't."

Blaise looked sick to his stomach at that realization. After a second, he shook his head. "Why can't we turn?"

"That would be the disturbing question of the moment, wouldn't it?"

Urian laughed nervously. "How do we get back?"

"There's always a portal of some kind." Falcyn turned a slow, small circle as he surveyed the land around them. "We just have to figure out where it is and what it looks like. You know . . . fun shit that, always."

"Yeah. Lots of fun." Urian's voice dripped with sarcasm. "And avoid stray magick and demons."

"And everything else," Medea added.

"Exactly what she said," Falcyn muttered under his breath.

"So glad I got up this morning." Blaise sighed heavily. "Hell, I even bathed."

Falcyn passed a smug sneer at him. "So glad I'm stuck here with all of you. Bitching and moaning."

"Blaise?" Medea whispered suddenly.

"Yeah ... I feel it."

Medea's dark eyes met his. "What is it?"

"Not sure." Falcyn saw nothing around them.

Suddenly, Urian heard it. A mere wisp of breath. So low as to be virtually inaudible.

With lightning reflexes honed by battle, Falcyn reached out and grabbed their pursuer.

"I mean you no harm!" The sound of a woman's voice shocked him.

Falcyn tightened his grip on what felt like a throat. "Show yourself."

She materialized in his grip. Large lavender eyes swallowed a face that appeared more girl than woman, and yet the fullness of her leather-wrapped body said that she was well into her twenties. Physically, anyway.

"What are you?"

She rubbed at his wrist to remind him that his death grip was cutting off her ability to speak. Another action that said she was older than a frightened teen.

Falcyn relaxed his hold, but not enough to allow her to escape. "I'm Brogan."

"Didn't ask your name. Don't really care. I asked *what* you are."

"Cursed. Exiled and damned. Please, let me go and I can help you."

She was hedging and Urian didn't like it. Creatures who played games usually had something to hide.

"Why?" Falcyn demanded.

"Why should you let me go? So that I can breathe."

Falcyn ground his teeth. "No, why should we trust you to help us?"

"Because I want out of here more than anything, but I lack the powers to break the seal or bargain for freedom. If you take me with you, I'll show you where a portal is."

Still suspicious, he released her. "And again, I ask what you are."

"A kerling Deathseer."

Falcyn conjured up a ball of fire and held it so that she knew her own death was imminent. "Deathseer or seeker?"

Urian agreed with that question, as there was a big difference between them. A seer saw death. A seeker caused it.

Holding her hands up, she stepped back from him. *"Seer,"* she said quickly, letting him know that she got the less-than-veiled threat in his actions. "Though ofttimes the Black Crom uses me to find his victims."

"And why is that?"

"I was sold to him for such."

Falcyn moved to kill her, but Blaise caught his arm.

"Don't hurt her."

Aghast, he stared at him. "Are you out of your mandrake mind?"

Blaise snorted. "All the time. But not about this." He held his hand out to the petite brunette. "Come, Brogan. I won't let him harm you."

Letting the fire in his hand die out, he scowled at Blaise. "Can you see her at all?"

Blaise shook his head. "I can only hear her voice. Why?"

Because she was exquisitely beautiful. Her long dark brown hair that had escaped her tight braids made perfect spirals around her elvish features and pointed ears. Enchanting features the fey often used to lure others to their doom. And that included her tight brown leather pants and corset that were covered by a flimsy green robe, and the fey stone necklace and diadem she wore.

But if Blaise couldn't see it, then it wasn't a trap for him.

"Why are you attracted to her?" Falcyn asked.

"Didn't say I was. I only hear the truth in her voice. She's not lying to us. So I think we should help her."

"And no good deed goes unpunished. You help her and you're likely to pay for it. In the worst way imaginable and at the worst possible time."

Blaise sighed heavily at Falcyn's mistrust, which had come from a lifetime of betrayal. "What I love most about you, Fal. Your never-ending optimism. It bowls me over."

For once, Urian was on Falcyn's side. He wouldn't be so quick to dismiss that sage advice. If he were Blaise, he'd be listening a little more closely.

Tucking down her gossamer wings so that they couldn't be seen, Brogan retrieved her knapsack. As she started past Falcyn, he stopped her. "You harm him ... or cause him to be harmed in any way—even a hangnail—and I will make sure you die in screaming agony."

Her eyes widened at his threat. "I see no death for him. You've no cause to threaten me on his behalf."

As she moved to walk beside Blaise, Medea dropped back to Falcyn's side. "What's a kerling?"

"A conjuring witch."

"That why you asked if she sought death?"

He nodded. "Kerlings can be a handful."

"Known many?"

"No, but I've killed my fair share."

Brogan gasped and glanced over her shoulder at Falcyn.

With a fake smile, he waved at her.

She let out a squeak and sidled closer to Blaise, who cast a fierce grimace in his direction. "What did you do?"

"I smiled."

"Ah, that explains it, then. It's such an unnatural act for you that you look like some questing beast whenever you try."

Falcyn screwed his face up as Blaise allowed the kerling to lead them.

They walked on while Urian listened to them bantering and tried to figure out if there was any truth to Xyn being alive. Or was it an elaborate lie by Kessar?

Wouldn't be the first time the demon had done such treachery. And a person could go mad thinking about it.

Once they reached their cave, Urian used his powers to seal them in.

Out of patience, Urian turned to Brogan. "You think if I called for Acheron he might hear me and come to the rescue?"

"You can try." Falcyn waited.

After a few seconds of trying, Urian growled again. "It was worth a shot."

"Anyone know a dark elf?" Falcyn glanced to Blaise, who made it his habit to party with them.

"None that I want to call."

Falcyn lit the cave with his fireballs. "Too bad we don't have Cadegan here. A dark hole like this is right up his alley."

"Illarion's, too." Urian reminded Falcyn of his other brother.

Falcyn nodded.

Medea gave him an arch stare. "I would have thought you were at home here, too."

Falcyn grimaced. "Stop with the stereotypes. Not all dragons hibernate in closed quarters. I lived on an island, on top of ruins. In the open and quite happy not to be penned in. My brother Max lives in a bar."

"Aye to that," Blaise chimed in. "My home was a castle."

Brogan cocked her head. "Most of the dragons here are cave-dwellers. They fire our forges. The rest hide so as not to be enslaved."

Clearing her own throat, Brogan motioned toward the backside of the cave. "There should be a tunnel that leads toward the underground channels where we might be able to find a path to the porch."

"The porch?" Medea asked.

"Aye. It's the plateau where the elders meet to watch the other realms. There's a portal there."

"Why do they do that?"

Brogan scoffed at her question. "In case you haven't noticed, my lady, there's not a lot to do here, other than survive and make weaponry for the gods and fey beings. So the elder wyrdlings look out, pick a happy mortal, and ruin their lives. For fun and wagering."

Medea gaped. "You're serious?"

Her features grim, Brogan nodded. "They call it the yewing. The mortal is randomly selected and his or her fate is up to whatever lot they draw from their skytel bag while they're watching them. They think it entertaining."

"I knew it!" Blaise growled. "I knew my life was nothing but a sick joke to the fey. And all of you said I was crazy." When no one commented, he drew up sullenly. "Well, you did. And I *was* right."

Falcyn snorted. "Anyway, let's find this porch and see if we can locate the portal back home."

Medea asked, "Can't we just teleport to the portal?"

Brogan shook her head. "I wouldn't advise it. Those powers tend to attract unwanted attention in this realm. The less magick used that they're unfamiliar with, the safer you'll be."

As they walked, Brogan drifted back to Medea's side. "They called you a Daimon?"

"Sort of."

"I don't know your species. Are you like the fey?"

"My people were created by the Greek god Apollo and then cursed by him."

"Why?"

Why indeed. That had been the question that had galled her the whole of her exceptionally long life as she explained it to the girl.

Medea sighed as she was driven against her will to remember the tragedy of her mother's mortal fate. Head over heels in love as a girl, she'd married Apollo's son without hesitation. And then pregnant with her, her mother had been forced to divorce Medea's father or see herself raped and murdered by the vengeful god.

Leaving her father had emotionally destroyed her mother. Had killed something deep inside her that hadn't come alive again until the day they'd reunited.

Centuries after Stryker had married and raised another family with another wife—Urian's surrogate mother.

And thus had begun the curse of her people as Stryker had made a bargain with an Atlantean goddess to save his family from his father's curse.

"That's horrible!" Brogan breathed as she finished the story.

"It is, indeed."

All of them had been damned by the god's anger for something they'd had no part in or any ability to stop.

"I'm so sorry, Medea."

She shrugged. "I got over it. Besides, I was six when he cursed us. I barely remember life before that day."

"You don't eat food?"

She shook her head.

Brogan fell silent for a moment. "But if you were to die at twenty-seven and you're not a Daimon now, how is it that you're still alive?"

"A bargain my mother made for my life."

Sadness turned her eyes a vivid purple. "Tell me of a mother who so loves her child. Is she beautiful? Wondrous?"

Medea nodded. "Beyond words." She pulled the locket from her neck and held it out to Brogan so that she could see the picture she had of her mother. "Her name is Zephyra."

"Like the wind?"

"Yes. Her eyes are black now, but when I was a girl, they were a most vivid green."

Brogan fingered the photo with a sad smile tugging at the edges of her lips. "You admire her."

"She's the strongest woman I've ever known. And I love her for it."

Closing the locket, she handed it back to Medea. "She looks like you."

"Thank you. But I think she's a lot more beautiful." Medea returned it to her neck. "What of your mother?"

A tear fell down her cheek. "My mother sold me to the Black Crom when I was ten-and-three. If she ever loved me, she never once showed it."

"I'm sorry."

Wiping at her cheek, she drew a ragged breath. "It's not so bad. She sold my siblings to much worse. At least I had Sight. Had I been born without anything, my fate would have been. . . . " She winced as if she couldn't bring herself to say more about it.

"What exactly is the Black Crom?" Medea asked, trying to distract her from the horror that lingered in the back of those lavender eyes.

"A headless Death Rider who seeks the souls of the damned or the cursed."

Medea jumped at Falcyn's voice in her ear.

"A kerling can sing to them to offer up a sacrifice before battle. Or summon them for a particular victim."

"Can," Brogan said, lifting her chin defiantly. There was something about her, fiery and brave. "But I don't. I hate the Crom. He springs from Annwn to claim the souls of his victims with a whip made from the bony spines of cowards. He rides a pale horse with fiery eyes that can incinerate the guilty and inno-cent alike should they happen upon him while he rides. None are safe in his path. To the very pit with him. I've no use for the likes of that beast. You've no idea what it's like to live in its shadow. Subject to its pitiless whims."

Though she'd just met her, Medea felt horrible for the woman. "Can you be freed?"

She shook her head. "Not even death can free me as I am bound to him for all eternity. What's done is done."

Suddenly, Brogan stopped moving.

Medea became instantly nervous at a look she was starting to recognize. "Is something wrong?"

"We're approaching the porch," she whispered.

"Is that bad?"

Urian gave her a droll stare.

She didn't answer the question except to say, "The Crom is here."

Urian looked up at her words to see the massive glowing horseman. At first, he appeared headless. Until one realized that his head was formed by mist at the end of the spiny whip he wielded as he rode. The white horse was giant in size ... almost as large as a Mack truck. An awful stench of sulfur permeated the cavern, choking them and sticking in their throats as if it had been created from thorns.

Even more disconcerting, the baying horse made the sound of twenty echoing beasts. And its hooves were thunderous—like an approaching train.

"I won't do it!" Brogan shouted. "I refuse you!"

The horse reared as the Crom cracked its whip in the air. Fire shot out from the whip's tip as more thunder echoed.

Unfazed and with fists clenched at her sides, Brogan stood stubbornly between them and the Crom. "Beat me all you like. I will not give you that power. Not again! Not over my new-found friends!"

"What's going on?" Medea asked.

Brogan kept her gaze locked stubbornly on her master. "He wants the ability to speak. But if I give it to him, then he can call out your name and claim your soul to take it with him to hell. And I will not allow it."

With a long, bony finger, he pointed at Brogan.

She shook her head at him. "Then take me, if you must. I'm all you'll be getting today! I won't let you have them! You hear me? No more!"

He charged at her.

In an act of absolute bravery, she stood her ground without flinching.

Blaise caught her an instant before the Crom would have mowed her down. Lifting her in his arms, the mandrake whirled her past the razor-sharp, blood-encrusted hooves that were mired with the remnants of the Crom's past victims.

Urian went charging in to cover them with Falcyn by his side.

Rolling her eyes at their brave stupidity since none of them were armed, Medea joined their cause. She manifested her sword and twirled it around her body. Urian unleashed his fireballs while she watched the fey creature turn around for another pass.

It started for them.

Until it saw her sword.

With one last shrieking cry, it vanished in a puff of pungent green smoke.

What the hell was that?

"Okay ... that was effing weird. Where did he go?" She glanced around, half-expecting him to manifest behind them. "What just happened?"

Brogan inclined her head to Medea's sword. "'Tis the gold of your blade and hilt. It's his weakness. With that, you could have maimed him."

Medea gaped at her. "You couldn't have told me that before he charged?"

"Wasn't allowed to say it until you found it on your own. I'm forbidden to."

"Well, that just sucks!"

Brogan smiled. "For me more than you, my lady. Believe me."

She had a point.

And Blaise had yet to set her back on her feet. In fact, he seemed reluctant to let her go.

"My lord?" Brogan blushed profusely.

Blaise hesitated. "Not sure I should let you down. You seem to keep finding trouble whenever I do."

Falcyn glared at them. "Blaise! Set her down! Now!"

Medea popped him on the arm as Brogan appeared stricken by his sharp tone. "What is your problem?"

Falcyn gestured at Brogan. "He doesn't know where she's been."

"Oh my God, Falcyn! He's not some two-year-old child and she's not a piece of candy he found on the floor that he stuck in his mouth!"

"Well, that's how he's acting. He looks at her like he could eat her up."

"And you're acting like a baby. Get over it. He's a grown dragon. He's allowed be nice to any woman he wants to. *Without* your permission or approval, you know?"

Falcyn's nose actually twitched and flared. "Doesn't mean I have to like it." He groused like that two-year-old she'd just mentioned.

Blaise rolled his eyes and shook his head. "He always acts like an old woman. I'm used to it."

Brogan laughed as Blaise finally set her back on her feet, but he kept her tucked by his side.

Before she could ask about it, Brogan drew their attention to the stones that, when they stepped back, Urian realized formed a half-broken demonic face suspended on pedestals over a deep, fiery abyss.

"Well, that's different." And the dais was impossible to reach ...

Medea arched a brow. "I take it that's the portal we're looking for?"

Brogan nodded. Her mood now was subdued and quiet. Gone was any hint of the playful sprite she'd been a few seconds ago.

Medea cast a dry stare to Falcyn. "This is when having a flying dragon would come in handy."

Falcyn snorted. "So would rope ... and a gag."

Medea swept a hot, seductive glance over his long, lush body. "A rope and a gag come in handy for *lots* of things, princess," she said suggestively.

Urian curled his lip. "Ew! Hey, brother over here and I do not approve of this entire line of conversation with my sister! Back to a G rating, folks."

Laughing, albeit a bit nervously, Brogan started toward the platform. She'd only taken a step before a light flashed and smoke exploded in front of them—this realm seemed to like that a lot. Apparently, the entire place had once doubled as a stage show for an Ozzy tour.

The peculiar portal in front of them churned into action, spinning and turning like a rusted nickelodeon. Light shot out from the demon's mouth and eyes, with a blinding intensity. Symbols twisted around it in a frenetic ballet that was painful to watch.

And out of that madness came more smoke and mist. As if an angry beast snorted at them with a furious hatred. Spiraling up and dancing to a jerky beat, the mist solidified into the shape of a tall hooded beast.

No, not a beast.

A man.

Urian hadn't seen a copián in a long, long time. At least not one who looked like that. At first glance, they looked more like a wizard of some kind. Or shaman. Indeed, his flowing feathered robes and chains, along with the braided black hair and the huge, elaborate raven-skull headdress, would have lent itself to that assumption. Especially since bells chimed as he moved and he held a blood-red torch staff in his left hand. One that belched more fire and smoke as it shot arcing balls of light upward around his head.

Yet they were far more powerful and ancient.

Timeless.

As he turned to face them, Urian saw that he'd painted a thick black band over his golden eyes that made their unusual color more vibrant. He stepped down the dais with the grace of a man half his age. And when he neared them, he flexed his dark gray gloved hand that held the staff, digging the wooden claws that were affixed to his fingertips into its leather-wrapped shaft. His gaze bored into them with the wisdom of the ages, and with the sharpness of daggers. As if he were cleaving secrets from their very souls.

"Kerling," he growled in the gruffest of tones. "What is this?"

Brogan curtsied to him. "They were brought here against their wills, copián. They don't belong in this realm. I seek to send them on their way."

A deep, fierce scowl lined his brow. The red light of his torch flared again and turned blue.

Confused, Medea leaned toward Falcyn. "What's a copián?"

"Hard to explain. They're time wardens and keepers of the portals."

She scowled. "Why don't we have one for the bolt-holes in Kalosis, then?"

"You do," the copián said, telling her what Urian already knew. "Braith, Verlyn, Cam, and Rezar were the first of our kind. They set the perimeters for the worlds and designed the portal gates between them. It's how they trapped Apollymi in her realm—by her own blood and design. It's why her son is the only one who can free her from her realm where she was imprisoned by her own sister and brother for crimes they imagined that she never committed."

Because Apollymi was the ancient goddess Braith. One of the very gods who'd first set the gates.

Another reason she sat at her pool and why Xyn had been put there as one of her servants and guardians.

Brogan gestured toward them. "As you can see, their presence disturbs the balance. This isn't their world and they shouldn't be here. We have to return them before they're discovered by the others."

Two lights shot out of his torch. They streaked up like the stray magick blasts had done earlier and circled around the old copián to land on each side of him. There they twisted up from the floor to create two tall, lean linen-wrapped plague doctors. With wide-brimmed cavalier hats, they stared out from their long-beaked, black linen masks from shiny ebony eyes. Soulless eyes that appeared to be bleeding around the corners. It was an eerie, macabre sight.

"What are those?" Medea asked.

Falcyn leaned down to whisper, "Zeitjägers."

"What do they do?"

"Guard time. But mostly they steal it."

She frowned. "How do you steal time?"

Falcyn laughed. "You ever been doing something ... look up and it's hours later and you can't figure out where the time went 'cause it feels like you just sat down?"

She nodded.

"Zeitjägers," he said simply. "Insidious bastards. They took that time from you and bottled it for their own means."

"Why?"

"So that we can sell it." The copián glanced to his companions. "Time is the most precious commodity in the entire universe. The most sacred. And yet it is the most often squandered. From the moment of our births, we're only allotted so much of it. And for even an hour more, there are those who are willing to give up anything for it." An evil smile curled his lips. "Even their immortal souls."

Urian shook his head at the truth.

The copián stepped down to approach Medea. "Surely a child of the Apollite race can understand that driving desperation better than most."

He was right about that. Nothing like being damned to only twenty-seven years for something you didn't do to make someone realize just how precious life was.

Even more so while watching everyone around you die long before their time.

For one more breath, their race was willing to take human lives and destroy their immortal souls. Unlike Urian, Medea's one saving grace was that her mother had sacrificed her own soul to save her from having to make that choice.

She'd never had to live like Urian and his siblings had. Medea had never made the hard choices they did.

The copián cocked his head. "You've heard the expression 'living on borrowed time'?"

"Yeah."

He gave Medea a crooked smile. "We're the ones you borrow it from."

But only an idiot played their game. Urian had heard too many horror stories about those who'd bargained with them and been burned.

There was never any such thing as a free lunch, and when you bargained with the paranormal, you always came up with the short end of the stick for it. The deck was stacked against you and they played with loaded dice.

The copián swept his sinister gaze over them. "My price is simple. An hour from each of you and I'll open the portal."

"An hour?" Falcyn sputtered. "How 'bout I just rip some heads off all y'all until you yield?"

Urian liked that idea.

The copián smirked. "You could do that, but you can't open the portal without me."

"Sure I could find someone."

"You really want to chance it?"

Falcyn's expression said he was willing to gamble.

The copián tsked at him. "So very violent from an immortal who can spare an hour with no problem whatsoever. Think of it like those humans who donate spare change for charity. An hour is but a penny and you have a jar full of them just sitting in your home that you'll never use. Why not give one to someone who could really use it?"

"Because you're assuming they'll use it for good, when I know for a fact that most people who barter with you don't have kindness in their hearts."

"True, but sometimes that trash they take out on their way to the grave is a service in and of itself, is it not?" He cast a pointed stare toward Urian.

You son of a whore. Urian could have done without that dig.

Blaise sucked his teeth in sharply. "Word of advice when dealing with these two? I wouldn't go for the twofers on the insults. Even with the zeitjägers as backup. I mean, let's face it. They're not being peaceful at the moment because they don't know how to be violent ... however, I'll be the first to say have at it if you can get us out of here. You can take two hours from me."

The copián scowled at Blaise. "Two?"

"Yeah. One for me and one for Brogan. I'll pay her fee."

She gasped at his offer. "Why would you do that?"

Blaise shrugged. "Being stuck here has been punishment enough for you. As noted, I won't miss two hours out of my life. I'd have just wasted them in a movie theater, anyway. And this way, I get to do something useful with them and be a hero to you. That's a twofer I can live with." He winked at her. "Besides, I don't intend to leave here without you."

"Suck-up, show-off," Falcyn muttered. Then louder, "Fine, take mine."

"So how do you take this time from us?" Medea glanced back to the zeitjägers.

The copián laughed. "It's already gone. As I said, you don't even miss it. You didn't even know we did it."

Falcyn leaned down to whisper in her ear. "Told you. Insidious bastards."

The copián walked toward the portal and lifted his staff up. The moment he did, the portal came alive with swirling, vibrant colors. He moved his staff through it until the mist began to mimic his movements.

Red fire shot out from the torch and was absorbed by the mist. "It's ready."

Urian grinned at Medea. For the first time in a long while, he enjoyed being the little brother. "Ladies first."

She rolled her eyes. "Like you'd know if I didn't make it."

"You might be polite and scream ... then again, it is you. Maybe Blaise should go first? I know he'd scream to warn us."

He turned an angry glare to Falcyn. "I thought you weren't going to tell anyone about my screaming fits?"

"I didn't. That was Max who outed you."

"Oh. ... Remind me to kill him later." Blaise headed for the portal. "Fine, I'll go through first."

Brogan took his hand. "I'll go with you."

Urian followed them into the stinging vortex. Damn it, he'd always hated stepping through one of these gates. They were similar to the one for Kalosis and Katateros.

Like him, Blaise held one of the keys that enabled the man-drake to travel to and from the veil world where the sorceress Merlin had pulled Avalon and Camelot out of time and place, so that she could protect the other worlds and realms from Morgen's evil.

Once more, Urian found himself landing on hard, crappy ground.

Falcyn landed a few feet away. "Blaise? You dead?"

"No." He didn't sound like he was in any better shape than Falcyn, though.

"Good. I want the pleasure of killing you myself, you bastard!"

Blaise snorted.

"Don't scoff, dragon." Urian was every bit as peeved. "Soon as I can move again, I intend to help with your murder and dismemberment."

Falcyn turned his head to the right, where Medea lay a few feet away from his side, unmoving on the grass. "Medea?"

She finally lifted a hand to brush her hair from her face. "Not dead, either."

"Brogan?"

"Just wishing I were." Shifting her legs, she made no move to rise. Rather she seemed content to lie on her back, staring up at the dismally gray sky. "Is it always this miserable to travel in such a manner?"

Blaise sighed. "Pretty much. Least I didn't slam into an invisible force field this time."

Rolling over, Falcyn pushed himself into a sitting position, then scowled as he caught sight of the dark, twisted trees around him. Trees that lined an equally screwed-up, bleak landscape.

"Hey, Blaise ... Why the hell are we in Val Sans Retour?"

Yeah. Urian rose slowly.

Sitting up immediately, Medea scowled. "The what?"

Falcyn let out another groan before he answered. "The Valley of No Return. So named because no one ever comes out of here *alive*. Like Blaise ... because I really am going to kill him as soon as I find my strength."

"Not true!" Blaise stood and took a defensive position. "I came out alive a few years back when I was here."

Falcyn made a rude noise at the reminder of the mandrake's less-than-stellar adventure.

Medea stood up and brushed herself off. "Did you?"

"Yeah."

His anger rising, Falcyn went to the mandrake. "But *why* are we here now, Blaise? How did we get here?"

Blaise quirked a sarcastic smirk. "Did you sleep through the part where we stepped into a magick portal and were sucked through a vortex?"

"Don't make me beat you with my shoe."

"Well, I'm just wondering. 'Cause you asked. I mean, you were there, were you not? You didn't miss that rather large, ghastly light we stepped into, did you?"

"Yeah, but I have a head injury right now. Maybe a concussion. Thinking some kind of serious brain damage. Definitely trauma of some sort. And a migraine the size of *you*."

Urian broke off Falcyn's tirade by jerking on his sleeve to get his attention so that he could show him the man who was quickly approaching their group.

"Who's that?"

Urian shrugged. "Don't know, but she seems to know him."

By the look on Blaise's face, he did, too.

And they weren't friends.

Falcyn narrowed his gaze on him. "Blaise?"

A tic started in his jaw. "I know that essence when I feel it. It's—"

"My brother Brandor!" Brogan shot to her feet and ran to him.

A tic started in the mandrake's jaw. "Are they kissing?"

Medea screwed her face up. "No, but she is hugging him like she hasn't seen him in a really, *really* long time."

Falcyn cocked his head. "Does kissing his cheek count?"

Medea popped him on the stomach as Blaise's expression turned into one of extreme pain. "That's mean! Don't torture the poor mandrake!"

With a fierce grimace, Falcyn and Urian stepped around her to confront Brogan and Brandor. "What's going on here?"

Brandor, who was the same height as Falcyn, put himself between Brogan and them. Even though his clothes were ragged and it was obvious he hadn't been living well, he kept one arm on Brogan as if to protect her while he braced his body to confront them.

Extremely tall, he had chiseled handsome features.

Yeah, the fey and demons had a lot in common.

His long, wavy black hair was matted from having been living in the woods on his own. Yet even so there was still rebellion in those hazel eyes that were so green they all but glowed with an unholy fire. By his predatorial stance, it was obvious he knew how to fight and wasn't afraid to bleed.

When he finally spoke, his words shocked Urian.

"I had Brogan bring you here so that I could speak with you."

"Excuse me?"

Brandor tensed, watching them for any hint of a coming attack. "I know you don't trust me. You've no reason to."

Brogan finally stepped away from him. She cast a sheepish glance toward Blaise. "I told you it could have been much worse. My brother's life makes a mockery of mine and my sisters' combined. To protect me from their fate, Bran gave up the bulk of his powers at puberty—transferred them to me so that I'd be stronger and have more value."

Sadness darkened Brandor's eyes. "I've been trying to help Ro for a long time."

"So what news do you have to share?" Medea asked.

"Apollo's after the goddess Apollymi and intends to use her army of Charonte to kill Acheron and take over the world and Olympus."

Urian scowled. That was all well and good, except for one thing. "And the Daimons protecting Apollymi?"

"Apollo has sent a plague to kill them and the gallu to punish them for their rebellion against him."

He looked over at his sister. Well, that explained the foreign illness that was tearing through their ranks. No wonder they couldn't fight it off.

Falcyn scratched at his chin. "Why do they want my dragonstone?"

"It's the only thing that can stop them."

"Yeah, well, they can rot." Falcyn shook his head. "I'm not about to help any of them."

Brandor gave him an arch stare. "Not even to save your own sister?"

Urian's heart skipped a beat at the mention of Xyn.

That cold steel hatred returned to Falcyn's eyes. "Don't go there."

Brandor glanced to Brogan. "I would never taunt anyone with such a cruelty. Family should never be used as a bartering tool. But it's what they will hold over you and use against you if you don't do what they want. It's why I told Ro to bring you here. I know where Sarraxyn is, and I will take you to her before they hurt her to get to you."

At the confirmation that he'd been too afraid to ask, Urian felt his knees go weak.

Xyn was alive.

For a moment he couldn't breathe. Those words slammed into him like a physical blow and left him reeling. Dear gods, was it true?

Even now, he could see her beautiful face. So much so that he barely registered their words.

"For what price?" Falcyn asked.

He took his sister's hand. "You've already paid it. You freed my sister from her realm and brought her to me so that I can protect her from her master. I'll help you free yours from hers. It's the least I can do."

Blaise shook his head. "Bullshit. I don't believe you."

Brogan's cheeks brightened with color. "You can trust him, Blaise. He's a good man."

"I don't trust anyone."

Urian sighed as he cast his gaze around each of them. "Yeah, I don't think anyone in this group can judge another for their past deeds." And he damn sure wasn't about to let them not give this bastard a shot if he really did have a way to free Xyn.

If there was any chance to see her again ...

He wanted it.

"This is all well and good, but let's not lose sight of the fact that

Urian and I aren't here on a vacation. I need your dragonstone, Falcyn. There's still the matter of the plague that's spreading through my people. I can't watch my parents and best friend die. I've had enough of death and I don't want any more of it."

Brandor scowled at her. "You're the daughter of Stryker?"

"How do you know that?"

"Apollo."

Falcyn narrowed his eyes on Brandor. "How much have you heard?"

"Everything."

"Well, if you know so much, any idea why we can't turn into dragons right now?"

"No, sorry."

"Blaise? Can you open the portal out of here?"

"My key doesn't work here."

Falcyn looked at him. "Urian?"

He made the sound of a warning buzzer. "Try again, Ringo."

Without a word to them, Blaise headed for the trees. "Sylph?"

One of the reddish-brown trees in a twisted form awakened to look at them. Blaise jumped away with a curse.

"What is it?" Urian asked.

Transforming into a bleeding, demonic body, the sylph advanced on them with a round of cursing and hissing.

Blaise turned pale before he grabbed Brogan to pull her back from the tree. "She's a gallu! Run!"

Light and sound exploded all around. It was as if the entire forest had come alive to consume them. Or at least tear them down. Everything was blowing up like some kind of sick heavy-metal light show.

They scattered into the fields.

For hours Urian and Blaise, with Brogan and Bran, searched for Falcyn and Medea. And as every minute passed, he worried more about Medea being alone with Falcyn. Though to be honest, he didn't know what concerned him most.

The fact that they might get along.

Or that they might kill each other.

But the one thing that weighed heaviest in his thoughts . . .

"Brandor?"

"Aye?"

"What you said about Xyn? Is it true? Is she a statue?"

He looked offended by Urian's question. "Why would I lie about that?"

"To manipulate Falcyn."

Blaise slowed as the air around him became statically charged. "That's not why you're asking, Daimon."

Urian threw up his own shields to keep the dragon from reading his thoughts.

But it was too late, judging by the intensity of Blaise's stare. "Why did you never tell us that you knew her?"

Urian flinched at the way he said *knew*. "To what purpose? I thought she was . . . " He couldn't say the word "dead." The pain was too much for it, even now.

Brogan reached out to touch Urian's arm. "You love her."

"It was a long time ago."

"Time doesn't harm love. Love conquers all."

Urian scoffed. "Love doesn't conquer all. Only a quick sword does that."

Brogan wrinkled her nose at him. "You can't lie to a kerling, my sweet. We see straight through you." She glanced over to her brother. "And Brandor isn't lying. I would tell you if he were. Especially about this. No one should hurt for love."

Urian inclined his head respectfully to her. She had a beautiful heart, and those things were rare enough that he knew to cherish the few people who managed to have them. "Thank you."

Even so, Urian was afraid to let himself hope. To dream. He'd lived so long now without either that he didn't know how to anymore.

He'd learned to function in a state of comfortably numb where nothing touched him anymore. As he often joked with Davyn, "Behold my fallow fields of the fucks I do not give."

Yeah, that was his current real estate, and he liked that address where pain didn't reside within him. Where agony didn't claim a permanent part of his soul.

And yet, even now if he closed his eyes, his skin tingled from the sweetest memories of Xyn's touch. His heart lightened at the prospect of hearing her laughter.

Seeing her vibrant green eyes light up when she saw him.

No one had ever made him feel like she did.

Strange how all the women of his life had played vastly different roles. Xanthia had used and kicked him. Sheba had treated him like a pet to be pampered and played with. Phoebe had loved and needed him and been dependent on him for her very survival. She had made him feel like some mythic hero.

And Xyn? She had stood at his side as an equal warrior. She had been his best friend.

He'd loved them all, but only Xanthia had ever taught him animosity because of her treachery and betrayal.

Brogan took his hand. "Are you all right?"

Urian swallowed hard against the raw fear and hope that choked him. Honestly? He hadn't been all right in a long time. And this new surge of bullshit after having buried his emotions for so long was really the last thing he needed. Especially right now. But he wasn't one to confide his feelings to anyone. Never mind someone he just met. "Sure."

The light in her eyes said that she knew better. Still, she smiled kindly. "If you say so." Squeezing his hand, she returned to Blaise to help him walk.

And Urian moved to stand near Brandor and keep him from harming Blaise for being so close to his sister. "I know, brother. Just remember, when we find Medea and Falcyn, you have to return the favor before I rip the dick off that bastard."

Brandor choked. "Pardon?"

"You heard me. Every time Falcyn looks at her, it takes everything I have not to do something completely suicidal."

*F*etch me Maddor. I don't care what whore you have to pry him off, bring him to me within the quarter hour or it's your balls I'll be dining on!" The fey bitch shoved him away, then headed away.

The captain of the guards turned on his companions with a hiss. "You heard her! Fetch the mandrake!"

"Fuck you." Varian du Fey slid his knife straight into the lung of the bastard in front of him and held him upright until he stopped struggling. Only then did he use his powers to remove all traces of the fey's existence.

"Damn, V. That's so cold."

Wiping the blood off on the sleeve of his jerkin, he sneered at his hellhound companion. "Oh, like you wouldn't have bitten his throat out, then licked your own balls."

"Probably the former, but never the latter. Too many others willing to do that for me." Kaziel grinned at him. "At any rate, killing an Adoni on an errand for your mother seems a bit reckless when we're supposed to be keeping a low profile. And to think Aeron and Nick accuse *me* of being rash."

"You *are* rash, my friend. So rash, it's actually creeping down your neck."

"Those are the hives I get from being this close to you when you're doing something profoundly stupid." Kaziel glanced down the hallway to make sure no one else was around. "Damn shame to be this near to your mother and she didn't recognize you."

"You've no idea. But I wouldn't put anything past her. The main thing for now is that we find Blaise and let him know what's going on. You go find them."

Kaziel hesitated. "What about you?"

"We still need more information. I'm after the dragons to see why my mother was so insistent on them, and especially Maddor. That's not like her. Which means there's something peculiar there and I intend to find out what."

Kaziel inclined his head to him. As he started away, Varian grabbed his wrist and pulled him into a dark alcove.

They'd barely vanished into the curtained shadows before two men came down the hallway, grumbling. They paused right in front of their hiding spot so that they could examine each other. "You don't think we're infected, do you?"

The dark-haired fey bit his lip. "I hope not. They're feeding the infected to the gallu."

Cursing, they went on their way.

Varian didn't move for several heartbeats as he digested that news. "Damn you, Apollo."

Something cold brushed against Varian. Quicker than he could think, he drew his dagger and lunged.

The shadow beside him solidified into a man who quickly disarmed him and tsked. "Careful, coz. I require dinner before someone daggers me."

He rolled his eyes at the shadowborn demon who had eyes of steel. And like his very soul, his shoulder-length hair that he wore pulled back into a short ponytail was neither light nor dark, but strands of varying shades that were trapped squarely between his two dueling natures. Shadow was fearless as a rule, and he was the most evil thing that stalked the darkness and called the deadliest night home. "Careful, demon. You tread on treacherous ground to be sneaking up on me."

"Sorry about that. But I'm here to let you know Apollo's closing the noose around the dragons, trying to get the dragonstone before Helios. Otherwise, all is lost."

"I already knew that."

Shadow growled at him. "I saved your life. Let's not forget the good part."

"Are you done harassing me?"

"Not even close." He flashed a cocky grin at Varian. "I'm also here for your portal key."

Varian laughed. Until he realized it wasn't a joke. "Are you crazy?" Without a key, he'd be trapped here.

"Probably. But our friends have no way to walk through the portals, back to their world."

"Can't you get them through on your own?"

He shook his head. "Shadow walkers can only pass through alone. Without a key, they'd be trapped and forced to wave at me on the other side."

"Well, that sucks."

"More than you know." Shadow held his hand out. "Give it up."

Grumbling, Varian pulled the dragon key from around his neck and handed it over. "How am I supposed to get back?"

After pocketing the key, Shadow clapped him on the arm. "You're resourceful. Surely you'll think of something. I hear that you're good in a crisis."

"You're such a bastard."

"'Course I am. Suckled on the tit of all evil itself."

There was never any shaming the rank demon. He thrived on insults for some unknown reason.

Disgruntled and annoyed, Varian sighed. "And here I thought you were some master thief who could steal a key from anyone you wanted."

"I can. Unfortunately, they tend to miss such an item quickly and form a search party for it. Last thing we need is them finding our comrades before us. If Falcyn's stone falls into our enemies' hands . . ."

There was that.

And Varian's stomach tightened at the thought. Shadow was right and he knew it.

Which also made him think of something else. "Question?"

"Not an oracle, but you're free to attempt it."

"How is it the sharoc can't detect you?" Varian had a hard enough time eluding their detection whenever he ventured here on his missions. He'd never understood how Shadow managed it.

"You want secrets I'm unwilling to give." He passed a gimlet stare to Kaziel, who was being unusually quiet. "The two of you aren't the only ones with pasts you don't want disclosed." And with that, he vanished.

Kaziel crossed his arms over his chest. "You trust him?"

"I don't trust anyone, other than my wife and children, but he's never given me a specific reason not to. Why?"

"Just thinking of something Aeron always says. I'd sooner trust my enemy than a friend, as I can afford to lose an enemy.

But killing a friend over betrayal burns twice as deep and thrice as long."

"Your point?"

"No point, really. Just something about that demon makes my hackles rise."

Varian couldn't agree more. "Don't worry. Like you, my bite is much worse than my bark." And he'd taken enough lives to prove it. If Shadow betrayed them, Varian would have no compunctions about laying open his throat.

Still, there was an evil presence here and for once it wasn't his mother.

No, this was something far more insidious. Like a blackness trying to devour the world. Like Níthöggur gnawing at the roots of Yggdrasill as he sought to free himself from his prison.

For now it was contained, but his gut said it wouldn't stay that way.

Kaziel scowled at him. "What's wrong?"

"Just a bad premonition."

"Of?"

"What the world would be like if we fail to stop Apollo."

Morgen *watched as* Apollo left her bed to dress. Exceptionally tall and golden fair from the top of his blond head all the way to his toes, he was exactly what one would expect of a god.

In and out of bed.

She pouted at him. "Why are you leaving?"

"It's taking too long to round up the dragon. I don't like this delay. We have to take care of this before Helios overthrows me and takes all my powers."

She scoffed at his concerns. "My men will handle it. They know better than to fail me."

He rinsed his mouth out and spat before he turned toward her, patting his chin dry. "And I know my son. He was ever resourceful. Not to mention, that bitch he serves. Apollymi hates me with a passion. As do her two sons. It took me too long to escape her after that bastard Styxx gift-wrapped me and handed me over. I have a staggering debt to repay them all."

"*Two* sons? I thought her one and only son was dead."

"I wish." He let out a bitter laugh. "Nay, my evil fey queen. Not dead. Acheron is hers by birth and conception. Brought back to life by my idiot of a twin sister who wanted to fuck him, and instead screwed the rest of us by her insatiable appetite for an ex-human whore. As for Styxx, he belongs to Apollymi by adoption. To that end, you can count my son as well. Indeed, she oft mothers Stryker more than she does her own."

"Really ... Any other brats I need know about?"

He dropped the towel and reached for his pants to pull them on. "You could almost count the Malachai. He is a direct descendent of her firstborn. Granted, a thousand times removed. And Urian. She pampers and protects him as well."

Five sons for Apollymi ...

Morgen rose up to lean against him. "Does she consider the current Malachai as one of hers?"

"Not as far as I know. Her loyalty to that end seems to have died with her original son, Monakribos."

"And what of his father? Was Kissare not supposed to be reborn so that he could return to her?"

Apollo froze in the middle of buttoning his shirt. He blinked slowly before he answered. "He was, indeed." A slow, evil grin spread across his face. "Why, Morgen, dearest evil bitchtress, I do believe you've found something."

"So he was reborn?"

Laughing, Apollo pulled her naked body against his. "I don't know. But I know who will."

The Fates.

He didn't say it, but Morgen knew the answer as well as he did. Those three whores knew everything about everyone. They were the greatest gossiping bitches ever born!

"And if he does live," Apollo whispered against her lips, "we will find him and gut him at her feet!"

"I don't follow. Wouldn't that be a bit anticlimactic? What's the point?"

He kissed her lips. "The point is that the goddess of all destruction and darkness has only had three weaknesses in the whole of her life. Kissare, Monakribos, and Acheron." He nipped at her lips. "Given how frigid a bitch she is, I'm willing to bet that they had more in common than just their mother."

Morgen's eyes widened as she finally understood. "You're thinking that Acheron's father is Kissare reincarnated?"

He actually drew blood from her bottom lip with his fangs as he pulled back and nodded. "It would explain so much. ... Archon swore he would never father a child with her, and he went to his nebulous state claiming Acheron wasn't his son. Had Apollymi truly loved him, she would never have allowed Styxx to end him. God knows, she suffered much to protect Kissare and their offspring."

"Then who's Acheron's real father?"

"Only Apollymi knows."

Morgen smiled at this newfound knowledge and what it signified. "And the Fates."

"If they don't, they will learn it." He gave her one last kiss, then stepped away.

She frowned at his actions. "Where are you off to?"

"To find my demon. I have another errand for him."

S*hake that moneymaker,* baby! You go! Make that barrier pay! Kick it! Show us more biceps! Spank it till it bleeds! C'mon, you can do it. Pound it harder!"

Urian growled at Medea and her sexual harassment.

Falcyn turned around to glare at Medea as she sat on the ground beside Brogan and catcalled to them while he, Urian, Blaise, and Brandor sought some way to break through the barrier. Hands on hips, he narrowed his gaze at her. "Not helpful."

Medea put her hand up to her lips before she leaned closer to Brogan to whisper rather loudly. "Neither are their attempts, but notice it doesn't stop them from trying."

Brogan laughed.

Falcyn arched a brow at their misplaced humor. "Instead of heckling, woman, you could try helping."

She flashed a grin to expose a hint of fang. "I am helping. I'm giving you encouragement, dragonfly."

His jaw out of joint, he turned toward Urian. "Would you consider *this* encouraging?"

"Coming from my sister? Yeah. She's not throwing things at you or directly insulting us and our parentage. Hell of an improvement, you ask me. Makes me wonder what you've done to her that she actually located some semblance of humor."

Medea shot a blast at Urian, who deftly dodged it.

Laughing, he returned it with one of his own, knowing she wouldn't let it hit her.

"Hey!" Falcyn snapped, shoving Urian aside. "Play nice! You hurt your sister and I'll fry your ass. Ash or no Ash."

Medea righted herself from where she'd dove to miss Urian's blast. "You tell him, sweet cheeks."

Urian scowled. "Is she drunk?" He glanced back at Blaise and Brandor. "What did you throw on her again?"

"Water." Brandor wiped at his brow.

Yeah, that wasn't the way she was acting. Urian was beginning to think a pod person had kidnapped her.

Medea scoffed. "I'm fine. We're just enjoying the sight of male stubbornness at its prime best, and wondering at what point the lot of you will cede defeat." She glanced over to Brogan. "How long have they been pounding this poor defenseless shell now?"

"At least an hour." Brogan wrinkled her nose.

Blaise shot a sudden blast at it that recoiled and hit Brandor squarely in the chest. The blast knocked him back fifteen feet and sent him head over heels until he landed on his side in a smoking heap.

Medea burst out laughing again.

With a groan, he pushed himself into a seated position to glare at Blaise. "Really, mandrake? Really?"

Squeaking in fear for her brother, Brogan scrambled to her

feet to check on Brandor and to make sure he didn't attack Blaise out of anger over his indignity.

"You know, Falcyn," Medea taunted. "I think that puts the wall over for bonus points on all your sorry hides."

"At least we're doing something. You could try your hand at it, you know?"

"Why? It's obviously not budging. If sheer force of will could open it, I'd give it to you and it would have surrendered ten hours ago."

"*One* hour ago."

"Tomayto, tomahto." Leaning on her side, she propped her head on her hand. "I should go ahead and take a nap while the lot of you waste your time."

Urian was ignoring their sniping banter. At least until a sharp light almost blinded him.

Summoning a god-bolt, he was about to release it when the shadow took the form of a man he knew well. And one he trusted not at all.

The moment he saw the glow engulfing their hands, Shadow drew up short and set fire to his own hands as if to retaliate. "Whoa! Down, boy!"

"What are you doing here?"

After allowing the fire in his hands to go out, Shadow tugged one of the three amulets he wore about his neck over his head. "I have a present for you."

"It's a portal key," Blaise said instantly. "I can feel it on him."

"The mandrake would be correct. Varian sent me to escort the lot of you out of here."

"We need to get back to Sanctuary," Medea rose to her feet. "We've wasted enough time."

"First we have to free the dragons at Camelot," Blaise reminded her.

Yeah, Urian was definitely on Blaise's side with this one.

Medea rolled her eyes. "They're statues, right? Been that way for centuries. What's a few more days? Meanwhile my people are dying even as we speak. We need to save them!"

Blaise approached her with angry strides. He stopped right in front of her so that he could speak in sharp staccato beats. "If they free the dragons, they'll tear through your Daimons. They'll die anyway."

Brandor growled at her. "And Falcyn's sister is among those being held. She'll be the first slaughtered should she wake her. Would you condemn her, too?"

Urian's heart stopped at those words.

Shit. He was being asked to choose between Davyn and Xyn. He couldn't make that call.

If either died because of him, he'd never be able to live with himself.

Shadow frowned as he listened to them arguing. After a second round of their escalating pitches, he whistled. "While this argument is really unamusing and unproductive, and I couldn't care less about the outcome, I feel obligated to mention something you might find interesting." He waited until all of them were facing him before he spoke again. "Why would Maddor be summoned for *this*? Seems a massive waste of his talents, if you ask me."

The color faded from Falcyn's face. "What delusions are you suffering?"

"No delusions, friend. Right before I left, they sent a guard after him and I'm sure it wasn't for coffee or tea, or for an afternoon snack. They usually only call him out for war."

Medea cursed under her breath and turned to face Falcyn. "They're planning to use him to lure you, aren't they?"

Falcyn nodded. "So it's a trap."

"Urian?" She pulled the ring from her pinkie and held it out to him. "Go to Davyn and make sure he's all right. Tell him I'll be there with the dragonstone as soon as I can. Please keep him safe for me."

Yeah, right. And leave Xyn alone? Was she insane?

No chance in hell.

Falcyn gave her a puzzled stare. "What are you doing?"

"I'm not about to let you walk into that nightmare without

someone at your back. God or whatever you are, you'll still need some support."

"What about your people?"

"They're not my son. But Maddor is yours." Tears blurred her vision. "For *that,* we march to hell itself." Urian suddenly realized just how deep Medea's feelings were for Falcyn, and he honestly didn't know how to feel at that moment.

Falcyn stepped around her. "Shadow, get Urian back to Sanctuary. We'll—"

"Ah, no," Urian said, interrupting him. "We stay together." He wasn't going any place until he knew Xyn was safe.

Shadow grimaced. "Oh yeah, 'cause a large, unfamiliar motley group sneaking through a castle would *never* get noticed. By anyone. Or get reported. Sounds like a great suicide plan to me. So glad Varian volunteered me for this happy venture into torture and hell. Bastard fey rat that he is!"

Falcyn draped his arm over Medea. "You sure about this? Shadow's right. Heading in there with us isn't the sanest bet."

She nodded.

"All right then, demon, off to see what trouble we can find."

Shadow let out a fierce groan. "Why do I always end up with the crazy ones?"

Urian smirked. "Birds of a feather?"

Shadow didn't appear the least bit amused. "Now I remember why I don't like you." He swept his gaze to Blaise and Falcyn. "Any of you, as far as that goes."

With a deep breath, Shadow cracked his knuckles. "All right, kids. Last chance. Those who want a ticket to Sanity, raise your hand and we go out the portal to your home realm."

He waited a full minute before he let out an exaggerated groan. "Okay then, suicide it is. Buckle up, buttercups. Keep your hands inside the cart at all times and try not to get your heads chopped off. Thank you for choosing to ride the Grand Stupidity today, and for dragging me into this when I'd much rather be at home, sorting my dirty underwear and watching the grass grow."

"Oh, stop whining." Blaise clapped him on the arm. "You love the excitement."

"Yeah, you keep believing those lies, mandrake, and inhaling those fumes." Shadow manifested a long rope.

Medea frowned as he stepped toward Brogan with it. "What are you doing?"

He paused to give her an irritated grimace. "Well, punkin, if we march in through the front doors, your enemies will descend on us like vultures on nummy roadkill. And while I do have more stupidity than the average man and a certain flair for theatrics, I can really do without a thorough gutting. Fact is, I'm doing my best to avoid the experience for the entirety of my exceptionally long life." He knotted the rope around Brogan's waist.

"You plan to take us through the Shadows." Brogan's voice was scarcely more than a whisper.

He nodded. "If we teleport in, Morgen will know instantly. Only safe way in or out is through my realm."

Medea was even more confused as Shadow moved to loop and tie Brogan to Brandor. "And so I ask again ... why the rope?"

"Keeps you from getting lost in the dark, princess." Shadow moved next to Blaise.

Her heart stopped beating as she finally understood. "The thread between the worlds?"

Shadow nodded. "Home sweet fucking home. The rope is to keep anything from snatching one of you away from me while we move through it."

Because to get lost there was to never be seen again. The darkness was ever hungry and sought any nourishment it could find.

Life being its number one sustenance.

Shadow roped everyone together and then double-checked the knots to make sure everyone was linked together.

He then lifted his arm and drew a series of symbols, reminiscent of an orchestra conductor directing a band only he could hear, and began a melancholic humming from deep inside his chest, haunting and thrumming. He picked up the crescendo and as he did so, the air around them stirred.

One moment they were standing outside, and in the next they were in a blurry, swirling world of dark sepia. It was like being trapped inside an old nickelodeon machine. Everything had a jerky, surreal feel to it, leaving them disoriented and a bit queasy.

"It'll take a few minutes to get your bearings." Shadow's voice sounded as distorted as the scenery.

"Why is everything so weird here?" Brogan asked.

"You're in the lining of the worlds. Think of it like a hollow realm." Shadow held his left hand up and a small porthole appeared to show them a bright sunny park where children played a game of chase. "From here, you can venture anywhere. Past. Present. Future. In all the worlds." He closed the porthole and opened one on his right that showed a storming sea.

It was both beautiful and terrifying.

Shadow walked forward, leading them through his eerie domain.

Time truly had no meaning here, and they couldn't tell if they had been walking for minutes or days when Shadow suddenly stopped and let out a foul curse as the sound of a howling came through the air.

They all turned and could suddenly now make out the sounds of the Crom's horse as he rushed toward them.

And he wasn't alone.

What appeared to be a hundred shadow dogs followed in his wake, with their yellow eyes glowing.

Urian curled his lip at the sight of them.

Shadow handed the rope to Falcyn. "Stay on the road. Move forward and I'll join you as soon as I can."

"What are you—"

"Go!" he roared at Falcyn. "Forward. Don't stop! If the barking dogs get to you, you're finished."

Falcyn rushed forward, dragging them in his wake. They ran up a small hill and turned back just in time to see Shadow overrun by the demonic dogs he'd sought to hold back from their heels.

Medea's eyes widened at the horrific sight. "We're dead."

Urian, Blaise, Falcyn, and Brandor took positions between Medea and Brogan as the rabid dogs approached them.

There was nothing left of where Shadow had been overrun by them.

Not even a drop of blood. It appeared as if he'd been completely devoured. Every last bit. Body and soul.

Louder and louder, the barking and snarling grew. Brogan reached out and took her hand. Then, just as the twisted demonic dogs reached them, the shadowed earth shot up at a right angle, forming a wall between them and the demonic beasts. They slammed into it and howled out in agony. Swirling and twisting like smoke, the ground formed a giant hand that sent the animals scattering and running off into the dark.

The Crom came in the next wave, on his eerie ghost steed. Rushing and snorting fire, the beast seemed every bit as determined to add them to its menu. Just as it would have reached their position, the hand bent around and curved up to form a huge beast of a man.

"You have no power here!" Though the voice was distorted in its inhuman growl and pitch, Urian still recognized it as Shadow's.

The Crom pulled his horse up short, causing it to rear and paw fire at the hand. "This kerling belongs to me!" The rasping voice came from Brogan.

Shite! Urian cursed as he saw that Brogan's eyes were now milky white with no iris or pupil whatsoever. Her skin was ice cold to the touch.

The Crom had obviously taken her over completely so that he could speak through her.

Blaise growled low in his throat. He must have realized what was going on. "You're not taking her!"

"B-b-b-b . . . " Brogan choked, then fell to her knees to clutch at her throat. It was obvious the Crom was commanding her to speak Blaise's name and she was refusing to give him the power of death over the mandrake.

Throwing her head back, Brogan let out a blood-chilling

screech. She pounded the ground until her fist was bloody and bruised.

"Stop it!" Blaise shifted into his dragon's body. He let loose a blast of fire toward the Crom.

Engulfed by the fire, he laughed through Brogan's throat. Then threw his whip of bones and skulls toward Blaise. The head at the end of it opened its mouth as if it were laughing at the mandrake.

Shadow caught it and threw it back toward the horse and rider. "Leave here or I will dine on you both!"

Yanking his whip free of Shadow's grasp, the Crom snapped it in the air, shooting sparks of fire in all directions. Sulfur rained down over them.

"I demand my property!" He cracked his whip for Brogan.

Urian caught it again and yanked the Crom from his horse. Faster than Medea could blink, Falcyn was on him.

He grabbed the Crom and pulled him up from the ground. "Renounce your claim on the kerling. Here and now. Give her her freedom or I will rid you of your essence for all eternity!"

The Crom struggled for several seconds until he realized that Falcyn wasn't about to give. More than that, he came to the startling and truthful conclusion that Falcyn indeed had the means and ability to carry out his not-so-empty threat. "Very well, my lord. I give the kerling her freedom."

No sooner did Brogan speak those words than she fell forward to lie in a heap. Blaise returned to his human form so that he could rush to her side and pull her into his arms.

"Ro?" His voice quivered from the strain of his fear. "Speak to me! Say something!"

Brandor knelt beside them. "Brogan, please don't leave me alone!"

Still, she didn't move. She didn't even appear to breathe. Her face turned pale, then blue.

Blaise cupped her cheek and cradled her against his shoulder. "Speak to me, my lady. I cannot live knowing I caused you harm."

When she didn't respond, Blaise choked on a sob and lifted her up. Her head fell back while Brandor took her hand and kissed it as if it were unspeakably precious. Tears fled down his cheeks.

Urian knew that love firsthand. He'd felt it the day Tannis had died, and it sucked to the outer reaches of hell itself. He wanted to scream and rage against the cosmos. It wasn't right or fair.

Damn them all!

Shadow swirled past them to Brogan and lightly touched her cheek.

No sooner did he withdraw his hand than her eyes fluttered open. Lost in their grief, neither Blaise nor Brandor saw it.

Not until Brogan pulled her hand from her brother's grasp and sank it deep into Blaise's pale hair. "They can take me by force and break every bone I have, but only you will ever have my heart, Blaise. For it alone is mine to give."

Laughing and crying, he pulled her to his lips so that he could kiss her.

Brandor quickly withdrew from them. And though it was obvious he didn't like to see his sister in the arms of another man, he didn't say a word as he moved to stand beside Medea. Facing the opposite direction.

Like Urian.

Snorting at their ridiculous actions, Medea wiped at her eyes. She drew a ragged, grateful breath.

More grateful than words could express that she was alive, Urian glanced at her with Falcyn, then over to Brandor. "Don't we feel like the odd ones out?"

Shadow manifested between them and draped his arms around their shoulders. "I feel your pain, my brothers. I'm always the oddest of the odd." He darted his gaze around them. "So which of you assholes destroyed my rope?"

When they finally reached their destination, Shadow slowed down. "We're here."

With his powers, he cut another hole into a small room from his shadow realm. Shadow stayed back while they walked through. Then he joined them and sealed the rupture tightly closed.

Medea gaped. "How do you do that?"

"That's like asking me how I breathe. I don't know. I just think it and it happens." Shadow gave her a sarcastic grin. "It's magick."

Rolling her eyes at his sarcasm, she shook her head at him. "You're a sick bastard."

"Always."

Urian stepped around them to scowl at the smear of blood on the floor. Even though there was no color in this room where they were—everything appeared as shades of black and white, like an old movie—he knew the looks of *that*. The smell of it.

"You're wounded?"

Shadow paused at Medea's question but didn't answer.

Then they all saw it. The huge, gaping wound in Shadow's side that was partially concealed by his cape.

Urian took a step toward him. "Shadow?"

His eyes rolled back into his head as his legs buckled. He would have hit the ground hard had Falcyn not caught him and lowered him slowly to the floor.

Yet no sooner did he pull back than the door opened to show a small group of fey. The rasping of metal filled the air as the Adoni unsheathed their swords. An instant later, they attacked.

Urian manifested his sword and shield and charged them before he attacked. With his skills honed by thousands of battles, he drove the fey back to cover them.

Brogan stayed by Shadow's side to defend him as they dealt with this newest assault.

Of course the fey sounded an alarm. 'Cause keeping quiet would just be too much to ask. Wouldn't it? Damn villains.

Urian glanced to Falcyn. "Well, this wasn't how I saw these events unfolding."

Falcyn snorted at his sarcasm. "I knew better than to get

involved with Daimons and Dark-Hunters. This is what I get for coming out of my hole."

With a grimace, Medea lopped the head off her fey opponent, then turned toward Falcyn before she engaged another enemy. "Stop whining, dragonfly! Why don't you shift and set fire to them? Make this a little easier on us? Eh?"

"Simple spatial awareness. If either Blaise or I changed right now, we'd kill the lot of you, as we'd take up this entire room and you'd be crushed beneath us. Still want me to shift, love?"

Medea flashed him a grin as she kicked her opponent back. "Please, don't."

"Thought you might feel that way."

Just as they finished off their Adoni and began to make sure there weren't more, the door flew open.

They turned as one solid group to face this new onslaught.

As tall as Urian, the newcomer was swathed in the gold and green armor of a fey guard. A thick leather hood covered his head. Muscled and fierce, he stood with the cocksure stance of a warrior who knew how to fight to the bitter end.

Yet he didn't draw his sword.

Rather he held his hands out to his sides as if amused by them and their predicament.

Urian lifted his shield and prepared for a psychic attack.

Instead, laughter greeted them. "Bet if I sneezed right now, I'd send the lot of you jumping straight to the ceiling like a glaring of cats."

Falcyn growled deep in his throat. "Varian, you worthless bastard! Get in here. Shadow's down."

The humor died instantly while the man shut the door, then lowered his hood to expose his long dark hair.

"What happened?" Varian knelt by Shadow's side.

Falcyn joined him there to help tend Shadow. "We were cornered by dire wolves."

"Dire wolves or gwyllgi?"

"Gwyllgi," Blaise answered.

Varian cursed. "Was the Crom with them?"

Blaise nodded without further comment.

Varian used his powers to strip Shadow's leather armor away. Then he lifted the linen shirt to inspect the damage.

Urian cringed in sympathetic pain at the sight of the festering wound and all the other deep, ridged scars that marred Shadow's cut and ripped abdomen and chest.

Again, Varian cursed—this time, more lewdly. "Damn, Shade. Can't you ever do anything halfway once in a while? No, you don't get a little wounded. You've got to get practically gutted."

Falcyn sat back on his heels. "If you hold him, I can heal him."

Varian stopped Falcyn. "If you're planning to tap what I think you are, don't. Apollo will feel it and jump all over you the minute you try." He worked to stop Shadow's bleeding. "I've got this. You have a mission to complete. But I should warn you . . ."

Urian's gut twisted over that tone.

Varian's gaze went to Blaise before he met Falcyn's stare. "There's a stairwell at the end of the hallway that will take you down to the catacombs. Be careful. They're expecting all of you to come here and be stupid."

Oh well, that they could do!

"Then far be it from us to disappoint them." Falcyn saluted him with the key that he had taken from Shadow. "Thanks." He rose and they left the chamber.

"Where does this lead?" Medea asked as they came up to a tunnel.

"Morgen's garden." Blaise's tone was flat and emotionless in the dim light.

"I don't understand. A garden underground?" No sooner had she finished the question than they slowed down.

Falcyn used his dragonfyre in his hand as a torch so that they could see what was around them.

The moment he raised his arm over his head and the light chased away the heavier shadows, Urian's heart stopped.

And so did he.

This was it . . .

Holy shit. The "garden" was massive and lined with giant

dragon statues that went on in an endless, eerie display. In every direction.

Brandor turned to look at Urian. "The light fog down here is from their breath. At least by that, we know they're still alive even if they are frozen by Merlin's spell."

Medea frowned. "I don't understand. If they're frozen, how can they breathe fog?"

Though he was blind in his human form, Blaise glanced toward Brogan and then Medea before he answered. "The gas we exhale. It causes that. Even when we're locked in by magick. Not sure why. Just a peculiar by-product."

"Do we have to free them all?" she asked.

Before Urian could explode with his answer, Falcyn headed for the largest beast over on his right. "It's the safest thing to do. That way, Morgen won't have any to rouse and use against us."

Urian was still too emotionally charged to speak. He was afraid if he did, he'd burst into tears.

Afraid if he moved, he'd fall to his knees.

Where was Xyn? He was desperate to find her.

Blaise left Brogan's side as he felt his way through the darkness. "I'm not sure how to use my father's ring to awaken them. Do you know?"

Falcyn reached out to take it from him.

Just as their fingers brushed, the dragon nearest them opened its eyes and growled. Falcyn pulled back as the beast by his side rose to do battle. Blaise took his arm and fisted his hand in his sleeve to stop him. "Don't! *That's* Maddor."

"Maddor ... " The name came out in an anguished breath. Maddor was Falcyn's son who'd been taken from him.

Finally in control of himself and able to focus on something, Urian splayed his hand against Falcyn's chest to stop him from approaching his child. "They have him pinned." He jerked his chin toward the chain that held Maddor in place. "I'm betting if you free the dragons, it'll kill him."

Because *that* was the kind of nasty tactics the gods specialized in. They were nothing if not cruel.

The chain ran straight into Maddor's chest and no doubt through his heart.

Damn Apollo for this!

And that wasn't all. He was muzzled, too. That combination of cruelty would have made Maddor insane. No dragon did well in captivity. Not even a mandrake. They were meant to roam free, not be bound in such a manner.

Stepping past Urian, Falcyn reached to touch his son's scales. "Maddor, calm yourself. We're here to help."

With a fiery hiss, Maddor lunged at him so that Falcyn couldn't make contact.

Maddor lashed at Blaise with his tail.

Falcyn barely pulled Blaise back before Maddor pierced him with a spike. "Stop! You don't want to harm us."

Of course I do. It's your fault I'm here! I intend to kill you both!

Falcyn winced at a truth he couldn't change. "I know and I'm sorry for that."

You're about to be even sorrier those three seconds before I kill you!

Suddenly, the floor rumbled under their feet. Like a 6.0 magnitude earthquake . . .

"Blaise? What the hell is going on here?"

"No idea. Flying hell-monkeys, maybe?"

Urian glanced around the room, trying to find the source. They should be so lucky. Instead of dramonk demons being unleashed, the cracks in the stone widened and a greenish smoke spiraled out. It was as if the entire dungeon were alive and moving.

No, not moving.

Breathing. That was exactly what it felt like. Smelled like. The way the floor and walls moved was in time to someone's intake of breath. In and out. Seismic. Rolling.

Jarring.

Urian sneered as he caught a whiff of some foul sulfuric stench. "Someone tell me these are vapors like the Delphian oracle used to get high on before she mumbled gibberish."

Medea shook her head. "Sorry, little brother. I actually visited her once. This ain't it."

True to her prediction, the smoke coiled into fierce warriors, complete with armor.

And swords.

They had a *lot* of swords.

"Damn it!" Urian summoned his sword and shield again. "We cannot catch a break."

"Hey, I gave you an easy way out," Falcyn reminded him. "You could be home right now, watching *Survivor*. But no, you chose to be here."

"What can I say? I'm an idiot. I'd blame it on the fact that I come from a long line of them, but my mom and dad would kick my ass for the insult. So I'll blame Stryker for raising me among them. Anyone have a clue who and what these assholes are?"

"It's the dungeon, enchanted to ensure their victims will live no matter what's done to them. Once they're finished with the torture, they take the lifeless body and add it to the catacombs. But the by-product of that cruelty and magick is that the dungeon absorbs the tortured soul and holds on to it forever. It makes the soul a part of it. After a time, *l'âme en peine* bonds with the others that are trapped here until they become one single entity."

"Okay." Falcyn glanced around at the forming warriors. "So they're ghosts?"

He shook his head. "No. The nature and strength of the residual magick combines with the souls. Instead of making individual ghosts, they become one single beast. Lombrey de la Mort."

Oh, just awesome. And here Urian had thought that Apollymi had the lion's share of fun toys. No, leave it to the fey bitch queen to have something known as the *Death Shadow*.

Falcyn stared at him. "Are you telling me that we're facing Shadow's evil twin?"

Brandor laughed. "His prince underling, actually. If Shadow were here, he could control Lombrey and force him into retreat. Or at least order him to stand down."

Why did those words make him sick to his stomach?

"Without him?" Urian asked.

Glancing around at the numerous warriors the darkness was spawning, Brandor sighed. "We're screwed. Lombrey's a nasty bastard. Filled with the screams and righteous agony of a million innocent victims. They say it's driven him mad and so he attacks everyone who comes into his domain. Indiscriminately."

Medea scowled. "Then how does Shadow quell him?"

"Hell if I know. For that matter, no one knows for sure. Only that he goes without fear into wherever it is that Lombrey lives and emerges victorious."

Falcyn growled in frustration. "Well, that's ... fucking useless."

Urian sighed heavily. They had to find some way to awaken Xyn. Get Maddor free without killing him. Awaken the other dragons.

And stop Lombrey from attacking them.

Or killing them.

Urian felt sick to his stomach.

We're doomed.

Falcyn coughed, "Um, guys, I have an idea that I'm pretty sure you're gonna hate."

H*ours later, Maddor* stepped back in uncertainty. "I-I don't understand."

"It's true, Maddor. At least I think you're Maddor." Provided the Crom was still in Maddor's dragon body and the gods hadn't screwed with them again.

'Cause that was how their luck was running. Ever the rubric of "solve one problem and create another."

"Falcyn sent me here to watch over you. I'm the one who goaded Medea into going to Falcyn, hoping he'd be able to get to you and help you out of here. I didn't count on his overreaction that would result in her death. Guess I should have."

Urian's breath caught in his throat as he heard that unexpected, sweet lilting voice that he'd thought was lost to his dreams.

Xyn.

He wanted to run to her. To hold her and kiss those lips. But this, right now, was between her and her brothers, so he stayed out of it.

Pale and standing on unsteady feet, she had one arm braced against the wall nearest her.

"Xyn? Is it really you?"

She gave Falcyn a wan smile. "Greetings, brother."

His own limbs shaking, he crossed the room to gather her into his arms. "How?"

"I don't know. One minute, I was frozen and then I was *here*. Wherever this is."

Falcyn fisted his hand in her long flame-red hair that parted to show off her pointed ears.

Urian couldn't move or breathe as her translucent, vibrant green gaze seared him. She was still one of the most beautiful women he'd ever seen.

Her presence staggered him. He fell back and leaned against a stone for support, because he didn't trust his legs to hold him. Not right now.

She pulled back to stare at Maddor. "Falcyn is your father, Maddor. Just as Blaise is your son."

That sucked every bit of the air from the room and had the same impact as a nuclear bomb detonating in their midst.

Blaise stumbled back. "W-w-w-what?"

Xyn nodded. "I was there when you were born. Your mother was furious, thinking your albinism had to do with Max's curse."

"What curse?"

Falcyn winced. "I never told Blaise the truth, Xyn. He had no idea about *that*."

Her jaw went slack. "I'm so sorry. I assumed he knew."

Falcyn shook his head. "By the time I learned about his birth, he was grown. I didn't have the heart to tell him then. Thanks, sister. You were always good at ratting me out."

Maddor sat down. "Blaise is my son? How?"

Xyn sighed. "Ormarra. She hid her pregnancy from you and was hoping to parlay Blaise's birth to her advantage."

"When I was born deformed, she tried to kill me."

Brogan moved to hold Blaise. "You're not deformed!"

"And I killed her for her actions against you, Blaise." Xyn said. "You were still wet from cracking open your egg when I took you to be raised by your adoptive father. The only truth you knew was that your father was the leader of the mandrakes."

He'd just assumed it was the mandrake before Maddor because only a tiny handful of fey knew Maddor was the first of their breed.

Another lie told that was meant only to wound and hurt, and divide a family.

Damn those who sought only to make mischief for mischief's sake. They were the root of all evil. Not greed or money.

Maddor growled at Xyn. "You should have told me about him!"

"I was planning to once I knew he was safe, but I was trapped here before I had the chance."

With a fierce roar, Maddor started for Xyn, only to be stopped by some unseen force.

"You can't harm her," Brogan reminded him. "I haven't given you her name."

"I hate all of you!" he roared.

Falcyn glared at him. "How dare *you!* Feel free to hate me all you want. I deserve it. Blaise, however, has never done anything to deserve your animosity for him. He's your son. One you've treated like hell and mocked over the centuries for no reason whatsoever. You owe him an apology."

Maddor gaped at Falcyn. "You're daring to lecture *me* on parenthood? Seriously?"

"Yeah and I'll bust your ass, boy! Don't ever think I can't take you in a fight. I promise you, I've eaten much tougher hides than yours and used their scales for shoes. If you want to act like a child, then I'll treat you like one."

The real Crom made a noise deep inside the dragon's body.

"What's going on, Brogan? He about to spew?"

She shook her head. "It's the strife between the two of you. It feeds him. Makes him—"

The Crom dissolved all the bonds that held his dragon's body and stood up.

"Stronger," she finished with a squeak.

Blaise took her hand and pulled her behind him. "What's he doing now?"

"Not sure." Falcyn put his hand out to stop Medea from engaging the beast as she moved in for an attack.

Because the Crom wasn't the only dragon rising.

All of them were and he wasn't sure what that signified. But with their luck, it wasn't a good thing.

"Maddor?" Falcyn glanced to his son. "You want to return to your real body?"

His whip sizzled as he turned a slow circle to survey the number of original dragons who were now a little more than just plain pissed off. And since they had no other target, they were circling the only enemy they found in the room.

Them.

The whole group. And that included their leader that they couldn't identify as a dragon since he was in the Crom's body and had no head.

"Yeah, I think I do."

Urian couldn't blame him there. Judging by the mood of the newly animated dragons, anything not one of their scaly clan was about to get eaten.

Lombrey rose up in an effort to block the dragons, but they passed right through his noncorporeal form.

Urian rolled his eyes. "Good to be a shadow, huh? Makes me wish I were one." He lifted his sword and shield and prepared to attack.

Just as Falcyn renewed that stupid incantation that had gotten them into this mess, a bright light flashed near them. It was intense and searing. So much so that it temporarily blinded them.

Until Acheron's demon companion Simi jumped out of it.

Dressed in her short purple skirt, black-and-red-striped leggings, and a matching corset, she drew up short as she surveyed everyone around her. Her red horns sprouted on top of her head as a tail came out from underneath her short skirt. A set of leathery bat wings sprang out, letting Urian know the not-so-little Charonte Goth demon meant business.

He laughed. Yeah, they had no idea what they were dealing with. *Hide your children. Hide your wife.*

Hide your pets.

Urian smiled at her. "Simi? What are you doing here?"

She shrugged. "Akri done told the Simi that you'd be acting all weird and funky lately, and that the Simi should be keeping her eyeball on you, akri-Uri. So ... your heart rate was picked up during my commercial break and it got my attention. Since I knew you wouldn't be with no heifer cowlike red-headed goddess creature doing things that make the Simi go blind, I thought you be troubled. So then I thought, Simi, you best be checking on that old ex-Daimon to make sure he okay and not about to get et by something not friendly."

Simi scowled as she put her finger to her cheek to consider her words. "No, that be wrong. Be *in* trouble." She grinned widely, flashing her fangs. "You in trouble, akri-Uri? Can the Simi eat your troubles? 'Cause I don't think these dragonlies be on the Simi no-eat list. Pretty sure akri won't mind if the Simi eats them up." She bit her lip with a childish enthusiasm that made Urian smile. Especially as she reached into her coffin backpack and pulled out her lobster bib and bottle of barbecue sauce to prepare.

The moment she did, the dragons backed away.

And that made Maddor nervous as hell. "What's going on?"

Xyn laughed. "Oh, hon, no one is dumb enough to tangle with a hungry Charonte. Don't you know?"

Simi gasped. "No! Say it no so! The Simi so-o-o-o-o hungry! It been a whole twenty minutes since the Simi ets her last diamond ... " She pouted as she turned around, looking for a meal.

More dragons shrank away.

"Yeah!" Urian blustered at them. "That's right! I've got a Charonte here and I'm not afraid to unleash her. Hah!"

A dragon sneezed beside him, blowing out fire that came a little too close to Urian.

Urian dashed to Simi's side, putting her between them. "Are you fireproof, Sim?"

"Bombproof, too." She belched and shot out a stream of fire that caused several dragons to scramble for cover. "See!"

"Ah, you bunch of hatchlings." With his hands on his hips, Falcyn finished putting Maddor back into his body.

The moment the Crom was himself again, he picked up his whip and went straight to Brogan.

Brogan held her hand up to let them know that it was all right. After a few seconds and a few whispered words in his ear, she nodded. "Peace to you, Crom."

With a curt jerk of his coat, he flashed himself onto the back of his horse and vanished.

"What did he say?" Blaise asked.

She smiled warmly. "That he never wants to be a dragon again. You can keep your smelly old body."

Urian scowled at Brogan. "That all?"

An evil light danced in her eyes. "I might have given him the name ... —Morgen."

Medea cleared her throat to remind them of the other dragons who were still glaring at them.

Xyn yawned. "How long have we slept?"

"Centuries," Blaise and Falcyn said simultaneously.

An unhappy murmur ran through the dragon horde.

"Simi eat them now since they all grumbly?" Her wings twitched with expectation.

The dragons quieted immediately.

Medea laughed. "Nice to know you don't just scare Daimons, Simi."

Simi pressed her finger to her lips and cocked her head in an adorable expression. She scowled, then smiled at Medea. "The

Simi knows you! I's seens you lots and lots. You're the evil princess who libs with the Simi's akra in Kalosis!"

"She's also my sister."

Simi gasped at Urian's words. Then caught herself. "Oh yeah. I should have ... but wait. Your daddy is fake-akri." She pressed her hands to her eyebrows. "The Simi is so confuseled!"

Urian laughed. "So am I most days." Sobering, he gently pulled one of her hands down until she opened her eyes to look at him. "Just remember that I was taken out of my mother's womb before I was born and put into the belly of another. So the Apollite who birthed me wasn't really my mother. And Stryker wasn't really my father. Styxx is my father and Bethany is my real mom."

"Ah! Like Simi you're adaptable!"

Urian's grin widened. "Yeah."

"Wait ... " Brandor scowled. "Does she mean adopted?"

"No, silly!" Arms akimbo, Simi rolled her eyes. "Even though we both were adopted, the Simi meant adaptable 'cause akri-Uri had to libs with people not his people. He not really a Daimon, he a demigod. Which is better. Sometimes, anyway." She tsked as she looked back at Urian. "I'm sorry, akri-Uri. That why you have sadness besides Phoebe-sadness?"

His eyes darkened. "No, Sim. Mostly I just have Phoebe-sadness."

She held her barbecue sauce out toward him. "Wanna eat a dragon? Make you feel all better. Give you warm and fuzzies in the belly."

And that succeeded in driving the dragons toward the shadows and Lombrey into a fit.

"No! No! No! You're not to hide in my domain! Get out, mangy beasts!"

Brandor cleared his throat to disguise his laughter. "You know, with all this noise, Morgen is bound to realize what's happened. We might want to think about getting out of here before she sends something or someone to investigate."

Falcyn nodded to his sister. "Granted, she should be a little preoccupied with the Crom after her—you still should take them to my island. Just to be safe."

She arched a brow at his order. "*All* of them? You really plan to tolerate us in your personal space?"

"It'll be the safest place for them."

Xyn kissed his cheek. "Love you."

"You, too."

She scoffed at his response. "I live for the day, Veles, when you can say that word without choking on it." And with that, she gathered the dragons and left through the portal.

Urian followed Xyn to Falcyn's island home, which was absolutely breathtaking. Open and airy, and yet technically a cavern, it was large and spacious with a stunning ocean view. The enchanted walls were crystal clear, so that he could look out but not be seen by anyone else. The transparency of the walls made them shimmer and sparkle from the daylight that burned the eyes, but not the skin. He could see why Falcyn had chosen it.

However, that was the last thing Urian had on his mind.

"Xyn?" He reached for her hand and pulled her into a dark alcove, away from the others.

Finally, they were alone.

And now that they were ... he was lost and unsure. Did she even remember him? She hadn't acted like it.

Maybe she'd suffered a head wound that had left her with amnesia. What did he say to her after all these years?

Sarraxyn trembled as she looked up into the bluest eyes she'd ever known. She'd forgotten what a huge, overwhelming beast Urian was. Which was shocking really, given that she was used to dragonswains, who were even larger and yet somehow he made them seem smaller.

Weaker.

There was an innate power to him that the others lacked. And at the same time, he was sexier than anyone she'd ever known because for all his power and ruthlessness, he would never harm her. He was a protector unlike anyone she'd ever met. He kept that vicious strength restrained and under control.

This close, you could feel the lethal killer inside him. The demon that salivated for blood. Yet he'd made love to her like a poet and touched her with the tenderest of care.

That was the beauty of her Daimon.

Love and happiness rushed through her and set her heart to pounding. But it wasn't enough to drown out her fear that he'd rebuff her after all this time.

She didn't know what to say to him after all this time. She'd just abandoned him. Not out of choice.

Still, did that matter? She could only imagine the hurt and pain he must have felt, thinking she'd just moved on. Or worse, that she'd died. So she did the only thing she could think of to do.

Stepping into his arms, she kissed him.

Urian growled at the taste of Xyn's lips. Of her sweet tongue sweeping against his as her arms wrapped around his waist. His body roared to life with a vengeance that was terrifying.

In the distance, he heard someone calling her name.

She deepened her kiss before she pulled away and nipped his chin. "Give me a few minutes?"

There wasn't enough blood left in his brain to form a coherent thought. "Um . . . okay."

Xyn laughed. "Urian?" She cupped his face and rubbed noses with him. "You'll be here when I get back?"

"I will." Nothing could make him leave.

"Okay."

With a ragged breath, he leaned back against the wall as she went to help the dragons settle in. Then he glanced down at the sizable lump in his jeans.

Damn, that was really obvious and embarrassing. He wasn't about to leave the shadows anytime in the near future.

At least you know it still works.

True. It'd been so long at this point, he had begun to wonder.

And that thought was still on his mind a few minutes later when Xyn returned as a faint whisper.

Laughing in his ear, she wrapped herself around him and

teleported him from his shadows into a bedroom. "What are you doing?"

She left him to lock the door, then returned to stand in front of him. Biting her lip in a way that only further inflamed him, she ran her finger down his chest, raising chill bumps the whole way. "Can you still use your magick to conjure clothes?"

"Yeah."

An evil grin broke across her face. "Good."

Before he could ask her why she wanted to know, she ripped open his shirt from hem to neck and attacked him as if she were starving and he was the last steak at a banquet.

Urian couldn't have been more floored had she set him on fire and used his balls for kindling. She ran her hands across his entire body while she licked and sucked his skin until he thought he'd go blind from it.

With her powers, she flipped him and tossed him onto the bed, then dissolved both their clothes.

Sucking his breath in, he surrendered himself completely to her fierce caresses. Never had a woman been so forceful with him. He loved it.

Xyn grazed Urian's throat with her teeth and licked his whiskers, allowing them to prick at her tongue. "I'm so glad you followed me and the others here."

He breathed against her ear as he tongued it and cupped her breast in his hand. His fingers toyed with her nipple in a way that had her wet and aching. "Oh, Xyn ... how could I not? I've missed you so!"

She nipped his chin while she fisted her hands against his muscular back and pressed her bare body into his. Ah gah, his skin felt so good. She wanted to cry at the peace she experienced by exploring him again. It was truly Katateros.

And it was then that she realized what was missing. How could she have missed it?

Shocked and amazed, she pulled back to scowl at his chest. "Uri? Where's your Daimon mark?"

He glanced down to where her hand rested over his heart.

"I'm not a Daimon anymore. I was . . . fixed—" Not exactly the correct word, but he couldn't think of anything better to use. "A long time ago."

"You're human?"

"No. I'm kind of unique."

"But you don't feed on souls?"

"Or blood."

She let out a peculiar half laugh. "You eat food?"

"I do."

Her eyes turned warm and adoring. "Oh, how I wish I'd been there the first time you ate to see your face."

"You didn't miss much. Other than a lot of cursing that followed the biting of my tongue."

Xyn laughed for real then at the image she had of him trying to figure out how to chew when he'd never had to do so before. "My Urian."

"That's me. Ever brain damaged."

"No. Definitely not." She kissed him, reveling in the miracle that was her Daimon. "I could just eat you up."

"I'm at your disposal."

She shook her head at these words as she nibbled his neck. He let out such a sound of pleasure that it honestly startled her. "Are you okay?"

He sucked his breath in sharply between his teeth. He cupped her head in his hands. "Depends. Is the truth going to be a buzzkill or a turn-on?"

"What do you mean?"

His gaze burned her as he sank his hand into her hair. "I haven't been with anyone in a long time, Xyn. My heart was broken one time too many."

Her gaze fell down to the tattoo on his arm where he bore the black tears that marked the passing of his loved ones. It was something all Daimons did to honor and remember those they'd lost.

Dipping her head down she kissed his mark. "Do you want me to leave?"

"No!"

She smiled, then nipped his chin.

Urian groaned as she slid her hand down to touch his cock. He felt his powers surge through him. Oh yeah, that was the most incredible pleasure. It'd been so long since anyone else had touched him that he'd forgotten what it felt like.

Capturing her lips, he pressed her hips closer to his.

She gave a low whistle of appreciation as she took him into her hand. Then she traced a line up to his tattoo of his father's shield pattern. "You've changed this, too?"

He nodded. "I made it look more like my father's."

"Stryker?"

Laughing, he shook his head. "You've missed so much. I'm the son of Styxx, not Stryker. Stryker and I are at war. But I don't want to talk about hate . . . not while I'm with you."

And not when she gave him that look right there that seared him to the core of his soul.

Xyn ran her hungry gaze over his tawny body. Every muscle was a study of sinewy grace and perfection. All man and all hot. His chest was dusted by golden hairs. Not too thick, just enough to be manly and appealing. Goodness, how she'd missed touching a man and being close to one like this.

Urian had always touched her in a way no one had—and not physically. Emotionally. A part of her was still timid to touch him for fear that her dragon powers would kick in and she'd scorch him, but the other part of her was desperate to be held. Just for a little while.

"You don't like false people, do you?"

He narrowed his gaze at her. "Are you reading my mind?"

"No. It's strictly from what you've said. I told you, I've never been able to read your thoughts and I don't know why." Which was so odd, because she normally could read those of others. Urian had always been different.

He gave her a cocky grin. "It doesn't take much to read them right now." He gave her a scorching once-over.

Xyn laughed until he dipped his fingers into the part of her that craved him most.

Urian stared down at her. A wicked light came into his eyes as he kissed his way down her body. He paused to lave her breasts. Ribbons of heated pleasure burned through her while his fingers continued to tease and play, and delve deep inside her.

Then ever so slowly, he continued south until he replaced his hand with his lips.

Xyn arched her back as her body twitched and ached in response to his masterful touch. Before she could draw another breath, her body shattered as one of the most intense orgasms of her life claimed her.

Still he continued to please her until he wrung another one from her spasming body. She sank her hand in his soft hair, tugging at it as he continued to tease her, over and over.

Urian growled at how good she tasted. It'd been way too long since he last had a woman. Hell, he'd had so little interest in them lately that he'd begun to fear he was broken. But there were no inhibitions or hesitation with her even though he should have them in spades.

They really needed to be focused on other things right now. But he didn't give a shit. Let them die and the world end. He didn't care. He needed her more than anything.

Unable to stand it anymore, he pulled back from her. He lifted her hips and drove himself deep inside her body.

She cried out his name.

Smiling, he thrust against her, seeking solace in her warm softness.

Xyn balled her fist in Urian's soft white hair as she buried her face in his neck to inhale the warm masculine scent of his skin. There was so much power in him, so much skill in the way he filled her and touched her. It was like he knew every way to wring as much pleasure from every thrust as he could. And to be able to have him again like this ... it was incredible.

For the first time in centuries, she felt human.

"Harder, baby," she purred in his ear, wanting him to love her with everything he had. This was the most incredible moment of her life and when he finally came, she joined him.

Completely spent and sated, she leaned back onto the bed

while he was still inside her. Her breathing ragged, she kept her legs wrapped around his waist while he stared into her eyes and toyed with her belly button. "That was incredible."

He flashed a devilish grin. "Glad I could oblige." He ran his hand around her breast, traced the line of her intricate tattoo, then gave it a light squeeze as he brushed her hardened nipple with his thumb. A smile curved his lips as he remembered when she'd had her tattoo done.

It was of a black sword wrapped with a pink rose for her strength. At the bottom was a redheaded pixielike woman and above her a half dragon rising up to shield and protect her.

The dragon matched his shield.

And beneath the dragon's wings she'd placed the words, *I am woman. Born of Pain. Hear me roar.* Done to remind herself that while she was dragon born and capable of extreme and utter violence, she was also capable of mercy and compassion.

But what made him smile were the words that had been added since the last time he'd seen her that went down the back of the sword. "You took my advice?"

She picked his hand up and lifted it to her lips so that she could nip his fingertips. "Only because I wanted something to remind me of you, and I love the way you see me. Don't agree, mind you. But I love that you think of me that way."

"That I do." He kissed the words that were there now. *I Am Invincible.* Then he shivered as her tongue darted between his fingers. He didn't know why, but it brought out a tenderness inside him. Something protective and scary.

But then she'd always done that. It was like the demon in him wanted to claim her and kill anyone who came near her. Anyone who hurt her or even looked at her wrong. It was feral and powerful.

And she owned that part of him. She always had.

Right now, he felt like his entire body was made of thrumming electricity that needed to ignite and explode. Sex with her had always heightened and strengthened his psychic abilities, but this was different.

He'd never felt anything like it before.

She nibbled his knuckle. "Is that one part about your Daimon-ness still true?"

"Yes. We all have a second penis hidden in our thigh."

She laughed out loud. "Where did that come from?"

"I don't know. You hear all kinds of stupidity coming out of the mouths of Dark-Hunters when you hang out with them. I'm always appalled and offended by about ninety percent of everything they say."

Xyn shook her head. "I mean can you still go all night and have multiple orgasms?"

He pressed himself deeper inside her so that she could tell he was already hard again and ready for more. "Oh, yes, ma'am. The one definite perk for my people." Which he'd always assumed had been done either as a punishment or a way to ensure that they could procreate in their exceedingly short life spans.

She tightened her thighs around him. "You telling me you're at the ready?"

He kissed her lightly on the lips. "Dearest Lady Dragon, I'm ready to go until neither of us can walk."

She sucked her breath in sharply as he teased her nipple with his tongue. Oh, he felt so good. "I intend to hold you to that."

"Then far be it from me to disappoint you ... "

Xyn had just finished her third orgasm when a strange buzzing started. "What is that?"

"Hold on a second." Urian used his powers to pull a peculiar thing to his hand that illuminated. He held it up to his ear. "Hey, little buddy, whatcha need?"

That was a strange tone she'd never heard him use before.

"Well, no. I can't kill your brother. I can give him a stern talking to for taking your Legos. What did your dad say?"

Xyn sat up and frowned as she tried to make sense of his conversation.

"I see. And Uncle Chris?"

Crossing her legs, she bit her lip at the perplexed frown on his face.

"No. No, Erik! Don't kill your brother. You might need bail

money one day and I might not be available for it, and Phoebe could hold that whole Barbie incident from last year against you. Just calm down and breathe. Your brother's life is worth more than a video game, I promise. I know it doesn't seem that way right now, but in an hour, you will move past this."

She heard someone yelling on the other end.

"Yeah, okay. I'll talk soon. Love you." Laughing, he lowered the little rectangle.

"Should I ask?"

He used his finger to swipe at the box, then held up a painting of a dark-haired boy with a huge, exaggerated smile on his face. "My nephew Erik."

"He's adorable."

"Some days." He pulled it back to swipe again. "He was about to kill this little guy." He showed a brown-haired boy with similar features who was a few years younger. "Tyr."

"Which of your brothers do they belong to?"

All the humor left his face then, and a deep, dark sadness swallowed the light in his eyes. The turmoil was so tragic that it made her gut tighten. "Urian?"

He flipped to another image. This one of a beautiful girl with reddish hair. "Little Phoebe."

"She's beautiful."

Urian drew a ragged breath. "I thought you were dead, Xyn."

"I know. You had no way of knowing what had happened." And then she saw the guilt in his eyes. "You found someone?"

He nodded.

Anger shot through her. For the merest instant she feared Urian had tricked her, but she caught herself before she reacted. Urian wouldn't do that. Granted, she'd been gone a long time. Still, integrity like his didn't vanish. And she had her own guilt to carry, even if it had been to help her family. She couldn't imagine the pain and sorrow that Urian had experienced for the centuries that they had been apart.

She knew that. Plus, he'd told her that he hadn't been with anyone. Not in a long while.

"What happened?"

"Phoebe died fourteen years ago." A tear slid from the corner of his eye and he quickly wiped it away.

Grateful she hadn't reacted, Xyn pulled him against her. "I'm so sorry."

"It's okay."

No, it wasn't. Not the way her Urian loved. She held him close and rubbed his back.

"Their mother is her sister."

"And you watch over them?"

He nodded. "I promised her I would."

"What of your brothers? How are they?"

Urian drew another ragged breath. "All gone."

"What?" she gasped in shock.

He nodded. "Atreus was the last to fall. I lost him in 1962 to a Dark-Hunter."

Sympathetic grief brought tears to her eyes as she brushed the hair back from his face. "I'm so sorry."

He kissed her hand. "It's okay. We're Daimons, right? Loss is what we're born for."

"So you've been alone all this time?"

"I still have Davyn," he said with a smile. But it quickly faded. "We've got to get your brother's egg. That's Davyn's only hope for a cure. I need you to talk sense into him, Xyn. Please?"

"A cure?"

Fury darkened his eyes as a tic started in his jaw. "Apollo sent a plague to wipe out the Daimons. Whatever it is, Davyn has it. I can't lose him."

"I won't let you." She kissed him. "Come. Let me go smack my brother around."

When she started to get up, Urian stopped her. She glanced back with a frown. "Something wrong?"

"I'm not a Daimon anymore. Do you remember what you said?"

"I remember."

"Good, because I plan to hold you to it."

Smiling, Xyn watched as he conjured his clothes and then handed her some the likes of which she'd never seen.

"What is this?"

"Modern clothing."

She wrinkled her nose at it. "Looks itchy."

"It is itchy. You'll get used to it. Besides, once we get this squared away, I intend to get you out of it as quickly as possible."

She arched a brow at his tone. "There better be a 'please' in that."

He snorted. "There will be as much begging in there as you require, I promise." He poked his lip out to prove it.

Laughing, she stood up on her tiptoes to draw his lip in between her teeth. "That's better."

Xyn swallowed as Urian stepped away and led her from the room. They had much left to talk about. A lot had happened to her since the last time she'd seen him.

Funny how promises were so easy to give.

And incredibly hard to keep.

S*itting at a* small round table at the Café Du Monde in New Orleans, Dikastas looked up from his coffee and beignets as a shadow fell over him and blocked his view of the pedestrian mall, where he liked to watch the tourists while they shopped and strolled along the busy street.

It was even worse than what he'd initially imagined for the interruption—some poor panhandler begging for spare change or an annoying ass wanting directions.

A pouting Girl Scout peddling some overly sweet cookies.

Oh no, those nightmares would be far preferable to this pestilent beast who brought with him a sickening sensation that caused Dikastas's jaw to fall slack. Indeed, he wouldn't have been more shocked or stunned to find Apollymi herself standing there, glaring hatred at him.

He choked down his bite of the sugary confection and took a

drink of coffee to clear his throat. "Apollo ... to what do I owe this ... " He searched for an appropriate word.

Honor definitely didn't fit.

Horror, not really.

Inconvenience would be the most apropos, but since Dikastas was the Atlantean god of justice, moderation, and order, he had a bit more tact than to say that out loud as it would cause conflict and strife. So he left it open to the Greek god's interpretation while he wiped his mouth with a paper napkin, then gestured at the small metal chair across from him.

Apollo accepted the invitation without hesitation. "What a peculiar place to find you. I actually thought Clotho was lying when she told me where you were living these days."

Little wonder that, given the fact that the vast majority of his pantheon was currently frozen as statues beneath Acheron's palace in Katateros. But since Dikastas had had the good sense not to cross Apollymi's wrath or Styxx's sword arm, he was one of the extreme few who'd been left free to roam the earth after they'd broken buck wild on them all a few years ago. "And how are my dear half-Greek nieces?"

"Worthless as always."

Dikastas didn't comment on that. Mostly, because he agreed about the three Fates. With their great stupidity and rash actions, they had accidentally damned the entire Atlantean race and pantheon in the blink of an eye. Jealous words spoken in a moment of fear against Acheron that had played out with devastating consequences for all the rest of them, especially the triplet goddesses.

He cleared his throat and pinned Apollo with a cool stare. "You still haven't told me why you're here."

After all, they weren't friends or even friendly. In fact, they hated each other with a fiery zeal. Their pantheons had been mortal enemies, back in the day. And the only thing the two of them had in common was their blond hair.

Literally.

And even it wasn't the same shade. Apollo's was far more golden and his tended toward brown.

"I want information."

Dikastas cocked his brow. "The Fates couldn't give you what you wanted?"

Apollo snorted. "As I said, they're basically worthless. What I need to know predates their births by a number of centuries and has to do with Apollymi and Kissare."

Interesting . . .

A waitress came up to ask Apollo for an order.

He sneered at her. "Do I look like I eat or drink shit? Begone from me, mortal scum!"

Dikastas sighed at his angry words. So much for Apollo being a god of temperance. "That was unnecessary."

"So is wasting my time!"

Yet Apollo had no problem intruding on his zen and wasting his. Typical. But then Apollo had always been a selfish prick that way.

All that mattered was his life and *his* wants.

Everyone else could go to Kalosis and rot.

Leaning back in his chair, Dikastas sipped his café au lait. "Well, if that's what you're after, the person you really want to talk to is Bet, as she'd have the most . . ." He trailed off as Apollo gave him a harsh stare and he realized the total stupidity of what he was suggesting.

"Ah," Dikastas said with a snide smile. "Guess you can't go there, can you?" Not after Apollo had screwed Bethany over in not one but two separate lifetimes. The Atlantean goddess of wrath and warfare wouldn't take kindly to Apollo going to her for anything other than a full disembowelment.

Followed with a thorough denutting.

And the sun itself would freeze over before she'd ever help the bastard who'd killed her beloved husband and cursed her to lose her son, Urian.

"She wouldn't have been there when Apollymi set up the Atlantean pantheon anyway. She hadn't been reborn yet, right?"

Again, courtesy of Apollo's *first* brutal betrayal against her and her husband . . .

Dikastas set his coffee cup down and reached for another beignet. "Correct."

Crossing his arms over his chest, Apollo stroked his chin as he thought about something. "So how did Archon convince the frigid bitch of all time to marry him and establish a pantheon with him as its king so that he could play ruler?"

Dikastas snorted at his assumption. "Apollymi isn't frigid. Therein is the problem. Her passions run deep and dark. She's ruthless and bloodthirsty, but that doesn't make her cold. She's as fiery as a volcano and even quicker to erupt, and far deadlier when she peaks."

"You still haven't answered my question. Why *him?* Why *then?*"

Dikastas shrugged. "Simple. Someone gave Archon the intel that Apollymi was awaiting the return of her precious Kissare, and she mistook the dull god as her Sephiroth come back to be with her. The spy fed Archon enough information that he was able to dupe her into thinking that he was her betrayed lover reborn as a god. That was why she agreed to set him up as her king and allowed him to rule over her. At least for a time."

"Are you sure he wasn't?"

"Yeah. Very much so. Kissare loved Apollymi. He gave his life for her and for their son. There was nothing altruistic about Archon. He was much like *you.*"

Apollo's eyes narrowed. But he chose to ignore the dig. "Who was he working with?"

"No one knows. Archon refused to betray his informant. He was too grateful to be the king of his own pantheon to ever give over the name of someone Apollymi would have surely gutted."

Apollo considered that for a few minutes. "Was Kissare ever reborn?"

"Again, no one knows. But I'd say he must have been."

"Why?"

"Because someone fathered Acheron. Knowing Apollymi as I do and how she is, I would lay my money and life that Kissare was the father of both her sons. You find out who Acheron's real father is and you will find out who Apollymi really loves."

"You think he's still alive?"

Dikastas cradled his coffee mug as he considered it. "That would be the question of the day, wouldn't it?"

Urian *growled as* he cowed the dragon bastard in front of him. He'd had it with the scaly beasts!

Xyn appeared between them. "Problem?"

The dragon raked a look over him that said he'd like to have a little Daimon barbecue. "No."

Urian scoffed. "Keep walking, Barney. Clubhouse is on your right."

Xyn screwed her face up at his words. "Barney?"

"Big purple bastard. Drives you insane with asinine bullshit, just like your friend there." He jerked his chin toward the lumbering dragon who'd left them.

Brushing her hand through his hair, she kissed his cheek. "I have so missed you."

Urian closed his eyes and savored her warmth. *"Kanis tin zoi mou pio omorfi."*

She smiled. "You make my life more beautiful, too."

And that was one of the things he adored most about her. She actually spoke his language.

Rubbing his stomach in a way that set him on fire, she stood way too close for his comfort. "Have you heard from Shadow yet?"

He shook his head. "He'll let us know as soon as he finds more housing."

That had been their first quest upon leaving the bedroom. Find new homes for their friends here, as they both knew Falcyn wouldn't be keen on sharing whenever he returned.

Speaking of . . .

They heard a sudden loud bellow as her brother and Medea returned.

"Fun times!" Xyn said with an overly exaggerated smile. "Let's go torment the big guy, shall we?"

Laughing, he followed her.

True to her words, she met Falcyn with a charming grin and grace that only she could pull off. "Like the new decorations? Wall-to-wall dragon?"

The grimace on her brother's face said that he didn't appreciate her attempt at humor. At all. "Ha. Hate you so much."

Xyn took his irritability in stride. "Ah, you're not fooling anyone. I know you missed me."

Falcyn made a disgruntled face at her. "Like a bleeding hemorrhoid."

Urian crossed his arms over his chest. While he didn't appreciate the tone, he'd stand down only out of respect for the fact that he understood sibling banter. There was no malice backing those words. Had anyone else said something like that to Xyn, he'd have handed them their throat.

And if Falcyn had hurt her feelings, they'd be having blows. Yet as long as she continued to laugh, he'd behave.

Falcyn grimaced. "So what do you plan to do with all of these beasts, Xyn? I'm not planning to let them move in, you know? Definitely not comfortable with them here."

Xyn smiled adoringly. "Why not? It's rather cozy, don't you think? That pink one really goes well with the decor. And it'd keep you from being lonely." She batted her eyelashes playfully.

It was all Urian could do not to double over with laughter.

Falcyn let out a sound of supreme disgust. "You know why. And don't start on me. As the old saying goes, door's on the wall."

She snorted like a horse. "Oh, relax, you old mangy beast. They're not planning to stay, anyway. We're just messing with you."

His relief was tangible.

Xyn met Medea's gaze and shook her head. "How do you put up with him?"

"I think he's hilarious."

She popped Falcyn on the stomach. "This one's a keeper, brother. You better not let her go."

Urian had just gone over to help one of the dragons who was having problems with his wings when a light dimmed near them.

The dragon tensed.

"Easy. It's just Shadow returning." He'd know that power surge anywhere.

Sure enough, Shadow popped in across the room, near Xyn. Inclining his head to Falcyn, he approached Xyn and Shadow. "Any luck?"

Shadow nodded. "Yeah. I have a few more willing to shelter dragons."

Falcyn let out an audible sigh. "Shadow ... you're my man."

Shadow let out a nervous laugh. "Since when?"

"Since I saved your ass. How are you feeling?"

"Like I had the hell beat out of me. ... And you're welcome."

Crossing his arms over his chest, Falcyn's expression said those words chafed him. Yet the gleam in his eyes betrayed his amusement. "How has Varian failed to gut you all these centuries?"

"Not from lack of effort on his part, I assure you. I'm just quicker than he is."

Falcyn shook his head. "Anyway, I'm glad to see you back on your feet."

"Glad to be back on my feet. Especially without Varian hovering over me like some great hairy mother. And I heard you made friends with little brother Lombrey."

"Yeah, you can keep him."

"Hmmm, so everyone keeps telling me. He's actually not so bad. Get him liquored up and laid, you can get about five or ten minutes of peace before he's in your face again."

Falcyn made a face of distaste. "So that's your secret."

"Basically. I find it works on most people."

Falcyn laughed. "And why is it that I think there's a little more to it than you're letting on?"

"Again, he's not so bad. You just have to understand where he's coming from. We're all creatures of the hell that birthed us. Are we not?"

"True." Falcyn stepped back as one of the dragons approached them.

"Are the sanctuaries ready?" he asked Shadow.

Shadow nodded. "They're being prepared."

"Thank you."

"Our pleasure."

He placed a kiss on Xyn's cheek, and Falcyn then turned toward Shadow. "Can I beg a favor?"

"Shoot you in the head? Sure."

Falcyn rolled his eyes and ignored that comment. "Can you get me back in, near my son?"

Shadow made a truly spectacular sound of scoffing disbelief. "And what level of special stupidity have you achieved, dragon? I know you took a significant hit to the head, but didn't realize it'd given you brain damage. Should we get you a CAT scan? Dog scan?"

"Ha ha. And I'm serious."

"Yeah ... so am I. I actually like having my bollocks attached to my body. While I don't get to use them as much as I'd like, I still prefer the comfy feeling of having them there over the alternative of seeing them in a jar on my desk."

"Then you'll help me or I know what to attack."

A tic started in Shadow's jaw. "Really hate you, dragon. ... Fine. But if you're caught, I don't know you. Never saw you and I have no idea how you got there. And I'm sending Lombrey to rescue or kill you, whichever. *His* choice."

"How have you managed to live so long without anyone killing you, again?"

"Told you, I'm fast on my feet." Shadow sighed. "So when do you want to partake of your suicide?"

Falcyn glanced around his crowded home. "Now would be a good time. It'll keep me from freaking out over my OCD."

Xyn scowled "OCD?"

"Overpopulated Communal Den." He pointed to the group. "Get rid of *that* while I'm gone."

She rolled her eyes at her brother. "Ugh, you big baby. You never did learn to share!"

"Oh, that's not true. I learned to share pain and misery early on."

"No, no. You learned to deliver pain and misery. *Big* difference. Being a carrier and deliverer isn't the same as sharing, *m'gios*. Do not confuse those terms."

"You're determined to annoy me, aren't you?"

Xyn smiled. "Always. Aren't you glad now that you woke me?"

"Thinking I should have overlooked *your* statue." Falcyn growled in the back of his throat. "Blaise! Why did we wake Xyn again?"

"You missed her!" he called out across the room.

"I lied!"

Xyn pushed him toward Shadow. "Go on and take him before he has a nervous breakdown. Or I kill him."

Medea laughed. "C'mon, dragonfly."

Urian went over to Xyn as they headed off. "Should I have gone?"

"Nah. They'll be fine. Besides, I like having you here."

He liked being here with her. For too long he'd been alone.

Xyn watched as Urian went to help the younger ones, and her heart broke for him. She had so much guilt over what she'd done. By helping her brothers, she'd abandoned him.

She hated the years that had been stolen from them. Damn Apollo for this.

Somehow she was going to make it up to Urian.

And pay Apollo with interest.

Apollo *froze as* he saw Morgen approaching his throne. Her hair was singed, her dress torn and filthy. "You look a little worse for the wear, love."

She actually shot a blast at him. "You bastard!"

He arched a brow at her. "Temper, temper. Be careful with that, lest I take offense."

"Take all you want! What happened to the dragonstone you promised me?"

"Patience. The game isn't over. Just a slight reset on the board."

She frowned. "What do you mean?"

He let out a long, weary sigh. "I forget that you're not a god. Playing with people's lives isn't something you've much experience with. Sometimes you have to let things run their course."

"Meaning?" she repeated.

"Meaning the good guys had all the dragons ... now they don't. And Urian holds the blood of Apollymi, Bet, Set, *and* Acheron ... "

Morgen sucked her breath in as she finally understood. "He's the key to bringing them all down."

"Isn't he, though. And you know what we've just discovered?"

A slow smile curved her lips. "The source of his undoing."

Apollo nodded slowly. With Phoebe under his control, he didn't need to find Acheron's father. He had something even better at his disposal.

Acheron's comeuppance.

Because that was the beauty of being a god of prophecy. He knew the future.

The final fate of the world ... of all humanity wasn't really in the hands of Acheron or even Apollymi.

It was in the bloodline of Urian's family.

And now it was in his.

October 28, 2017

Medea had dreaded this moment for days. But it was something that had to be done and something that she didn't want Urian to discover on his own. Better the news come from someone he loved than to be dumped on him by accident.

How she'd allowed Falcyn to talk her into doing this in Acheron's palace on Katateros, she had no idea. She definitely loved the beast. Only that could account for this level of insanity.

But in the end, he was right. It was better that Urian be comfortable and surrounded by family when he learned the truth than to be blindsided and surrounded by strangers. That wouldn't bode well for anyone.

Still . . .

This was nerve-racking. The huge marble palace was awe-inspiring, as one would expect the home of ancient gods to be. It had been built to impress, and she was definitely not immune to its austerity.

Acheron's throne was set off to her right on a massive dais where several small little dragonlike creatures were currently curled around and napping with Acheron's two sons. The way the creatures were entwined, she wasn't even sure how many of them there were.

Simi and her Charonte sister were on the floor to her left, watching some shopping network channel on a massively huge monitor that was mounted to the wall on her left. Completely content, they were eating barbecue-drenched popcorn out of a bowl they shared that was perched between them while Acheron's steward, Alexion, and his wife, Danger, kept it filled to capacity.

Urian's father, Styxx, met her and Falcyn in the doorway. At almost seven feet in height, he was an impressively handsome beast. Dressed in a casual blue button-down shirt and jeans, he was a far cry from Ash's preferred Goth style. "Yeah, we know. But it keeps them out of trouble and stops them from putting horns on the babies' heads."

Medea laughed as she saw that Urian's birth mother, Bethany, was holding their youngest son in her arms and cooing to the toddler. "So this is the little Aricles I keep hearing about from big brother Urian."

With her black spiral curls pulled away from her face in a ponytail, Bethany rubbed her son's back. Her caramel skin was flawless over sharply chiseled features. "Would you like to hold him?"

"I might keep him if I do."

Ari smiled as he looked up at her. "Mimi?"

Completely sunk, Medea took him and was lost the moment he wrapped his arms around her neck and hugged her with a giddy squeal and bounce. It'd been so long since she last held a baby that she'd forgotten just how wonderful it felt to have such unbounded affection.

That was the hardest part about being around Daimons; they couldn't have children. Only Apollites could.

Falcyn brushed his hand through her hair. "You okay?"

She nodded. "You're screwed, though. Word of warning. I want a bunch of these again."

He wrinkled his nose as Aricles squeezed Falcyn's finger and bit it. "I don't know. He's kind of smelly and leaking out both ends."

Bethany laughed. "It doesn't bother you when it's yours who smells that way."

"If you say so." He met Styxx's gaze doubtfully.

Styxx cleared his throat. "I'm agreeing with Beth. All the way."

"That's because my brother is not a fool." Acheron came in and clapped his hands on Styxx's shoulders.

Medea froze at the sight of them together. While she knew they were identical, except for their eye color and hair color—and that only because Acheron artificially colored his black and red—it was still shocking to see them side-by-side like this.

If the two of them put their minds to it, there would really be no way to tell them apart.

Spooky.

"Dear gods, who's dead?"

They all froze as Urian came into the room to catch them gathered there.

"Please tell me it's Stryker." There was no missing the hopeful tone in Urian's voice.

"Not funny." Medea handed Aricles back to Bethany as she braced herself for the last thing she wanted to do. How in the world was she going to tell Urian about Phoebe . . .

Now she wished she'd taken Davyn up on his offer to be here for this confrontation. But then she wasn't a coward and Urian was her brother.

I can do this.

Falcyn put his hand on her shoulder to let her know that he was with her. She took comfort in his presence. And with a deep breath, she braced herself for what was going to be a horrible reaction.

Real bad.

"There's something I need to tell you, Urian. Something you're not going to believe."

"I've won the lottery?"

She rolled her eyes at his misplaced and extremely irritating humor. "No. It's about Phoebe."

The color faded from his cheeks. When he spoke, his tone was brittle. "What about her?"

There was no easy way to do this. So she settled on just ripping the Band-Aid off as quickly and mercifully as possible. "Stryker didn't kill her that night. She's still alive."

Gah, that sounded harsh even to her own ears. She could kick her own ass.

Delicate, thy name is not Medea.

He staggered back into his father's arms and would have fallen had Styxx not been there. "What?"

"Breathe," Styxx whispered in his ear. "I've got you."

Urian shook his head. "It's not possible."

I feel that, brother.

But she had to be strong for him. And she had no choice now except to see this through. "Both Davyn and I saw her. She's alive, Urian. Just not the same."

Urian's head spun from the emotions that took turns assaulting him. Disbelief. Anger. Pain. Betrayal. He couldn't even settle on one. As soon as he thought he had one emotion, it melted into another.

He glared at Acheron. "Did you know?"

"I swear on my mother's life, I had no idea. She's not human, so I can't see her fate. It's beyond my powers. If I'd known, I'd have told you."

Urian blinked and blinked again as he slowly digested her news. "Stryker knew?"

She nodded weakly.

Of course the bastard knew. Why would he think otherwise? "Why didn't he tell me?"

"He didn't want you to feel guilty for what she's become. For what she did."

What? He scowled at her. "What she did?"

Medea looked away as if she couldn't bear to tell him that part. "She went trelos, Uri. She attacked the commune where you had her housed."

No. They'd have told him.

She was lying.

He glanced over at the one person who would know. "Ash . . . if this is true, is there any way to get her back?"

Acheron shook his head. "Not that I know. But I'm a god of fate. Not one of souls." He looked to Styxx's wife.

She shook her head. "Wrath, warfare, misery, and the hunt. You need someone hunted down and killed with extreme prejudice, I'm your girl. But I was never in charge of souls, either. Sorry."

Falcyn sighed. "And I'm a war god, too. What a worthless lot, we are."

"Although ..."

They turned to stare at Acheron.

Ash bit his lip as he considered something. "This is a long shot. I mean Hail Mary pass of all time."

"What?" Urian stepped away from his father.

"I might know somebody who can help with this. ... Xander."

Urian considered that. Xander was a Dark-Hunter currently stationed in New Orleans. Part sorcerer, he was one of the darkest powers. So much so that Artemis had only gotten a part of his soul.

"Who is he?" Medea asked.

Acheron sighed. "He deals with transmutations and is the only nondemon I know who can bargain with Jaden and Thorn. If anyone can help you, he'll be your best bet."

Medea looked hopeful. "You think he'll do it?"

Ash let out a nervous laugh. "I don't know. He's a tricky sonofabitch. But he does have a weakness."

"And that is?"

Urian already knew before Ash spoke.

"Brynna Addams and Kit Baughy. They can talk him into most things. Maybe, just maybe they can talk him into this."

And if they didn't, Urian would drag him out and kick his ass.

At least that was his thought until he turned and saw Xyn standing in the hallway that led to his bedroom where they'd been when Medea had arrived.

The instant his gaze met hers, he knew she'd heard every word of this exchange.

And the hurt in her eyes hit him like a sledgehammer to the groin. *What the hell, Fates? Were you bitches bored?* For the majority of his life, he'd been bitterly alone.

In his life he'd only had two women he'd ever really loved.

How could he choose between them?

Torn and terrified, he headed toward her. She stepped back into the shadows.

Urian rushed after her, praying she didn't use her powers to vanish. If she ran, he wouldn't be able to track her. "Xyn?"

Thankfully, she stopped and turned to face him. "You should go to her."

He heard the tears in her voice. "Talk to me."

"You don't want me to talk to you, Uri. I'm drakomai. In the mood I'm in, I might hurt you." Her eyes flashed to their serpentine dragon form. "I know this isn't your fault. That you didn't know. But the dragon in me doesn't care." Her breathing turned ragged. "This is why we couldn't be together when you were a Daimon. Because what lives in me is as dangerous as the demon in you. And it doesn't share. You're too close to me, and a dragon will kill what it loves before it shares it. We are not selfless creatures." Her skin was turning into scales.

Urian cupped her face in his hands and kissed her.

The moment he did, she calmed and stopped turning. Tears swam in her eyes.

"You're my first love, Sarraxyn. My best friend."

"And Phoebe owns your heart. Don't think I haven't heard the others speak of it. How you've pined for her."

He winced. "You think I didn't mourn you, too? Every bit as badly? Ask Davyn." He looked back toward the throne room. "They don't speak of it because they weren't there when you vanished. Davyn was. My brothers were. It was the same when you were gone. I was a shell of pain for a century!"

"Aye, and telling me you got over it in the arms of another—"

"Isn't what I'm saying. God, Xyn, please have mercy. If Phoebe is trelos, I'm to blame for it. Think of how I feel. *I* did this to her. *I* killed her."

"Then we will sort this out."

That shocked him. "You'll help me?"

"No. I'm going to kick your ass for getting into this mess." She glared at him, then kissed his lips tenderly. "Why do I love you? You make me so crazy!"

"S'a—"

"Don't!" She cut his words off sharply. "You don't even say that until we have Phoebe. And this—" She indicated her body.

"Off limits, buddy. You're stewing in your juices. And you better be grateful I'm not adding fire to the kettle!"

He was a sick bastard that he found her amusing. If anyone else talked to him like that, even Acheron, he'd have their ass on a platter. "Yes, ma'am."

Her green eyes flashed emerald fire. "You better be damn glad you have the finest ass I've ever seen on any man."

"Are you sexually harassing me?"

"And you better be glad I am 'cause that's the closest thing to sex you're getting until we get this matter settled."

Someone cleared their throat.

Urian glanced over his shoulder to find his father standing there with a frown.

"Well, I guess that answers my question as to whether you're all right. The way you took off, I was worried. I can see there was no need."

Urian cringed. "This was not how I meant for you two to meet." Clearing his throat, he stepped aside so that his father could see Sarraxyn, who was dressed in a pair of jeans and a tight black T-shirt. Her long red hair was a mass of thick curls that hung to her waist. "Xyn, my father, Styxx."

"It's an honor, sir." She held her hand out to him.

"Likewise." The amused glint in his father's eyes darkened as he turned her hand over and examined the tattoo on the inside of her forearm just above her wrist. It was a dragonmark similar to the one Falcyn had, but different. "You're a Were-Hunter?"

"Please don't insult me. Drakomai. Much older than they are."

"Are you related to Falcyn?"

"We're all related. My mother's Lilith. My father's Helios."

Urian's eyes widened at a fact he never knew. "The Titan?"

She nodded. "We don't converse, though. We had a falling-out a long time ago. I wasn't as fortunate as Urian when it came to my father. I was unfortunately stuck with just a penis."

Shocked, Urian felt his jaw drop, but thankfully his father laughed at her words.

He clapped Urian on the arm. "I adore her. Trust me, your

mother said something far more shocking to my father when she met him. And at least neither of you were naked when you met me."

"Pardon?" Urian scowled at that weirdness.

"Ask your grandfather about the day we met." And with that he wandered back to the others.

"Not sure I want to." He turned back toward Xyn. "Do I?"

Xyn let out a long, tired sigh as she stared at those perfectly sculpted features that she'd always thought were identical to Stryker's. However, now that she'd met Styxx, she realized Urian favored his real father a lot more. "Probably not."

Irritated, and torn between wanting to slap him and hug him, she reached up to run her hand through his hair. Then she yanked it. "Why does my relationship with you have to be so complicated?"

"What can I say? The gods hate me."

"Indeed. A Daimon forced to work with the Dark-Hunters . . . if that's not hatred, I don't know what is."

Xyn *had no* idea how true those words would prove to be until a short time later when they knocked on the door of a peculiar dark purple shotgun shack in the heart of the French Quarter. Fanning herself with her hands, she blew out a deep breath to help alleviate the fierce, oppressive heat. "Isn't it supposed to be winter here?"

Urian laughed. "Welcome to one of New Orleans's infamous heat waves. If you don't like the weather, wait a minute."

"Huh?"

He winked at her. "Meaning that's how fast it changes. Like a teenage Gemini chugging Red Bull on a party line."

That reference was completely lost on her.

Ash shook his head before he knocked on the door.

An instant later, it opened of its own accord. Most people might think that odd or creepy, but where they lived, it was just par for the course, normal.

Ash stood back for Urian to go first. *"Entrez."*

Urian laughed at Acheron's invitation. "Um, yeah, I don't think so. First Daimon in the door usually gets staked. How you think I've lived this long? I'm not about to walk into a Dark-Hunter's house uninvited." He smacked Ash on the arm. "Just because you can, doesn't mean you should." He clicked his tongue at him.

Ash appeared less than amused. "Don't make me rip out your esophagus and beat you with it."

"That threat would carry more weight, *Uncle,* if we weren't related now." Urian grinned at him. *"Après-vous."*

Ash passed a smirk to Xyn. "Tell me something. Is or was he ever sweet and cuddly?"

She shrugged. "Only after sex."

With a visible shudder, Ash led the way in. "Oh, so not going there." Then under his breath, he said, "No wonder you two get along. Sheez!"

Laughing, Urian pulled Xyn into his arms and put her in front of him.

"What are you doing?"

"Equality, my lady dragon. You're my meat shield because I know the Hunter can't harm you." He kissed the back of her head playfully as the door behind them slammed shut with an eerie thud.

Xyn would be offended but for the fact that she knew Urian better. If anything were to happen, he'd be the first to trade his life for hers. "Umm-hmm, Daimon. Keep talking. I'll throw you out in daylight."

"Not a threat anymore. Uncle Ash made me dayproof."

"Really?"

"Yeah, I did. Am regretting it now. Should have crispy-fried his ass before I released my brother from captivity and learned Urian's mother was a goddess of equal power who really likes him." As if he were guided there by something unseen, Ash headed down the narrow hallway that led the length of the house, to the far back left room on the first floor.

Following along, Xyn ran her finger down the flocked dark burgundy wallpaper. She'd never seen any place decorated like this before.

"The style's called Victorian and brocade." Urian pointed up at the black chandelier over their heads, which hung off the main staircase. "They had a morbid fascination with the occult, hence the jet crystals. You slept through a lot of changes."

Indeed, she had.

Ash knocked three times on the door, which opened alone, just as the front one had.

"It's not dusk, Ancient Wonder." The thickly accented voice came from the center of a four-poster bed that had thick burgundy draperies pulled closed around it. "Why are you here, Ash, and bringing friends no less?"

Xyn could feel the man's powers. Very few had the essence of his. These were more akin to Shadow's than Acheron's or Urian's or even hers.

Unnaturally born.

His had been inherited after birth and finely honed by years of practice. Yet beneath that, she sensed that some of them had been stolen.

Who was this man?

"Sorry to disturb, Xander, but we need your expertise."

He let out a soft growl before he parted the curtains. Only he didn't touch them. As with the doors. They flew back so that he could look at them while he lay in bed on his side. "I wasn't a morning person when I was human. That hasn't improved since my conversion to a Dark-Hunter." He stretched languidly, then yawned.

Suddenly, he froze. "You want me to do what?"

Xyn glanced around. No one had spoken.

"We'll wait for you in the parlor." Ash's tone wasn't a question. It was a definite "get dressed and move."

As they walked, Xyn took Urian's hand and rubbed his chest, amazed at what an incredibly handsome creature he was. His features were so elegantly sculpted. And the way he wore his pale hair pulled back into a tight ponytail only accentuated their chiseled perfection. He was flawless in his beauty.

And that loose-limbed way he walked . . .

Total confidence and all predator. Even when he was unsure, he still exuded this aura of power that was delectable.

The only time there was ever a chink in his feral armor was when they were alone, or whenever he was around family he was completely comfortable with.

Which showed her what he thought of Acheron. Ash was one of the chosen few who knew the real Urian. And she wondered if he understood what a privilege it was for Urian to show his playful humor or to let down his guard.

Her Daimon didn't do that lightly. His life had been too harsh.

Something that became immediately apparent when Xander entered the room. Urian let go of her hand and crossed his arms over his chest. He took one step in front of her and widened his stance to provide a shield for her. Not to be rude. It was an instinctive need he had to protect what he cared about.

He gave her plenty of freedom to maneuver, but his stance made it clear that in order to get to her, someone would have to go through him first. He was also positioned to cover Ash's vulnerable side, with his back to the wall and his gaze facing the window and door.

Ever a predator. Ingrained to the very core of his soul.

And the Dark-Hunter picked up on it, too. He was dressed in a pair of black jeans and a black T-shirt, his skin a rich, golden arrowwood. His head was shaved, but by the stubble lining his chiseled features, she could tell it must be raven black.

Given his coloring, she would have assumed him to have dark eyes, yet his were definitely not.

In fact, they were as spectacular as Acheron's and Urian's. The right one was a light, icy green, rimmed with a darker shade of moss, whereas his left eye was a kaleidoscope of amber and rust bisected by shades of yellow and green. Unnerving in their beauty, those eyes seemed ageless and betrayed a deep-seated tragic past that tugged at her heart.

Like Urian, he was a creature of secrets and power, and it bled from every pore of his body.

"So," Xander said slowly. "What's up, Daimon-not-Daimon and Dark-Hunter-not-Dark-Hunter, and lady dragon so beautiful I won't even categorize you because that would be a disservice to one of your grace."

Urian cleared his throat. "Her name is Xyn, and eyes to me if you want to keep them."

"No fear. I only have eyes for one lady, and I would never shame her. That being said, even though I adore my house and have no personal interest in any other, it doesn't mean that I can't appreciate that which someone else calls home."

Xyn had to give it to the man, he was slick and charming. She could only imagine how many women had lost themselves to those eyes and that honeyed tongue.

And Urian slid a look to her that said he suspected she might not be immune to it.

She blinked innocently. "You need to be taking notes, buddy." Smiling, she stepped forward to wrap her arms around his waist and squeeze him tight. While she normally didn't play into anyone's insecurities, she knew that it wasn't in Urian's nature to be like that. Nor was he jealous.

However, Xanthia's infidelity had left a vicious scar on his soul, and the last thing she wanted was to open that wound and make it bleed.

Urian placed a gentle hand over hers. "We have a little situation. How much do you know about soul exchanges?"

He let out a dark laugh. "Second only to Jaden. Why?"

Urian paused as he considered where to begin. This was so complicated. He didn't even know how to start. "My wife ... whom I thought was dead, has apparently gone trelos. Is there any way to pull the souls out of her and restore her?"

Actually, that wasn't as complicated as he'd thought.

Xander narrowed his eyes on Ash. "You want me to help a Daimon?"

"Yeah. Believe it or not."

"That's a tough one." He flicked his fingers open. Fire lit the tips as he held his left hand out. A book flew from the shelves to land on the desk in front of him. It opened itself and turned to a page. The fire left his fingers to swirl around the blank pages for several heartbeats but didn't burn them. Instead, the fire revealed the words as if someone or something unseen were writing.

Urian stepped closer to read over his shoulder. However, he'd never seen anything like that alphabet. It wasn't alchemy or any of the ancient languages he knew.

Xander made all kinds of strange noises. "You people don't believe in making things easy, do you?"

"Not really. We could try Psyche, but last I rang her bell, she came with a two-hundred-pound tumor."

Xander scowled at Acheron. "Pardon?"

"Eros. She came with Eros."

He shook his head. "This is useless." He threw his hand out and the book skittered back to the shelf. The flames on his fingers went out. "Simple answer is, I don't know. Where is she?"

"In Kalosis."

Xander let out a deep guffaw. Until he realized they weren't joking. "Wait ... you're asking a Dark-Hunter to descend into Daimon Central to save a trelos Daimon that even Daimons fear? Are you fucking kidding me?"

Urian gestured to Xyn. "We've got a dragon."

"And I *don't* have a head injury. Or a fatal dose of stupidity. Nor am I suicidal."

"What if I said pretty please?"

"Nice, Daimon. Real nice. You're an effing comedian. And while that might get you a guest appearance on someone's late show, it's not going to get me down your daddy's bolt-hole."

"But you *will* do it for me."

Xander let out a fierce growl at Acheron. "I'm reassessing this favor you think I owe you."

"Don't think. I know. And remember that Urian is my nephew. I would be terribly put out if anything happened to him."

Xander raked a slow hand over his face. "On one condition."

"That is?" Ash cocked his hip as he waited.

He counted them off on his fingers. "I want Simi, with a fresh bottle of barbecue sauce."

"I can do that. I'd planned to send her with you anyway to keep a certain goddess from eating your head for breaching her portal."

"Good." Xander stepped back, clapped his hands together, and made a sound like a hollow cymbal. It echoed through the room with an ethereal recoil. "Shadow!" The call was low and deep. Not the typical kind of shout.

Oddly enough, particles in the air began to swim about as if caught in a vortex. Light formed a cone.

An instant later Shadow appeared. He glanced around the four of them, then grimaced. "Why? Why is it never Emma Stone? Gal Gadot? Hell, I'd settle for Artemis. Nah ... it's always one of you losers whining for me." He looked up at the ceiling. "Why, Lord? Why?"

"Stop ... we have a favor."

"Of course you do. Figured you didn't want a weather report, and I know you didn't call because you were worried about my health or wanted to play Parcheesi. You're all a bunch of selfish assholes. So what can I do you for?"

"We need to get into Kalosis."

He laughed a much higher-pitched sound than Xander's. "What? You're serious? Who's been knocking back Drano shots?" He narrowed his glare on Urian. "Remember what happened the last time I opened a portal for you? Didn't end well for me. I'm still bleeding through my T-shirts."

"True. Would it help if I said I appreciate you?"

"Not even a little. I thought you had a sister for this?"

"She's preoccupied with *her* brother." Urian indicated Xyn.

Shadow growled. "Have I said today how much I hate Hunters?"

Urian grinned. "Yeah, but we're not listening."

"Hope you all get eaten by Apollymi." Shadow looked to Acheron. "Except for you. You're to stay here. 'Cause I don't want the world to end. It might suck, but not as bad as it would if she and her kin were in charge."

"No worries. I know the drill." Ash winked. "Simi? Human form."

The tattoo on his forearm peeled itself off to manifest before them into Ash's teen Goth, demon daughter who was wearing an adorable panda onesie. She blinked at all of them, yawned, and then changed into her typical skirt and corset wear, complete with a set of purple and black cyber falls. "Are we having a party, akri?"

"No, Simikee. Sorry. I need you to go with them to visit Apollymi. Do you mind?"

"Not at all! The Simi loves her goddess-akra. She's the bestest!"

Ash nodded, then paused as he met Xander's gaze. "What?"

"Just thinking ... this would be better if we had a kerling going in." He looked at Shadow. "I know you don't, but do you have any friends?"

"I do have friends, for your information." Shadow turned toward Urian. "Think we can pry Brogan off Blaise for a little soiree?"

He pulled his phone out of his pocket. "It's worth a try."

Xyn was still baffled by that little device. It was quite impressive.

Meanwhile, Simi came over and took her arm. "What's your favorite people to eat, akra-Dragon?"

"You know, Simi, I haven't eaten any in a while."

"Oh. Akri has you on a diet, too. That's just so wrong. He won't let me eat hardlies anythings. It's just so hard. But is how I maintains this girlie figure at my age."

Before she could comment, Urian slid his phone back into his pocket.

"I have good news and bad news."

Xander made a face that said he felt a bit sick at the prospect. "What?"

An instant later, Blaise and Brogan both appeared.

"I got your kerling, but she comes with a two-hundred-pound tumor."

Blaise appeared baffled by his comment. "What?"

Acheron snickered as he clapped him on the back. "Inside joke at your expense. Sorry, Blaise."

"What else is new, Ash? Everyone takes a potshot at the dragon. We're low-hanging fruit. So large, we're easy to hit. So everyone takes a shot."

Brogan lowered her hood to expose her braided dark hair. The petite fey witch was absolutely exquisite. Like Simi, she appeared so frail and harmless and yet was capable of extreme and utter violence.

She held her hand out toward Xander. "You must be the reason Urian called. I'm Brogan."

"Xander."

"And this is Blaise."

Xander smiled. "A kerling Deathseer who commands a mandrake *and* a Crom. That's something I've never seen before." He clicked his tongue. "I take back what I said, Shadow. You have impressive friends."

"Yeah, remember that next time you insult me."

As they made ready, Xyn caught the look in Urian's eyes. She stepped over to him. "Are you all right?"

He nodded, but she knew better.

And as they headed into Kalosis she had a bad feeling that things were about to go all kinds of wrong. Something about this wasn't right. Trouble was, she'd been dormant for so long that a lot of her powers weren't reliable yet.

She still felt weak from whatever spell had been used on her.

Urian hung back from the others. He let them go through the portal. But when Xyn started to go, he kept her with him.

She looked up with a questioning brow. He sensed that she wasn't at her full strength. Yet she said nothing about it.

For him, she was going into this not knowing what they'd face. He didn't take that act of loyalty lightly. Nor was he willing to risk her lightly.

Summoning his powers, he let them flow into his arm, then lifting her chin, he kissed her.

Xyn felt the surge Urian gave her and it wasn't just from his kiss. He'd handed over a portion of his strength to her, as well. "What have you done?"

He smiled down at her. "I'm trained to fight at half strength. You're not."

And with that, he fell back into the portal.

Stunned, she met Acheron's swirling silver gaze.

He shrugged at her. "Tory thinks I'm headstrong? I've got nothing on that one. I haven't been able to do anything with that dumbass since the day I met him. May the gods have mercy on you."

Rolling her eyes, she went in after Urian, cursing him with every sickening twist of the vortex. Which thanks to Shadow, didn't drop them into the main hall at Stryker's feet.

Because Shadow was able to manipulate the Nether Realm between the worlds, he took them in so that they arrived not far from her old cave. She actually envied him for the powers ... in a way.

They would be nice to hold for a bit, but with them came a profound loneliness and solitude that made what a dragon endured seem kind in comparison.

As soon as they landed, she caught the look on Shadow's face. Feeling for the dark demon, she went over and kissed his cheek. "Thank you."

Startled, he stepped back from her.

Xyn scowled at his reaction. "You act as if no one's ever thanked you before."

"They don't normally. Not sure how to handle kindness. It terrifies me."

That was the biggest tragedy of their kind. Or perhaps that was the biggest indictment against humanity. When kindness and decency became so rare that people no longer knew how to respond to it, or when having witnessed a kind act they felt the need to comment on something that really should be so common-place that it never should be newsworthy.

If anything should ever be so common as to be taken for granted, surely in the name of the gods, it should be kindness and not cruelty.

Shadow glanced around the dull gray landscape. "Ahh, I see today's forecast is gloomy with an overcast of doom and despair. I like it. Should we build a summer home?"

Blaise laughed. "My soulmate! We should hang out more."

Brogan appeared offended by that. "You fickle beast. I thought I was your soulmate? Now you're making overtures to Shadow? I can't leave you alone for five minutes." She sighed heavily.

"Would it help if I said he's not as cute as you?"

"Not really. Damage done."

Xander sighed. "I'm thinking this might have been a mistake."

Shaking his head, Urian laughed. "Brother, I think that every day. Shall we?"

Ash *had just* returned home when he found Styxx waiting for him.

"Where's Urian?"

"Oh shit" didn't quite capture the feeling of dread that ripped through him as he realized just how badly he'd screwed up. Because he was used to dealing with Dark-Hunters, he wasn't used to thinking about the fact that Urian now had "parents."

More to the point, he wasn't used to remembering that Urian had a mother and father who would kick his ass if anything happened to him.

Ash gave his twin a nervous grin. "Um . . . "

"That's a bad sound, brother. That's the kind of sound you normally make that precedes my desire to hurt you." Styxx crossed his arms over his chest as he pinned him with a gimlet stare.

"Let me remind you before you kill me that in order to get to your son, you'll have to go into the domain where my mother resides, and she won't be happy if you harm me."

The look of disgust on his face might actually have been amusing if Ash hadn't felt so bad about causing it.

"What did you do?"

"He wanted to go after Phoebe."

Ash hadn't been cussed out that effectively or colorfully in ancient Greek in a number of centuries. It was impressive.

Styxx finally stopped long enough to issue one fierce command. "Open the portal to Kalosis!"

"The one I control will take you straight to Stryker."

"I don't give a shit where it goes. Get me down there so I can find my child. Now!"

Bethany appeared instantly. "What's going on?"

Styxx gestured at Ash. "He let our child loose in Kalosis to go after his gallu-infected wife."

And now Ash was being cussed in ancient Egyptian and Atlantean. Which brought Tory out of the main room, into the hall where they were gathered.

"What in the world is going on? Is that Egyptian?"

Ash gestured at them. "I pissed off my family again ... and yes, First Dynasty."

Bethany's eyes flared to red. "Tory? Can you please watch Ari for a bit? I have to go find my oldest and drag him home before he does something stupid."

"Sure."

"Open the portal, Acheron," Styxx repeated.

"Stryker—"

"Won't stand in *my* way." Bethany immediately pulled her hair back into a ponytail.

While Ash would argue with his brother, he was going to cede that point to Bethany. Given the fury in her eyes and tone, he had no doubt that Stryker would get his ass kicked effectively. "All right, then." He opened the portal. "Urian has friends with him. Please try not to skewer Simi."

That seemed to calm Styxx a little. "Thank you for sending her with him."

"You really think I wouldn't?"

"I didn't think you'd send *him!*"

"Stop arguing!" Bethany snapped. "Get to my baby!" She pushed Styxx toward the portal. "I'm going to beat both of you later."

As soon as Ash closed the portal, he turned to see Tory's perturbed grimace. "What did I do to piss you off?"

Smiling, she pulled him into her arms. "Nothing. You look like you could use a hug."

Finally, someone who wasn't mad at him. "I really didn't mean to put him in harm's way."

"I know, sexy baby. It's all good."

S*tryker was used* to unexpected visitors dropping through their portal. Over the centuries, they'd had quite a few interesting creatures.

Dark-Hunters. Were-Hunters.

A couple of gods. Demons. Forest creatures. A large number of trelos.

Stupid humans by the dozens, especially in the nineties during the height of the vampire craze. He couldn't count how many Goth counterculture members had dropped in, taken one look at them, and said, "Bite me!" and not in a bad way. They'd wanted to join them.

They'd always provided a quick and easy snack for his Spathi warriors.

Even his wife had dropped in at his feet a decade ago.

But this ... *this* was a first.

An ancient Greek hero and an Egyptian goddess who landed on their feet with a searing glare that would have sent a lesser man scurrying for cover.

As it was, Stryker remained seated and only lifted one insolent brow at the temerity of confronting him in his own living room, as it were. He tilted his head toward his wife, who came forward to lean against his throne that was made out of the bones of gods Misos had defeated long ago.

"Hmm, Phyra. I'm trying to decide if I should be flattered by their visit or pissed."

Crossing her arms over her chest, she shrugged. "If they're bringing tribute, flattered. Any other reason ... I say we skewer them where they stand."

Bethany scoffed. "Try it and I'll use your guts for shoelaces."

Styxx cleared his throat as he placed a gentle hand on his bloodthirsty wife's shoulder. "What my nondiplomatic better half is trying to say is that we're here on a mission of peace. And it's one that concerns you, too, Stryker."

"How so? Since the last time I looked, we were enemies?"

"Enemies or not, we have a common interest ... Urian."

At the mention of his son, Stryker felt a rush of pain and anger. One that made him want to lash out as he remembered that Urian wasn't really *his* son.

He was *theirs*.

"What of him?"

"He's here. Seeking Phoebe."

Those words went through Stryker like ice. He came off his throne before he'd even realized he'd moved. "What do you mean, he's here?"

"As I said. And I'm not a fool, Stryker. You don't stop loving a child. He came here to find her and help her."

Damn him for the truth of that statement. Like it or not, he did still love the boy, even if he did want to beat him senseless. Stryker glanced to Zephyra. She was his strength.

When she met his gaze, she gave a subtle nod. "We have to find our son before he's harmed. Where would he be?"

And that was why he loved her.

"I don't know. But we'll find him." Stryker ground his teeth in frustration as he glared at Zolan. "Fetch Davyn and Medea. One of them might know something."

Bethany stopped Stryker as he started past her. "Was he really so hard to raise?"

He let out a frustrated sigh. "He was a nightmare unimagined ... and my greatest joy and pride."

Tears gathered in her eyes. She lifted her hand toward his cheek. "May I?"

Stryker knew she was asking if she could share his memories of Urian's childhood. A part of him was selfish enough that he wanted to keep them for himself and deny her request. But then, he wasn't quite that big a bastard. The rational part of him knew that he wouldn't have had so great a gift if not for his two enemies.

So the real crime wasn't in the anger that lay between him and Urian now so much as in the fact that they had never known their son at all.

He couldn't imagine a worse horror than what they'd experienced. To have the son they'd wanted so desperately ripped from their lives and given to another. His gaze went to the scars on Styxx's arm where he'd carved the name they'd intended to give Urian on his birth ... Galen.

No, he wouldn't be that cruel to anyone. Enemies or not. So he nodded and braced himself for her intrusion.

Closing her eyes, she laid her warm hand to his cheek, then reached to touch Styxx with her other hand. It wasn't until Styxx gasped that Stryker realized she was sharing the memories with him as well.

His head spun as he felt Bethany picking through his mind with a master skill.

Strangely enough, she revived things inside him that he'd forgotten. Precious moments spent with Urian as a child when he'd once thought the world of Stryker. The night when Urian had picked up his battle helm for the first time, and tried it on.

It'd fit over his head like a bell, and sat askew to the point where the poor child had been unable to see. Still, Urian had stumbled his way into Stryker's bedroom to proclaim himself ready to battle by his side. He'd stood there, completely naked save for that helm and his wooden sword and a towel he'd knotted around his neck.

"I'm ready, Solren! Take me with you to battle the human vermin!"

Another time when Urian had stolen the laces from his armor to make a present for Paris.

"Why, Urian? Why would you do this?"

"I didn't want you to fight and get hurt, Solren, and I wanted a present for Paris. So it seemed like a good way to accomplish both goals."

How many times had he been on the brink of strangling the boy only to have Urian turn around with a logic so sweet and loving that it pulled him back from homicide?

Until the day he'd learned the staggering truth.

Trates had been as nervous as always. Flittering about in his study.

"What are you doing?"

"I have news, *kyrios*. Distressing news."

"About Acheron or the Dark-Hunters?"

"Neither."

That had stopped Stryker cold. "What then?"

Trates had swallowed hard and hesitated. "Urian."

By then, Urian had been his last surviving child. Stryker had lost all of his grandchildren and great-grandchildren. And two unofficial "spouses" he'd refused to marry lest he give the women some false hope that they might claim a part of him that he was incapable of offering them. Since he knew he'd never love them, it just seemed wrong to marry them under a lie.

So many of his family had fallen that his heart had grown to ice and his blood had turned to pure venom.

He was dead inside and he knew it.

Except for Urian.

His son alone held his love and devotion.

Stryker had thought himself above being hurt until Trates spoke. "Your son has married a daughter of the heiress's bloodline."

"What?"

"It's true, *kyrios*." Trates had shown him the pictures. Of Phoebe and Urian. "He's running interference between our searchers and her sister, Cassandra. He's been helping to cover her tracks."

And still a part of Stryker had refused to believe it. In the back of his mind, he'd convinced himself that Urian's enemies had concocted a lie to put distance in his heart for his son. To spread discord in their house. After all, it was just the sort of thing they would do.

That was easier to believe than his son had betrayed him.

But he hadn't been able to let it go. And so he'd gone to Elysia and there he'd met Phoebe himself.

The stupid chit had no idea who he was. She'd sat one afternoon and talked to him about the most asinine of topics until he'd wanted to strangle her. Why Urian had wanted to marry her, he couldn't imagine. While she was pretty enough, she was immature and insipid. Gossipy about Hollywood starlets and soap operas. Things Urian would know nothing about and care even less for.

He'd tried to understand their relationship and had left even more baffled.

Then he'd waited for Urian to tell him the truth.

Stryker had dropped hints that he knew. But Urian had deftly turned the topic to something else.

Until that fateful night ...

Everything had gone wrong.

He'd learned about Acheron being the true son of Apollymi and her lies to him. That had hit him like a sledgehammer. All these years, he'd thought Apostolos was dead and that he was her chosen son.

Instead, he'd found out that he was a puppet and Acheron was her beloved child. It had gutted him. Worse, Urian had killed their own to protect the bitch he knew Stryker wanted dead.

So when Shanus's call had come in while Urian was out that Phoebe had gone trelos ...

Stryker had been torn between his duty as a father and to his people, and his fury over being betrayed. When he'd gone there, his intention had been to kill Phoebe. To unleash his wrath on her for the lives she'd taken.

They'd fought and fought.

In the end, he'd been unable to do it. For the first time in his life, Stryker had shown mercy. Instead of killing her, he'd brought her back to Kalosis and locked her up. His intention had been to tell Urian later and let him deal with her.

Then when they'd faced Acheron and Wulf in Dante's Inferno ... he'd absolutely lost his fucking mind. Acheron, a two-bit whore, loved by Apollymi in spite of turning against her and her cause, surrounded by countless Hunters who were loyal and willing to die for him, in all his smugness. For Acheron to stand there, taunting and judging him when all he was trying to do was save his people. ... And Apollymi with her taunting him about Urian's betrayal when he'd done nothing to deserve it.

Because in the end, Stryker had only had one person in his entire life he could depend on. One person he could love. One person who loved him. And the gods had taken her from him.

Everyone else used him and lied while they did so. They tried to kill him or threw him away like he was garbage. Or worse, the gods took them from him and left him barren and alone.

Except for Urian. He was the only one Stryker had depended on and needed.

Then to find out that the one and only person he thought he could rely on was also a fraud ...

It'd shattered him. The pain of losing that sole person in his world who loved him had been more than he could bear. It had destroyed him and so he'd lashed out and done to Urian what the entire world had done to him since the moment he'd been violently thrust from his mother's womb into the cold and unfeeling hands of a wet nurse who'd rather see him dead than fed.

But even then, he'd known that Acheron wouldn't let his son die. Stryker had merely severed their bond so that Urian couldn't hurt him anymore.

Because Stryker knew that Urian was the one and only person who would always have the power to bring him to his knees.

He was his son. His beautiful boy. Regardless of what Urian did or how badly he hurt him.

The bastard was his son. And Stryker would always love him. No matter what pain Urian gave him, he wouldn't care.

It was why he'd kept Phoebe alive. Even though Stryker knew

he should kill her. That so long as she lived, she was a danger. He couldn't do it. He could lie to himself and everyone else about why he'd done what he'd done. He could lie about what happened to Phoebe. Tell them all that he'd killed her and cut Urian's throat.

It changed nothing. Because he couldn't kill what his son loved. And though he could cut his son's throat, he couldn't kill his boy.

Worse, Stryker had relived that day a million times over and had lashed himself with guilt and remorse. With so many could-haves and should-haves. He would sell his soul for one chance to go back and change what he'd done to them.

That was why he didn't believe hell was real. Life *was* hell. It existed solely to torment the living, and death was the reward for having endured it.

Stryker choked on tears he hadn't realized were falling until Bethany dropped her hand from his face, released from the nightmares of his past.

At some point during the horrors, Zephyra had pressed herself against his back to comfort him and had buried her hand in his hair.

His breathing ragged, Stryker wasn't sure what to expect from Styxx and Bethany. Given the memories of Urian he'd just passed to them, he half-expected both Styxx and Bethany to gut him where he stood.

Instead, Styxx jerked him forward into a fierce embrace. When he whispered in his ear, his voice was thick with emotion. "From this day forward, we are brothers, Stryker. I will never again consider you my enemy."

Swallowing hard, he nodded.

Likewise, Bethany wiped away her own tears. "Thank you for loving my son so. I am honored to share him with you. Now let's find him so we can both set his ass on fire."

W*hat do you* mean, we're lost?" Urian glared at Davyn. They had barely gotten to him in time with the dragonstone before the gallu had struck and killed him. Even so, their rescue wasn't going quite as planned.

"I'm still weak from my attack, so my tracking abilities are down."

"Why isn't he a gallu?" Blaise asked. "I thought everyone they attacked converted."

"Not if you eat one of them first." Davyn flashed him a grin. "You get all kinds of perks, we learned. Ability to walk in daylight. And a freaky immunity to their bites."

Xander scowled. "So it's like a cure?"

"If we have enough gallu to go around, yeah. That's why we've been leaving Dark-Hunters alone these last few years. You're not our primary targets anymore. The gallu are."

Xander gaped and turned toward Urian. "Did you know that?"

"Yeah. Doesn't everyone?"

"No, they don't." Xander's phone started ringing. The shocked expression on his face was quite comic. "There's cell service in hell?"

Davyn laughed. "We have cable and Internet, too. Hell would not be complete without reality TV and telemarketers."

Snorting at his sarcasm, Xander answered his phone. And the soft, tender way the tough guy spoke made them all stop and stare at him.

"Hey, baby. No, I'm sorry. I should have left a note, but it was Ash and it came up suddenly. Yeah, I'm a thoughtless ass, you know that." He paused to glare at them. "Be back soon ... you, too. Bye." In a huff, he hung it up and slid it into his pocket. "What, you jackals?"

Davyn's eyes widened. "Thought Dark-Hunters couldn't have a girlfriend?"

"Could be my boyfriend, you don't know." Xander pushed past him.

Davyn let out an evil laugh. "Actually, *I* do. And if you were family, brother, I'd be all over *that*—" He glanced down to Xander's ass. "Believe you me. Anytime you're ready to turn, give me a shout."

Rolling his eyes, Xander cast his gaze around at the lot of them. "It's none of anyone's business."

Urian passed a knowing look to Xyn. He knew that level of pissed off. That was a man who had a serious relationship with someone he wasn't supposed to and didn't want to discuss it.

Wow . . .

And he thought *he* had problems.

Which he did, hence this trip through hell.

"Where exactly are we?" Blaise asked.

"A dark and bitter forest."

He snorted at Xyn's answer. "Ha ha, sis. Ha ha. Not what I meant. What is this place used for?"

"This is a no-man's-land." Urian pointed toward the dark wall to their left that was covered with steeled thorns. "What you want to avoid is crossing to the barrier lands where the souls of the damned reside. Those are some nasty bastards. Back in the day, some of the stronger Apollites tried to feed off their souls."

"Did not go well for them." Davyn shuddered.

"Yeah. We had a huge problem with trelos outbreaks. But when you're desperate enough . . . you do dumb shit."

Xander stopped dead in his tracks to stare at them. "So what? Your people ate the souls that were here?"

Urian nodded. "Not like we had a lot of choice." He jerked his chin toward the barrier. "My father, with Apollymi's help, erected that barrier when we were teens to help confine the most corrupt souls that he feared our people couldn't handle."

A strange glow came over Xander's body. He turned a slow circle.

"Not all the gods are dead here."

Shadow drew up short. "He's right. I feel it, too."

Urian sensed nothing. He turned toward Xyn.

"I've got nothing. It feels the same as it always has."

Xander held his hand out toward Shadow. Without hesitation, Shadow took it. The two of them grew quiet as a breeze began to blow around their small group.

Urian moved to cover Xyn and Brogan, along with Blaise and

Davyn. His arm began to glow even though he couldn't sense whatever they were picking up on.

"I'm still getting nothing."

Shadow looked at that wall. "I think it's coming from in *there*."

"Could a god have gotten in?"

Xyn had a bad feeling when Brogan asked her question. "Or was she or he already inside when they were put there?"

And made stronger.

That was a terrifying thought.

"Anyone else getting an ulcer?" Blaise gulped audibly.

"Mine just had twins," Shadow said with a sigh. "Mazel tov!"

"Let's back away from the barrier." Xyn grabbed Urian and pulled him toward the city where the Daimons lived.

"You think Phoebe might have taken refuge there?"

Urian really didn't like Xander's question. "It's possible. But—" He broke off as he felt the strangest sensation.

Like something slithering up his legs. His head began to spin. "Urian?"

He heard Xyn, but he couldn't respond. Or move. His breathing turned thick and ragged. Everything spun.

One moment he was reaching for Xyn and the next . . .

He was in a vortex. Only he hadn't summoned a portal. Rushing winds filled his ears as he tried to get his bearings to figure out where he was going and how he'd stumbled into one when he hadn't been moving.

When he hit the ground, it was so hard it broke the band holding his hair, causing it to spill out over his shoulders. Worse, he smacked his head against the concrete hard enough to momentarily rattle his senses.

He hadn't been hit that hard since Archie had sucker-punched him. Damn, he'd forgotten how bad it hurt to be hit unexpectedly. Pushing himself up, he blinked and scanned the huge, cold room to find himself inside an ancient temple similar to Apollymi's.

Only this one was made of deep, glittering obsidian. Large

jade pots were set apart every few feet so that they could burn with an unholy green fire that cast eerie shadows on the walls.

"I would apologize for the rough landing, but I only wish it'd been harder for you."

Urian froze at the sound of Phoebe's bitter voice. Shocked, he turned around to find her sitting on a throne almost identical to Stryker's. That was stunning enough.

But it wasn't the most jaw-dropping element.

Oh no . . . not by a long shot. Gone was his timid, sweet little wife. The woman on that throne had her golden hair teased up and braided in an elaborate, ancient Atlantean style. Dressed in a sheer, shimmering gown, she was a thing of exquisite beauty who had more in common with Apollymi than his shy bride.

"Charonte got your tongue?"

She wasn't trelos . . . or was she?

This Phoebe reminded him of that first trelos he'd killed as a boy. The one who'd been so freakishly lucid and in command of himself.

"You've changed."

"Really? That's all you have to say to me?"

"Well, you did drop me on my head and rattle my brains, love."

She stood up from her throne with fury in her eyes. That was a look that used to herald a thorough tongue-lashing for him, and not the kind that he looked forward to. The kind that left him hard up and pissed off.

"You broke your word to me, Urian."

Wiping at the blood on his face, he gaped at her. "You mean when Stryker cut my throat?"

"I called for you and you didn't come!"

"I came as soon as I could. And I was told you were dead."

She ran at him and shoved him back. "How could you not know!"

"I wasn't a Daimon anymore, Phoebe. I don't have the same powers now that I had then."

"You left me!" she shrieked, repeating her accusation.

Urian caught her against him. "I thought you were dead."

"How could you not know? I was right here!"

"Again, Phee, Stryker cut my throat. I've been banned from Kalosis. I was protecting your sister like I promised you."

"What else have you been doing, huh?"

He scowled. "What?"

She slapped him. "How long until you found your dragon bitch and crawled back into her bed?"

Anger tore through him at her accusation. "Oh my God, Phoebe! I haven't gone near a woman in years! I've lived in hell because of you. Are you kidding?"

"Then why aren't you glad to see me?"

"You dropped me on my head!" He enunciated each word slowly. "You attacked me. You *slapped* me! Why do you think?" Furious beyond endurance, he gestured at the door. "I came here to help you, even though I'm banned. I aligned myself to the Dark-Hunters whom you know I hate. How much more could I do to prove to you that I loved you?"

She grabbed him then and sank her fangs into his neck.

Urian hissed in pain. Damn, he'd forgotten how much *that* hurt, and now that he was no longer an Apollite or Daimon, he didn't get the adrenaline or sexual surge from it. All he felt was the agony.

Apparently, so did Phoebe. Shrieking even louder than before, she lifted her head and shoved him back. "What did they do to you?"

"I told you. Stryker killed me because I helped you and Cassandra."

That finally seemed to get through to her. She blinked at him. "Your father killed you?"

"Yeah. How many times do I have to tell you that? Why do you think I don't live here anymore?" Grimacing, he wiped at the blood on his neck.

The fury returned to her eyes. "*You* murdered my grandparents, you bastard!"

He did do that. Urian couldn't deny it. "You weren't born then."

"You think that makes it okay?"

"No, but—"

"You lied to me about so many things!" When she moved to slap him again, he caught her wrist.

"I'm not your whipping boy, Phoebe."

"You used me!"

He shook his head. "I protected you and I loved you."

She bared her fangs at him. "You're incapable of love."

Those words lashed his heart and left it bleeding. "You're wrong about that."

She snatched her hand from his grasp. "Had you loved me, you would have told me the truth. You wouldn't have allowed me to care about a monster who destroyed my family. What? Did you laugh at us? Did you think it funny that you kept me like a toy while your father killed us off, one by one?"

"Oh my God, Phoebe! I lived in hell the entire time I was with you. I loved my father and because of you, I was forced to lie to him."

She shook her head. "No. You *chose* to lie to him." She punctuated her words by poking him in his chest. "You chose, Urian. You could have left him at any time and stayed with me, but no. You must have enjoyed the lies or you wouldn't have gone crawling back to him constantly."

"It's not that simple. He was my father!"

"And yet you live with your enemy now? How quickly you got over it, huh?"

This was insane! She wasn't making any sense.

"And you could have told me at any time you were still alive. Why didn't you?"

"Look around!" She threw her arms out to indicate the walls around her. "Your father locked me in this hellhole and threw away the key." She shoved him again. "I screamed and screamed for *you*. I kept thinking that surely you could hear me. That you would love me enough to come. *You never did!*"

Her shrieks tore through him. Not just the words, but the fear that he had heard her and had dismissed it as nightmare hauntings.

Because she was supposed to be dead. He'd heard so many voices in his head for so long. How was he to know that hers was real?

"What do want me to do, Phoebe? Apologize? I'm sorry! I never meant to hurt you."

"But you did." Tears welled in her eyes. "And I refuse your apology. There are some things that 'sorry' doesn't fix!"

"Fine. I'll take you to Cassandra, and—"

She cut his words off with a bitter laugh. "You don't tell me what to do, and you don't own me. Remember we're Apollites. You carry *my* last name, Urian *Peters*."

That was their custom. Since paternity was never an absolute given, but everyone knew who the mother was who birthed a child, it was Apollite tradition to trace lineage through the mother's family and to assume the wife's name upon marriage. As the Apollite saying went, "Mama's baby, Daddy's maybe." He wasn't sure where she was going with that.

Not until the thorns around the room began to thicken.

"What are you doing?" Urian summoned his sword.

She laughed darkly. "Planning to use that on me?"

"No." He hoped. "But what's going on?"

A cold, sinister smile curled her lips. "You left me here to rot, Urian. I'm returning the favor."

The floor below his feet buckled and released the souls he'd warned the others about. They rushed him with a screeching howl.

"Apollo!" she called out. "See our bargain met. Behold the son of your enemy! I deliver him to you in exchange for my freedom!"

Shadow? *What do* you mean you can't get through? That's your schtick! You're a cockroach. You get into places no one can."

With an offended scowl, he turned to face Blaise. "Really, mandrake? Cockroach? Least I don't lick my own balls. And for your information, whoever constructed that barrier did a bang-up job of it!"

"That would be me."

They all turned to see Apollymi in the mist.

Xyn went cold at the ethereal beauty of the ancient goddess who eyed them all with malice. Her black gown blended in perfectly with the darkness, but her white hair and eyes seemed to glow, making her appear even more haunting and frightening.

Her gaze went to Styxx, Stryker, and Bethany, who had found the others. Then to Xyn. "I should be furious."

She narrowed her gaze on Xander. "Beyond rage ... and if this were anyone other than Urian, I'd skewer the lot of you for being here. As it is ... " Apollymi threw out her arms and the walls opened.

"Wish you'd joined the party sooner." Bethany had the audacity to admonish her.

Apollymi's jaw dropped.

"Yes, I yelled at you. I have not forgotten the ass-whipping I still owe you. Remember that I was pregnant at our last encounter. Not pregnant now, Pol. You want a rematch ... *Any* time."

"Beth, Beth, Beth." Styxx pulled her gently away from Apollymi. "Let's not anger the nice goddess who opened the door so that we could get our son. Okay? Focus on Uri. Your baby needs you. Save the whup-ass for the bad guys who have our child."

She pointed her finger at Apollymi before she nodded. "Okay."

Xyn expected Apollymi to blast her. Instead, the goddess actually smiled.

When she realized Xyn was watching her, she gave her a smirk. "What? I've always admired Bet'anya."

Xyn wasn't about to get in the middle of that. Besides, she had more important things to think about. Like finding Urian. Running to catch up with the others, she quickly learned why this wasn't the side to be on.

Holy evil ...

The screams that echoed on this side were deafening. Xyn covered her ears. Even Simi was grimacing.

Xander looked at Stryker. "Why don't you eat some of these and shut them up?"

"Really? You just went there?"

"Given how loud this is? Yeah."

"Shield your ears," Apollymi warned.

Xyn knew what was coming. She transformed into a dragon an instant before Apollymi let loose with a sonic blast so loud, it shattered two of the walls around them. She barely extended her wings in time to shield her charges from the rubble of the ceiling that rained down on them.

Styxx was the first to recover from it. "Thank you, Xyn."

"Yes." Bethany petted her on the wing. "Thank you so much!"

"No problem." She carefully lifted her other wing to make sure everyone was safe. Luckily no one had been harmed.

"What? No one thanks me for stopping the noise?" Apollymi shook her head. "Ingrates! I'm always surrounded by ingrates!"

Bethany grimaced at her. "We wouldn't be ungrateful, Polli, if you hadn't dropped a house down on top of us."

"There's just no pleasing you."

Slack-jawed, Bethany looked at her husband. "Why did you stop your conquest? One more day . . . just one more friggin' day!"

"Don't go there."

Xyn changed back into her human form and moved to stand next to Brogan, who was being strangely silent. "You have something?"

"I'm not sure." She had that glassy, odd look about her that she got anytime she was communing with the aether.

Then Brogan's eyes cleared. "We have to hurry." She took off at a dead run.

They followed.

By the time they reached the other side of the barrier, Xyn was both proud and horrified as she saw her Daimon in all his bloody glory. There were bodies everywhere. Urian stood with his shield and sword as he held them off, but they were about to overrun him.

Closing her eyes, Xyn used her powers to cover him with her armor while she summoned her own gear for herself. She ran into the fray and rolled to come up behind him and catch the Adoni who was about to attack him there.

"What kept you?"

"Had to get my nails done."

Urian laughed at her answer. "Should have got your hair done while you were at it. You're getting split ends."

"Like you're one to talk. When was the last time you had a trim? And what's that growth on your face? You a man or a goat?"

She stabbed over his shoulder to catch the one in front of him, then twirled to catch a second one and then a third.

Urian stopped her before she could go after a fourth. He had a cut on his face that made her heart sink. "Thank you." With a quick kiss, he let go and stabbed an assailant on her right.

"Uri?"

He paused to look back at her.

"S'agapo."

In the past, he'd never allowed her to tell him that she loved him before. She wasn't sure how he'd take it.

He reached out to touch her cheek. *"Ise to alo mou miso."* *You are my other half.*

Nothing could have meant more to her. Because she knew he didn't speak those words lightly.

"Damn, Daimon! Who did you piss off!" Xander shouted. "Where are these things coming from?"

"Yeah!" Shadow concurred. "Who opened the gate?"

Blaise kicked his opponent back. "Better yet, how do we close it?"

The only one happy was Simi, who was making barbecue of them.

"You have Apollo and Morgen to thank for this. Apollo stole Hades's scepter."

Apollymi cursed under her breath. "The one that opens the portals between the worlds?"

"Yeah, that's the one."

Xander growled. "Back to my question ... how do we close it?"

"Blood of Apollo and Apollymi." Urian faced them. "In other words. Me."

Xyn had a bad feeling as she heard that note in his voice. It was one she'd heard a few other times, right before he'd done something dramatically stupid. Usually for one of his brothers.

Or sister.

"Don't you do it!" she growled. "So help me, Uri! Don't you make me drag you from hell to beat your ass."

"We can't leave it open, Xyn."

Then she saw.

Time slowed down as she held her breath. He was going for the stupid win. Her soul screamed out as her fear paralyzed her.

And before she could gather her wits to do anything to stop him, Stryker teleported. He grabbed Urian and disarmed him, then flipped him into her arms.

An instant later, he let them take him in Urian's place.

Xyn fell to the ground with Urian on top of her. She wasn't sure which of them was the most shocked as they stared at each other. All she knew was how delighted she was to have him here.

Urian couldn't believe he was still alive or that he was cushioned by his dragon. But his relief was short-lived.

Panic replaced it as he remembered what Stryker had done. Pushing himself up, he quickly surveyed the battlefield, which was now eerily quiet. Shadow and Xander were turning around, looking for more enemies. Brogan was holding Blaise. Simi was . . .

Well, she was snacking.

And his parents were heading for . . .

No.

Urian couldn't breathe as he saw Stryker on the ground. In that moment, he forgot all the anger and hate he bore the man. Forgot the fact that he'd wanted him dead and had plotted his murder.

All he saw was the man who'd held him when he was a boy. The one who used to chase monsters from under his bed. His father who'd taught him to tie his sandals. To walk with pride and integrity.

The one who'd thrown himself to his enemies to save his life.

"Baba!" Urian ran to him. "Baba, no!" Tears filled his eyes as he fell to his knees by Stryker's side and gently rolled him over.

He was covered in blood. His breathing ragged, he was barely alive. *"Eisai oti kalutero uparxei, m'gios."* You are the best thing on earth, my son. "I'm so sorry I ever hurt you."

Urian grabbed him by the shirt with both fists. "Don't you dare die on me, you bastard! Don't you do this to me or Medea!" Summoning every bit of his determination, grit, and fire, Urian heated his arm until it glowed bright and burned like wildfire. By the gods, he was not going to let Stryker go. The gods and fate had taken enough from him. He was not going to let them rip another fucking thing from his life.

Not again!

Not like this!

He was done with it!

Blinded by tears, he sent everything he had into his father. His strength. His powers.

Most of all, he sent his love. In spite of everything that had happened between them, they were still family. "Please, please, Baba." Weeping, Urian laid his head down on his chest.

But there was no heartbeat.

Damn you gods! Damn you all!

And then he felt it. His father's hand in his hair. The softest beat of his heart against his ear, followed by a deep intake of breath.

Urian let out a nervous laugh as he lifted his head to meet Stryker's gaze.

He smiled at him the way he used to when he was a boy. "Goodness, child. Does this mean you're talking to me again?"

Unable to speak past the pain and relief he felt, Urian nodded.

"Well hell, son, if I'd known this was all it'd take to make you forgive me, I'd have killed myself a decade ago."

"You're not funny, Baba."

Stryker wiped away his tears and kissed his forehead. "And

I'm not your only father, either." He jerked his chin toward Styxx and Bethany.

Xyn helped Urian up while Styxx helped Stryker to his feet.

Styxx let out a deep sigh. "Again, Stryker. We are family."

Stryker nodded. "We are. Now where's Phoebe?"

Snorting, Urian pulled his hair back into a ponytail to secure it. "Not where she thought she'd be."

Xander looked around. "What do you mean?"

Simi came over with her barbecue sauce. "He means that's his Phoebe's in the corner rocking like she's gots the rabies."

"Pardon?"

Simi pointed with her bottle.

His arm glowing, Urian headed for Phoebe. While he didn't know exactly where she was, he had a good idea of the vicinity.

It didn't take long to find her. As Simi said, she had the rabies. And the minute she saw Urian, she had a bit more.

She started to run away, but Urian caught her.

"I'm not going to hurt you." Although he *really* felt like it.

Her eyes appeared wild as she glanced from him to his companions. "What are you going to do?"

"Honestly? I feel sorry for you." And for the fact that Apollo had lied to her. He looked over his shoulder at the others. "Apollo promised to free her if she gave him some of my blood. I don't know what he needed it for. Once he had it, he sicced those bastards on me and left her here."

Apollymi scoffed. "Apollo lying. Imagine that?"

"Yeah. Anyway, now that we know you're not completely trelos, I'm thinking that since Acheron fixed me, we might be able to fix you."

Phoebe gaped. "You're forgiving me?"

"No, no, no. You attacked Davyn. You let Apollo infect my father and stepmother with a virus that almost wiped them out."

"Although *I* thank you for that because I got Brogan out of it," Blaise murmured.

"Shut up, Blaise."

"Well, I'm just saying, we don't *all* hate her."

Urian glared at him. Then returned to the topic at hand. "You attempted to feed me to them. So—"

"I want a divorce, Urian."

He arched a brow at that.

"I've been caged my whole life. First by my father, then my mother. By you and here. I want to be on my own in the real world. I'm tired of being tied to other people and living by someone else's rules. I just want to have my own life for me."

Urian held his hands up in surrender. "You got it. I won't argue. I'll make sure you're provided for."

Phoebe laughed. "Peters heiress, remember? Don't need it. I have my own funds."

"Fair enough. Do you at least want your sister's address?"

She nodded. "That I do want."

Urian handed her his phone and unlocked it. "Press two and it'll ring Cassandra."

While she went off alone, he turned toward the others. "I think our crisis of the moment is over."

Shadow burst out laughing. "No, it's not, princess. Apollo has a scepter that can open portals. And your blood. That's a recipe for extreme disaster. My ulcer just had quads."

Xander nodded. "He's right. This is going to get bad."

"We need to pool resources to stop him." Stryker sighed heavily.

"Is what he said true?" Xander jerked his chin toward Davyn. "Your Daimons don't live on souls anymore?"

"It's true. Why?"

"Then I'm thinking we should enter an official truce."

Stryker nodded. "One caveat. We're not the only Daimons out there. We're only one small group."

"But I can mark them," Apollymi offered. "That way the Dark-Hunters can tell my Spathi from the others. I'll give them a mark that no one else can copy or duplicate. It'll be seen only by the Hunters' eyes so that they won't be able to hurt them."

"That'll work."

Bethany smiled. "Who would have ever thought we'd be on the same side?"

Grimacing, Styxx scratched nervously at his neck. "I have to say, I'm not comfortable bedding down with Atlanteans."

Bethany smacked him on the stomach. "Hey now!"

He laughed. "You don't count."

Stryker stepped aside with Urian. "Are we good again?"

"I don't know, Solren ... you did cut my throat. I am kind of fucked up." Urian cracked a smile. "But I'm your son, so I think normality and sanity sailed away a long time ago. Given that, I guess we are."

Stryker pulled him into his arms and fisted his hand in his hair like he did when Urian was young. "I've missed you so much." Those gruff words were growled against his ear.

"Missed you, too."

For a minute, Urian didn't think he'd let go. Finally, he pounded him on the back and stepped away.

Then Stryker paused. "You're welcome to come and go. I've kept your place just as you left it. No one's bothered any of your things."

And that told Urian more than anything how much his father loved him. "Thank you."

"All right, I'm off to tell my Daimons to stop killing Dark-Hunters. That might take a while to sink in. Eleven thousand years of instinct is hard to reset."

Davyn nodded. "He's not wrong. I still want to crap my pants every time I see Acheron." He glanced over to Styxx. "Or you, because you look like him."

Simi let out a horselike snort. "Oh, poo on that! Akri a sweetie. He not kill no Daimon what he don't gotta!" She hiccupped. "Ooo, that one bit me back!"

Phoebe came over and returned Urian's phone. She sniffed back the tears from her face. "Thank you."

"You all right?"

She nodded. "Can you help me get to Minnesota?"

"Sure. I'll go right now, if you want."

I'll see the others back. Xyn passed her thoughts to him. *You take care of Phoebe. I'll see you later.*

Urian nodded before he headed to the portal with Phoebe so that he could see her settled.

It didn't take long to see her to Cassandra and Wulf's. The moment they arrived, Cassandra let out a shriek he was surprised didn't orbit the world a thousand times.

Even their dog whined over it.

And when Phoebe saw the kids, she burst into a round of tears that was truly stellar, especially over little Phoebe.

Wulf clapped him on the back. "Guess you'll be relocating here, after all."

Urian shook his head. "We're not back together."

"What?"

"Long story."

"Man, I'm sorry."

Wishing he felt as bad about it as Wulf did, Urian sighed. "Appreciate it."

"Uri, Uri, Uri!" Jeff came running in to take a flying leap into his arms.

"Umph!" Urian barely caught him. "Dang, boy! What have you been eating? Rocks?"

Laughing, he hugged his neck. "Are you staying long?"

"Nah, sorry. I have to get back. Did you meet your aunt Phoebe?"

"Yeah, but they're talking about girl stuff. It's boring."

Cassandra and Phoebe came into the room to give him the same look most people gave to three-day-old cheese they'd left out in their car in August.

Urian set Jeff back on his feet and patted him on the head. "Well, on that note, I better run before my testicles crawl any further into my body. I might one day want to use them again."

He left before it got any uglier or more awkward.

But then, he was used to not feeling like he belonged. In all the centuries he'd lived—all the places he'd called home—never once had he felt comfortable or at peace. Never had he felt that sense of utter belonging.

Nowhere.

That was probably the strangest part of it all. Medea had moved in with his father and found her groove right away in Kalosis, along with her mother. Davyn and Paris had synced right up the moment they met. Even Danger had shown up at Acheron's temple with Alexion and the two of them had set up a home as if she'd always been there. Even the demon Xirena had moved right in with Simi and been fine.

Now Phoebe was at home with her sister in a way Urian had never felt welcome.

And he was . . .

Lost still.

Adrift in his own loneliness.

He felt weird in Kalosis with Stryker and Zephyra. While he spent most of his time in Katateros, he was isolated in one room.

Forever solitude.

It was all he'd ever known.

Oh well. It was what it was. At least he didn't have the guilt anymore. That was something new, at least.

Those were his thoughts until he opened the door to his room to find it completely empty. As in *stark* empty. Like a buffet after Simi and her sister went through it.

What the hell?

Had they cleared out his stuff for another baby?

Stunned and a little pissed off, Urian turned around and went to find Alexion. "Where's my stuff? Did we get robbed?"

Alexion stared at him as if *he'd* lost his mind. "Xyn came and got it. I assumed you knew."

That only confused him more. "Where'd she take it?"

He shrugged.

Seriously? The bastard had no comment? Double hell.

Frustrated that they'd play this game, Urian pulled out his phone and called her. "Xyn? Where's my stuff?"

He'd barely finished the question before he was teleported to her cavern. Urian hung up his phone as he glanced around the fancy massive place she'd made for herself. Glittering and open, it held all manner of high-end electronics and expensive furnishings. His dragonswan had exquisite taste. But then, she always had.

In the center was what appeared to be a giant tree staircase. And when Xyn came down it wearing a slinky green negligee, he felt his throat go dry and a part of his anatomy stand to attention in great appreciation of her lush curves that had always set his body on fire.

"You okay?" she asked as she slowed her pace.

"Not sure ... am I in the right place?"

She laughed as she closed the distance between them. "Is this not what you wanted? Did I read you wrong?"

"I don't know. What did you read?"

Her cheeks turned bright pink. "Oh my God, Urian! Are you back with your wife?"

Why was she so pissed off at him? "Ex-wife! No!" He caught her arm as she started away and he finally realized what she'd done. "You moved me in with you?"

She gave him a no-duh glare. "Isn't that where we were headed?"

Before Phoebe had shown up, yeah. But after that ... "I thought you'd changed your mind."

Her features softened to a tenderness that made his heart beat faster. "We don't change our minds." She kissed him tenderly, then took his hand to lead him toward the sofa. "I put your console there with your headset. And I bought you a comfy gaming chair."

Unable to believe his eyes, Urian stopped her as he realized how much attention she paid to the smallest details of his habits and likes. Tenderness choked him.

"Sarraxyn?"

"Yes?"

"Love you. And I won't take you for granted. Thank you."

"For what?"

For the one thing he'd never had in his entire existence. A place where he felt wanted. Where he belonged. "For giving me what I've never had before ... a home."

EPILOGUE

Xander shrugged his jacket off. What a screwed-up night. The Dark-Hunters were now allied to the Daimons.

Hell had frozen over.

Yeah. He'd finally lived long enough to be shocked. His mother and Confucius were right. If you sat by the river long enough, you would eventually see the bodies of your enemies float by.

Strange, strange, strange.

"Brynna! You're not going to believe the shit that happened tonight!"

He frowned when he didn't find her waiting up for him.

Weird. She always waited up for him to come home.

"Brynna?"

Xander went through the house, looking for his Squire. "Bryn?"

Was she ill? A bad feeling came over him. This wasn't normal. Suddenly scared, he pulled his phone out to check voice mail.

The first two were junk. But the third one ...

It made his blood run cold.

The voice was one he didn't know.

We have your Squire, Dark-Hunter. It's a brave new world. And if you don't do what we say, we'll send her back to you in pieces.

Do you love fiction with a supernatural twist?

Want the chance to hear news about your favourite authors (and the chance to win free books)?

Keri Arthur
Kristen Callihan
P.C. Cast
Christine Feehan
Jacquelyn Frank
Larissa Ione
Darynda Jones
Sherrilyn Kenyon
Jayne Ann Krentz and Jayne Castle
Lucy March
Martin Millar
Tim O'Rourke
Lindsey Piper
Christopher Rice
J.R. Ward
Laura Wright

Then visit the Piatkus website
www.piatkus.co.uk

And follow us on Facebook and Twitter
www.facebook.com/piatkusfiction | @piatkusbooks

piatkus